SECRETS OF CAMP WHATEVER

THE DOORS TO NOWHERE

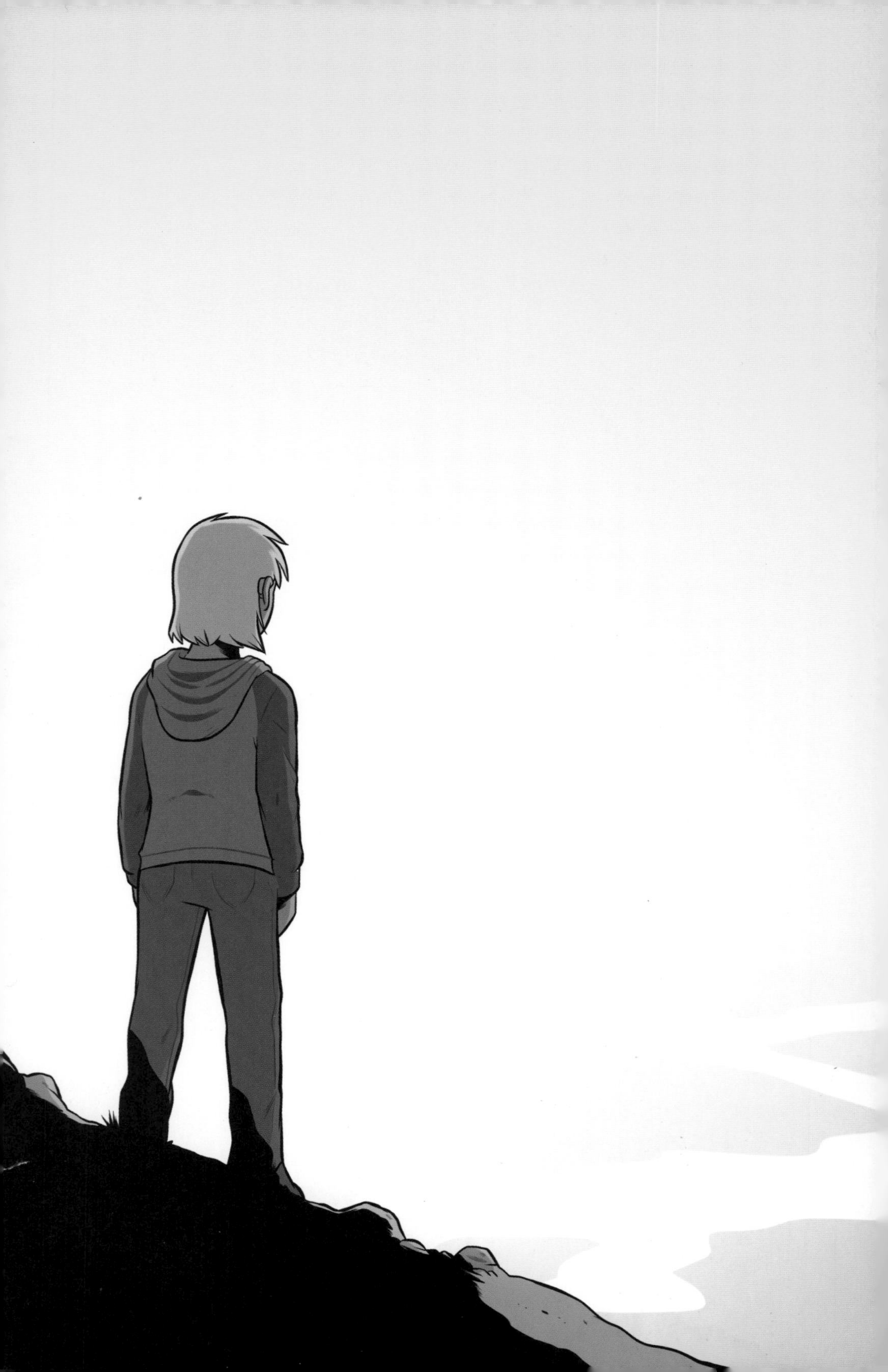

SECRETS OF CAMP WHATEVER

THE DOORS TO NOWHERE

By **CHRIS GRINE**

Designed by **KATE Z. STONE**
Edited by **SHAWNA GORE**
Consulting Reader **ALEXANDREA GILL**

AN ONI PRESS PUBLICATION

PUBLISHED BY ONI-LION FORGE PUBLISHING GROUP, LLC.

James Lucas Jones, president & publisher • Charlie Chu, e.v.p. of creative & business development • Steve Ellis, s.v.p. of games & operations • Alex Segura, s.v.p of marketing & sales • Michelle Nguyen, associate publisher • Brad Rooks, director of operations • Amber O'Neill, special projects manager • Margot Wood, director of marketing & sales • Katie Sainz, marketing manager • Henry Barajas, sales manager • Tara Lehmann, publicist • Holly Aitchison, consumer marketing manager • Troy Look, director of design & production • Angie Knowles, production manager • Kate Z. Stone, senior graphic designer • Carey Hall, graphic designer • Sarah Rockwell, graphic designer • Hilary Thompson, graphic designer • Vincent Kukua, digital prepress technician • Chris Cerasi, managing editor • Jasmine Amiri, senior editor • Shawna Gore, senior editor • Amanda Meadows, senior editor • Robert Meyers, senior editor, licensing • Desiree Rodriguez, editor • Grace Scheipeter, editor • Zack Soto, editor • Ben Eisner, game developer • Jung Lee, logistics coordinator • Kuian Kellum, warehouse assistant

Joe Nozemack, publisher emeritus

onipress.com
facebook.com/onipress
twitter.com/onipress
instagram.com/onipress

Chrisgrine.com
instagram.com/grinetastic
twitter.com/chrisgrine

First Edition: May 2022

ISBN 978-1-63715-036-8
eISBN 978-1-63715-052-8

Library of Congress Control Number: 2021949323

1 2 3 4 5 6 7 8 9 10

To Violet

Please clean your room
before your mom gets home
or we'll both be in trouble.

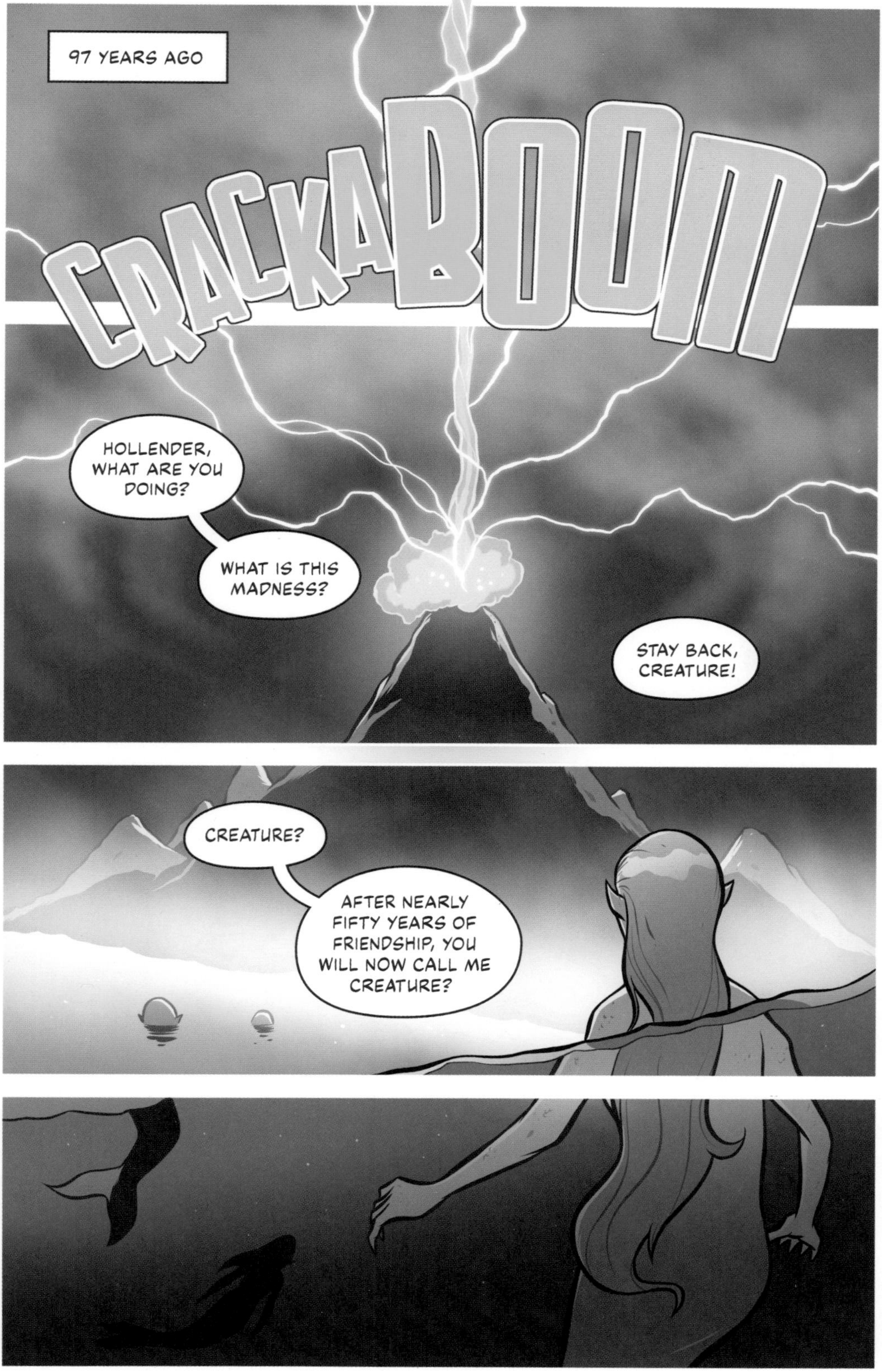
97 YEARS AGO
CRACKABOOM
HOLLENDER, WHAT ARE YOU DOING?
WHAT IS THIS MADNESS?
STAY BACK, CREATURE!
CREATURE?
AFTER NEARLY FIFTY YEARS OF FRIENDSHIP, YOU WILL NOW CALL ME CREATURE?

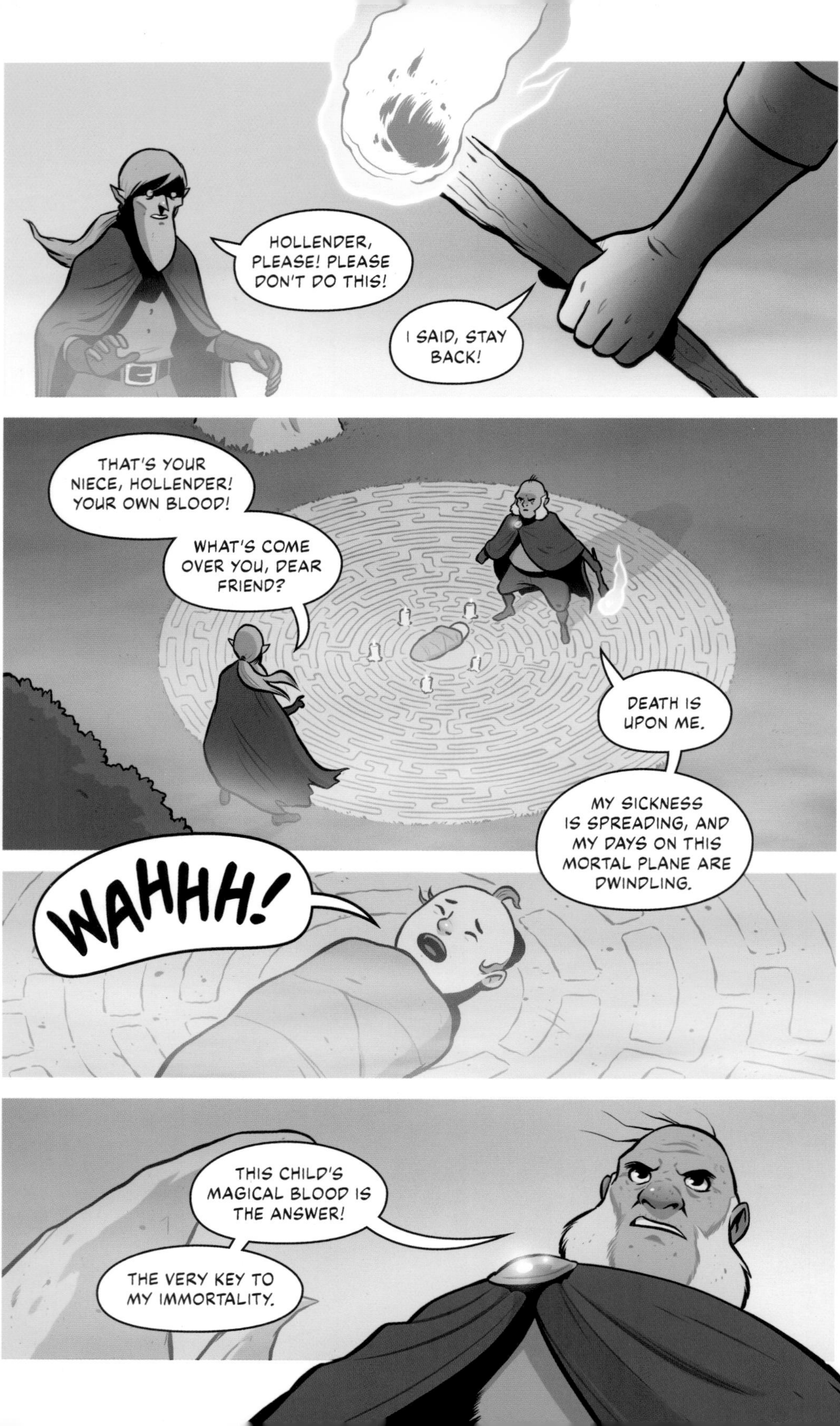
HOLLENDER, PLEASE! PLEASE DON'T DO THIS!
I SAID, STAY BACK!
THAT'S YOUR NIECE, HOLLENDER! YOUR OWN BLOOD!
WHAT'S COME OVER YOU, DEAR FRIEND?
DEATH IS UPON ME.
MY SICKNESS IS SPREADING, AND MY DAYS ON THIS MORTAL PLANE ARE DWINDLING.
WAHHH!
THIS CHILD'S MAGICAL BLOOD IS THE ANSWER!
THE VERY KEY TO MY IMMORTALITY.

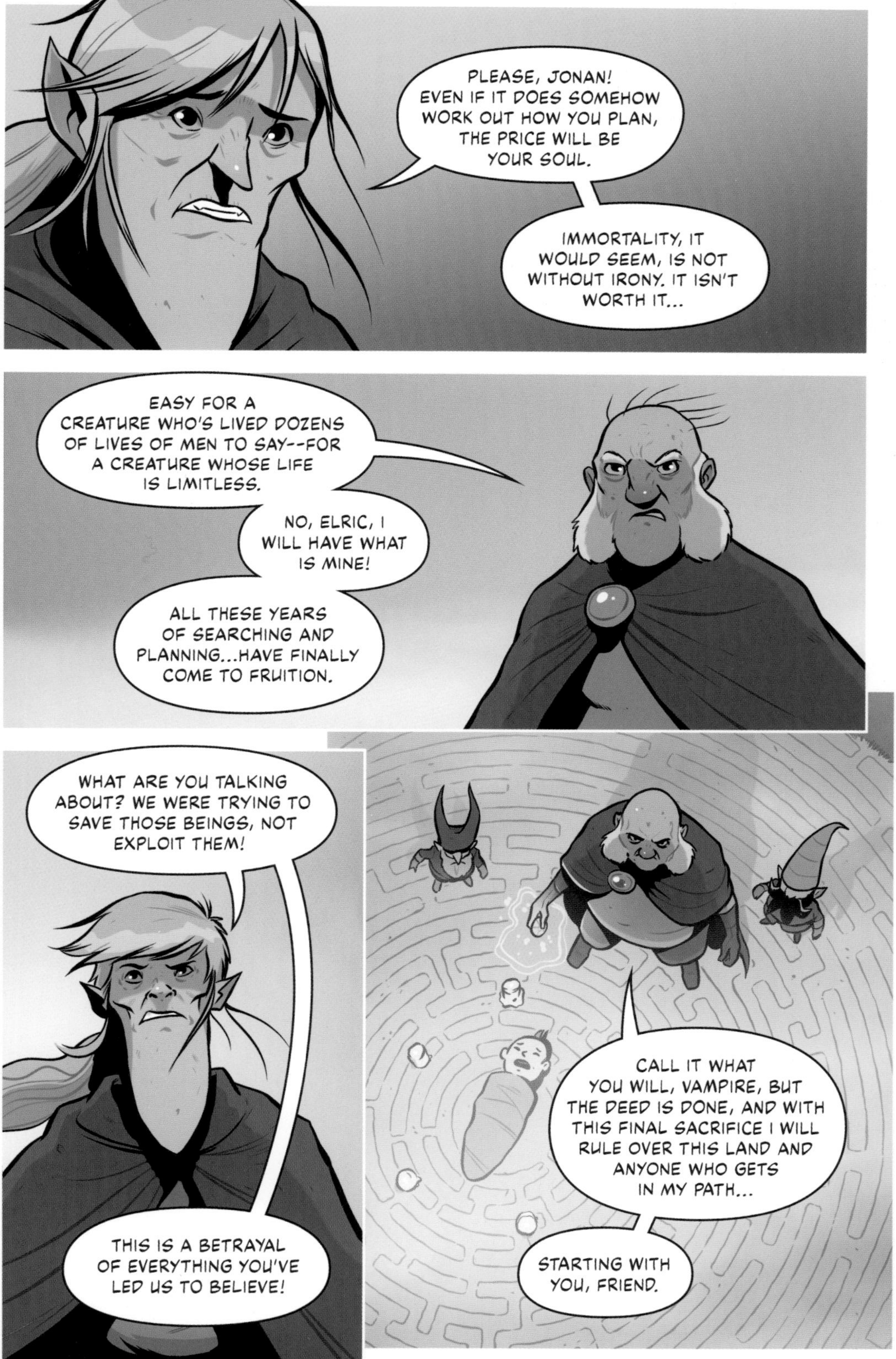
PLEASE, JONAN! EVEN IF IT DOES SOMEHOW WORK OUT HOW YOU PLAN, THE PRICE WILL BE YOUR SOUL.
IMMORTALITY, IT WOULD SEEM, IS NOT WITHOUT IRONY. IT ISN'T WORTH IT...
EASY FOR A CREATURE WHO'S LIVED DOZENS OF LIVES OF MEN TO SAY--FOR A CREATURE WHOSE LIFE IS LIMITLESS.
NO, ELRIC, I WILL HAVE WHAT IS MINE!
ALL THESE YEARS OF SEARCHING AND PLANNING...HAVE FINALLY COME TO FRUITION.
WHAT ARE YOU TALKING ABOUT? WE WERE TRYING TO SAVE THOSE BEINGS, NOT EXPLOIT THEM!
THIS IS A BETRAYAL OF EVERYTHING YOU'VE LED US TO BELIEVE!
CALL IT WHAT YOU WILL, VAMPIRE, BUT THE DEED IS DONE, AND WITH THIS FINAL SACRIFICE I WILL RULE OVER THIS LAND AND ANYONE WHO GETS IN MY PATH...
STARTING WITH YOU, FRIEND.

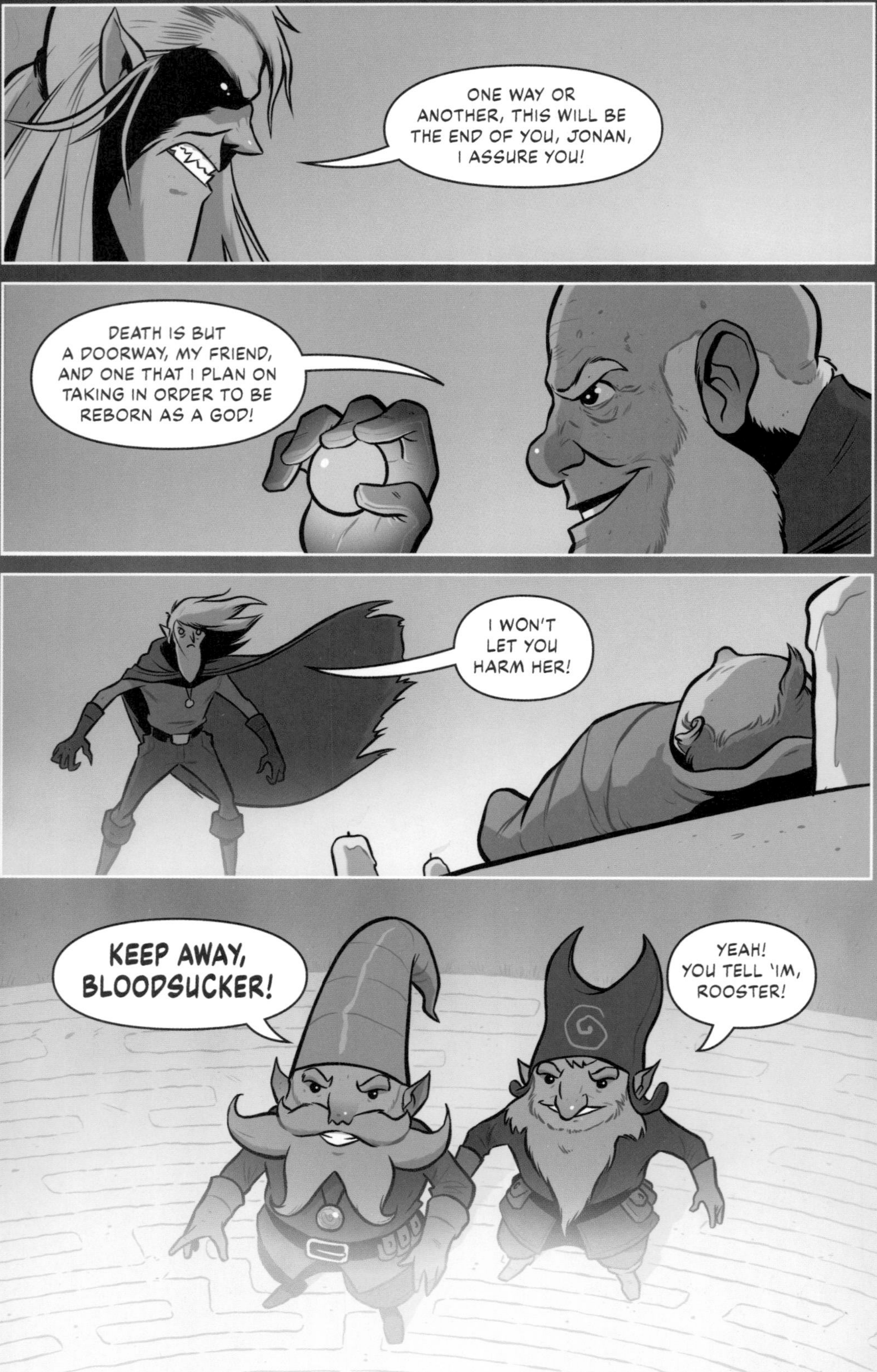
ONE WAY OR ANOTHER, THIS WILL BE THE END OF YOU, JONAN, I ASSURE YOU!
DEATH IS BUT A DOORWAY, MY FRIEND, AND ONE THAT I PLAN ON TAKING IN ORDER TO BE REBORN AS A GOD!
I WON'T LET YOU HARM HER!
KEEP AWAY, BLOODSUCKER!
YEAH! YOU TELL 'IM, ROOSTER!

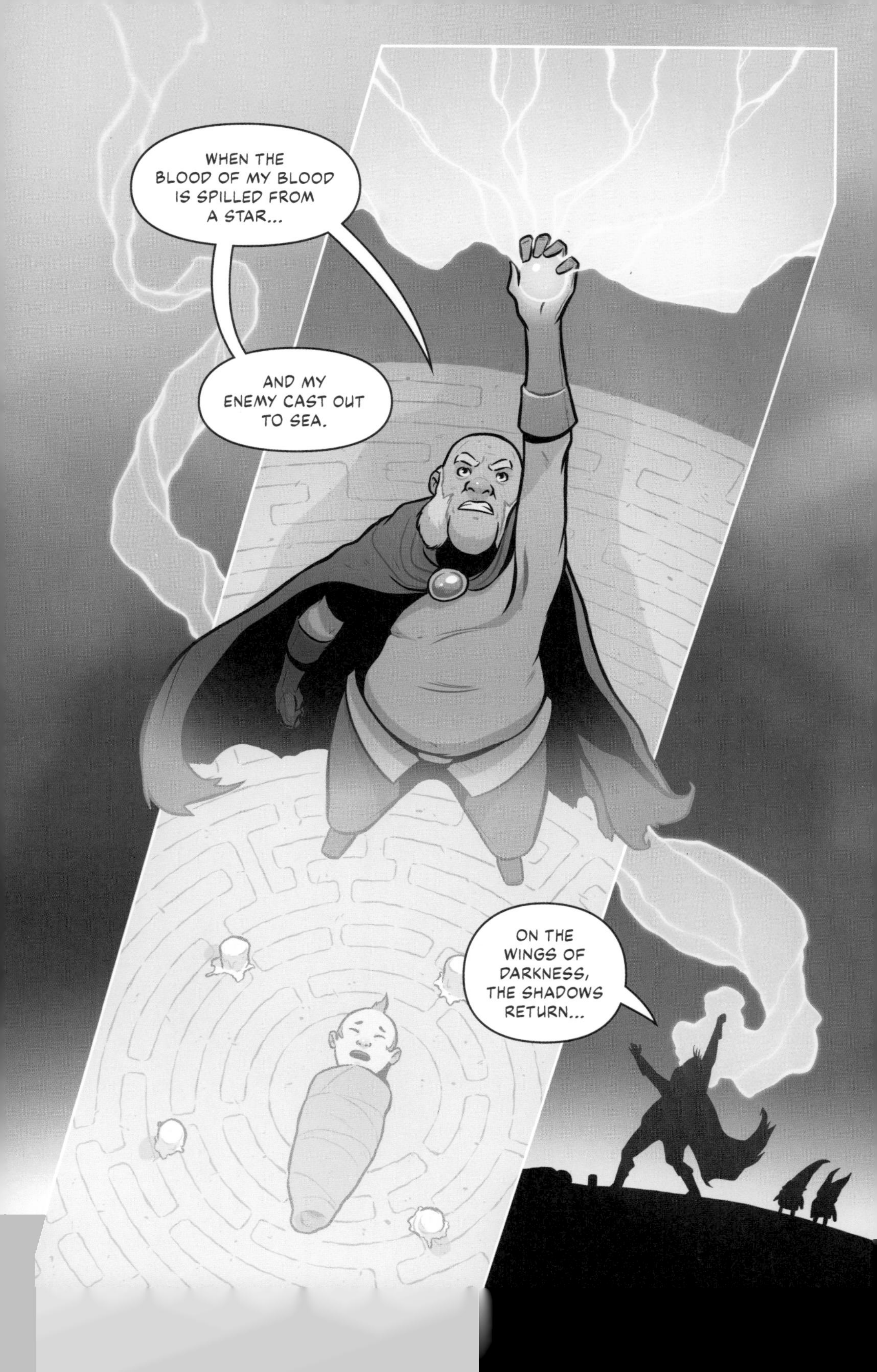
WHEN THE BLOOD OF MY BLOOD IS SPILLED FROM A STAR...
AND MY ENEMY CAST OUT TO SEA.
ON THE WINGS OF DARKNESS, THE SHADOWS RETURN...

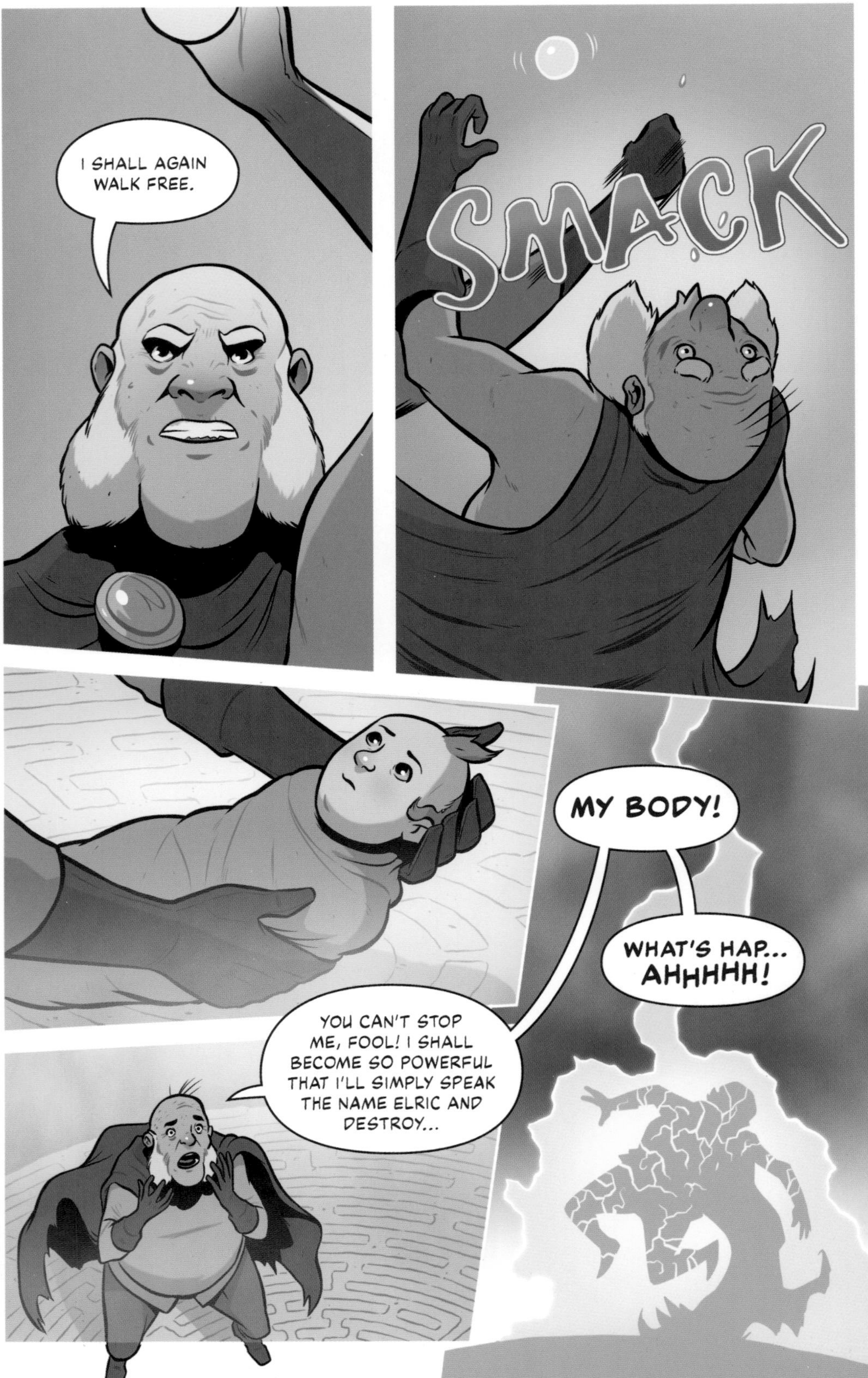
I SHALL AGAIN WALK FREE.
SMACK
MY BODY!
WHAT'S HAP... AHHHHH!
YOU CAN'T STOP ME, FOOL! I SHALL BECOME SO POWERFUL THAT I'LL SIMPLY SPEAK THE NAME ELRIC AND DESTROY...

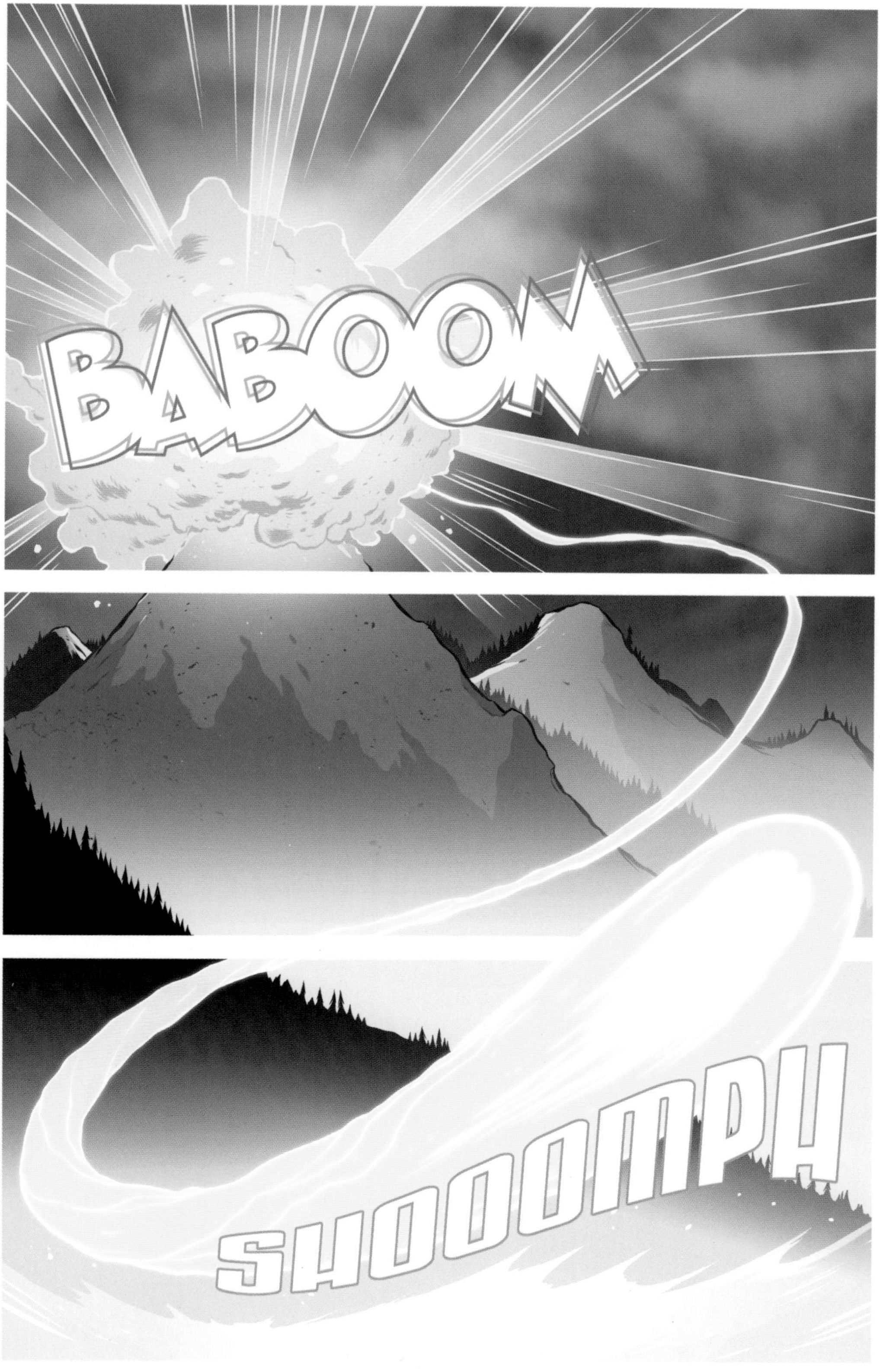
BABOOM
SHOOOMPH

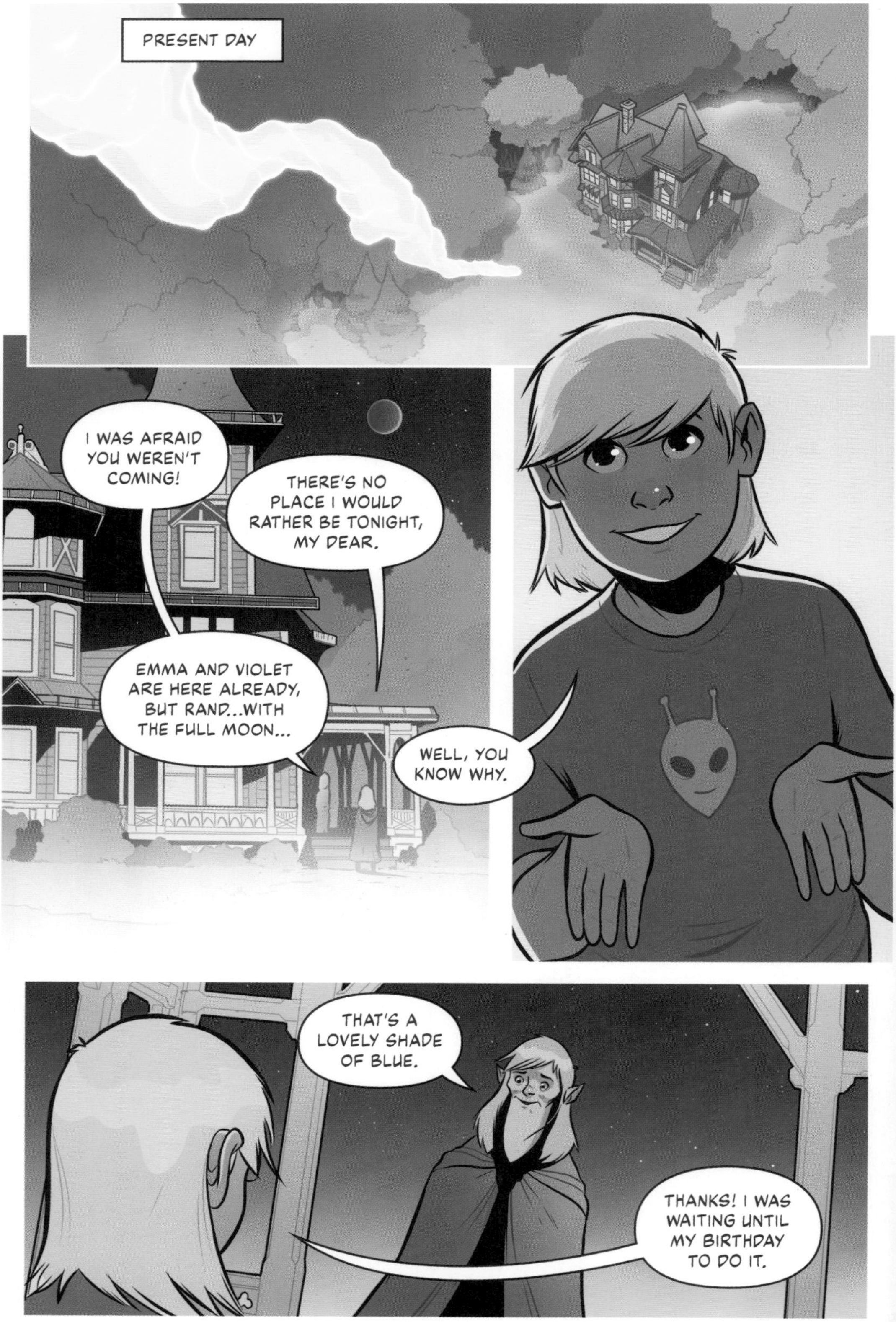
PRESENT DAY
I WAS AFRAID YOU WEREN'T COMING!
THERE'S NO PLACE I WOULD RATHER BE TONIGHT, MY DEAR.
EMMA AND VIOLET ARE HERE ALREADY, BUT RAND...WITH THE FULL MOON...
WELL, YOU KNOW WHY.
THAT'S A LOVELY SHADE OF BLUE.
THANKS! I WAS WAITING UNTIL MY BIRTHDAY TO DO IT.

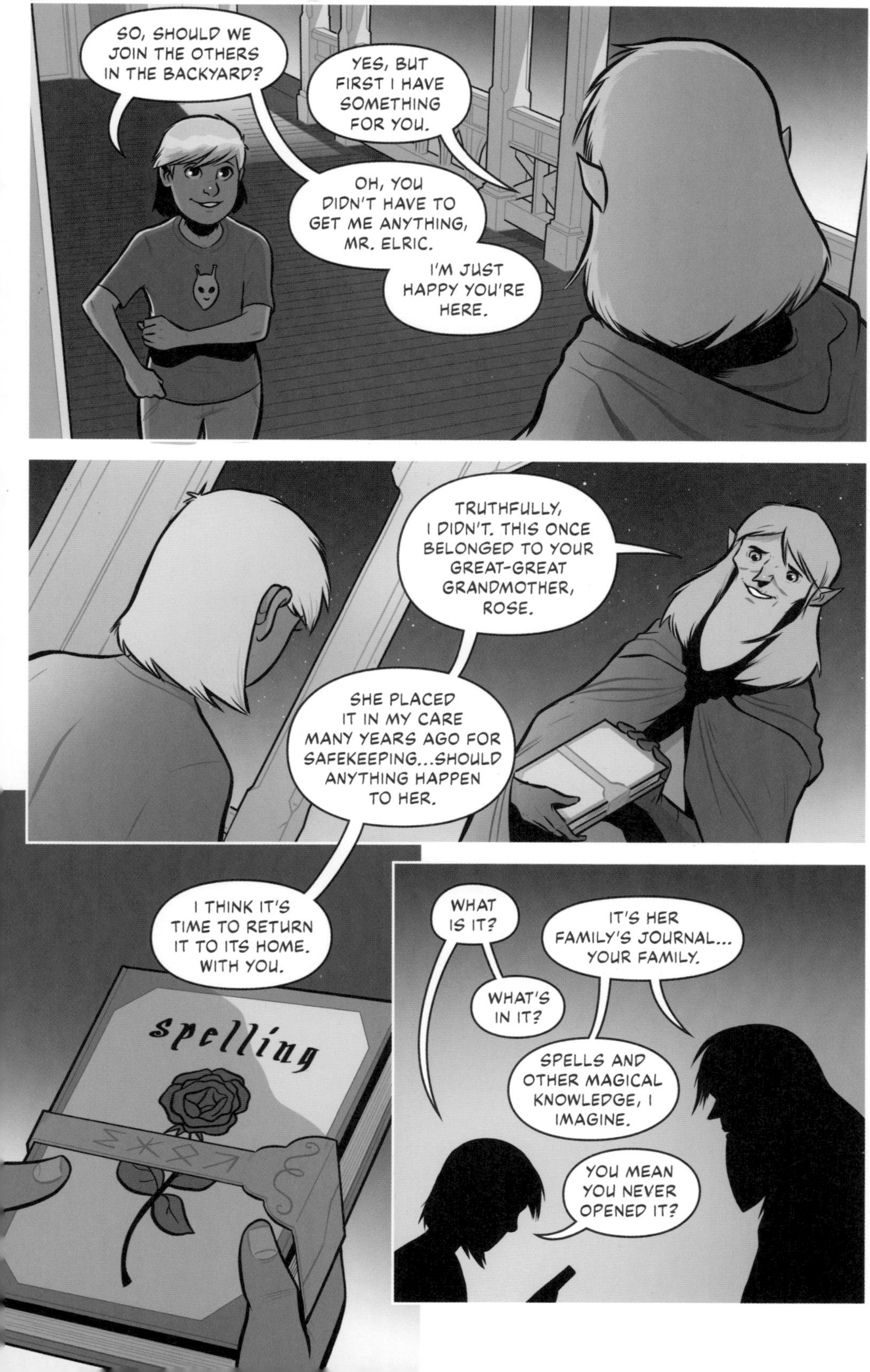
SO, SHOULD WE JOIN THE OTHERS IN THE BACKYARD?
YES, BUT FIRST I HAVE SOMETHING FOR YOU.
OH, YOU DIDN'T HAVE TO GET ME ANYTHING, MR. ELRIC.
I'M JUST HAPPY YOU'RE HERE.
TRUTHFULLY, I DIDN'T. THIS ONCE BELONGED TO YOUR GREAT-GREAT GRANDMOTHER, ROSE.
SHE PLACED IT IN MY CARE MANY YEARS AGO FOR SAFEKEEPING...SHOULD ANYTHING HAPPEN TO HER.
I THINK IT'S TIME TO RETURN IT TO ITS HOME. WITH YOU.
spelling
WHAT IS IT?
WHAT'S IN IT?
IT'S HER FAMILY'S JOURNAL... YOUR FAMILY.
SPELLS AND OTHER MAGICAL KNOWLEDGE, I IMAGINE.
YOU MEAN YOU NEVER OPENED IT?

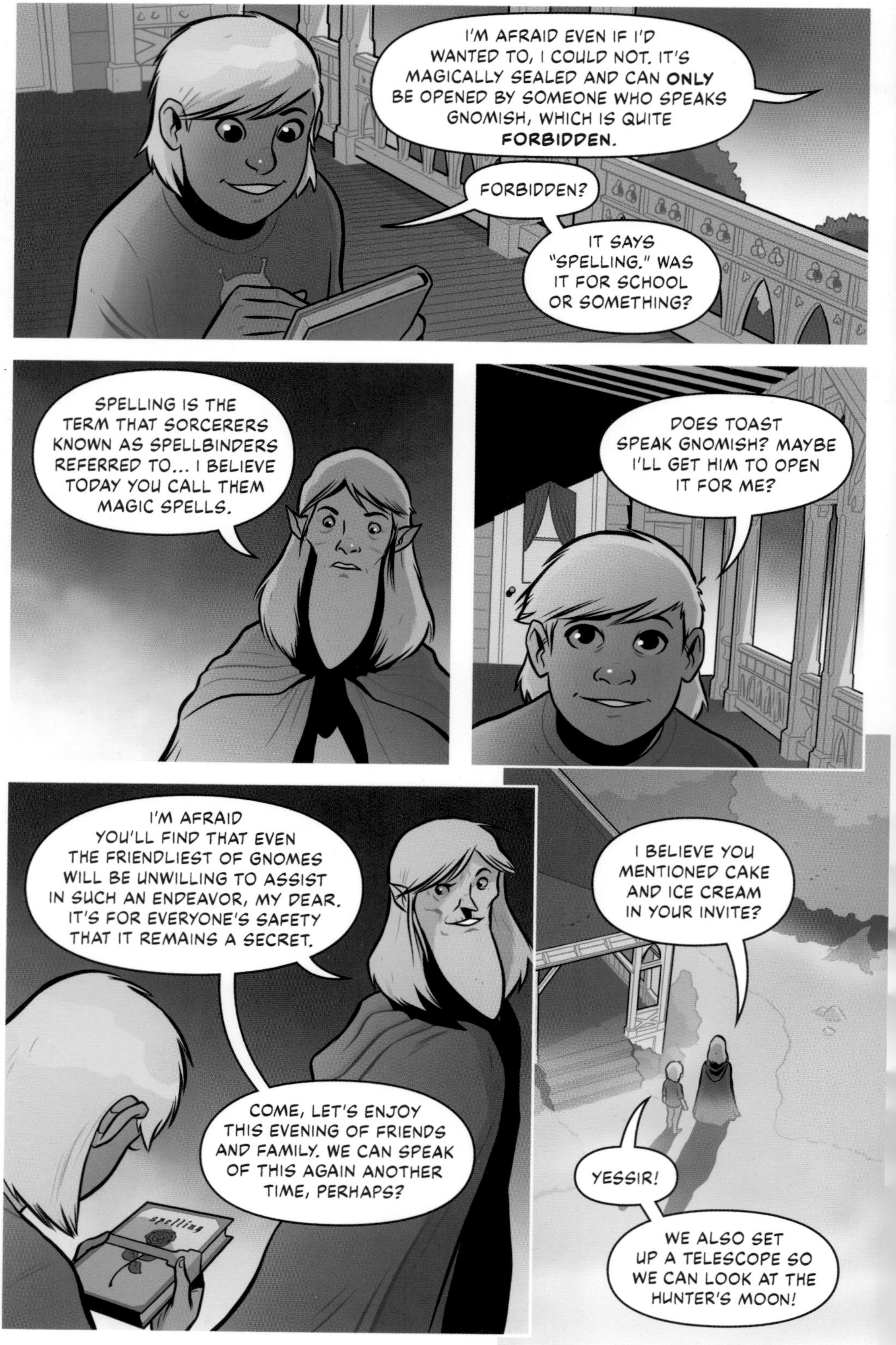
I'M AFRAID EVEN IF I'D WANTED TO, I COULD NOT. IT'S MAGICALLY SEALED AND CAN **ONLY** BE OPENED BY SOMEONE WHO SPEAKS GNOMISH, WHICH IS QUITE **FORBIDDEN.**
FORBIDDEN?
IT SAYS "SPELLING." WAS IT FOR SCHOOL OR SOMETHING?
SPELLING IS THE TERM THAT SORCERERS KNOWN AS SPELLBINDERS REFERRED TO... I BELIEVE TODAY YOU CALL THEM MAGIC SPELLS.
DOES TOAST SPEAK GNOMISH? MAYBE I'LL GET HIM TO OPEN IT FOR ME?
I'M AFRAID YOU'LL FIND THAT EVEN THE FRIENDLIEST OF GNOMES WILL BE UNWILLING TO ASSIST IN SUCH AN ENDEAVOR, MY DEAR. IT'S FOR EVERYONE'S SAFETY THAT IT REMAINS A SECRET.
COME, LET'S ENJOY THIS EVENING OF FRIENDS AND FAMILY. WE CAN SPEAK OF THIS AGAIN ANOTHER TIME, PERHAPS?
spelling
I BELIEVE YOU MENTIONED CAKE AND ICE CREAM IN YOUR INVITE?
YESSIR!
WE ALSO SET UP A TELESCOPE SO WE CAN LOOK AT THE HUNTER'S MOON!

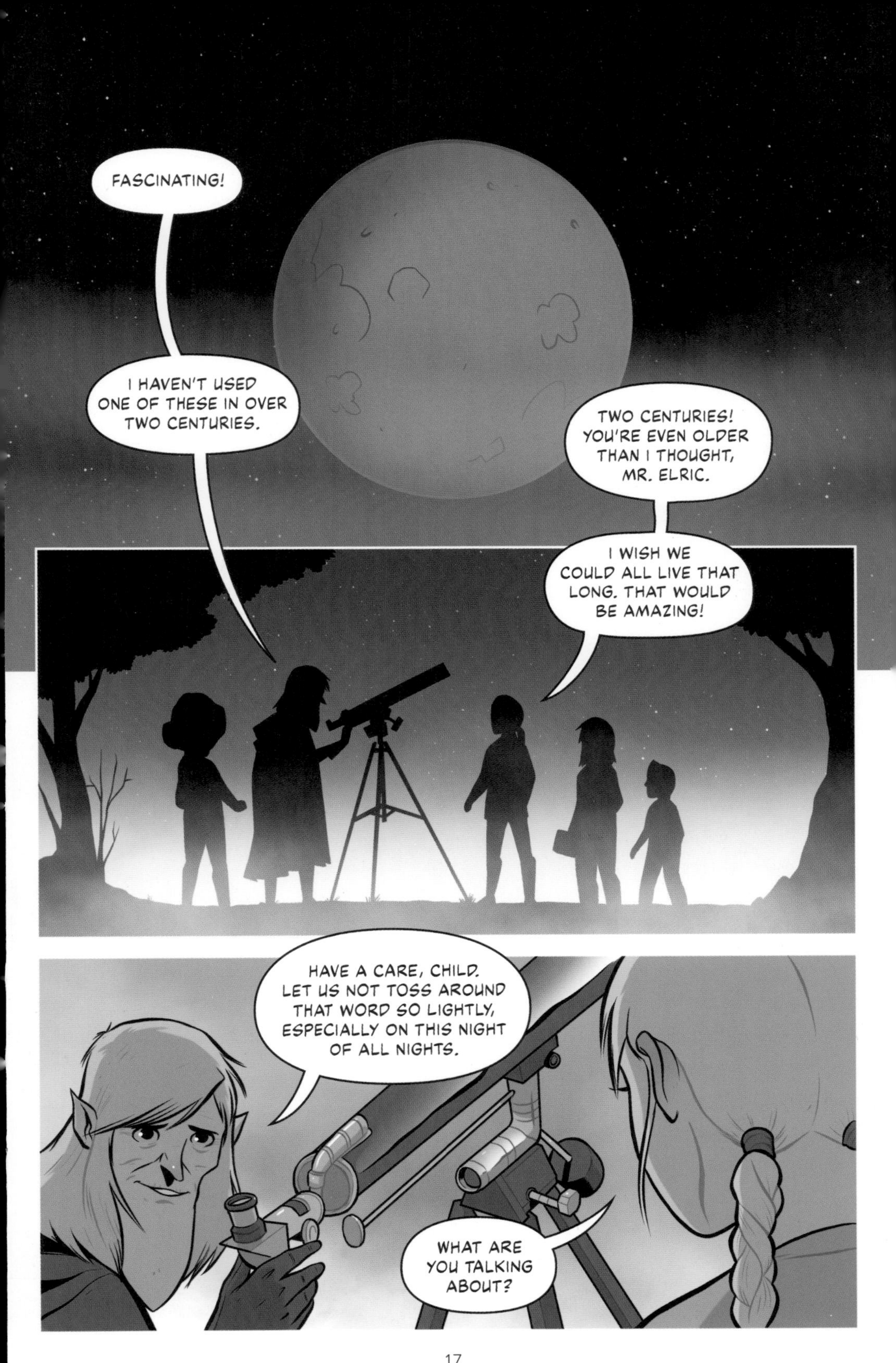
FASCINATING!
I HAVEN'T USED ONE OF THESE IN OVER TWO CENTURIES.
TWO CENTURIES! YOU'RE EVEN OLDER THAN I THOUGHT, MR. ELRIC.
I WISH WE COULD ALL LIVE THAT LONG. THAT WOULD BE AMAZING!
HAVE A CARE, CHILD. LET US NOT TOSS AROUND THAT WORD SO LIGHTLY, ESPECIALLY ON THIS NIGHT OF ALL NIGHTS.
WHAT ARE YOU TALKING ABOUT?

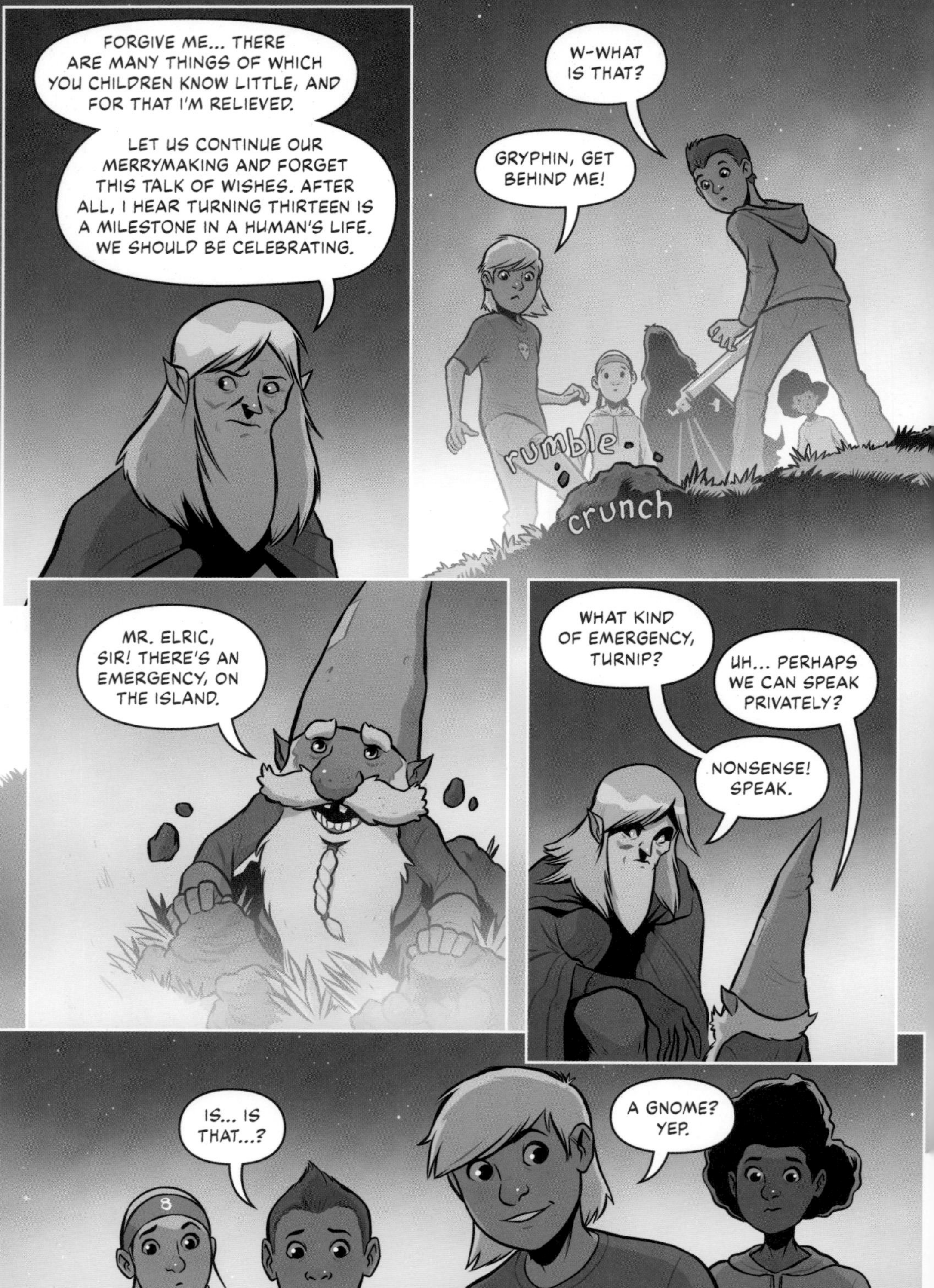
FORGIVE ME... THERE ARE MANY THINGS OF WHICH YOU CHILDREN KNOW LITTLE, AND FOR THAT I'M RELIEVED.
LET US CONTINUE OUR MERRYMAKING AND FORGET THIS TALK OF WISHES. AFTER ALL, I HEAR TURNING THIRTEEN IS A MILESTONE IN A HUMAN'S LIFE. WE SHOULD BE CELEBRATING.
W-WHAT IS THAT?
GRYPHIN, GET BEHIND ME!
rumble
crunch
MR. ELRIC, SIR! THERE'S AN EMERGENCY, ON THE ISLAND.
WHAT KIND OF EMERGENCY, TURNIP?
UH... PERHAPS WE CAN SPEAK PRIVATELY?
NONSENSE! SPEAK.
IS... IS THAT...?
A GNOME? YEP.

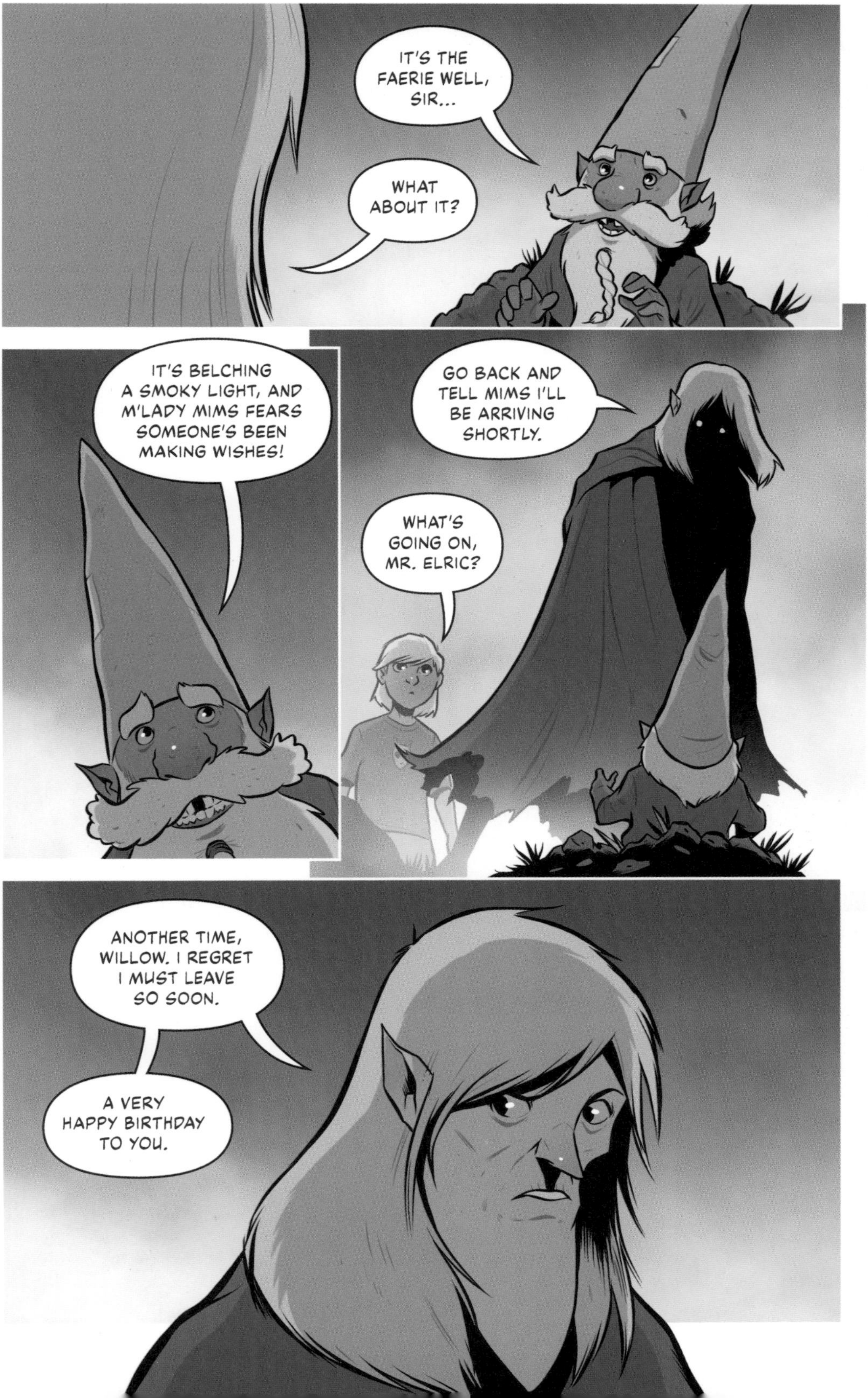
IT'S THE FAERIE WELL, SIR...
WHAT ABOUT IT?
IT'S BELCHING A SMOKY LIGHT, AND M'LADY MIMS FEARS SOMEONE'S BEEN MAKING WISHES!
GO BACK AND TELL MIMS I'LL BE ARRIVING SHORTLY.
WHAT'S GOING ON, MR. ELRIC?
ANOTHER TIME, WILLOW. I REGRET I MUST LEAVE SO SOON.
A VERY HAPPY BIRTHDAY TO YOU.

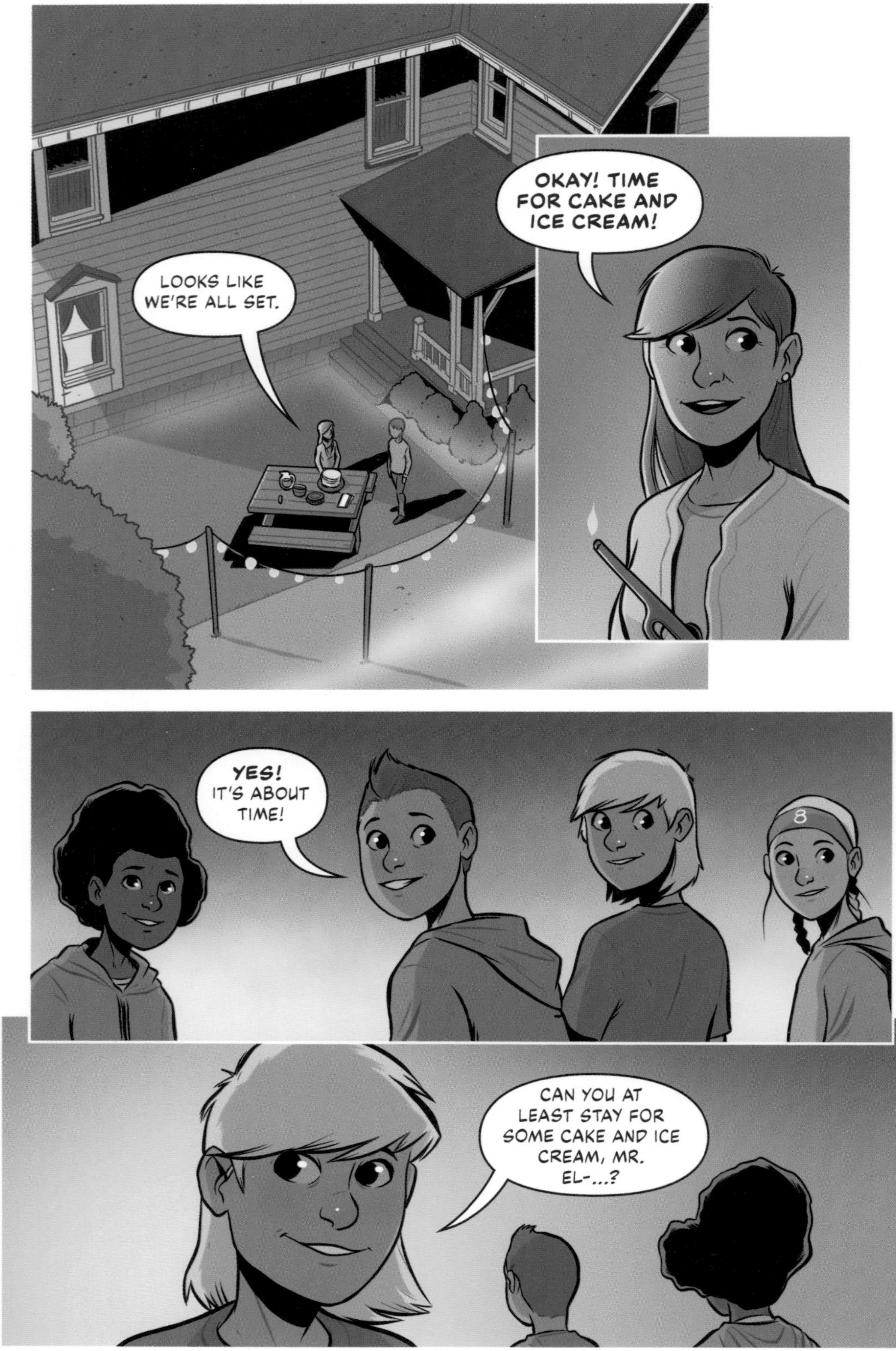
LOOKS LIKE WE'RE ALL SET.
OKAY! TIME FOR CAKE AND ICE CREAM!
YES! IT'S ABOUT TIME!
8
CAN YOU AT LEAST STAY FOR SOME CAKE AND ICE CREAM, MR. EL-...?

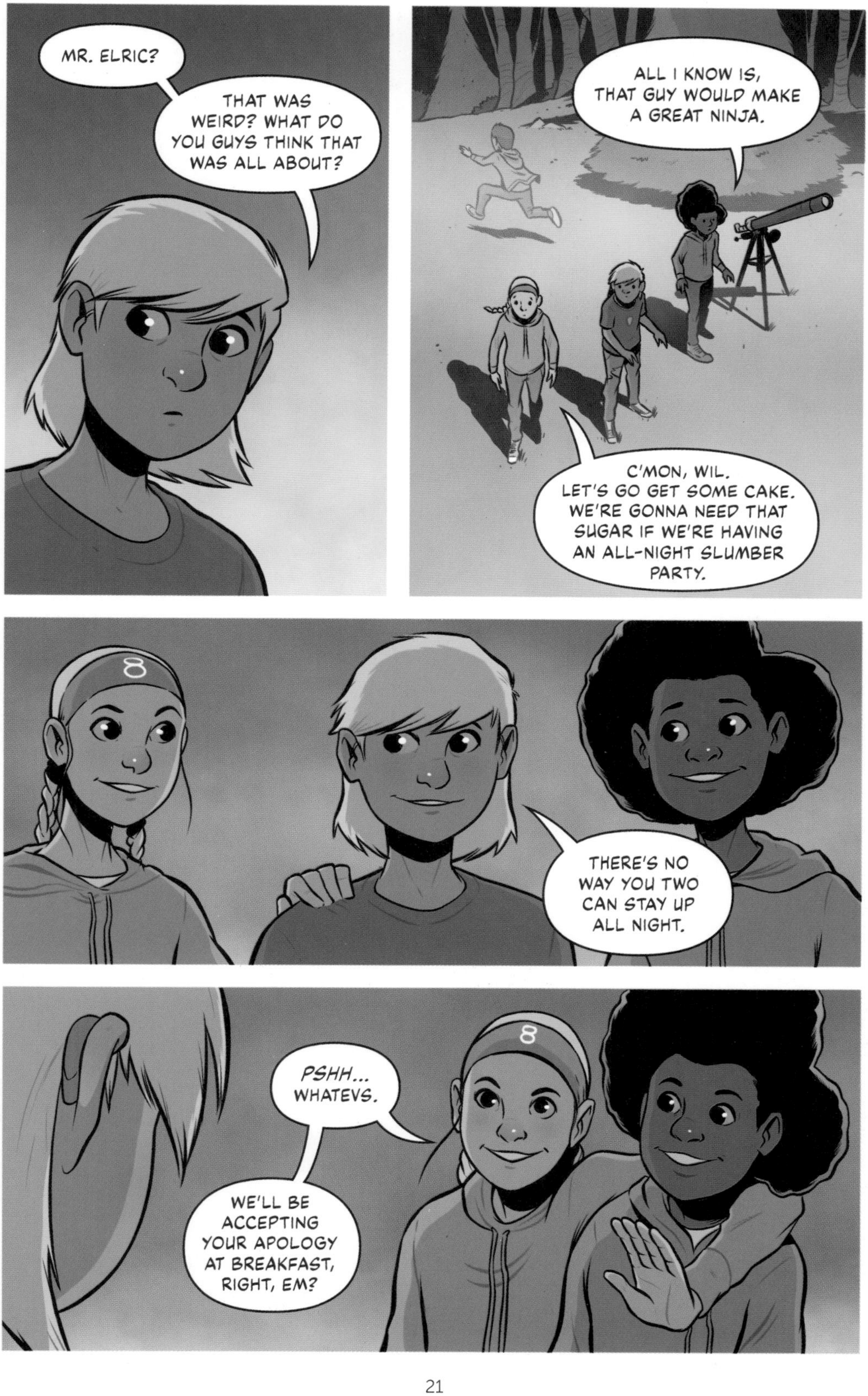
MR. ELRIC?
THAT WAS WEIRD? WHAT DO YOU GUYS THINK THAT WAS ALL ABOUT?
ALL I KNOW IS, THAT GUY WOULD MAKE A GREAT NINJA.
C'MON, WIL. LET'S GO GET SOME CAKE. WE'RE GONNA NEED THAT SUGAR IF WE'RE HAVING AN ALL-NIGHT SLUMBER PARTY.
THERE'S NO WAY YOU TWO CAN STAY UP ALL NIGHT.
PSHH... WHATEVS.
WE'LL BE ACCEPTING YOUR APOLOGY AT BREAKFAST, RIGHT, EM?

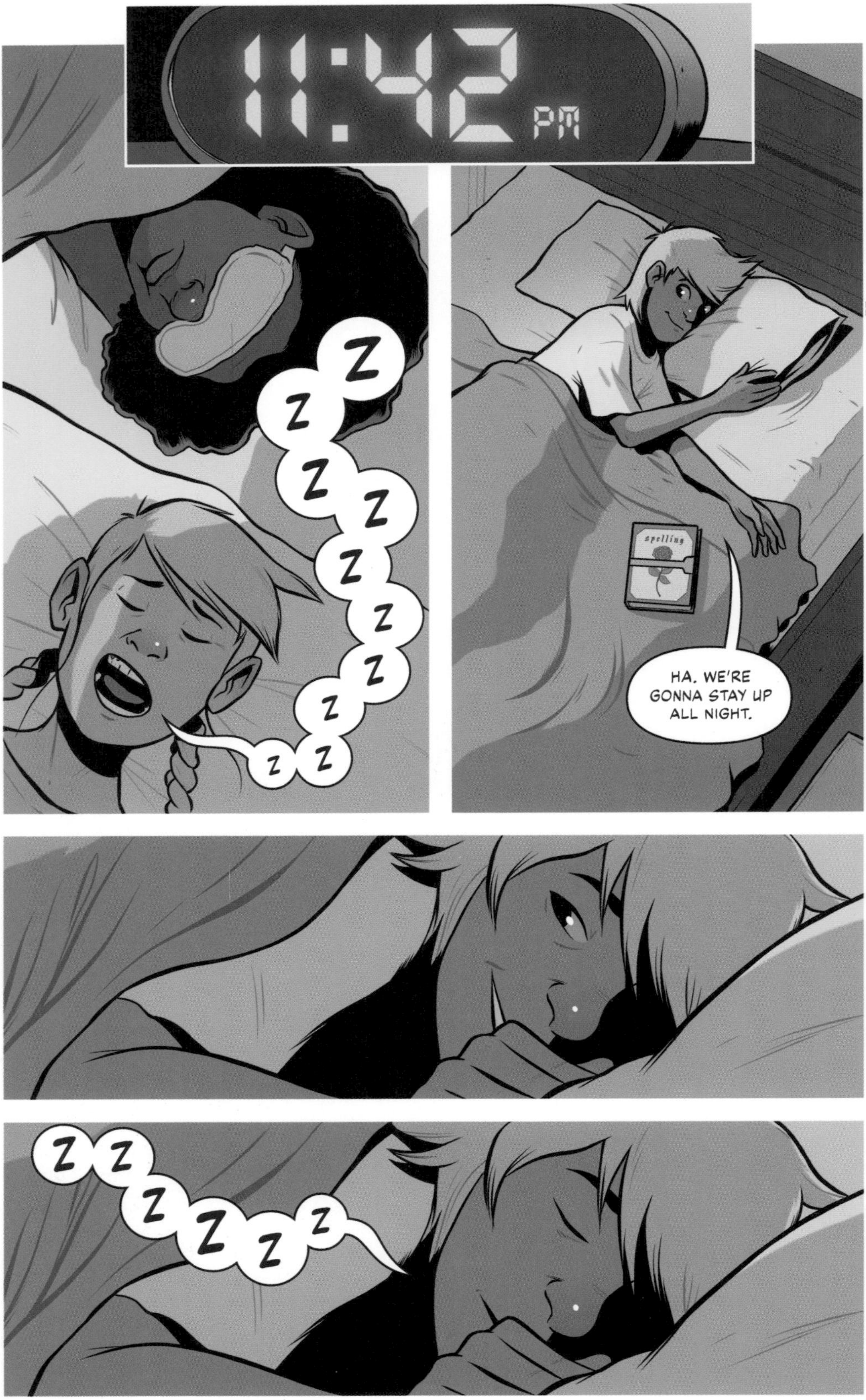
11:42 PM
Z Z Z Z Z Z Z Z Z Z
spelling
HA. WE'RE GONNA STAY UP ALL NIGHT.
Z Z Z Z Z Z Z

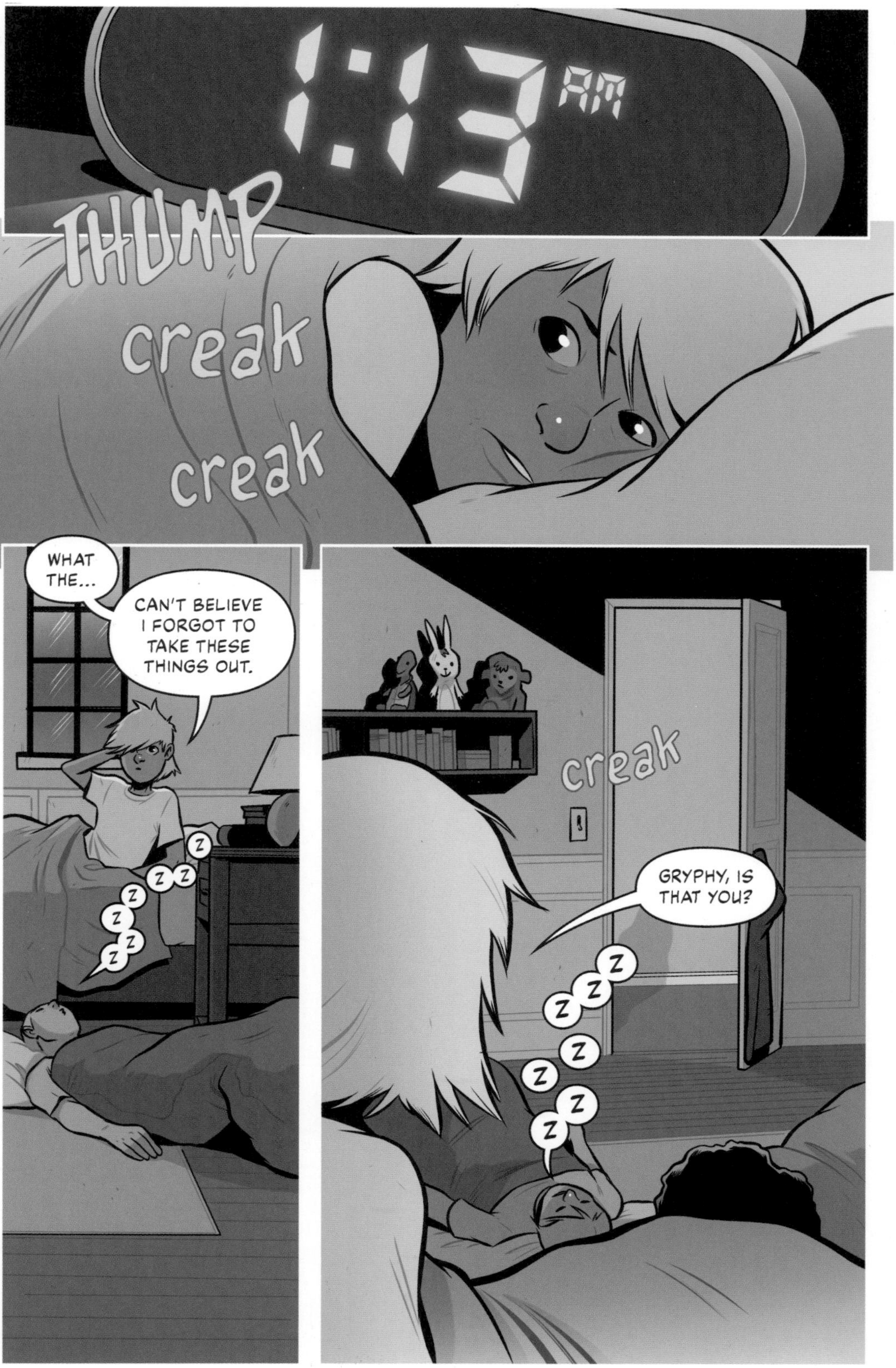
1:13 AM
THUMP
creak
creak
WHAT THE...
CAN'T BELIEVE I FORGOT TO TAKE THESE THINGS OUT.
creak
GRYPHY, IS THAT YOU?

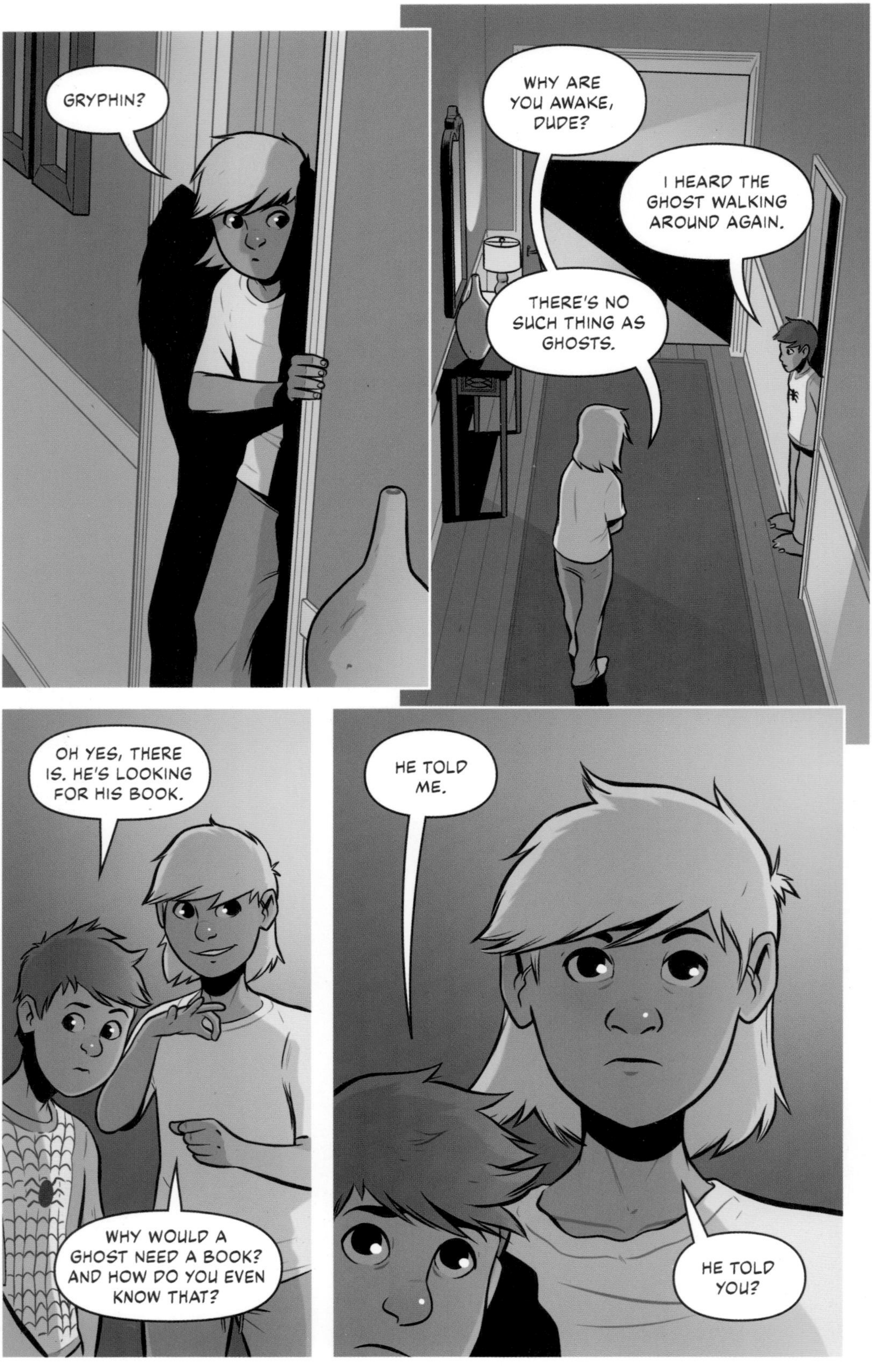
GRYPHIN?
WHY ARE YOU AWAKE, DUDE?
I HEARD THE GHOST WALKING AROUND AGAIN.
THERE'S NO SUCH THING AS GHOSTS.
OH YES, THERE IS. HE'S LOOKING FOR HIS BOOK.
WHY WOULD A GHOST NEED A BOOK? AND HOW DO YOU EVEN KNOW THAT?
HE TOLD ME.
HE TOLD YOU?

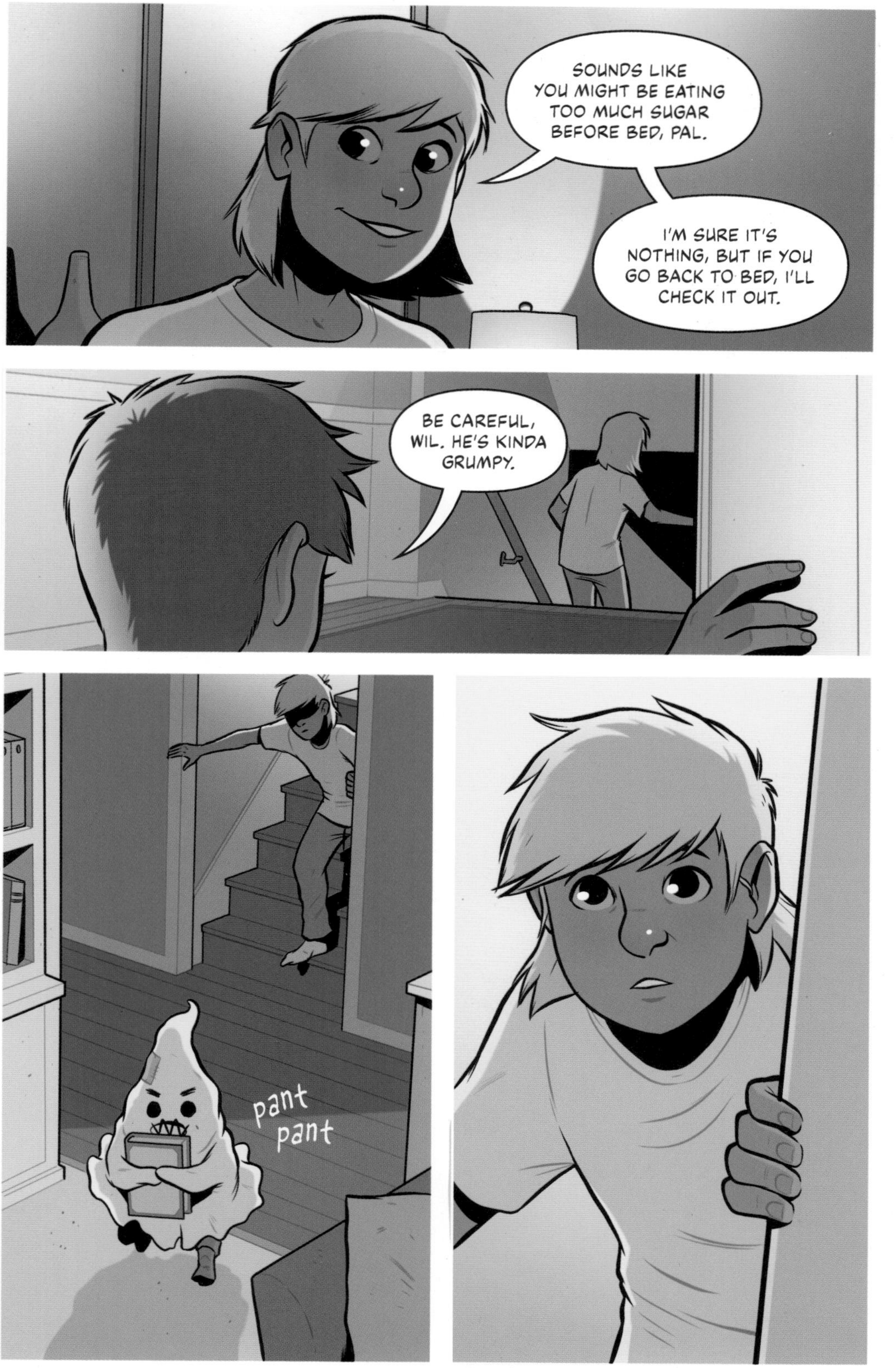
SOUNDS LIKE YOU MIGHT BE EATING TOO MUCH SUGAR BEFORE BED, PAL.
I'M SURE IT'S NOTHING, BUT IF YOU GO BACK TO BED, I'LL CHECK IT OUT.
BE CAREFUL, WIL. HE'S KINDA GRUMPY.
pant pant

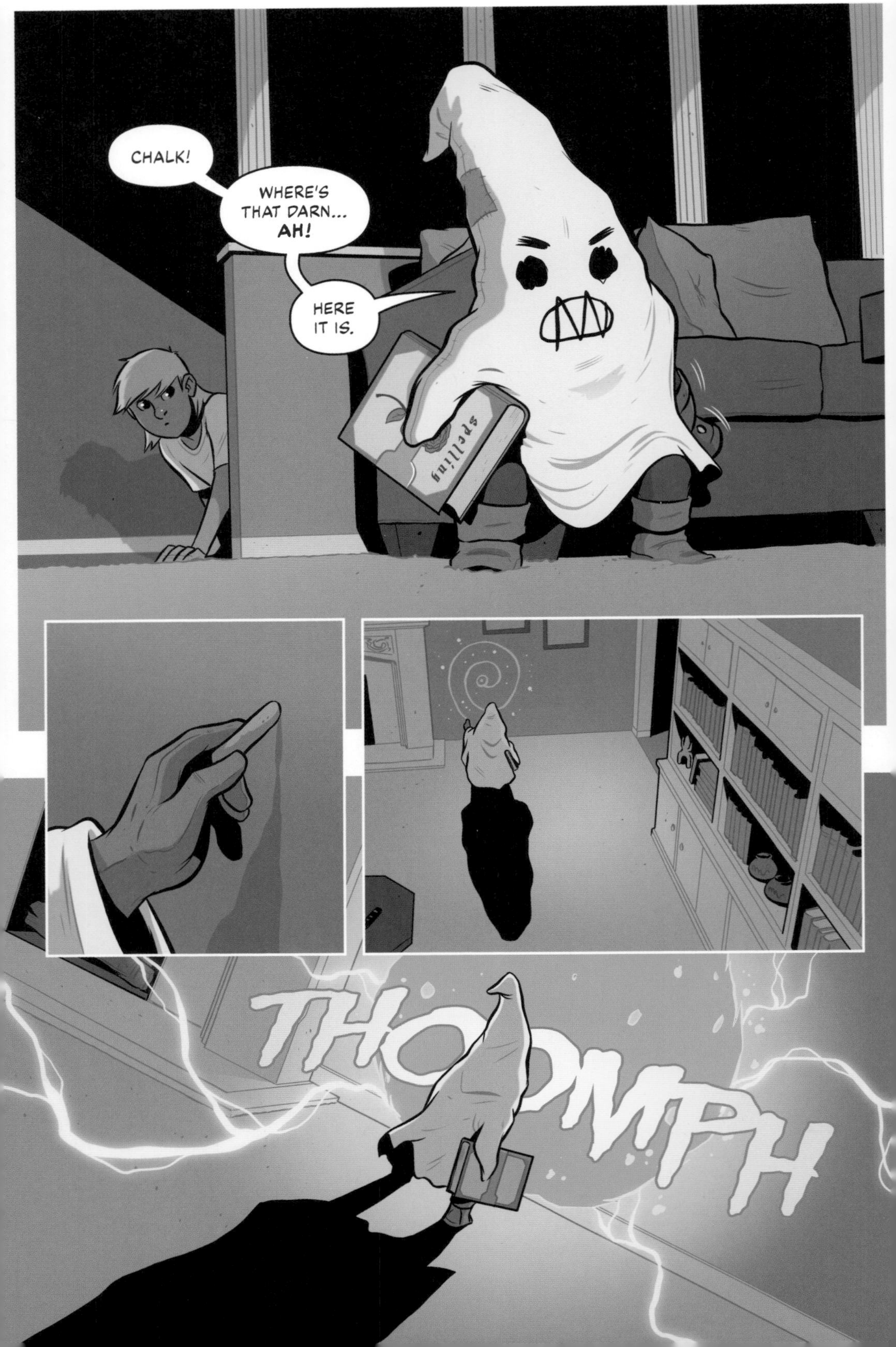
CHALK!
WHERE'S THAT DARN... AH!
HERE IT IS.
spelling
THOOMPH

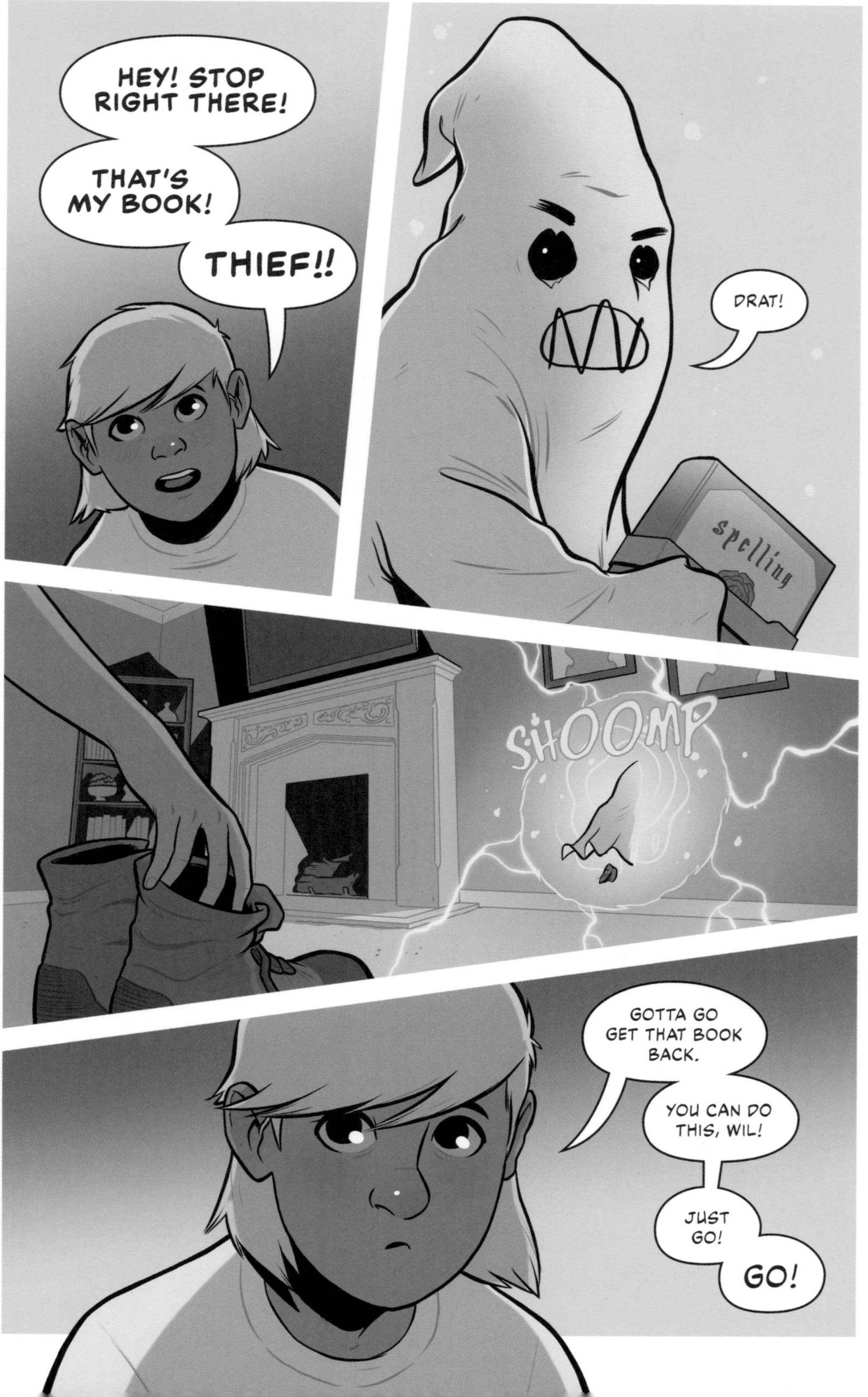
HEY! STOP RIGHT THERE!
THAT'S MY BOOK!
THIEF!!
DRAT!
Spelling
SHOOMP
GOTTA GO GET THAT BOOK BACK.
YOU CAN DO THIS, WIL!
JUST GO!
GO!

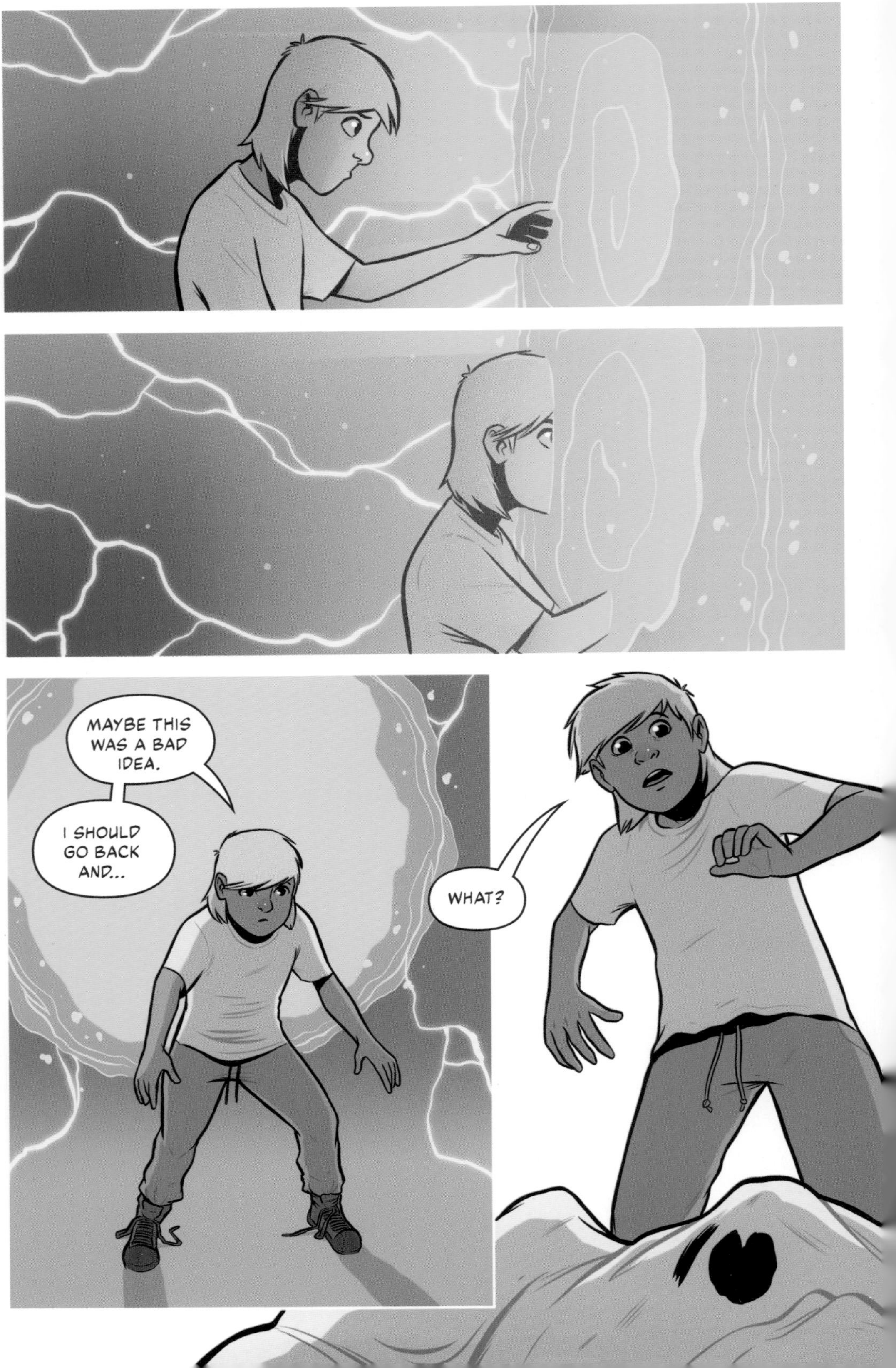
MAYBE THIS WAS A BAD IDEA.
I SHOULD GO BACK AND...
WHAT?

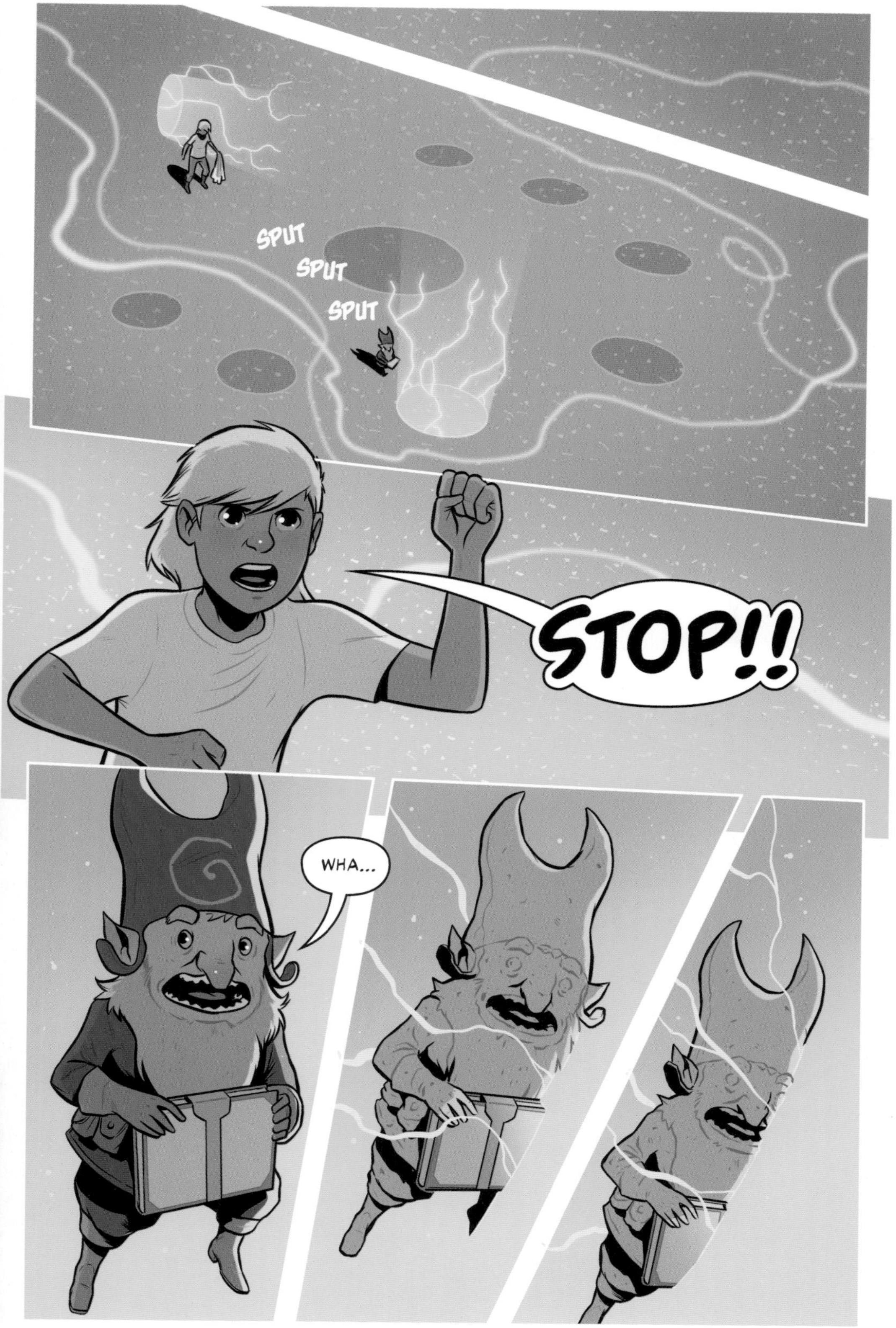
SPUT
SPUT
SPUT
STOP!!
WHA...

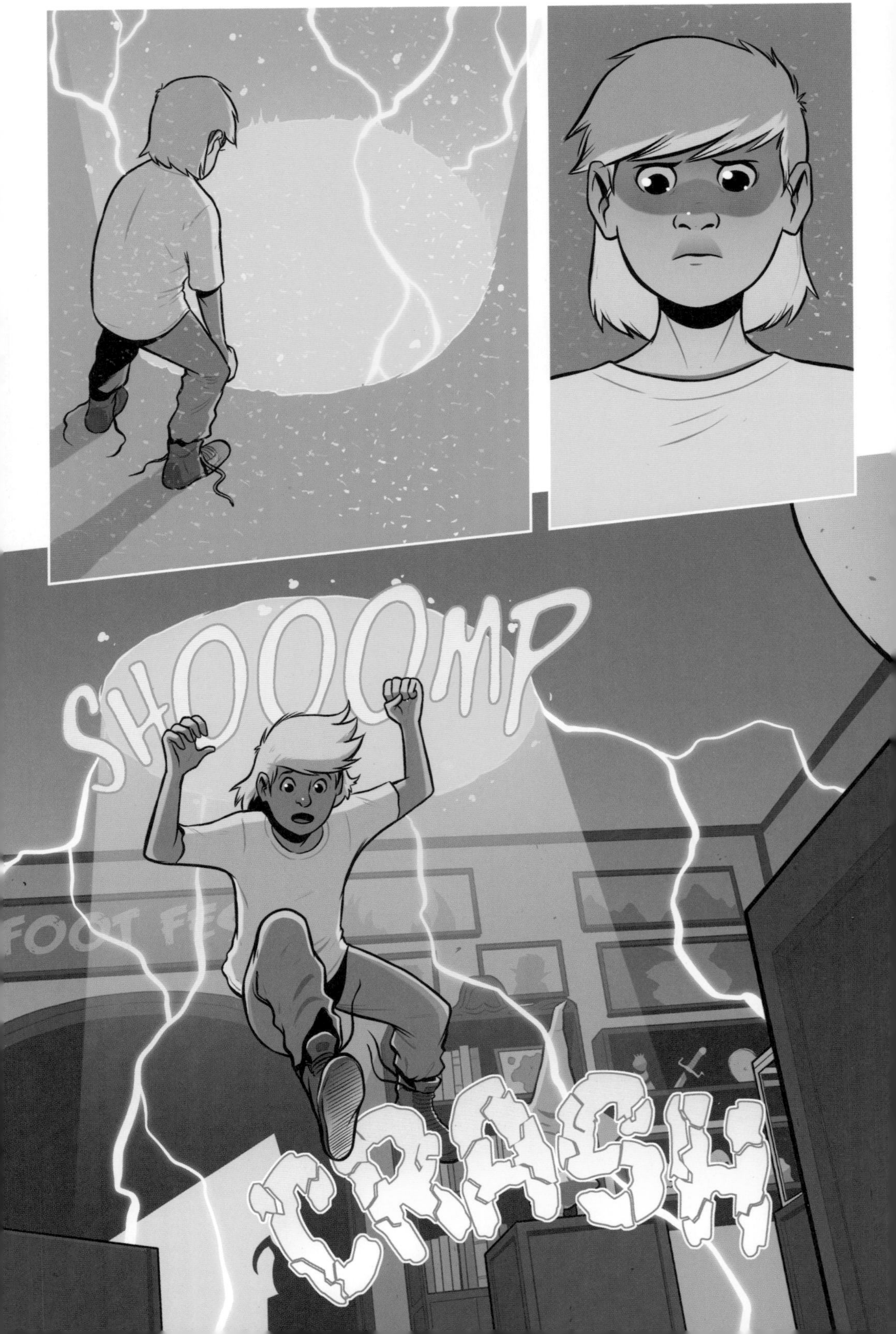
SHOOOMP
FOOT FE
CRASH

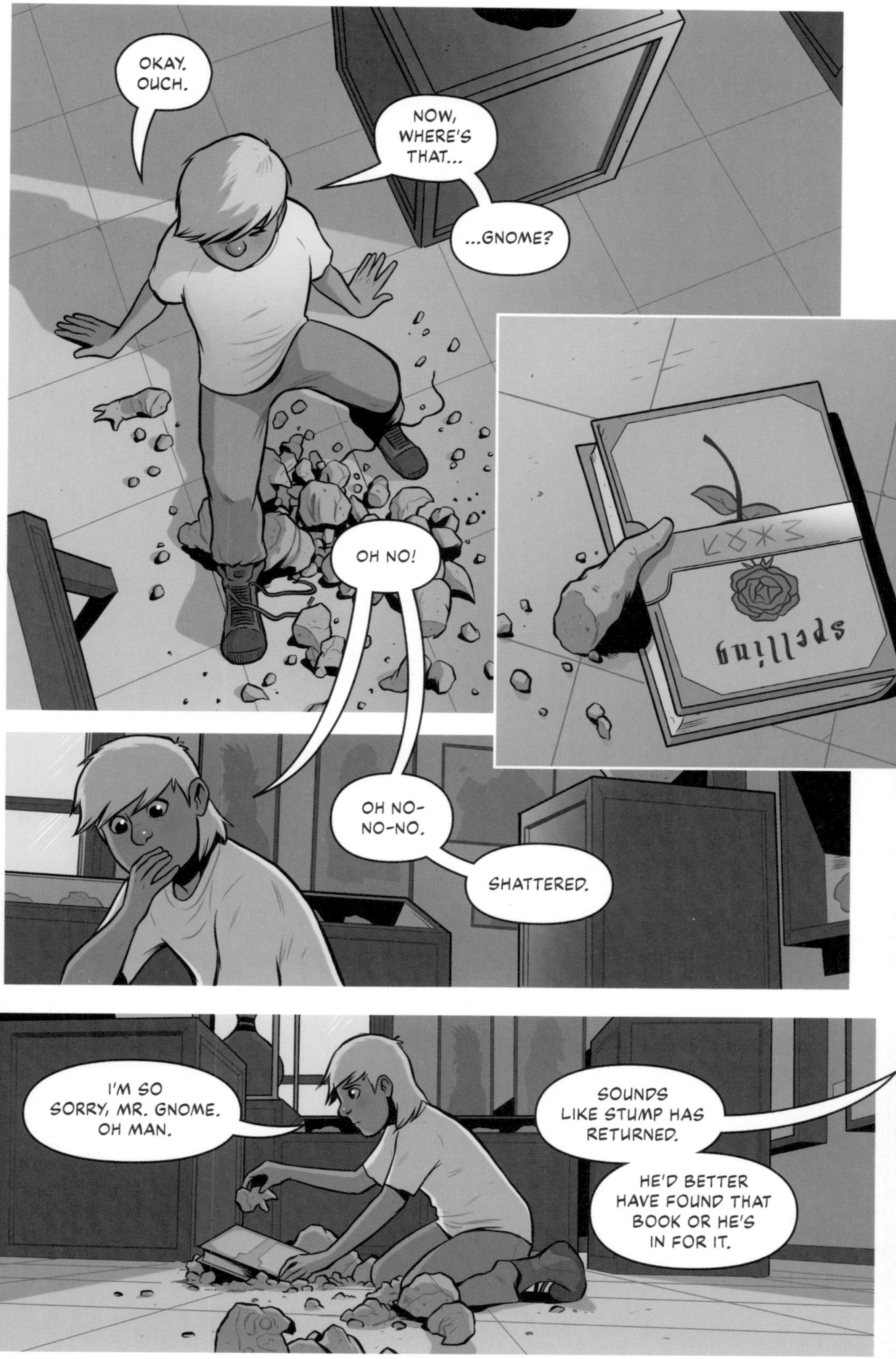
OKAY. OUCH.
NOW, WHERE'S THAT...
...GNOME?
spelling
OH NO!
OH NO-NO-NO.
SHATTERED.
I'M SO SORRY, MR. GNOME. OH MAN.
SOUNDS LIKE STUMP HAS RETURNED.
HE'D BETTER HAVE FOUND THAT BOOK OR HE'S IN FOR IT.

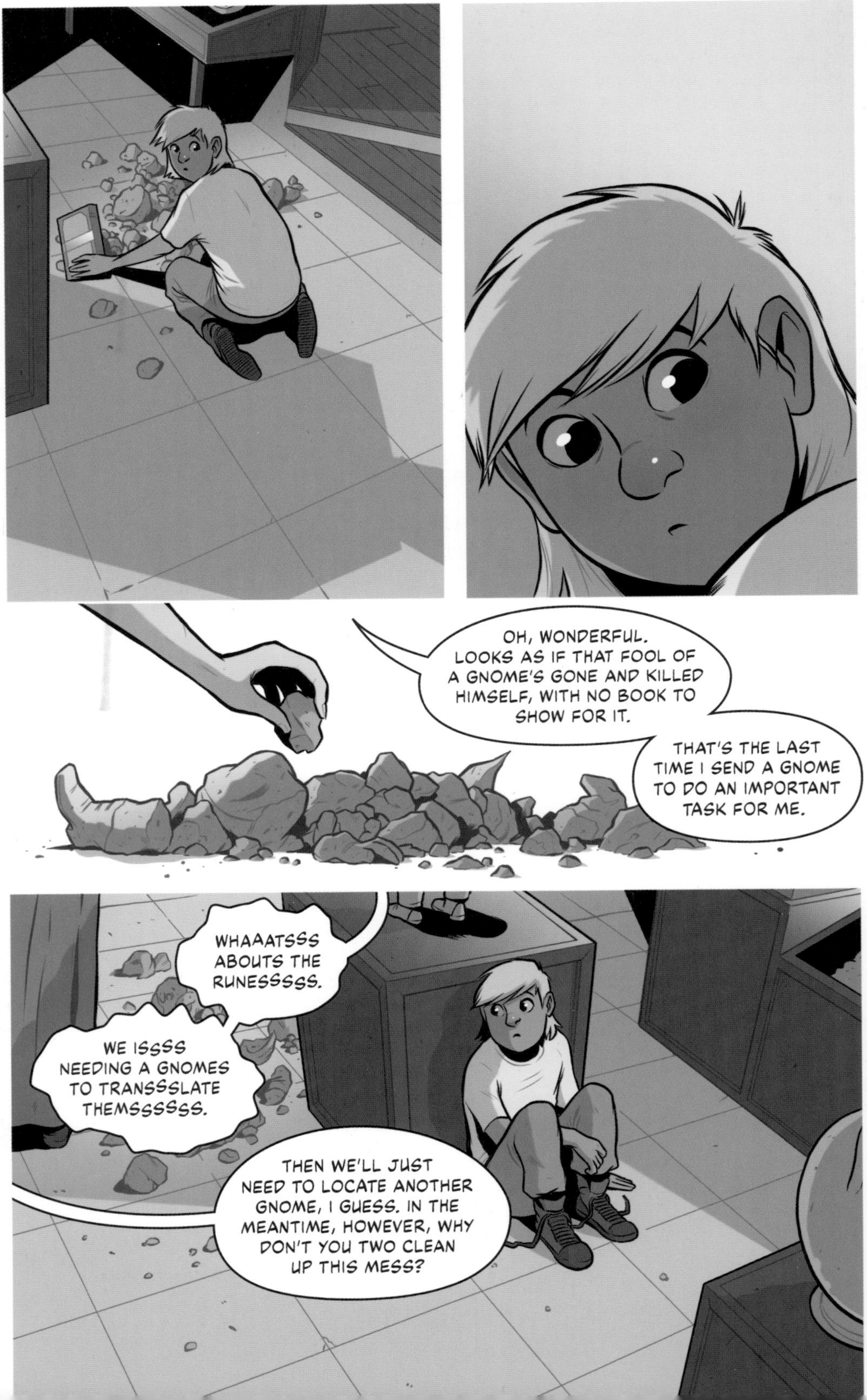
OH, WONDERFUL. LOOKS AS IF THAT FOOL OF A GNOME'S GONE AND KILLED HIMSELF, WITH NO BOOK TO SHOW FOR IT.
THAT'S THE LAST TIME I SEND A GNOME TO DO AN IMPORTANT TASK FOR ME.
WHAAATSSS ABOUTS THE RUNESSSSS.
WE ISSSS NEEDING A GNOMES TO TRANSSSLATE THEMSSSSSS.
THEN WE'LL JUST NEED TO LOCATE ANOTHER GNOME, I GUESS. IN THE MEANTIME, HOWEVER, WHY DON'T YOU TWO CLEAN UP THIS MESS?

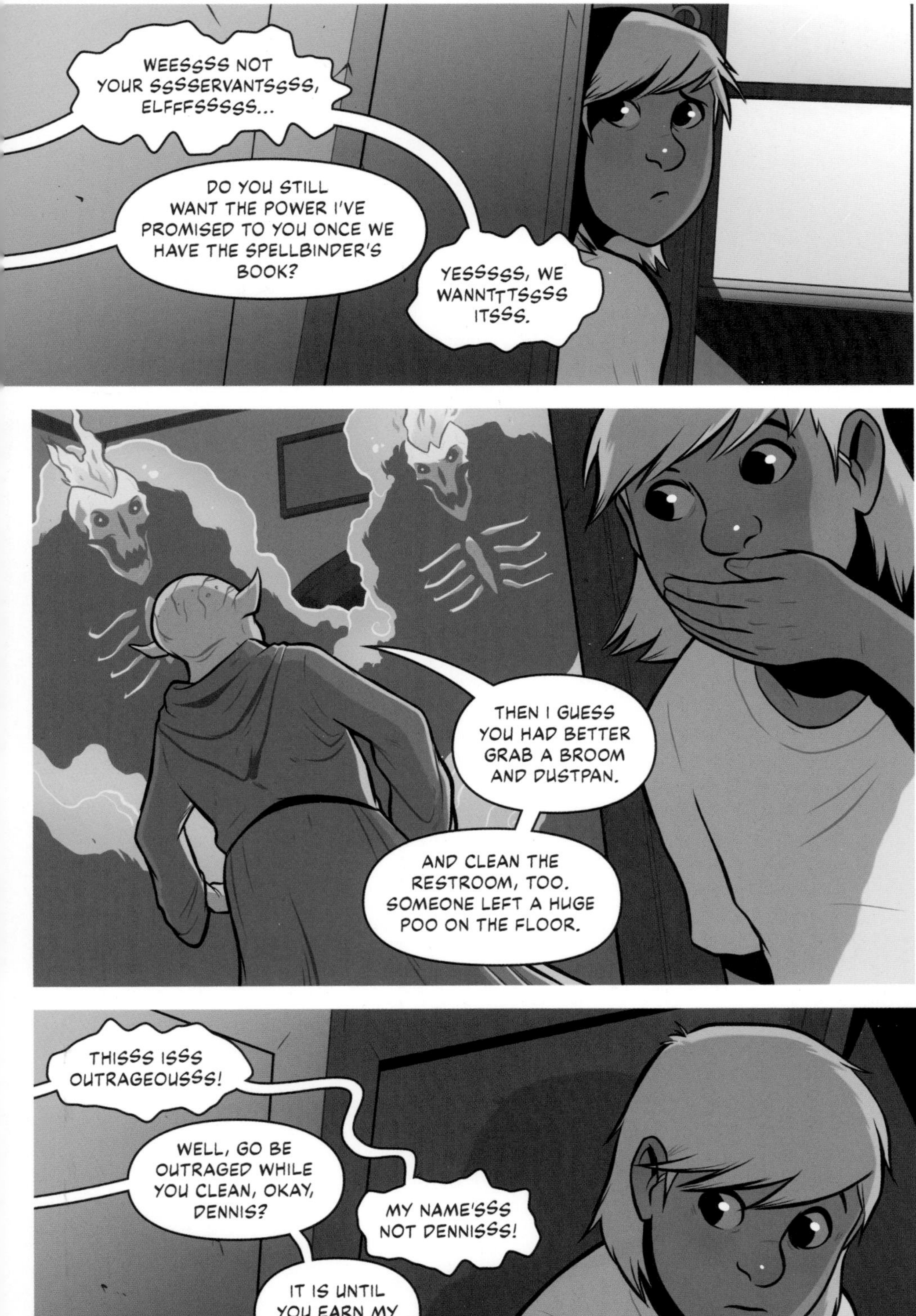
WEESSSS NOT YOUR SSSSERVANTSSSS, ELFFFSSSSS...
DO YOU STILL WANT THE POWER I'VE PROMISED TO YOU ONCE WE HAVE THE SPELLBINDER'S BOOK?
YESSSSS, WE WANNTTTSSSS ITSSS.
THEN I GUESS YOU HAD BETTER GRAB A BROOM AND DUSTPAN.
AND CLEAN THE RESTROOM, TOO. SOMEONE LEFT A HUGE POO ON THE FLOOR.
THISSS ISSS OUTRAGEOUSSS!
WELL, GO BE OUTRAGED WHILE YOU CLEAN, OKAY, DENNIS?
MY NAME'SSS NOT DENNISSS!
IT IS UNTIL YOU EARN MY RESPECT.

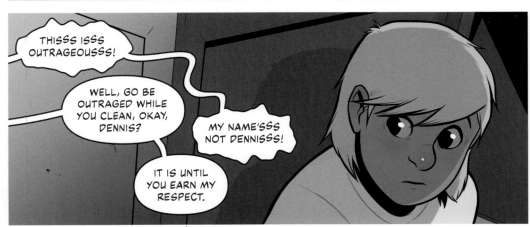

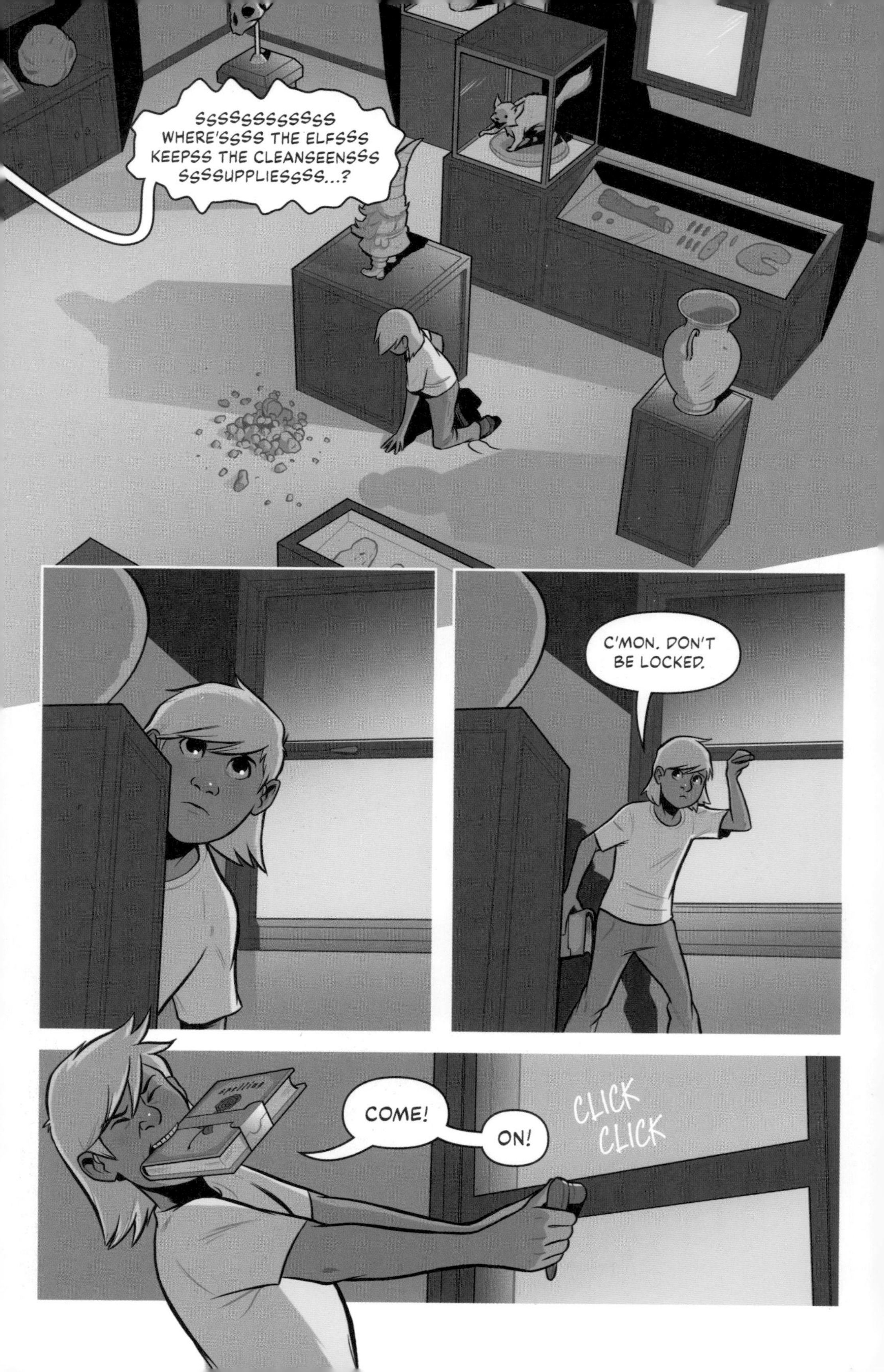
SSSSSSSSSSSS
WHERE'SSSS THE ELFSSS
KEEPSS THE CLEANSEENSSS
SSSSUPPLIESSSS...?
C'MON. DON'T
BE LOCKED.
COME!
ON!
CLICK
CLICK

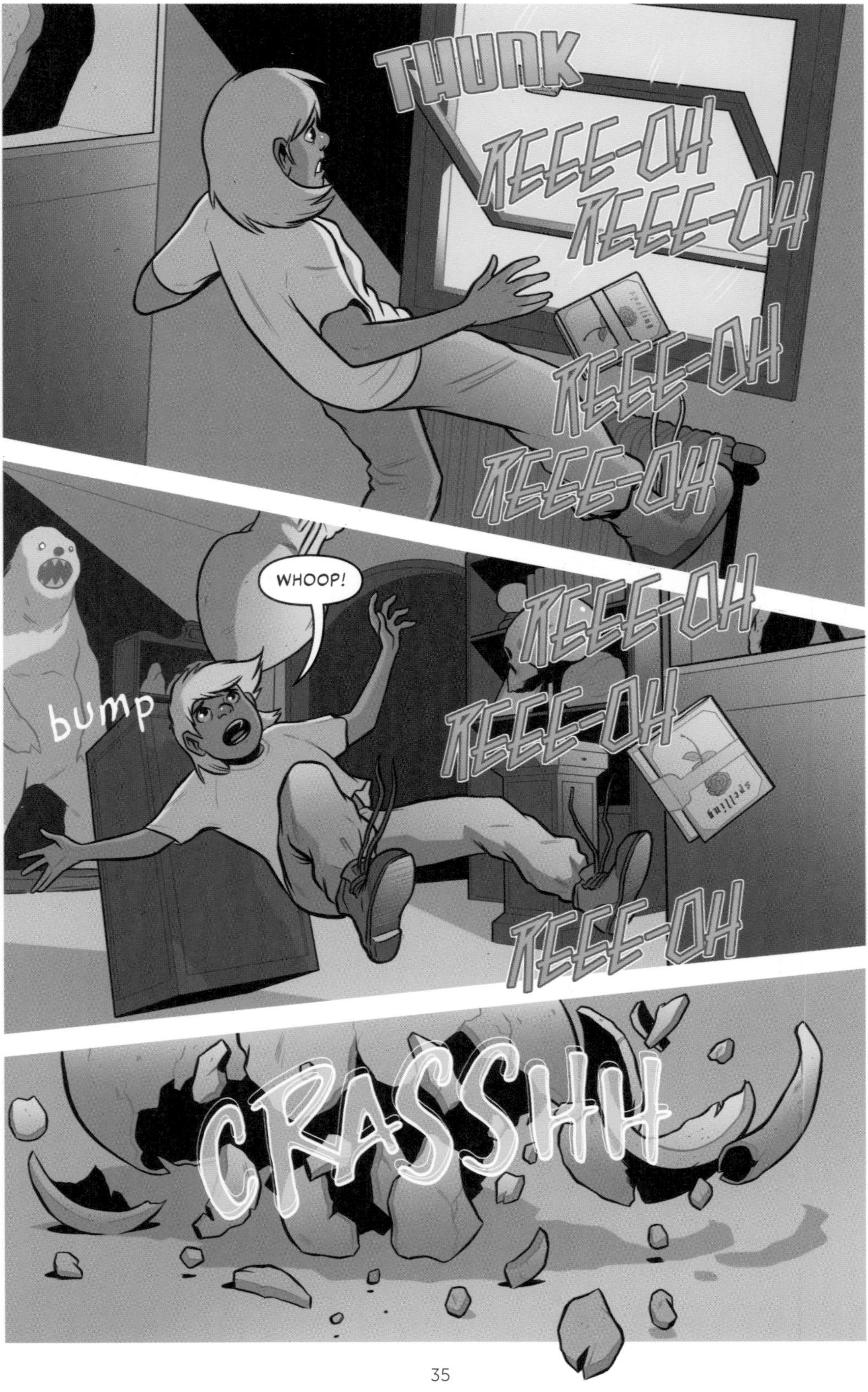
THUNK
REEE-OH
REEE-OH
REEE-OH
REEE-OH
WHOOP!
REEE-OH
bump
REEE-OH
spelling
REEE-OH
CRASSHH

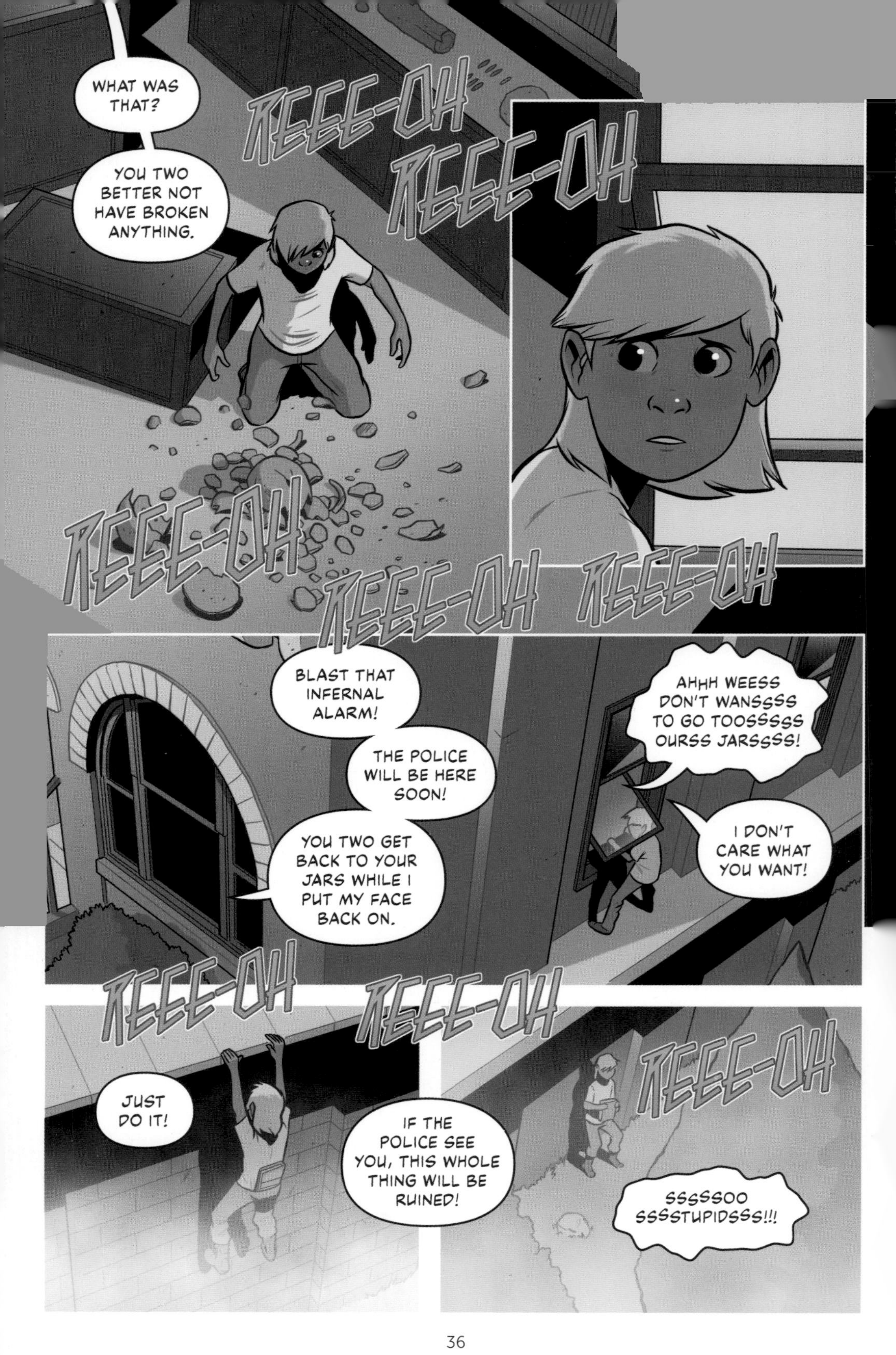
WHAT WAS THAT?
YOU TWO BETTER NOT HAVE BROKEN ANYTHING.
REEE-OH
REEE-OH
REEE-OH
REEE-OH
REEE-OH
BLAST THAT INFERNAL ALARM!
THE POLICE WILL BE HERE SOON!
YOU TWO GET BACK TO YOUR JARS WHILE I PUT MY FACE BACK ON.
AHHH WEESS DON'T WANSSSS TO GO TOOSSSSS OURSS JARSSSS!
I DON'T CARE WHAT YOU WANT!
REEE-OH
REEE-OH
JUST DO IT!
IF THE POLICE SEE YOU, THIS WHOLE THING WILL BE RUINED!
REEE-OH
SSSSSOO SSSSTUPIDSSS!!!

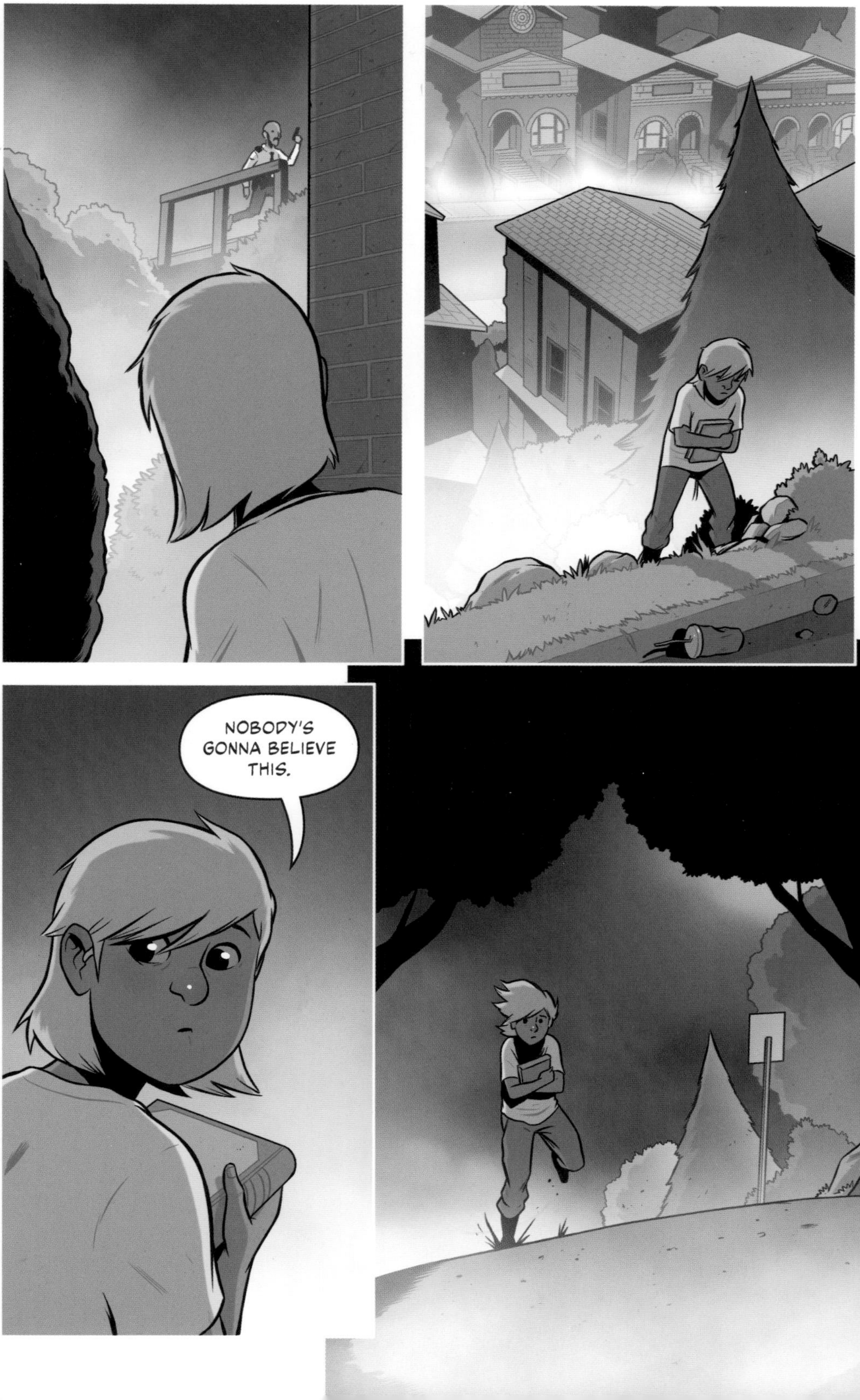
NOBODY'S GONNA BELIEVE THIS.

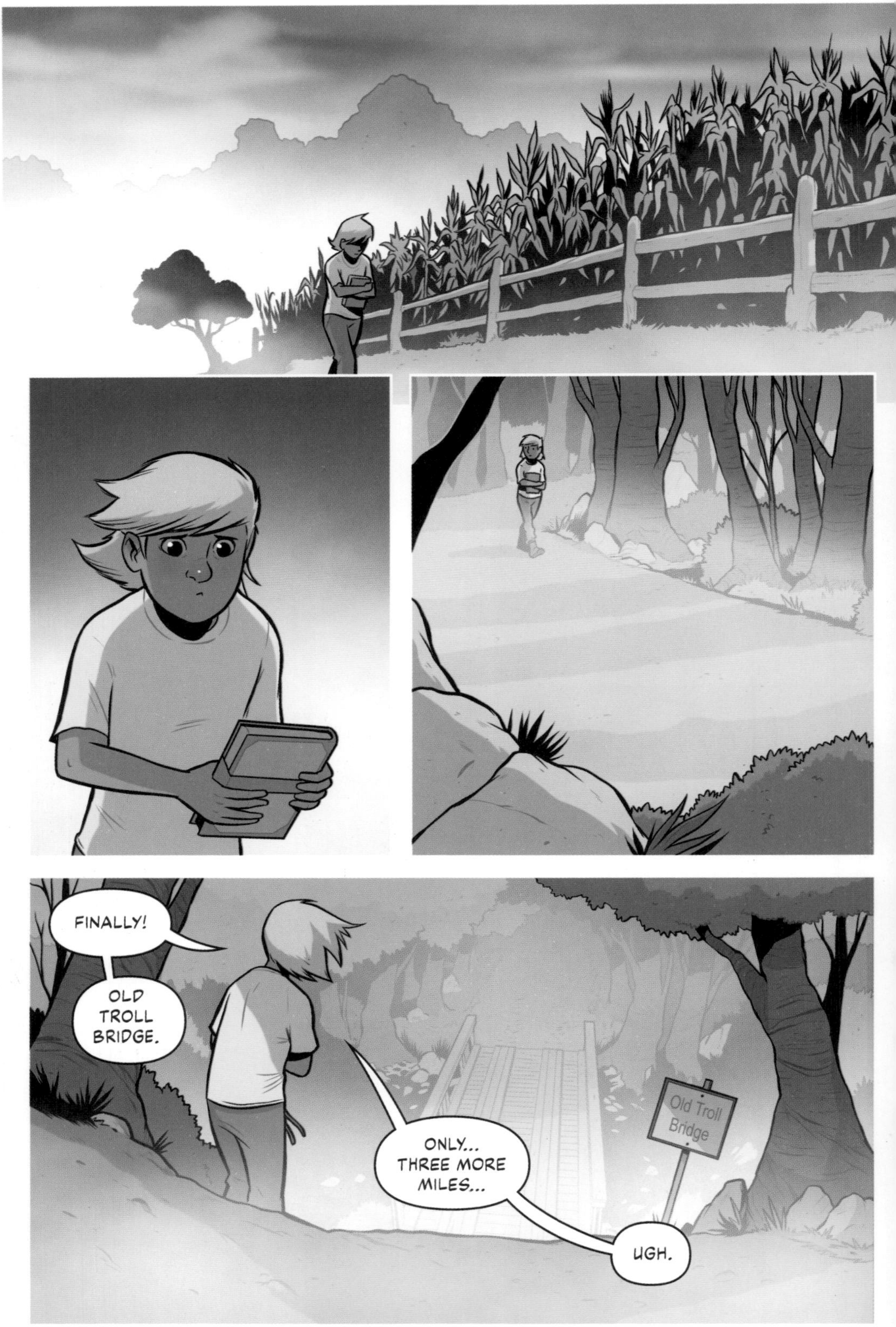
FINALLY!
OLD TROLL BRIDGE.
Old Troll Bridge
ONLY... THREE MORE MILES...
UGH.

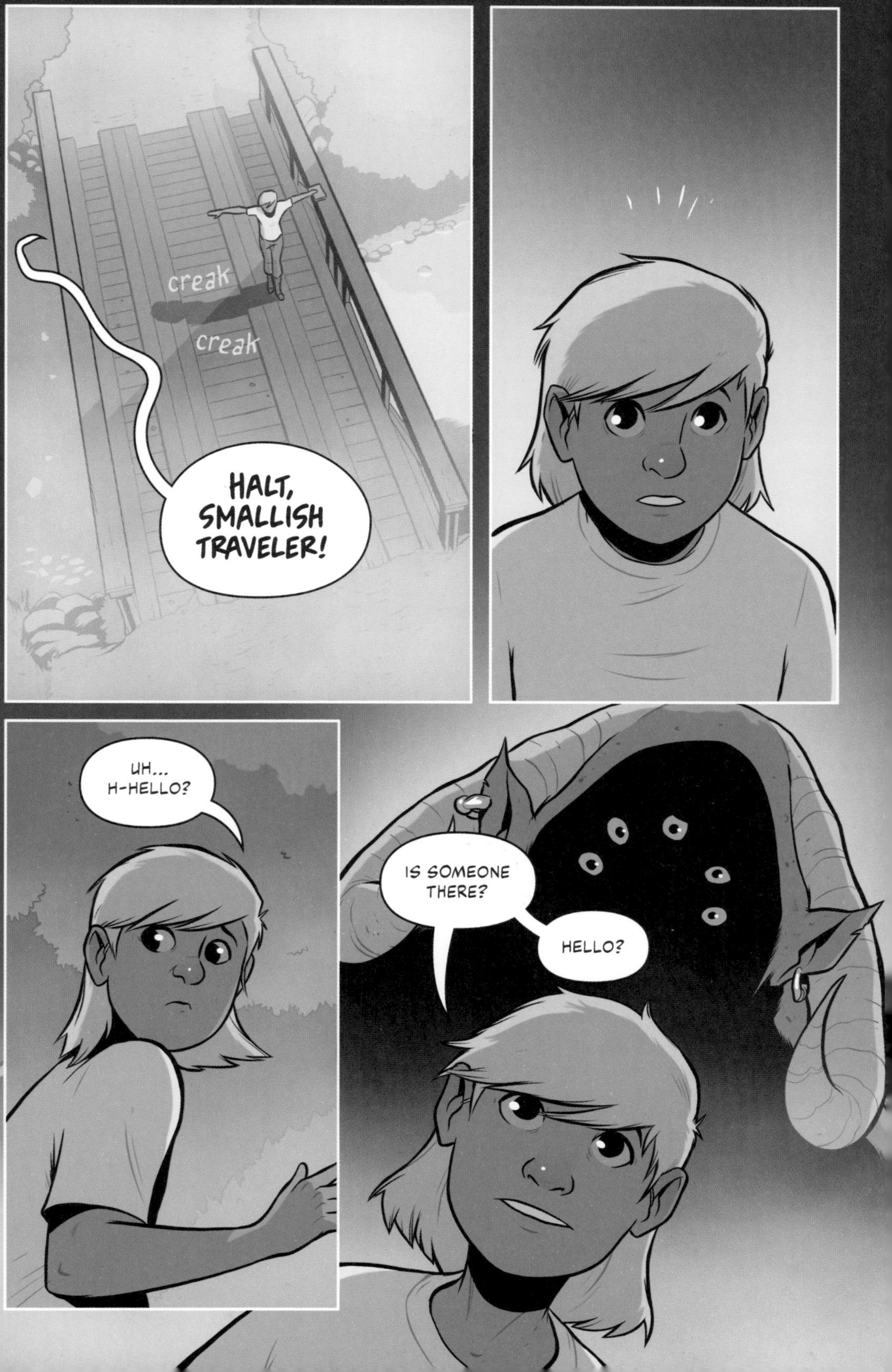
creak
creak
HALT, SMALLISH TRAVELER!
UH... H-HELLO?
IS SOMEONE THERE?
HELLO?

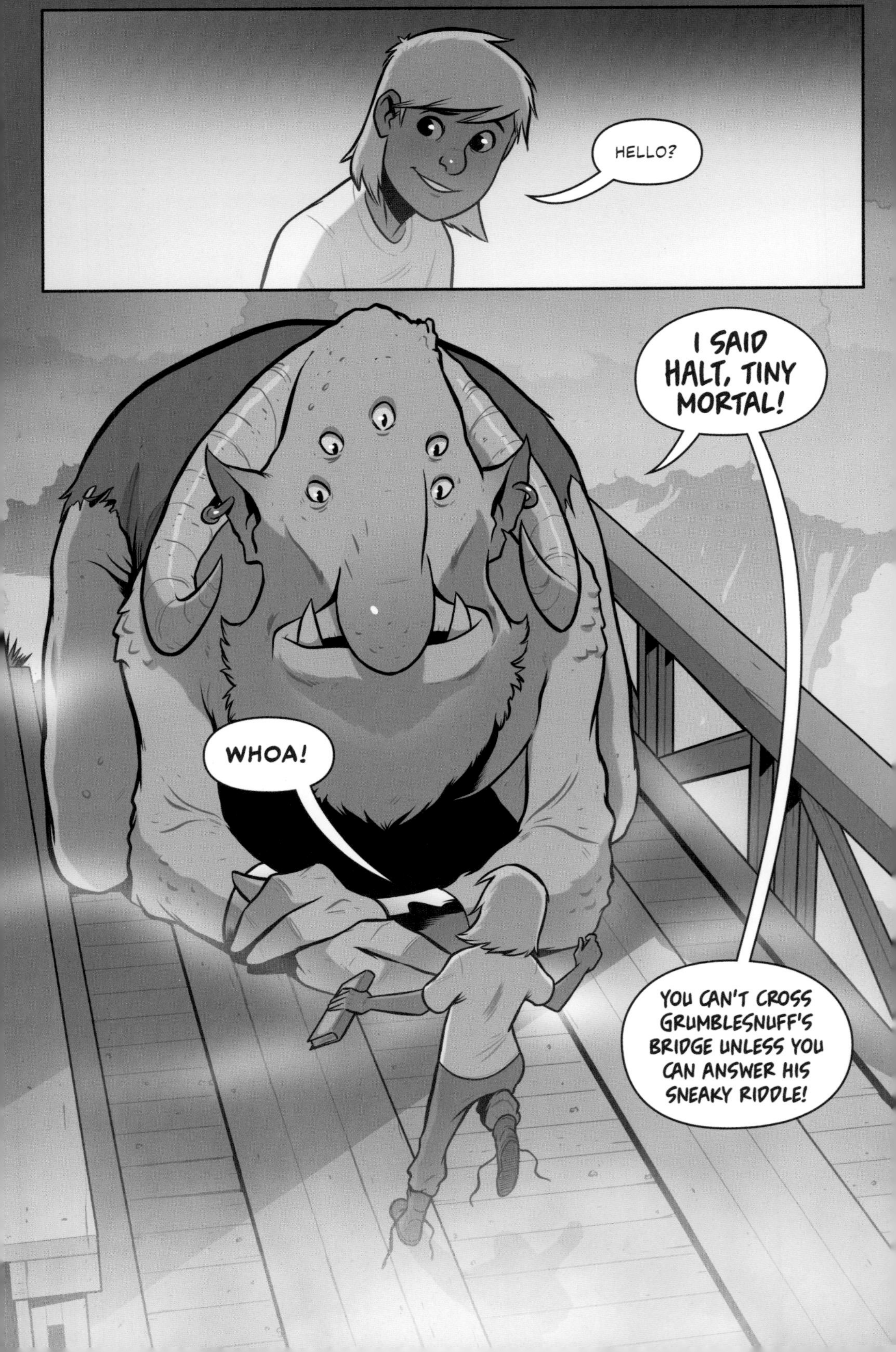
HELLO?
I SAID HALT, TINY MORTAL!
WHOA!
YOU CAN'T CROSS GRUMBLESNUFF'S BRIDGE UNLESS YOU CAN ANSWER HIS SNEAKY RIDDLE!

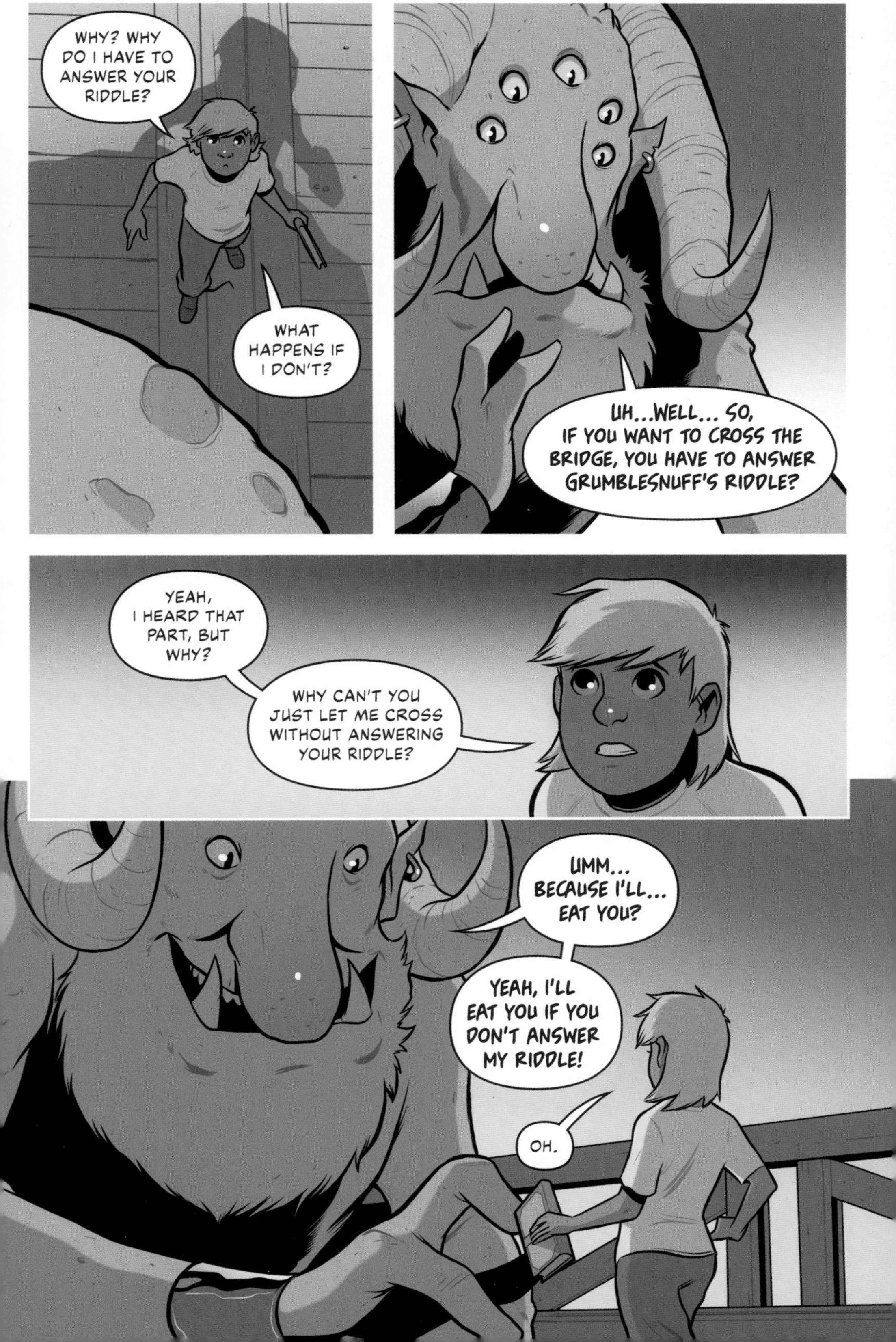
WHY? WHY DO I HAVE TO ANSWER YOUR RIDDLE?
WHAT HAPPENS IF I DON'T?
UH...WELL... SO, IF YOU WANT TO CROSS THE BRIDGE, YOU HAVE TO ANSWER GRUMBLESNUFF'S RIDDLE?
YEAH, I HEARD THAT PART, BUT WHY?
WHY CAN'T YOU JUST LET ME CROSS WITHOUT ANSWERING YOUR RIDDLE?
UMM... BECAUSE I'LL... EAT YOU?
YEAH, I'LL EAT YOU IF YOU DON'T ANSWER MY RIDDLE!
OH.

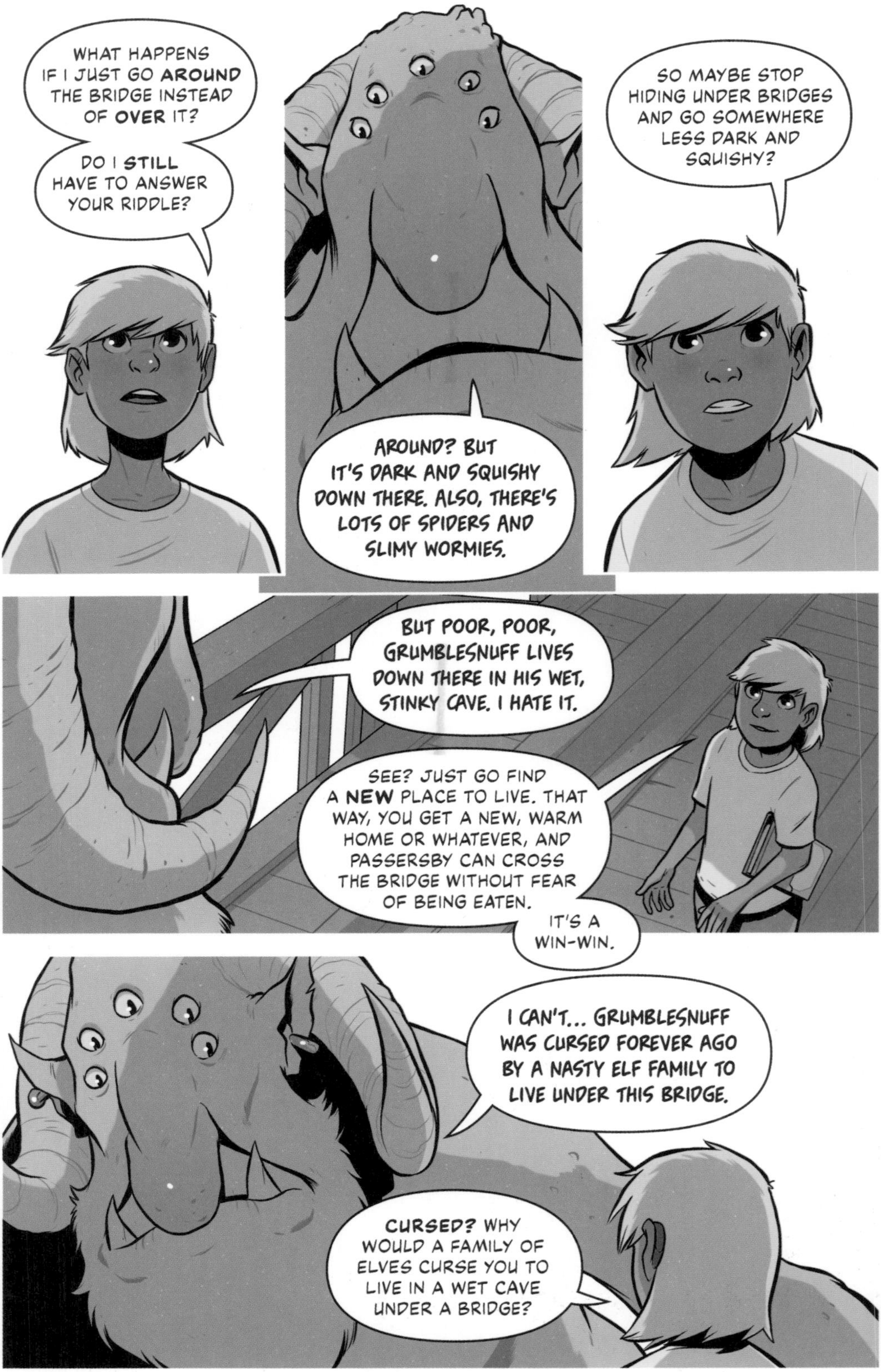
WHAT HAPPENS IF I JUST GO AROUND THE BRIDGE INSTEAD OF OVER IT?
DO I STILL HAVE TO ANSWER YOUR RIDDLE?
AROUND? BUT IT'S DARK AND SQUISHY DOWN THERE. ALSO, THERE'S LOTS OF SPIDERS AND SLIMY WORMIES.
SO MAYBE STOP HIDING UNDER BRIDGES AND GO SOMEWHERE LESS DARK AND SQUISHY?
BUT POOR, POOR, GRUMBLESNUFF LIVES DOWN THERE IN HIS WET, STINKY CAVE. I HATE IT.
SEE? JUST GO FIND A NEW PLACE TO LIVE. THAT WAY, YOU GET A NEW, WARM HOME OR WHATEVER, AND PASSERSBY CAN CROSS THE BRIDGE WITHOUT FEAR OF BEING EATEN.
IT'S A WIN-WIN.
I CAN'T... GRUMBLESNUFF WAS CURSED FOREVER AGO BY A NASTY ELF FAMILY TO LIVE UNDER THIS BRIDGE.
CURSED? WHY WOULD A FAMILY OF ELVES CURSE YOU TO LIVE IN A WET CAVE UNDER A BRIDGE?

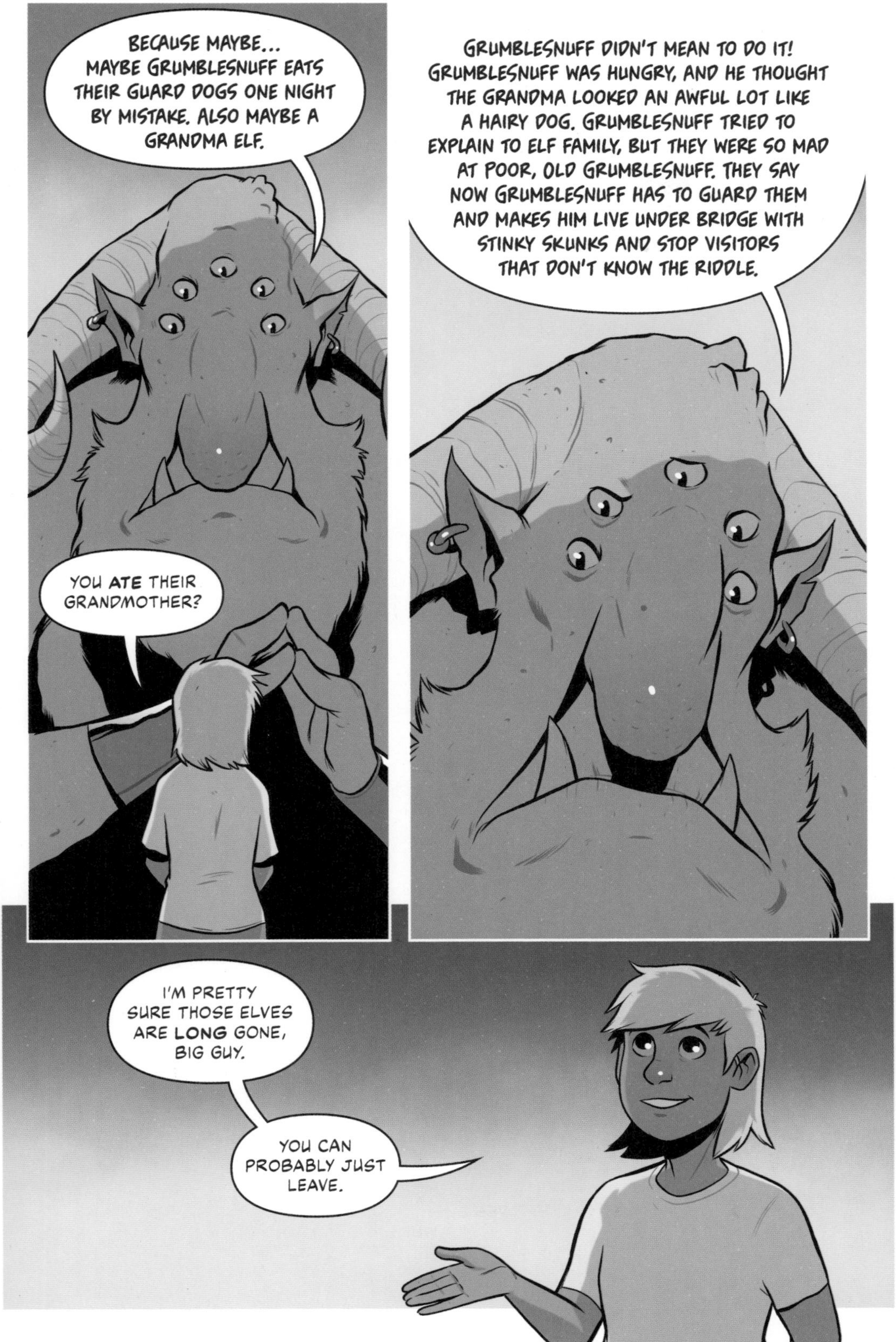
BECAUSE MAYBE... MAYBE GRUMBLESNUFF EATS THEIR GUARD DOGS ONE NIGHT BY MISTAKE. ALSO MAYBE A GRANDMA ELF.
YOU **ATE** THEIR GRANDMOTHER?
GRUMBLESNUFF DIDN'T MEAN TO DO IT! GRUMBLESNUFF WAS HUNGRY, AND HE THOUGHT THE GRANDMA LOOKED AN AWFUL LOT LIKE A HAIRY DOG. GRUMBLESNUFF TRIED TO EXPLAIN TO ELF FAMILY, BUT THEY WERE SO MAD AT POOR, OLD GRUMBLESNUFF. THEY SAY NOW GRUMBLESNUFF HAS TO GUARD THEM AND MAKES HIM LIVE UNDER BRIDGE WITH STINKY SKUNKS AND STOP VISITORS THAT DON'T KNOW THE RIDDLE.
I'M PRETTY SURE THOSE ELVES ARE **LONG** GONE, BIG GUY.
YOU CAN PROBABLY JUST LEAVE.

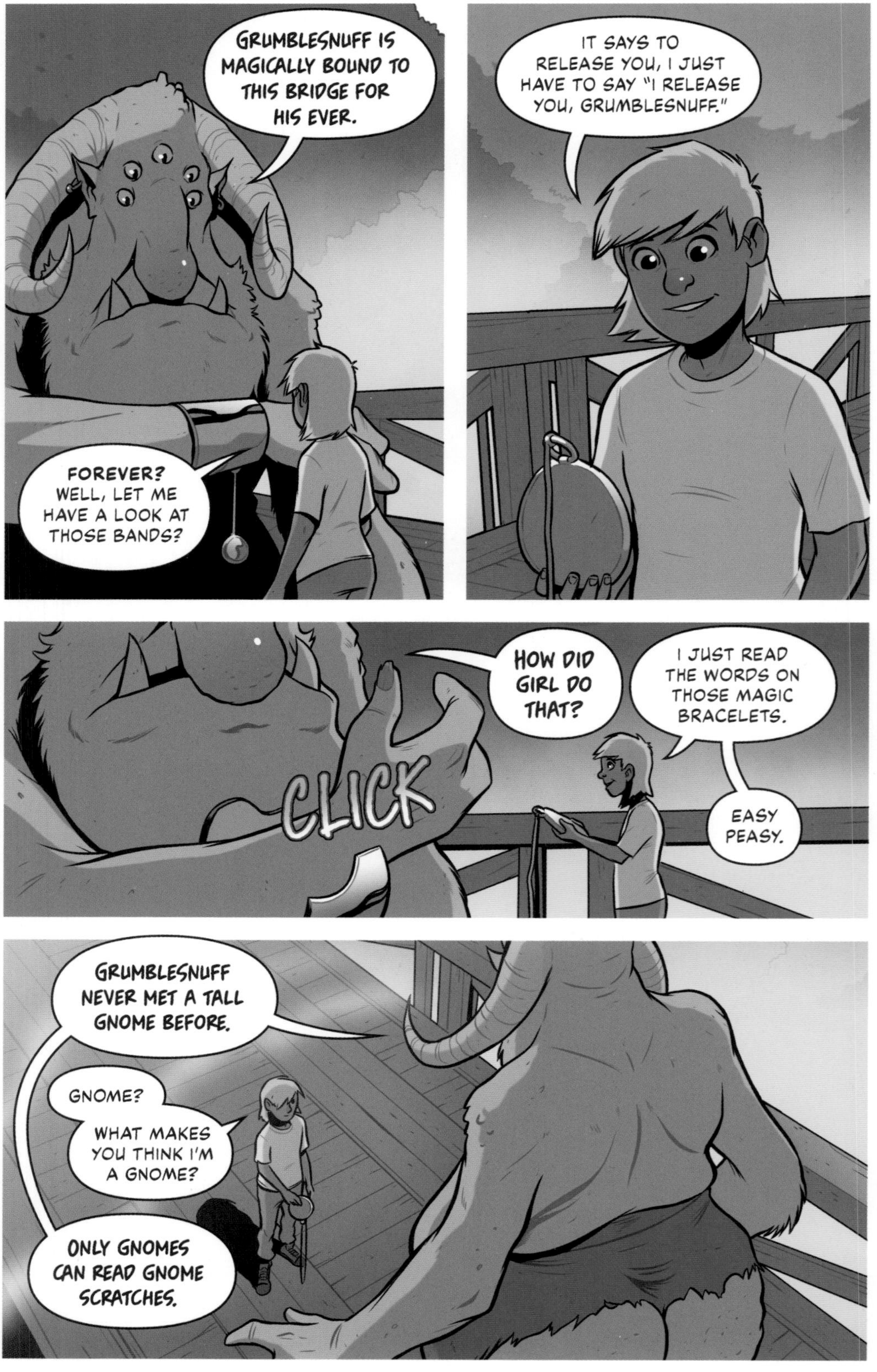
GRUMBLESNUFF IS MAGICALLY BOUND TO THIS BRIDGE FOR HIS EVER.
FOREVER? WELL, LET ME HAVE A LOOK AT THOSE BANDS?
IT SAYS TO RELEASE YOU, I JUST HAVE TO SAY "I RELEASE YOU, GRUMBLESNUFF."
CLICK
HOW DID GIRL DO THAT?
I JUST READ THE WORDS ON THOSE MAGIC BRACELETS.
EASY PEASY.
GRUMBLESNUFF NEVER MET A TALL GNOME BEFORE.
GNOME?
WHAT MAKES YOU THINK I'M A GNOME?
ONLY GNOMES CAN READ GNOME SCRATCHES.

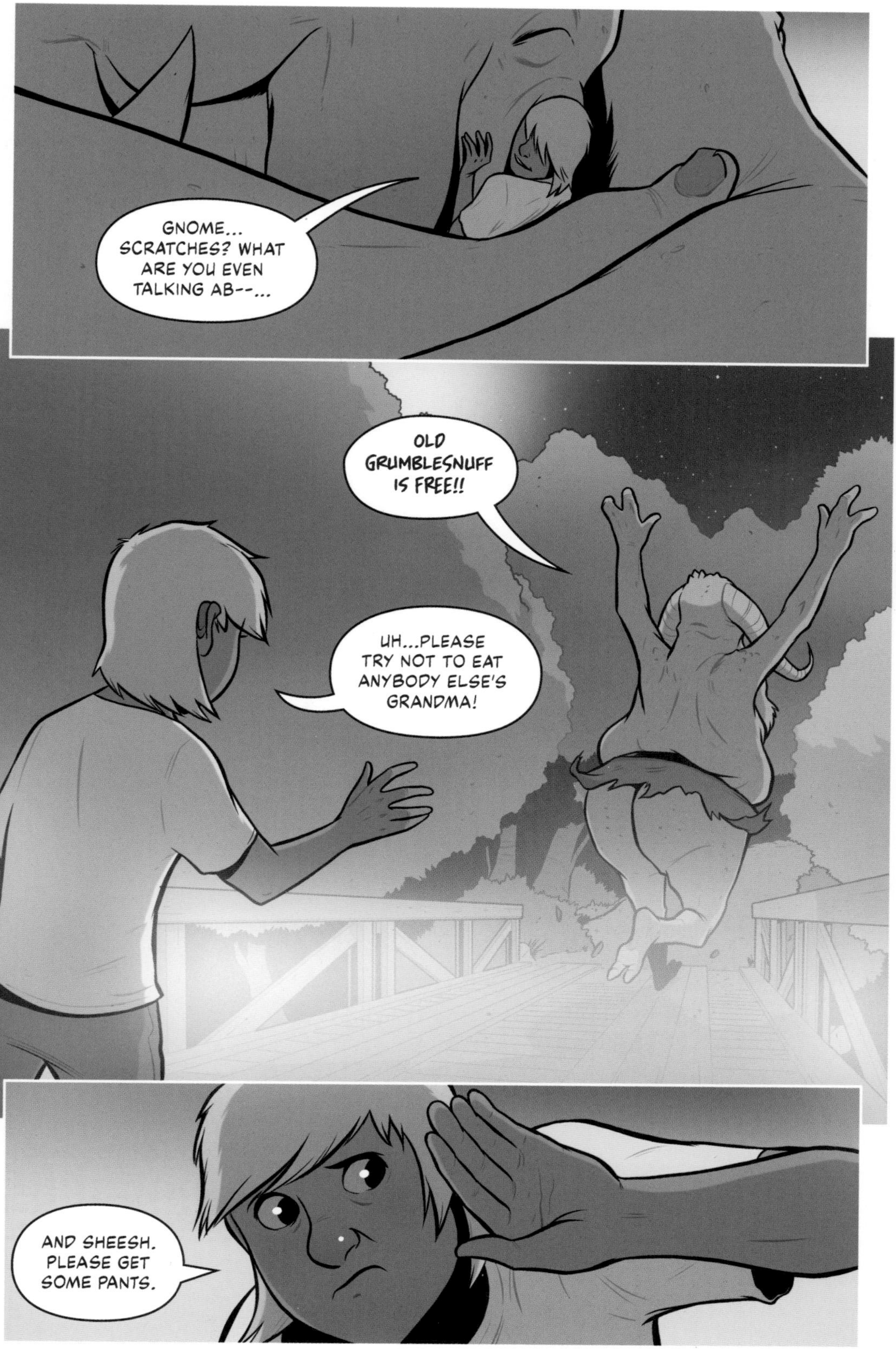
GNOME... SCRATCHES? WHAT ARE YOU EVEN TALKING AB--...
OLD GRUMBLESNUFF IS FREE!!
UH...PLEASE TRY NOT TO EAT ANYBODY ELSE'S GRANDMA!
AND SHEESH. PLEASE GET SOME PANTS.

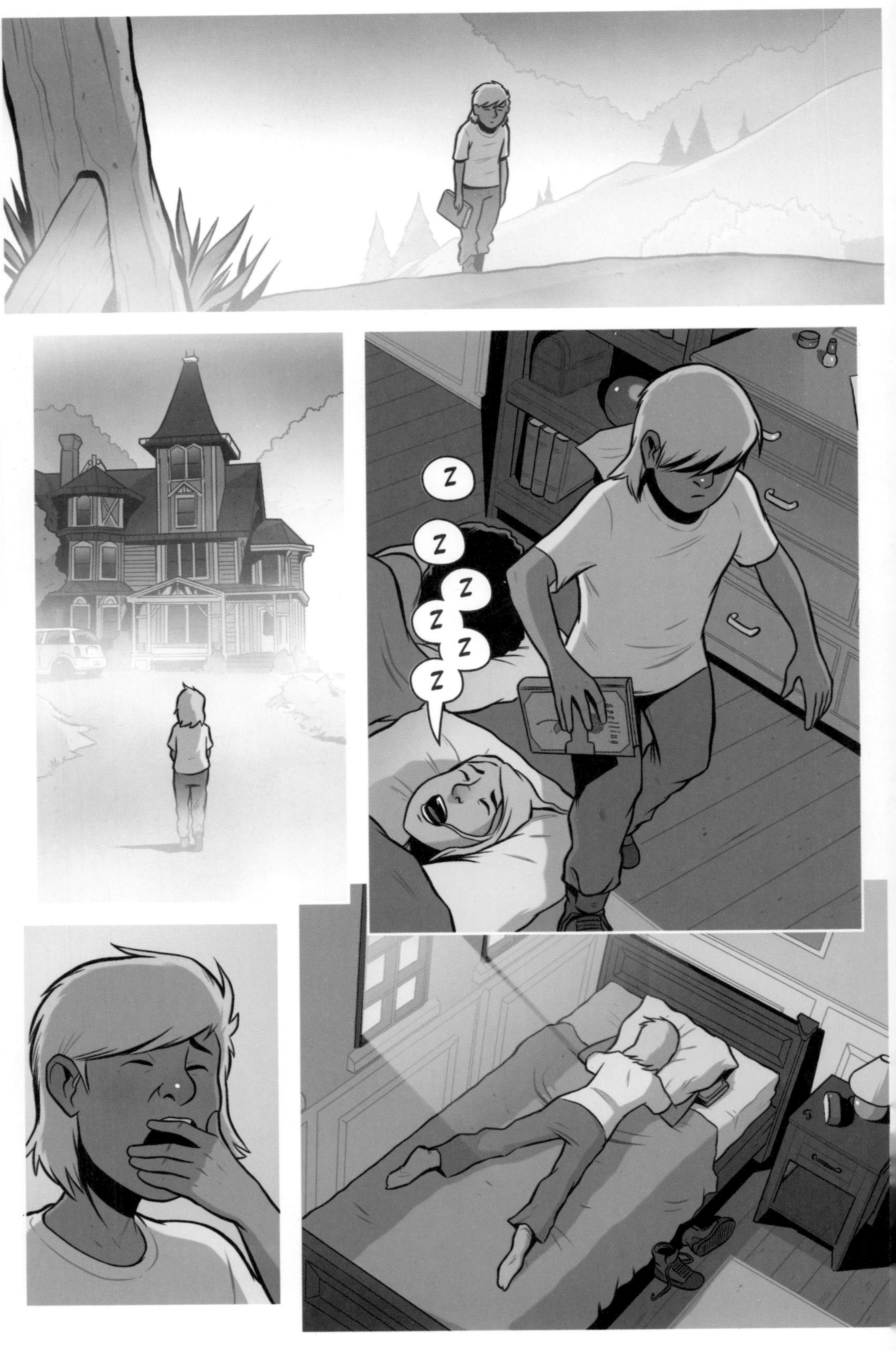
Z
Z
Z
Z
Z
Z
spelling

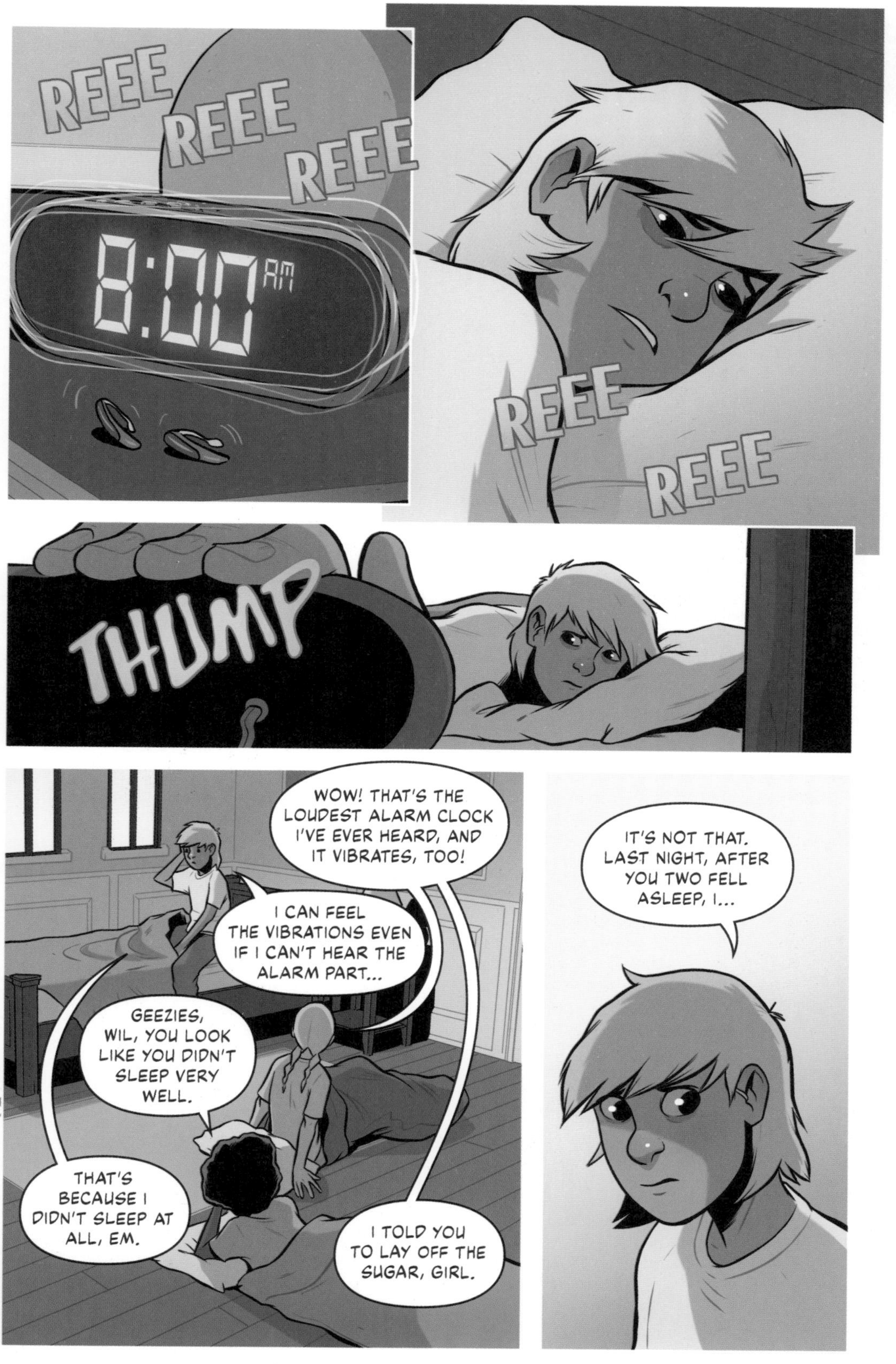
REEE
REEE
REEE
8:00 AM
REEE
REEE
THUMP
WOW! THAT'S THE LOUDEST ALARM CLOCK I'VE EVER HEARD, AND IT VIBRATES, TOO!
I CAN FEEL THE VIBRATIONS EVEN IF I CAN'T HEAR THE ALARM PART...
GEEZIES, WIL, YOU LOOK LIKE YOU DIDN'T SLEEP VERY WELL.
THAT'S BECAUSE I DIDN'T SLEEP AT ALL, EM.
I TOLD YOU TO LAY OFF THE SUGAR, GIRL.
IT'S NOT THAT. LAST NIGHT, AFTER YOU TWO FELL ASLEEP, I...

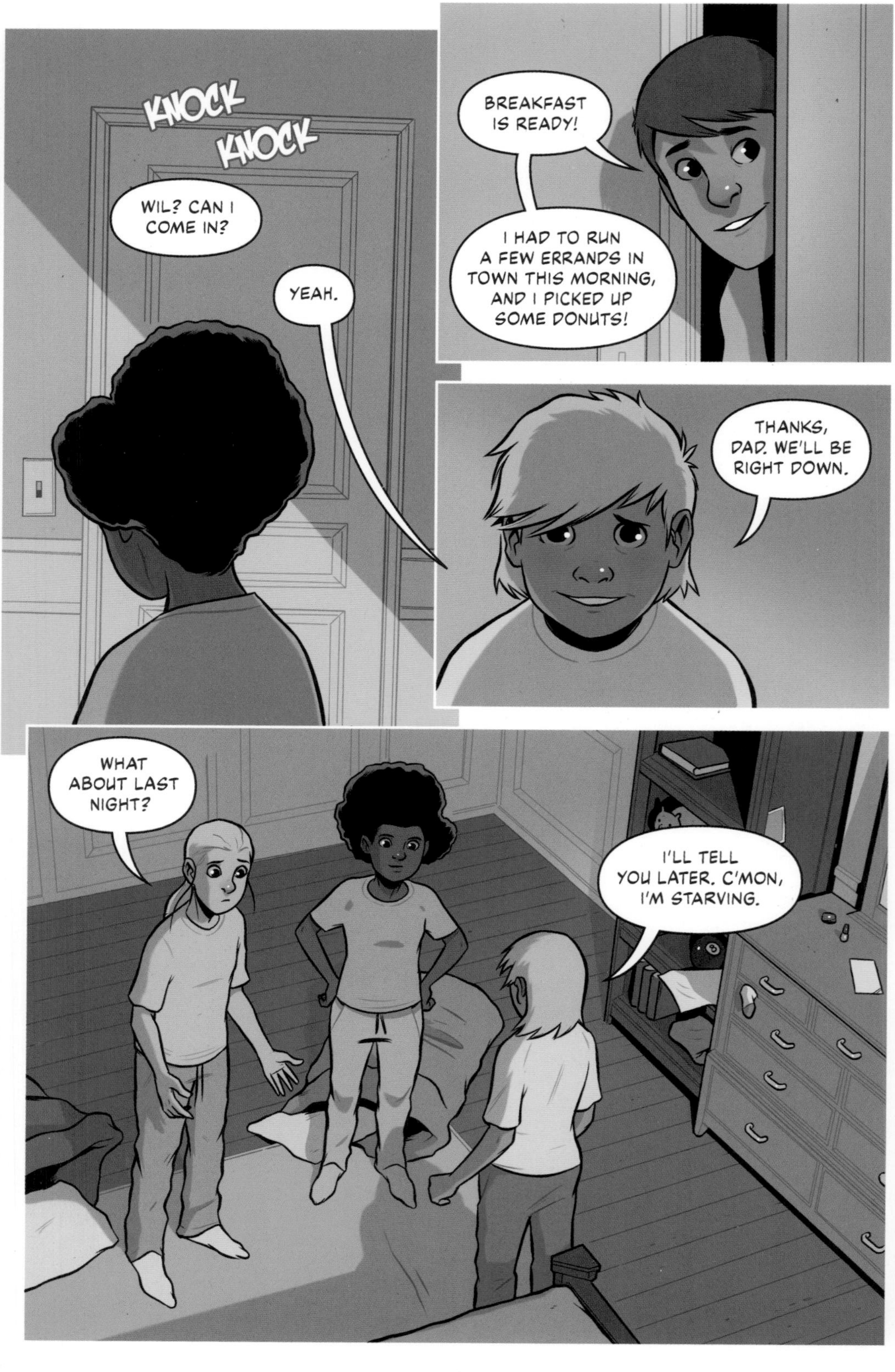
KNOCK KNOCK
WIL? CAN I COME IN?
YEAH.
BREAKFAST IS READY!
I HAD TO RUN A FEW ERRANDS IN TOWN THIS MORNING, AND I PICKED UP SOME DONUTS!
THANKS, DAD. WE'LL BE RIGHT DOWN.
WHAT ABOUT LAST NIGHT?
I'LL TELL YOU LATER. C'MON, I'M STARVING.

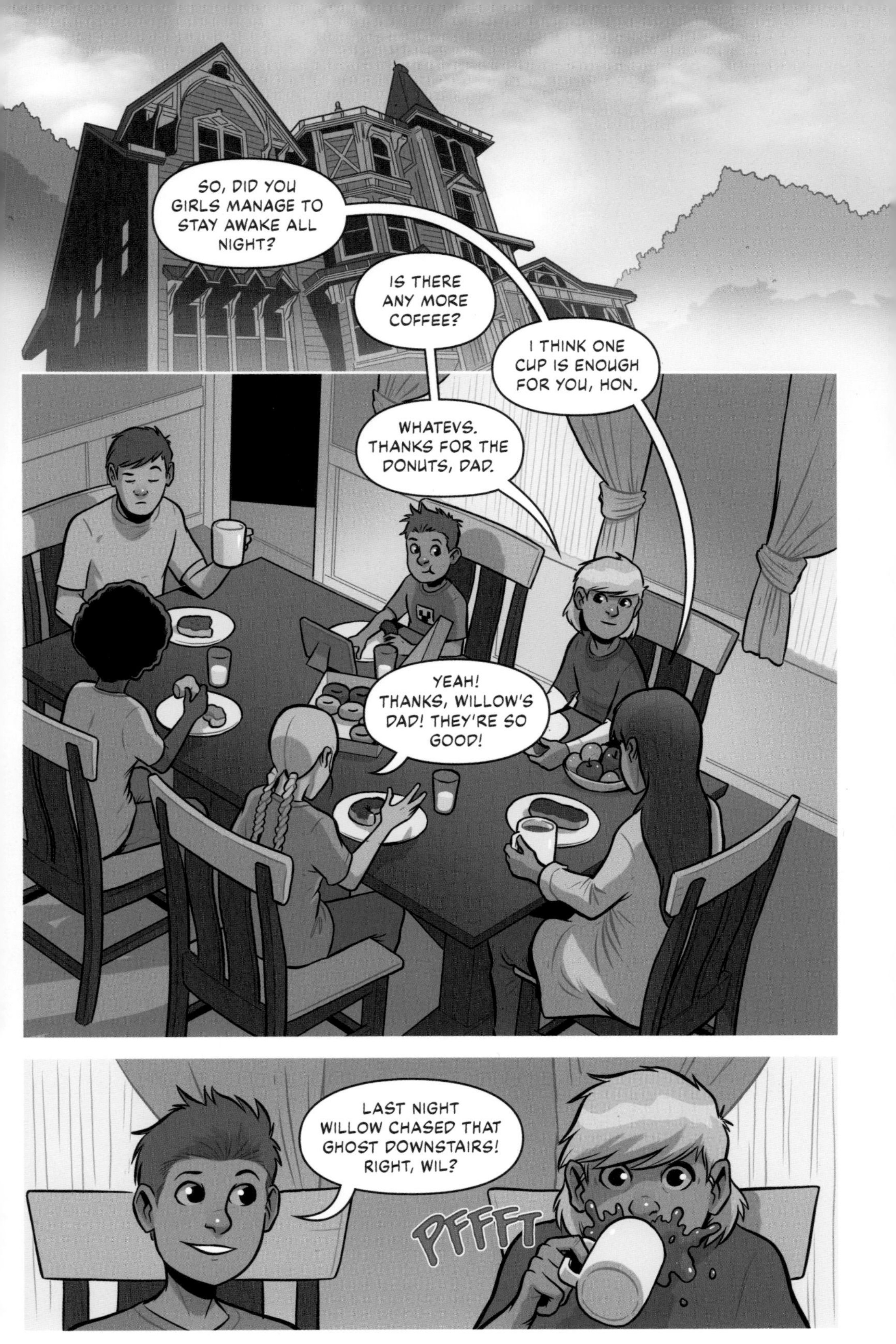
SO, DID YOU GIRLS MANAGE TO STAY AWAKE ALL NIGHT?
IS THERE ANY MORE COFFEE?
I THINK ONE CUP IS ENOUGH FOR YOU, HON.
WHATEVS. THANKS FOR THE DONUTS, DAD.
YEAH! THANKS, WILLOW'S DAD! THEY'RE SO GOOD!
LAST NIGHT WILLOW CHASED THAT GHOST DOWNSTAIRS! RIGHT, WIL?
PFFFT

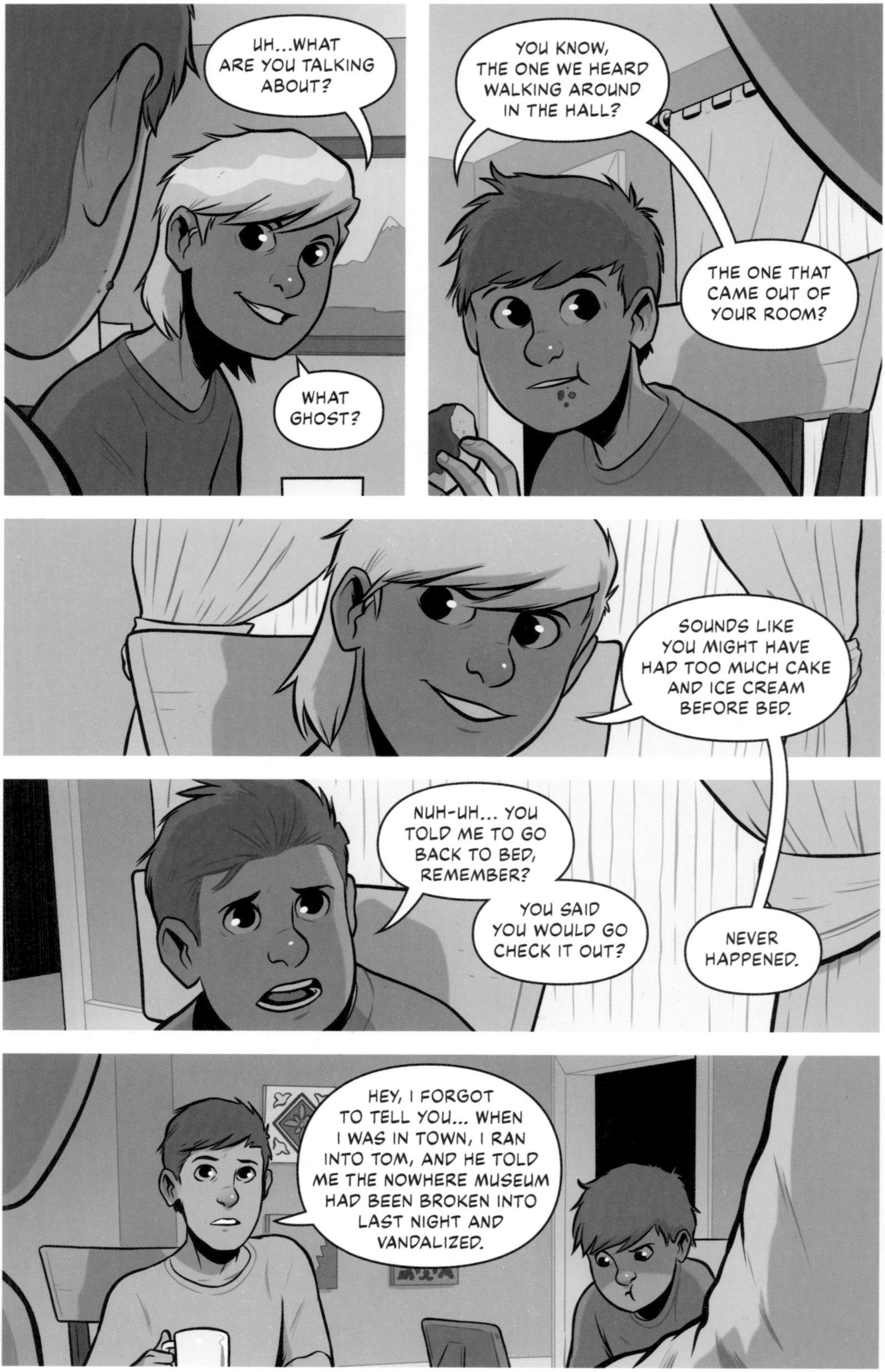
UH...WHAT ARE YOU TALKING ABOUT?
WHAT GHOST?
YOU KNOW, THE ONE WE HEARD WALKING AROUND IN THE HALL?
THE ONE THAT CAME OUT OF YOUR ROOM?
SOUNDS LIKE YOU MIGHT HAVE HAD TOO MUCH CAKE AND ICE CREAM BEFORE BED.
NUH-UH... YOU TOLD ME TO GO BACK TO BED, REMEMBER?
YOU SAID YOU WOULD GO CHECK IT OUT?
NEVER HAPPENED.
HEY, I FORGOT TO TELL YOU... WHEN I WAS IN TOWN, I RAN INTO TOM, AND HE TOLD ME THE NOWHERE MUSEUM HAD BEEN BROKEN INTO LAST NIGHT AND VANDALIZED.

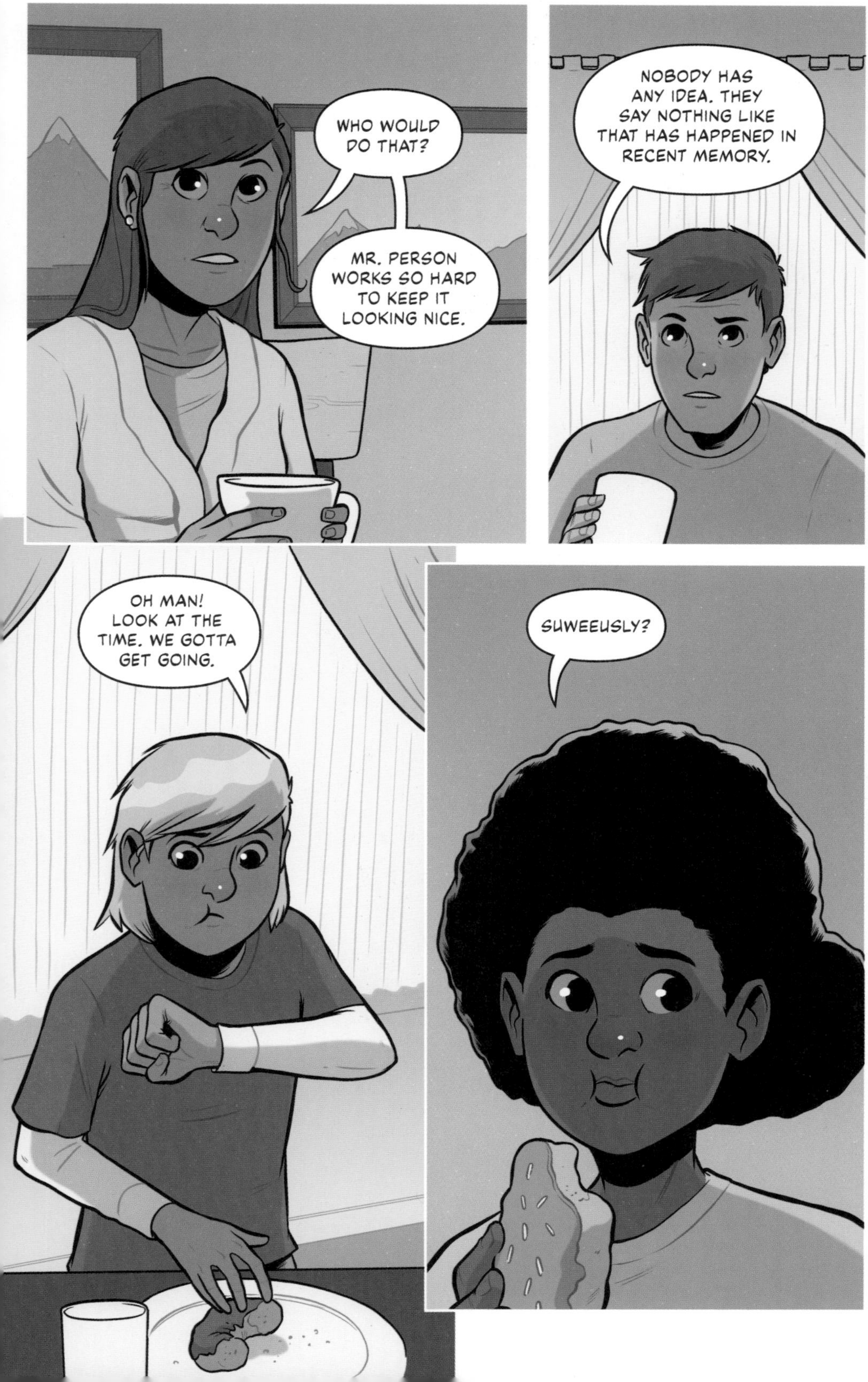
WHO WOULD DO THAT?
MR. PERSON WORKS SO HARD TO KEEP IT LOOKING NICE.
NOBODY HAS ANY IDEA. THEY SAY NOTHING LIKE THAT HAS HAPPENED IN RECENT MEMORY.
OH MAN! LOOK AT THE TIME. WE GOTTA GET GOING.
SUWEEUSLY?

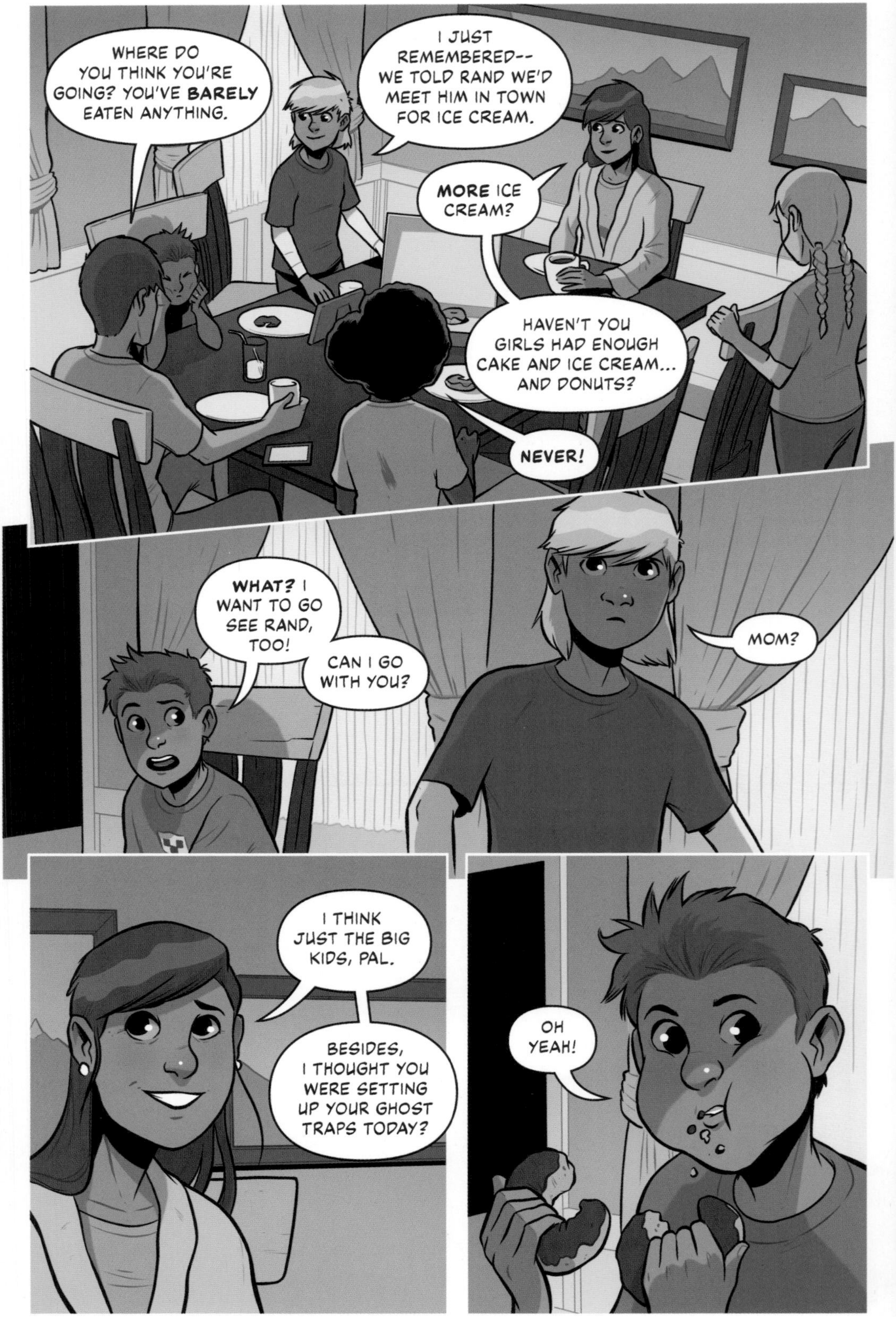
WHERE DO YOU THINK YOU'RE GOING? YOU'VE **BARELY** EATEN ANYTHING.
I JUST REMEMBERED-- WE TOLD RAND WE'D MEET HIM IN TOWN FOR ICE CREAM.
MORE ICE CREAM?
HAVEN'T YOU GIRLS HAD ENOUGH CAKE AND ICE CREAM... AND DONUTS?
NEVER!
WHAT? I WANT TO GO SEE RAND, TOO!
CAN I GO WITH YOU?
MOM?
I THINK JUST THE BIG KIDS, PAL.
BESIDES, I THOUGHT YOU WERE SETTING UP YOUR GHOST TRAPS TODAY?
OH YEAH!

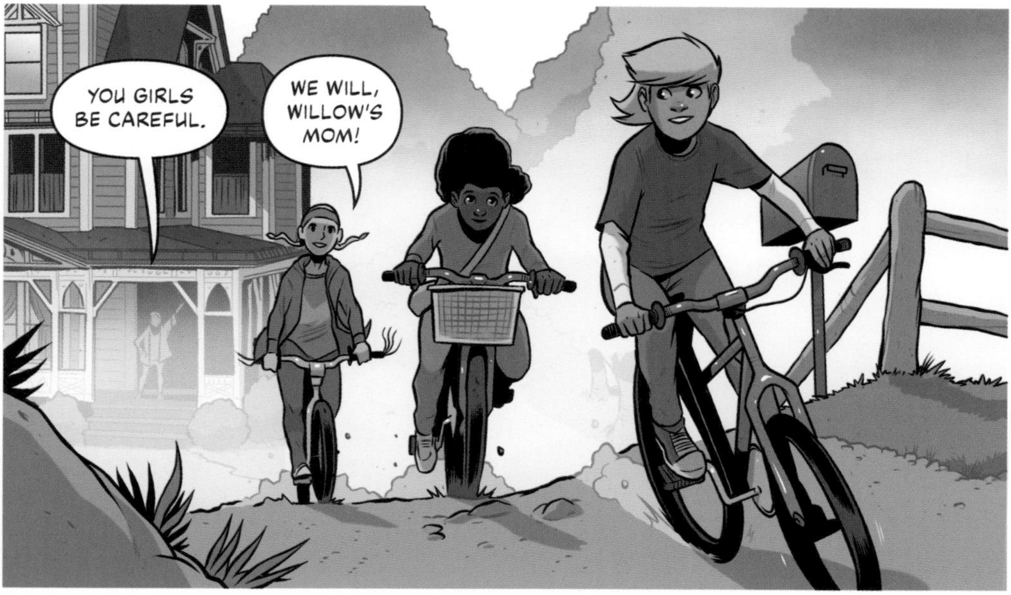
YOU GIRLS BE CAREFUL.
WE WILL, WILLOW'S MOM!

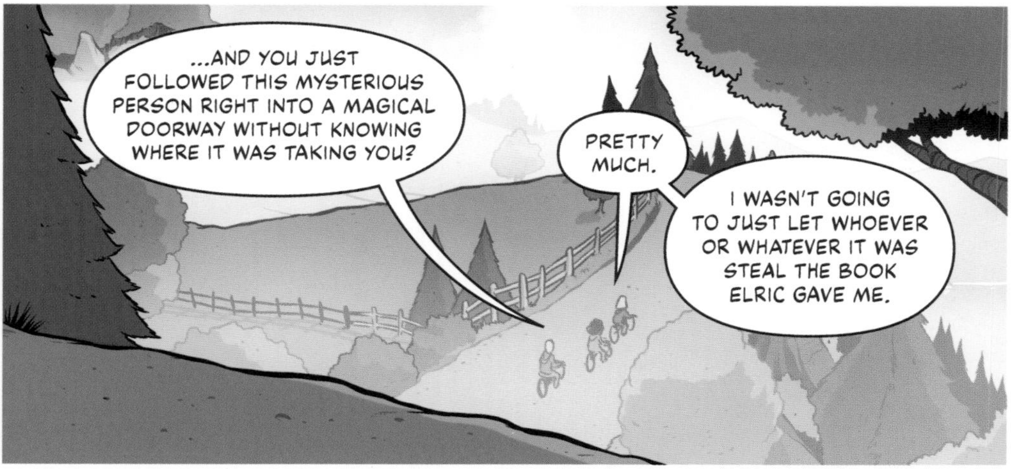
...AND YOU JUST FOLLOWED THIS MYSTERIOUS PERSON RIGHT INTO A MAGICAL DOORWAY WITHOUT KNOWING WHERE IT WAS TAKING YOU?
PRETTY MUCH.
I WASN'T GOING TO JUST LET WHOEVER OR WHATEVER IT WAS STEAL THE BOOK ELRIC GAVE ME.

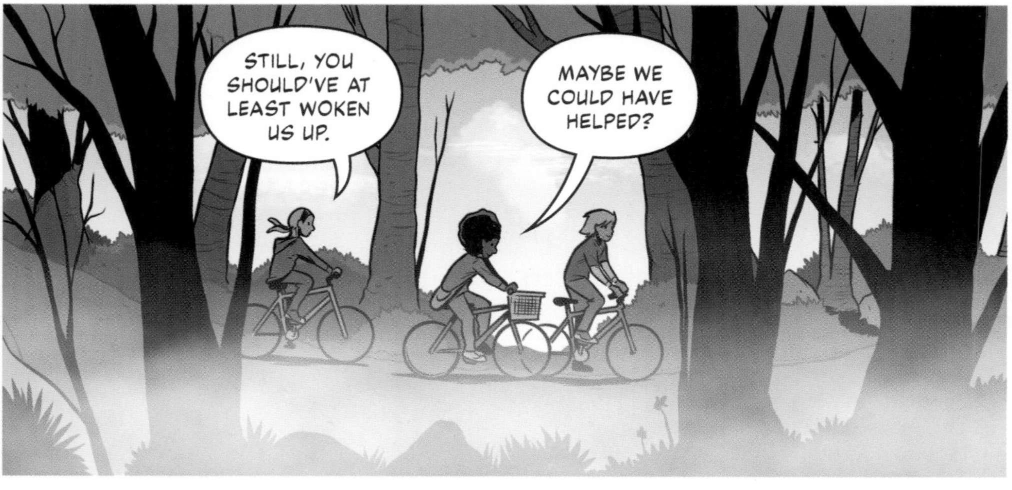
STILL, YOU SHOULD'VE AT LEAST WOKEN US UP.
MAYBE WE COULD HAVE HELPED?

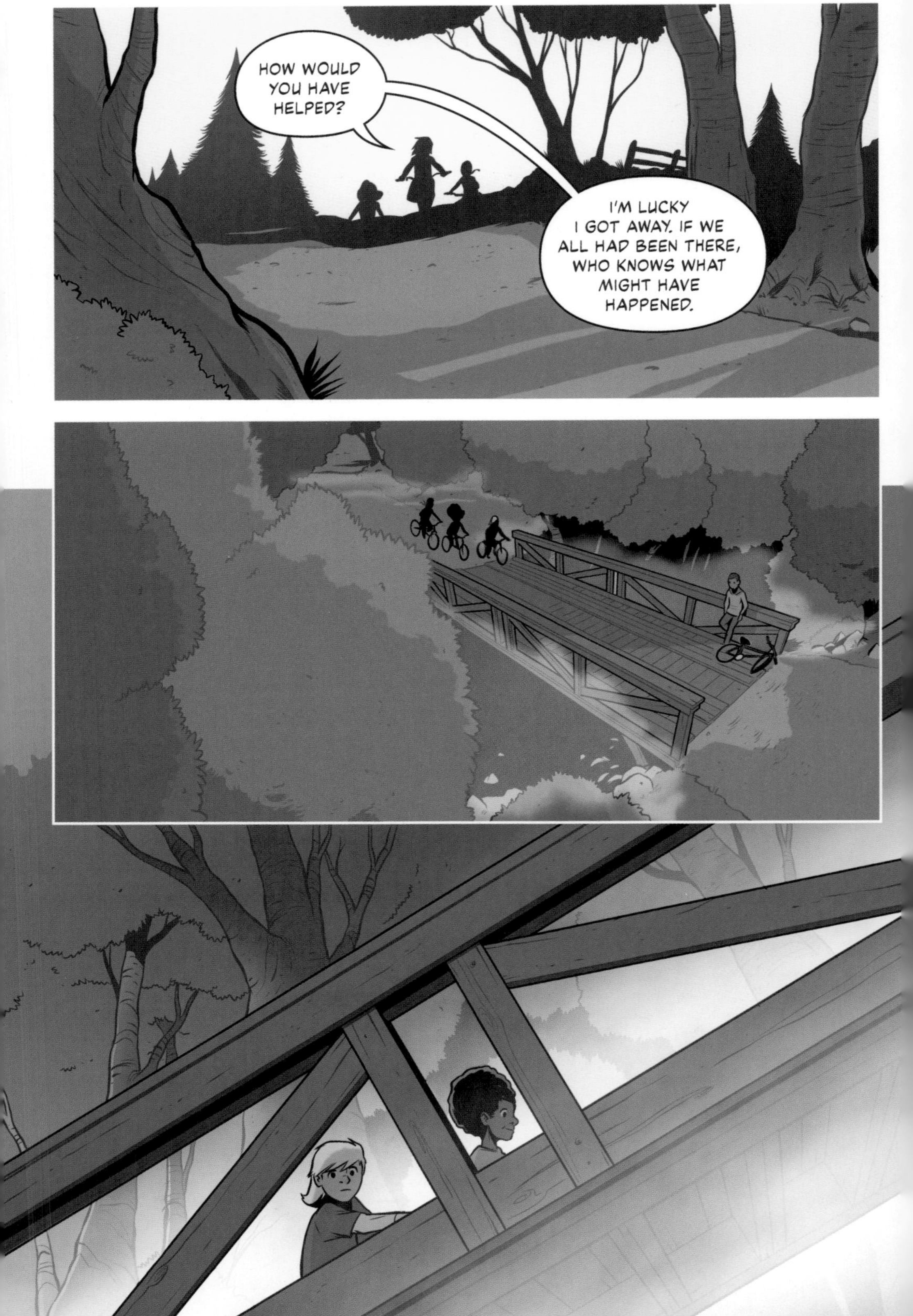
HOW WOULD YOU HAVE HELPED?
I'M LUCKY I GOT AWAY. IF WE ALL HAD BEEN THERE, WHO KNOWS WHAT MIGHT HAVE HAPPENED.

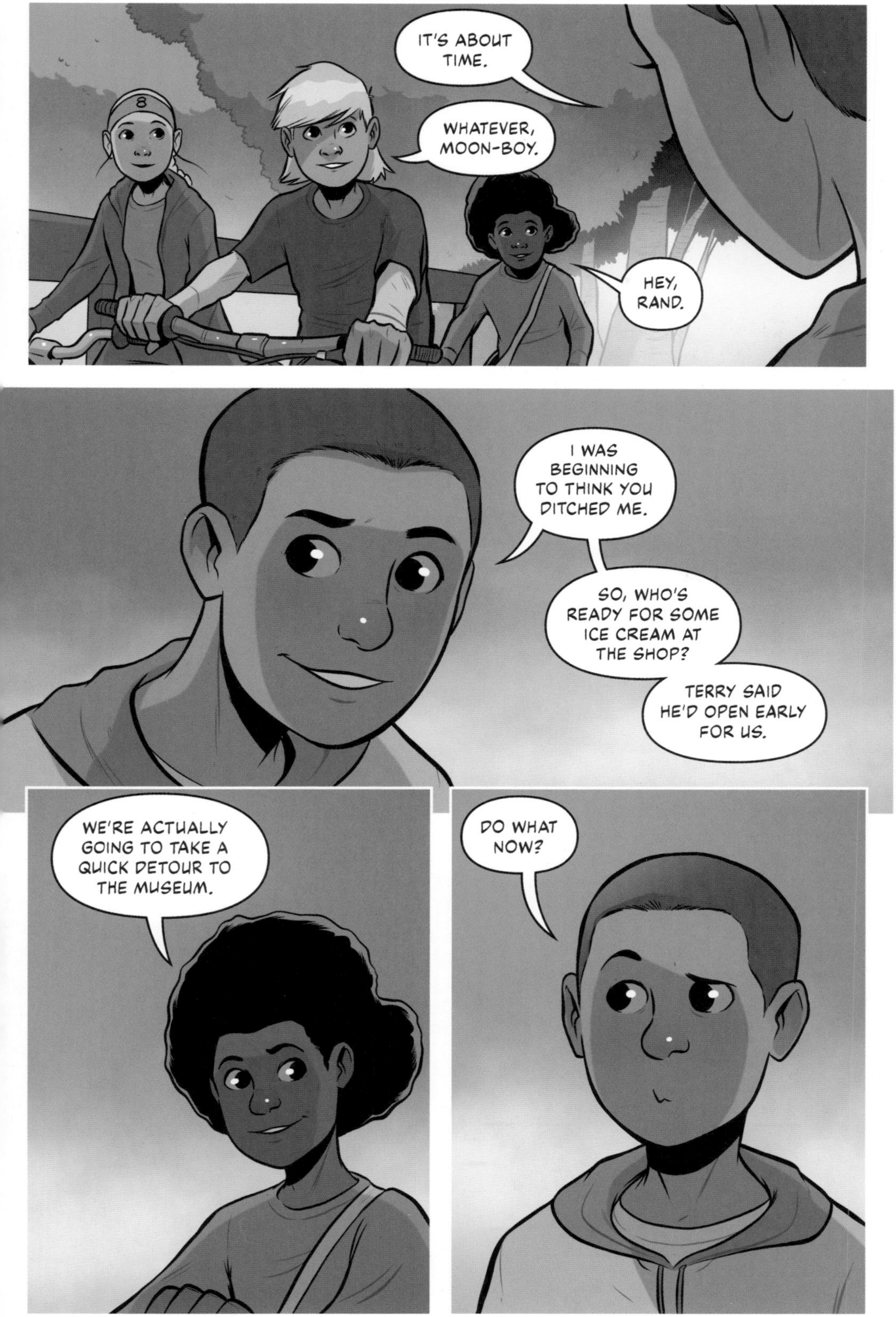
IT'S ABOUT TIME.
WHATEVER, MOON-BOY.
HEY, RAND.
I WAS BEGINNING TO THINK YOU DITCHED ME.
SO, WHO'S READY FOR SOME ICE CREAM AT THE SHOP?
TERRY SAID HE'D OPEN EARLY FOR US.
WE'RE ACTUALLY GOING TO TAKE A QUICK DETOUR TO THE MUSEUM.
DO WHAT NOW?

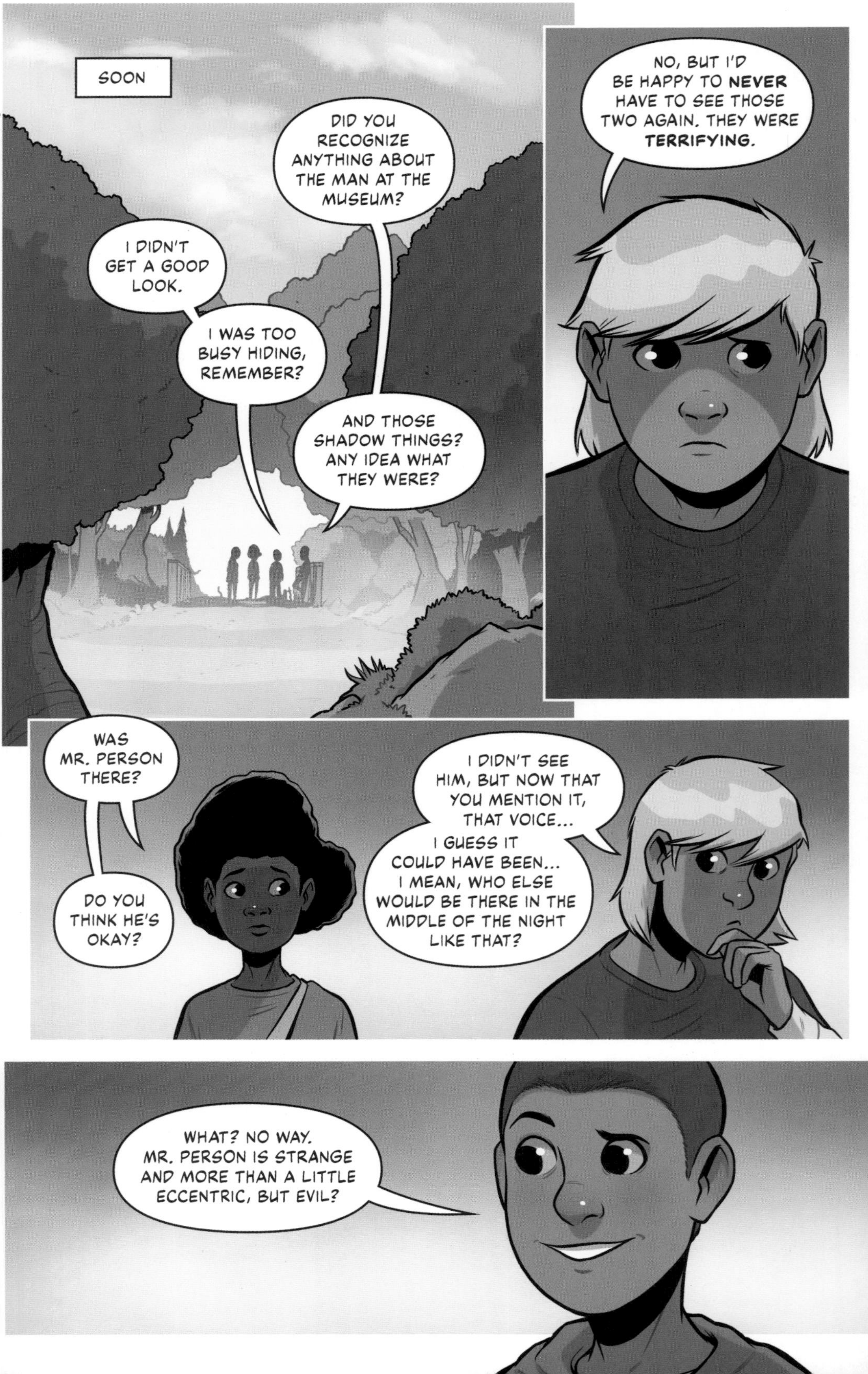
SOON
DID YOU RECOGNIZE ANYTHING ABOUT THE MAN AT THE MUSEUM?
I DIDN'T GET A GOOD LOOK.
I WAS TOO BUSY HIDING, REMEMBER?
AND THOSE SHADOW THINGS? ANY IDEA WHAT THEY WERE?
NO, BUT I'D BE HAPPY TO NEVER HAVE TO SEE THOSE TWO AGAIN. THEY WERE TERRIFYING.
WAS MR. PERSON THERE?
DO YOU THINK HE'S OKAY?
I DIDN'T SEE HIM, BUT NOW THAT YOU MENTION IT, THAT VOICE...
I GUESS IT COULD HAVE BEEN... I MEAN, WHO ELSE WOULD BE THERE IN THE MIDDLE OF THE NIGHT LIKE THAT?
WHAT? NO WAY. MR. PERSON IS STRANGE AND MORE THAN A LITTLE ECCENTRIC, BUT EVIL?

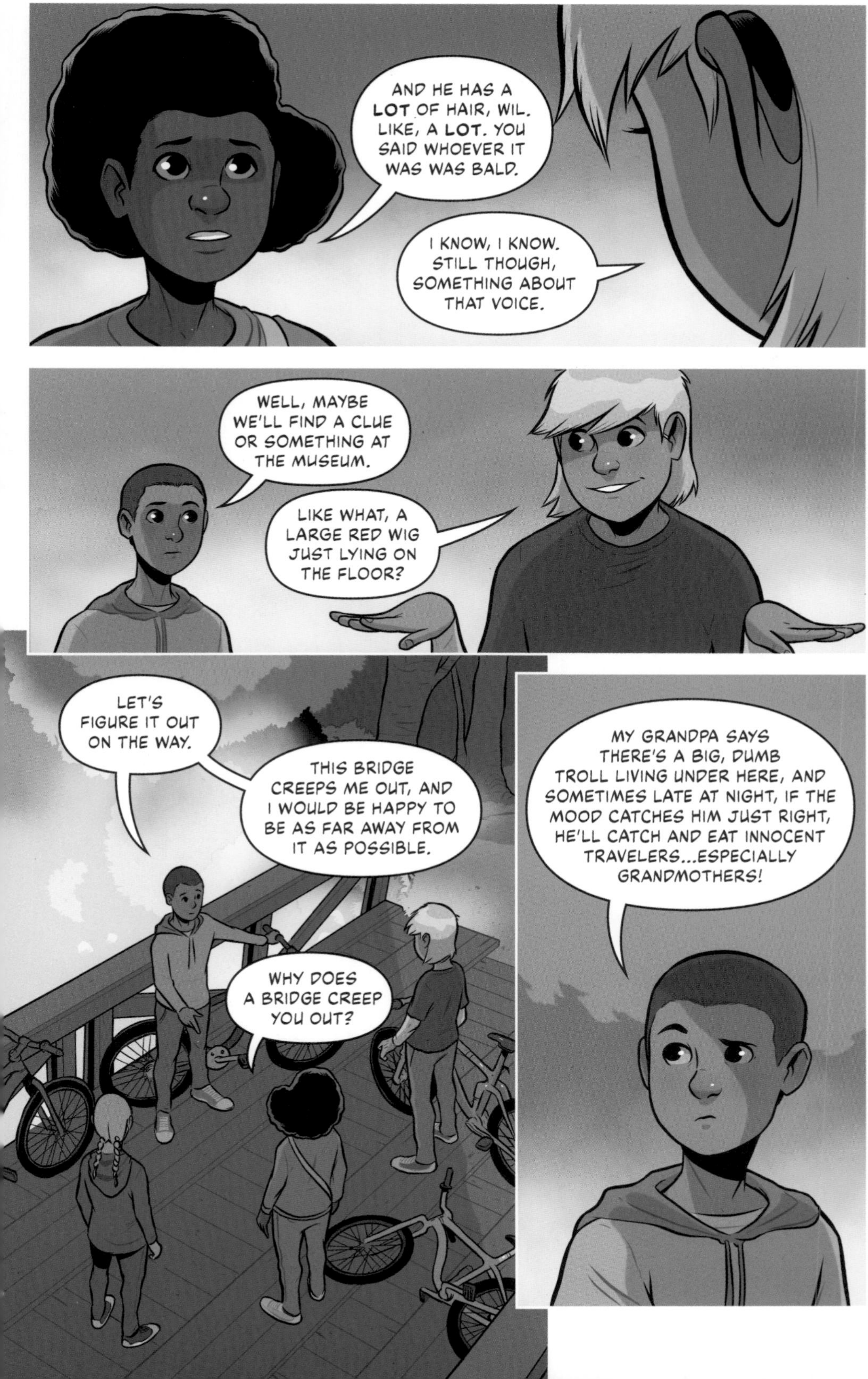
AND HE HAS A **LOT** OF HAIR, WIL. LIKE, A **LOT**. YOU SAID WHOEVER IT WAS WAS BALD.
I KNOW, I KNOW. STILL THOUGH, SOMETHING ABOUT THAT VOICE.
WELL, MAYBE WE'LL FIND A CLUE OR SOMETHING AT THE MUSEUM.
LIKE WHAT, A LARGE RED WIG JUST LYING ON THE FLOOR?
LET'S FIGURE IT OUT ON THE WAY.
THIS BRIDGE CREEPS ME OUT, AND I WOULD BE HAPPY TO BE AS FAR AWAY FROM IT AS POSSIBLE.
WHY DOES A BRIDGE CREEP YOU OUT?
MY GRANDPA SAYS THERE'S A BIG, DUMB TROLL LIVING UNDER HERE, AND SOMETIMES LATE AT NIGHT, IF THE MOOD CATCHES HIM JUST RIGHT, HE'LL CATCH AND EAT INNOCENT TRAVELERS...ESPECIALLY GRANDMOTHERS!

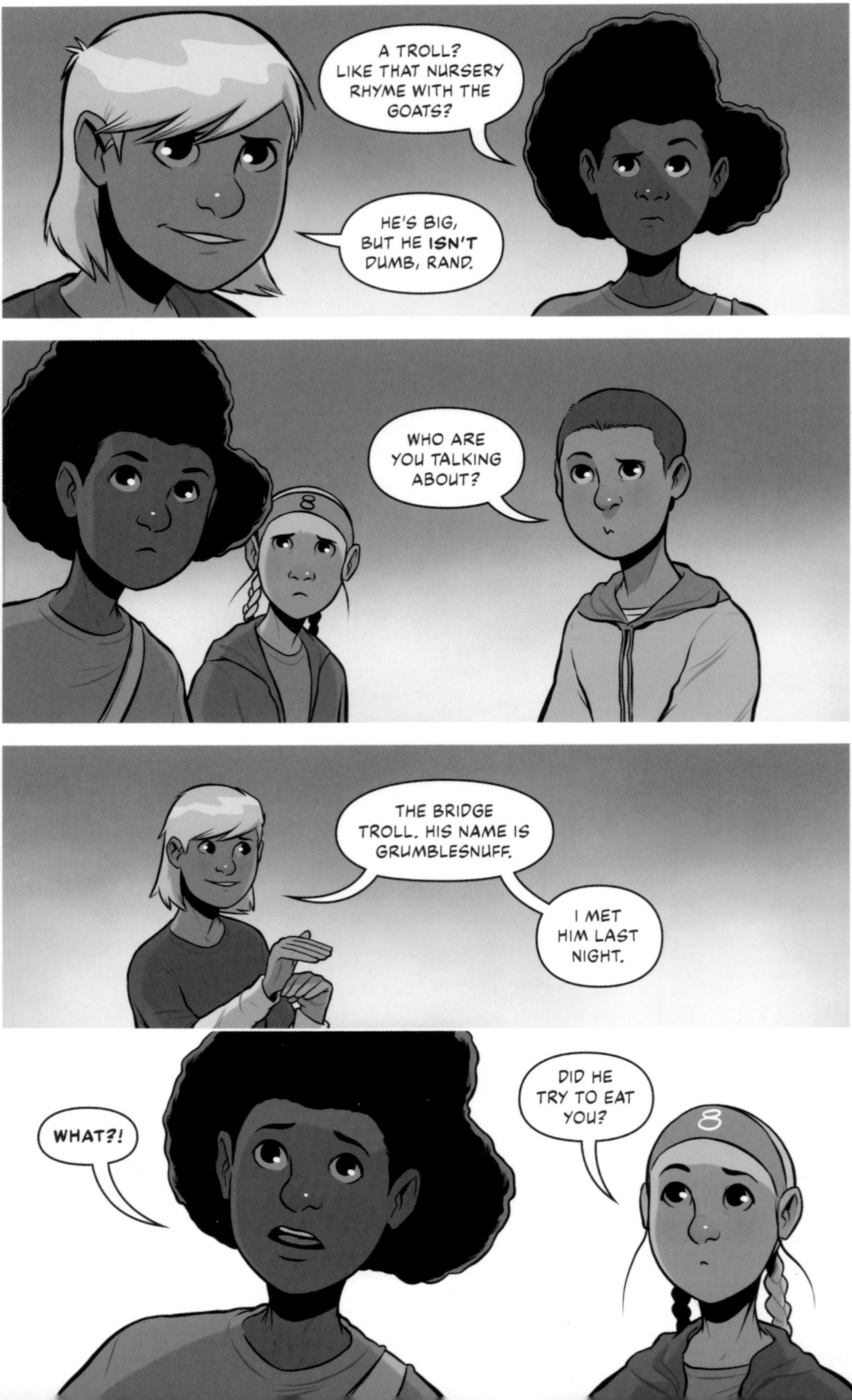
A TROLL? LIKE THAT NURSERY RHYME WITH THE GOATS?
HE'S BIG, BUT HE **ISN'T** DUMB, RAND.
WHO ARE YOU TALKING ABOUT?
THE BRIDGE TROLL. HIS NAME IS GRUMBLESNUFF.
I MET HIM LAST NIGHT.
WHAT?!
DID HE TRY TO EAT YOU?

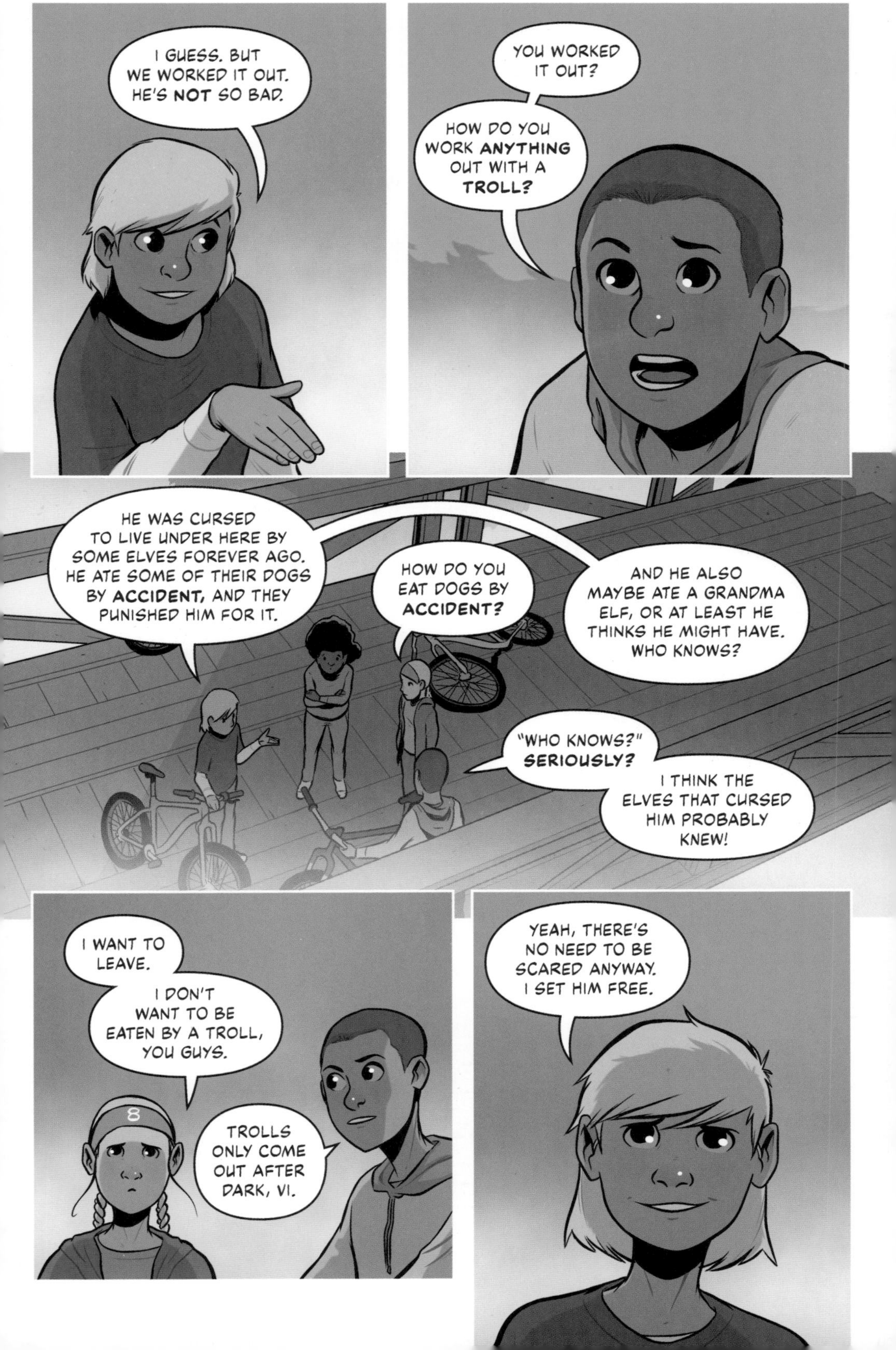
I GUESS. BUT WE WORKED IT OUT. HE'S **NOT** SO BAD.
YOU WORKED IT OUT?
HOW DO YOU WORK **ANYTHING** OUT WITH A **TROLL?**
HE WAS CURSED TO LIVE UNDER HERE BY SOME ELVES FOREVER AGO. HE ATE SOME OF THEIR DOGS BY **ACCIDENT,** AND THEY PUNISHED HIM FOR IT.
HOW DO YOU EAT DOGS BY **ACCIDENT?**
AND HE ALSO MAYBE ATE A GRANDMA ELF, OR AT LEAST HE THINKS HE MIGHT HAVE. WHO KNOWS?
"WHO KNOWS?" **SERIOUSLY?**
I THINK THE ELVES THAT CURSED HIM PROBABLY KNEW!
I WANT TO LEAVE.
I DON'T WANT TO BE EATEN BY A TROLL, YOU GUYS.
TROLLS ONLY COME OUT AFTER DARK, VI.
YEAH, THERE'S NO NEED TO BE SCARED ANYWAY. I SET HIM FREE.

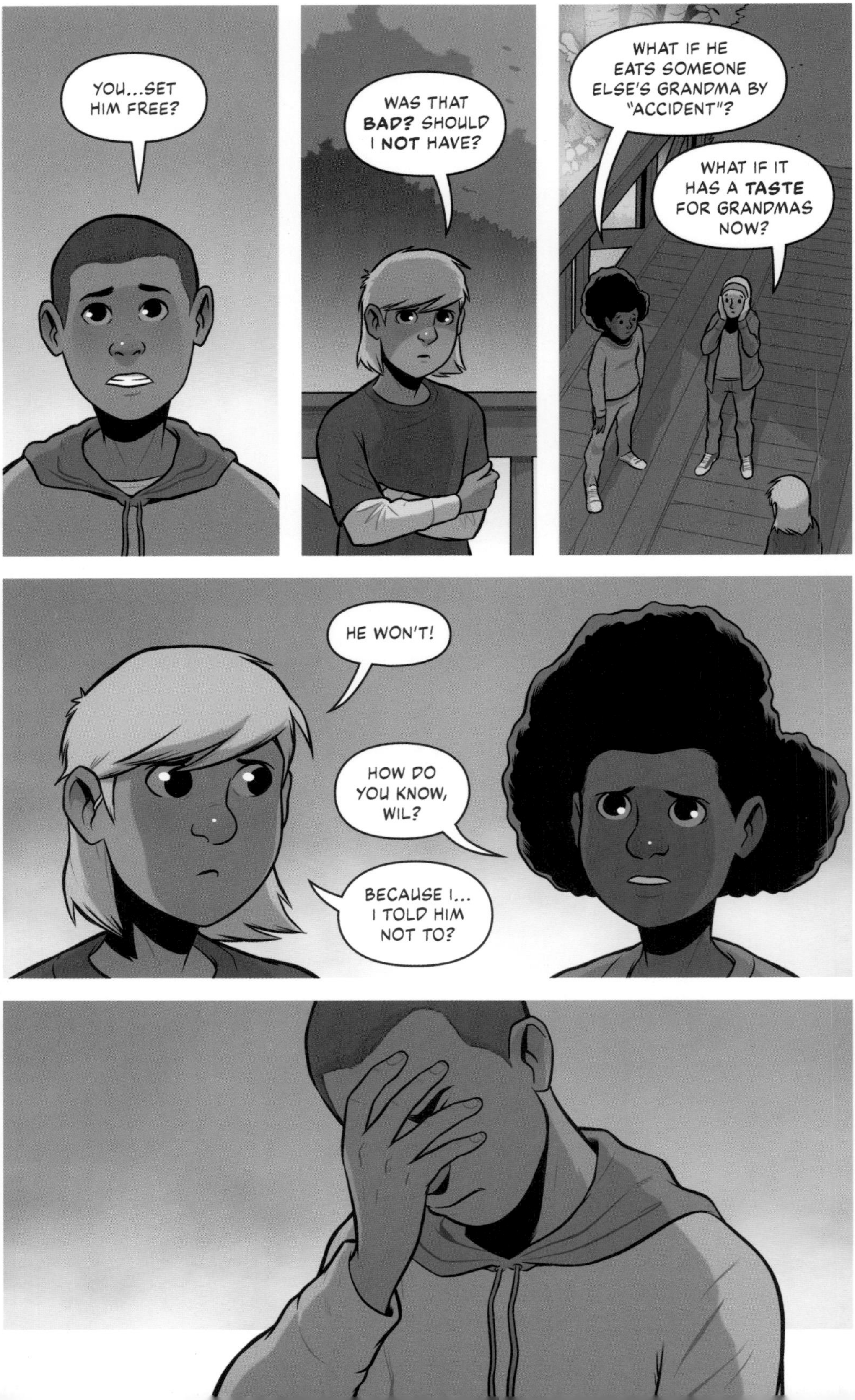
YOU...SET HIM FREE?
WAS THAT BAD? SHOULD I NOT HAVE?
WHAT IF HE EATS SOMEONE ELSE'S GRANDMA BY "ACCIDENT"?
WHAT IF IT HAS A TASTE FOR GRANDMAS NOW?
HE WON'T!
HOW DO YOU KNOW, WIL?
BECAUSE I... I TOLD HIM NOT TO?

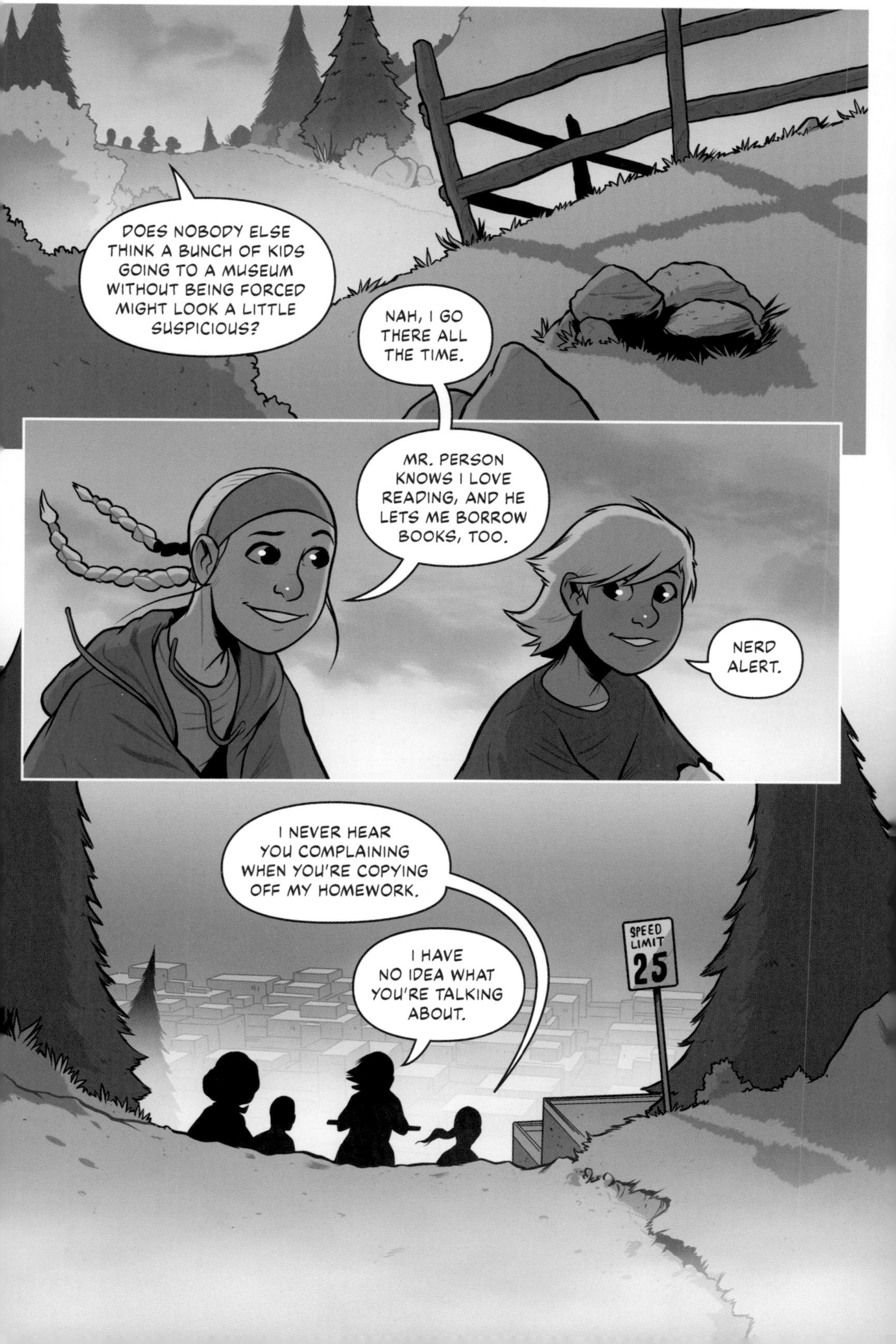
DOES NOBODY ELSE THINK A BUNCH OF KIDS GOING TO A MUSEUM WITHOUT BEING FORCED MIGHT LOOK A LITTLE SUSPICIOUS?
NAH, I GO THERE ALL THE TIME.
MR. PERSON KNOWS I LOVE READING, AND HE LETS ME BORROW BOOKS, TOO.
NERD ALERT.
I NEVER HEAR YOU COMPLAINING WHEN YOU'RE COPYING OFF MY HOMEWORK.
I HAVE NO IDEA WHAT YOU'RE TALKING ABOUT.
SPEED LIMIT 25

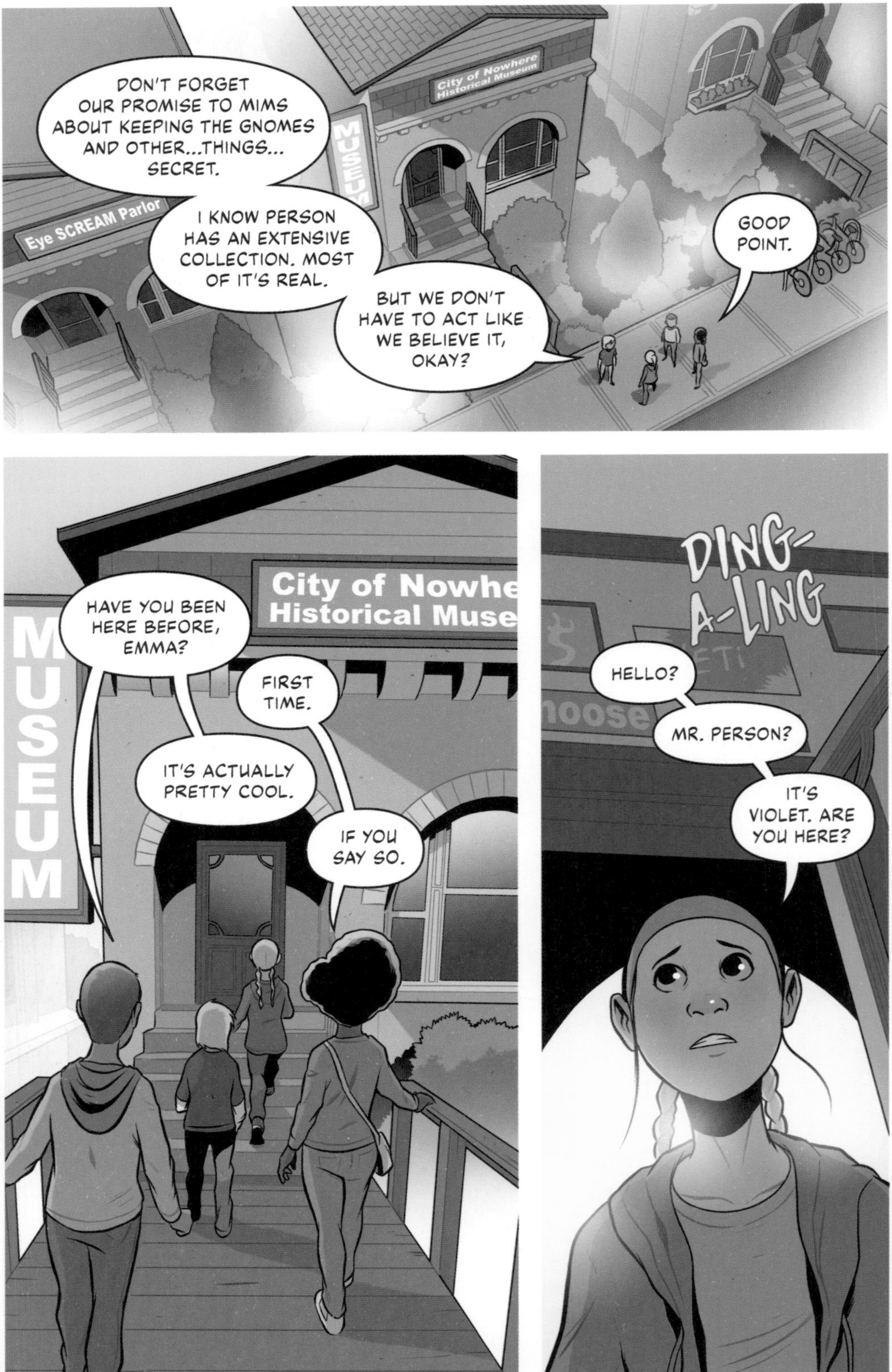
City of Nowhere Historical Museum
MUSEUM
Eye SCREAM Parlor
DON'T FORGET OUR PROMISE TO MIMS ABOUT KEEPING THE GNOMES AND OTHER...THINGS... SECRET.
I KNOW PERSON HAS AN EXTENSIVE COLLECTION. MOST OF IT'S REAL.
BUT WE DON'T HAVE TO ACT LIKE WE BELIEVE IT, OKAY?
GOOD POINT.
MUSEUM
City of Nowhe
Historical Muse
HAVE YOU BEEN HERE BEFORE, EMMA?
FIRST TIME.
IT'S ACTUALLY PRETTY COOL.
IF YOU SAY SO.
DING-A-LING
HELLO?
MR. PERSON?
IT'S VIOLET. ARE YOU HERE?

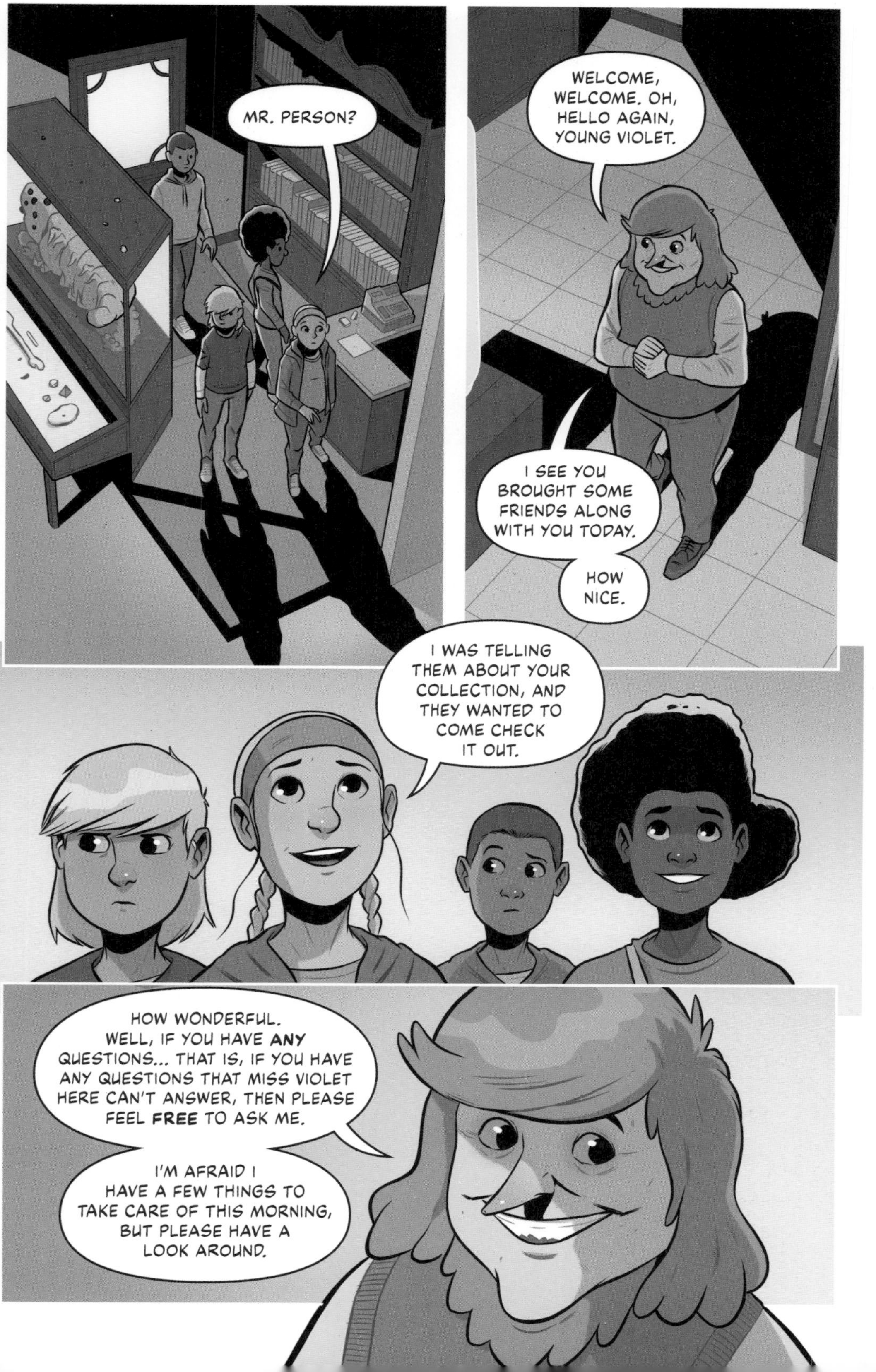
MR. PERSON?
WELCOME, WELCOME. OH, HELLO AGAIN, YOUNG VIOLET.
I SEE YOU BROUGHT SOME FRIENDS ALONG WITH YOU TODAY.
HOW NICE.
I WAS TELLING THEM ABOUT YOUR COLLECTION, AND THEY WANTED TO COME CHECK IT OUT.
HOW WONDERFUL. WELL, IF YOU HAVE **ANY** QUESTIONS... THAT IS, IF YOU HAVE ANY QUESTIONS THAT MISS VIOLET HERE CAN'T ANSWER, THEN PLEASE FEEL **FREE** TO ASK ME.
I'M AFRAID I HAVE A FEW THINGS TO TAKE CARE OF THIS MORNING, BUT PLEASE HAVE A LOOK AROUND.

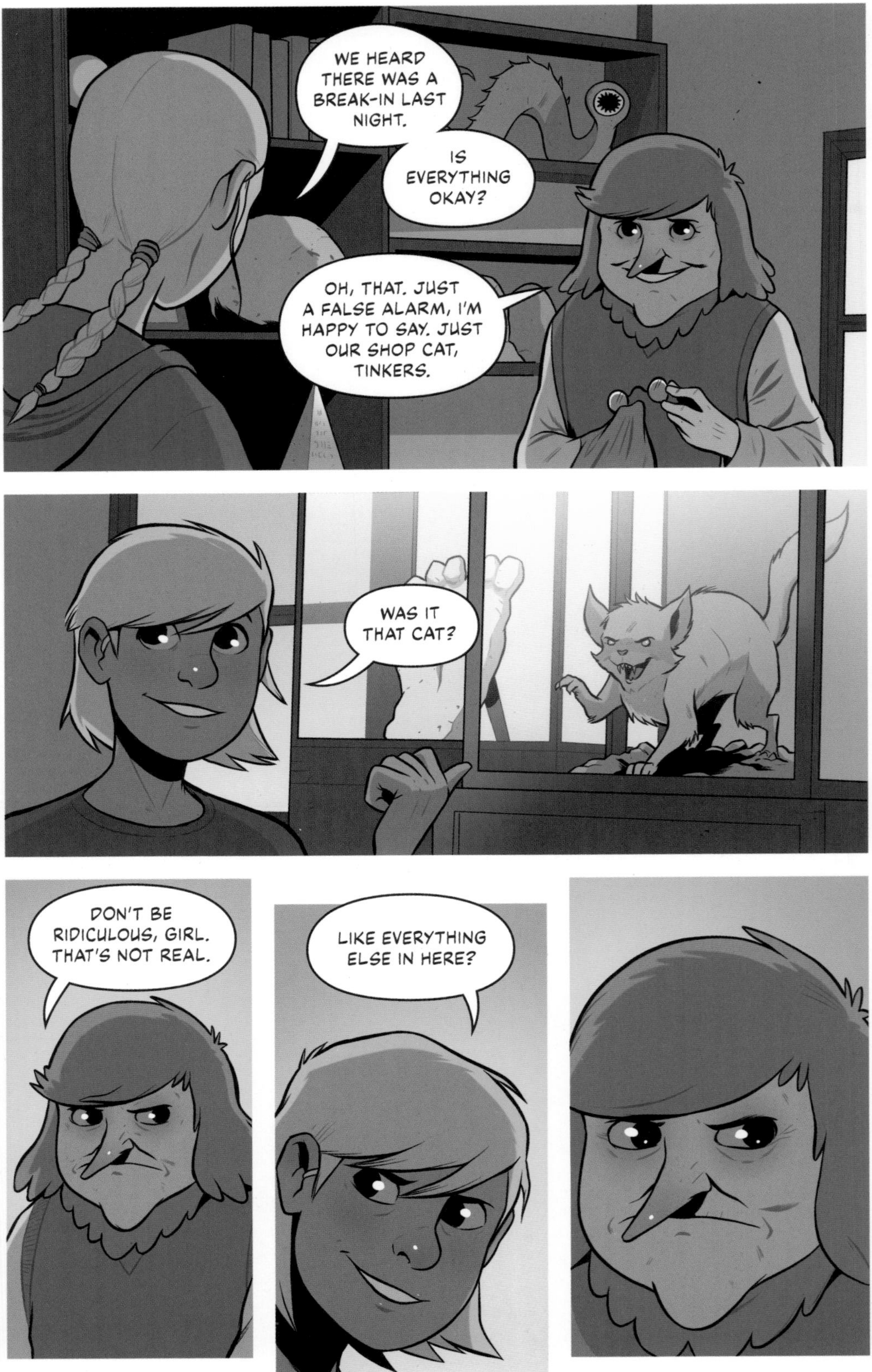
WE HEARD THERE WAS A BREAK-IN LAST NIGHT.
IS EVERYTHING OKAY?
OH, THAT. JUST A FALSE ALARM, I'M HAPPY TO SAY. JUST OUR SHOP CAT, TINKERS.
WAS IT THAT CAT?
DON'T BE RIDICULOUS, GIRL. THAT'S NOT REAL.
LIKE EVERYTHING ELSE IN HERE?

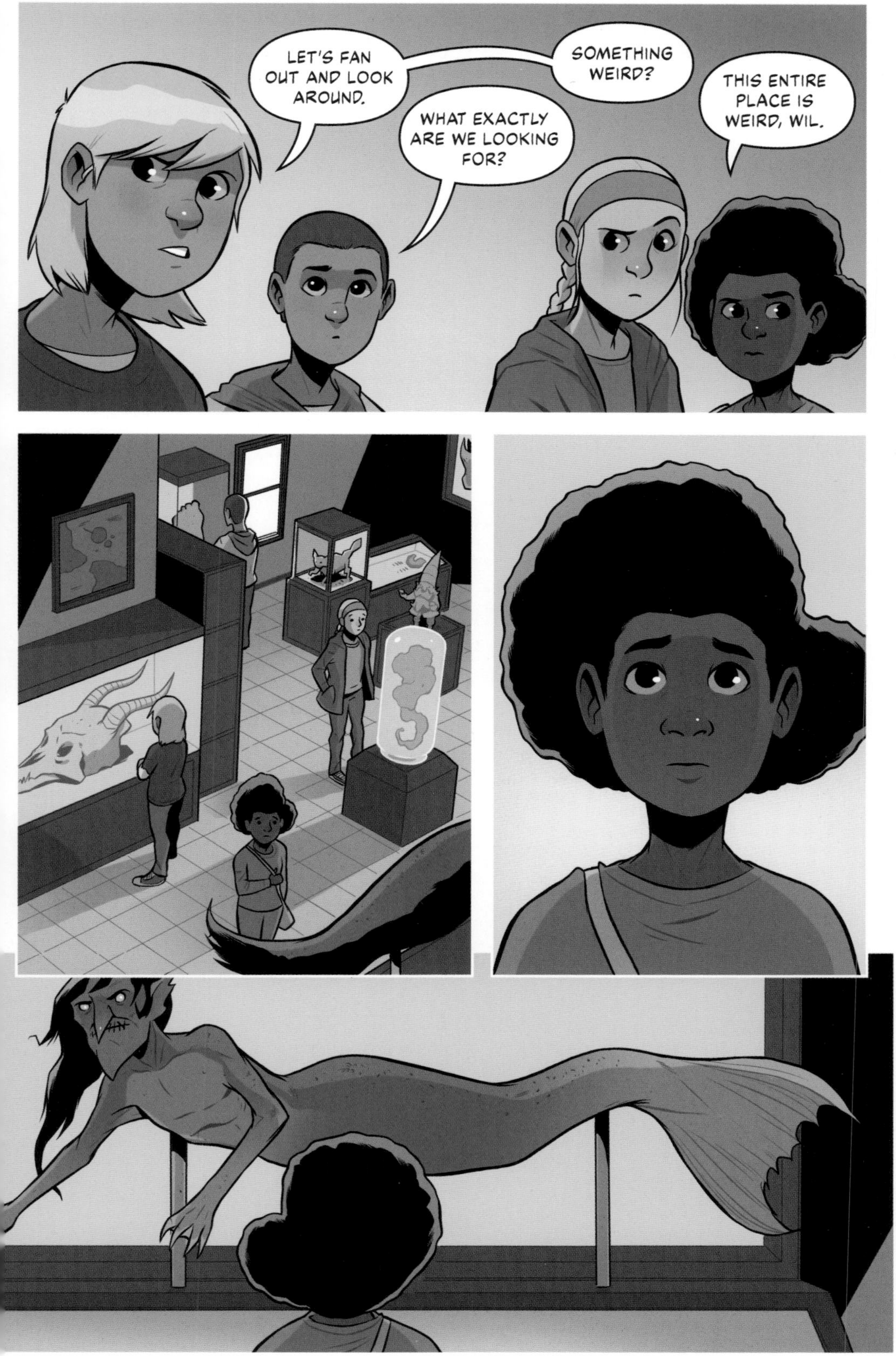
LET'S FAN OUT AND LOOK AROUND.
SOMETHING WEIRD?
WHAT EXACTLY ARE WE LOOKING FOR?
THIS ENTIRE PLACE IS WEIRD, WIL.

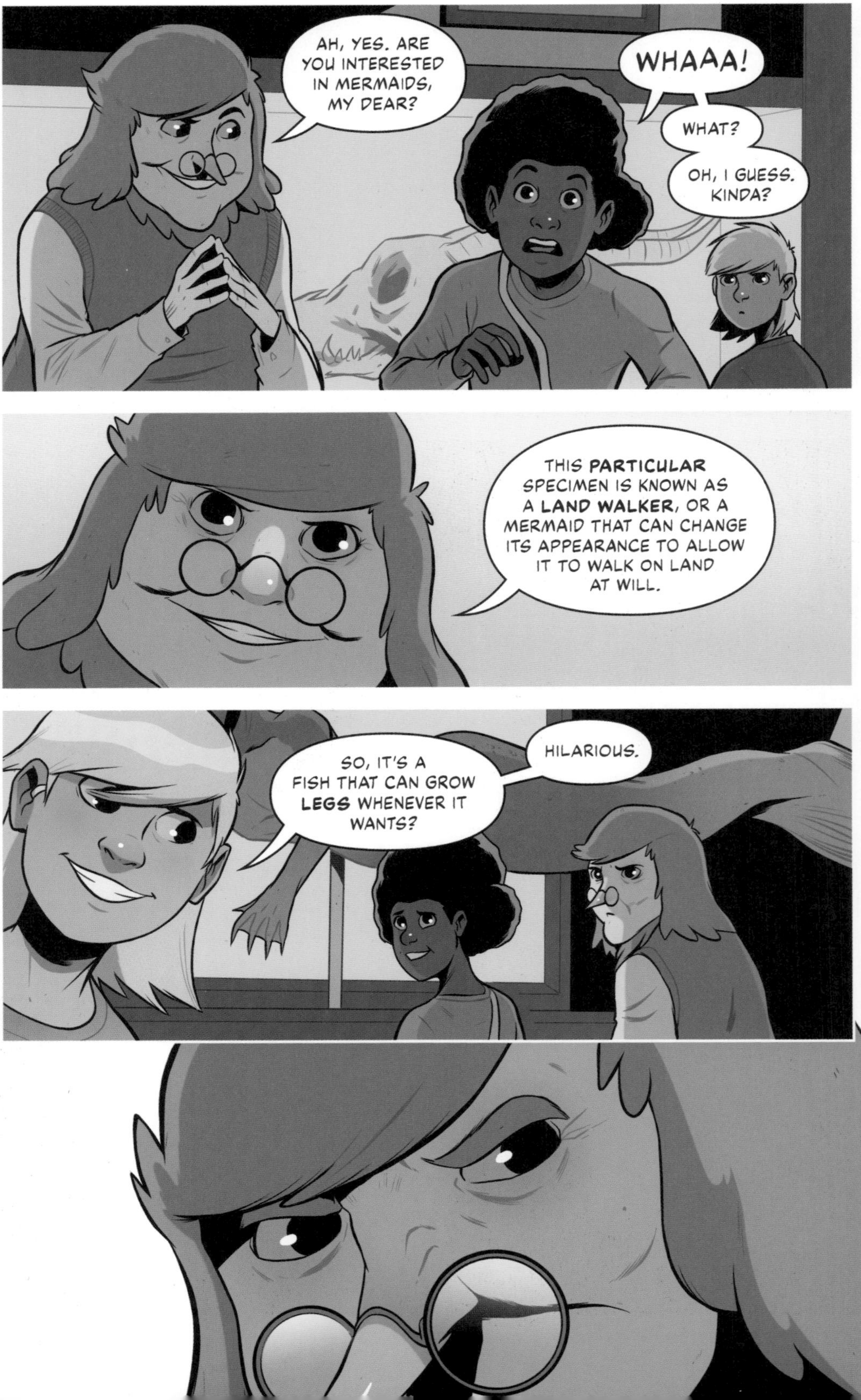
AH, YES. ARE YOU INTERESTED IN MERMAIDS, MY DEAR?
WHAAA!
WHAT?
OH, I GUESS. KINDA?
THIS **PARTICULAR** SPECIMEN IS KNOWN AS A **LAND WALKER**, OR A MERMAID THAT CAN CHANGE ITS APPEARANCE TO ALLOW IT TO WALK ON LAND AT WILL.
SO, IT'S A FISH THAT CAN GROW **LEGS** WHENEVER IT WANTS?
HILARIOUS.

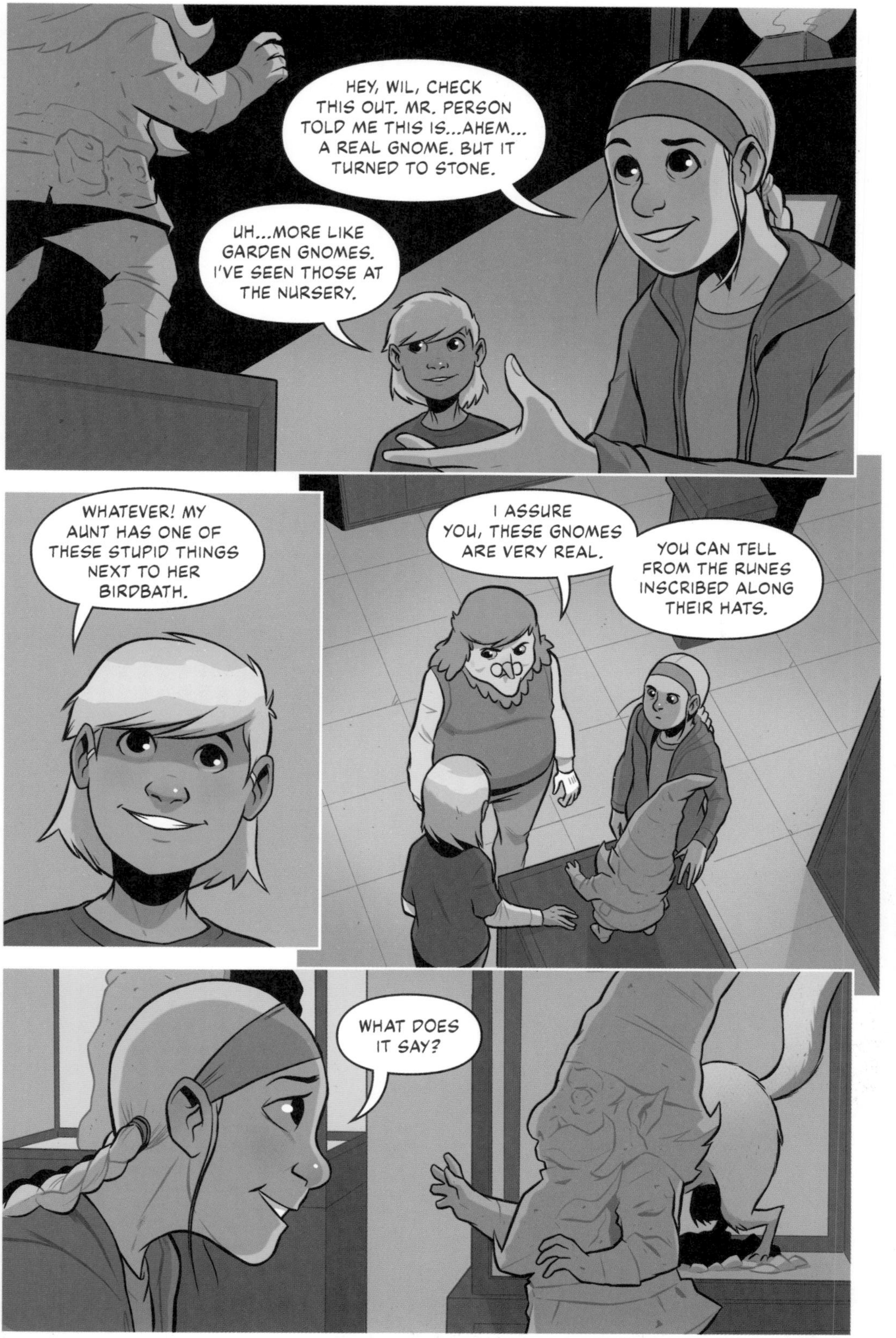
HEY, WIL, CHECK THIS OUT. MR. PERSON TOLD ME THIS IS...AHEM... A REAL GNOME. BUT IT TURNED TO STONE.
UH...MORE LIKE GARDEN GNOMES. I'VE SEEN THOSE AT THE NURSERY.
WHATEVER! MY AUNT HAS ONE OF THESE STUPID THINGS NEXT TO HER BIRDBATH.
I ASSURE YOU, THESE GNOMES ARE VERY REAL.
YOU CAN TELL FROM THE RUNES INSCRIBED ALONG THEIR HATS.
WHAT DOES IT SAY?

NOBODY KNOWS. AT LEAST, NOBODY WHO DOESN'T SPEAK GNOMISH, THAT IS.

YOU DON'T KNOW GNOMISH, MR. PERSON?

GOOD HEAVENS, NO.

IT'S QUITE **FORBIDDEN** FOR ANYONE BUT A **GNOME** TO HAVE THAT KNOWLEDGE.

WHY IS THAT?

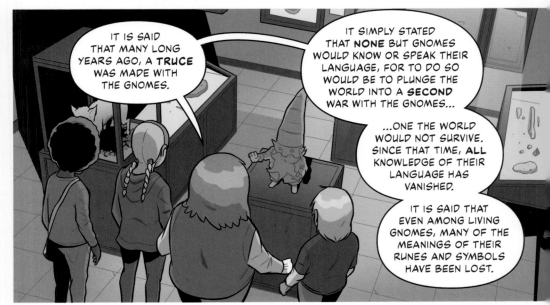

IT IS SAID THAT MANY LONG YEARS AGO, A **TRUCE** WAS MADE WITH THE GNOMES.

IT SIMPLY STATED THAT **NONE** BUT GNOMES WOULD KNOW OR SPEAK THEIR LANGUAGE, FOR TO DO SO WOULD BE TO PLUNGE THE WORLD INTO A **SECOND** WAR WITH THE GNOMES...

...ONE THE WORLD WOULD NOT SURVIVE. SINCE THAT TIME, **ALL** KNOWLEDGE OF THEIR LANGUAGE HAS VANISHED.

IT IS SAID THAT EVEN AMONG LIVING GNOMES, MANY OF THE MEANINGS OF THEIR RUNES AND SYMBOLS HAVE BEEN LOST.

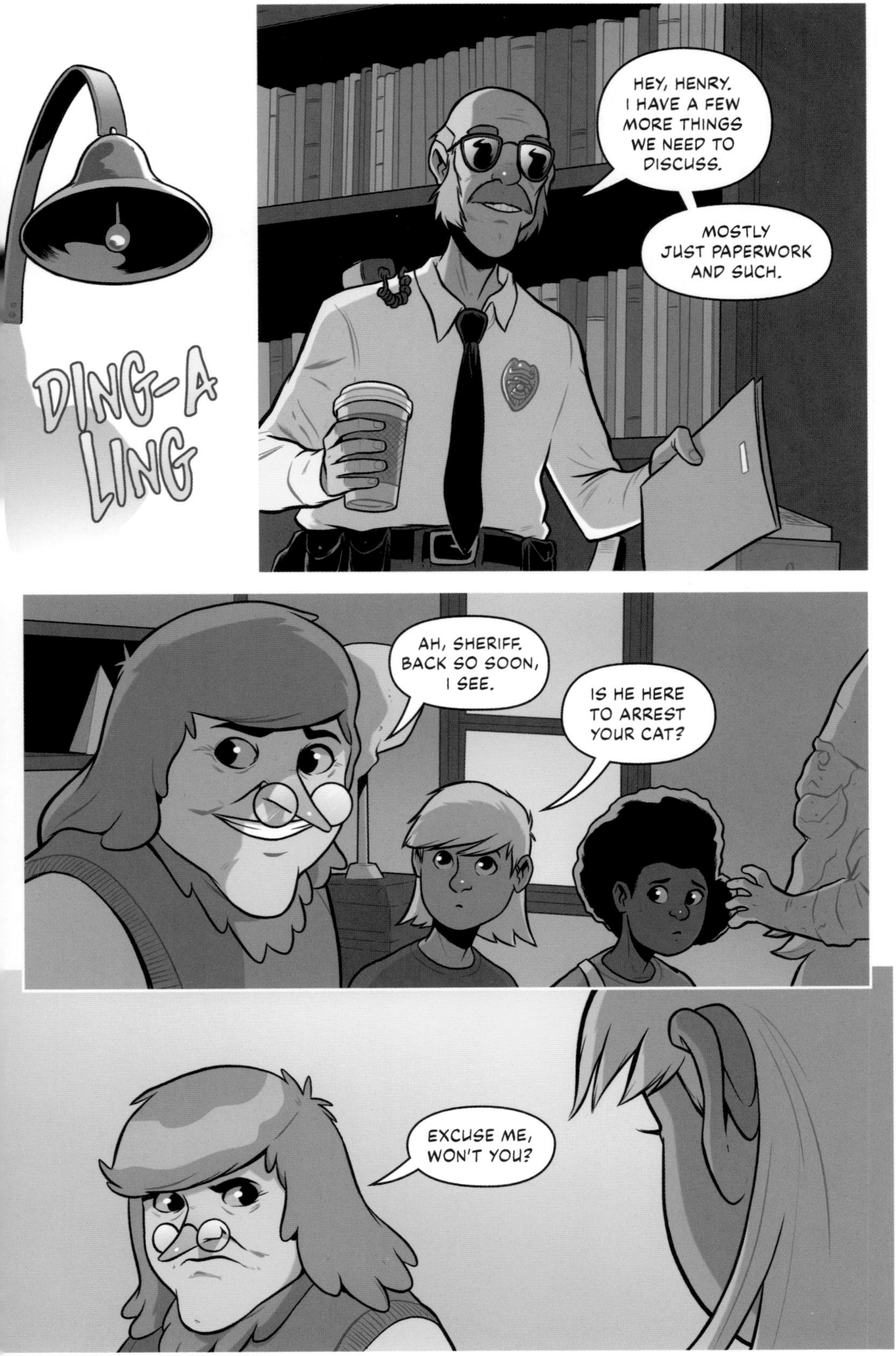
DING-A LING
HEY, HENRY. I HAVE A FEW MORE THINGS WE NEED TO DISCUSS.
MOSTLY JUST PAPERWORK AND SUCH.
AH, SHERIFF. BACK SO SOON, I SEE.
IS HE HERE TO ARREST YOUR CAT?
EXCUSE ME, WON'T YOU?

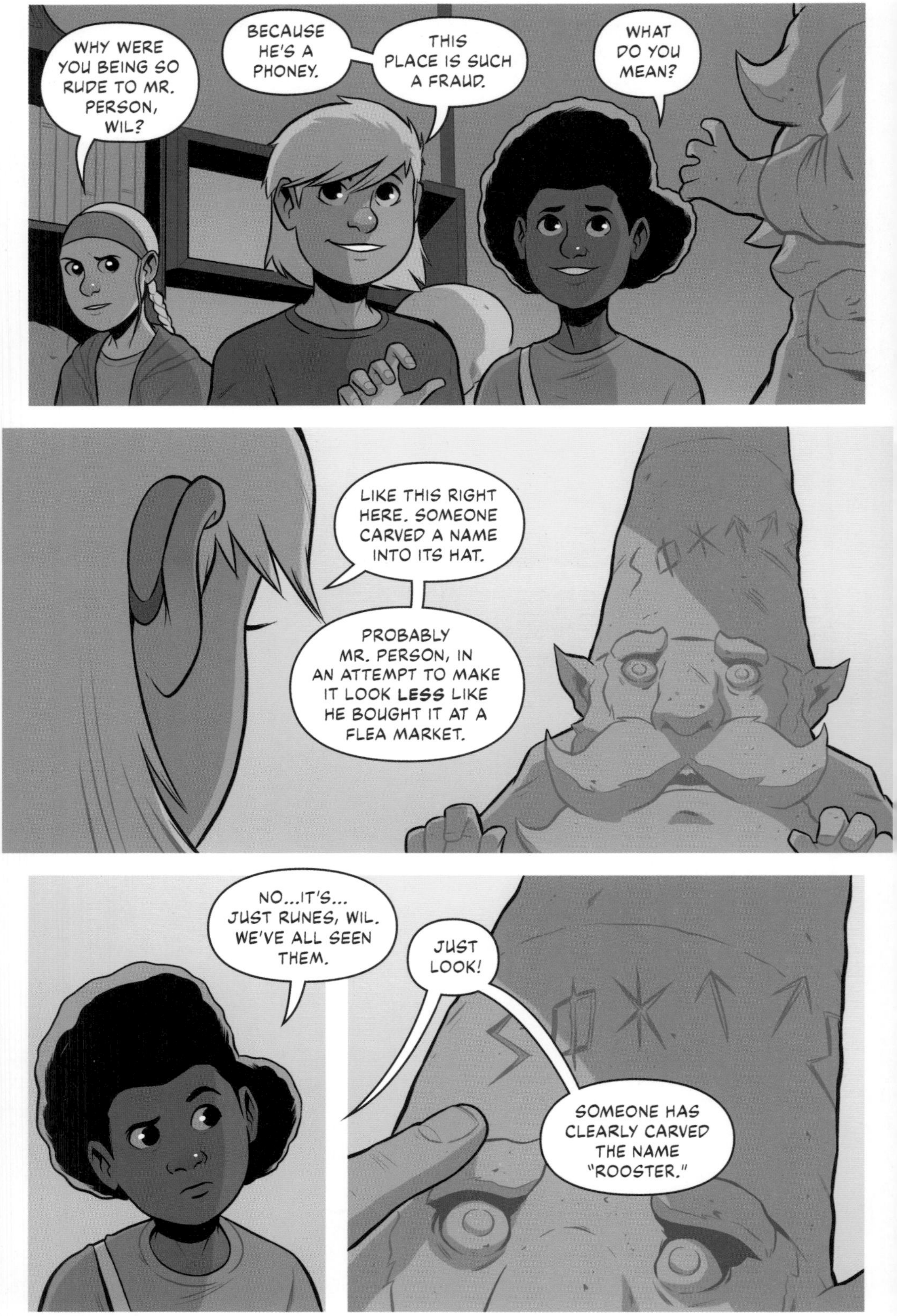
WHY WERE YOU BEING SO RUDE TO MR. PERSON, WIL?
BECAUSE HE'S A PHONEY.
THIS PLACE IS SUCH A FRAUD.
WHAT DO YOU MEAN?
LIKE THIS RIGHT HERE. SOMEONE CARVED A NAME INTO ITS HAT.
PROBABLY MR. PERSON, IN AN ATTEMPT TO MAKE IT LOOK **LESS** LIKE HE BOUGHT IT AT A FLEA MARKET.
NO...IT'S... JUST RUNES, WIL. WE'VE ALL SEEN THEM.
JUST LOOK!
SOMEONE HAS CLEARLY CARVED THE NAME "ROOSTER."

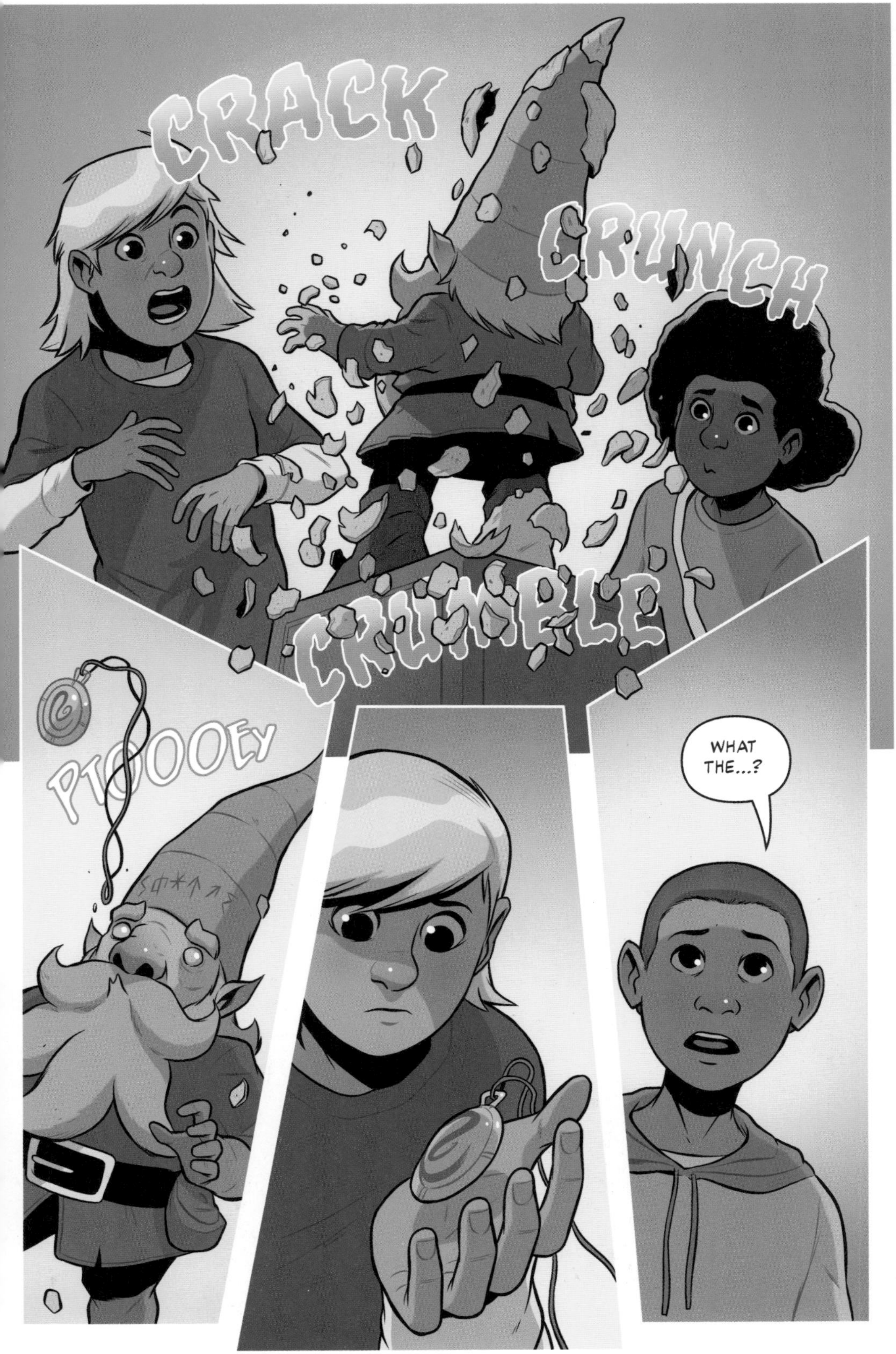
CRACK
CRUNCH
CRUMBLE
PTOOOEy
WHAT THE...?

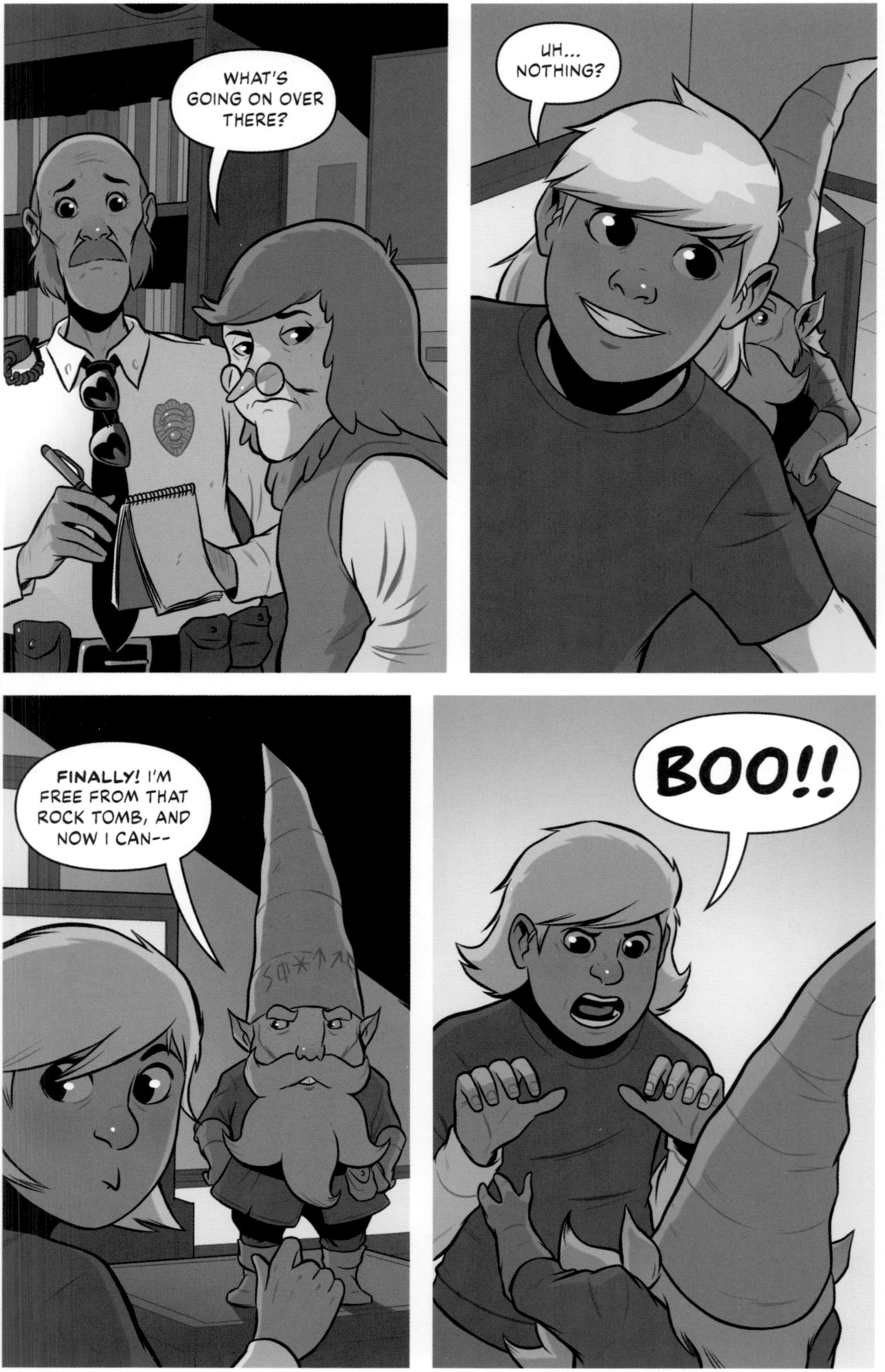
WHAT'S GOING ON OVER THERE?
UH... NOTHING?
FINALLY! I'M FREE FROM THAT ROCK TOMB, AND NOW I CAN--
BOO!!

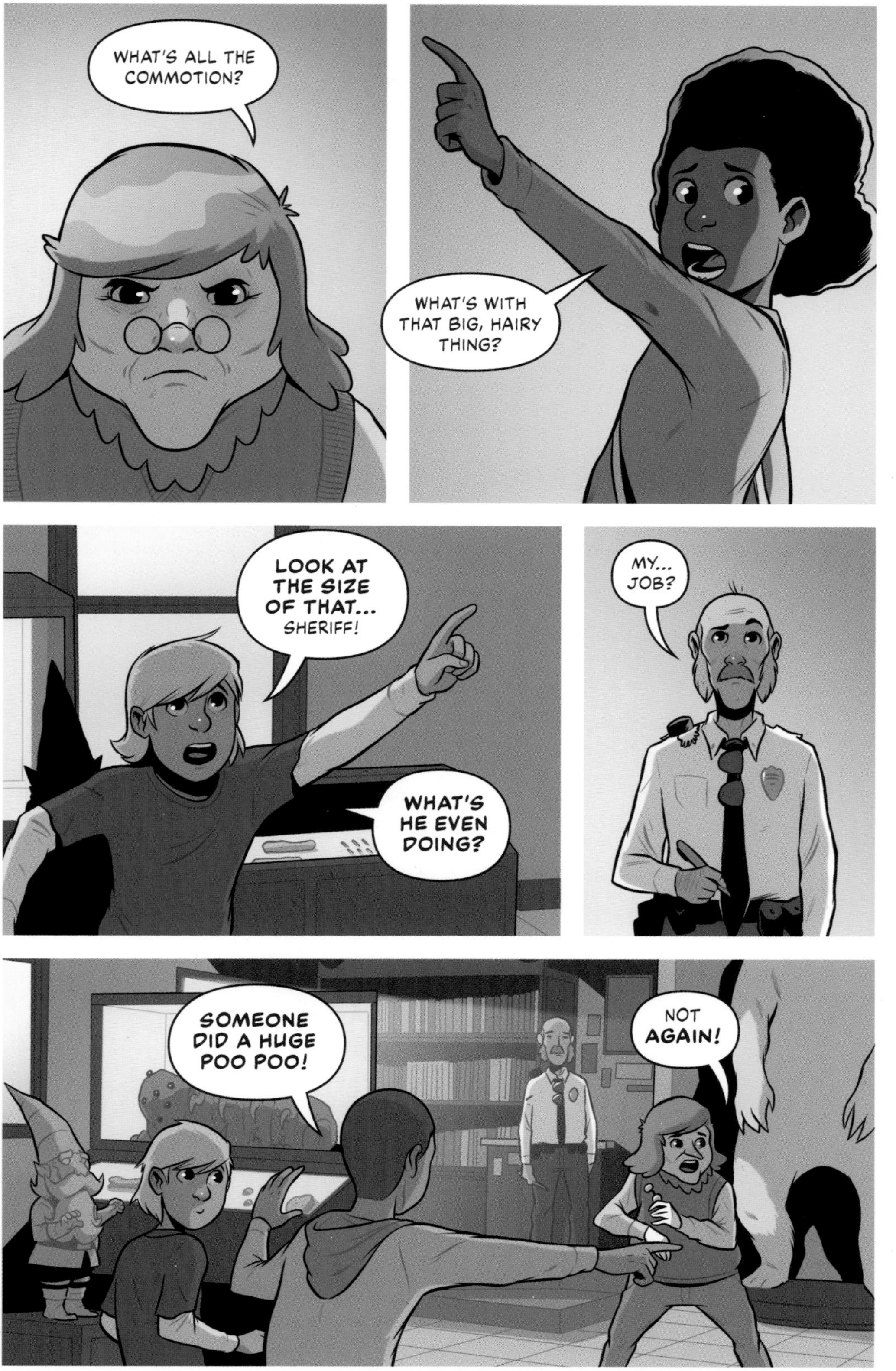
WHAT'S ALL THE COMMOTION?
WHAT'S WITH THAT BIG, HAIRY THING?
LOOK AT THE SIZE OF THAT... SHERIFF!
WHAT'S HE EVEN DOING?
MY... JOB?
SOMEONE DID A HUGE POO POO!
NOT AGAIN!

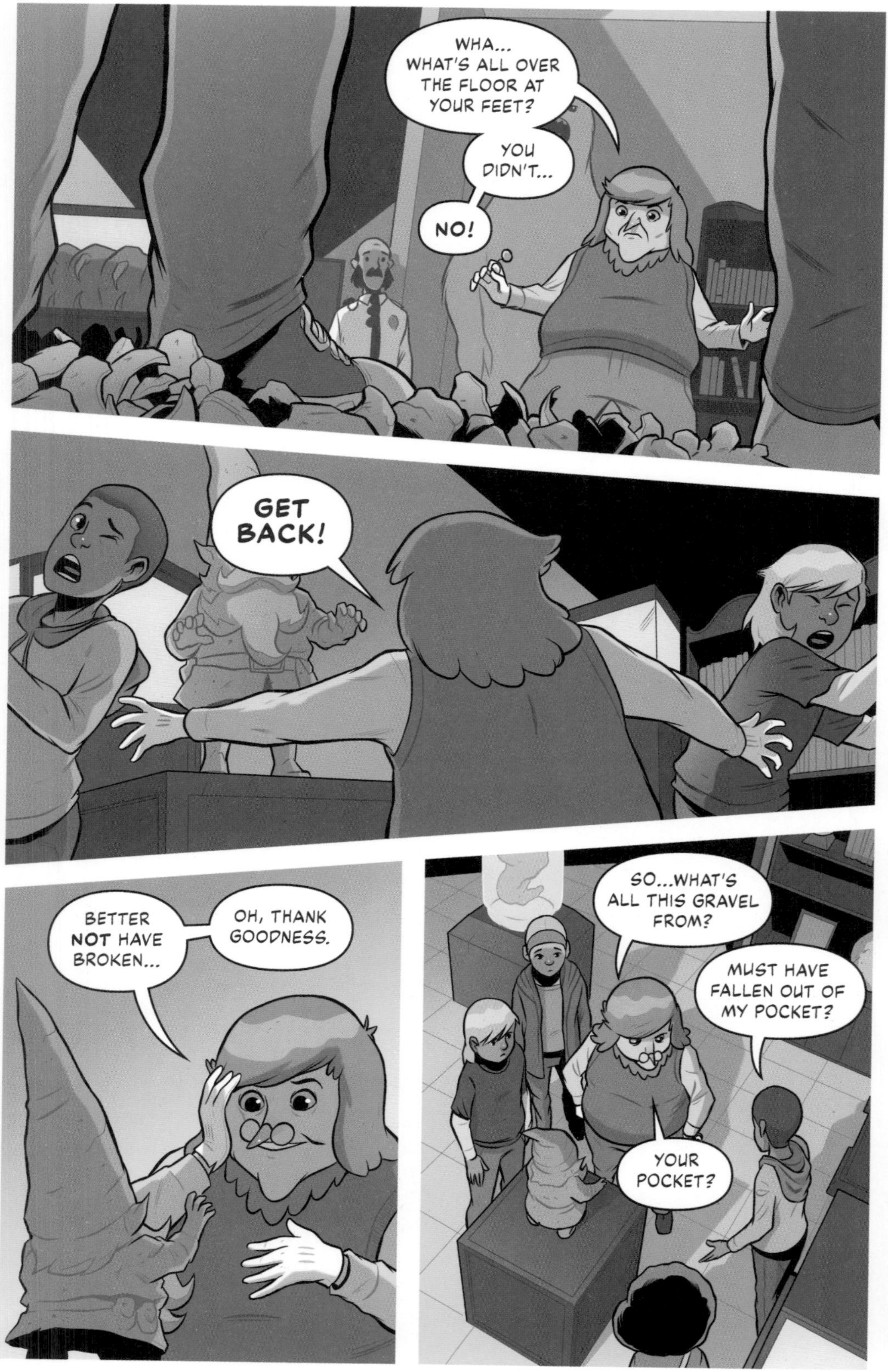
WHA... WHAT'S ALL OVER THE FLOOR AT YOUR FEET?
YOU DIDN'T...
NO!
GET BACK!
BETTER **NOT** HAVE BROKEN...
OH, THANK GOODNESS.
SO...WHAT'S ALL THIS GRAVEL FROM?
MUST HAVE FALLEN OUT OF MY POCKET?
YOUR POCKET?

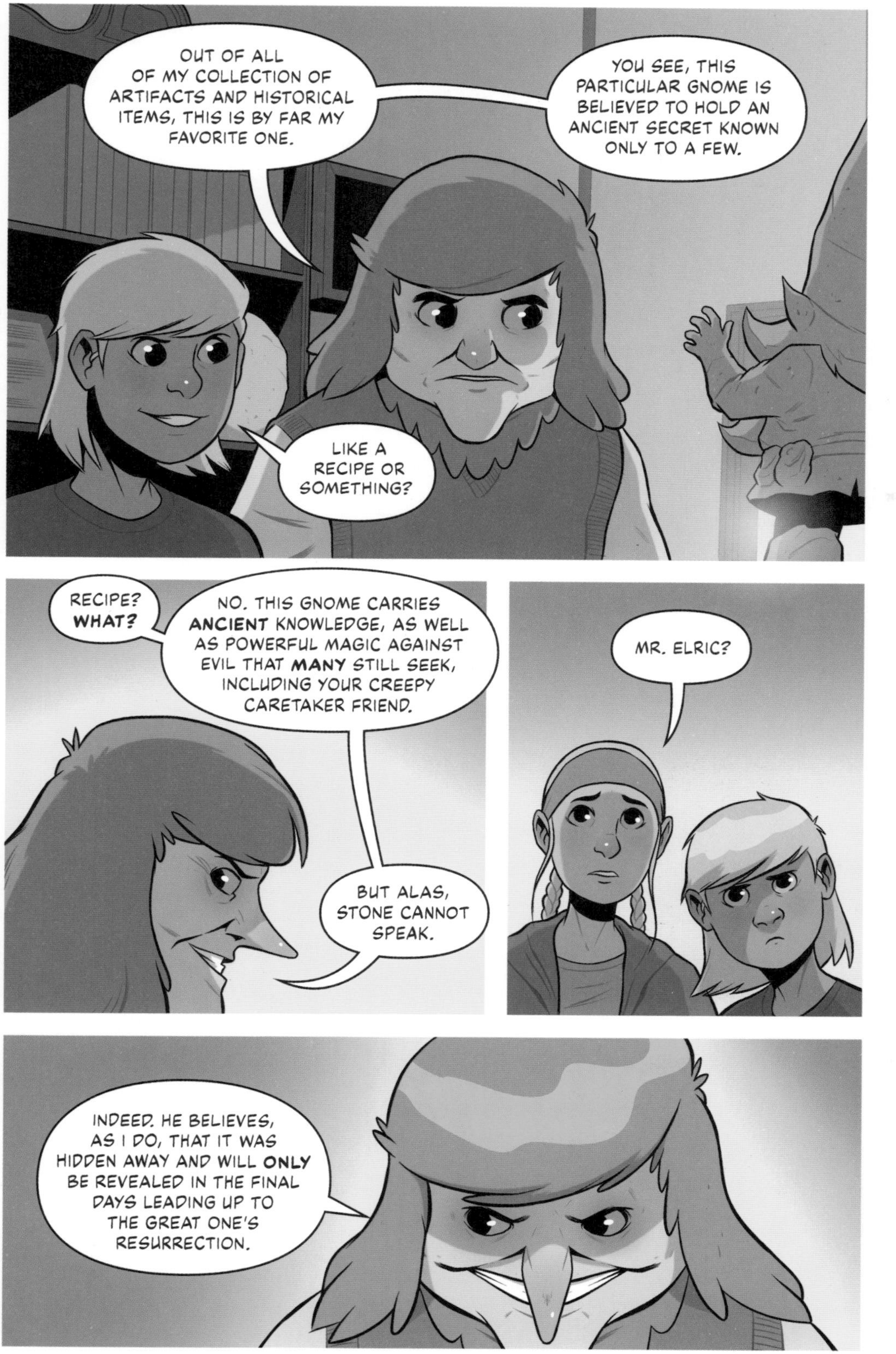
OUT OF ALL OF MY COLLECTION OF ARTIFACTS AND HISTORICAL ITEMS, THIS IS BY FAR MY FAVORITE ONE.
YOU SEE, THIS PARTICULAR GNOME IS BELIEVED TO HOLD AN ANCIENT SECRET KNOWN ONLY TO A FEW.
LIKE A RECIPE OR SOMETHING?
RECIPE? **WHAT?**
NO. THIS GNOME CARRIES **ANCIENT** KNOWLEDGE, AS WELL AS POWERFUL MAGIC AGAINST EVIL THAT **MANY** STILL SEEK, INCLUDING YOUR CREEPY CARETAKER FRIEND.
BUT ALAS, STONE CANNOT SPEAK.
MR. ELRIC?
INDEED. HE BELIEVES, AS I DO, THAT IT WAS HIDDEN AWAY AND WILL **ONLY** BE REVEALED IN THE FINAL DAYS LEADING UP TO THE GREAT ONE'S RESURRECTION.

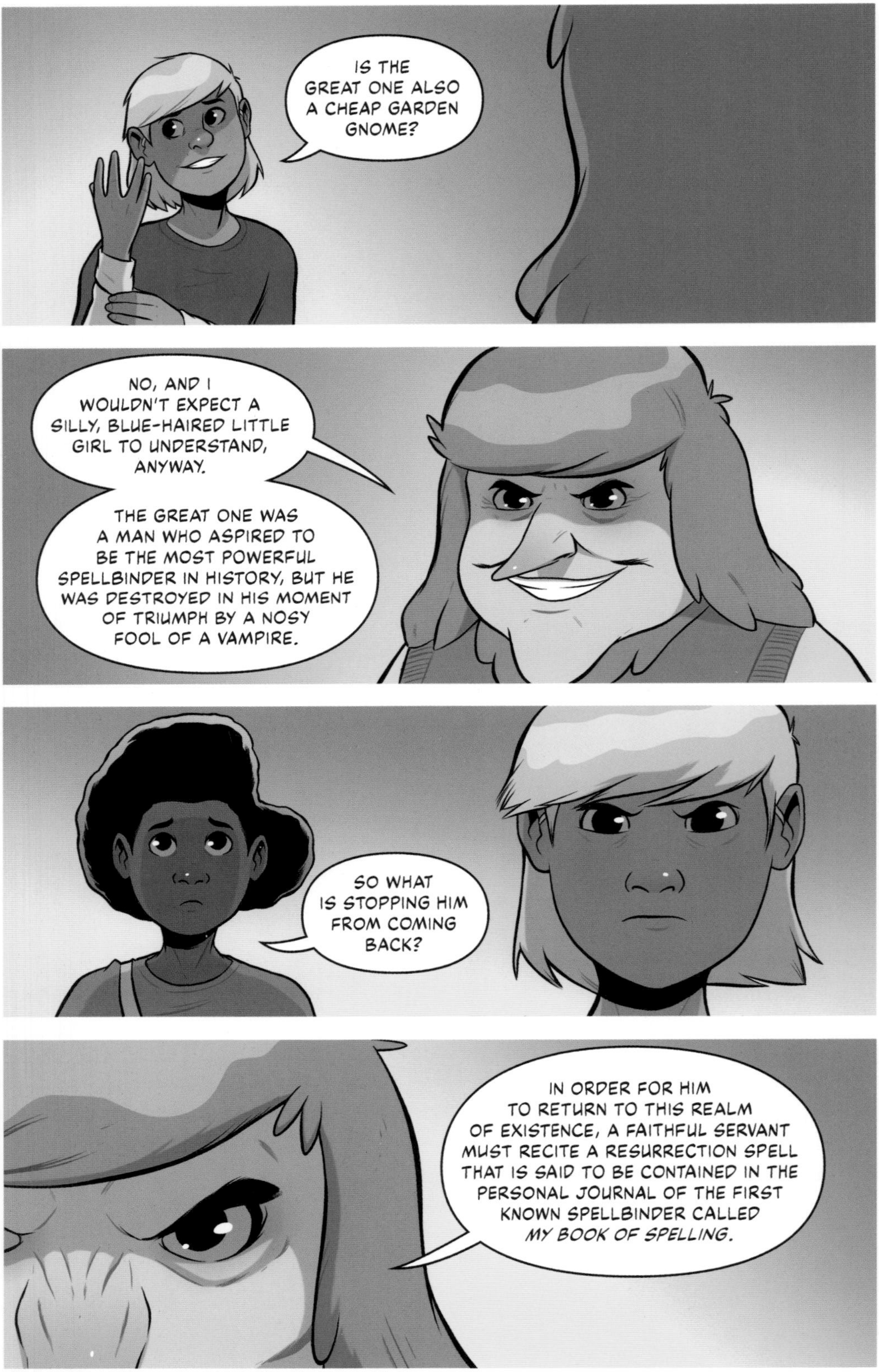
IS THE GREAT ONE ALSO A CHEAP GARDEN GNOME?
NO, AND I WOULDN'T EXPECT A SILLY, BLUE-HAIRED LITTLE GIRL TO UNDERSTAND, ANYWAY.
THE GREAT ONE WAS A MAN WHO ASPIRED TO BE THE MOST POWERFUL SPELLBINDER IN HISTORY, BUT HE WAS DESTROYED IN HIS MOMENT OF TRIUMPH BY A NOSY FOOL OF A VAMPIRE.
SO WHAT IS STOPPING HIM FROM COMING BACK?
IN ORDER FOR HIM TO RETURN TO THIS REALM OF EXISTENCE, A FAITHFUL SERVANT MUST RECITE A RESURRECTION SPELL THAT IS SAID TO BE CONTAINED IN THE PERSONAL JOURNAL OF THE FIRST KNOWN SPELLBINDER CALLED *MY BOOK OF SPELLING*.

HA HA HA

A SPELLING BOOK?

IT'S **NOT** THAT KIND OF SPELLING, VI.

IT'S A SPELL-BOOK.

THEY JUST CALLED IT SPELLING BACK THEN. IT'S WEIRD, I KNOW.

THAT'S... CORRECT, WILLOW, WAS IT?

THE JOURNAL IS MAGICALLY SEALED ALONG WITH THE BODY OF THE SPELLBINDER, IN HIS TOMB.

UNFORTUNATELY, THE LOCATION OF THIS TOMB HAS BEEN **LOST** TO HISTORY AND CAN ONLY BE DISCOVERED WITH THE HELP OF A **KEY**.

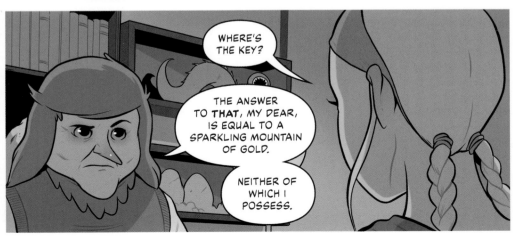

WHERE'S THE KEY?

THE ANSWER TO **THAT**, MY DEAR, IS EQUAL TO A SPARKLING MOUNTAIN OF GOLD.

NEITHER OF WHICH I POSSESS.

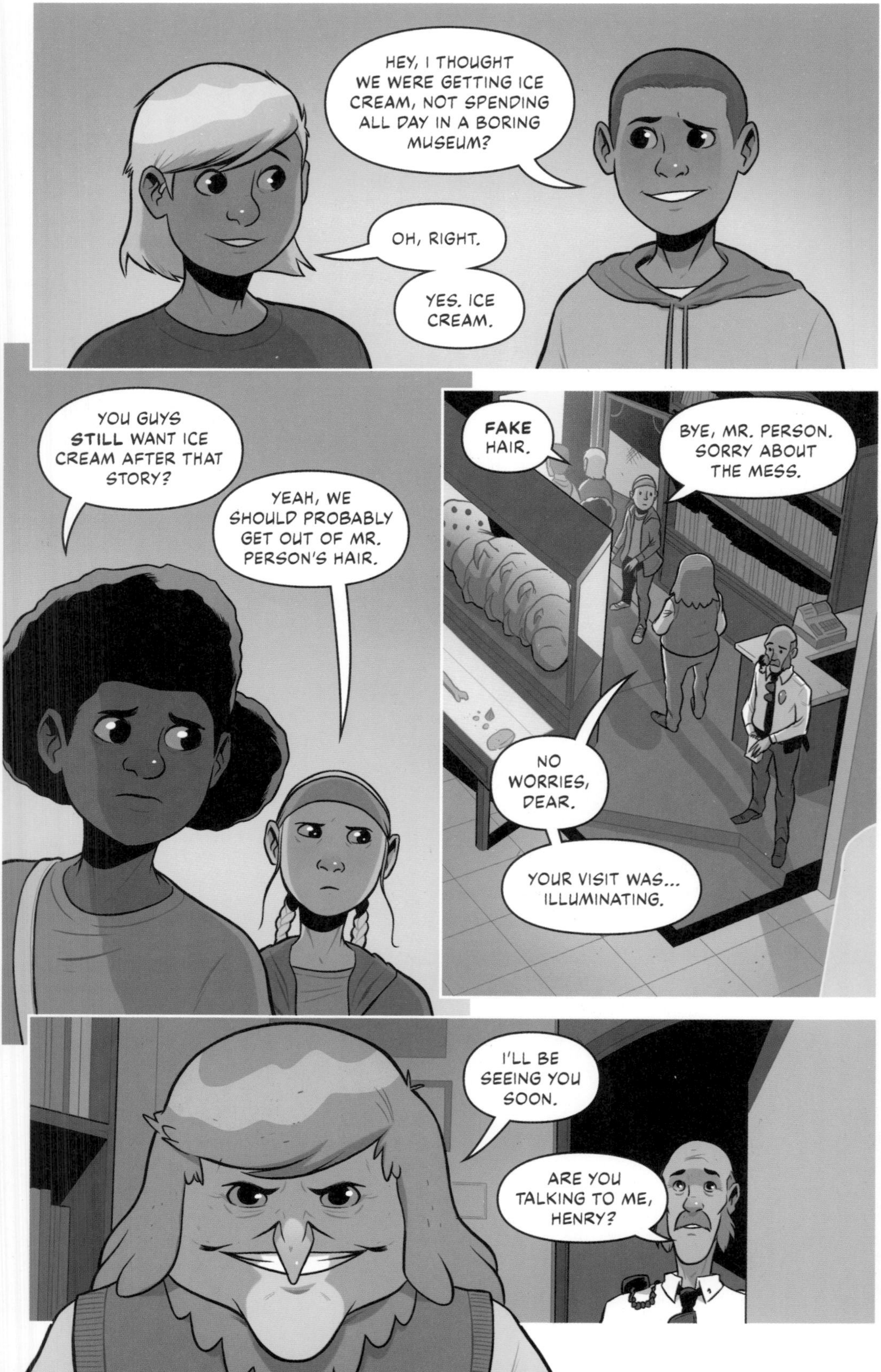
HEY, I THOUGHT WE WERE GETTING ICE CREAM, NOT SPENDING ALL DAY IN A BORING MUSEUM?
OH, RIGHT.
YES. ICE CREAM.
YOU GUYS **STILL** WANT ICE CREAM AFTER THAT STORY?
YEAH, WE SHOULD PROBABLY GET OUT OF MR. PERSON'S HAIR.
FAKE HAIR.
BYE, MR. PERSON. SORRY ABOUT THE MESS.
NO WORRIES, DEAR.
YOUR VISIT WAS... ILLUMINATING.
I'LL BE SEEING YOU SOON.
ARE YOU TALKING TO ME, HENRY?

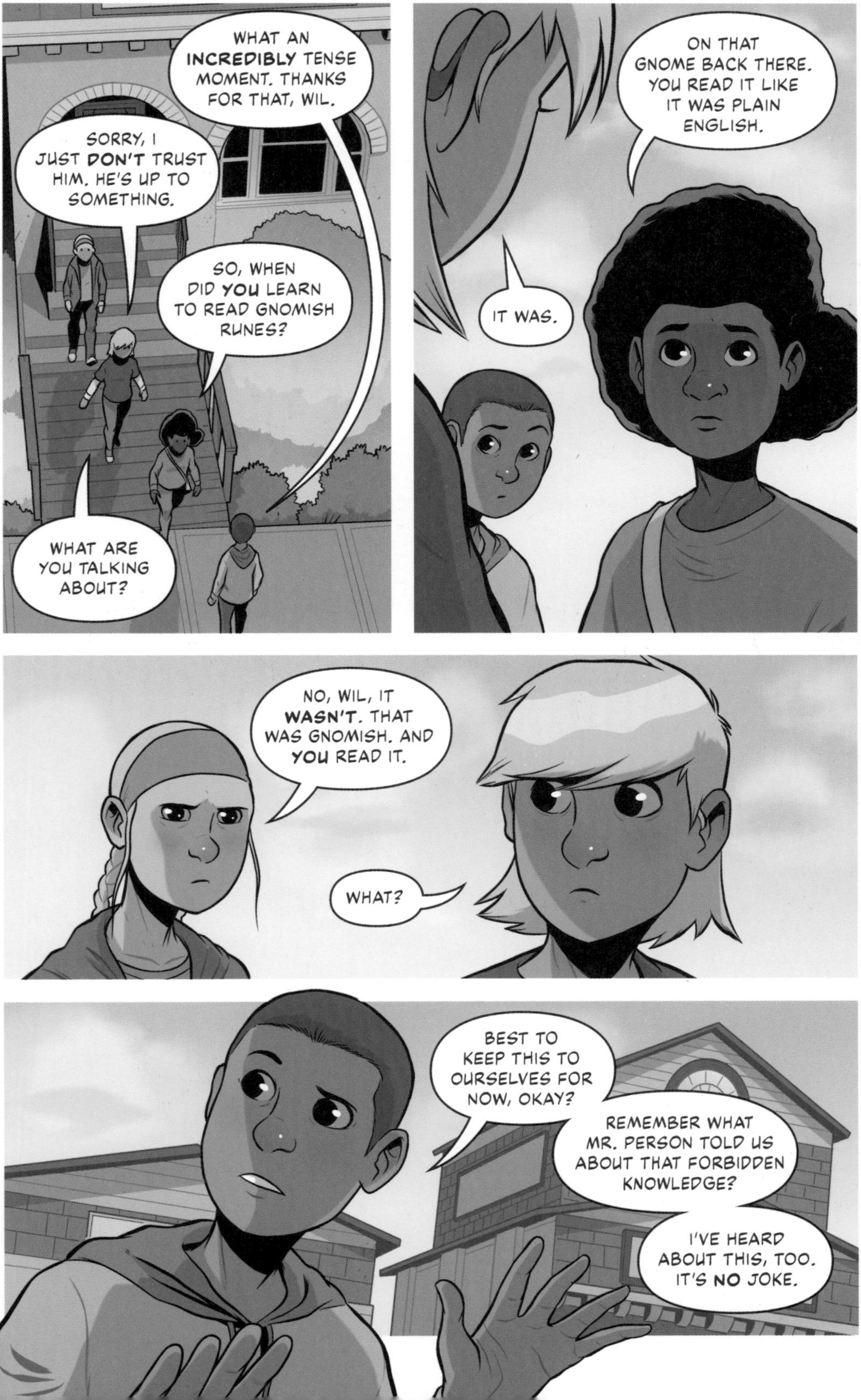
WHAT AN INCREDIBLY TENSE MOMENT. THANKS FOR THAT, WIL.
SORRY, I JUST DON'T TRUST HIM. HE'S UP TO SOMETHING.
SO, WHEN DID YOU LEARN TO READ GNOMISH RUNES?
WHAT ARE YOU TALKING ABOUT?
ON THAT GNOME BACK THERE. YOU READ IT LIKE IT WAS PLAIN ENGLISH.
IT WAS.
NO, WIL, IT WASN'T. THAT WAS GNOMISH. AND YOU READ IT.
WHAT?
BEST TO KEEP THIS TO OURSELVES FOR NOW, OKAY?
REMEMBER WHAT MR. PERSON TOLD US ABOUT THAT FORBIDDEN KNOWLEDGE?
I'VE HEARD ABOUT THIS, TOO. IT'S NO JOKE.

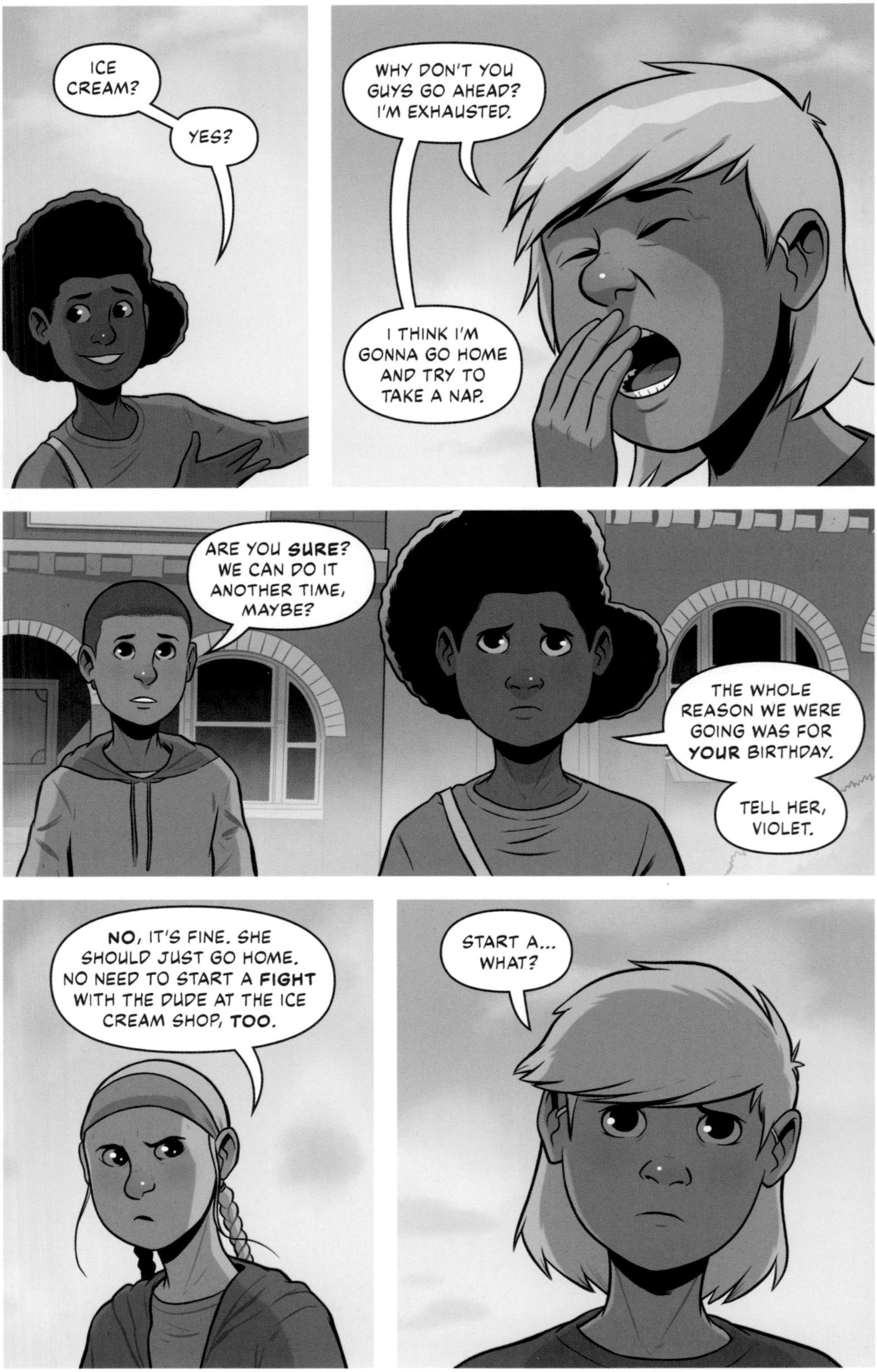
ICE CREAM?
YES?
WHY DON'T YOU GUYS GO AHEAD? I'M EXHAUSTED.
I THINK I'M GONNA GO HOME AND TRY TO TAKE A NAP.
ARE YOU SURE? WE CAN DO IT ANOTHER TIME, MAYBE?
THE WHOLE REASON WE WERE GOING WAS FOR YOUR BIRTHDAY.
TELL HER, VIOLET.
NO, IT'S FINE. SHE SHOULD JUST GO HOME. NO NEED TO START A FIGHT WITH THE DUDE AT THE ICE CREAM SHOP, TOO.
START A... WHAT?

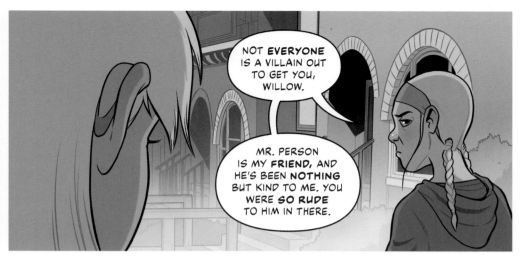

NOT **EVERYONE** IS A **VILLAIN** OUT TO GET YOU, WILLOW.

MR. PERSON IS MY **FRIEND**, AND HE'S BEEN **NOTHING** BUT KIND TO ME. YOU WERE **SO RUDE** TO HIM IN THERE.

HE'S UP TO SOMETHING, VIOLET! WE **ALL** KNOW IT!

RIGHT, EMMA? RAND?

I DON'T KNOW, WIL. HE SEEMS PRETTY **HARMLESS** TO ME.

COME HAVE ICE CREAM WITH US. IT'S MY TREAT.

NO. GO HAVE SOME FUN. I'LL CATCH UP WITH YOU LATER, I GUESS.

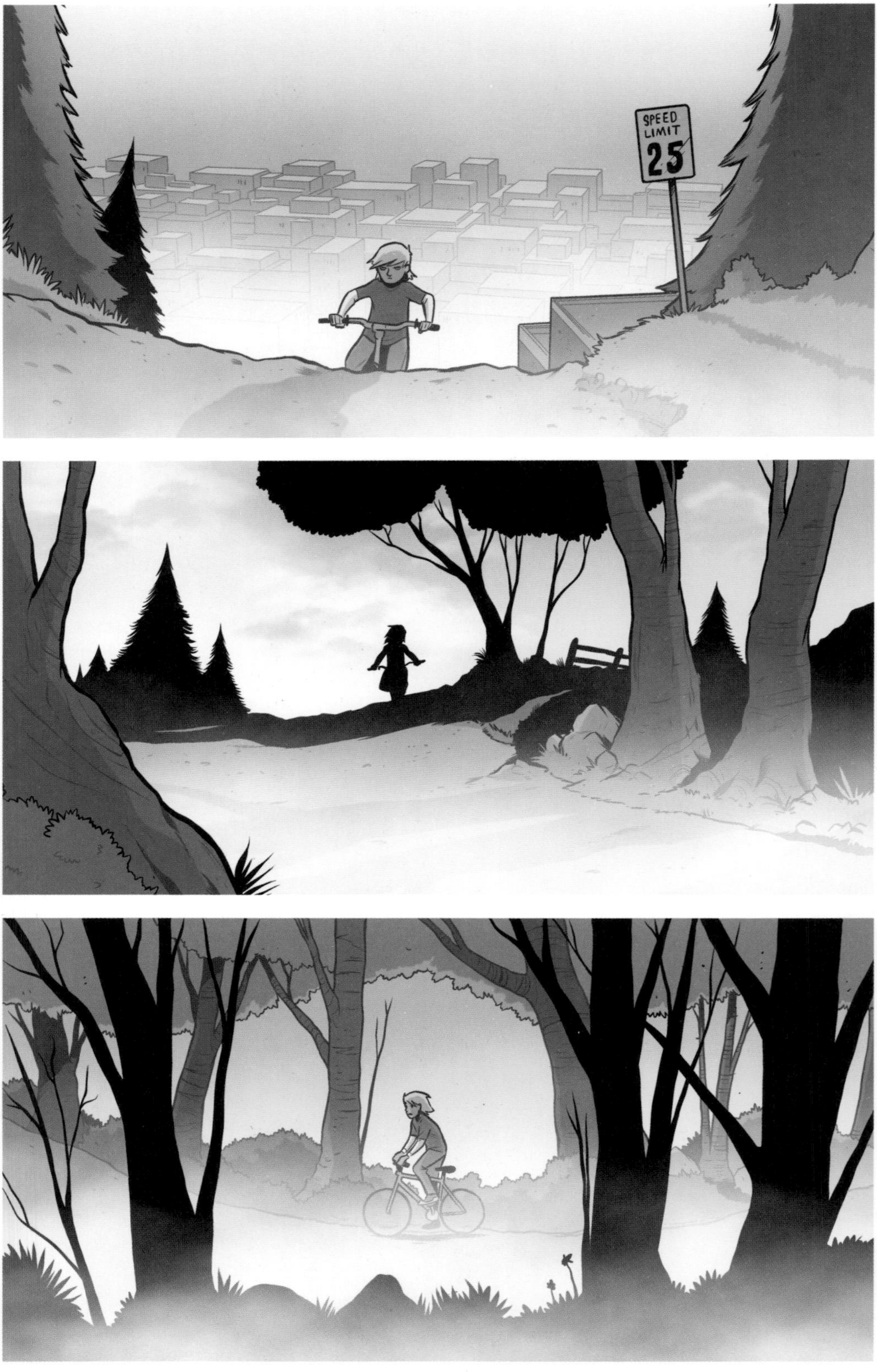
SPEED
LIMIT
25

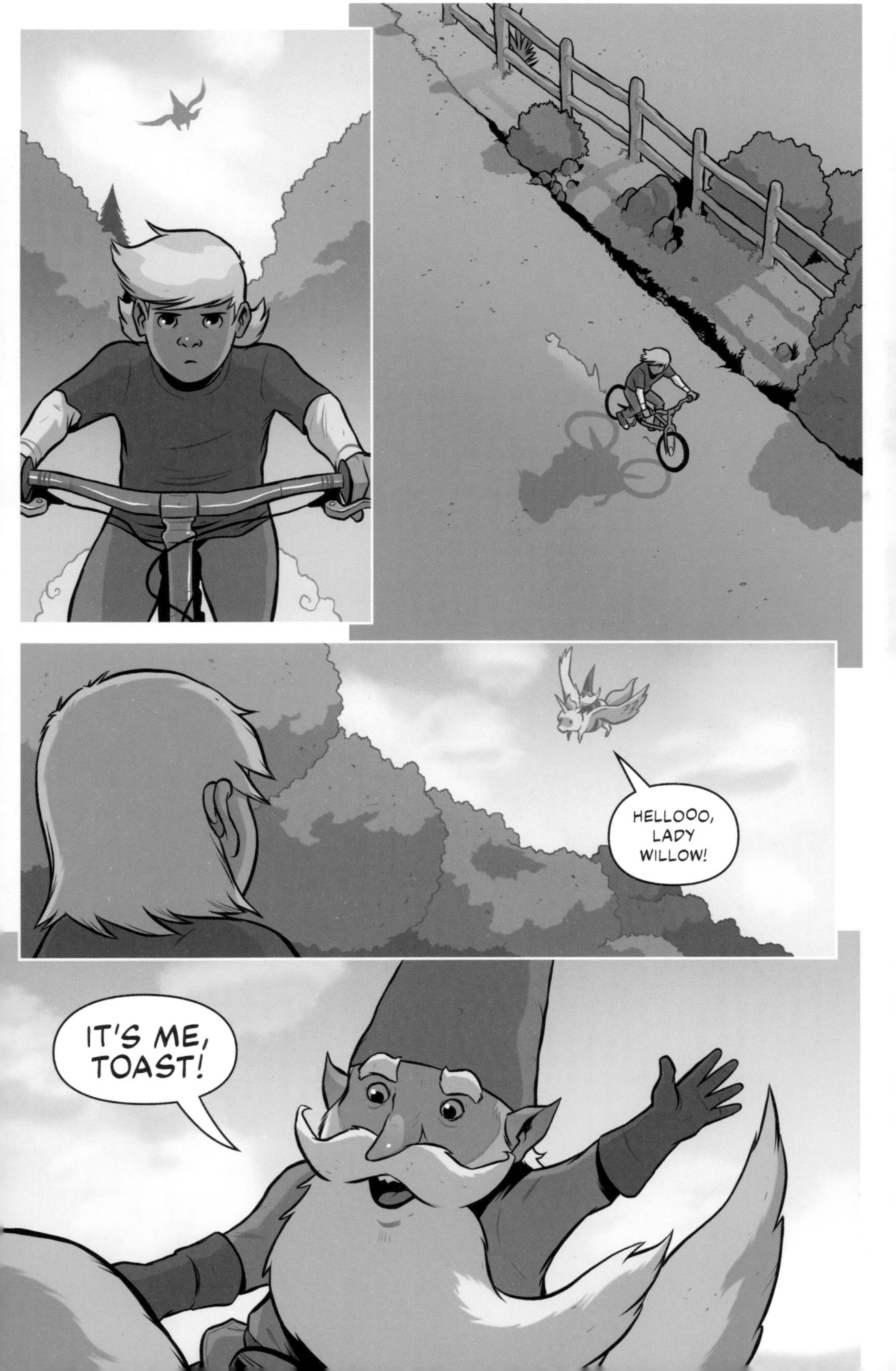
HELLOOO, LADY WILLOW!
IT'S ME, TOAST!

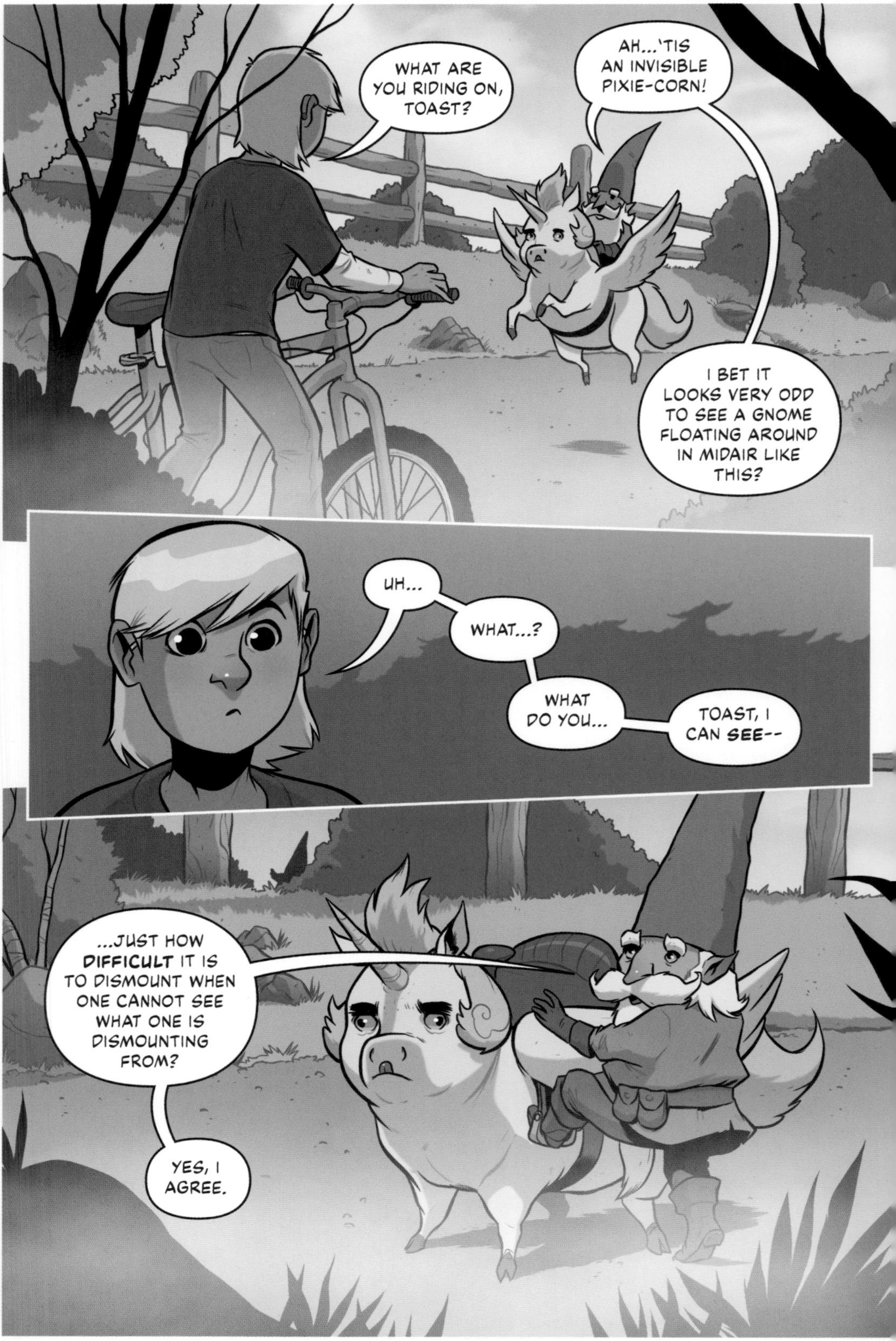
WHAT ARE YOU RIDING ON, TOAST?
AH...'TIS AN INVISIBLE PIXIE-CORN!
I BET IT LOOKS VERY ODD TO SEE A GNOME FLOATING AROUND IN MIDAIR LIKE THIS?
UH...
WHAT...?
WHAT DO YOU...
TOAST, I CAN **SEE**--
...JUST HOW **DIFFICULT** IT IS TO DISMOUNT WHEN ONE CANNOT SEE WHAT ONE IS DISMOUNTING FROM?
YES, I AGREE.

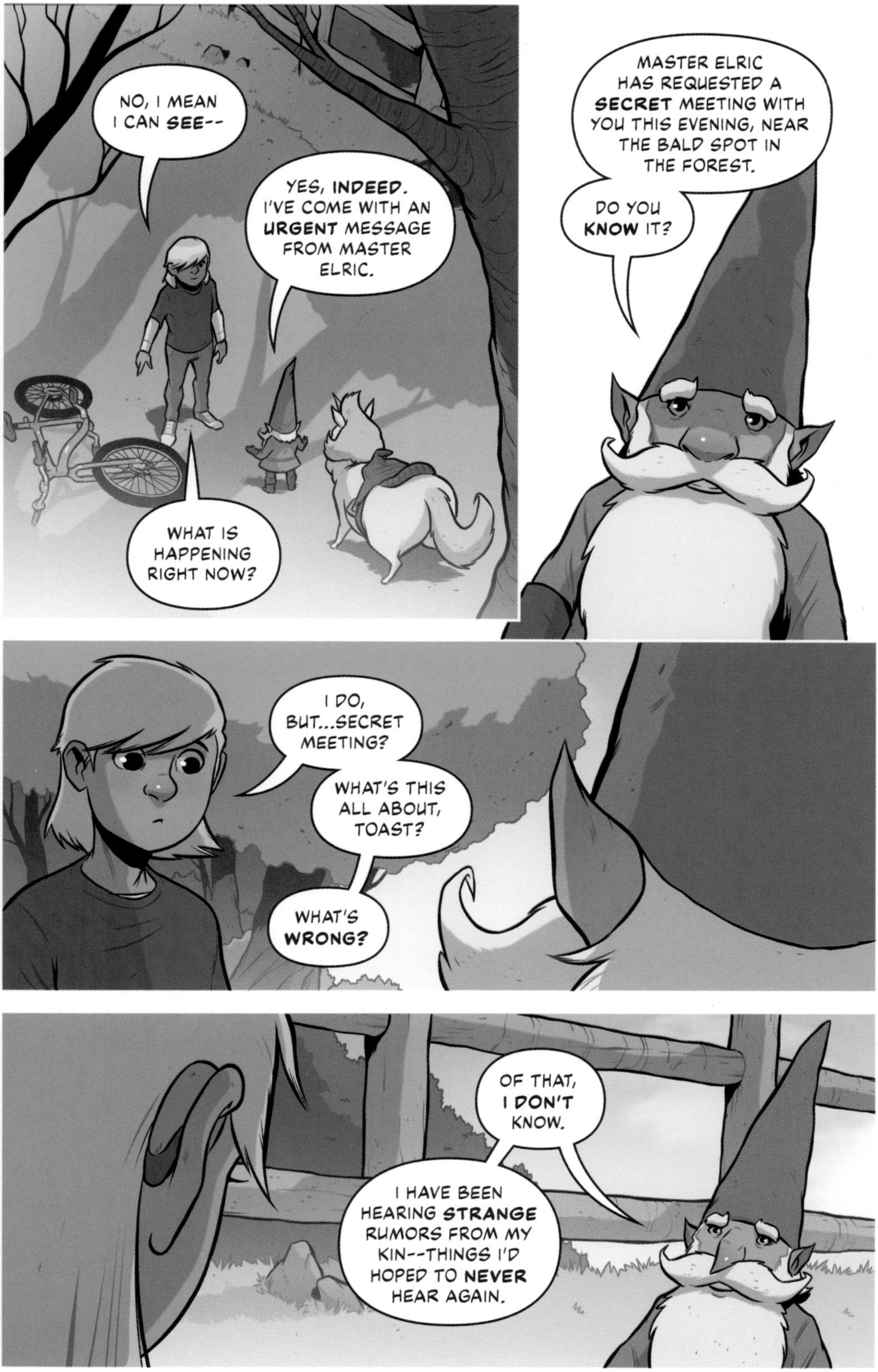

NO, I MEAN I CAN **SEE**--
YES, **INDEED.** I'VE COME WITH AN **URGENT** MESSAGE FROM MASTER ELRIC.
WHAT IS HAPPENING RIGHT NOW?
MASTER ELRIC HAS REQUESTED A **SECRET** MEETING WITH YOU THIS EVENING, NEAR THE BALD SPOT IN THE FOREST.
DO YOU **KNOW** IT?
I DO, BUT...SECRET MEETING?
WHAT'S THIS ALL ABOUT, TOAST?
WHAT'S **WRONG?**
OF THAT, **I DON'T** KNOW.
I HAVE BEEN HEARING **STRANGE** RUMORS FROM MY KIN--THINGS I'D HOPED TO **NEVER** HEAR AGAIN.

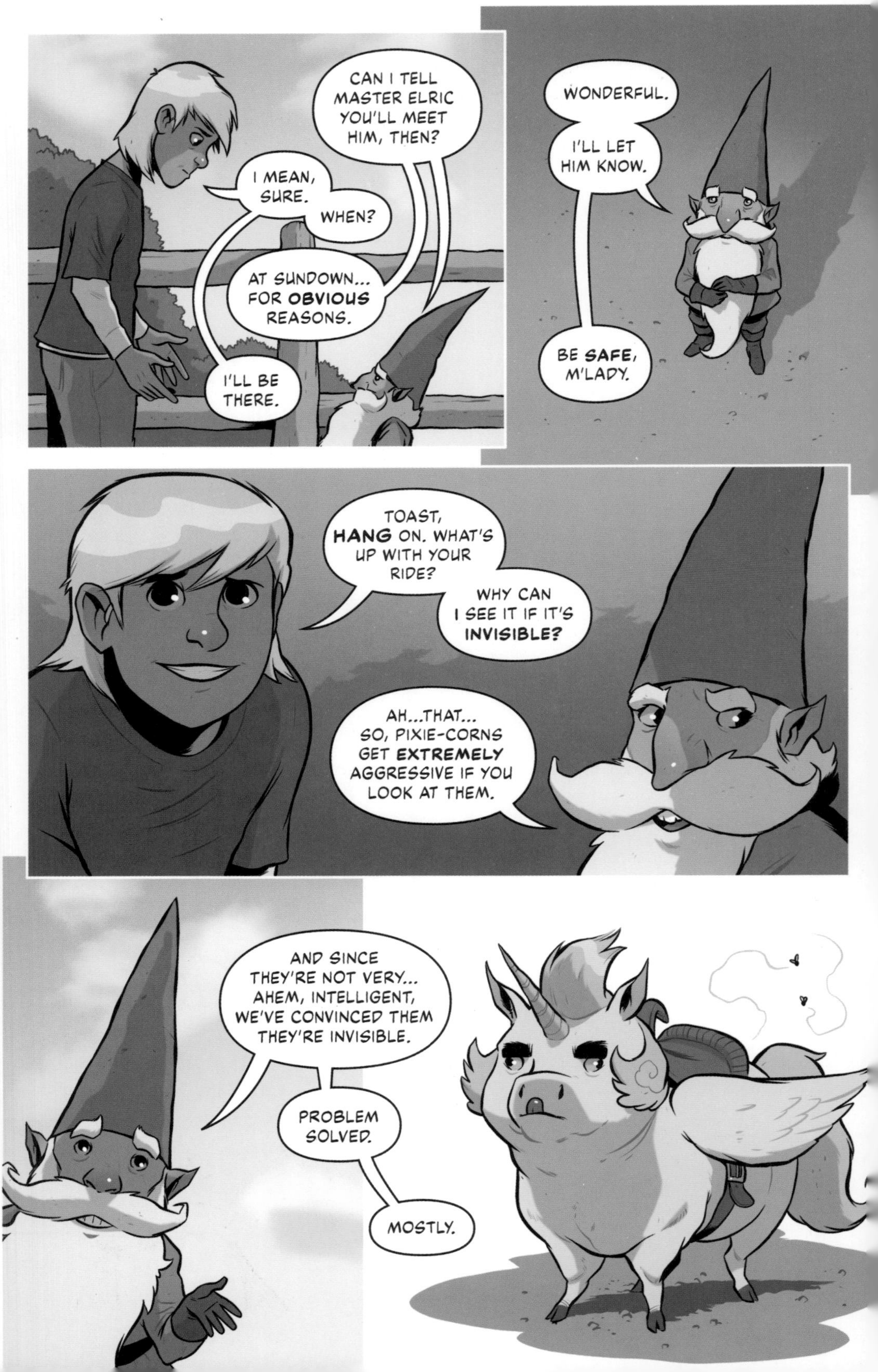
I MEAN, SURE.
WHEN?
CAN I TELL MASTER ELRIC YOU'LL MEET HIM, THEN?
AT SUNDOWN... FOR **OBVIOUS** REASONS.
I'LL BE THERE.
WONDERFUL.
I'LL LET HIM KNOW.
BE **SAFE**, M'LADY.
TOAST, **HANG** ON. WHAT'S UP WITH YOUR RIDE?
WHY CAN I SEE IT IF IT'S **INVISIBLE?**
AH...THAT... SO, PIXIE-CORNS GET **EXTREMELY** AGGRESSIVE IF YOU LOOK AT THEM.
AND SINCE THEY'RE NOT VERY... AHEM, INTELLIGENT, WE'VE CONVINCED THEM THEY'RE INVISIBLE.
PROBLEM SOLVED.
MOSTLY.

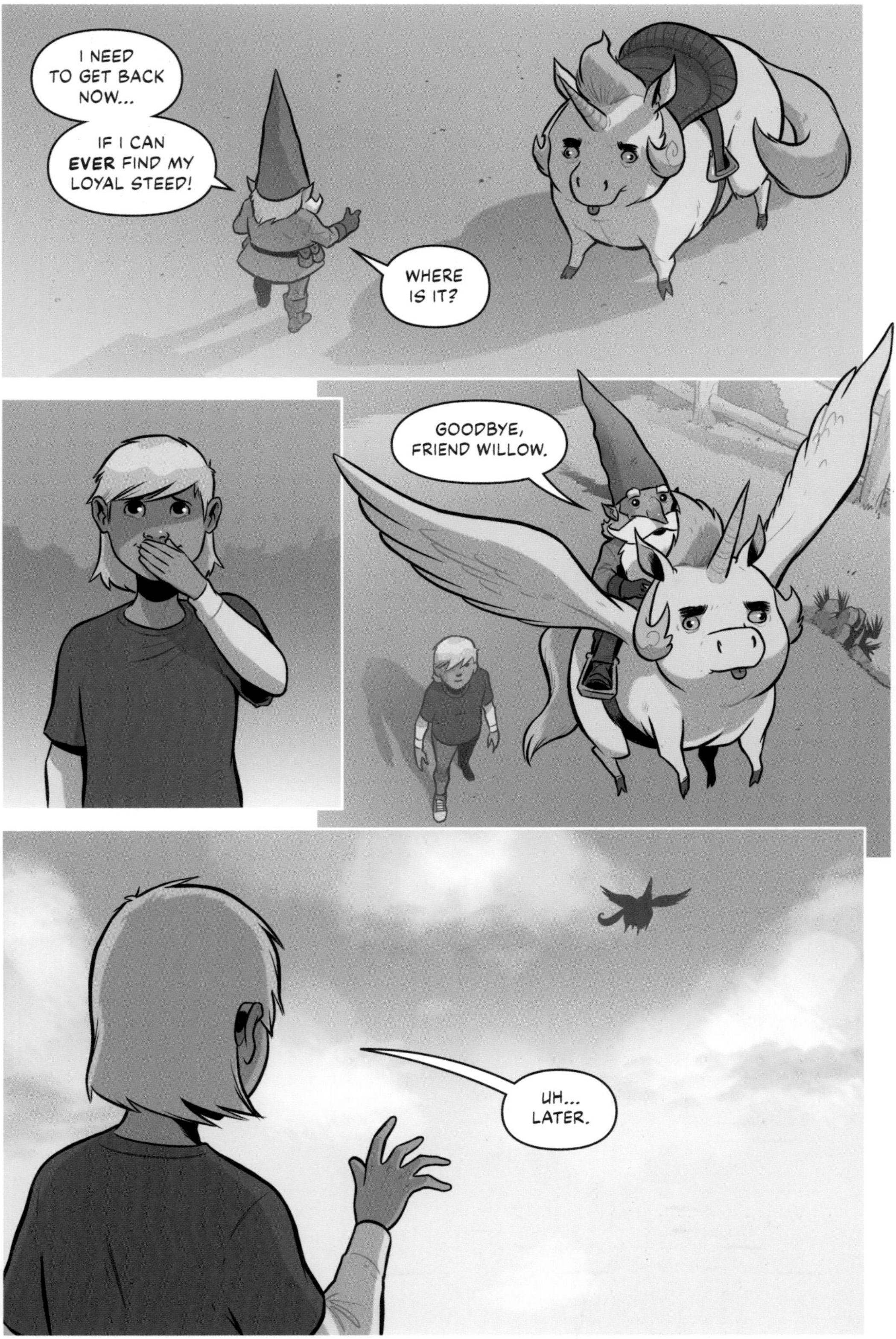
I NEED TO GET BACK NOW...
IF I CAN **EVER** FIND MY LOYAL STEED!
WHERE IS IT?
GOODBYE, FRIEND WILLOW.
UH... LATER.

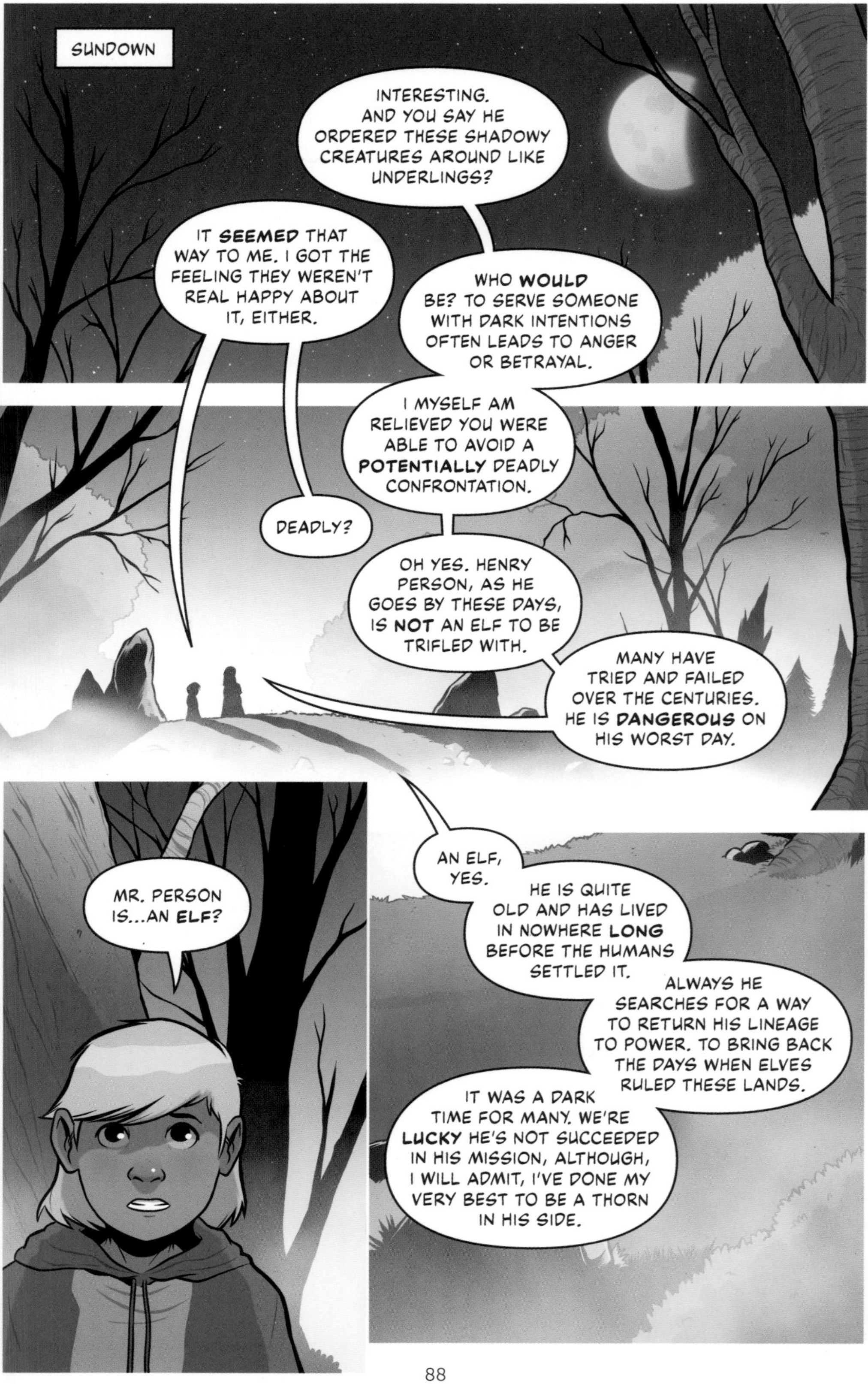
SUNDOWN
INTERESTING. AND YOU SAY HE ORDERED THESE SHADOWY CREATURES AROUND LIKE UNDERLINGS?
IT **SEEMED** THAT WAY TO ME. I GOT THE FEELING THEY WEREN'T REAL HAPPY ABOUT IT, EITHER.
WHO **WOULD** BE? TO SERVE SOMEONE WITH DARK INTENTIONS OFTEN LEADS TO ANGER OR BETRAYAL.
I MYSELF AM RELIEVED YOU WERE ABLE TO AVOID A **POTENTIALLY** DEADLY CONFRONTATION.
DEADLY?
OH YES. HENRY PERSON, AS HE GOES BY THESE DAYS, IS **NOT** AN ELF TO BE TRIFLED WITH.
MANY HAVE TRIED AND FAILED OVER THE CENTURIES. HE IS **DANGEROUS** ON HIS WORST DAY.
MR. PERSON IS...AN **ELF**?
AN ELF, YES.
HE IS QUITE OLD AND HAS LIVED IN NOWHERE **LONG** BEFORE THE HUMANS SETTLED IT.
ALWAYS HE SEARCHES FOR A WAY TO RETURN HIS LINEAGE TO POWER. TO BRING BACK THE DAYS WHEN ELVES RULED THESE LANDS.
IT WAS A DARK TIME FOR MANY. WE'RE **LUCKY** HE'S NOT SUCCEEDED IN HIS MISSION, ALTHOUGH, I WILL ADMIT, I'VE DONE MY VERY BEST TO BE A THORN IN HIS SIDE.

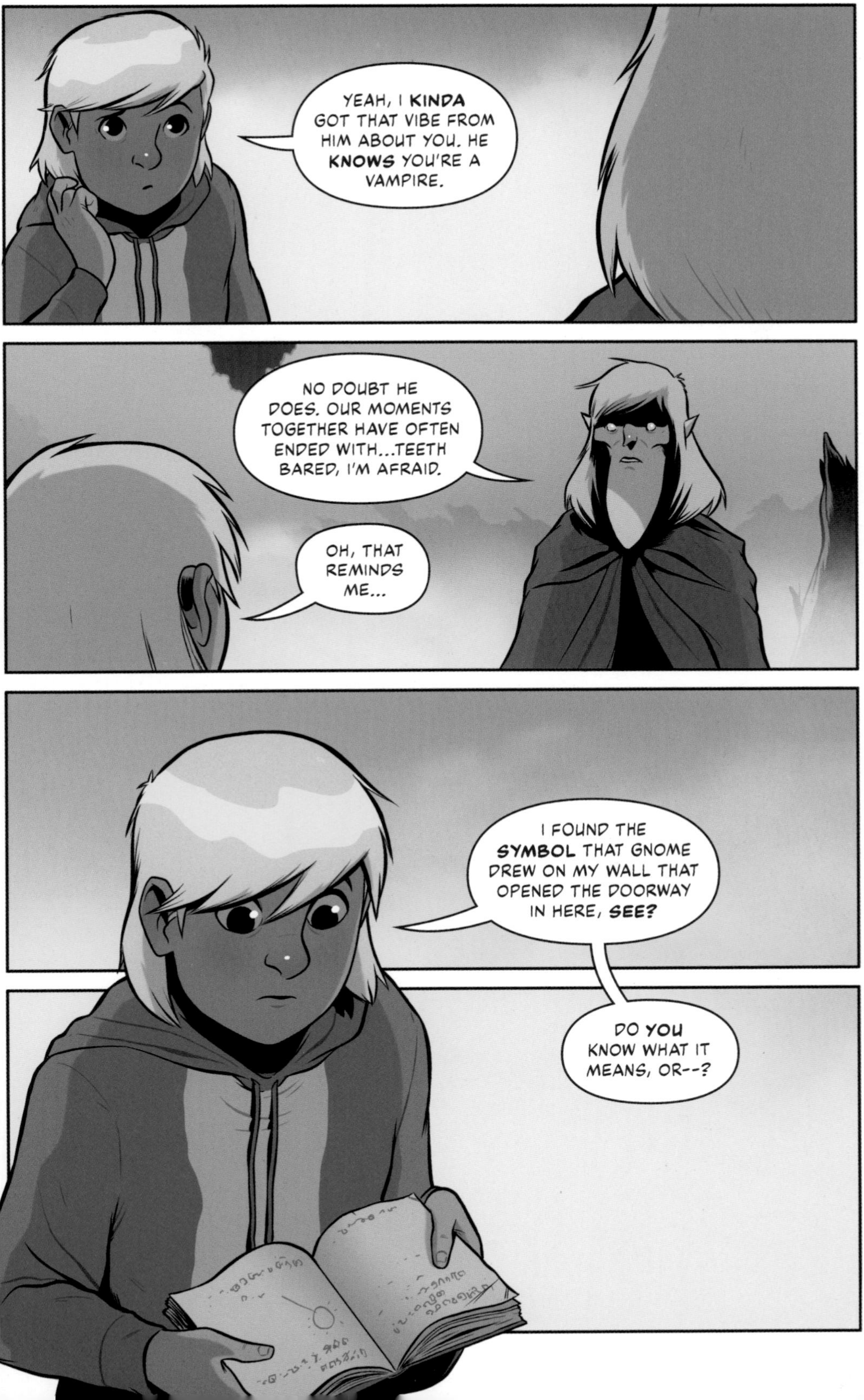
YEAH, I KINDA GOT THAT VIBE FROM HIM ABOUT YOU. HE KNOWS YOU'RE A VAMPIRE.
NO DOUBT HE DOES. OUR MOMENTS TOGETHER HAVE OFTEN ENDED WITH...TEETH BARED, I'M AFRAID.
OH, THAT REMINDS ME...
I FOUND THE SYMBOL THAT GNOME DREW ON MY WALL THAT OPENED THE DOORWAY IN HERE, SEE?
DO YOU KNOW WHAT IT MEANS, OR--?

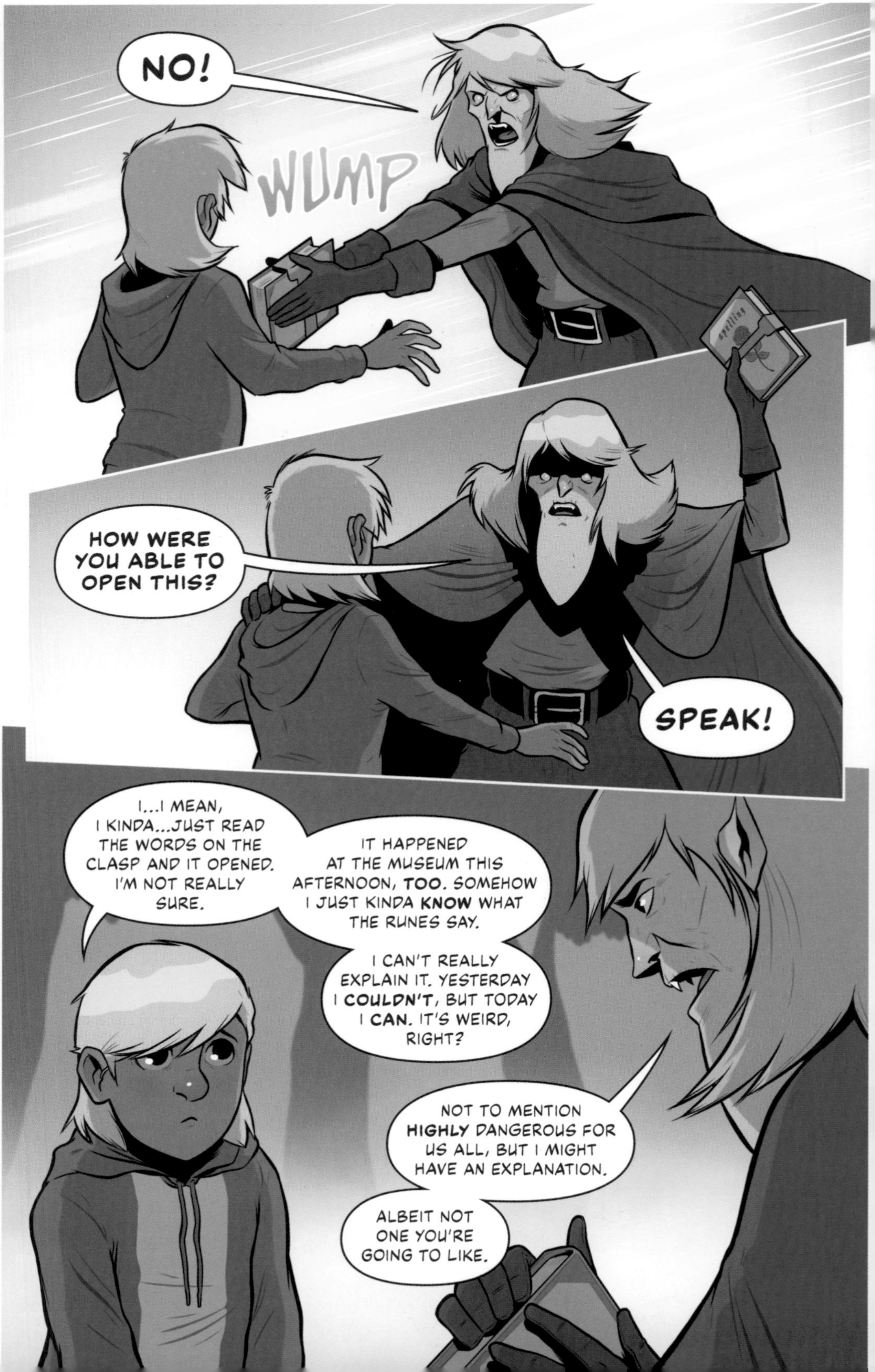
NO!
WUMP
spelling
HOW WERE YOU ABLE TO OPEN THIS?
SPEAK!
I...I MEAN, I KINDA...JUST READ THE WORDS ON THE CLASP AND IT OPENED. I'M NOT REALLY SURE.
IT HAPPENED AT THE MUSEUM THIS AFTERNOON, **TOO**. SOMEHOW I JUST KINDA **KNOW** WHAT THE RUNES SAY.
I CAN'T REALLY EXPLAIN IT. YESTERDAY I **COULDN'T**, BUT TODAY I **CAN**. IT'S WEIRD, RIGHT?
NOT TO MENTION **HIGHLY** DANGEROUS FOR US ALL, BUT I MIGHT HAVE AN EXPLANATION.
ALBEIT NOT ONE YOU'RE GOING TO LIKE.

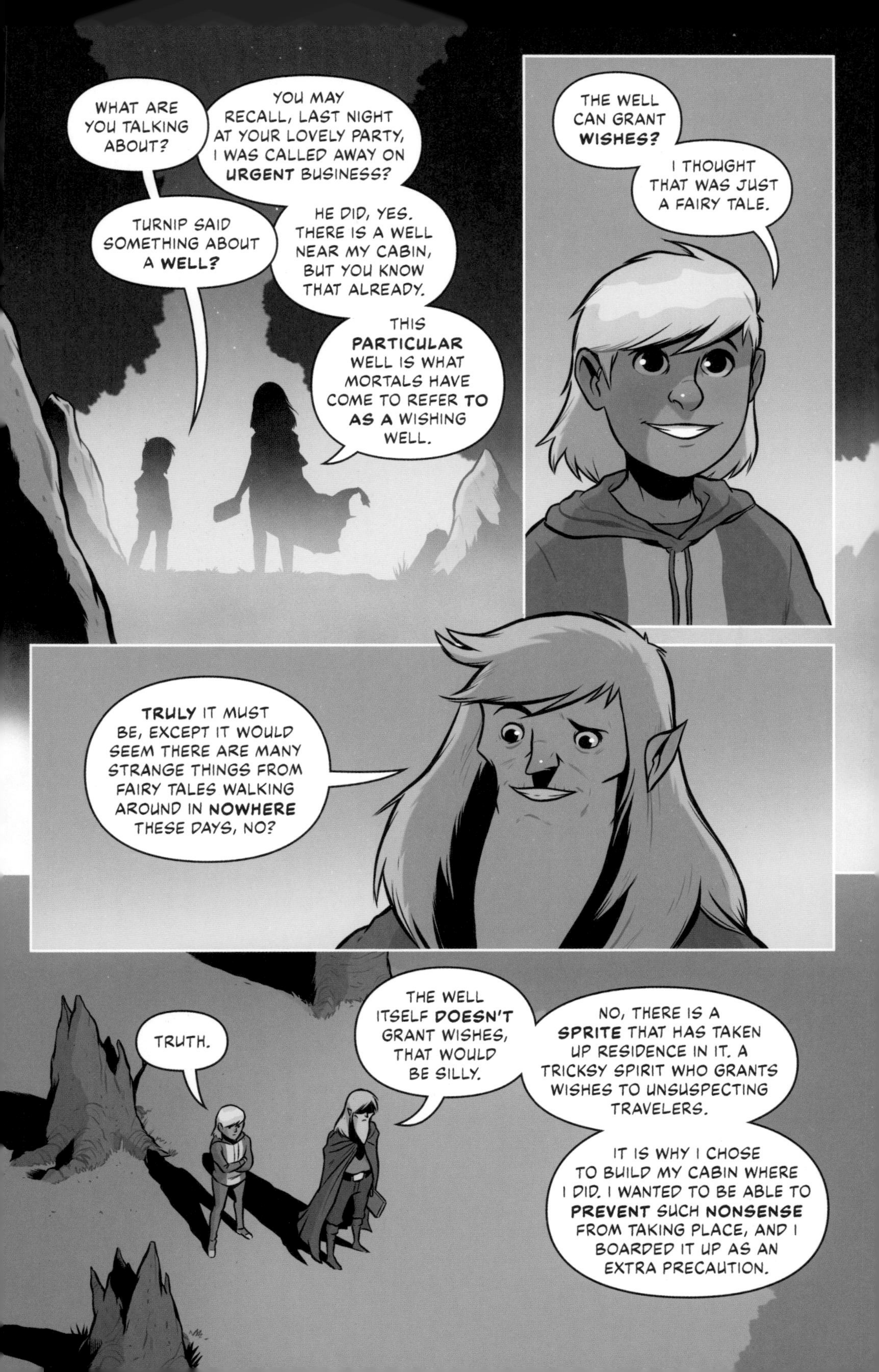

WHAT ARE YOU TALKING ABOUT?
YOU MAY RECALL, LAST NIGHT AT YOUR LOVELY PARTY, I WAS CALLED AWAY ON **URGENT** BUSINESS?
TURNIP SAID SOMETHING ABOUT A **WELL?**
HE DID, YES. THERE IS A WELL NEAR MY CABIN, BUT YOU KNOW THAT ALREADY.
THIS **PARTICULAR** WELL IS WHAT MORTALS HAVE COME TO REFER **TO AS A** WISHING WELL.
THE WELL CAN GRANT **WISHES?**
I THOUGHT THAT WAS JUST A FAIRY TALE.
TRULY IT MUST BE, EXCEPT IT WOULD SEEM THERE ARE MANY STRANGE THINGS FROM FAIRY TALES WALKING AROUND IN **NOWHERE** THESE DAYS, NO?
TRUTH.
THE WELL ITSELF **DOESN'T** GRANT WISHES, THAT WOULD BE SILLY.
NO, THERE IS A **SPRITE** THAT HAS TAKEN UP RESIDENCE IN IT. A TRICKSY SPIRIT WHO GRANTS WISHES TO UNSUSPECTING TRAVELERS.
IT IS WHY I CHOSE TO BUILD MY CABIN WHERE I DID. I WANTED TO BE ABLE TO **PREVENT** SUCH **NONSENSE** FROM TAKING PLACE, AND I BOARDED IT UP AS AN EXTRA PRECAUTION.

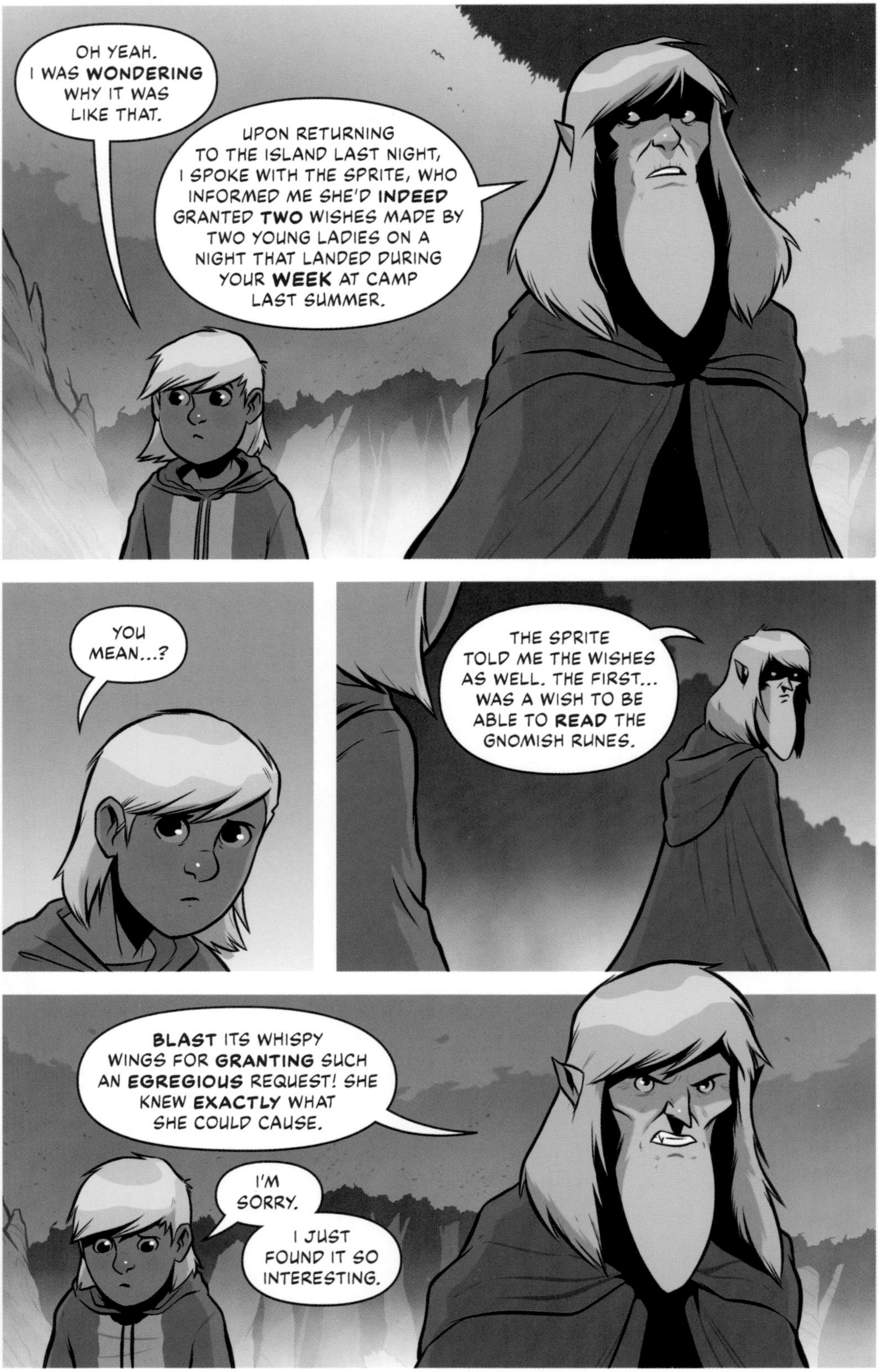
OH YEAH. I WAS WONDERING WHY IT WAS LIKE THAT.
UPON RETURNING TO THE ISLAND LAST NIGHT, I SPOKE WITH THE SPRITE, WHO INFORMED ME SHE'D INDEED GRANTED TWO WISHES MADE BY TWO YOUNG LADIES ON A NIGHT THAT LANDED DURING YOUR WEEK AT CAMP LAST SUMMER.
YOU MEAN...?
THE SPRITE TOLD ME THE WISHES AS WELL. THE FIRST... WAS A WISH TO BE ABLE TO READ THE GNOMISH RUNES.
BLAST ITS WHISPY WINGS FOR GRANTING SUCH AN EGREGIOUS REQUEST! SHE KNEW EXACTLY WHAT SHE COULD CAUSE.
I'M SORRY.
I JUST FOUND IT SO INTERESTING.

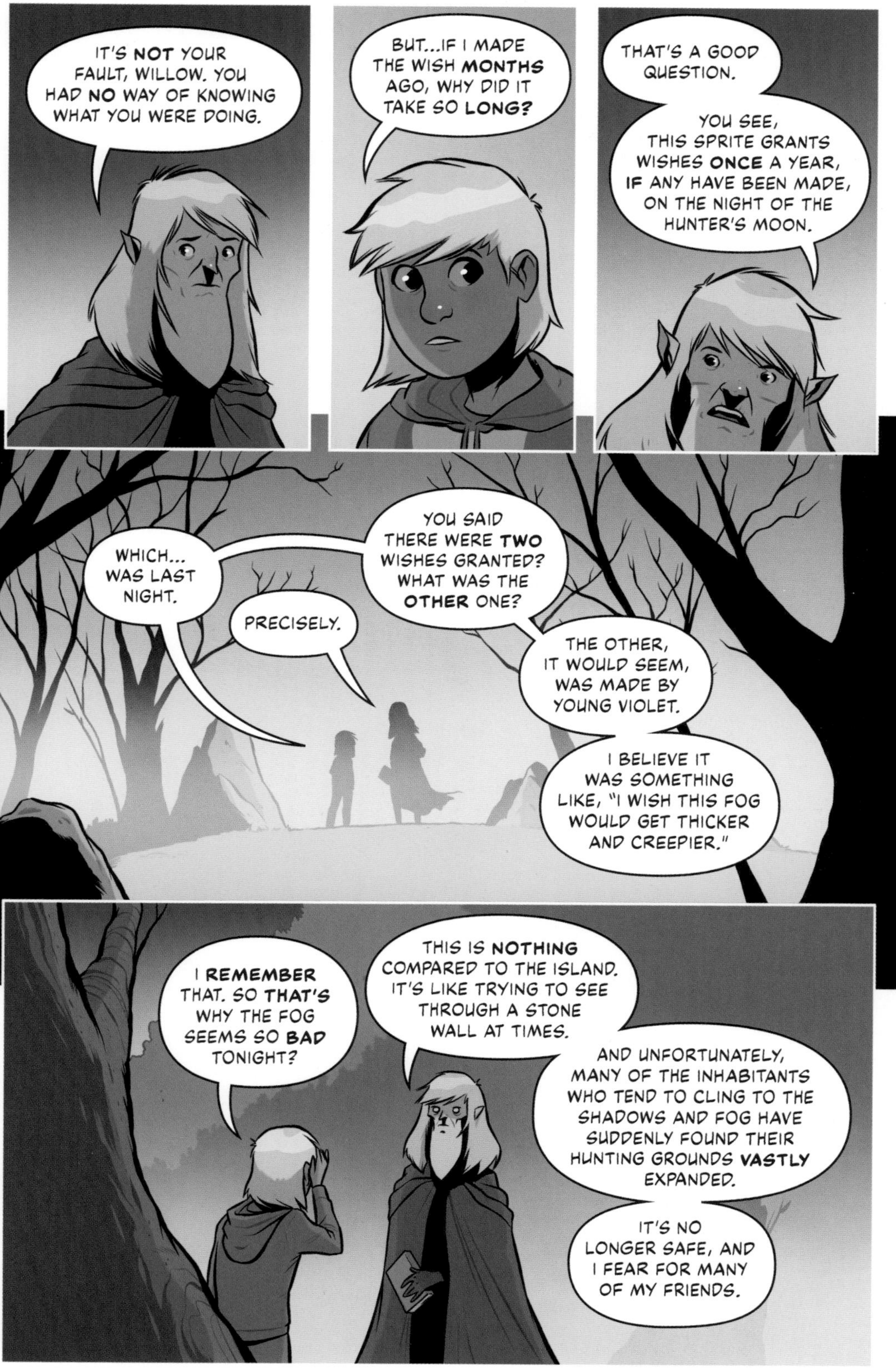
IT'S **NOT** YOUR FAULT, WILLOW. YOU HAD **NO** WAY OF KNOWING WHAT YOU WERE DOING.
BUT...IF I MADE THE WISH **MONTHS** AGO, WHY DID IT TAKE SO **LONG?**
THAT'S A GOOD QUESTION.
YOU SEE, THIS SPRITE GRANTS WISHES **ONCE** A YEAR, **IF** ANY HAVE BEEN MADE, ON THE NIGHT OF THE HUNTER'S MOON.
WHICH... WAS LAST NIGHT.
PRECISELY.
YOU SAID THERE WERE **TWO** WISHES GRANTED? WHAT WAS THE **OTHER** ONE?
THE OTHER, IT WOULD SEEM, WAS MADE BY YOUNG VIOLET.
I BELIEVE IT WAS SOMETHING LIKE, "I WISH THIS FOG WOULD GET THICKER AND CREEPIER."
I **REMEMBER** THAT. SO **THAT'S** WHY THE FOG SEEMS SO **BAD** TONIGHT?
THIS IS **NOTHING** COMPARED TO THE ISLAND. IT'S LIKE TRYING TO SEE THROUGH A STONE WALL AT TIMES.
AND UNFORTUNATELY, MANY OF THE INHABITANTS WHO TEND TO CLING TO THE SHADOWS AND FOG HAVE SUDDENLY FOUND THEIR HUNTING GROUNDS **VASTLY** EXPANDED.
IT'S NO LONGER SAFE, AND I FEAR FOR MANY OF MY FRIENDS.

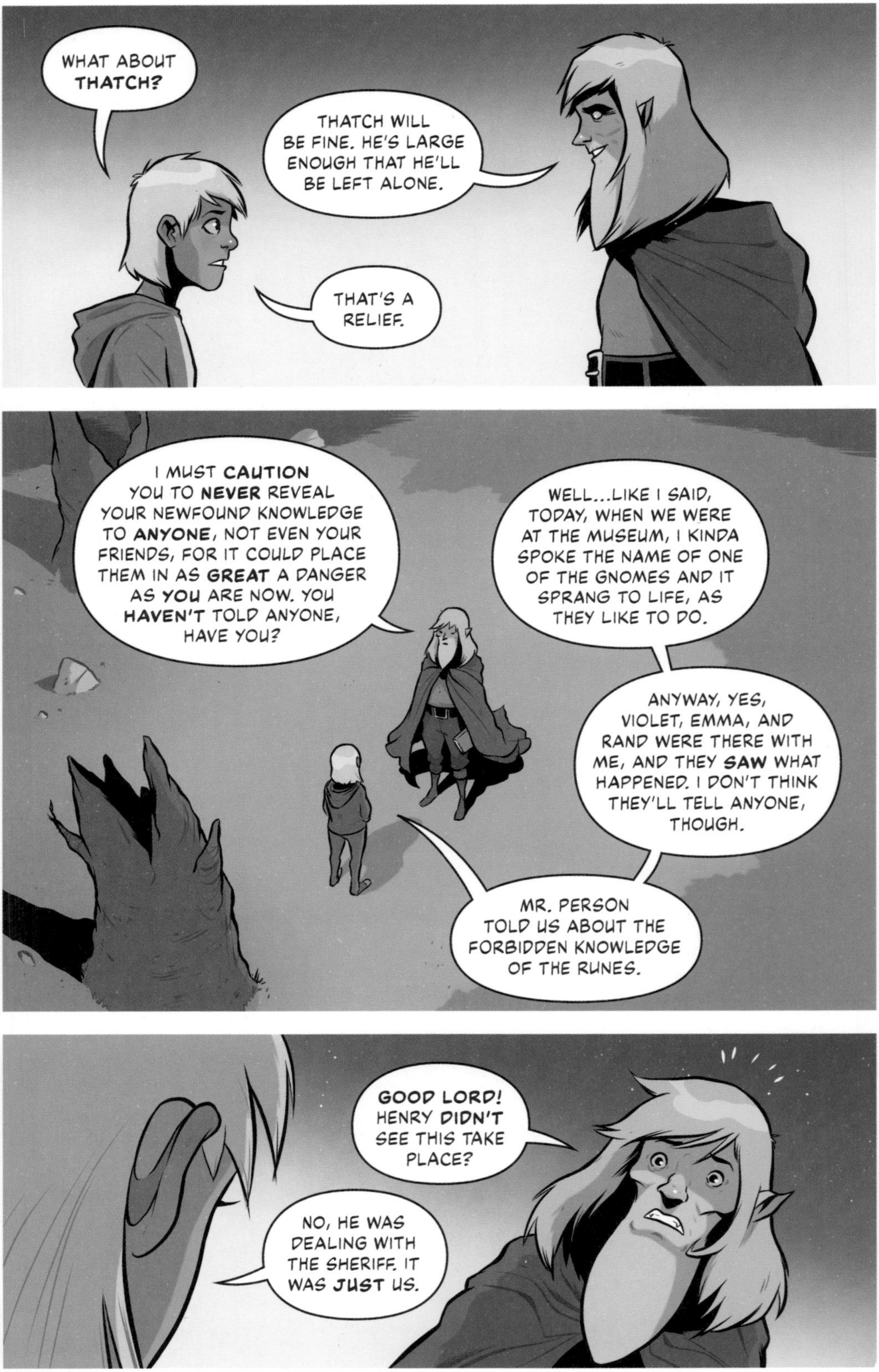
WHAT ABOUT THATCH?
THATCH WILL BE FINE. HE'S LARGE ENOUGH THAT HE'LL BE LEFT ALONE.
THAT'S A RELIEF.
I MUST CAUTION YOU TO NEVER REVEAL YOUR NEWFOUND KNOWLEDGE TO ANYONE, NOT EVEN YOUR FRIENDS, FOR IT COULD PLACE THEM IN AS GREAT A DANGER AS YOU ARE NOW. YOU HAVEN'T TOLD ANYONE, HAVE YOU?
WELL...LIKE I SAID, TODAY, WHEN WE WERE AT THE MUSEUM, I KINDA SPOKE THE NAME OF ONE OF THE GNOMES AND IT SPRANG TO LIFE, AS THEY LIKE TO DO.
ANYWAY, YES, VIOLET, EMMA, AND RAND WERE THERE WITH ME, AND THEY SAW WHAT HAPPENED. I DON'T THINK THEY'LL TELL ANYONE, THOUGH.
MR. PERSON TOLD US ABOUT THE FORBIDDEN KNOWLEDGE OF THE RUNES.
GOOD LORD! HENRY DIDN'T SEE THIS TAKE PLACE?
NO, HE WAS DEALING WITH THE SHERIFF. IT WAS JUST US.

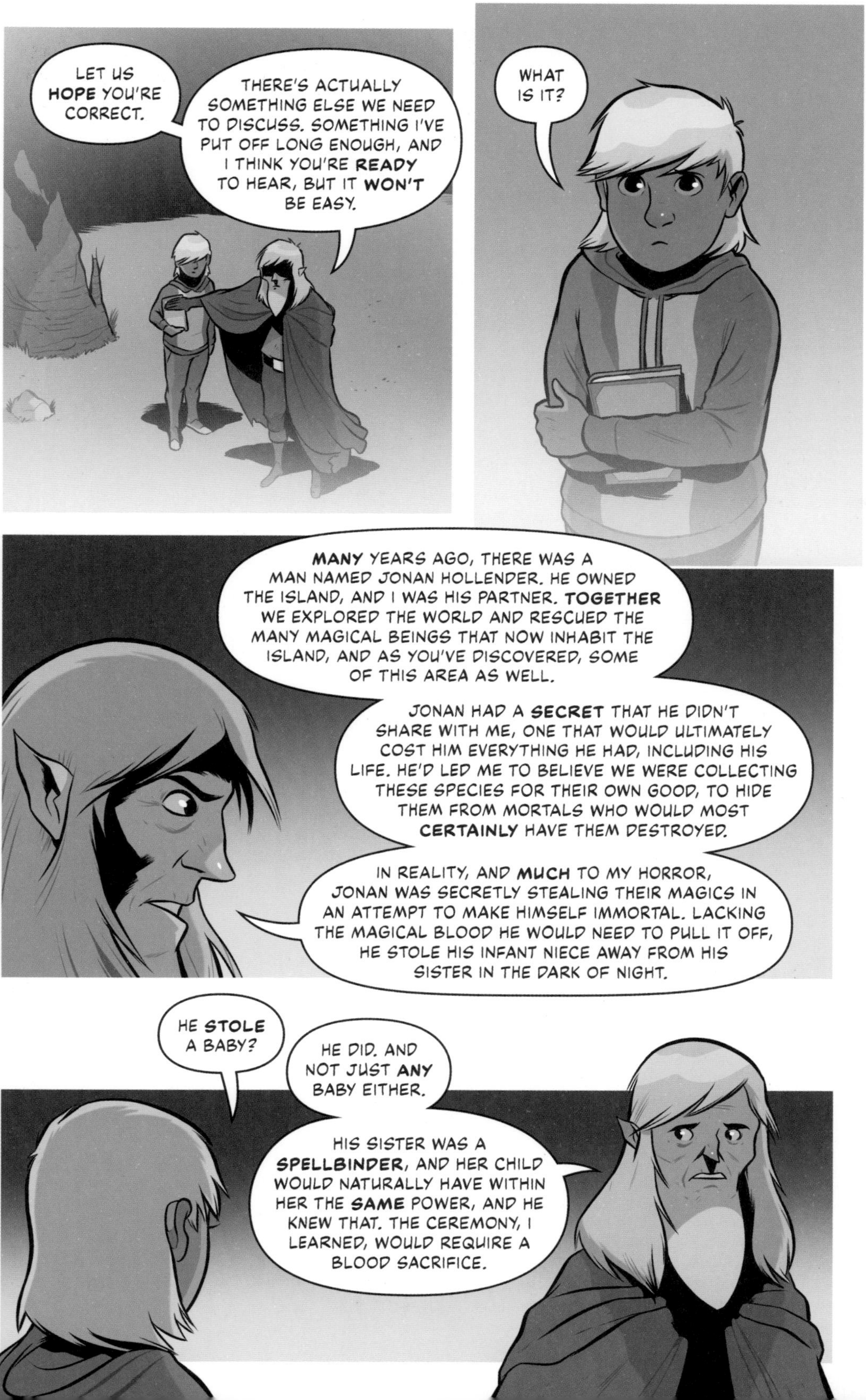
LET US **HOPE** YOU'RE CORRECT.
THERE'S ACTUALLY SOMETHING ELSE WE NEED TO DISCUSS. SOMETHING I'VE PUT OFF LONG ENOUGH, AND I THINK YOU'RE **READY** TO HEAR, BUT IT **WON'T** BE EASY.
WHAT IS IT?
MANY YEARS AGO, THERE WAS A MAN NAMED JONAN HOLLENDER. HE OWNED THE ISLAND, AND I WAS HIS PARTNER. **TOGETHER** WE EXPLORED THE WORLD AND RESCUED THE MANY MAGICAL BEINGS THAT NOW INHABIT THE ISLAND, AND AS YOU'VE DISCOVERED, SOME OF THIS AREA AS WELL.
JONAN HAD A **SECRET** THAT HE DIDN'T SHARE WITH ME, ONE THAT WOULD ULTIMATELY COST HIM EVERYTHING HE HAD, INCLUDING HIS LIFE. HE'D LED ME TO BELIEVE WE WERE COLLECTING THESE SPECIES FOR THEIR OWN GOOD, TO HIDE THEM FROM MORTALS WHO WOULD MOST **CERTAINLY** HAVE THEM DESTROYED.
IN REALITY, AND **MUCH** TO MY HORROR, JONAN WAS SECRETLY STEALING THEIR MAGICS IN AN ATTEMPT TO MAKE HIMSELF IMMORTAL. LACKING THE MAGICAL BLOOD HE WOULD NEED TO PULL IT OFF, HE STOLE HIS INFANT NIECE AWAY FROM HIS SISTER IN THE DARK OF NIGHT.
HE **STOLE** A BABY?
HE DID. AND NOT JUST **ANY** BABY EITHER.
HIS SISTER WAS A **SPELLBINDER**, AND HER CHILD WOULD NATURALLY HAVE WITHIN HER THE **SAME** POWER, AND HE KNEW THAT. THE CEREMONY, I LEARNED, WOULD REQUIRE A BLOOD SACRIFICE.

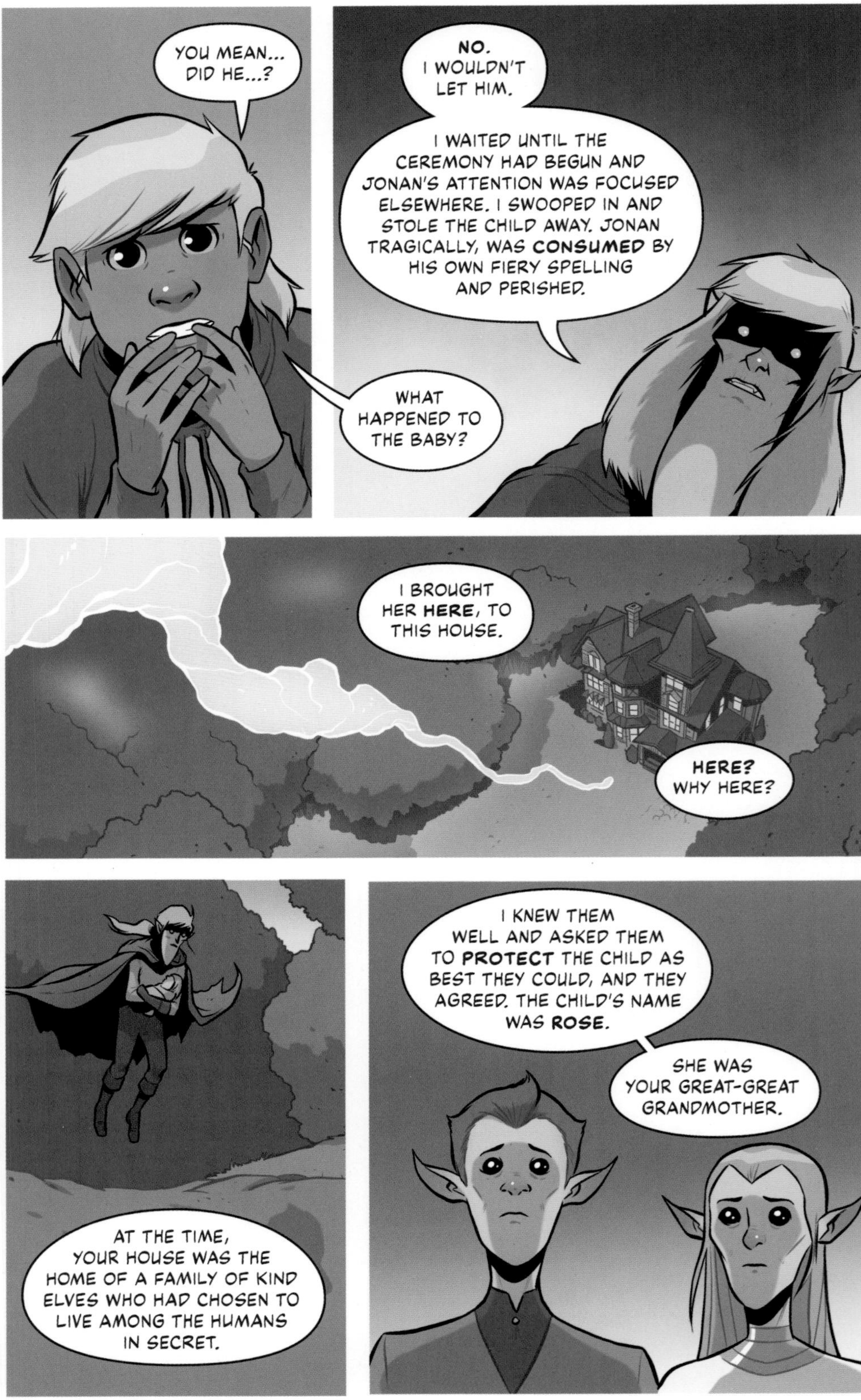
YOU MEAN... DID HE...?
NO. I WOULDN'T LET HIM.
I WAITED UNTIL THE CEREMONY HAD BEGUN AND JONAN'S ATTENTION WAS FOCUSED ELSEWHERE. I SWOOPED IN AND STOLE THE CHILD AWAY. JONAN TRAGICALLY, WAS CONSUMED BY HIS OWN FIERY SPELLING AND PERISHED.
WHAT HAPPENED TO THE BABY?
I BROUGHT HER HERE, TO THIS HOUSE.
HERE? WHY HERE?
AT THE TIME, YOUR HOUSE WAS THE HOME OF A FAMILY OF KIND ELVES WHO HAD CHOSEN TO LIVE AMONG THE HUMANS IN SECRET.
I KNEW THEM WELL AND ASKED THEM TO PROTECT THE CHILD AS BEST THEY COULD, AND THEY AGREED. THE CHILD'S NAME WAS ROSE.
SHE WAS YOUR GREAT-GREAT GRANDMOTHER.

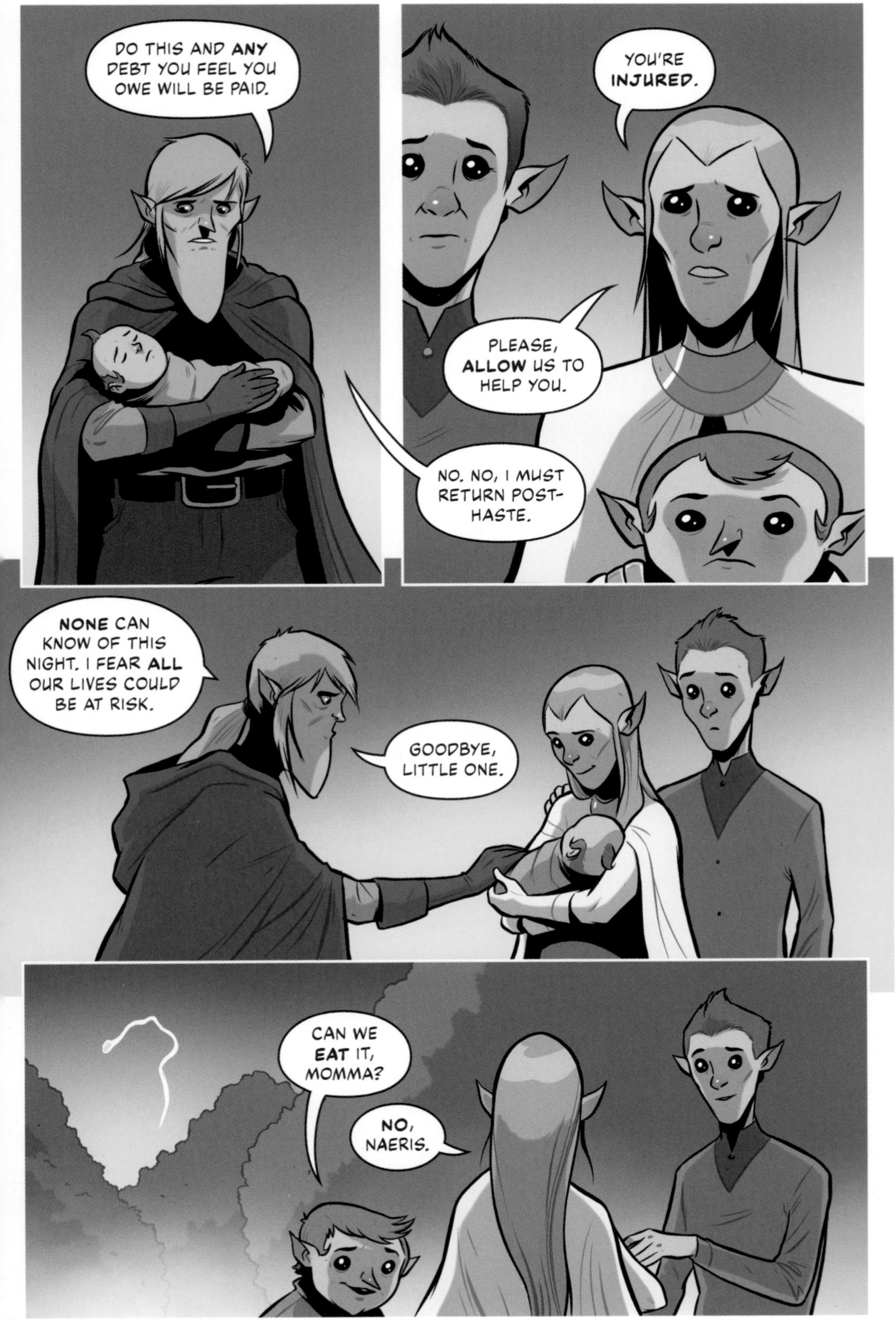
DO THIS AND ANY DEBT YOU FEEL YOU OWE WILL BE PAID.
YOU'RE INJURED.
PLEASE, ALLOW US TO HELP YOU.
NO. NO, I MUST RETURN POST-HASTE.
NONE CAN KNOW OF THIS NIGHT. I FEAR ALL OUR LIVES COULD BE AT RISK.
GOODBYE, LITTLE ONE.
CAN WE EAT IT, MOMMA?
NO, NAERIS.

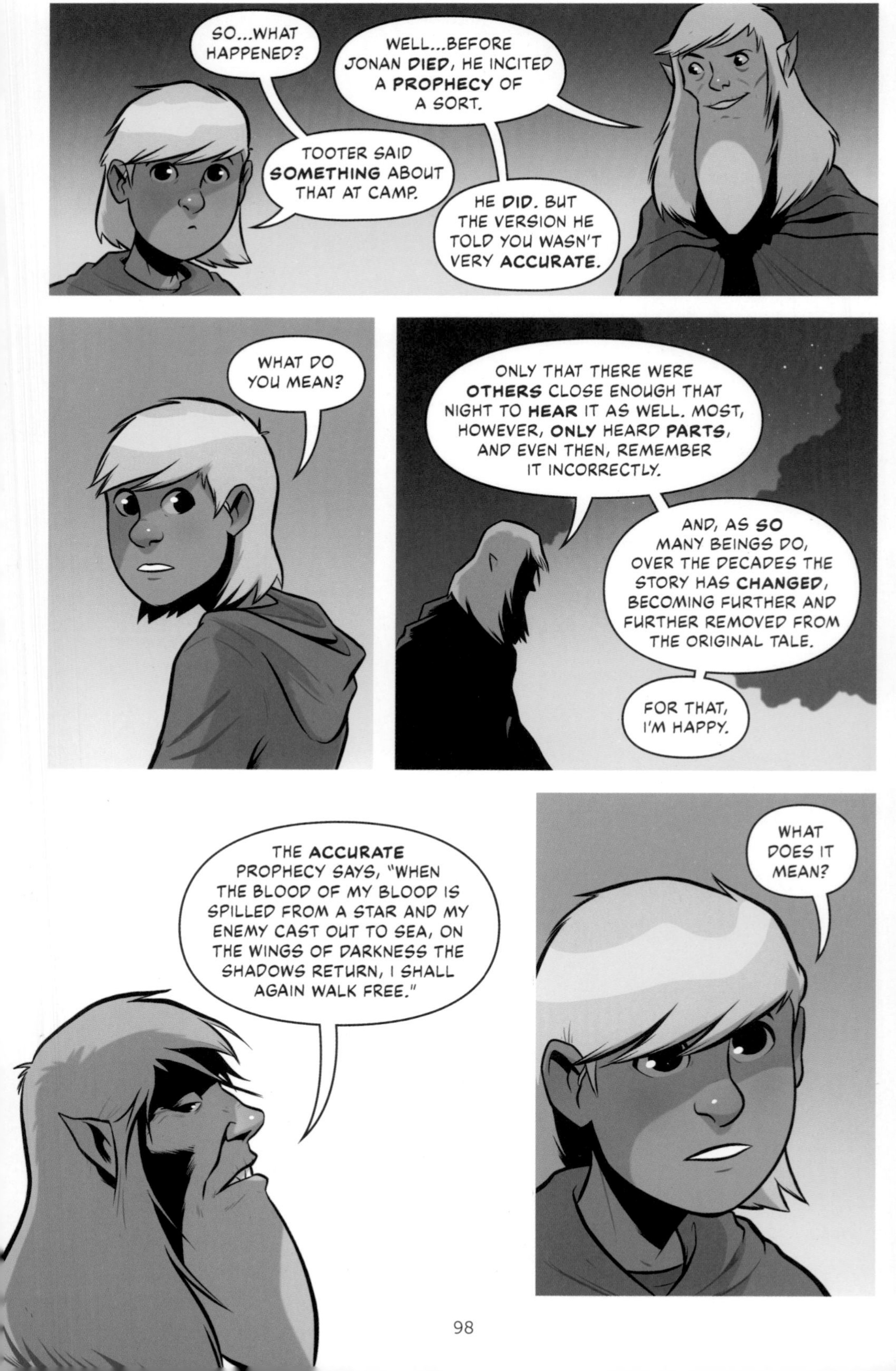

SO...WHAT HAPPENED?
WELL...BEFORE JONAN DIED, HE INCITED A PROPHECY OF A SORT.
TOOTER SAID SOMETHING ABOUT THAT AT CAMP.
HE DID. BUT THE VERSION HE TOLD YOU WASN'T VERY ACCURATE.
WHAT DO YOU MEAN?
ONLY THAT THERE WERE OTHERS CLOSE ENOUGH THAT NIGHT TO HEAR IT AS WELL. MOST, HOWEVER, ONLY HEARD PARTS, AND EVEN THEN, REMEMBER IT INCORRECTLY.
AND, AS SO MANY BEINGS DO, OVER THE DECADES THE STORY HAS CHANGED, BECOMING FURTHER AND FURTHER REMOVED FROM THE ORIGINAL TALE.
FOR THAT, I'M HAPPY.
THE ACCURATE PROPHECY SAYS, "WHEN THE BLOOD OF MY BLOOD IS SPILLED FROM A STAR AND MY ENEMY CAST OUT TO SEA, ON THE WINGS OF DARKNESS THE SHADOWS RETURN, I SHALL AGAIN WALK FREE."
WHAT DOES IT MEAN?

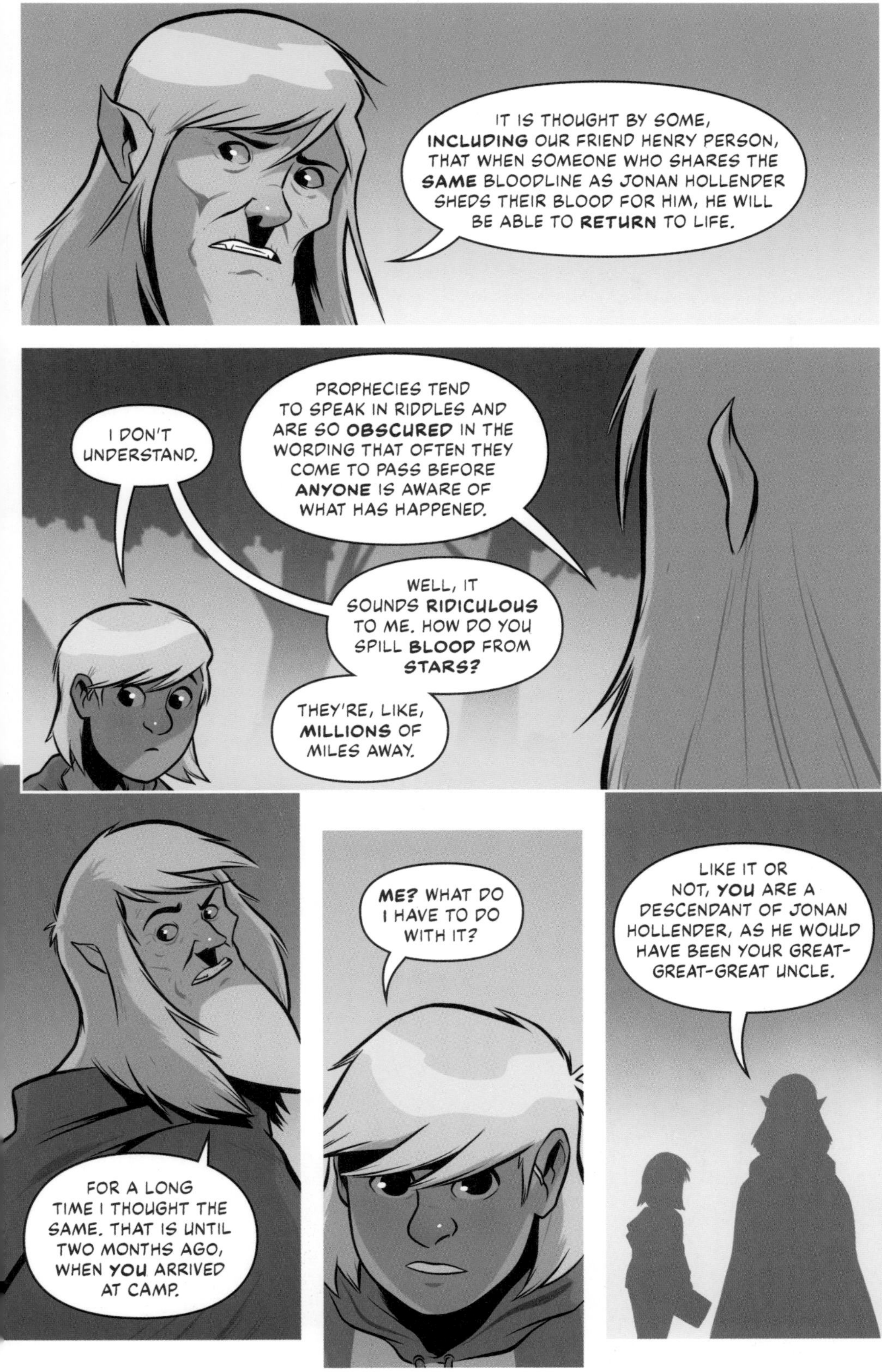

IT IS THOUGHT BY SOME, **INCLUDING** OUR FRIEND HENRY PERSON, THAT WHEN SOMEONE WHO SHARES THE **SAME** BLOODLINE AS JONAN HOLLENDER SHEDS THEIR BLOOD FOR HIM, HE WILL BE ABLE TO **RETURN** TO LIFE.
I DON'T UNDERSTAND.
PROPHECIES TEND TO SPEAK IN RIDDLES AND ARE SO **OBSCURED** IN THE WORDING THAT OFTEN THEY COME TO PASS BEFORE **ANYONE** IS AWARE OF WHAT HAS HAPPENED.
WELL, IT SOUNDS **RIDICULOUS** TO ME. HOW DO YOU SPILL **BLOOD** FROM **STARS?**
THEY'RE, LIKE, **MILLIONS** OF MILES AWAY.
FOR A LONG TIME I THOUGHT THE SAME. THAT IS UNTIL TWO MONTHS AGO, WHEN **YOU** ARRIVED AT CAMP.
ME? WHAT DO I HAVE TO DO WITH IT?
LIKE IT OR NOT, **YOU** ARE A DESCENDANT OF JONAN HOLLENDER, AS HE WOULD HAVE BEEN YOUR GREAT-GREAT-GREAT UNCLE.

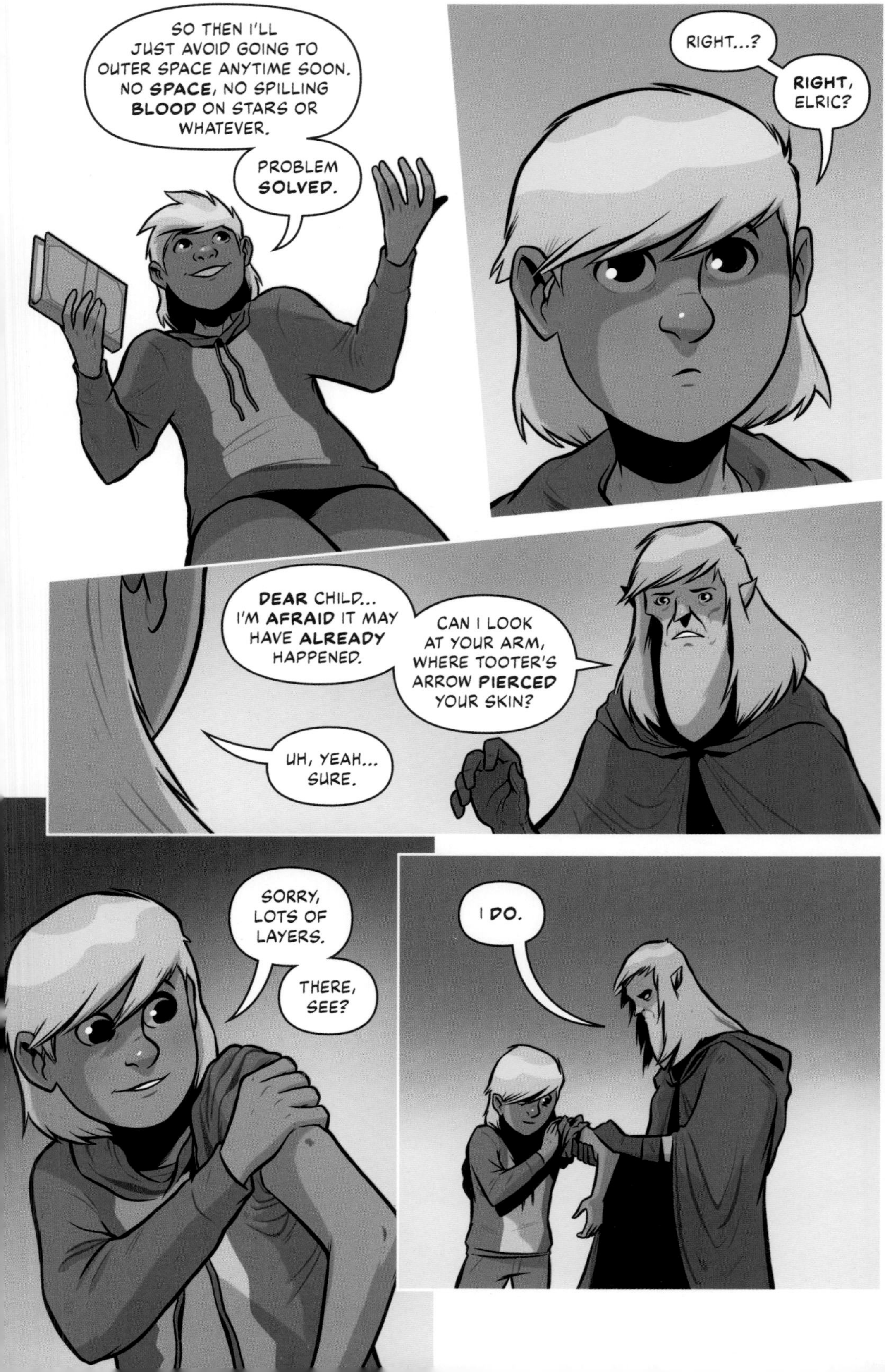
SO THEN I'LL JUST AVOID GOING TO OUTER SPACE ANYTIME SOON. NO **SPACE**, NO SPILLING **BLOOD** ON STARS OR WHATEVER.
PROBLEM **SOLVED**.
RIGHT...?
RIGHT, ELRIC?
DEAR CHILD... I'M **AFRAID** IT MAY HAVE **ALREADY** HAPPENED.
CAN I LOOK AT YOUR ARM, WHERE TOOTER'S ARROW **PIERCED** YOUR SKIN?
UH, YEAH... SURE.
SORRY, LOTS OF LAYERS.
THERE, SEE?
I **DO**.

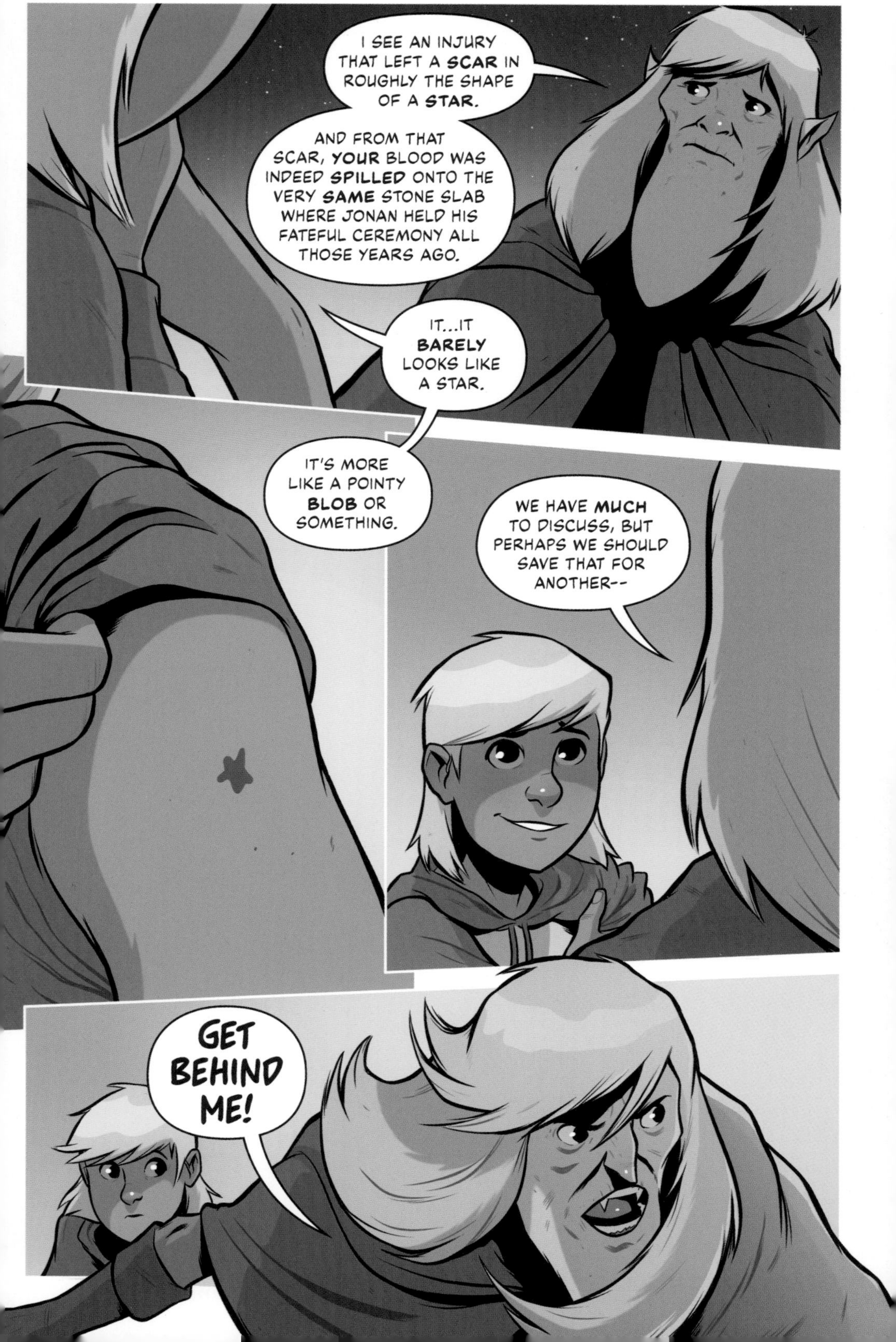
I SEE AN INJURY THAT LEFT A **SCAR** IN ROUGHLY THE SHAPE OF A **STAR.**
AND FROM THAT SCAR, **YOUR** BLOOD WAS INDEED **SPILLED** ONTO THE VERY **SAME** STONE SLAB WHERE JONAN HELD HIS FATEFUL CEREMONY ALL THOSE YEARS AGO.
IT...IT **BARELY** LOOKS LIKE A STAR.
IT'S MORE LIKE A POINTY **BLOB** OR SOMETHING.
WE HAVE **MUCH** TO DISCUSS, BUT PERHAPS WE SHOULD SAVE THAT FOR ANOTHER--
GET BEHIND ME!

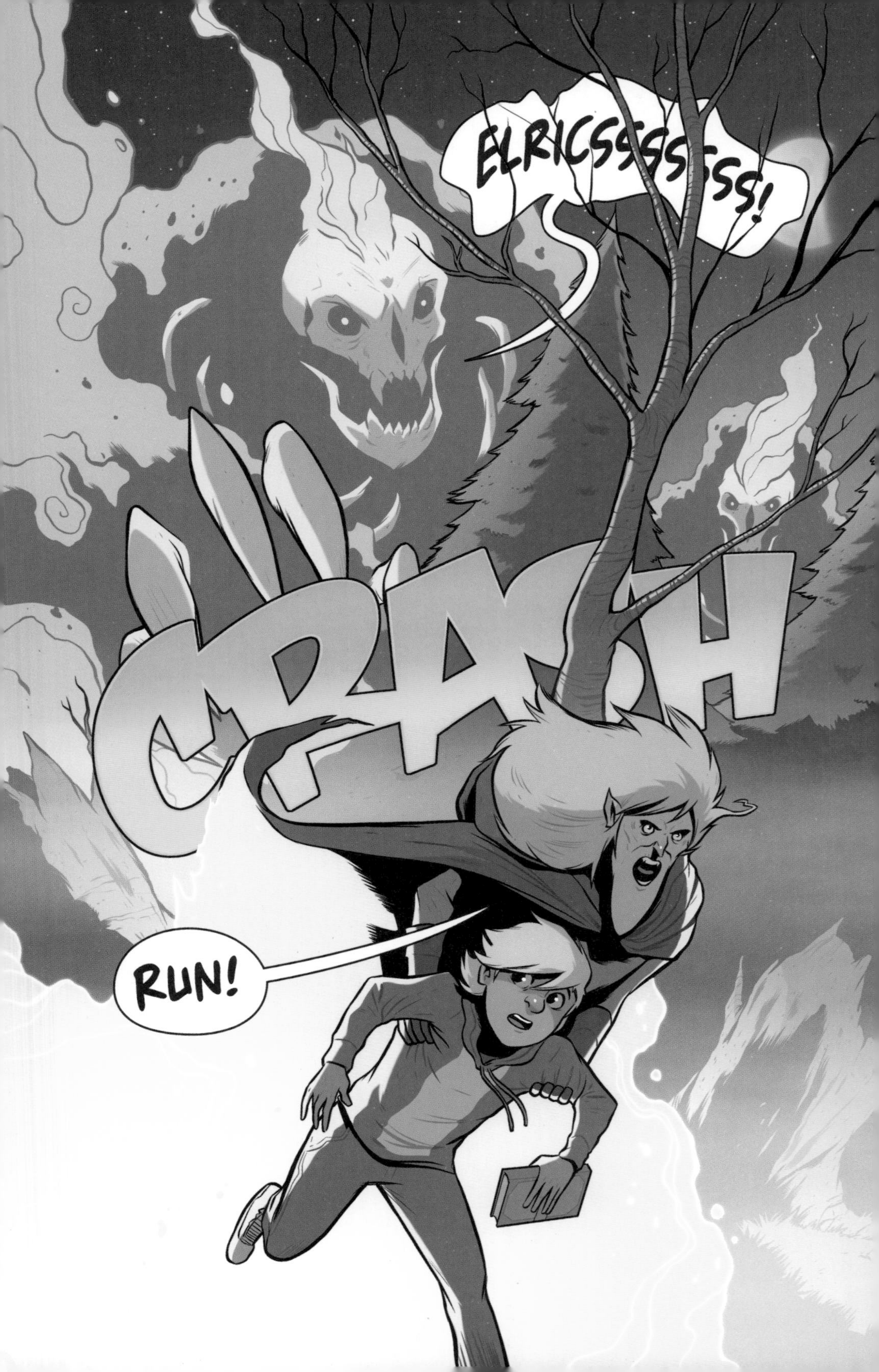
ELRICSSSSSSSS!
CRASH
RUN!

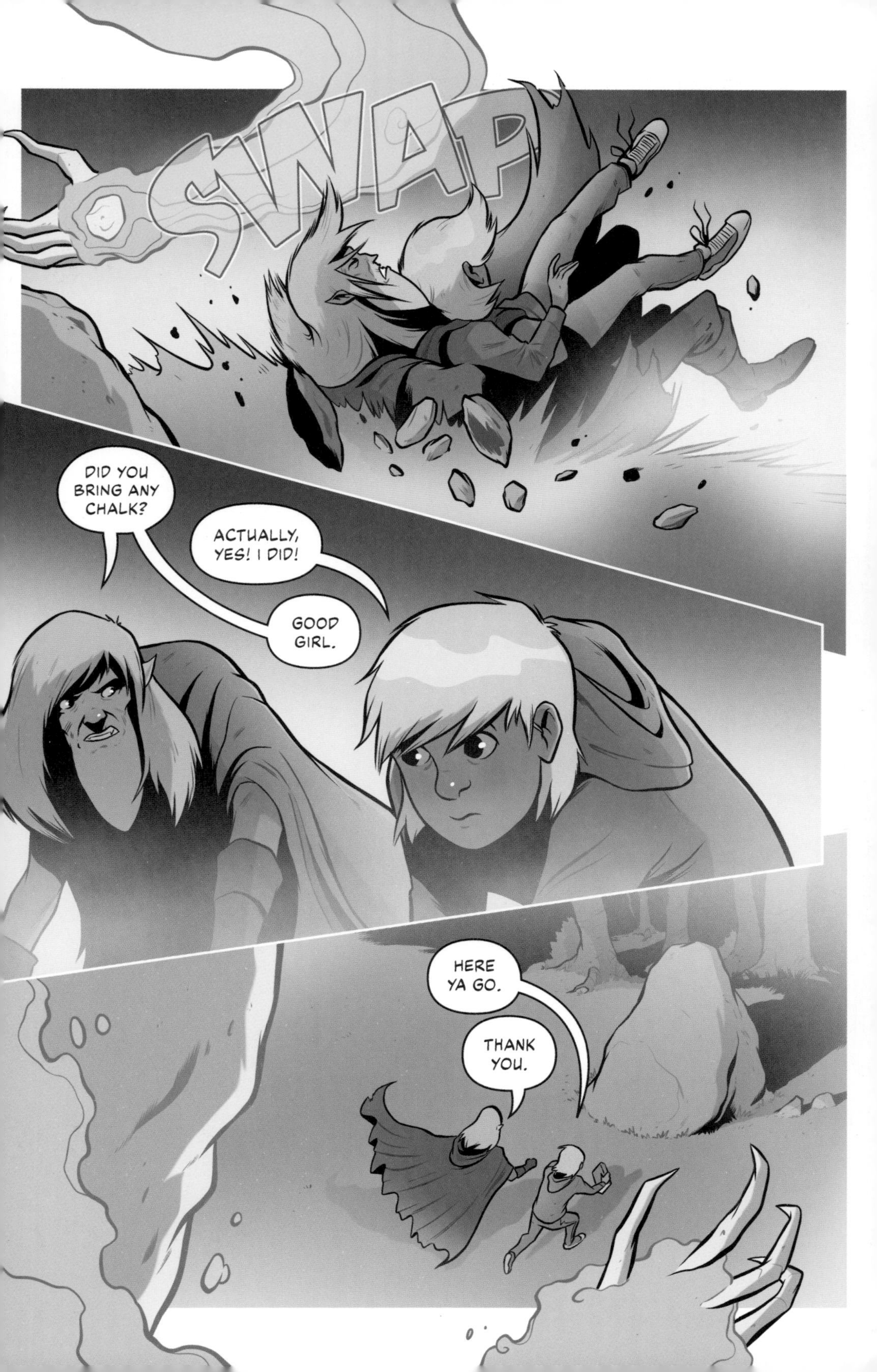
SWAP
DID YOU BRING ANY CHALK?
ACTUALLY, YES! I DID!
GOOD GIRL.
HERE YA GO.
THANK YOU.

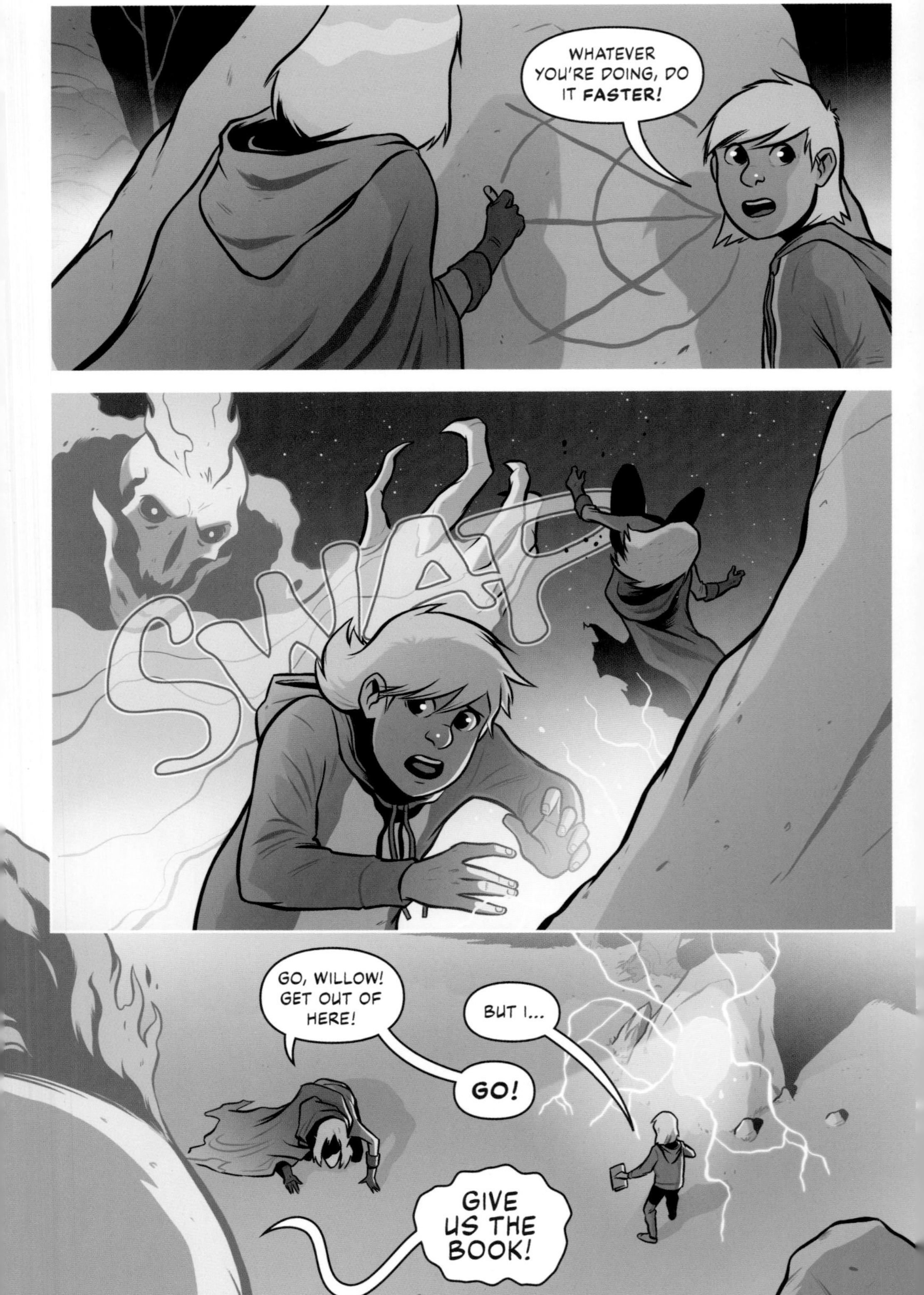
WHATEVER YOU'RE DOING, DO IT **FASTER!**
SWAP
GO, WILLOW! GET OUT OF HERE!
BUT I...
GO!
GIVE US THE BOOK!

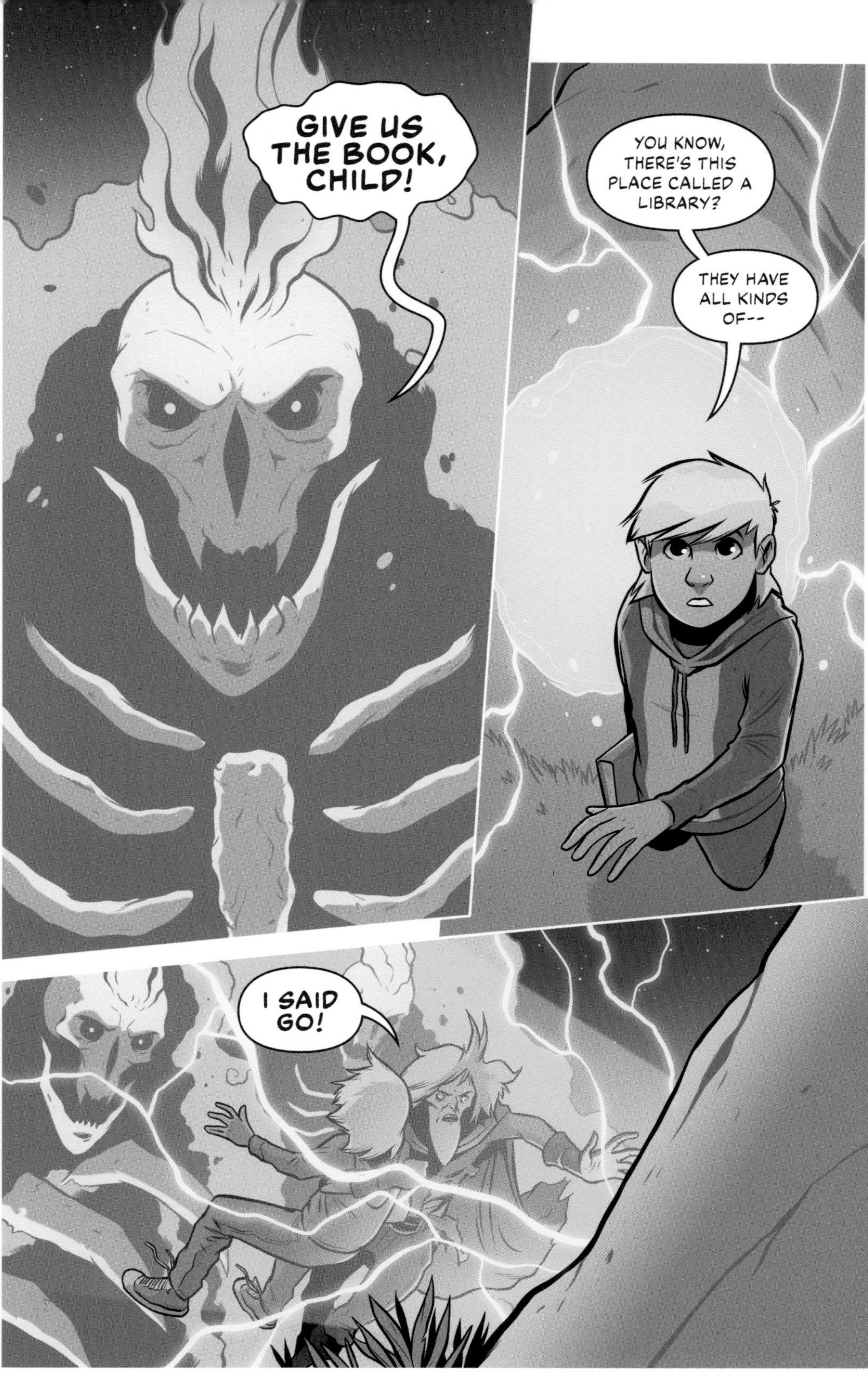
GIVE US THE BOOK, CHILD!
YOU KNOW, THERE'S THIS PLACE CALLED A LIBRARY?
THEY HAVE ALL KINDS OF--
I SAID GO!

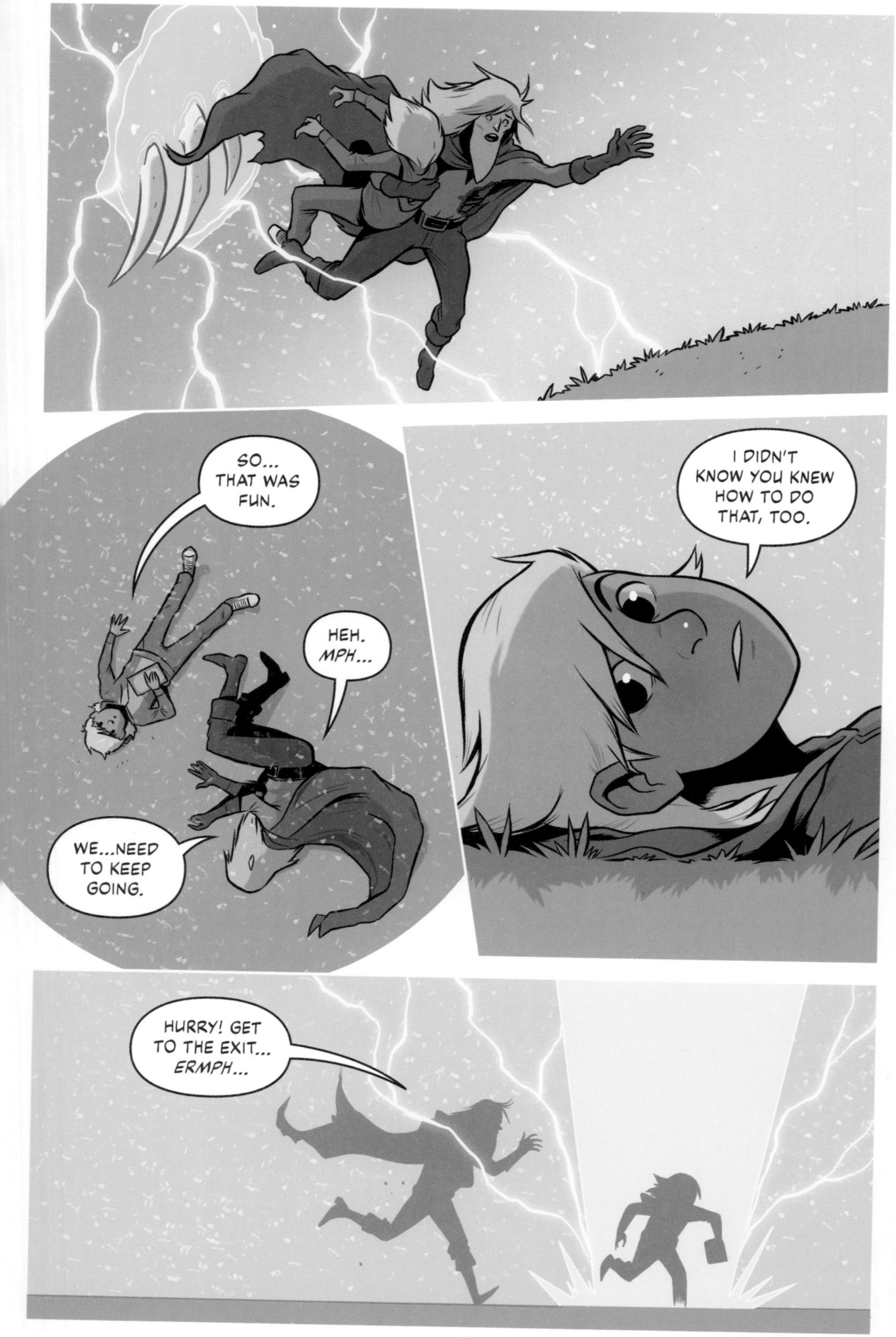
SO... THAT WAS FUN.
HEH. *MPH...*
WE...NEED TO KEEP GOING.
I DIDN'T KNOW YOU KNEW HOW TO DO THAT, TOO.
HURRY! GET TO THE EXIT... *ERMPH...*

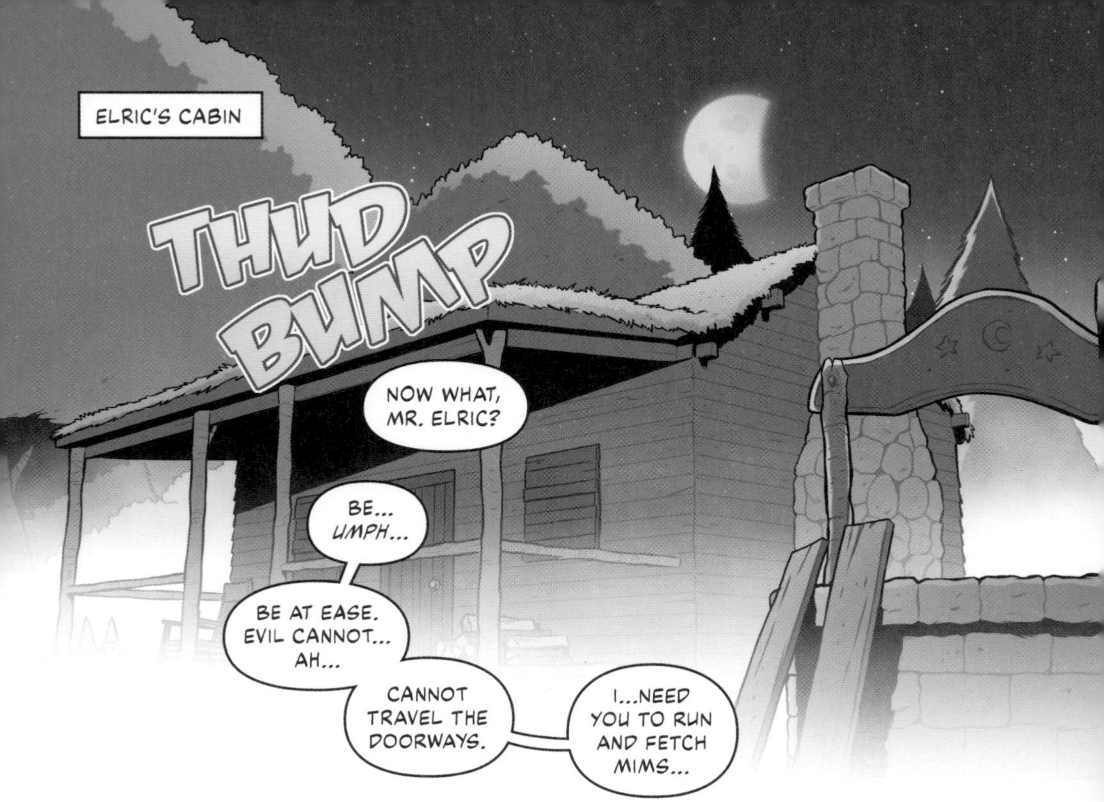
ELRIC'S CABIN
THUD
BUMP
NOW WHAT, MR. ELRIC?
BE... UMPH...
BE AT EASE. EVIL CANNOT... AH...
CANNOT TRAVEL THE DOORWAYS.
I...NEED YOU TO RUN AND FETCH MIMS...

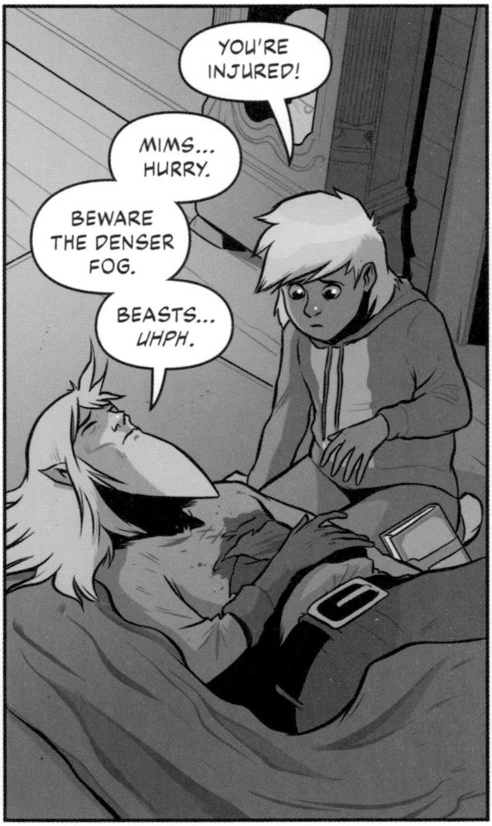
YOU'RE INJURED!
MIMS... HURRY.
BEWARE THE DENSER FOG.
BEASTS... UHPH.

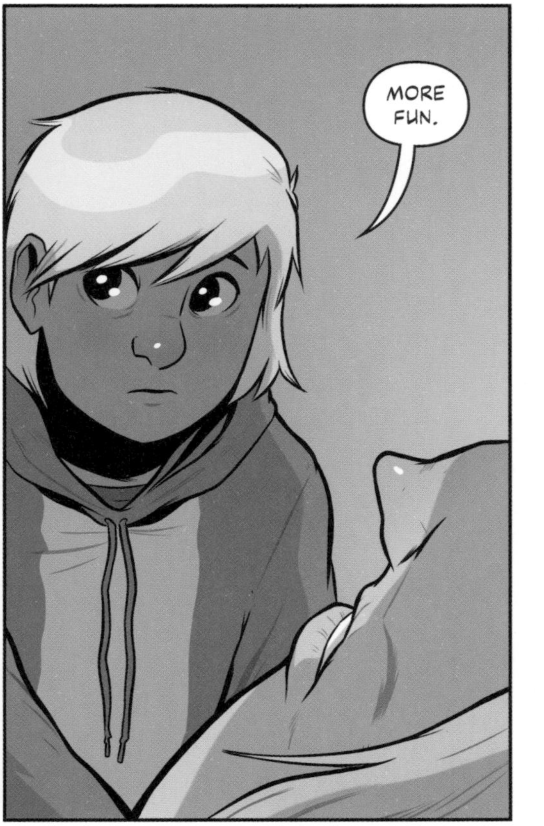
MORE FUN.

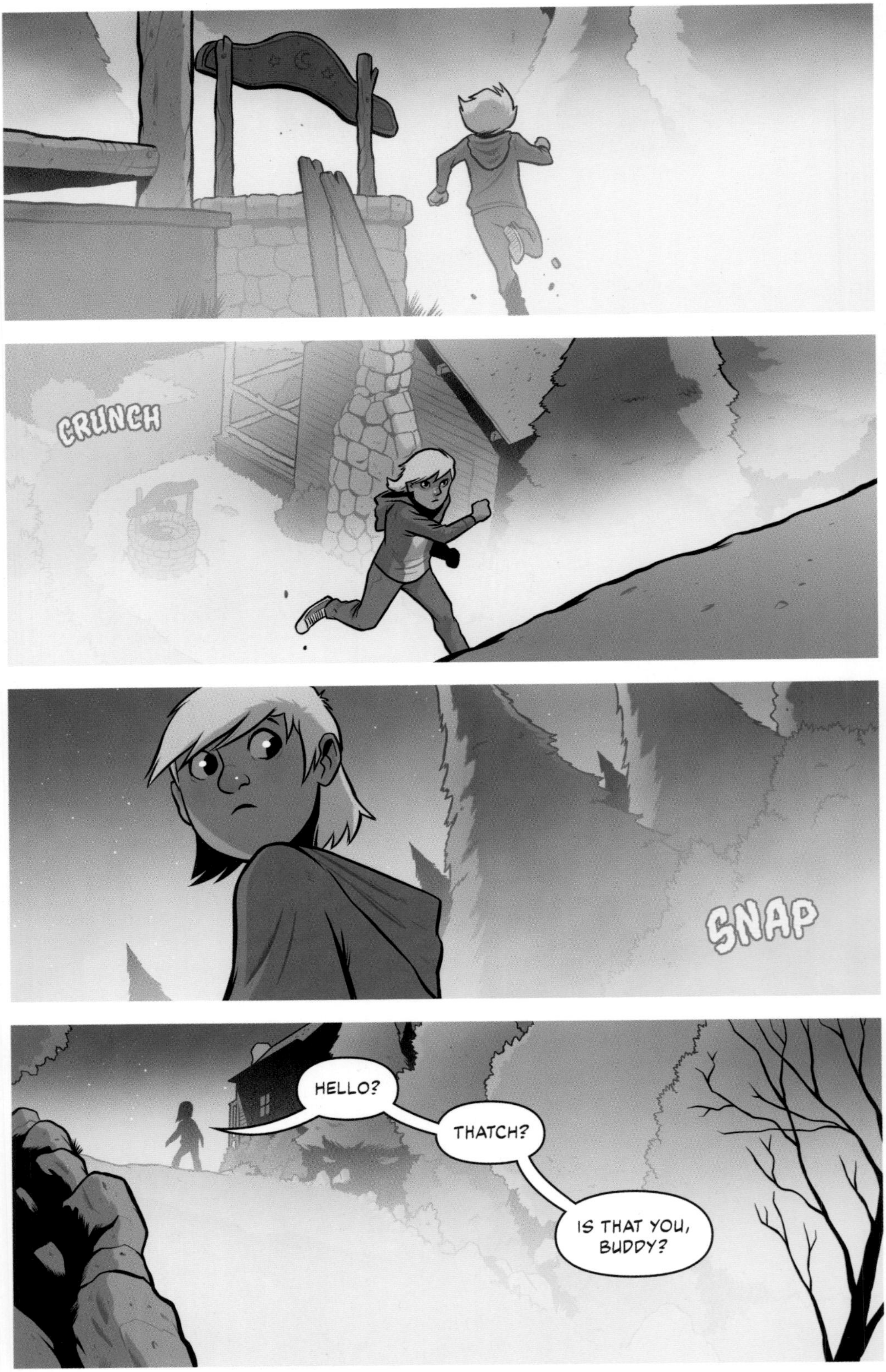
CRUNCH
SNAP
HELLO?
THATCH?
IS THAT YOU, BUDDY?

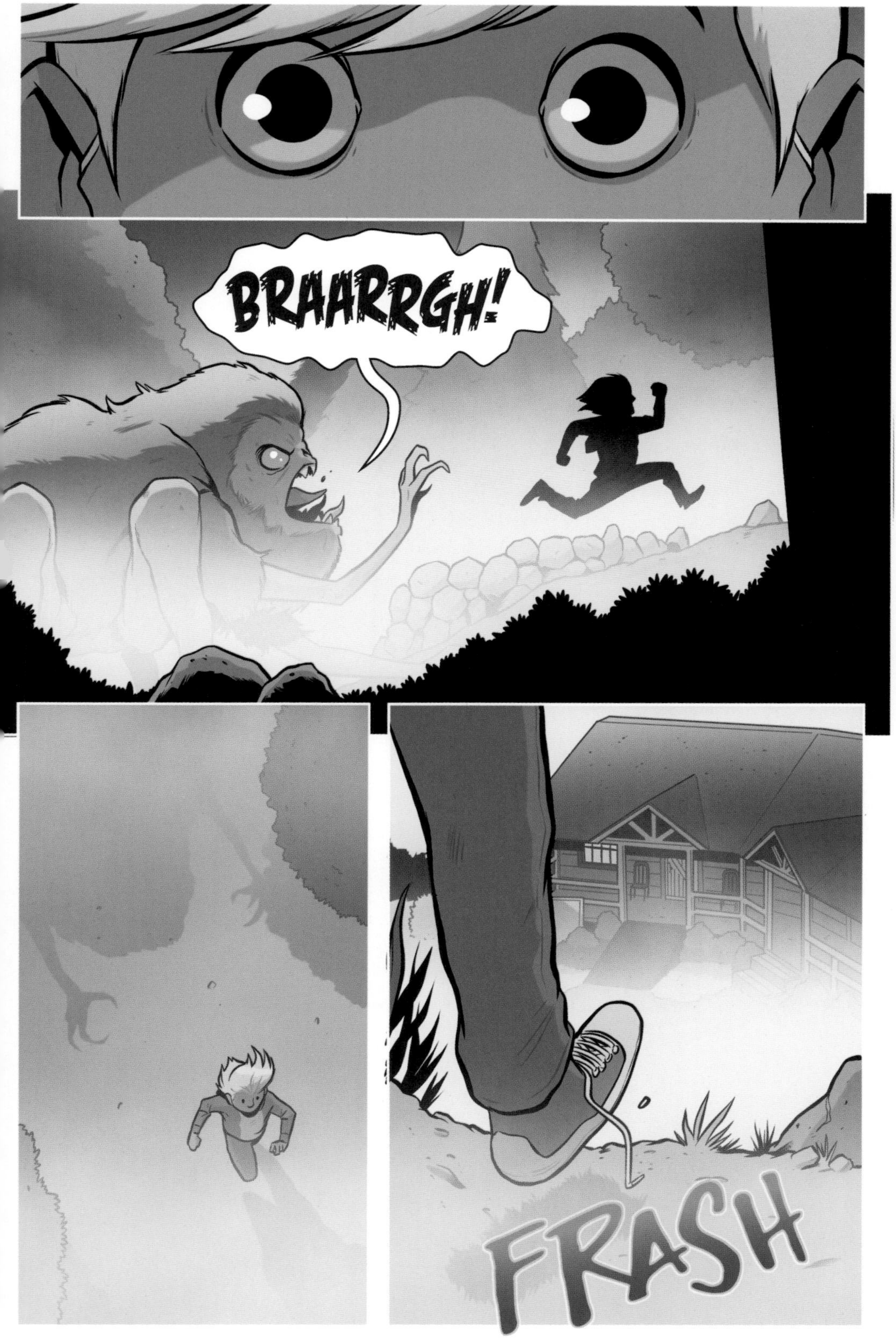
BRAARRGH!
FRASH

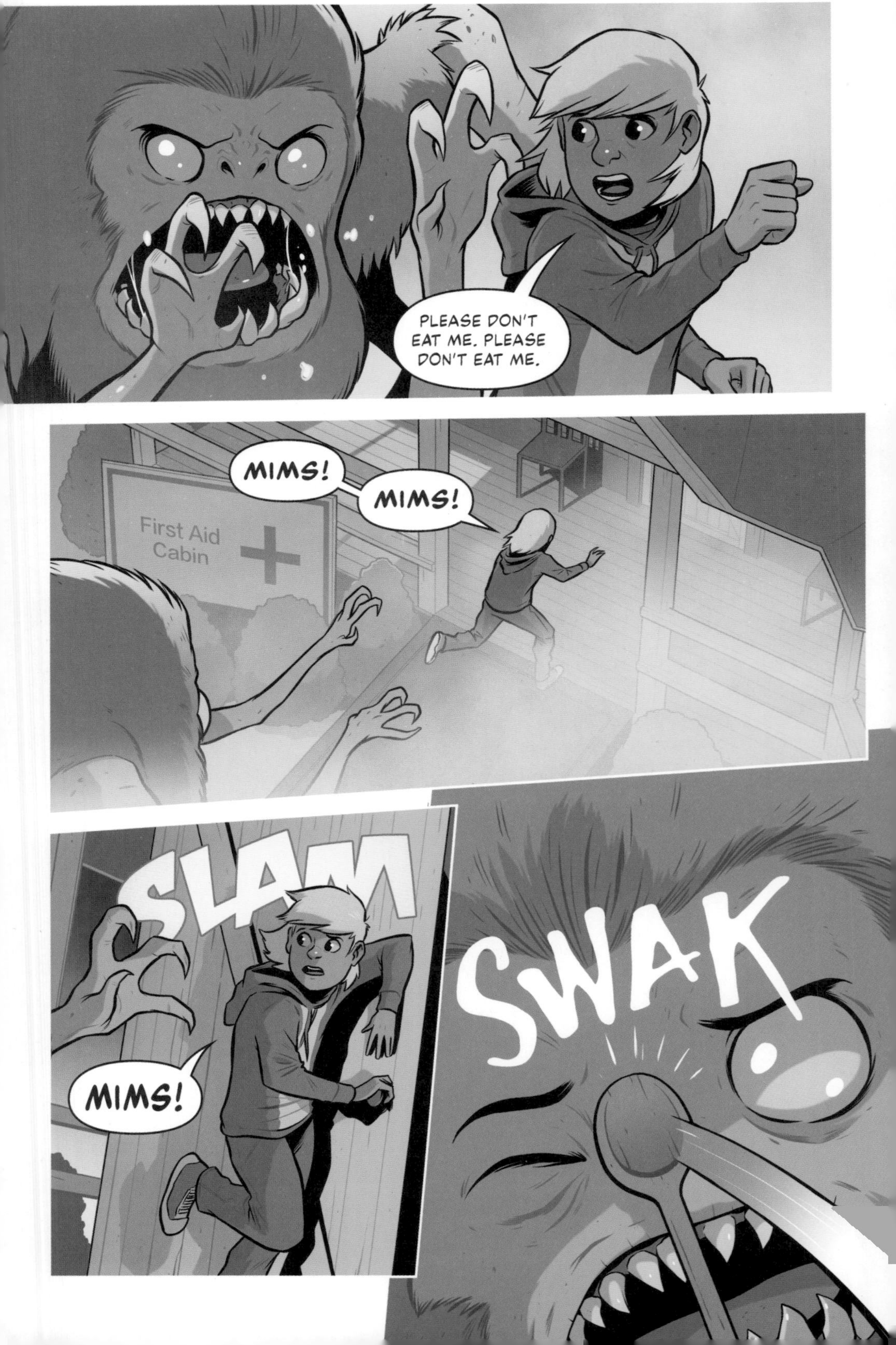
PLEASE DON'T EAT ME. PLEASE DON'T EAT ME.
MIMS!
MIMS!
First Aid Cabin
SLAM
MIMS!
SWAK

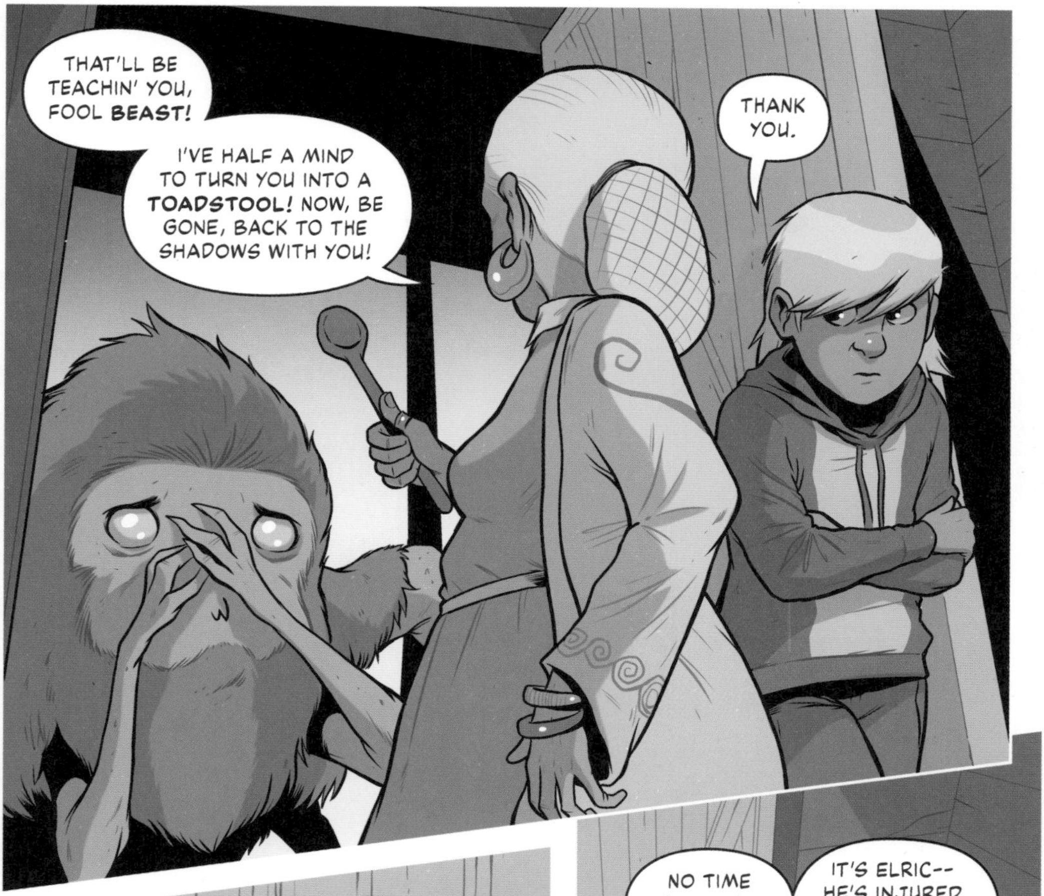
THAT'LL BE TEACHIN' YOU, FOOL BEAST!
I'VE HALF A MIND TO TURN YOU INTO A TOADSTOOL! NOW, BE GONE, BACK TO THE SHADOWS WITH YOU!
THANK YOU.

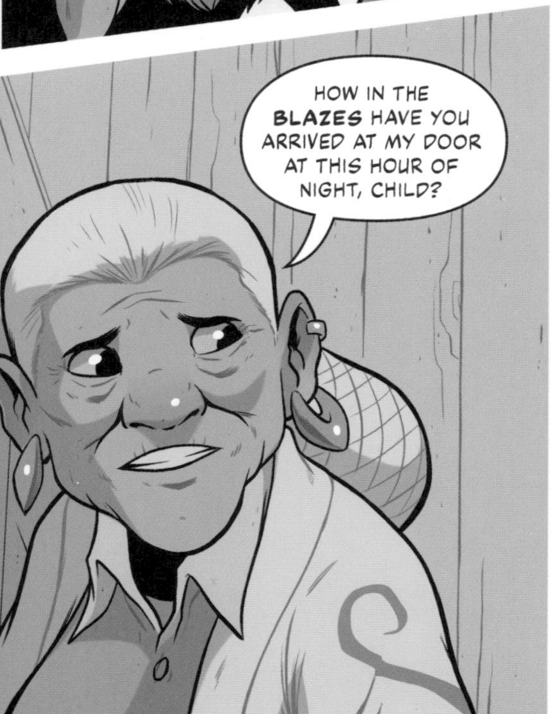
HOW IN THE BLAZES HAVE YOU ARRIVED AT MY DOOR AT THIS HOUR OF NIGHT, CHILD?

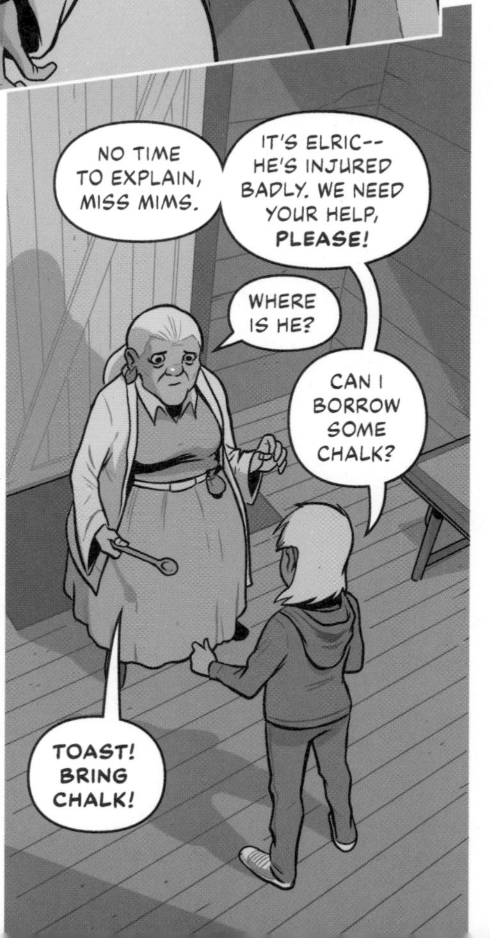
NO TIME TO EXPLAIN, MISS MIMS.
IT'S ELRIC-- HE'S INJURED BADLY. WE NEED YOUR HELP, PLEASE!
WHERE IS HE?
CAN I BORROW SOME CHALK?
TOAST! BRING CHALK!

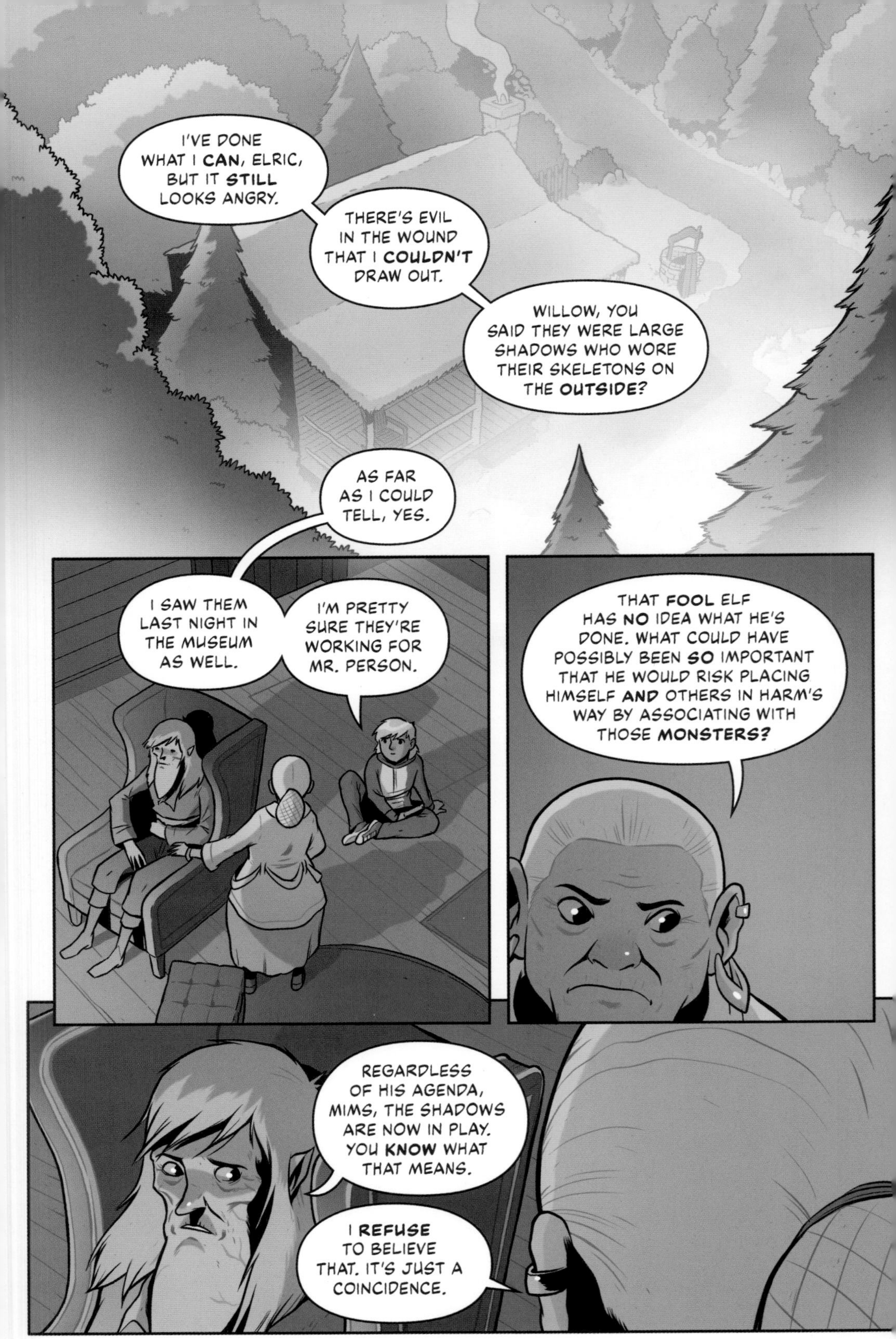
I'VE DONE WHAT I CAN, ELRIC, BUT IT STILL LOOKS ANGRY.
THERE'S EVIL IN THE WOUND THAT I COULDN'T DRAW OUT.
WILLOW, YOU SAID THEY WERE LARGE SHADOWS WHO WORE THEIR SKELETONS ON THE OUTSIDE?
AS FAR AS I COULD TELL, YES.
I SAW THEM LAST NIGHT IN THE MUSEUM AS WELL.
I'M PRETTY SURE THEY'RE WORKING FOR MR. PERSON.
THAT FOOL ELF HAS NO IDEA WHAT HE'S DONE. WHAT COULD HAVE POSSIBLY BEEN SO IMPORTANT THAT HE WOULD RISK PLACING HIMSELF AND OTHERS IN HARM'S WAY BY ASSOCIATING WITH THOSE MONSTERS?
REGARDLESS OF HIS AGENDA, MIMS, THE SHADOWS ARE NOW IN PLAY. YOU KNOW WHAT THAT MEANS.
I REFUSE TO BELIEVE THAT. IT'S JUST A COINCIDENCE.

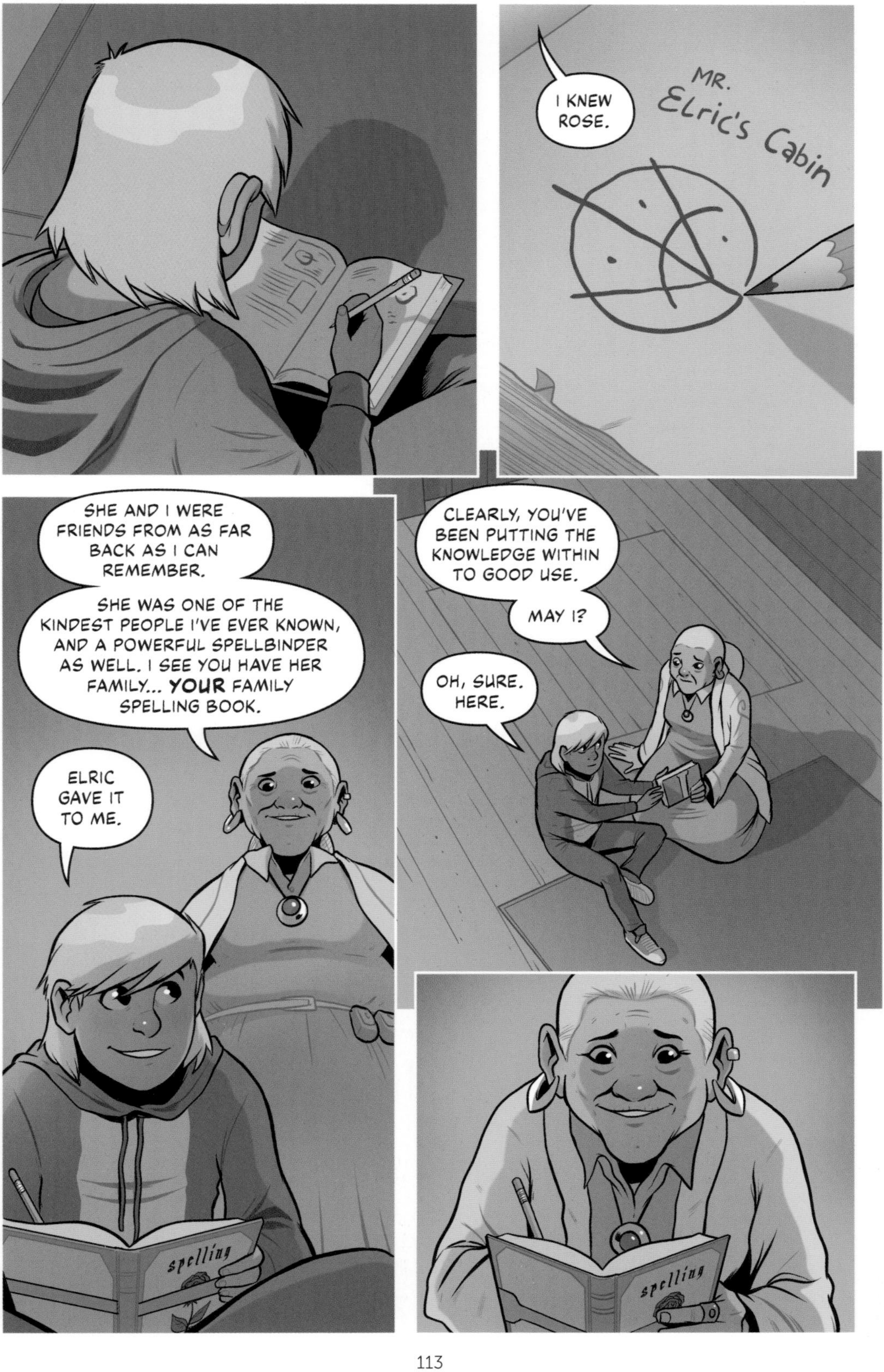
I KNEW ROSE.
MR. Elric's Cabin
SHE AND I WERE FRIENDS FROM AS FAR BACK AS I CAN REMEMBER.
SHE WAS ONE OF THE KINDEST PEOPLE I'VE EVER KNOWN, AND A POWERFUL SPELLBINDER AS WELL. I SEE YOU HAVE HER FAMILY... YOUR FAMILY SPELLING BOOK.
ELRIC GAVE IT TO ME.
spelling
CLEARLY, YOU'VE BEEN PUTTING THE KNOWLEDGE WITHIN TO GOOD USE.
MAY I?
OH, SURE. HERE.
spelling

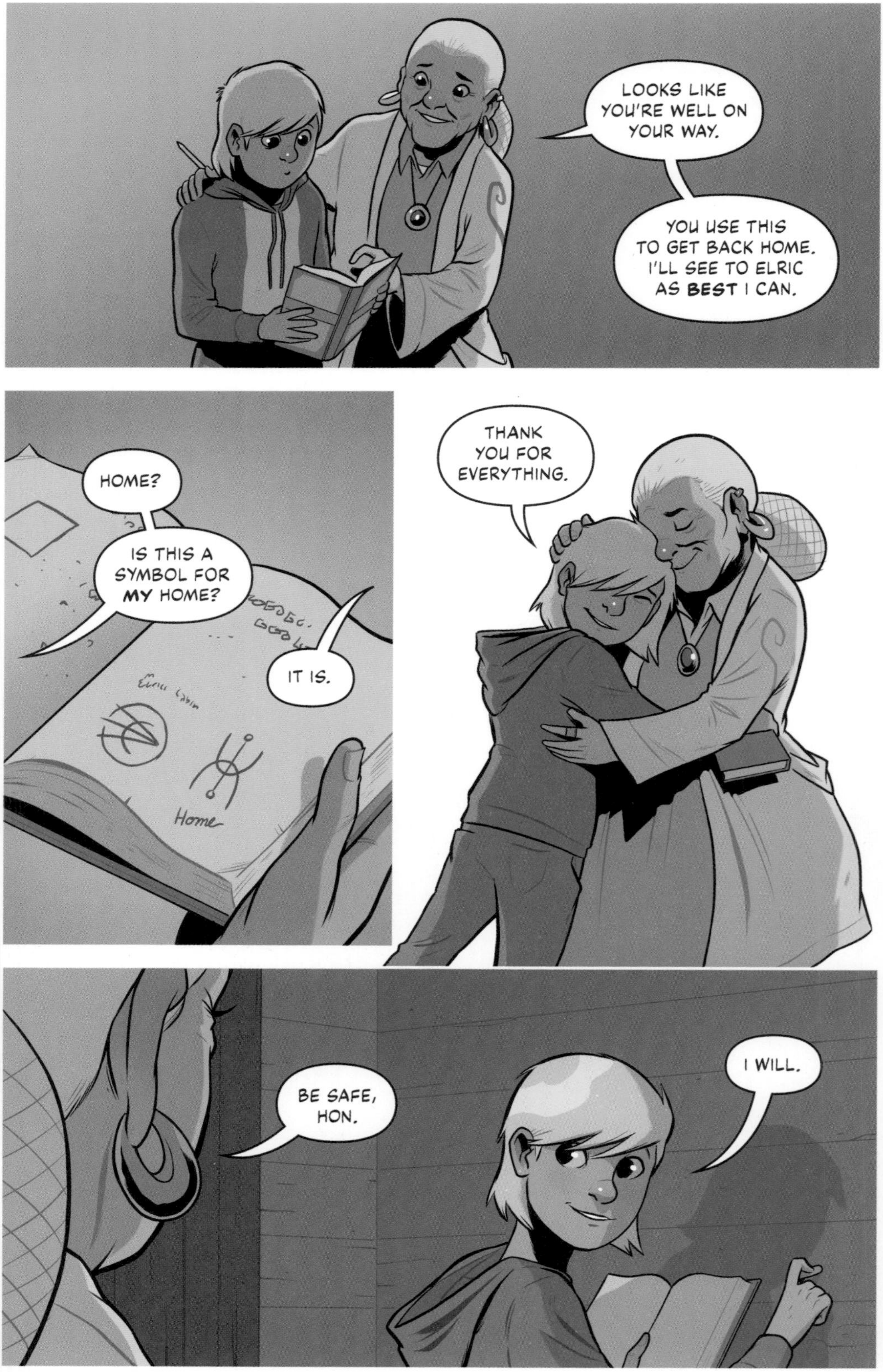
LOOKS LIKE YOU'RE WELL ON YOUR WAY.
YOU USE THIS TO GET BACK HOME. I'LL SEE TO ELRIC AS **BEST** I CAN.
HOME?
IS THIS A SYMBOL FOR **MY** HOME?
IT IS.
Home
THANK YOU FOR EVERYTHING.
BE SAFE, HON.
I WILL.

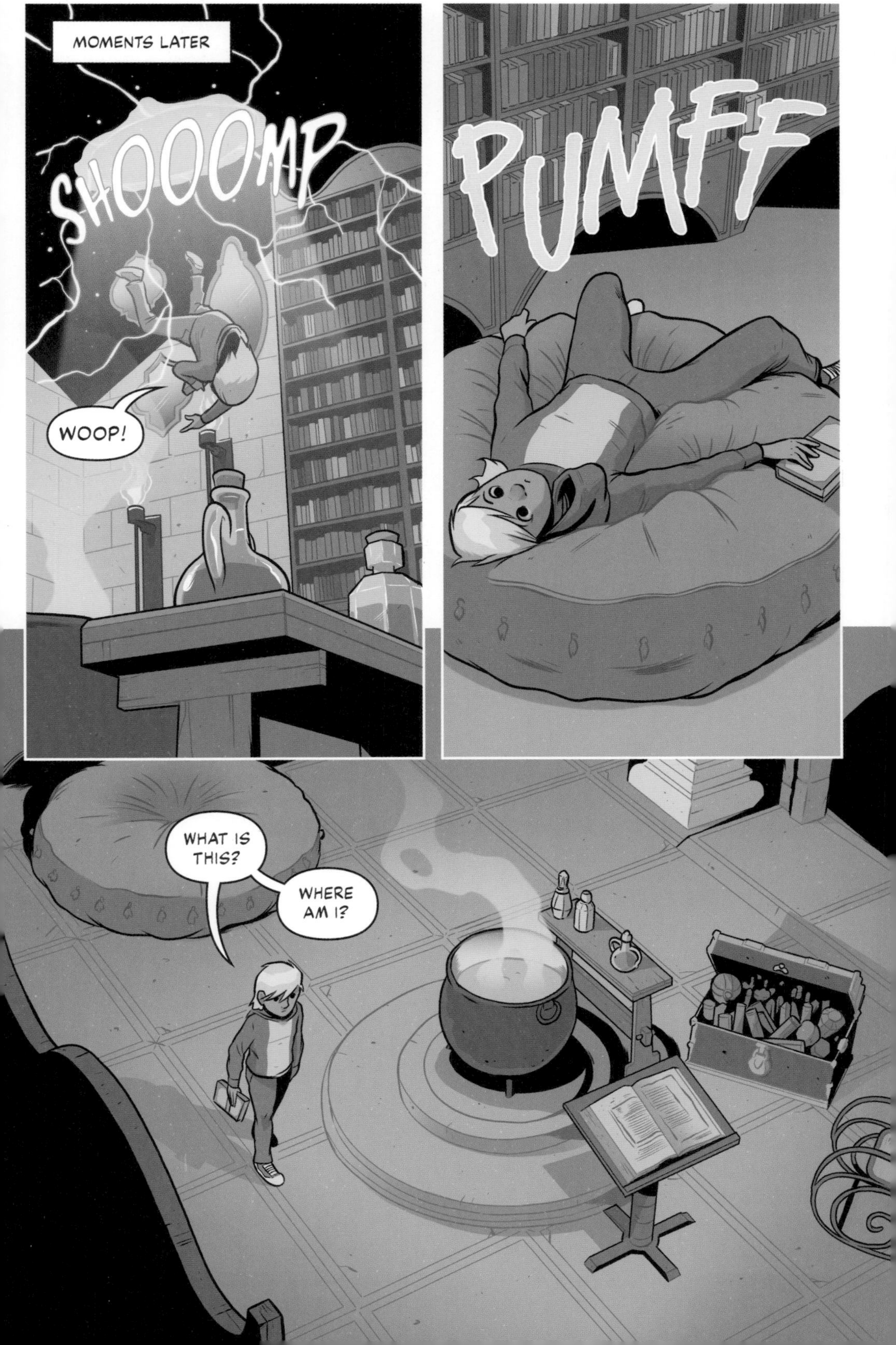
MOMENTS LATER
SHOOOMP
WOOP!
PUMFF
WHAT IS THIS?
WHERE AM I?

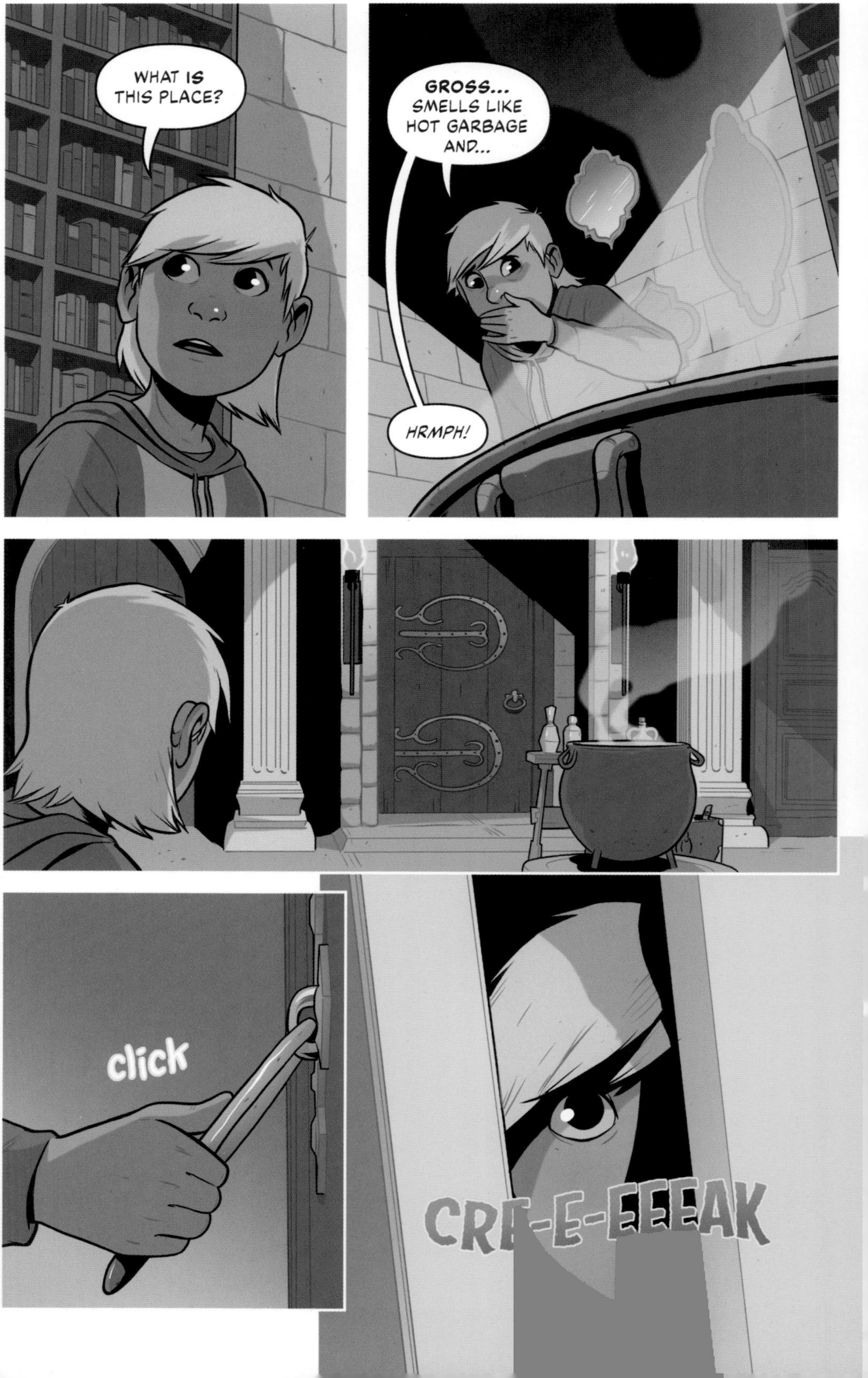
WHAT IS THIS PLACE?
GROSS... SMELLS LIKE HOT GARBAGE AND...
HRMPH!
click
CRE-E-EEEAK

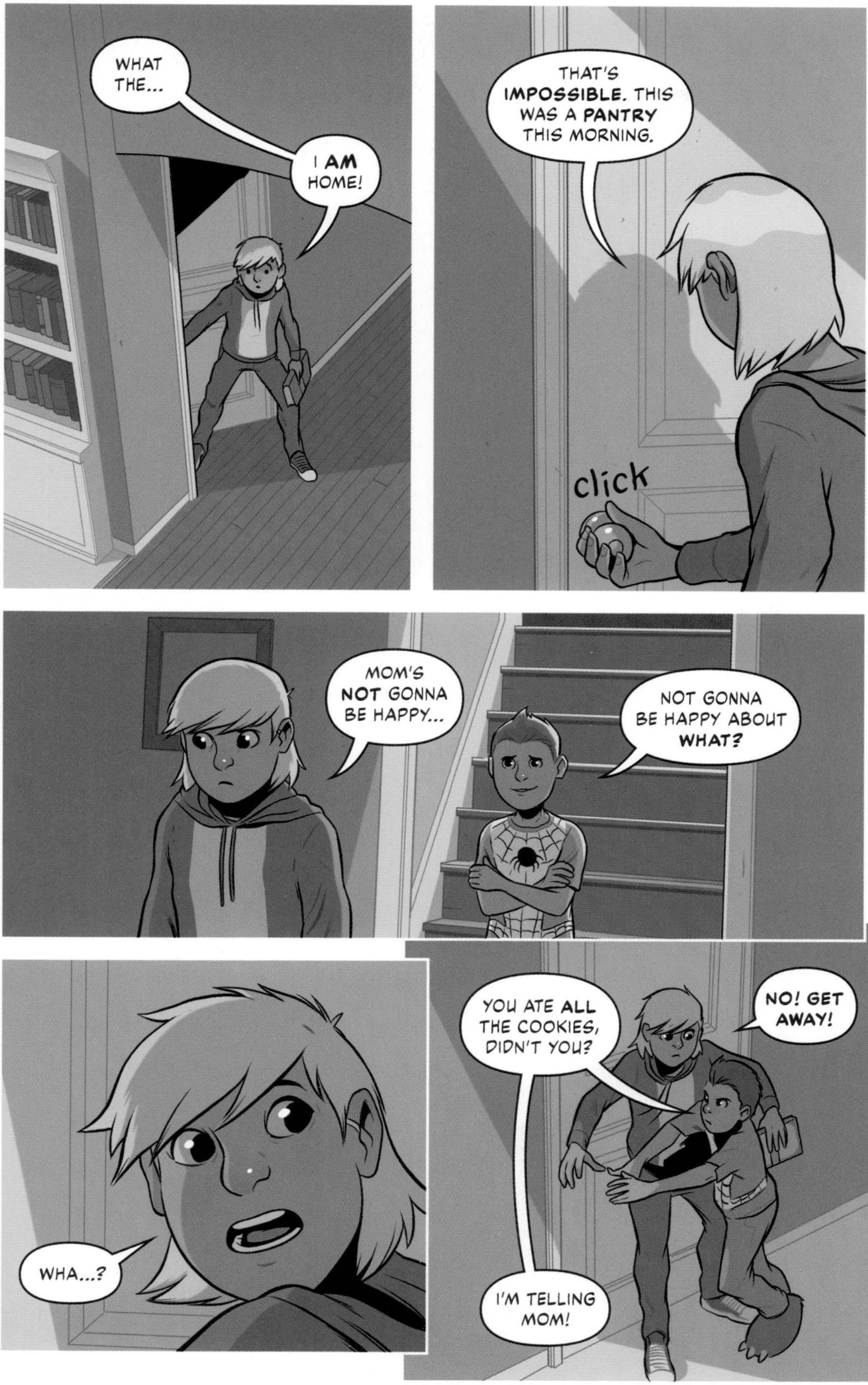
WHAT THE...
I **AM** HOME!
THAT'S **IMPOSSIBLE.** THIS WAS A **PANTRY** THIS MORNING.
click
MOM'S **NOT** GONNA BE HAPPY...
NOT GONNA BE HAPPY ABOUT **WHAT?**
WHA...?
YOU ATE **ALL** THE COOKIES, DIDN'T YOU?
NO! GET AWAY!
I'M TELLING MOM!

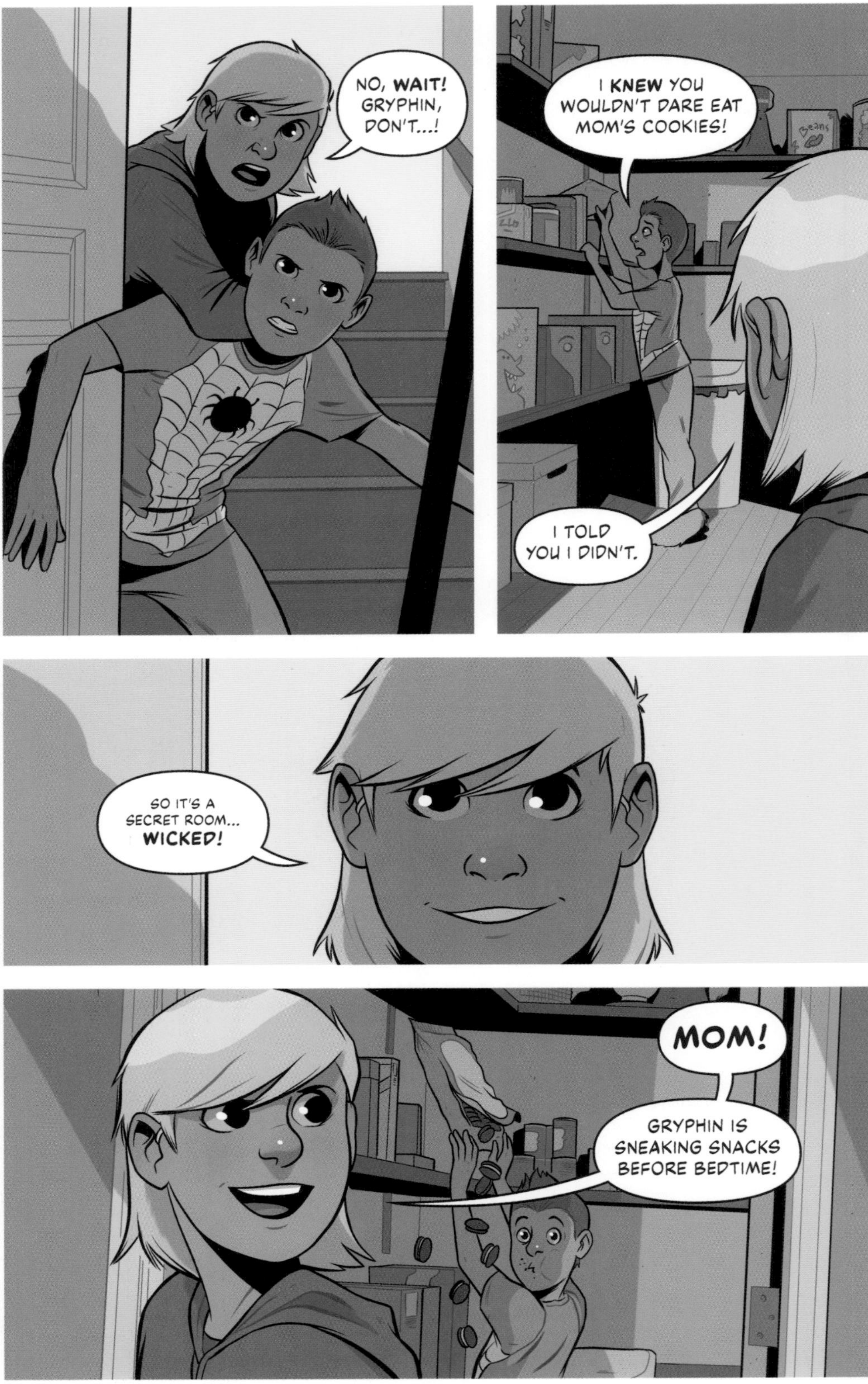
NO, WAIT! GRYPHIN, DON'T...!
I KNEW YOU WOULDN'T DARE EAT MOM'S COOKIES!
I TOLD YOU I DIDN'T.
SO IT'S A SECRET ROOM... WICKED!
MOM!
GRYPHIN IS SNEAKING SNACKS BEFORE BEDTIME!

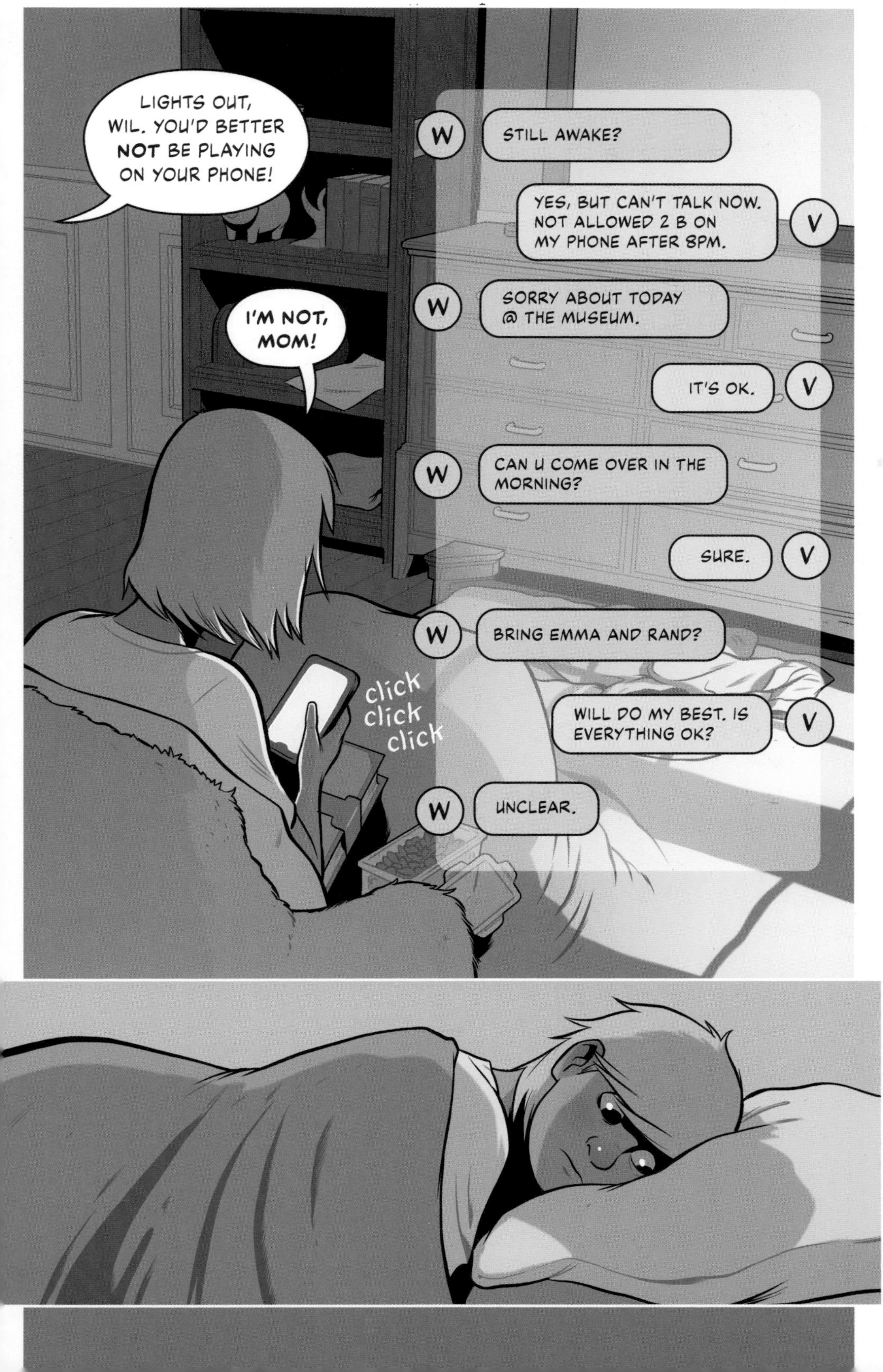
LIGHTS OUT, WIL. YOU'D BETTER **NOT** BE PLAYING ON YOUR PHONE!
I'M NOT, MOM!
W STILL AWAKE?
YES, BUT CAN'T TALK NOW. NOT ALLOWED 2 B ON MY PHONE AFTER 8PM. V
W SORRY ABOUT TODAY @ THE MUSEUM.
IT'S OK. V
W CAN U COME OVER IN THE MORNING?
SURE. V
W BRING EMMA AND RAND?
WILL DO MY BEST. IS EVERYTHING OK? V
W UNCLEAR.
click click click

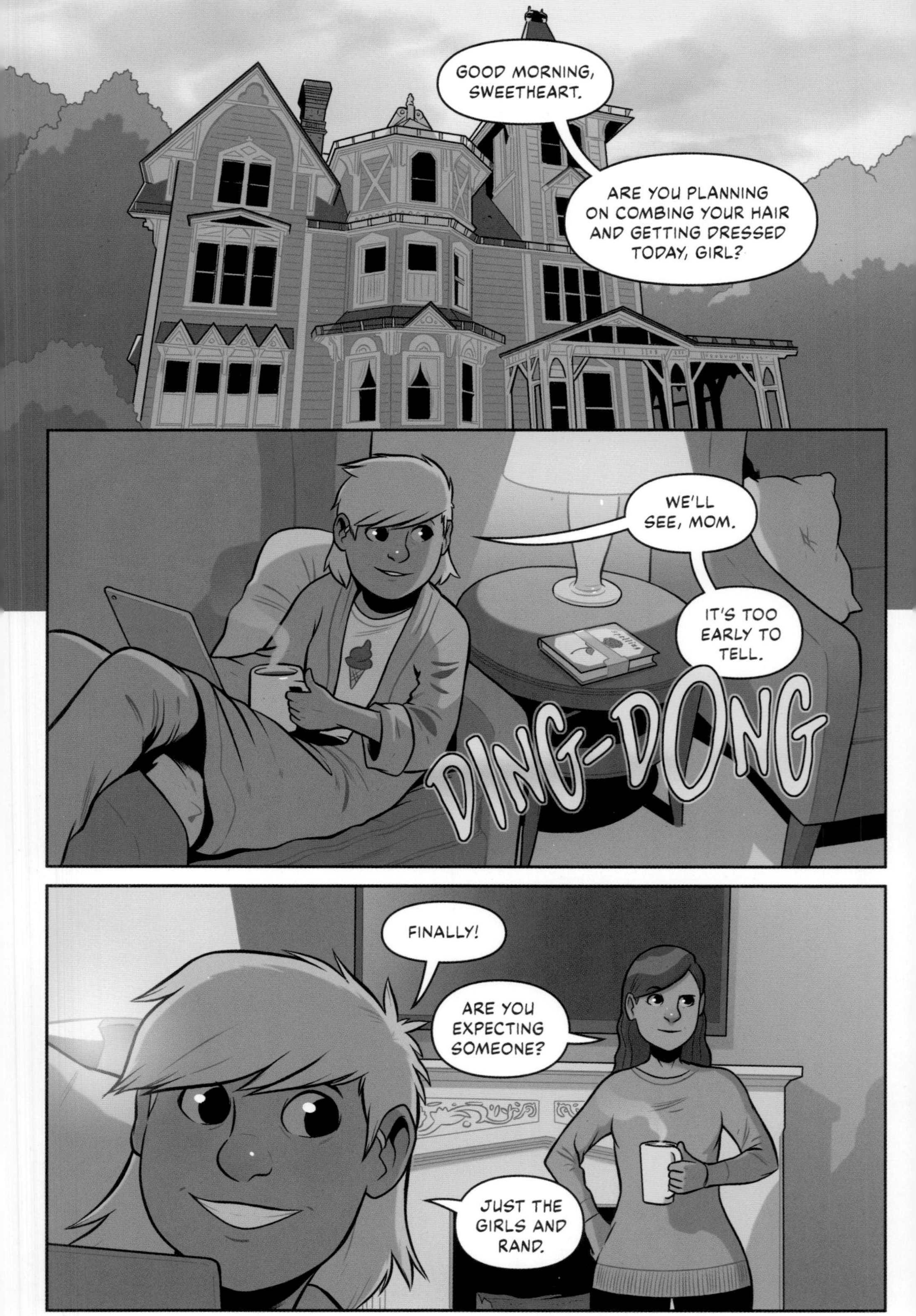
GOOD MORNING, SWEETHEART.
ARE YOU PLANNING ON COMBING YOUR HAIR AND GETTING DRESSED TODAY, GIRL?
WE'LL SEE, MOM.
IT'S TOO EARLY TO TELL.
DING-DONG
FINALLY!
ARE YOU EXPECTING SOMEONE?
JUST THE GIRLS AND RAND.

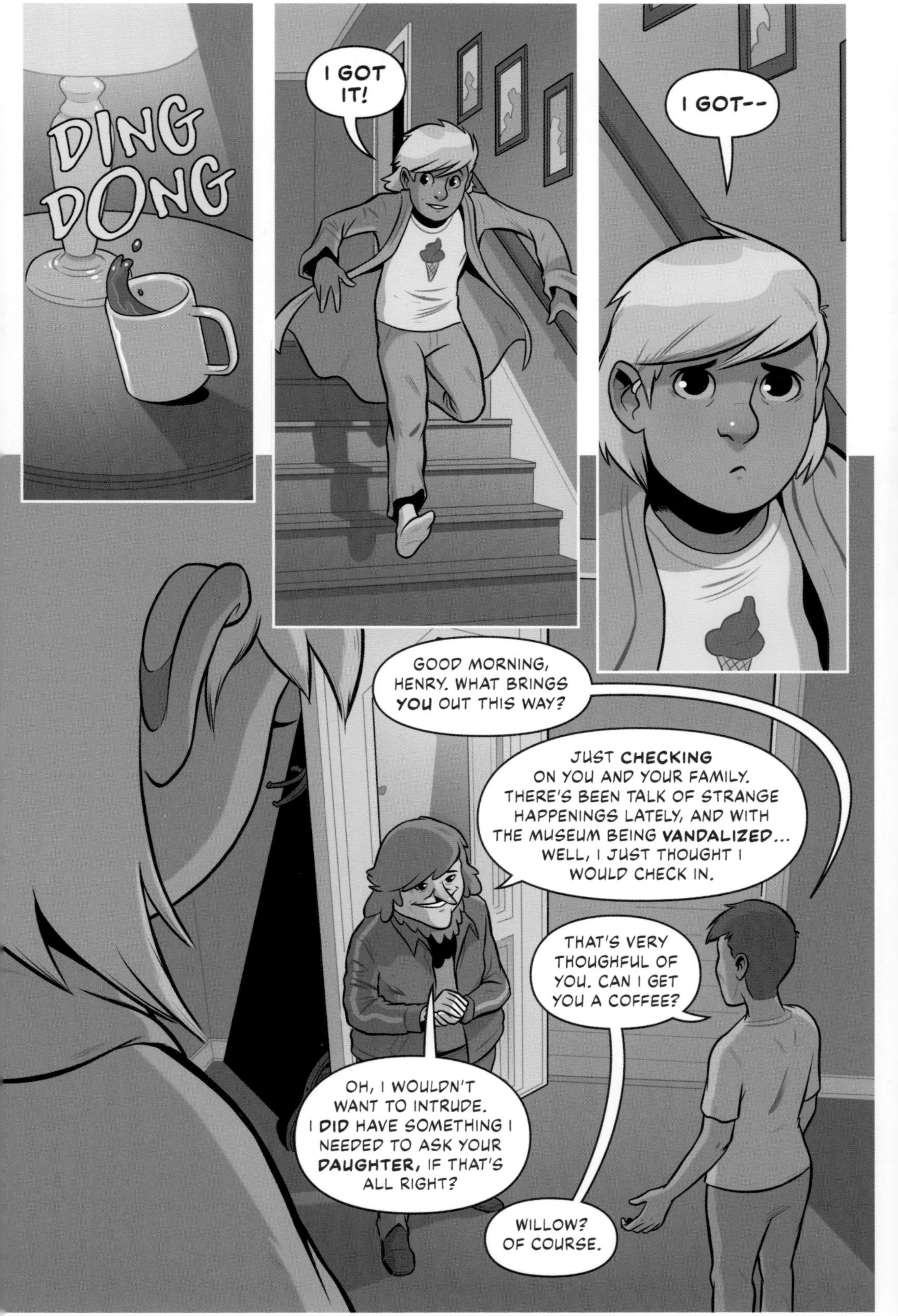
DING DONG
I GOT IT!
I GOT--
GOOD MORNING, HENRY. WHAT BRINGS **YOU** OUT THIS WAY?
JUST **CHECKING** ON YOU AND YOUR FAMILY. THERE'S BEEN TALK OF STRANGE HAPPENINGS LATELY, AND WITH THE MUSEUM BEING **VANDALIZED**... WELL, I JUST THOUGHT I WOULD CHECK IN.
THAT'S VERY THOUGHFUL OF YOU. CAN I GET YOU A COFFEE?
OH, I WOULDN'T WANT TO INTRUDE. I **DID** HAVE SOMETHING I NEEDED TO ASK YOUR **DAUGHTER**, IF THAT'S ALL RIGHT?
WILLOW? OF COURSE.

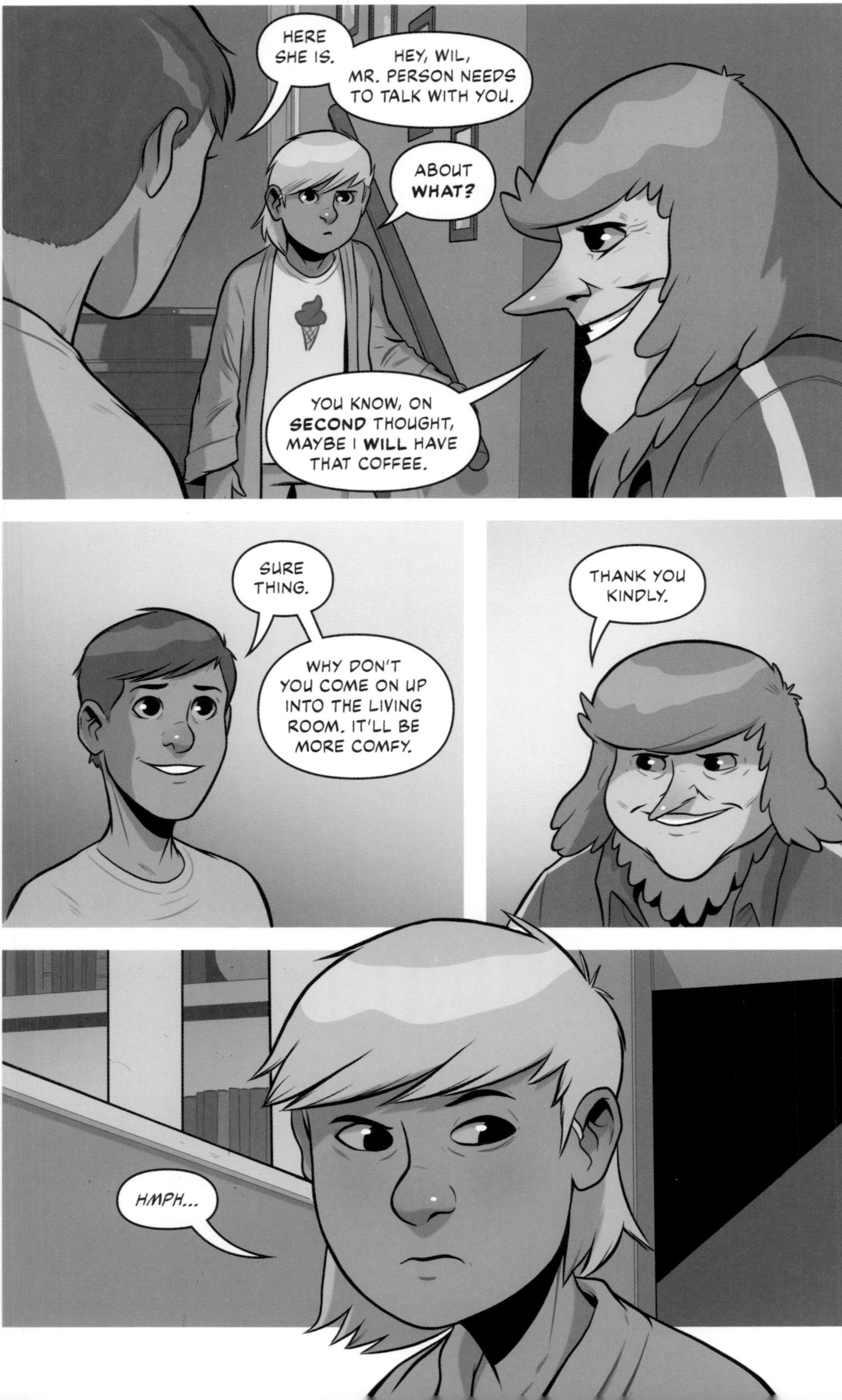
HERE SHE IS.
HEY, WIL, MR. PERSON NEEDS TO TALK WITH YOU.
ABOUT **WHAT?**
YOU KNOW, ON **SECOND** THOUGHT, MAYBE I **WILL** HAVE THAT COFFEE.
SURE THING.
WHY DON'T YOU COME ON UP INTO THE LIVING ROOM. IT'LL BE MORE COMFY.
THANK YOU KINDLY.
HMPH...

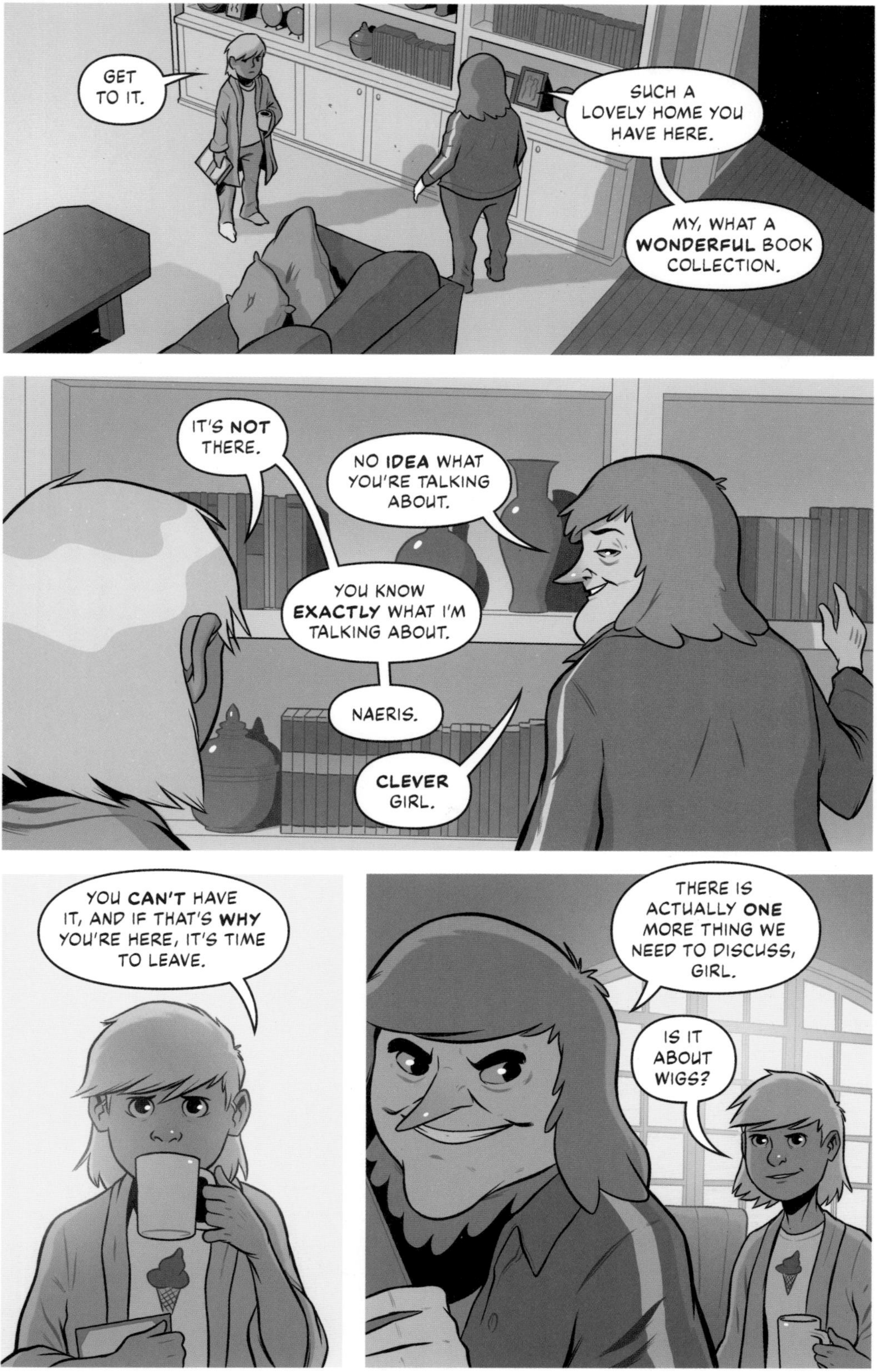
GET TO IT.
SUCH A LOVELY HOME YOU HAVE HERE.
MY, WHAT A **WONDERFUL** BOOK COLLECTION.
IT'S **NOT** THERE.
NO **IDEA** WHAT YOU'RE TALKING ABOUT.
YOU KNOW **EXACTLY** WHAT I'M TALKING ABOUT.
NAERIS.
CLEVER GIRL.
YOU **CAN'T** HAVE IT, AND IF THAT'S **WHY** YOU'RE HERE, IT'S TIME TO LEAVE.
THERE IS ACTUALLY **ONE** MORE THING WE NEED TO DISCUSS, GIRL.
IS IT ABOUT WIGS?

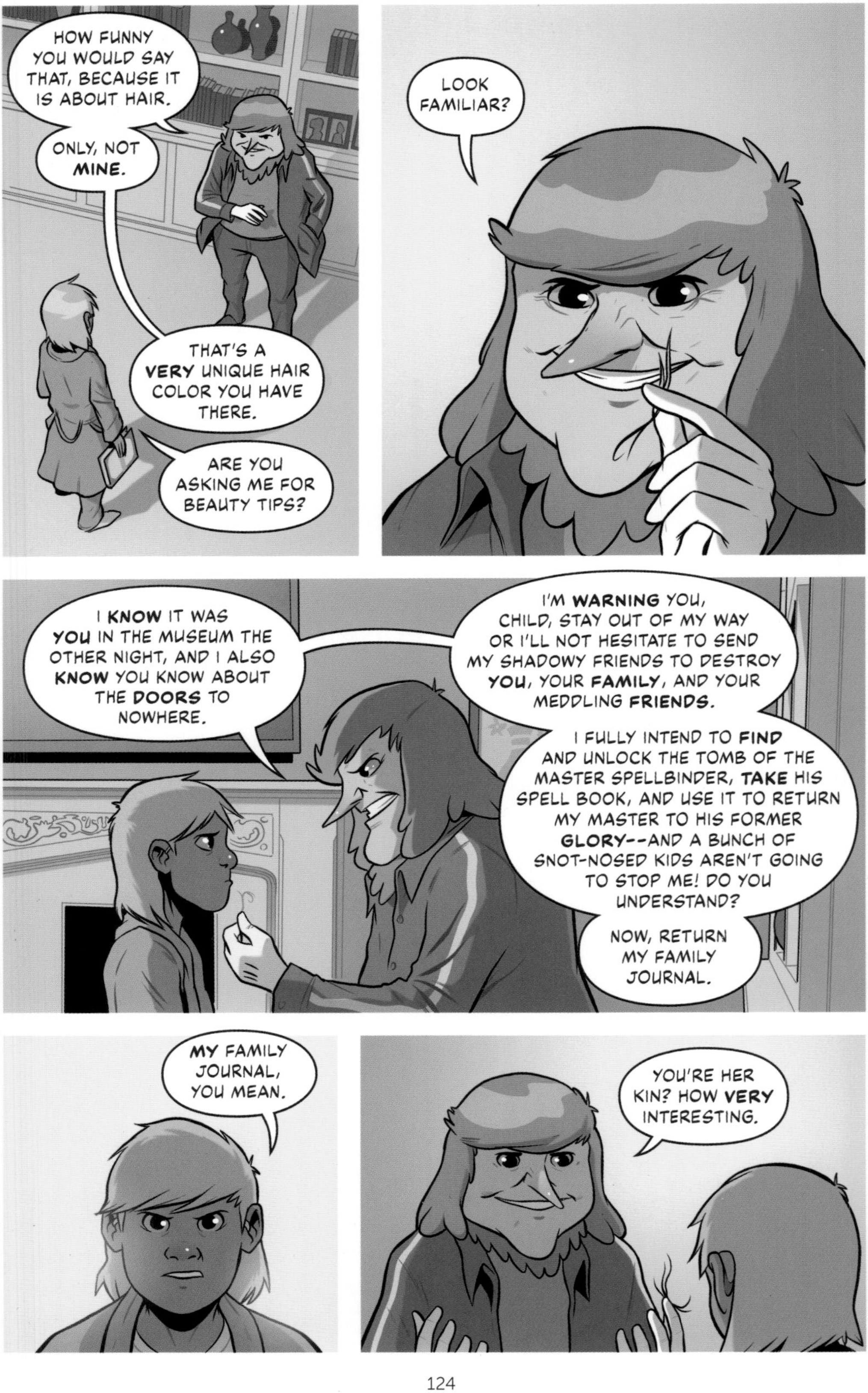
HOW FUNNY YOU WOULD SAY THAT, BECAUSE IT IS ABOUT HAIR.
ONLY, NOT **MINE**.
THAT'S A **VERY** UNIQUE HAIR COLOR YOU HAVE THERE.
ARE YOU ASKING ME FOR BEAUTY TIPS?
LOOK FAMILIAR?
I **KNOW** IT WAS **YOU** IN THE MUSEUM THE OTHER NIGHT, AND I ALSO **KNOW** YOU KNOW ABOUT THE **DOORS** TO NOWHERE.
I'M **WARNING** YOU, CHILD, STAY OUT OF MY WAY OR I'LL NOT HESITATE TO SEND MY SHADOWY FRIENDS TO DESTROY **YOU**, YOUR **FAMILY**, AND YOUR MEDDLING **FRIENDS**.
I FULLY INTEND TO **FIND** AND UNLOCK THE TOMB OF THE MASTER SPELLBINDER, **TAKE** HIS SPELL BOOK, AND USE IT TO RETURN MY MASTER TO HIS FORMER **GLORY**--AND A BUNCH OF SNOT-NOSED KIDS AREN'T GOING TO STOP ME! DO YOU UNDERSTAND?
NOW, RETURN MY FAMILY JOURNAL.
MY FAMILY JOURNAL, YOU MEAN.
YOU'RE HER KIN? HOW **VERY** INTERESTING.

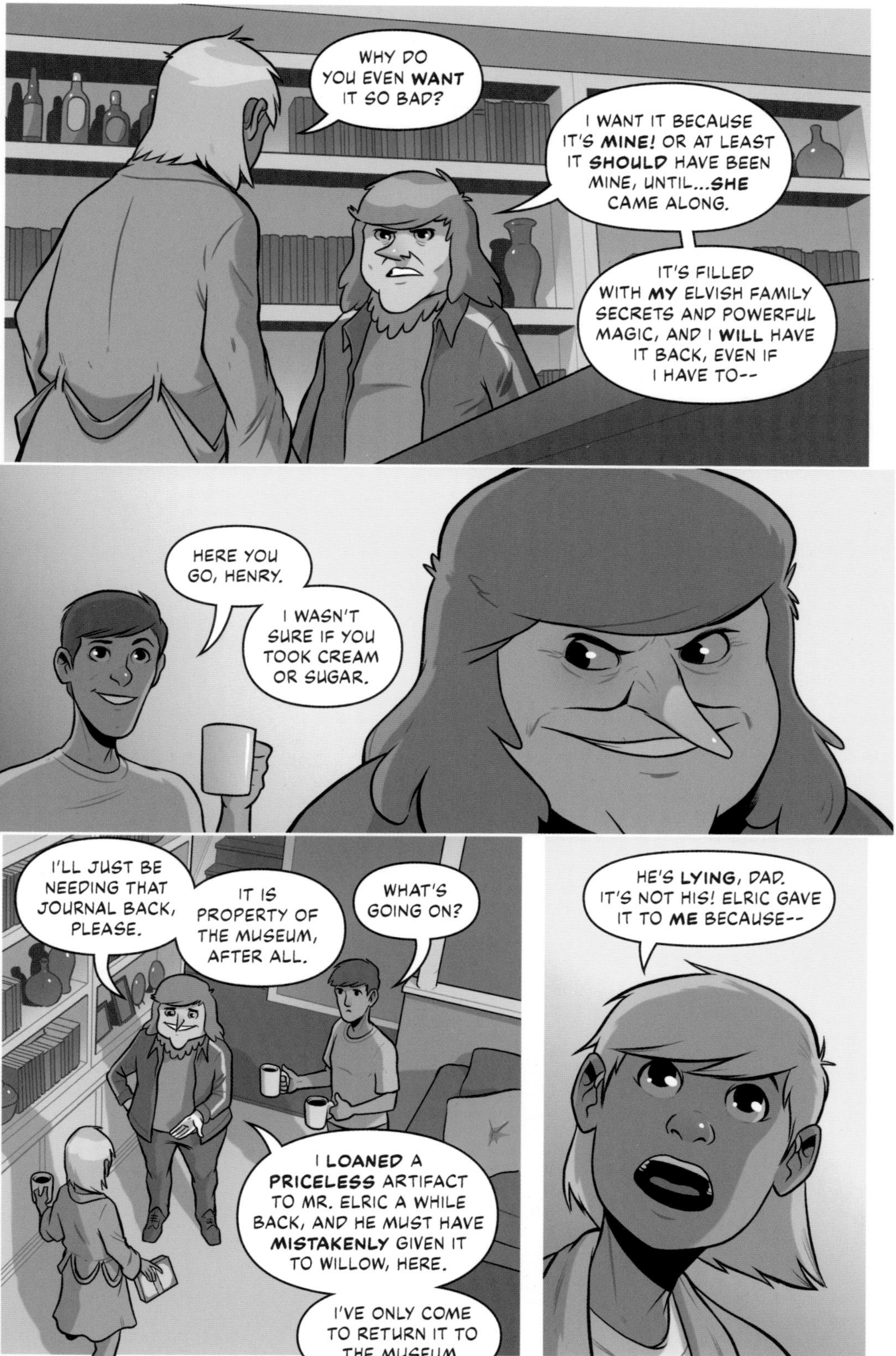
WHY DO YOU EVEN **WANT** IT SO BAD?
I WANT IT BECAUSE IT'S **MINE!** OR AT LEAST IT **SHOULD** HAVE BEEN MINE, UNTIL...**SHE** CAME ALONG.
IT'S FILLED WITH **MY** ELVISH FAMILY SECRETS AND POWERFUL MAGIC, AND I **WILL** HAVE IT BACK, EVEN IF I HAVE TO--
HERE YOU GO, HENRY.
I WASN'T SURE IF YOU TOOK CREAM OR SUGAR.
I'LL JUST BE NEEDING THAT JOURNAL BACK, PLEASE.
IT IS PROPERTY OF THE MUSEUM, AFTER ALL.
WHAT'S GOING ON?
I **LOANED** A **PRICELESS** ARTIFACT TO MR. ELRIC A WHILE BACK, AND HE MUST HAVE **MISTAKENLY** GIVEN IT TO WILLOW, HERE.
I'VE ONLY COME TO RETURN IT TO THE MUSEUM.
HE'S **LYING**, DAD. IT'S NOT HIS! ELRIC GAVE IT TO **ME** BECAUSE--

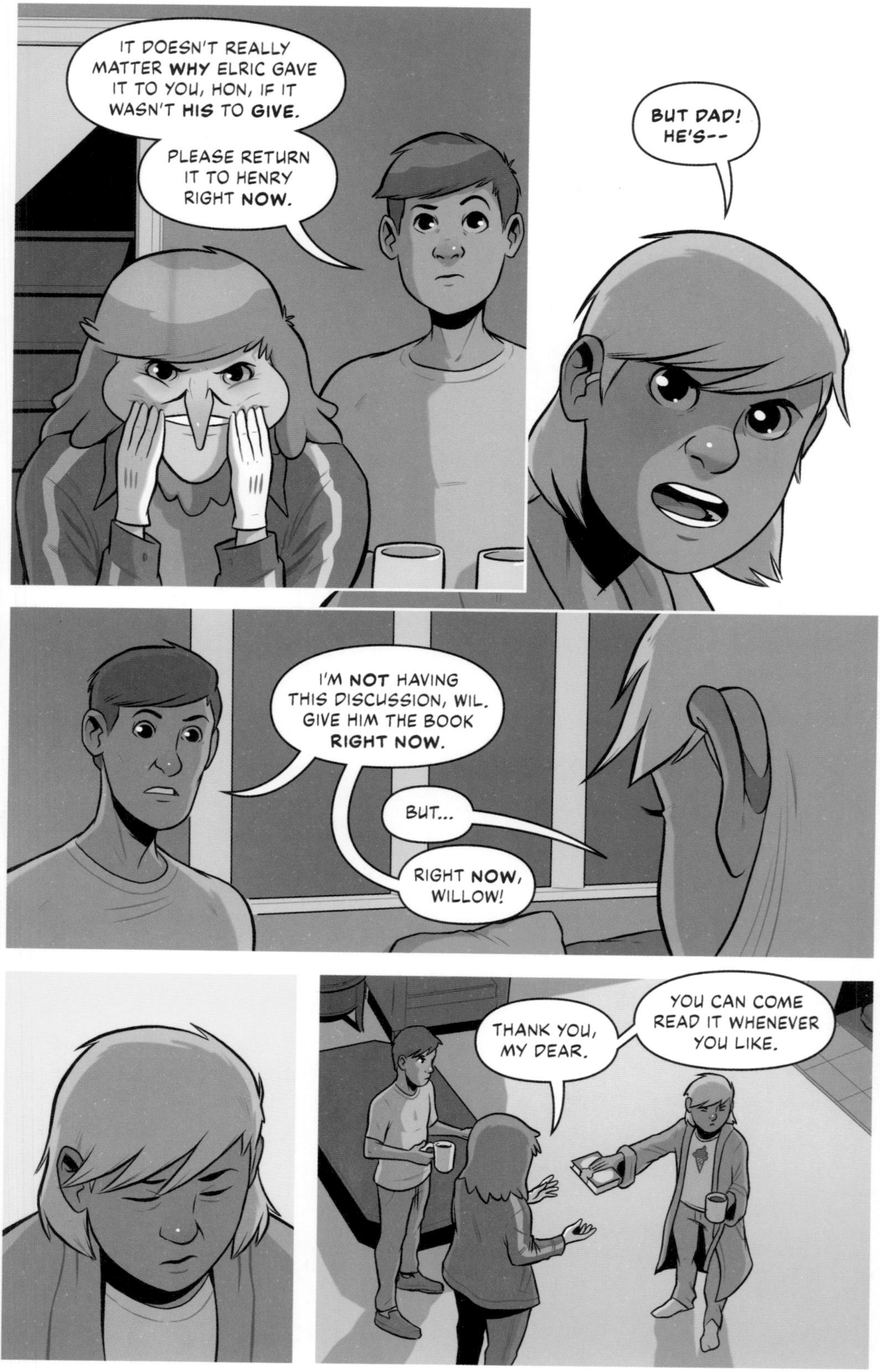
IT DOESN'T REALLY MATTER WHY ELRIC GAVE IT TO YOU, HON, IF IT WASN'T HIS TO GIVE.
PLEASE RETURN IT TO HENRY RIGHT NOW.
BUT DAD! HE'S--
I'M NOT HAVING THIS DISCUSSION, WIL. GIVE HIM THE BOOK RIGHT NOW.
BUT...
RIGHT NOW, WILLOW!
THANK YOU, MY DEAR.
YOU CAN COME READ IT WHENEVER YOU LIKE.

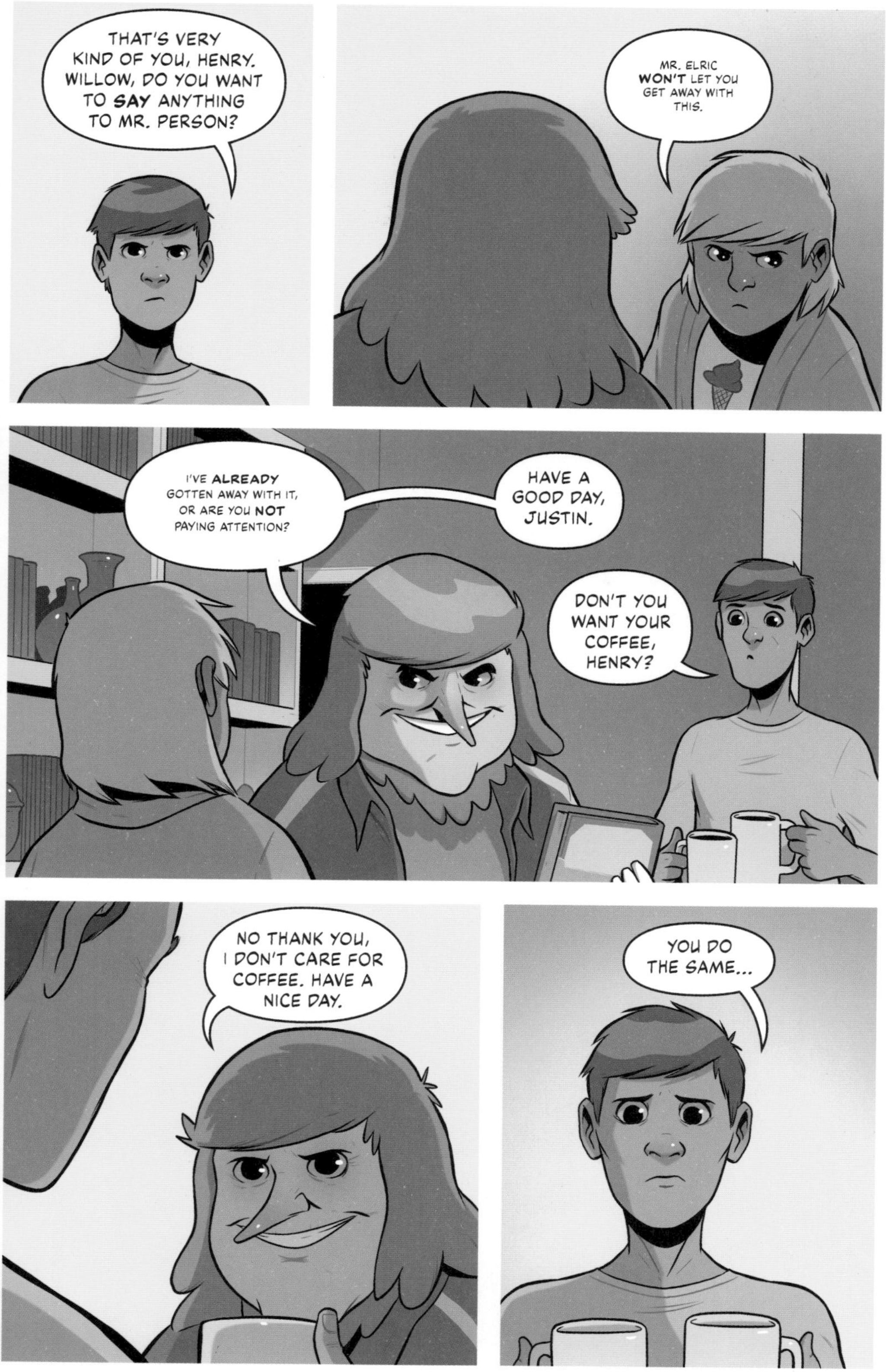
THAT'S VERY KIND OF YOU, HENRY. WILLOW, DO YOU WANT TO SAY ANYTHING TO MR. PERSON?
MR. ELRIC WON'T LET YOU GET AWAY WITH THIS.
I'VE ALREADY GOTTEN AWAY WITH IT, OR ARE YOU NOT PAYING ATTENTION?
HAVE A GOOD DAY, JUSTIN.
DON'T YOU WANT YOUR COFFEE, HENRY?
NO THANK YOU, I DON'T CARE FOR COFFEE. HAVE A NICE DAY.
YOU DO THE SAME...

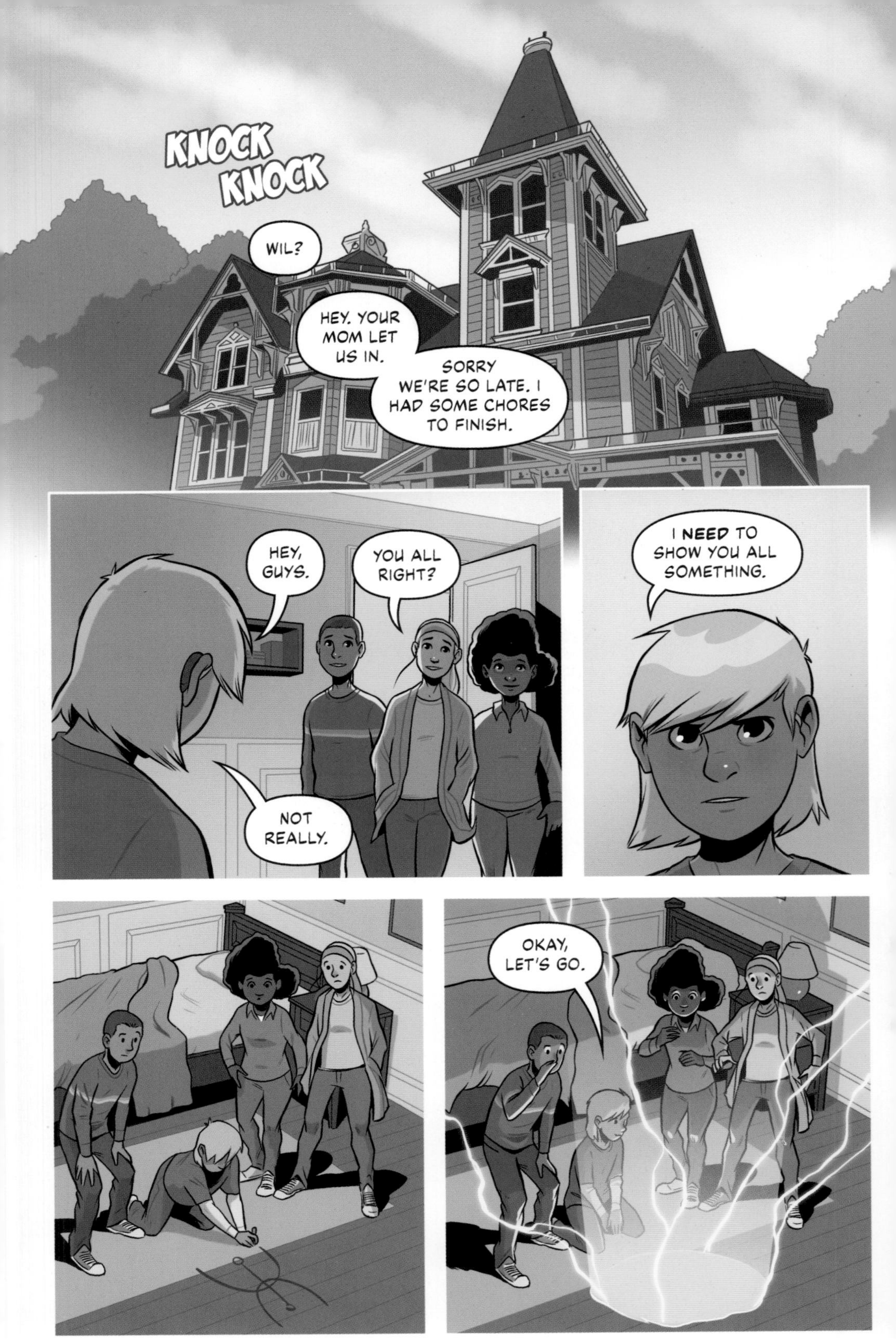
KNOCK KNOCK
WIL?
HEY. YOUR MOM LET US IN.
SORRY WE'RE SO LATE. I HAD SOME CHORES TO FINISH.
HEY, GUYS.
YOU ALL RIGHT?
NOT REALLY.
I **NEED** TO SHOW YOU ALL SOMETHING.
OKAY, LET'S GO.

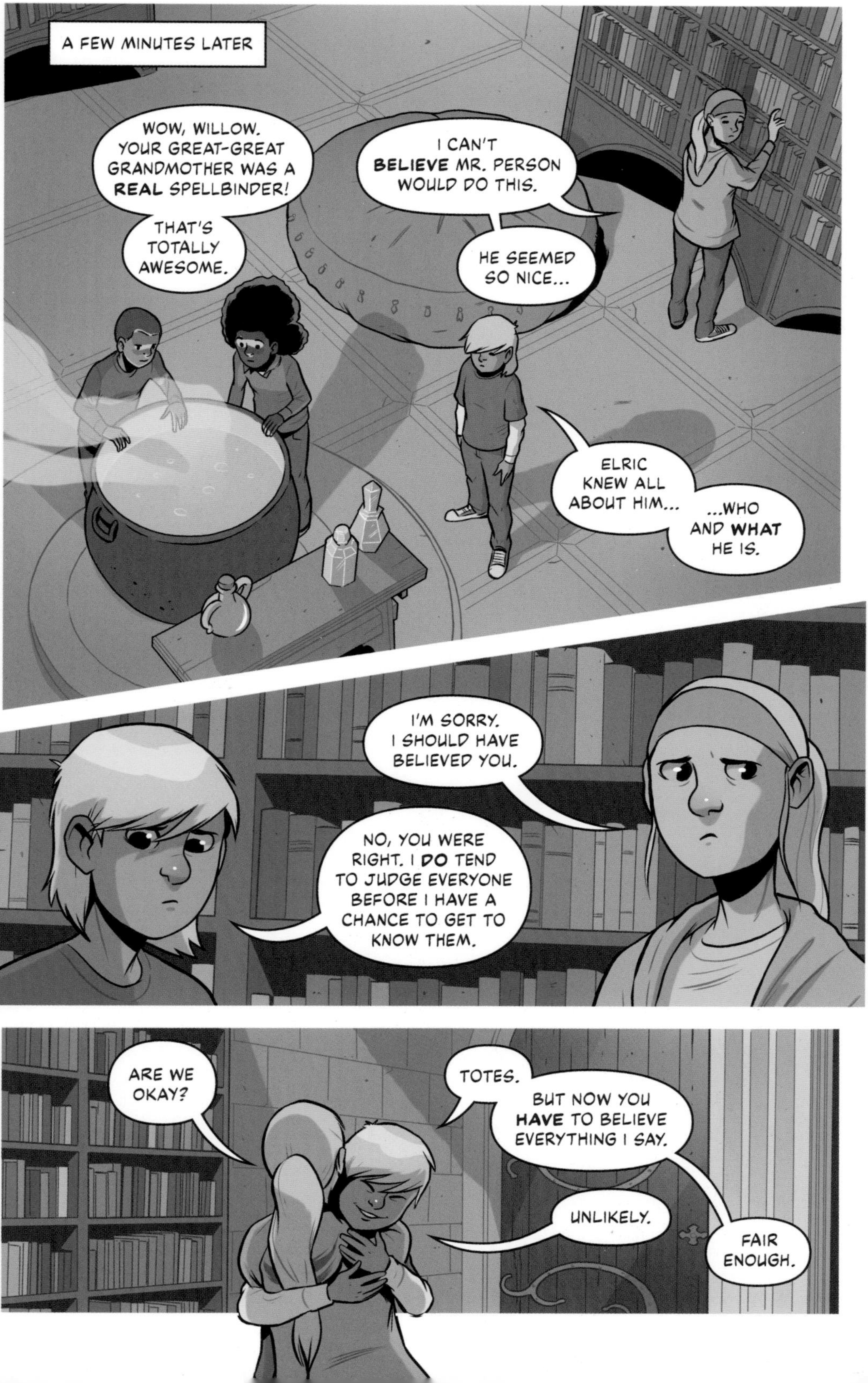

A FEW MINUTES LATER
WOW, WILLOW. YOUR GREAT-GREAT GRANDMOTHER WAS A REAL SPELLBINDER!
THAT'S TOTALLY AWESOME.
I CAN'T BELIEVE MR. PERSON WOULD DO THIS.
HE SEEMED SO NICE...
ELRIC KNEW ALL ABOUT HIM...
...WHO AND WHAT HE IS.
I'M SORRY. I SHOULD HAVE BELIEVED YOU.
NO, YOU WERE RIGHT. I DO TEND TO JUDGE EVERYONE BEFORE I HAVE A CHANCE TO GET TO KNOW THEM.
ARE WE OKAY?
TOTES.
BUT NOW YOU HAVE TO BELIEVE EVERYTHING I SAY.
UNLIKELY.
FAIR ENOUGH.

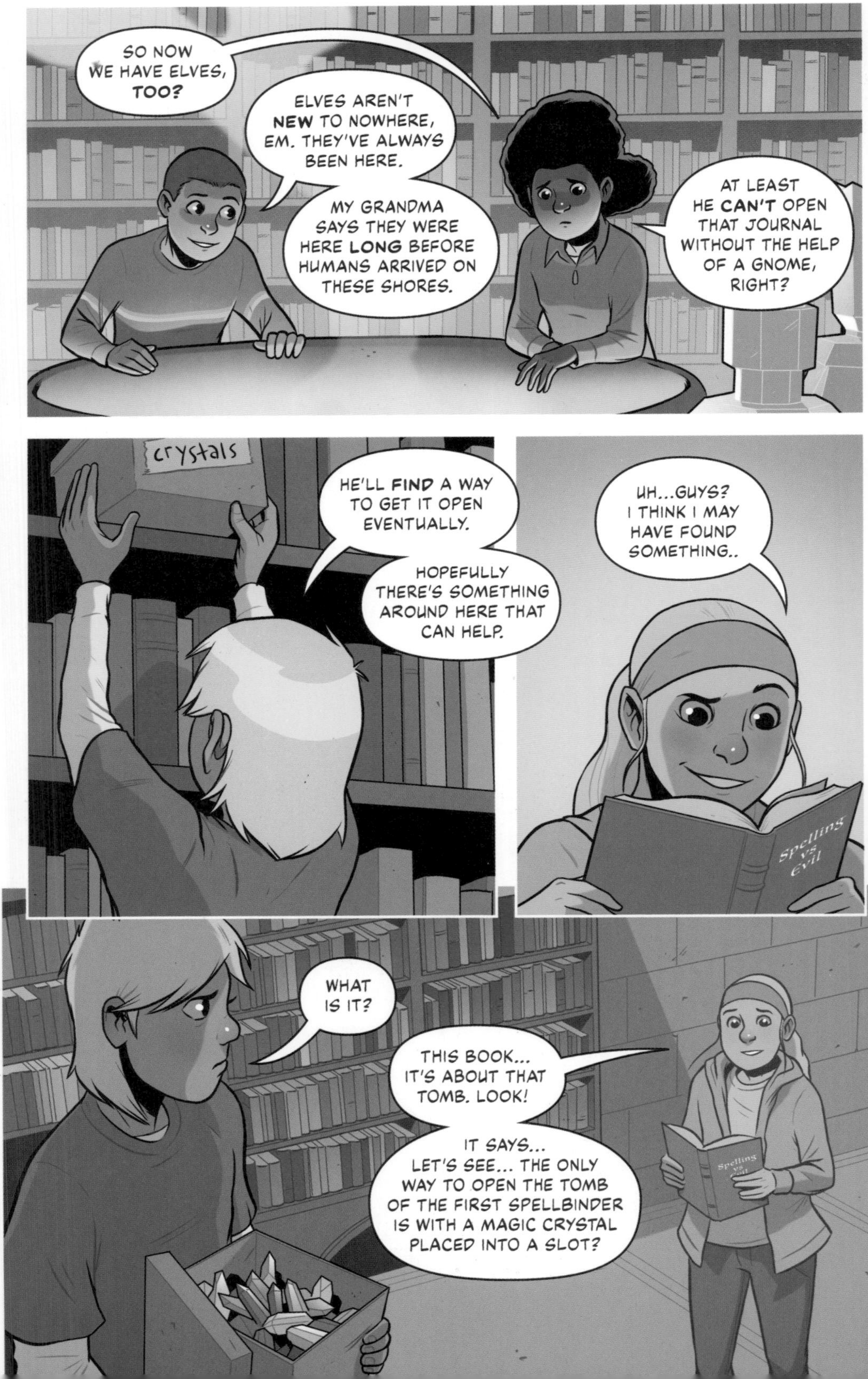
SO NOW WE HAVE ELVES, **TOO?**
ELVES AREN'T **NEW** TO NOWHERE, EM. THEY'VE ALWAYS BEEN HERE.
MY GRANDMA SAYS THEY WERE HERE **LONG** BEFORE HUMANS ARRIVED ON THESE SHORES.
AT LEAST HE **CAN'T** OPEN THAT JOURNAL WITHOUT THE HELP OF A GNOME, RIGHT?
crystals
HE'LL **FIND** A WAY TO GET IT OPEN EVENTUALLY.
HOPEFULLY THERE'S SOMETHING AROUND HERE THAT CAN HELP.
UH...GUYS? I THINK I MAY HAVE FOUND SOMETHING..
Spelling vs Evil
WHAT IS IT?
THIS BOOK... IT'S ABOUT THAT TOMB. LOOK!
IT SAYS... LET'S SEE... THE ONLY WAY TO OPEN THE TOMB OF THE FIRST SPELLBINDER IS WITH A MAGIC CRYSTAL PLACED INTO A SLOT?

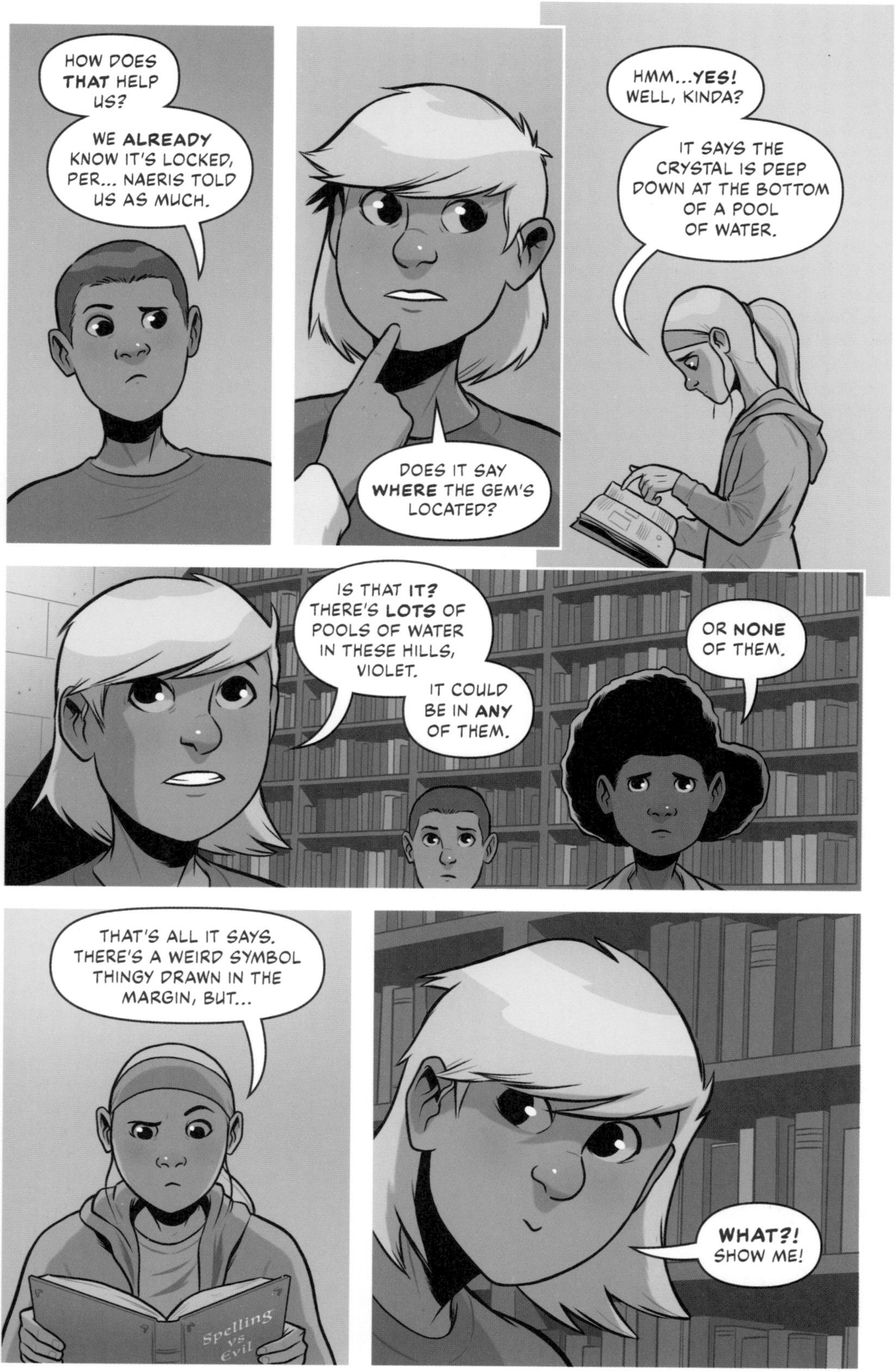
HOW DOES THAT HELP US?
WE ALREADY KNOW IT'S LOCKED, PER... NAERIS TOLD US AS MUCH.
DOES IT SAY WHERE THE GEM'S LOCATED?
HMM...YES! WELL, KINDA?
IT SAYS THE CRYSTAL IS DEEP DOWN AT THE BOTTOM OF A POOL OF WATER.
IS THAT IT? THERE'S LOTS OF POOLS OF WATER IN THESE HILLS, VIOLET.
IT COULD BE IN ANY OF THEM.
OR NONE OF THEM.
THAT'S ALL IT SAYS. THERE'S A WEIRD SYMBOL THINGY DRAWN IN THE MARGIN, BUT...
Spelling vs Evil
WHAT?! SHOW ME!

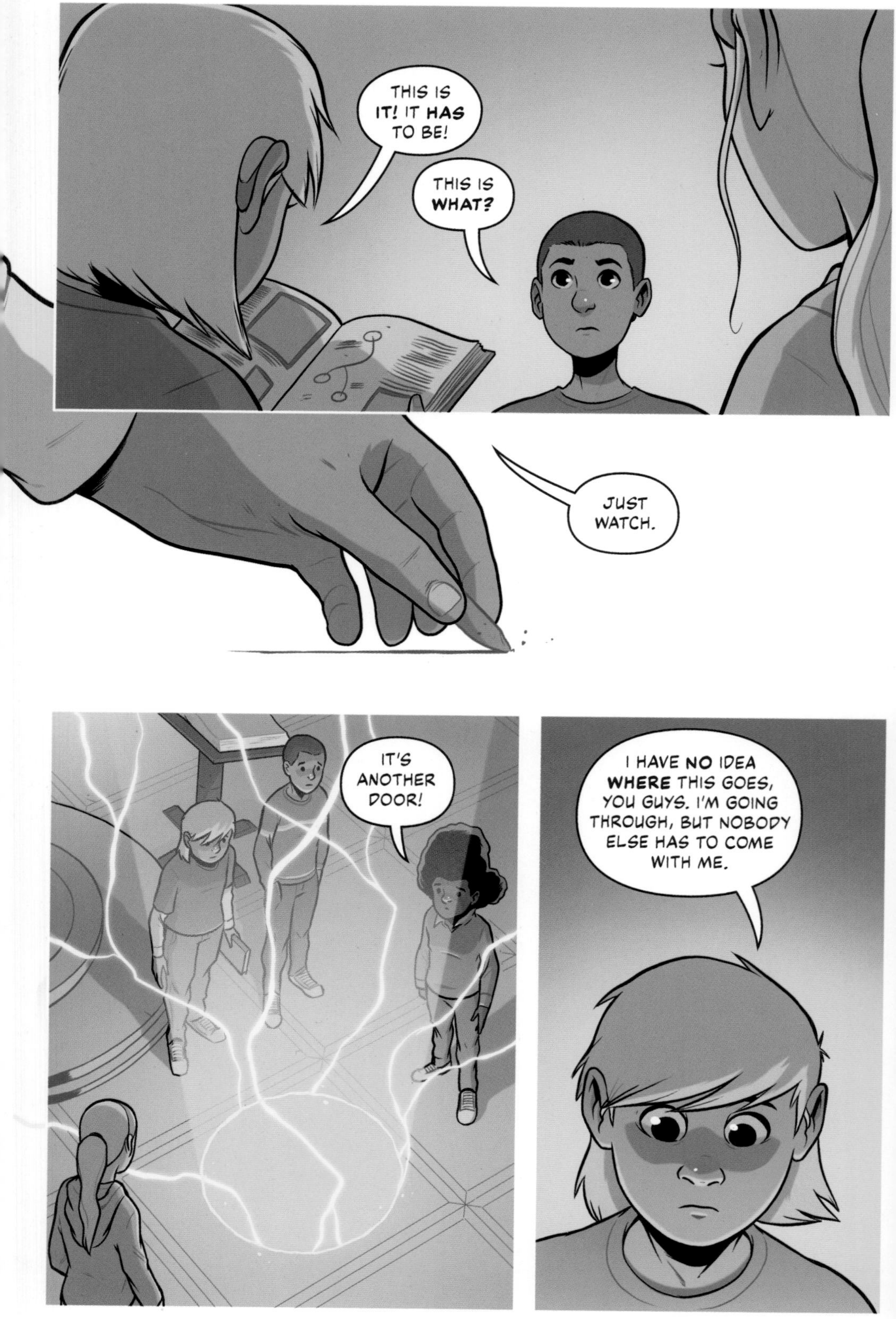
THIS IS IT! IT HAS TO BE!
THIS IS WHAT?
JUST WATCH.
IT'S ANOTHER DOOR!
I HAVE NO IDEA WHERE THIS GOES, YOU GUYS. I'M GOING THROUGH, BUT NOBODY ELSE HAS TO COME WITH ME.

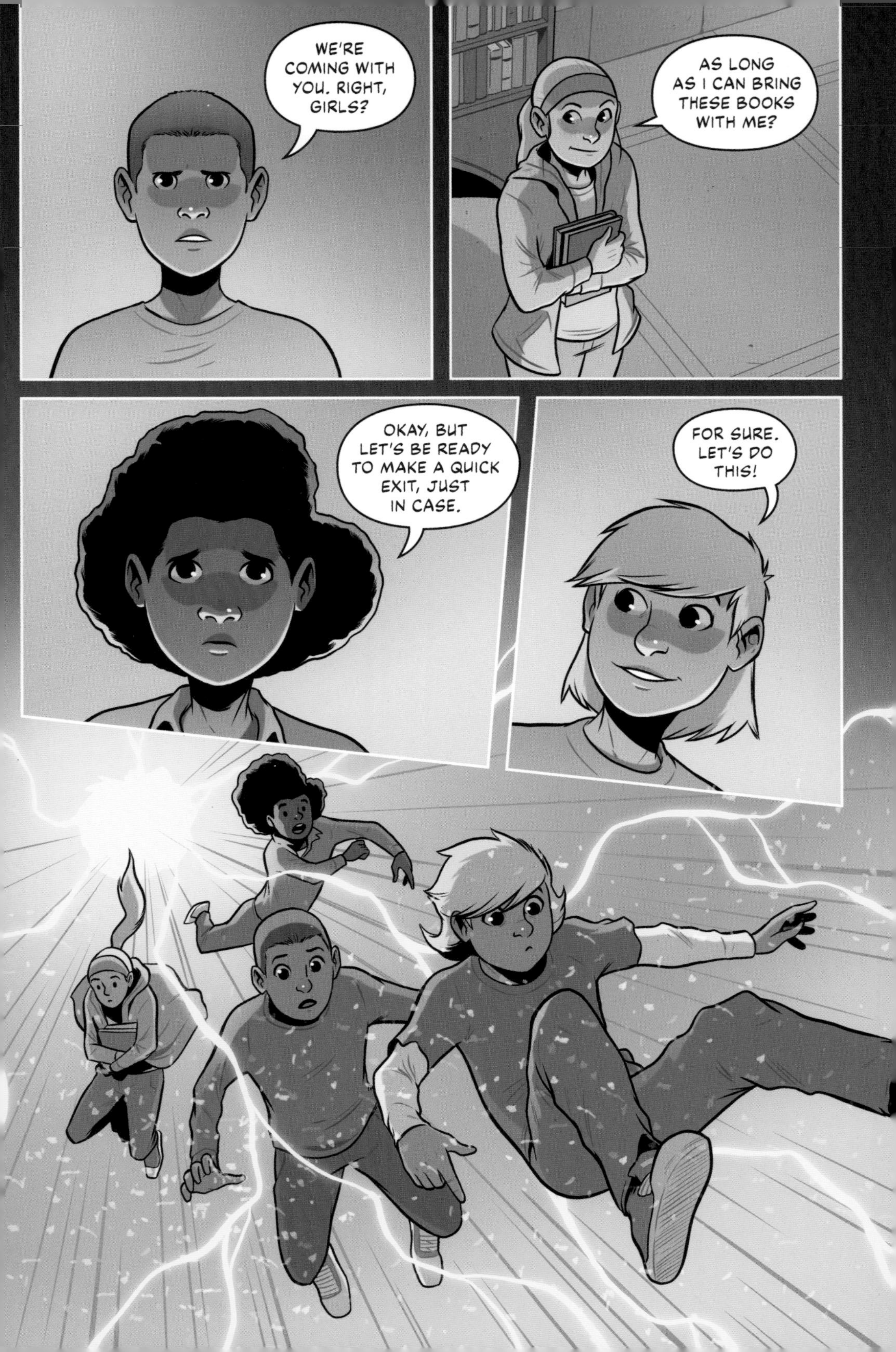
WE'RE COMING WITH YOU. RIGHT, GIRLS?
AS LONG AS I CAN BRING THESE BOOKS WITH ME?
OKAY, BUT LET'S BE READY TO MAKE A QUICK EXIT, JUST IN CASE.
FOR SURE. LET'S DO THIS!

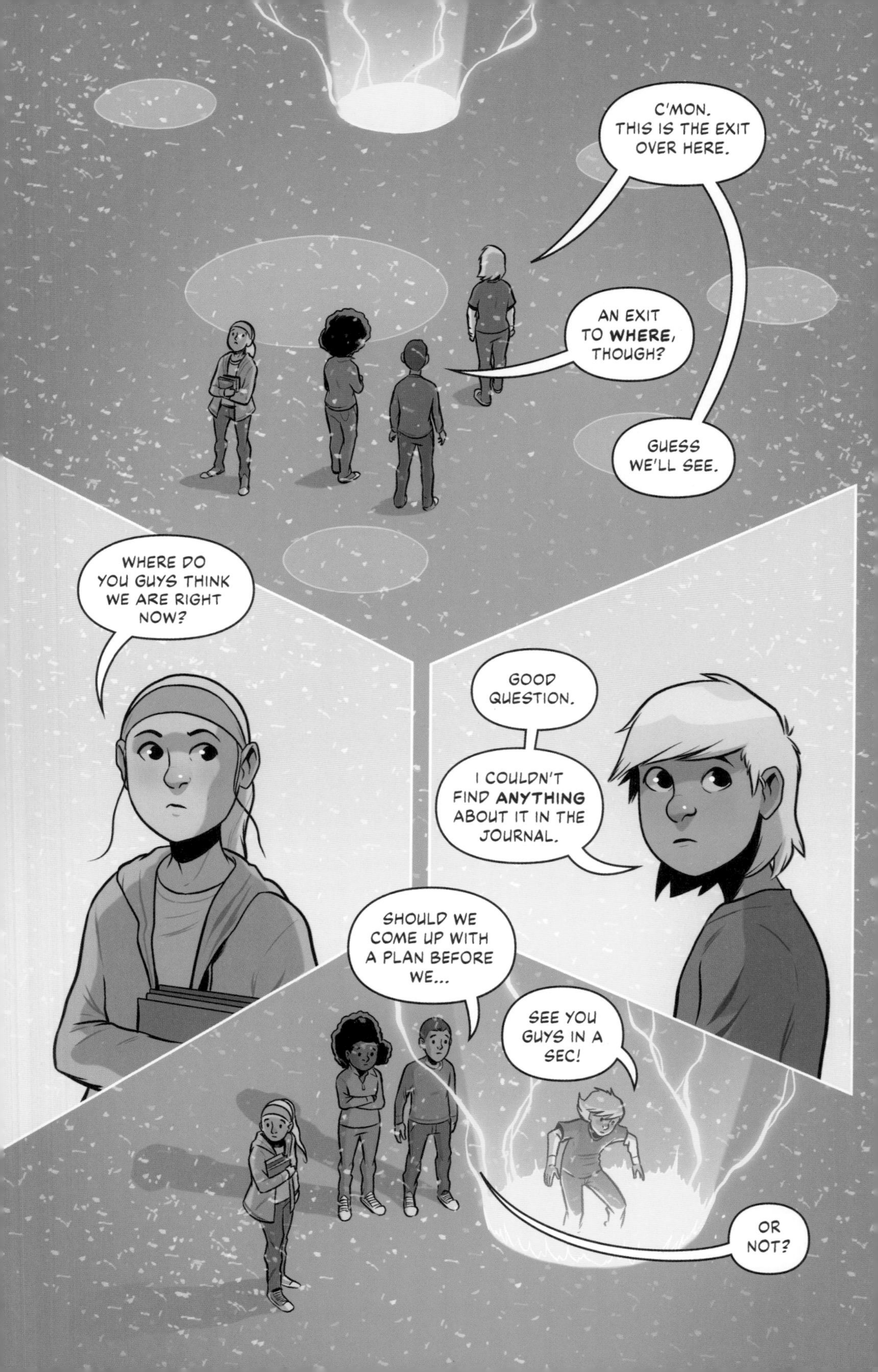
C'MON. THIS IS THE EXIT OVER HERE.
AN EXIT TO **WHERE**, THOUGH?
GUESS WE'LL SEE.
WHERE DO YOU GUYS THINK WE ARE RIGHT NOW?
GOOD QUESTION.
I COULDN'T FIND **ANYTHING** ABOUT IT IN THE JOURNAL.
SHOULD WE COME UP WITH A PLAN BEFORE WE...
SEE YOU GUYS IN A SEC!
OR NOT?

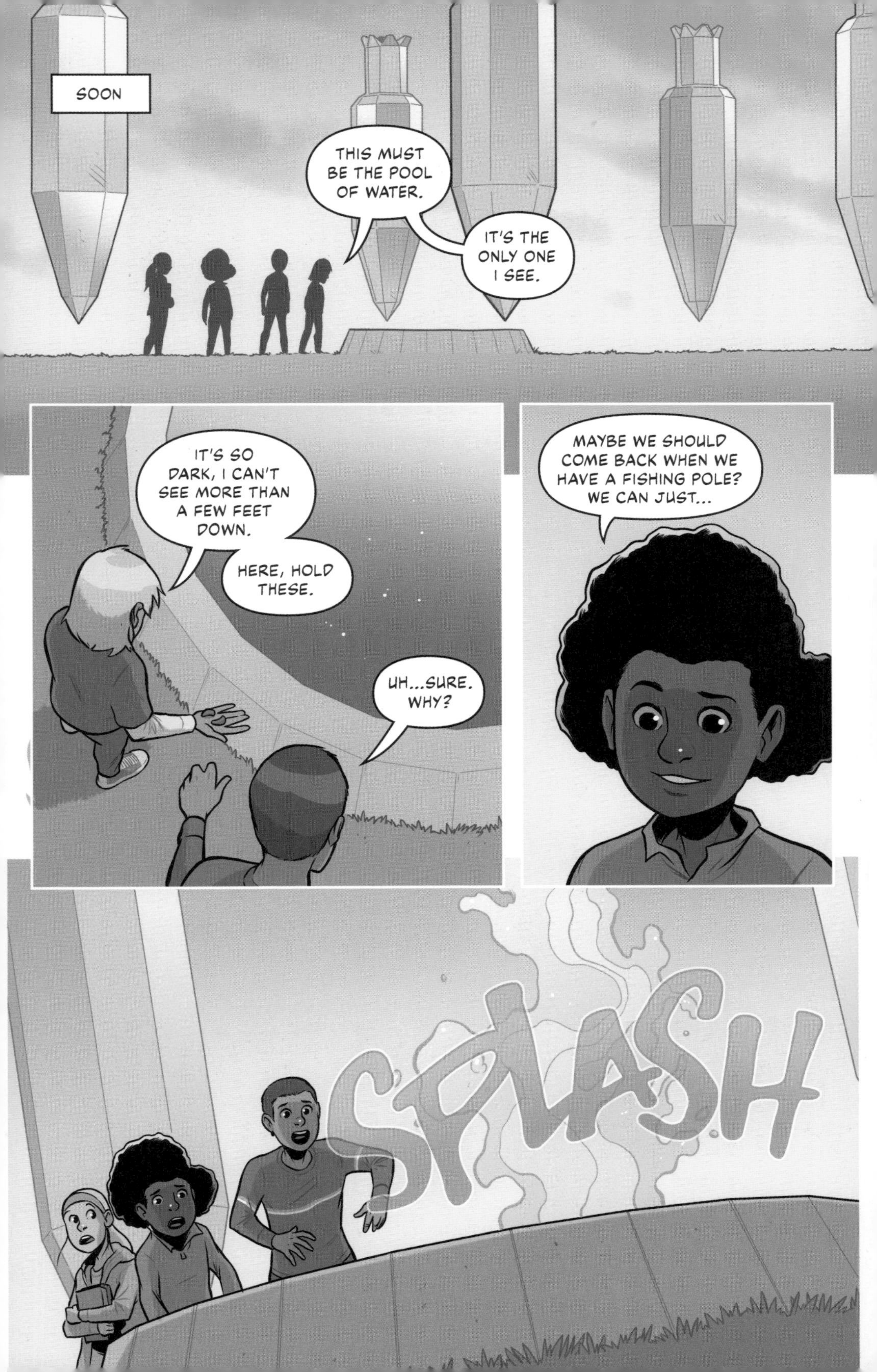
SOON
THIS MUST BE THE POOL OF WATER.
IT'S THE ONLY ONE I SEE.
IT'S SO DARK, I CAN'T SEE MORE THAN A FEW FEET DOWN.
HERE, HOLD THESE.
UH...SURE. WHY?
MAYBE WE SHOULD COME BACK WHEN WE HAVE A FISHING POLE? WE CAN JUST...
SPLASH

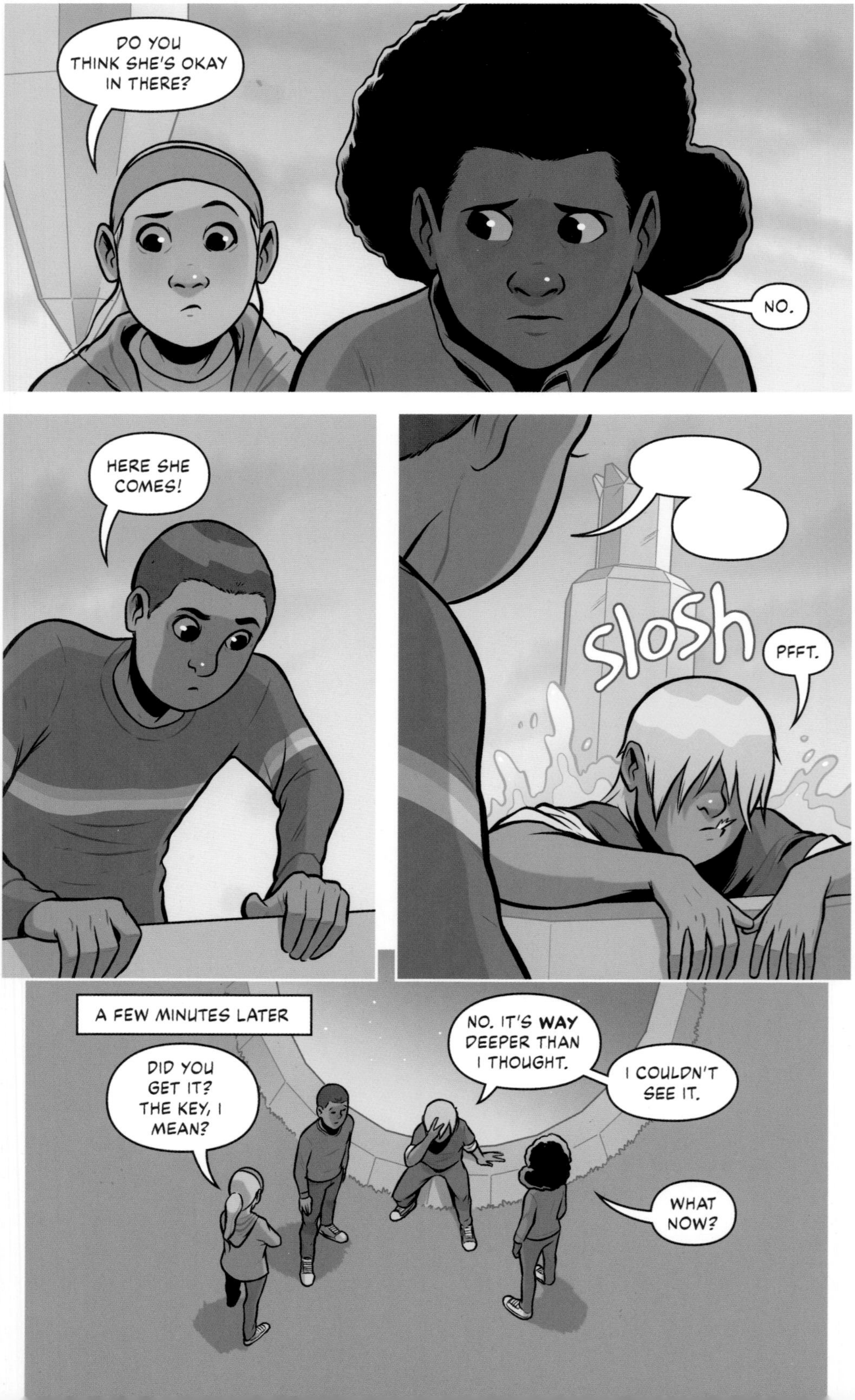
DO YOU THINK SHE'S OKAY IN THERE?
NO.
HERE SHE COMES!
SLOSH
PFFT.
A FEW MINUTES LATER
DID YOU GET IT? THE KEY, I MEAN?
NO. IT'S **WAY** DEEPER THAN I THOUGHT.
I COULDN'T SEE IT.
WHAT NOW?

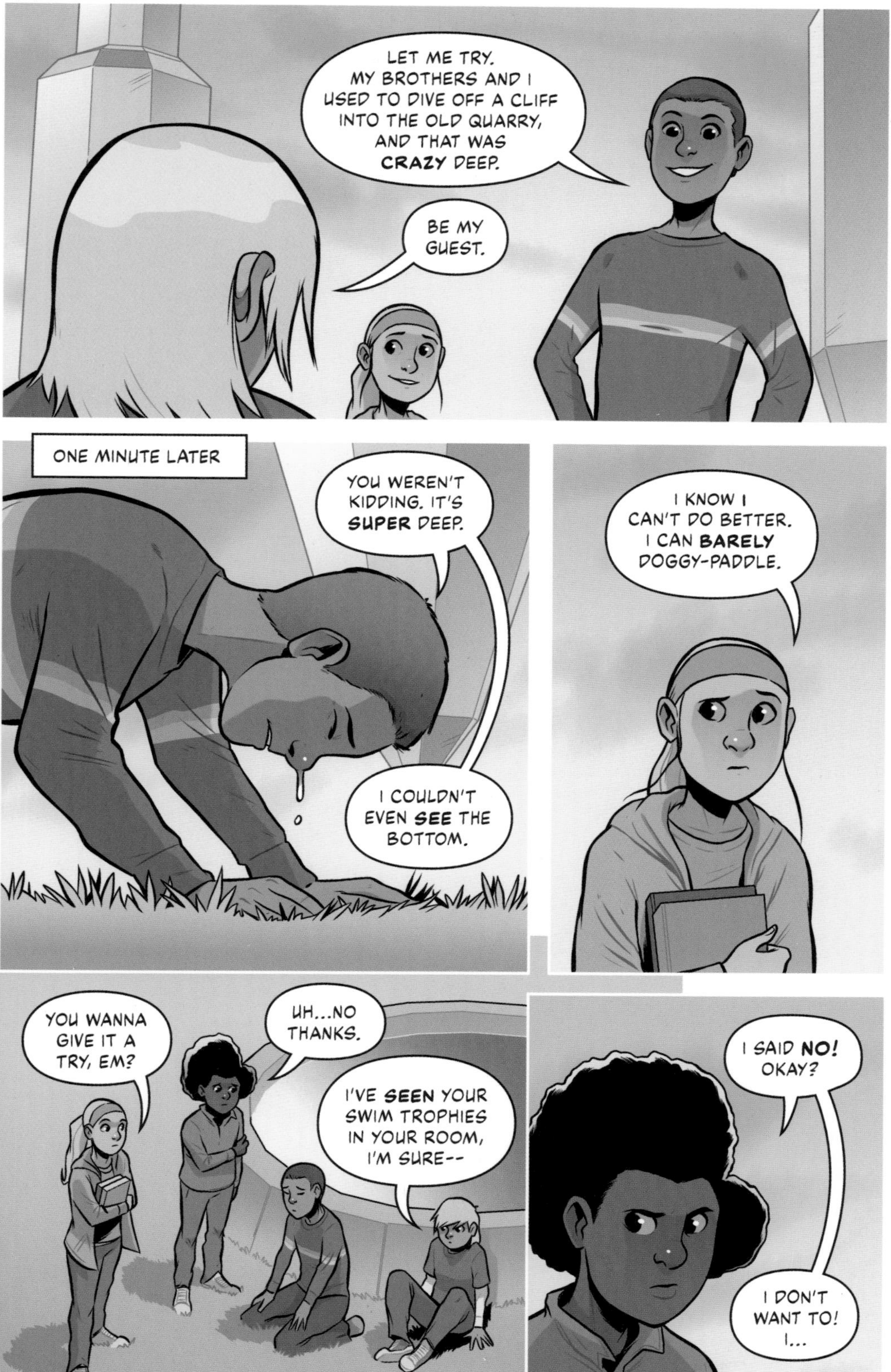
LET ME TRY. MY BROTHERS AND I USED TO DIVE OFF A CLIFF INTO THE OLD QUARRY, AND THAT WAS **CRAZY** DEEP.
BE MY GUEST.
ONE MINUTE LATER
YOU WEREN'T KIDDING. IT'S **SUPER** DEEP.
I COULDN'T EVEN **SEE** THE BOTTOM.
I KNOW I CAN'T DO BETTER. I CAN **BARELY** DOGGY-PADDLE.
YOU WANNA GIVE IT A TRY, EM?
UH...NO THANKS.
I'VE **SEEN** YOUR SWIM TROPHIES IN YOUR ROOM, I'M SURE--
I SAID **NO!** OKAY?
I DON'T WANT TO! I...

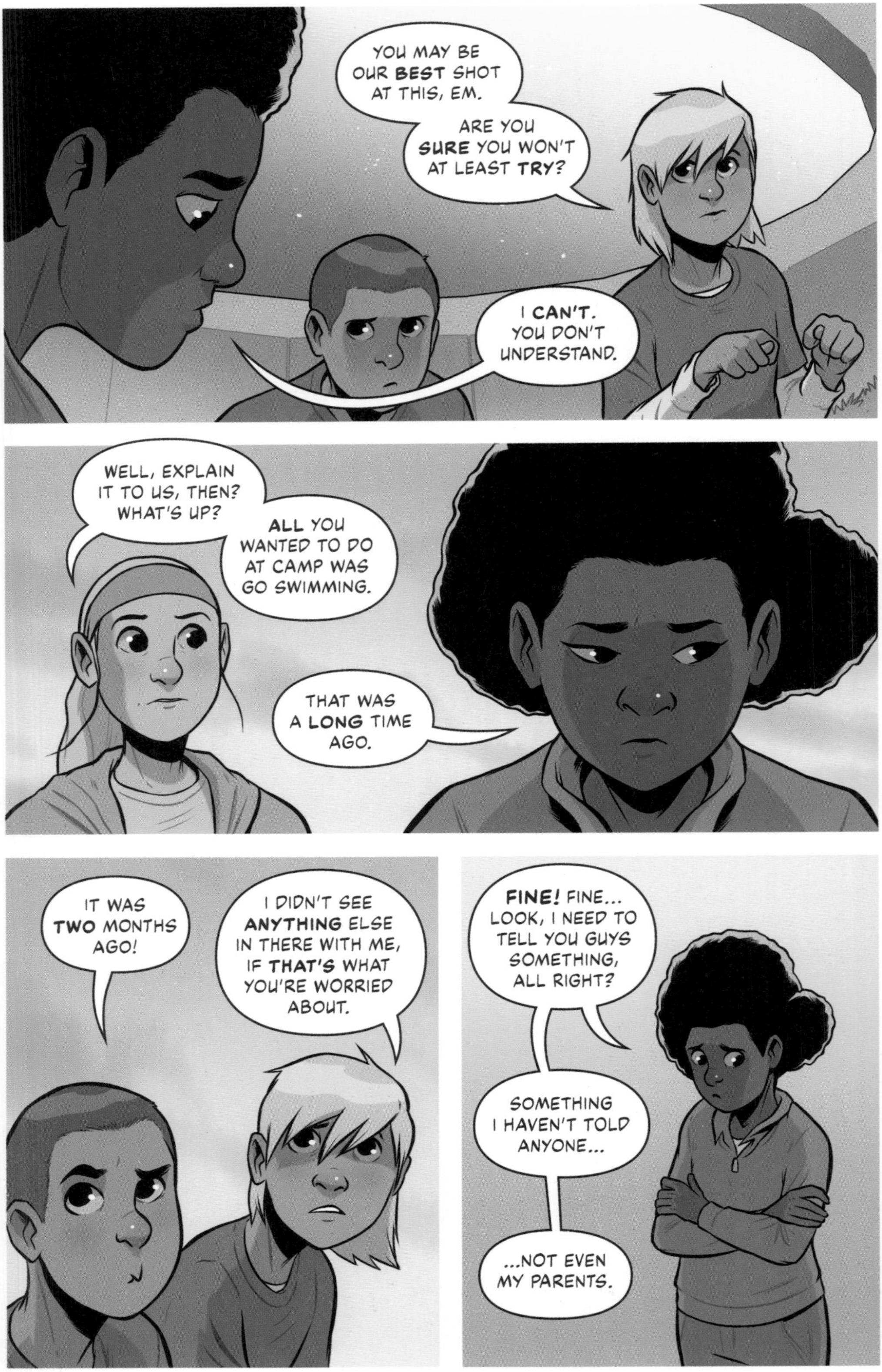
YOU MAY BE OUR BEST SHOT AT THIS, EM.
ARE YOU SURE YOU WON'T AT LEAST TRY?
I CAN'T. YOU DON'T UNDERSTAND.
WELL, EXPLAIN IT TO US, THEN? WHAT'S UP?
ALL YOU WANTED TO DO AT CAMP WAS GO SWIMMING.
THAT WAS A LONG TIME AGO.
IT WAS TWO MONTHS AGO!
I DIDN'T SEE ANYTHING ELSE IN THERE WITH ME, IF THAT'S WHAT YOU'RE WORRIED ABOUT.
FINE! FINE... LOOK, I NEED TO TELL YOU GUYS SOMETHING, ALL RIGHT?
SOMETHING I HAVEN'T TOLD ANYONE...
...NOT EVEN MY PARENTS.

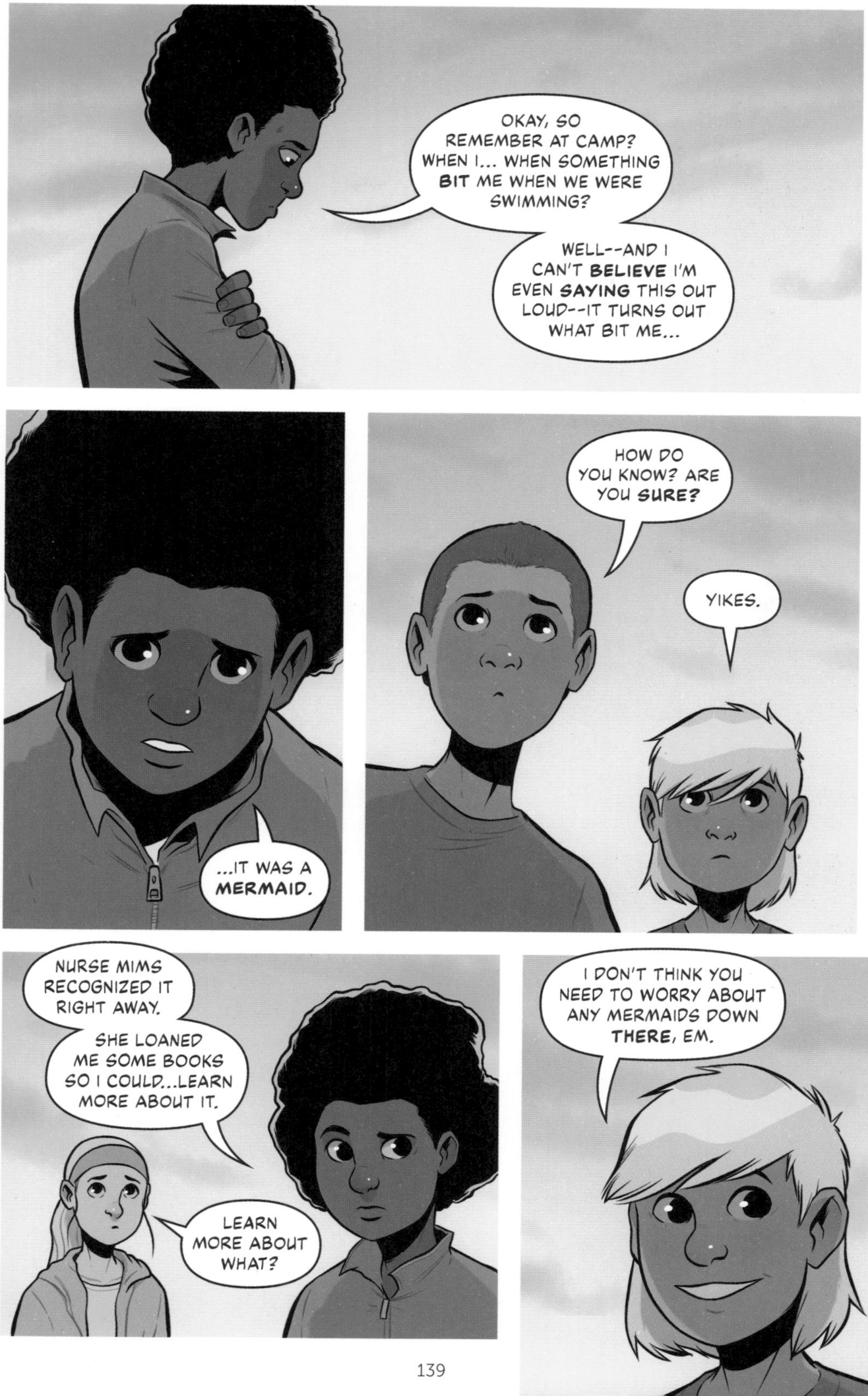

OKAY, SO REMEMBER AT CAMP? WHEN I... WHEN SOMETHING **BIT** ME WHEN WE WERE SWIMMING?
WELL--AND I CAN'T **BELIEVE** I'M EVEN **SAYING** THIS OUT LOUD--IT TURNS OUT WHAT BIT ME...
...IT WAS A **MERMAID.**
HOW DO YOU KNOW? ARE YOU **SURE?**
YIKES.
NURSE MIMS RECOGNIZED IT RIGHT AWAY.
SHE LOANED ME SOME BOOKS SO I COULD...LEARN MORE ABOUT IT.
LEARN MORE ABOUT WHAT?
I DON'T THINK YOU NEED TO WORRY ABOUT ANY MERMAIDS DOWN **THERE**, EM.

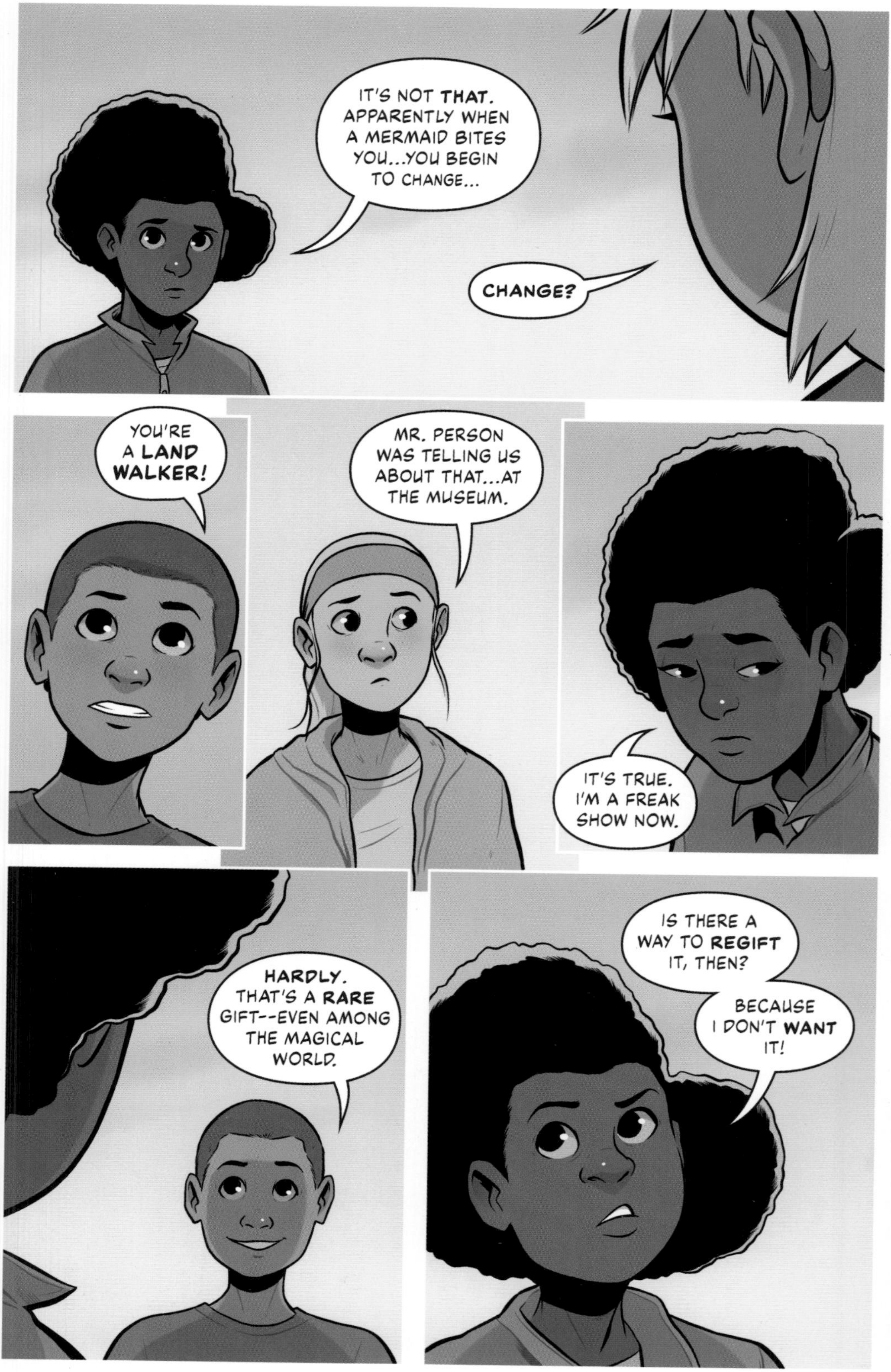
IT'S NOT THAT. APPARENTLY WHEN A MERMAID BITES YOU...YOU BEGIN TO CHANGE...
CHANGE?
YOU'RE A LAND WALKER!
MR. PERSON WAS TELLING US ABOUT THAT...AT THE MUSEUM.
IT'S TRUE. I'M A FREAK SHOW NOW.
HARDLY. THAT'S A RARE GIFT--EVEN AMONG THE MAGICAL WORLD.
IS THERE A WAY TO REGIFT IT, THEN?
BECAUSE I DON'T WANT IT!

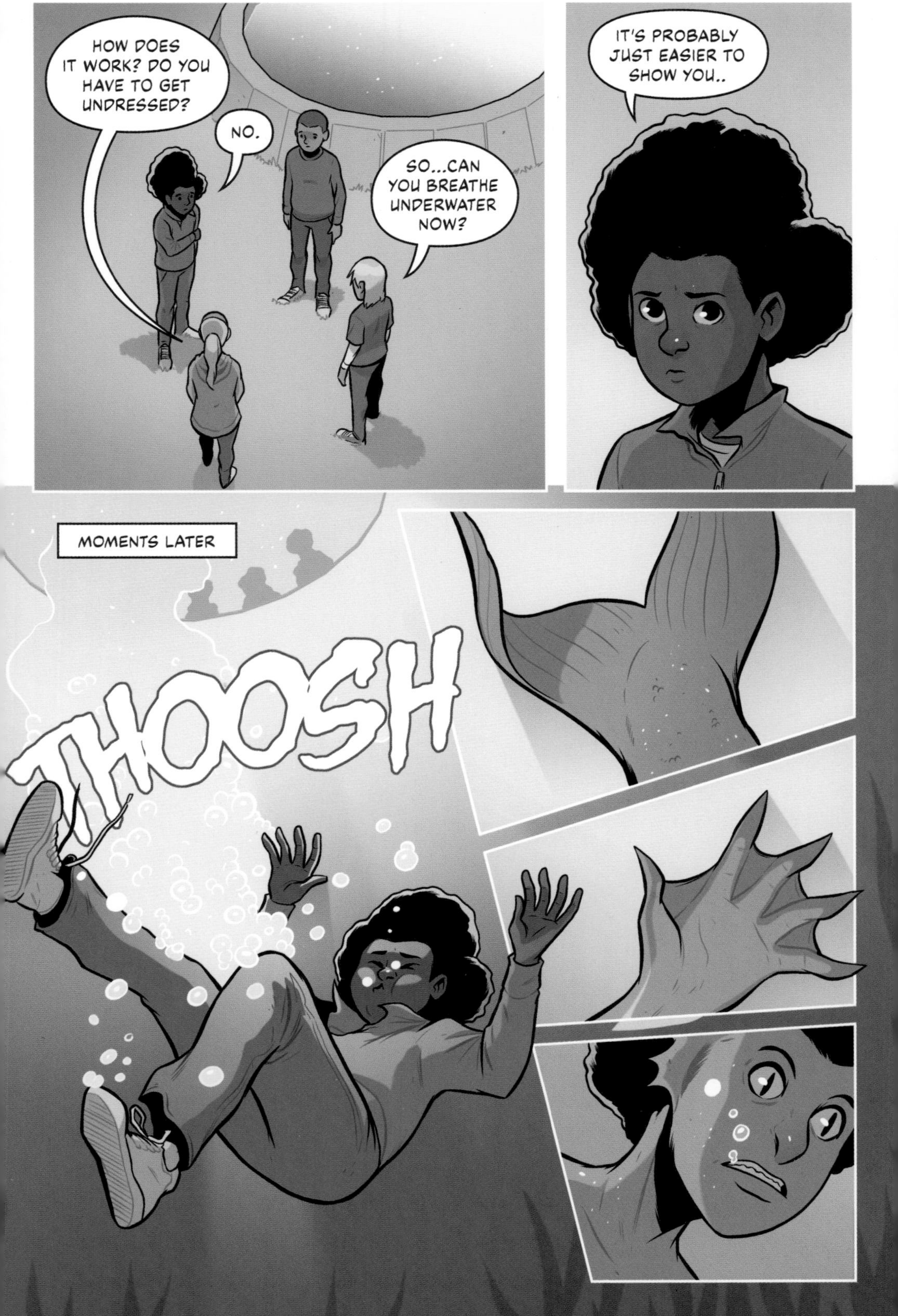
HOW DOES IT WORK? DO YOU HAVE TO GET UNDRESSED?
NO.
SO...CAN YOU BREATHE UNDERWATER NOW?
IT'S PROBABLY JUST EASIER TO SHOW YOU..
MOMENTS LATER
THOOSH

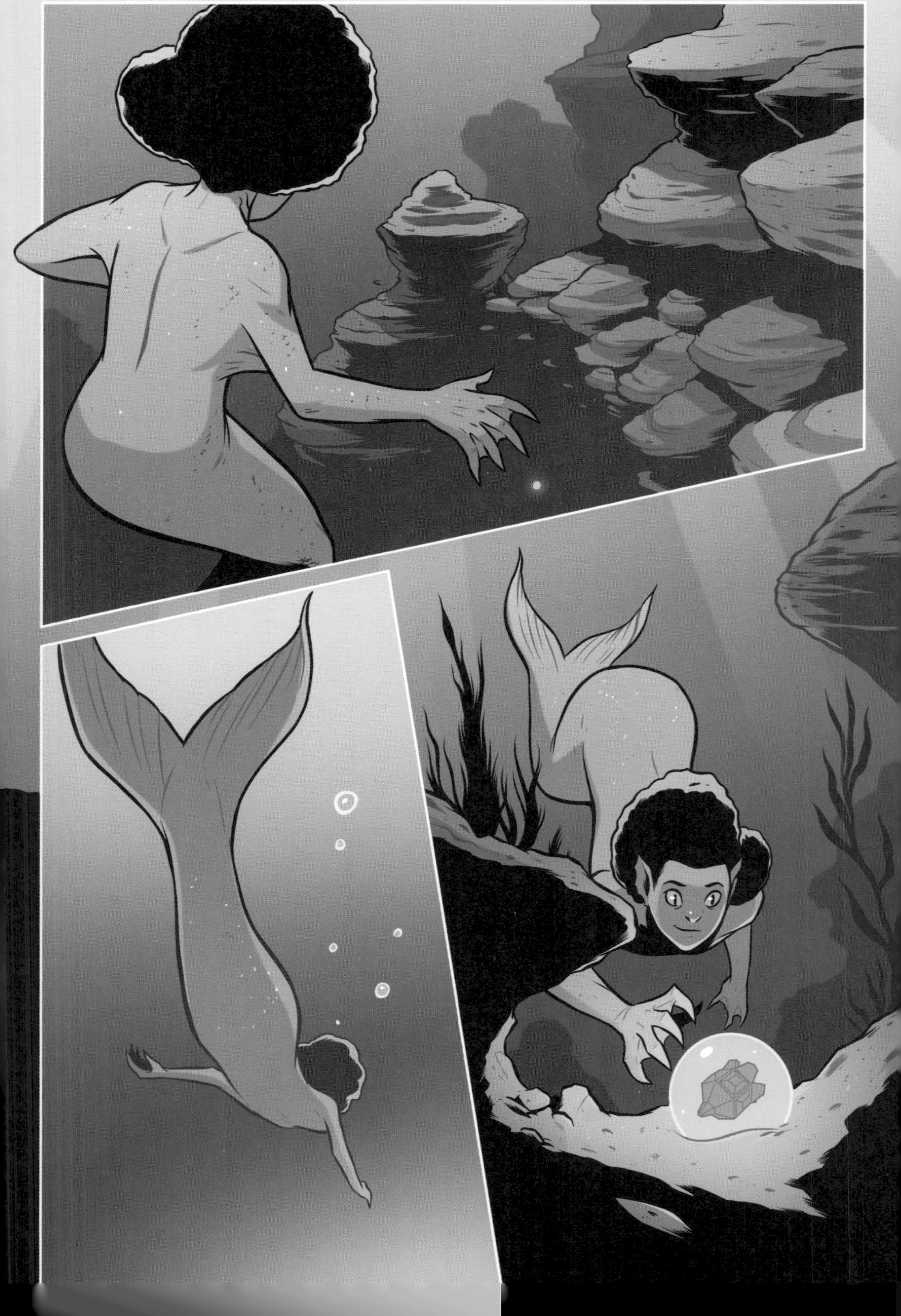

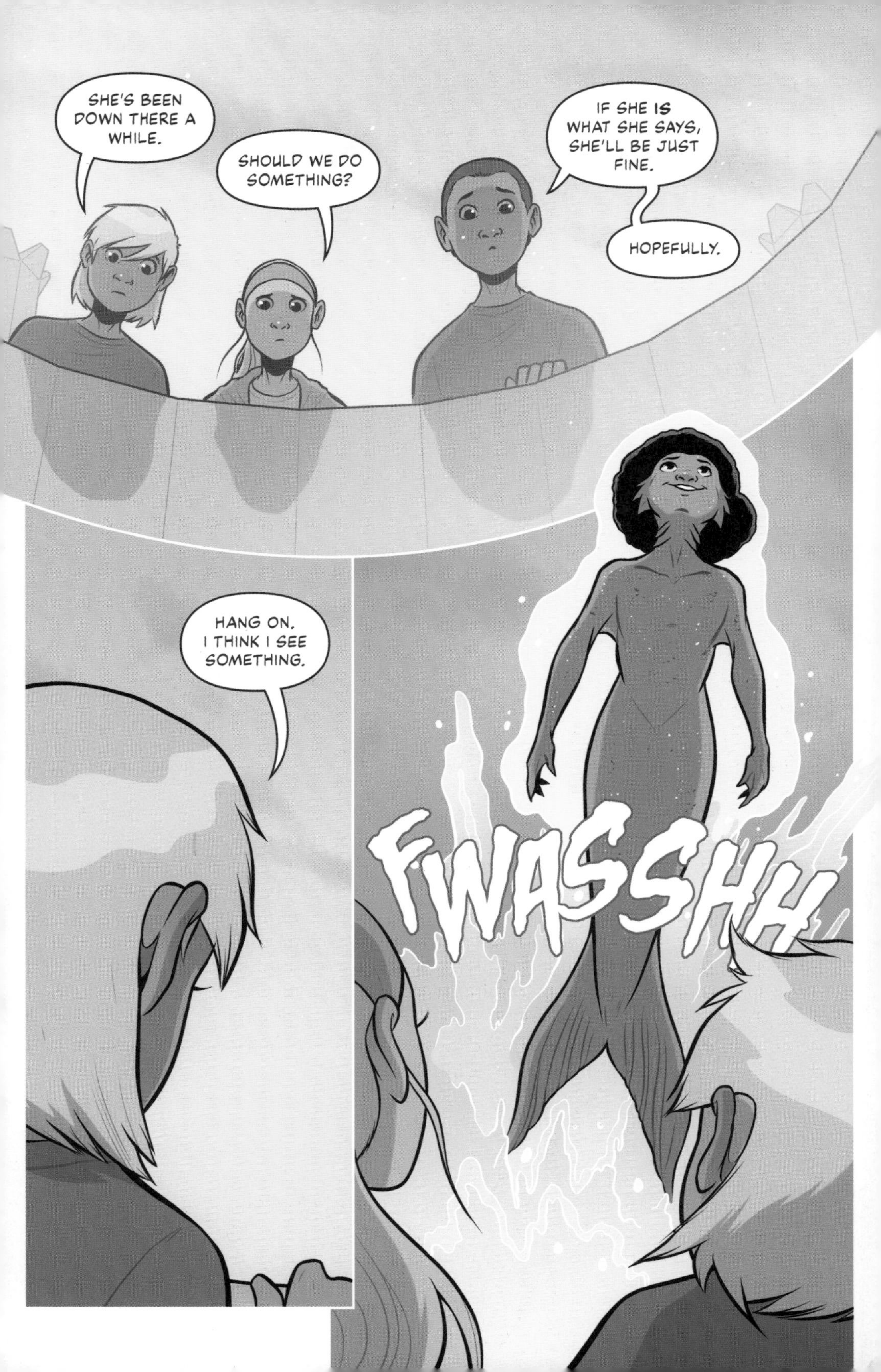
SHE'S BEEN DOWN THERE A WHILE.
SHOULD WE DO SOMETHING?
IF SHE **IS** WHAT SHE SAYS, SHE'LL BE JUST FINE.
HOPEFULLY.
HANG ON. I THINK I SEE SOMETHING.
FWASSHH

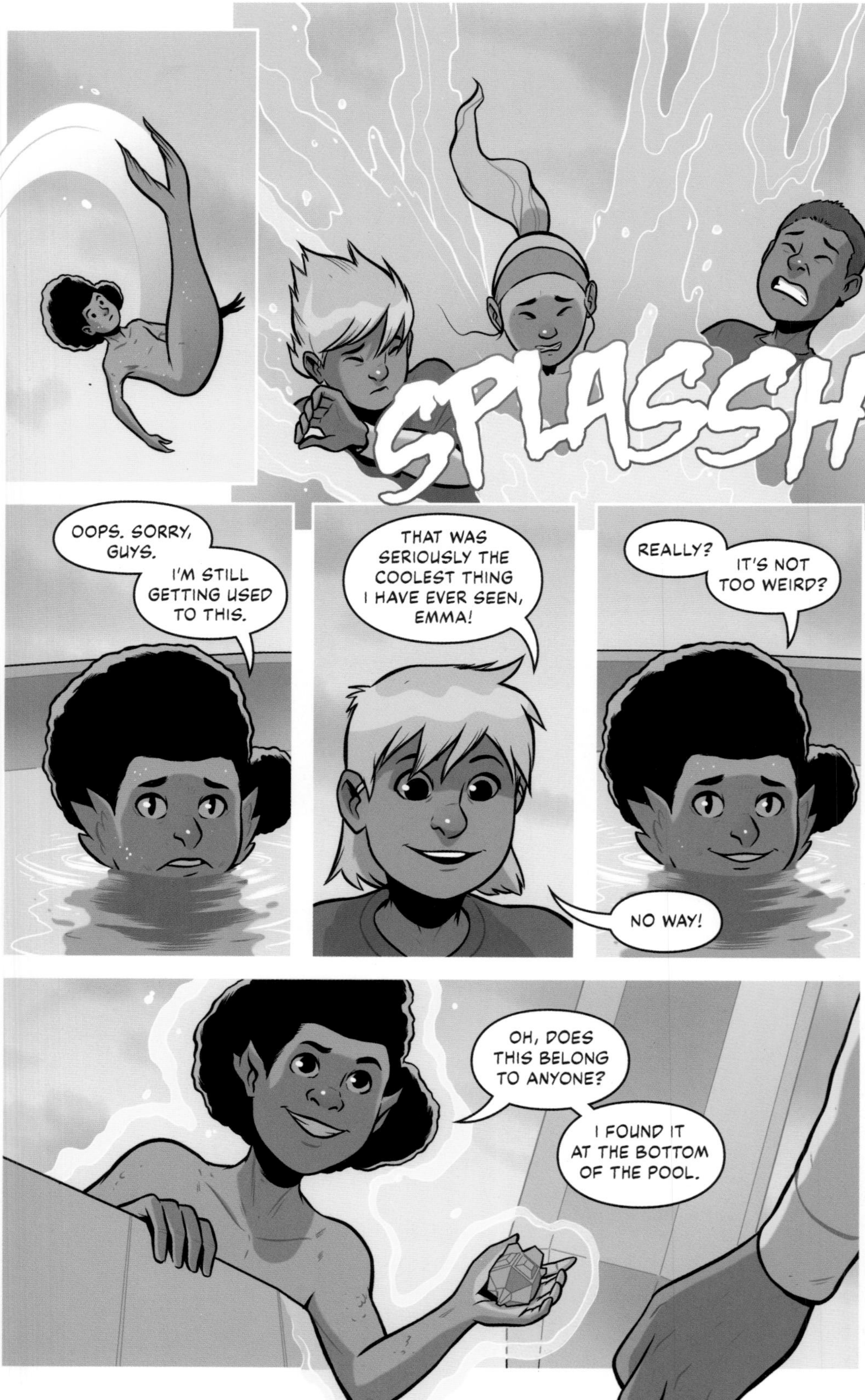
SPLASSH
OOPS. SORRY, GUYS.
I'M STILL GETTING USED TO THIS.
THAT WAS SERIOUSLY THE COOLEST THING I HAVE EVER SEEN, EMMA!
REALLY?
IT'S NOT TOO WEIRD?
NO WAY!
OH, DOES THIS BELONG TO ANYONE?
I FOUND IT AT THE BOTTOM OF THE POOL.

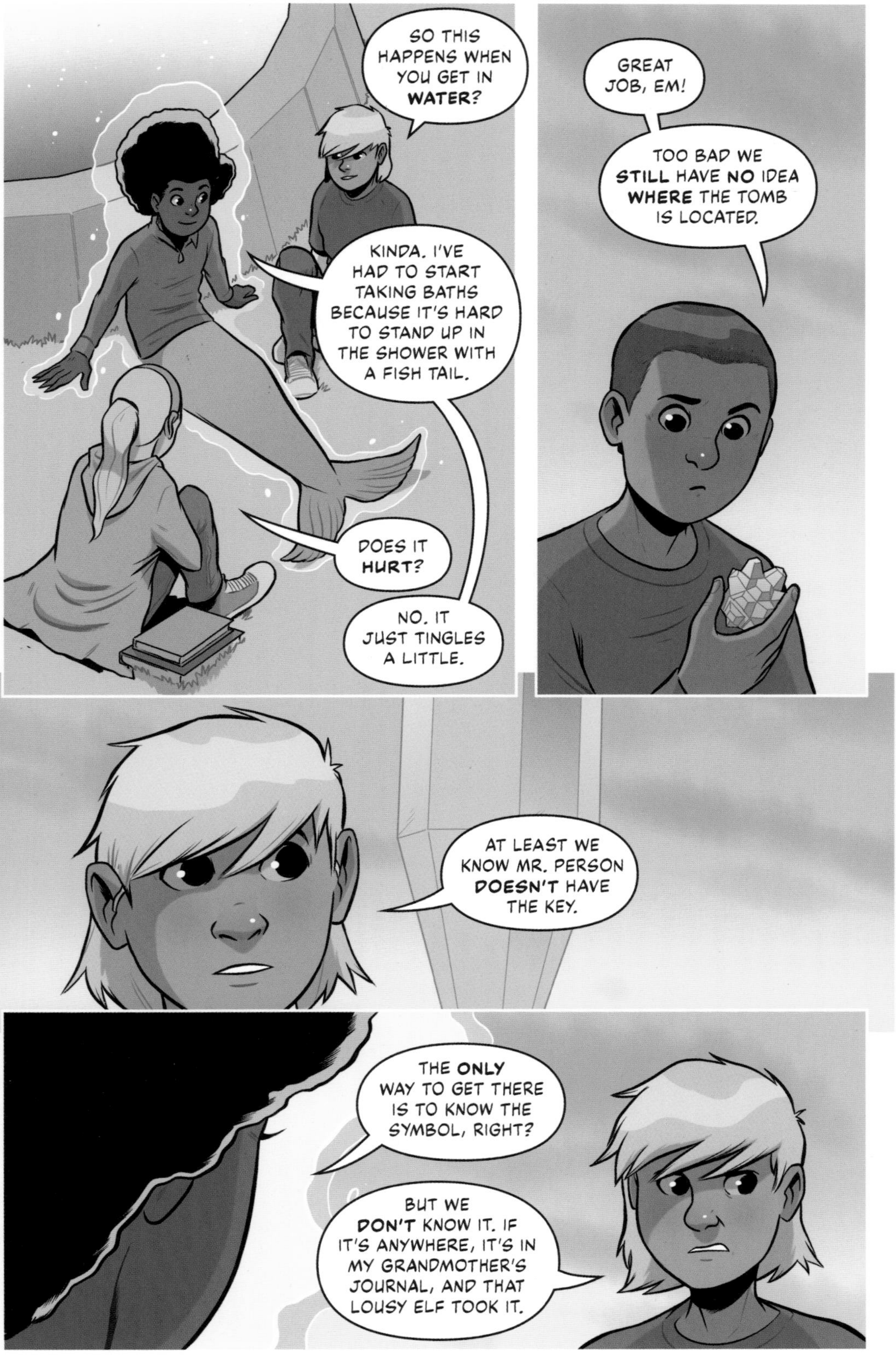
SO THIS HAPPENS WHEN YOU GET IN **WATER**?
KINDA. I'VE HAD TO START TAKING BATHS BECAUSE IT'S HARD TO STAND UP IN THE SHOWER WITH A FISH TAIL.
DOES IT **HURT**?
NO. IT JUST TINGLES A LITTLE.
GREAT JOB, EM!
TOO BAD WE **STILL** HAVE **NO** IDEA **WHERE** THE TOMB IS LOCATED.
AT LEAST WE KNOW MR. PERSON **DOESN'T** HAVE THE KEY.
THE **ONLY** WAY TO GET THERE IS TO KNOW THE SYMBOL, RIGHT?
BUT WE **DON'T** KNOW IT. IF IT'S ANYWHERE, IT'S IN MY GRANDMOTHER'S JOURNAL, AND THAT LOUSY ELF TOOK IT.

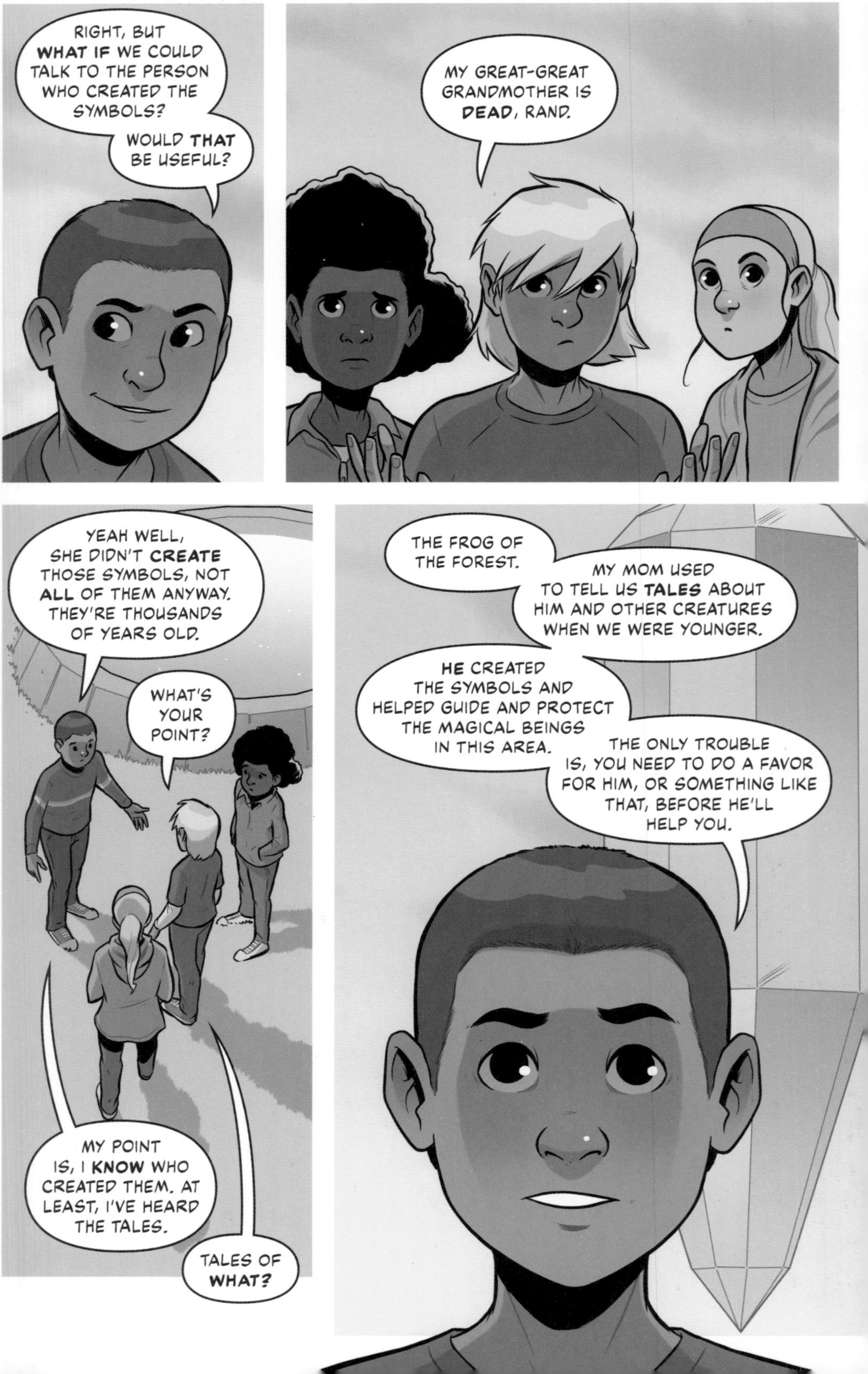

RIGHT, BUT **WHAT IF** WE COULD TALK TO THE PERSON WHO CREATED THE SYMBOLS?
WOULD **THAT** BE USEFUL?
MY GREAT-GREAT GRANDMOTHER IS **DEAD**, RAND.
YEAH WELL, SHE DIDN'T **CREATE** THOSE SYMBOLS, NOT **ALL** OF THEM ANYWAY. THEY'RE THOUSANDS OF YEARS OLD.
WHAT'S YOUR POINT?
MY POINT IS, I **KNOW** WHO CREATED THEM. AT LEAST, I'VE HEARD THE TALES.
TALES OF **WHAT?**
THE FROG OF THE FOREST.
MY MOM USED TO TELL US **TALES** ABOUT HIM AND OTHER CREATURES WHEN WE WERE YOUNGER.
HE CREATED THE SYMBOLS AND HELPED GUIDE AND PROTECT THE MAGICAL BEINGS IN THIS AREA.
THE ONLY TROUBLE IS, YOU NEED TO DO A FAVOR FOR HIM, OR SOMETHING LIKE THAT, BEFORE HE'LL HELP YOU.

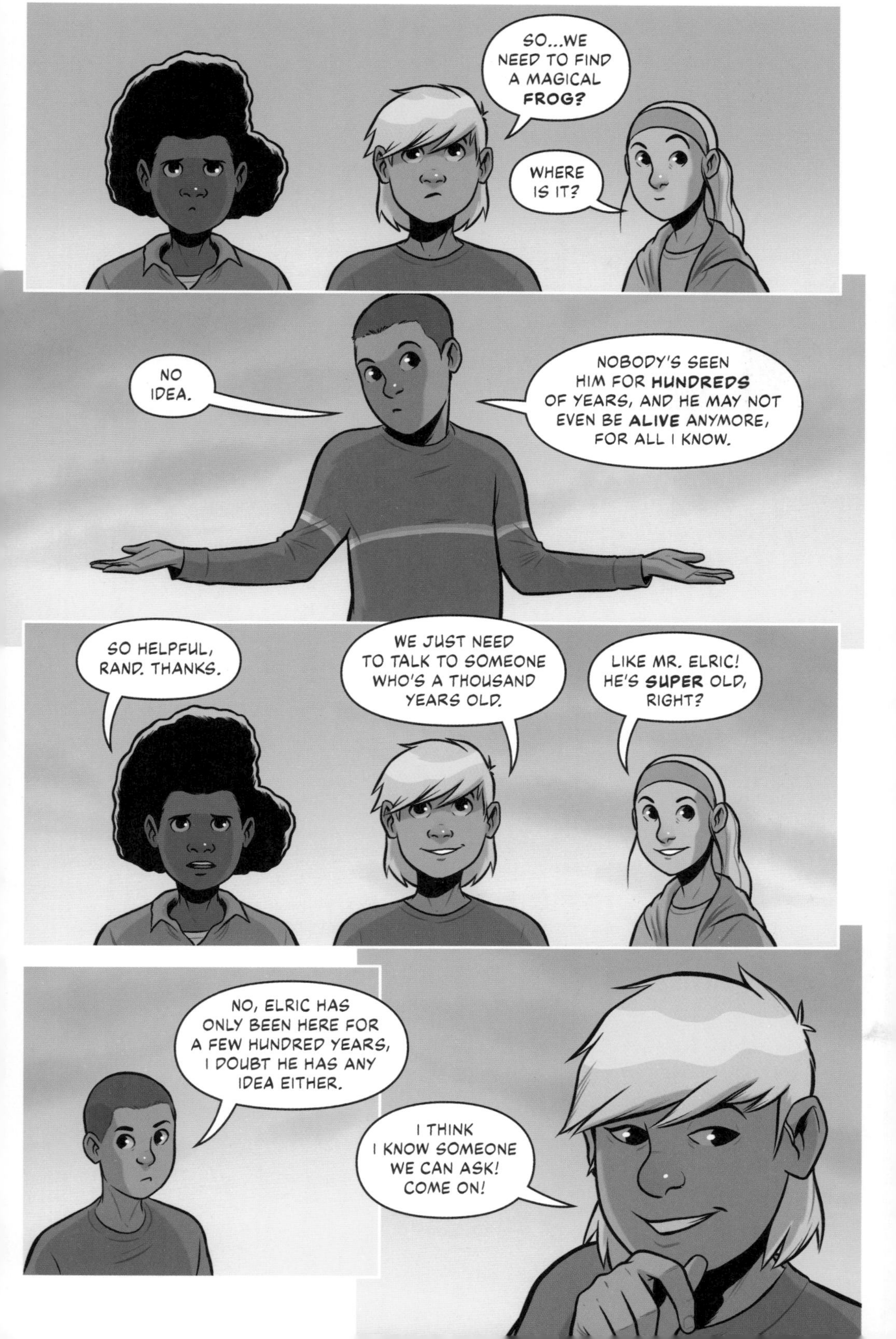
SO...WE NEED TO FIND A MAGICAL **FROG?**
WHERE IS IT?
NO IDEA.
NOBODY'S SEEN HIM FOR **HUNDREDS** OF YEARS, AND HE MAY NOT EVEN BE **ALIVE** ANYMORE, FOR ALL I KNOW.
SO HELPFUL, RAND. THANKS.
WE JUST NEED TO TALK TO SOMEONE WHO'S A THOUSAND YEARS OLD.
LIKE MR. ELRIC! HE'S **SUPER** OLD, RIGHT?
NO, ELRIC HAS ONLY BEEN HERE FOR A FEW HUNDRED YEARS, I DOUBT HE HAS ANY IDEA EITHER.
I THINK I KNOW SOMEONE WE CAN ASK! COME ON!

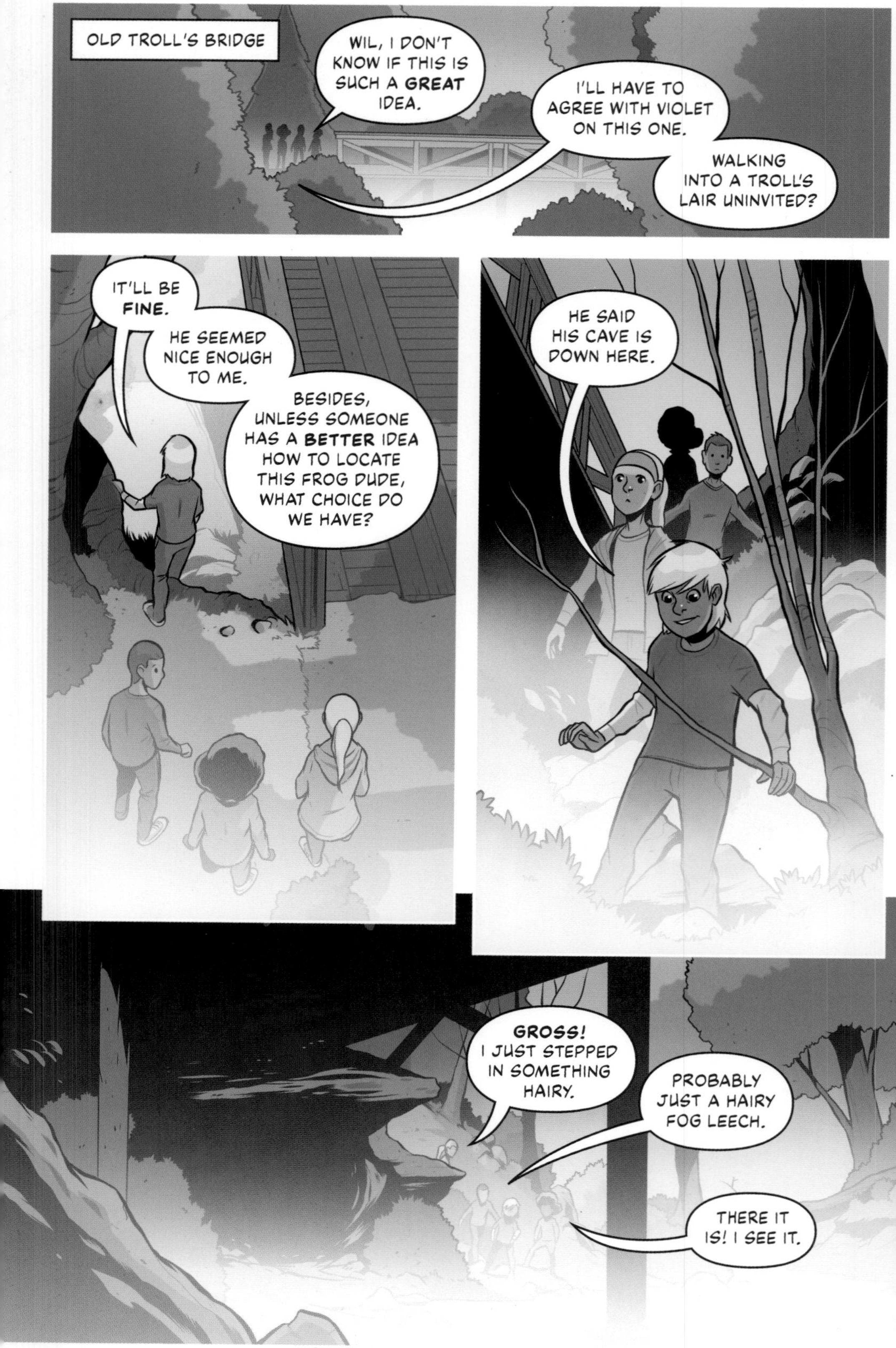
OLD TROLL'S BRIDGE
WIL, I DON'T KNOW IF THIS IS SUCH A **GREAT** IDEA.
I'LL HAVE TO AGREE WITH VIOLET ON THIS ONE.
WALKING INTO A TROLL'S LAIR UNINVITED?
IT'LL BE **FINE.**
HE SEEMED NICE ENOUGH TO ME.
BESIDES, UNLESS SOMEONE HAS A **BETTER** IDEA HOW TO LOCATE THIS FROG DUDE, WHAT CHOICE DO WE HAVE?
HE SAID HIS CAVE IS DOWN HERE.
GROSS! I JUST STEPPED IN SOMETHING HAIRY.
PROBABLY JUST A HAIRY FOG LEECH.
THERE IT IS! I SEE IT.

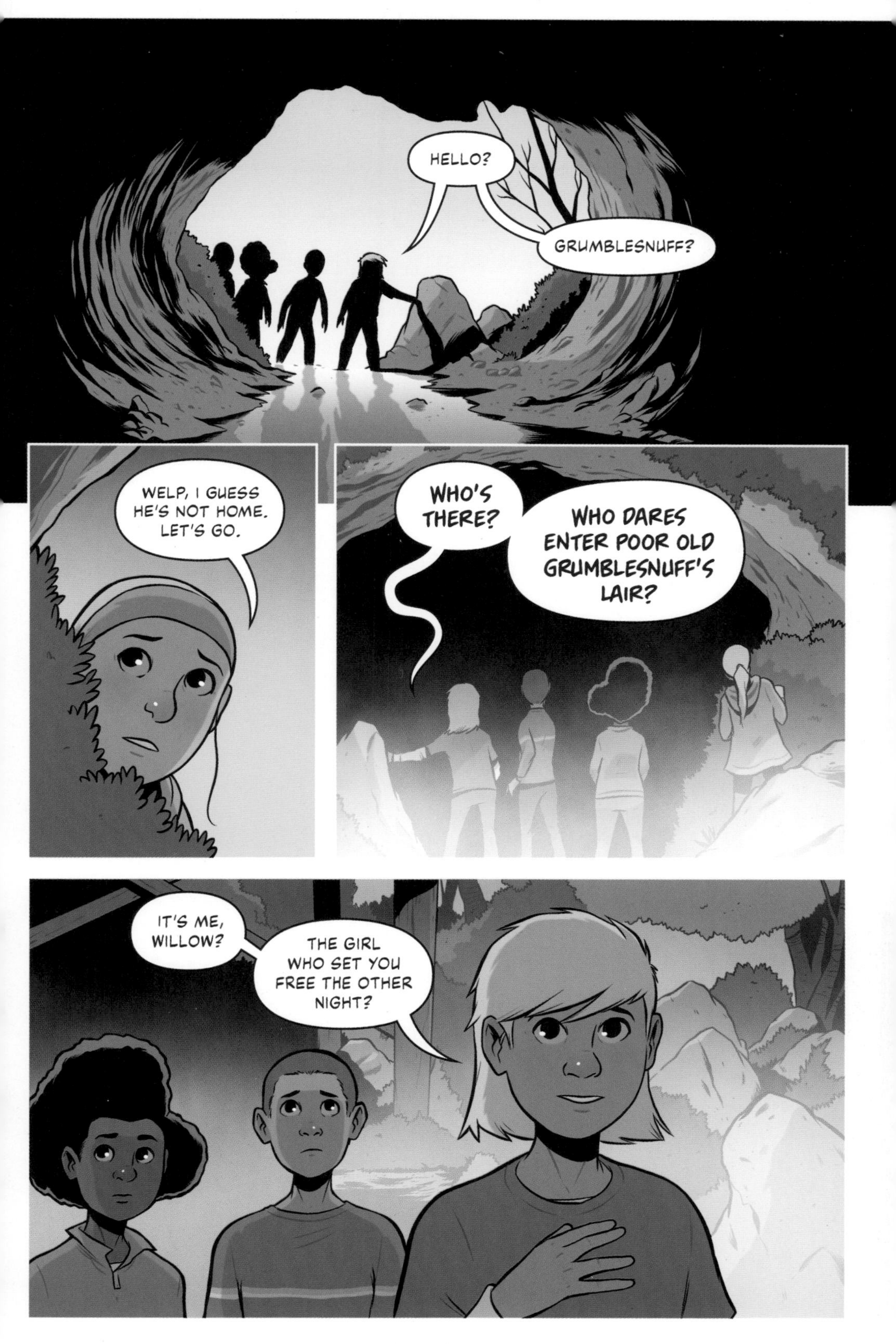
HELLO?
GRUMBLESNUFF?
WELP, I GUESS HE'S NOT HOME. LET'S GO.
WHO'S THERE?
WHO DARES ENTER POOR OLD GRUMBLESNUFF'S LAIR?
IT'S ME, WILLOW?
THE GIRL WHO SET YOU FREE THE OTHER NIGHT?

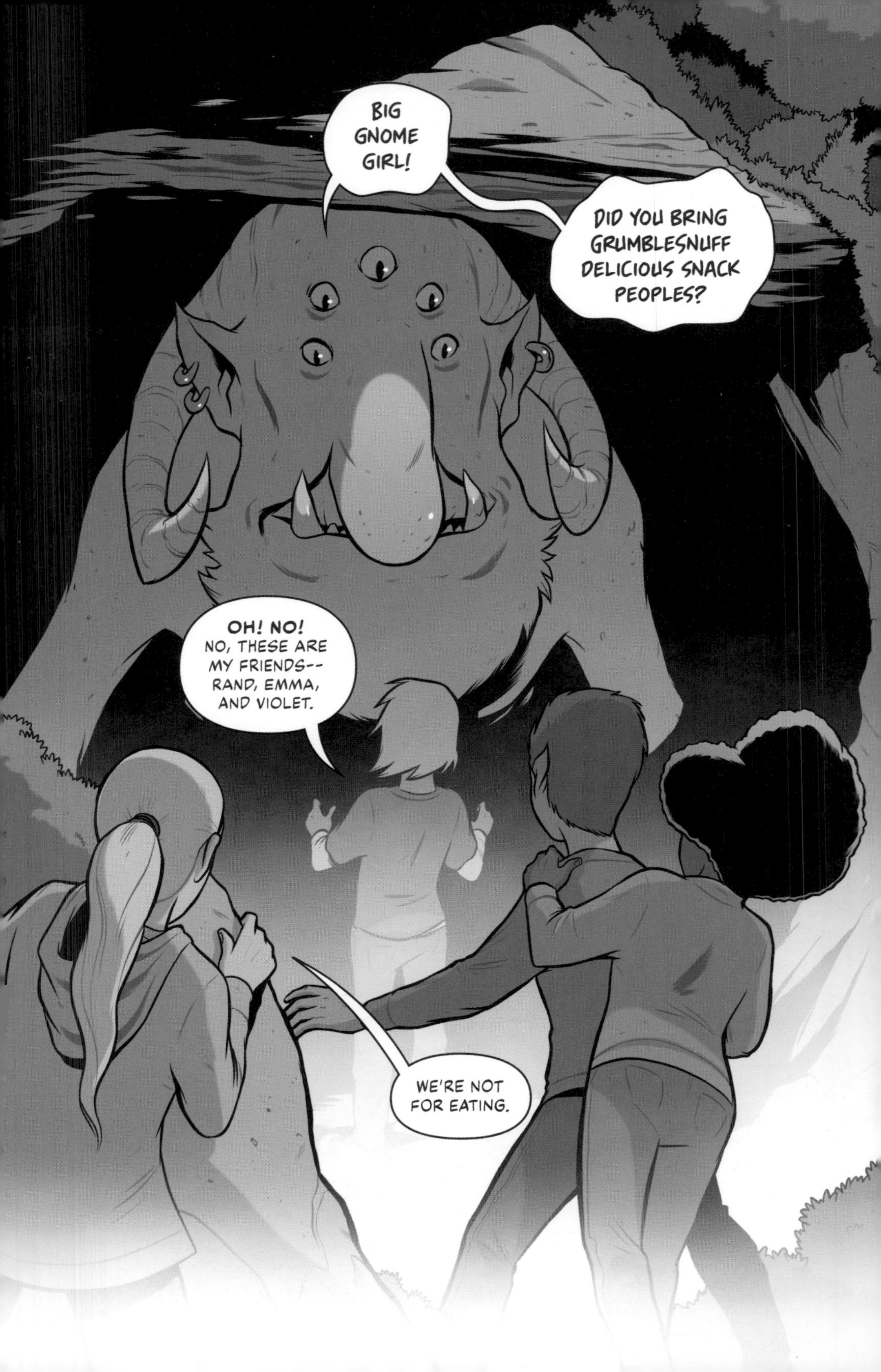
BIG GNOME GIRL!
DID YOU BRING GRUMBLESNUFF DELICIOUS SNACK PEOPLES?
OH! NO! NO, THESE ARE MY FRIENDS-- RAND, EMMA, AND VIOLET.
WE'RE NOT FOR EATING.

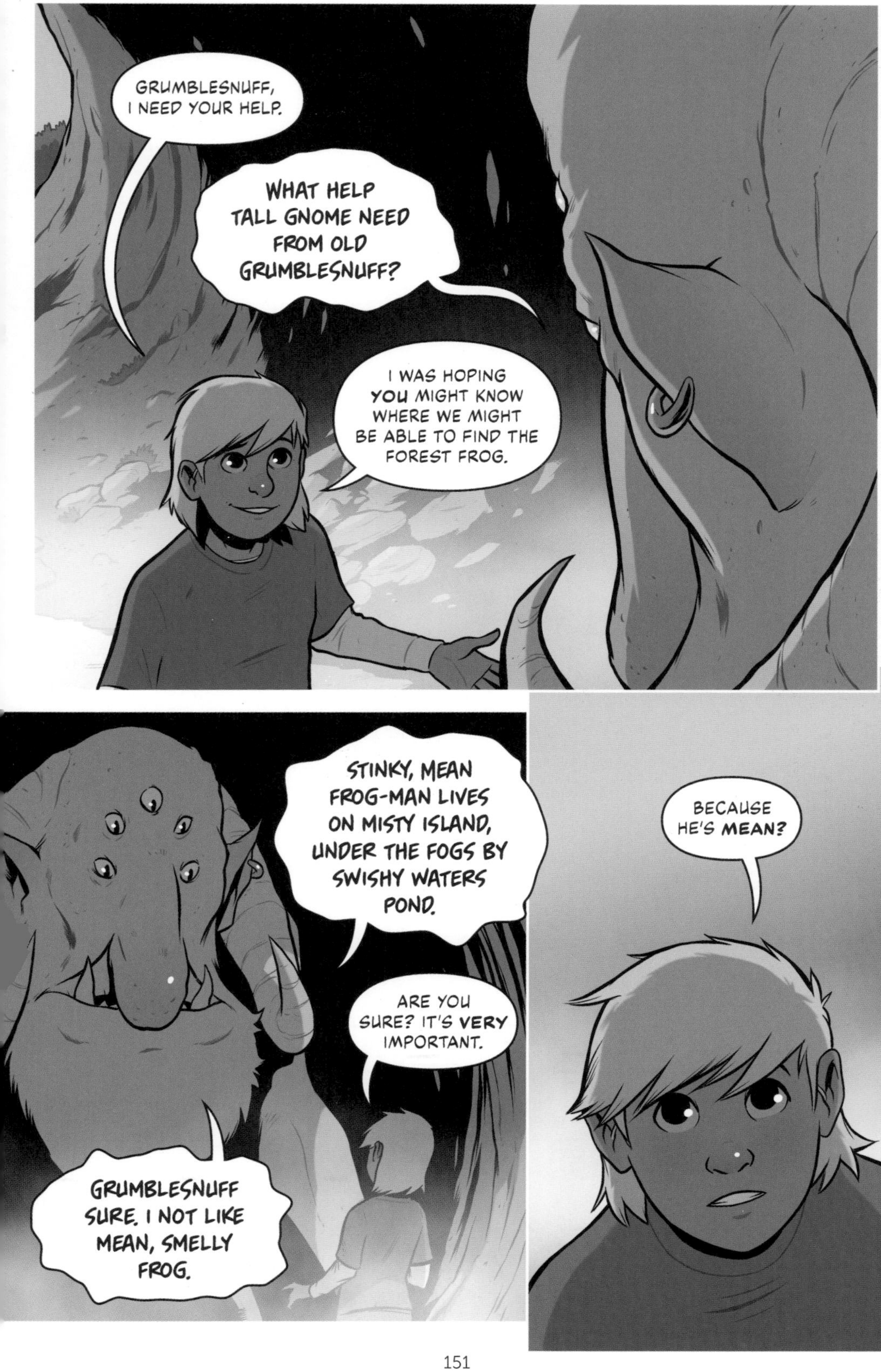
GRUMBLESNUFF, I NEED YOUR HELP.
WHAT HELP TALL GNOME NEED FROM OLD GRUMBLESNUFF?
I WAS HOPING **YOU** MIGHT KNOW WHERE WE MIGHT BE ABLE TO FIND THE FOREST FROG.
STINKY, MEAN FROG-MAN LIVES ON MISTY ISLAND, UNDER THE FOGS BY SWISHY WATERS POND.
ARE YOU SURE? IT'S **VERY** IMPORTANT.
GRUMBLESNUFF SURE. I NOT LIKE MEAN, SMELLY FROG.
BECAUSE HE'S **MEAN**?

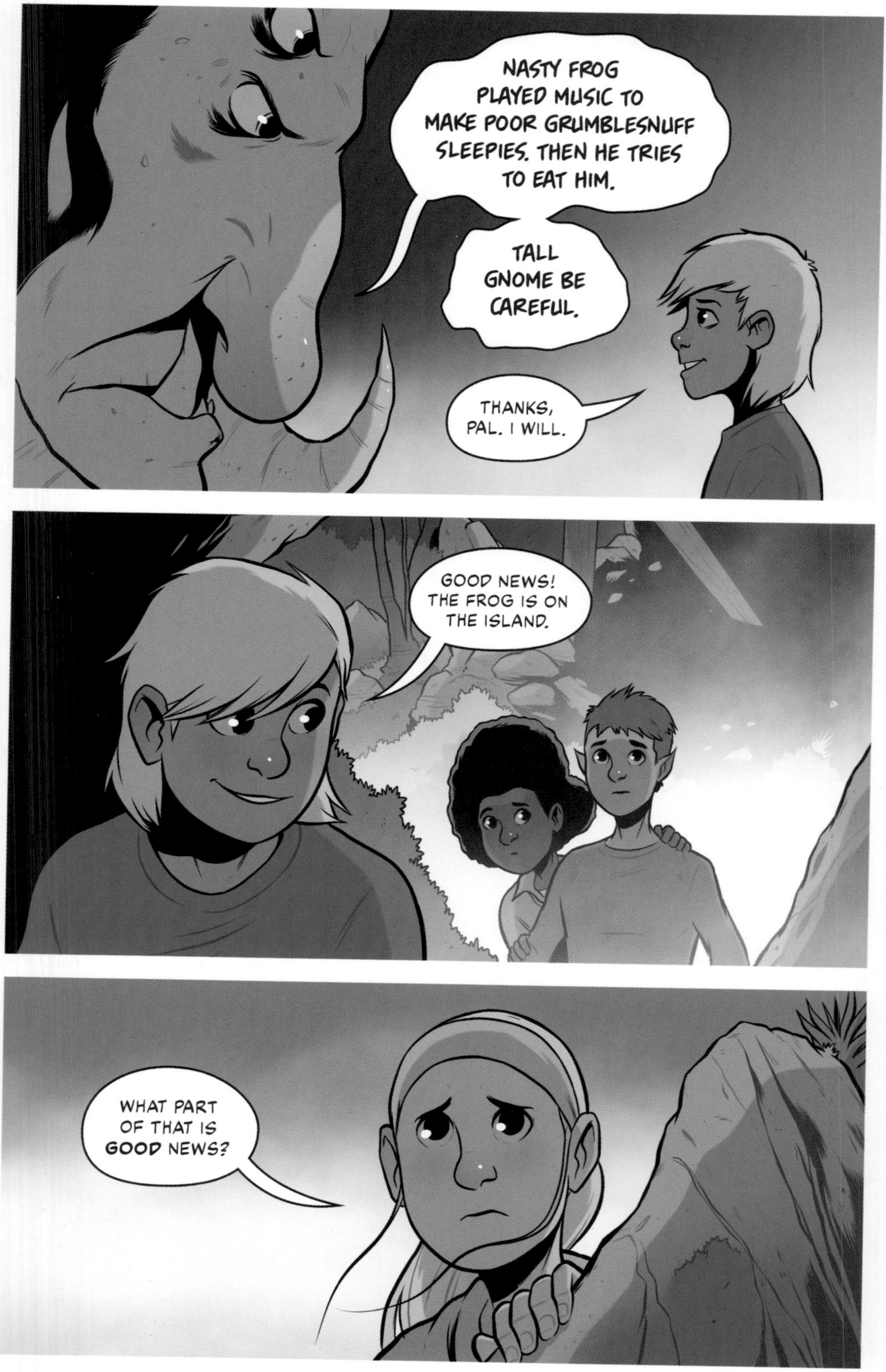
NASTY FROG PLAYED MUSIC TO MAKE POOR GRUMBLESNUFF SLEEPIES. THEN HE TRIES TO EAT HIM.
TALL GNOME BE CAREFUL.
THANKS, PAL. I WILL.
GOOD NEWS! THE FROG IS ON THE ISLAND.
WHAT PART OF THAT IS GOOD NEWS?

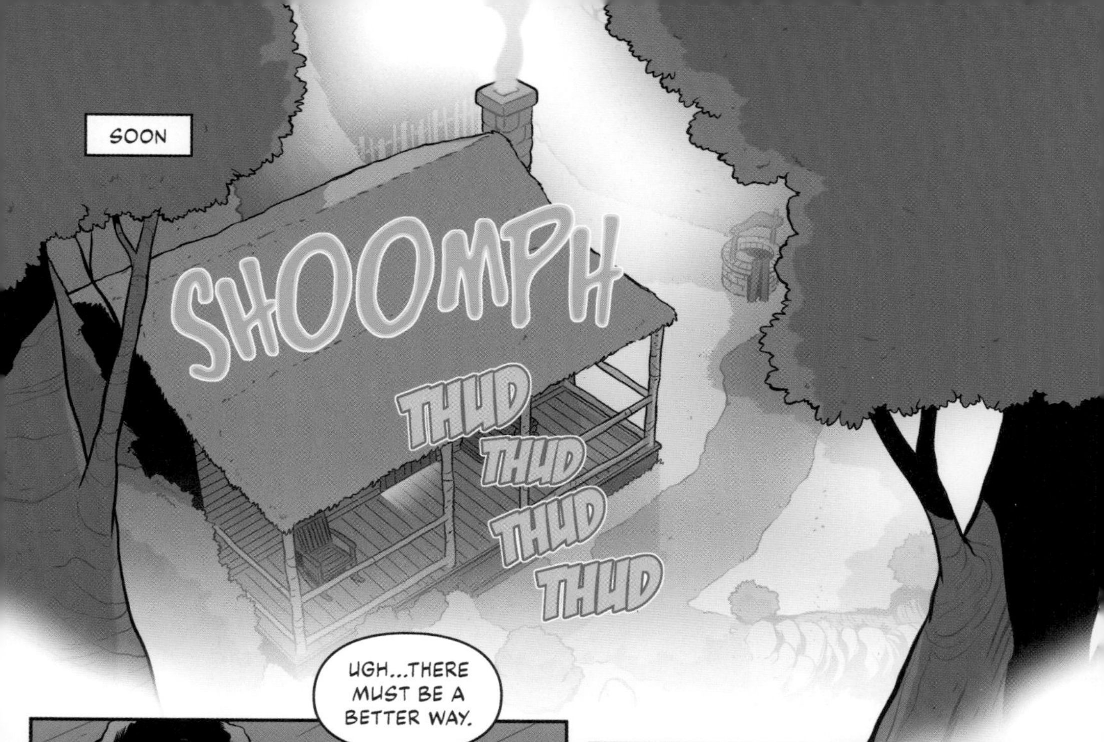
SOON
SHOOMPH
THUD
THUD
THUD
THUD

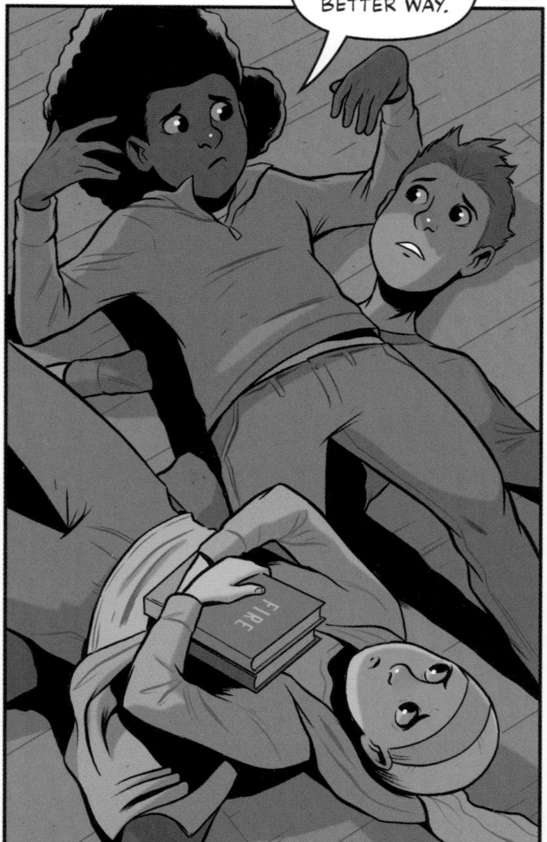
UGH...THERE MUST BE A BETTER WAY.
FIRE

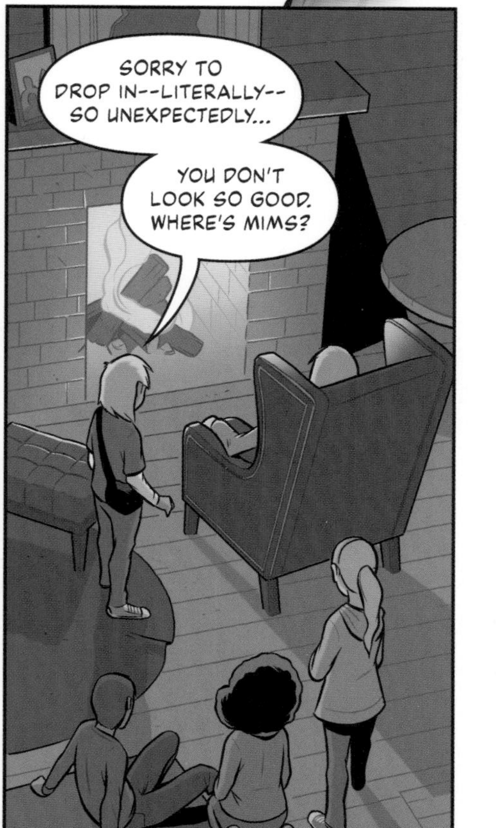
SORRY TO DROP IN--LITERALLY--SO UNEXPECTEDLY...
YOU DON'T LOOK SO GOOD. WHERE'S MIMS?

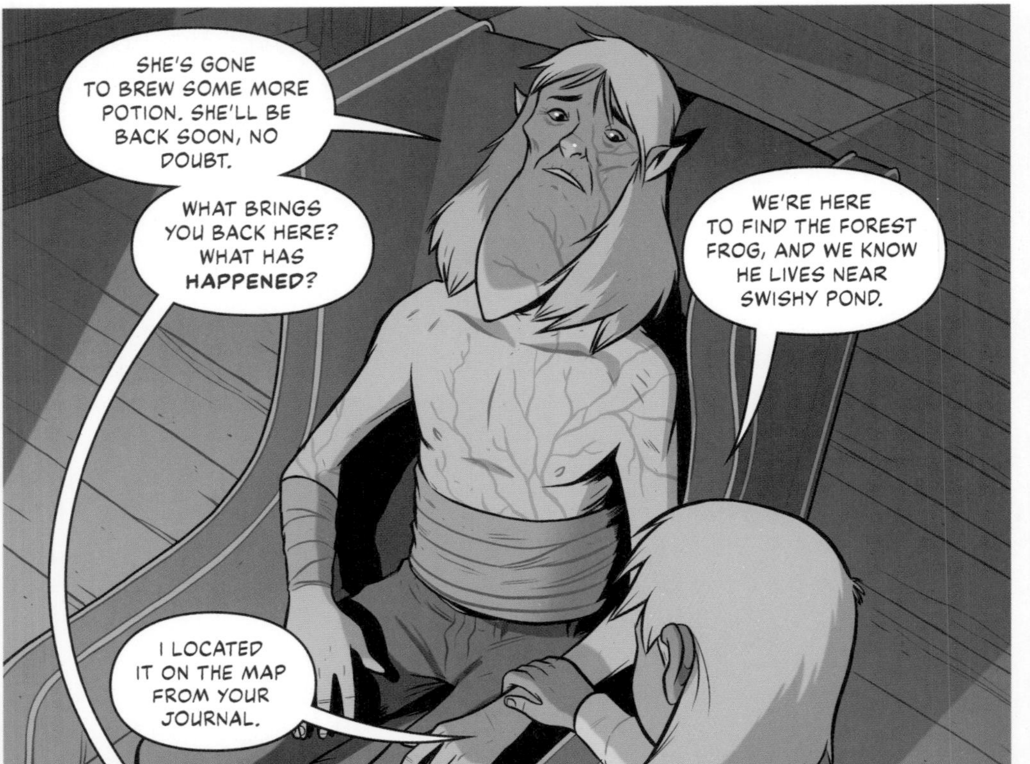
SHE'S GONE TO BREW SOME MORE POTION. SHE'LL BE BACK SOON, NO DOUBT.
WHAT BRINGS YOU BACK HERE? WHAT HAS **HAPPENED?**
WE'RE HERE TO FIND THE FOREST FROG, AND WE KNOW HE LIVES NEAR SWISHY POND.
I LOCATED IT ON THE MAP FROM YOUR JOURNAL.
YOU MUSTN'T GO ALONE. NO, THE FOREST HAS GROWN **RESTLESS.** THE FOG IS...

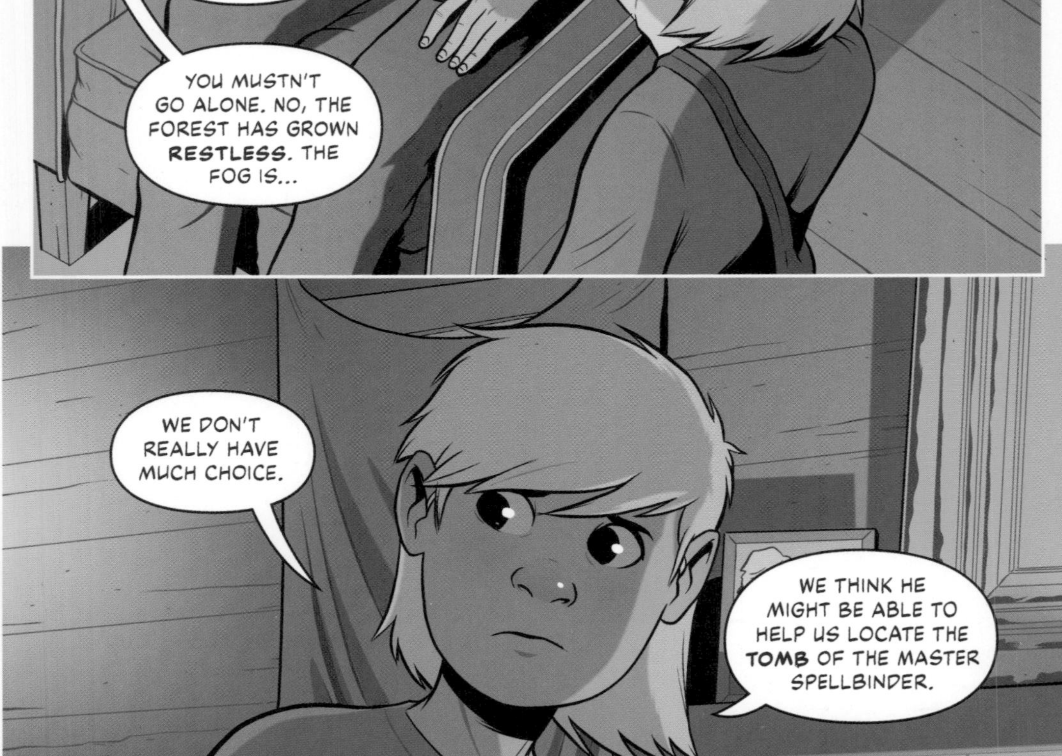
WE DON'T REALLY HAVE MUCH CHOICE.
WE THINK HE MIGHT BE ABLE TO HELP US LOCATE THE **TOMB** OF THE MASTER SPELLBINDER.

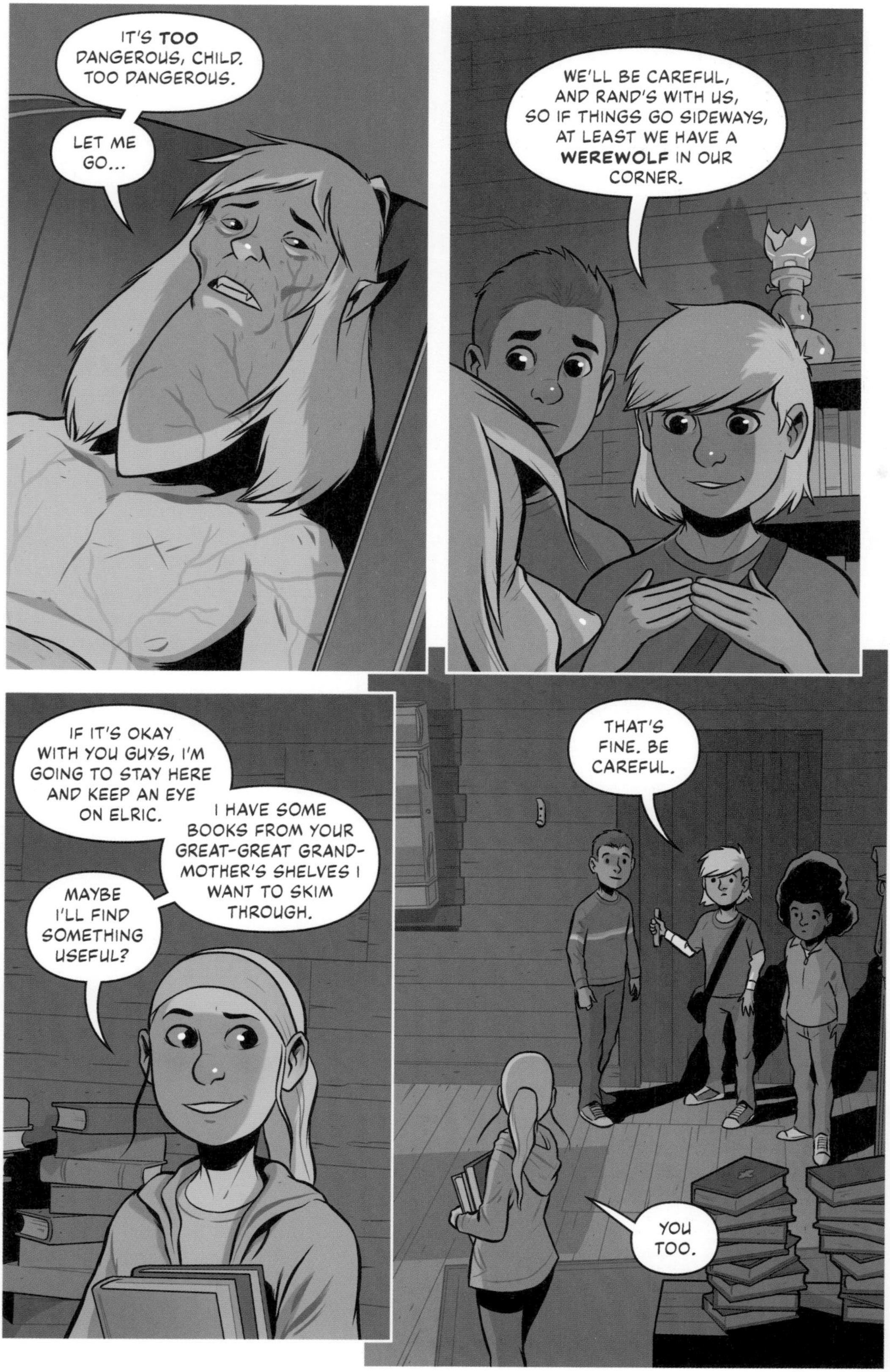
IT'S **TOO** DANGEROUS, CHILD. TOO DANGEROUS.
LET ME GO...
WE'LL BE CAREFUL, AND RAND'S WITH US, SO IF THINGS GO SIDEWAYS, AT LEAST WE HAVE A **WEREWOLF** IN OUR CORNER.
IF IT'S OKAY WITH YOU GUYS, I'M GOING TO STAY HERE AND KEEP AN EYE ON ELRIC.
I HAVE SOME BOOKS FROM YOUR GREAT-GREAT GRAND-MOTHER'S SHELVES I WANT TO SKIM THROUGH.
MAYBE I'LL FIND SOMETHING USEFUL?
THAT'S FINE. BE CAREFUL.
YOU TOO.

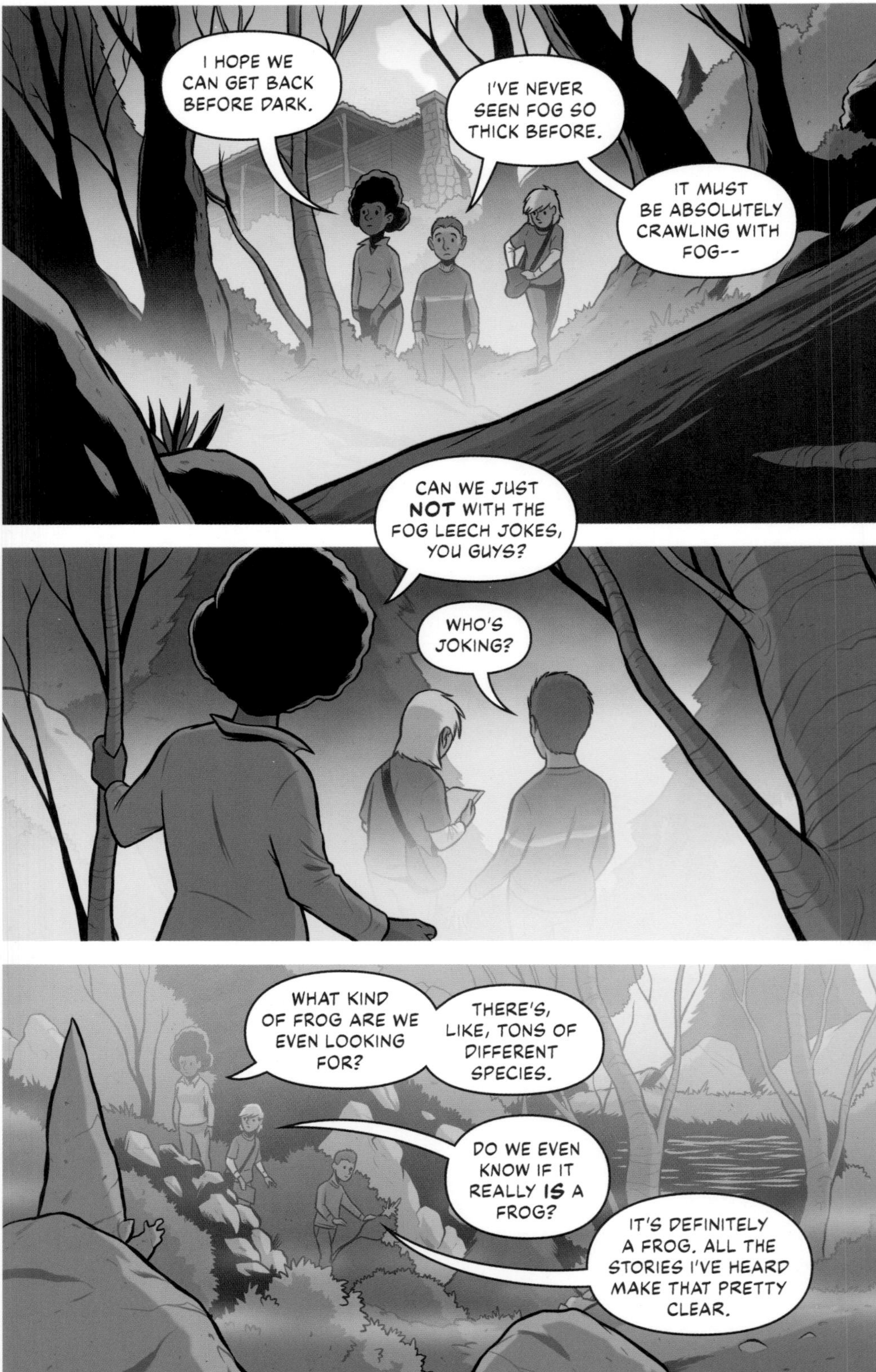
I HOPE WE CAN GET BACK BEFORE DARK.
I'VE NEVER SEEN FOG SO THICK BEFORE.
IT MUST BE ABSOLUTELY CRAWLING WITH FOG--
CAN WE JUST **NOT** WITH THE FOG LEECH JOKES, YOU GUYS?
WHO'S JOKING?
WHAT KIND OF FROG ARE WE EVEN LOOKING FOR?
THERE'S, LIKE, TONS OF DIFFERENT SPECIES.
DO WE EVEN KNOW IF IT REALLY **IS** A FROG?
IT'S DEFINITELY A FROG. ALL THE STORIES I'VE HEARD MAKE THAT PRETTY CLEAR.

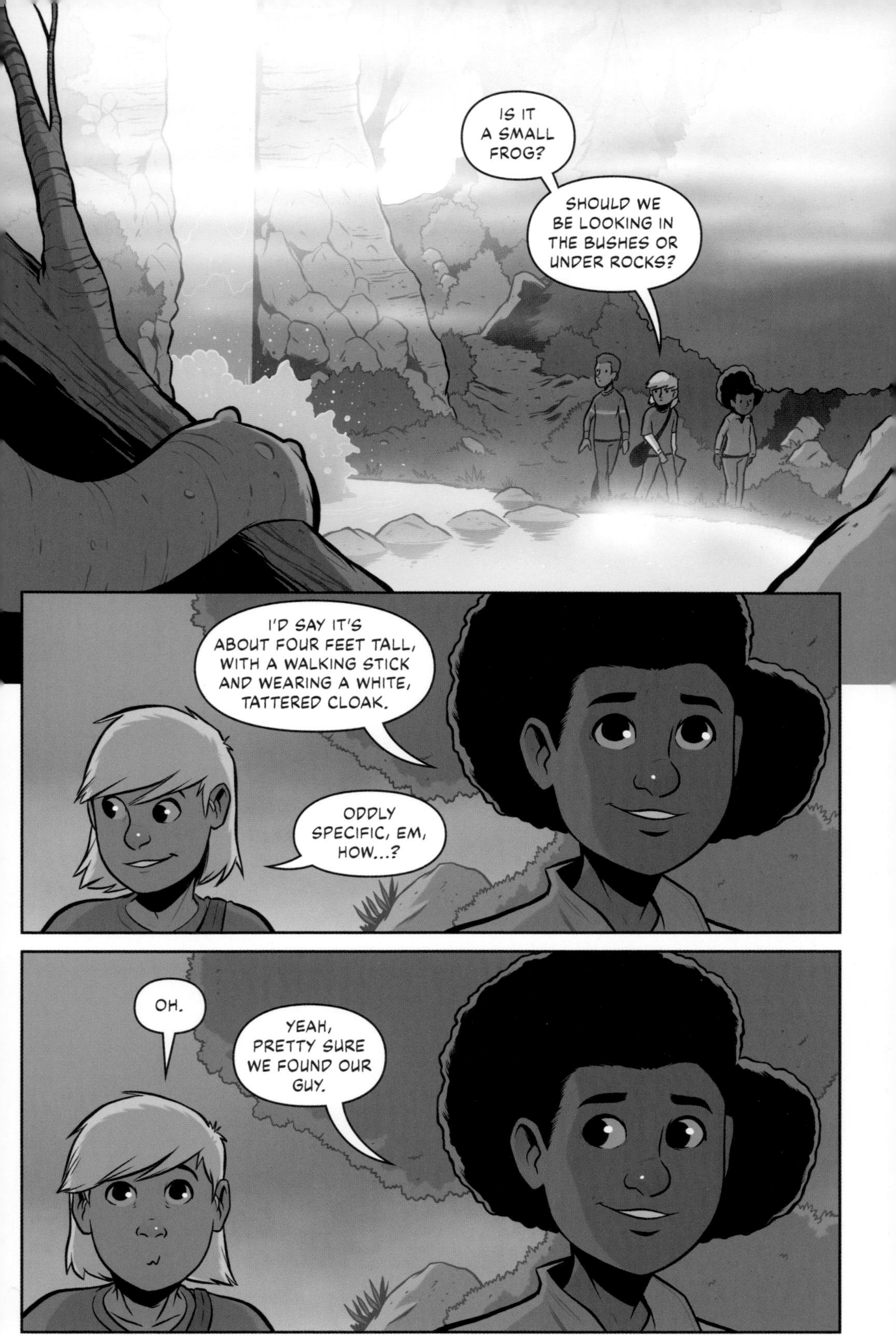

IS IT A SMALL FROG?
SHOULD WE BE LOOKING IN THE BUSHES OR UNDER ROCKS?
I'D SAY IT'S ABOUT FOUR FEET TALL, WITH A WALKING STICK AND WEARING A WHITE, TATTERED CLOAK.
ODDLY SPECIFIC, EM, HOW...?
OH.
YEAH, PRETTY SURE WE FOUND OUR GUY.

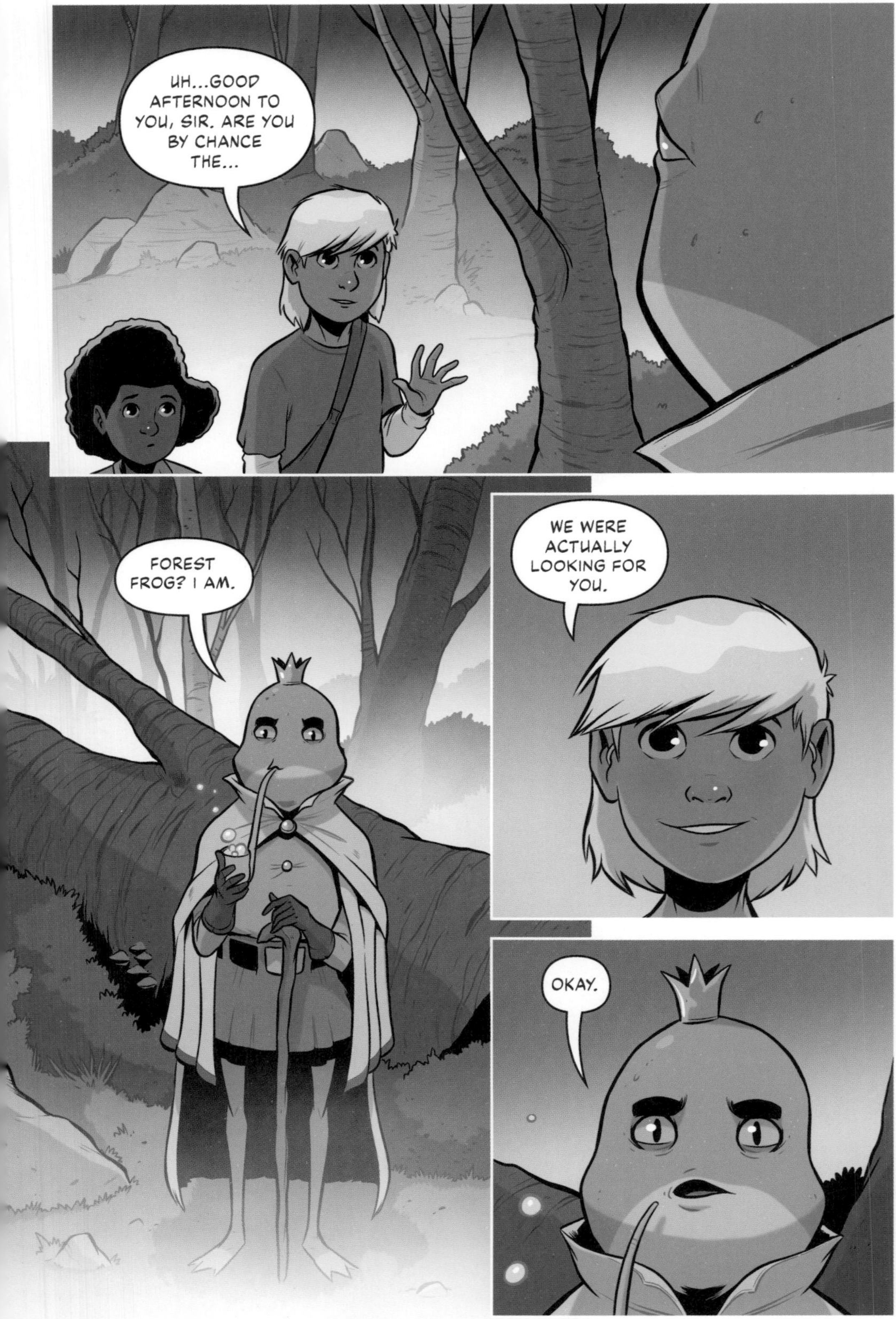
UH...GOOD AFTERNOON TO YOU, SIR. ARE YOU BY CHANCE THE...
FOREST FROG? I AM.
WE WERE ACTUALLY LOOKING FOR YOU.
OKAY.

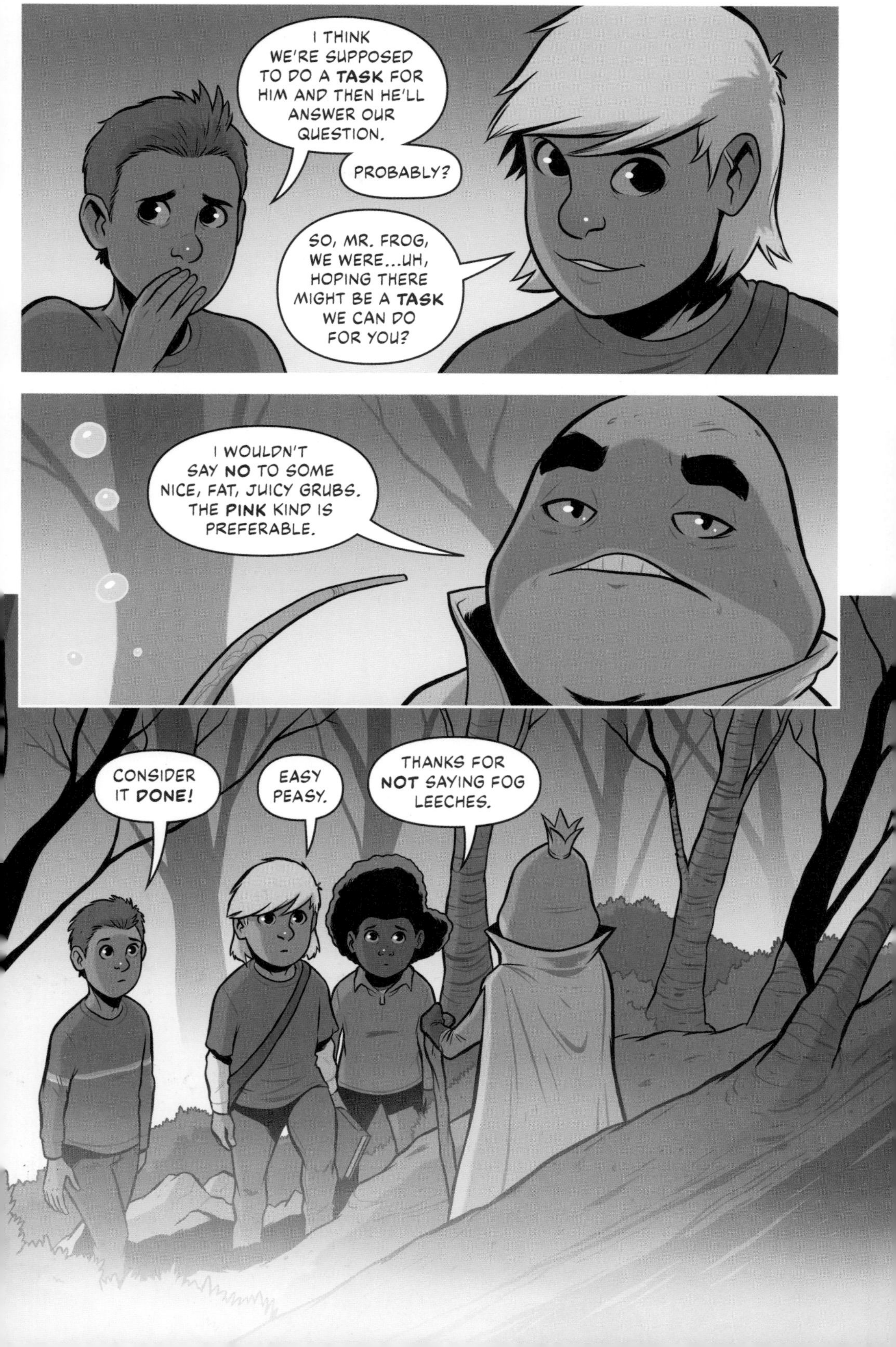
I THINK WE'RE SUPPOSED TO DO A TASK FOR HIM AND THEN HE'LL ANSWER OUR QUESTION.
PROBABLY?
SO, MR. FROG, WE WERE...UH, HOPING THERE MIGHT BE A TASK WE CAN DO FOR YOU?
I WOULDN'T SAY NO TO SOME NICE, FAT, JUICY GRUBS. THE PINK KIND IS PREFERABLE.
CONSIDER IT DONE!
EASY PEASY.
THANKS FOR NOT SAYING FOG LEECHES.

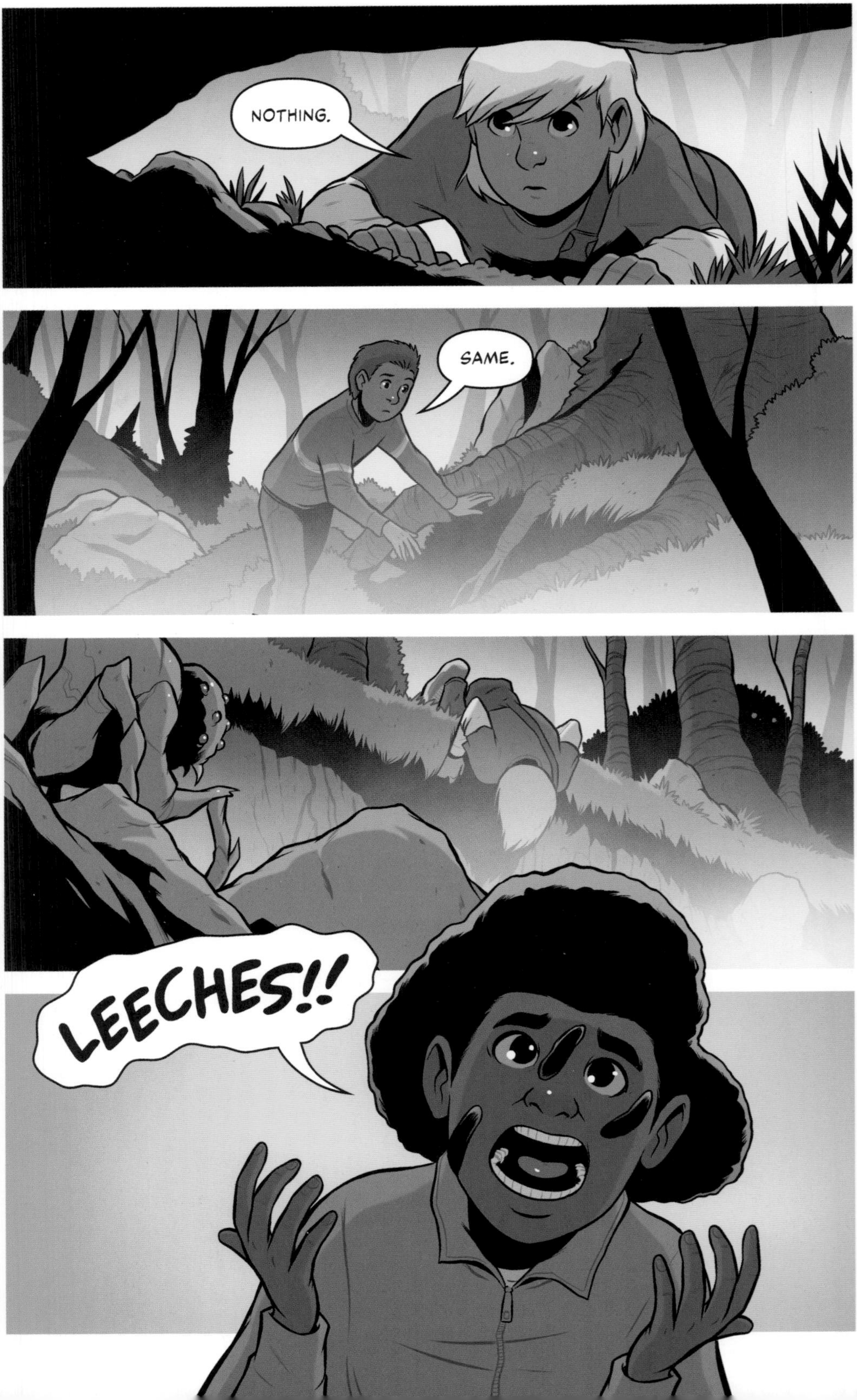
NOTHING.
SAME.
LEECHES!!

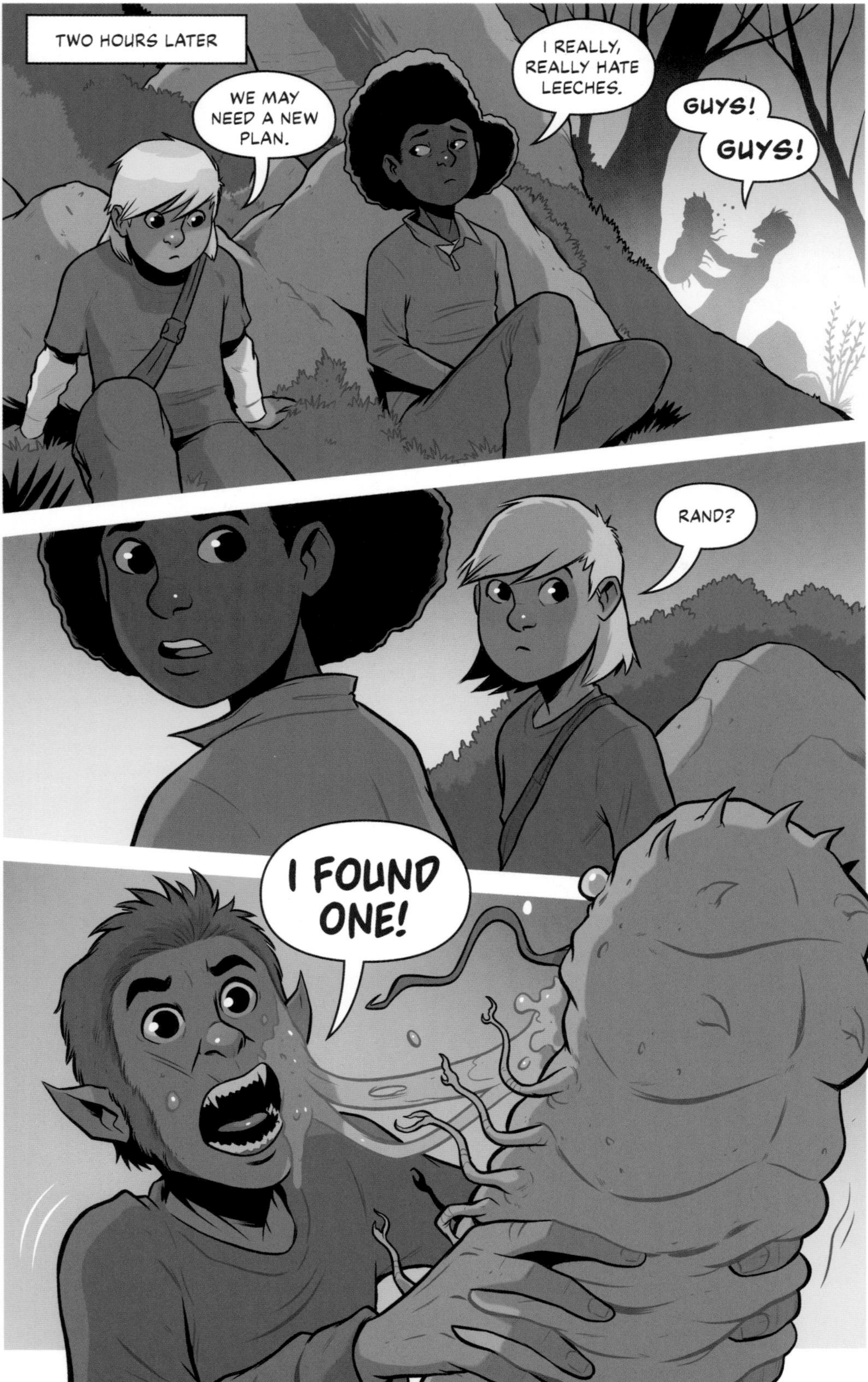
TWO HOURS LATER
WE MAY NEED A NEW PLAN.
I REALLY, REALLY HATE LEECHES.
GUYS!
GUYS!
RAND?
I FOUND ONE!

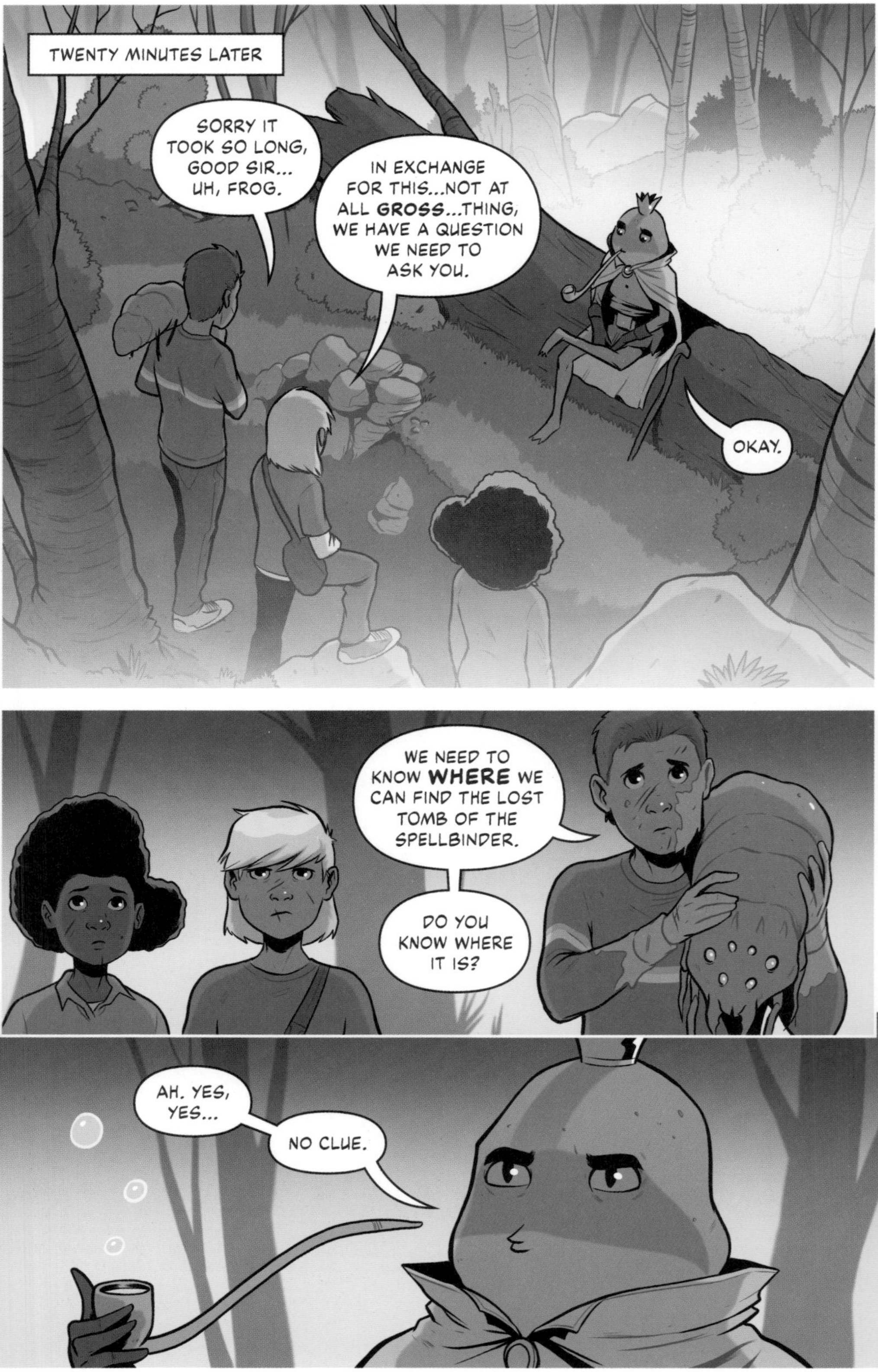
TWENTY MINUTES LATER
SORRY IT TOOK SO LONG, GOOD SIR... UH, FROG.
IN EXCHANGE FOR THIS...NOT AT ALL GROSS...THING, WE HAVE A QUESTION WE NEED TO ASK YOU.
OKAY.
WE NEED TO KNOW WHERE WE CAN FIND THE LOST TOMB OF THE SPELLBINDER.
DO YOU KNOW WHERE IT IS?
AH. YES, YES...
NO CLUE.

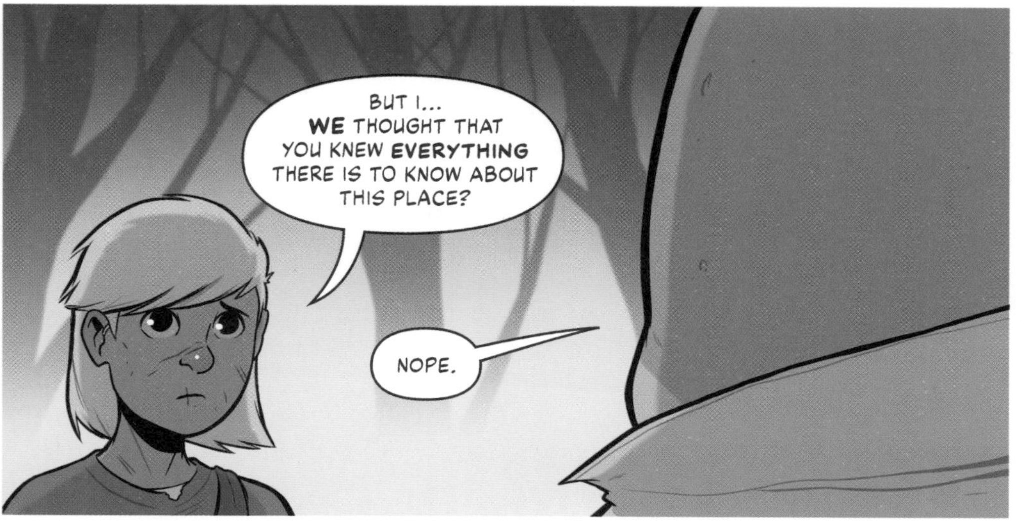
BUT I...
WE THOUGHT THAT YOU KNEW **EVERYTHING** THERE IS TO KNOW ABOUT THIS PLACE?
NOPE.

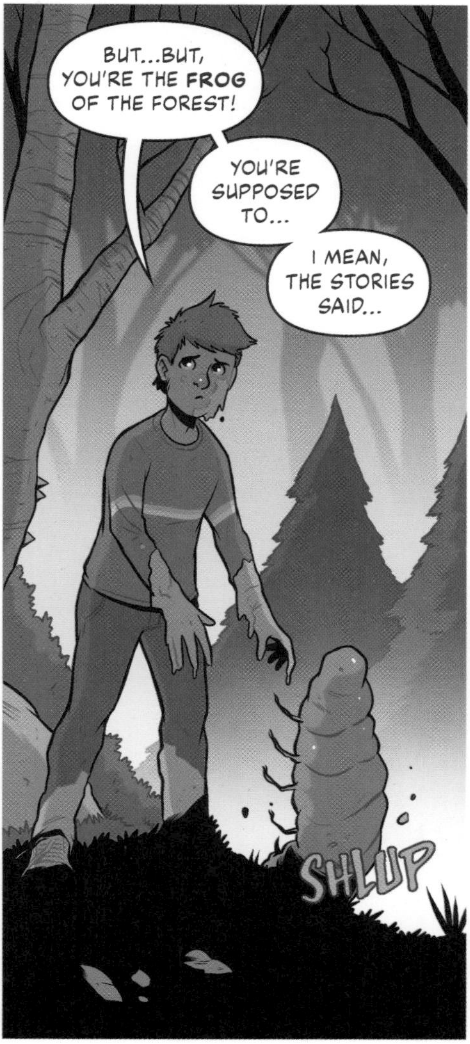
BUT...BUT, YOU'RE THE **FROG** OF THE FOREST!
YOU'RE SUPPOSED TO...
I MEAN, THE STORIES SAID...
SHLUP

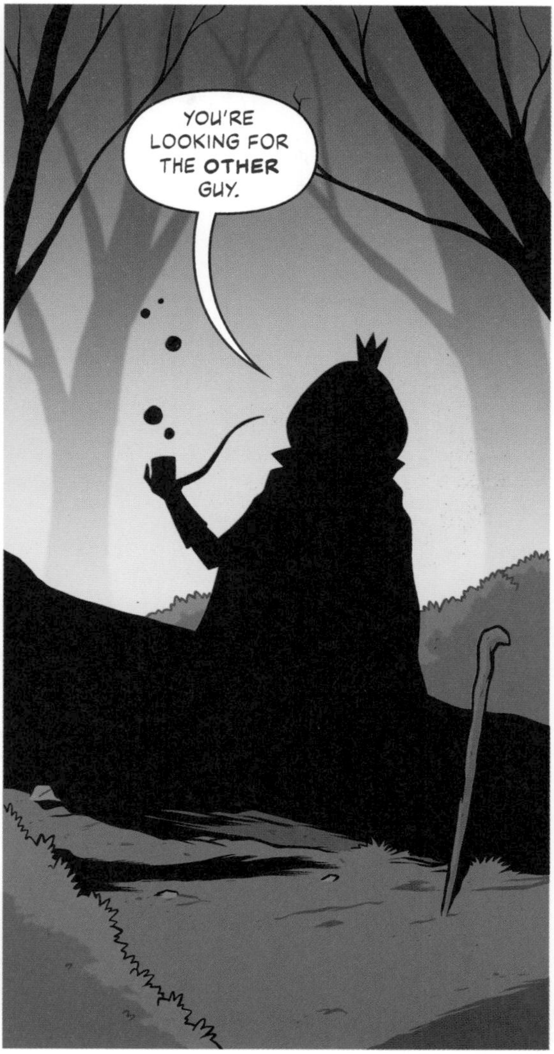
YOU'RE LOOKING FOR THE **OTHER** GUY.

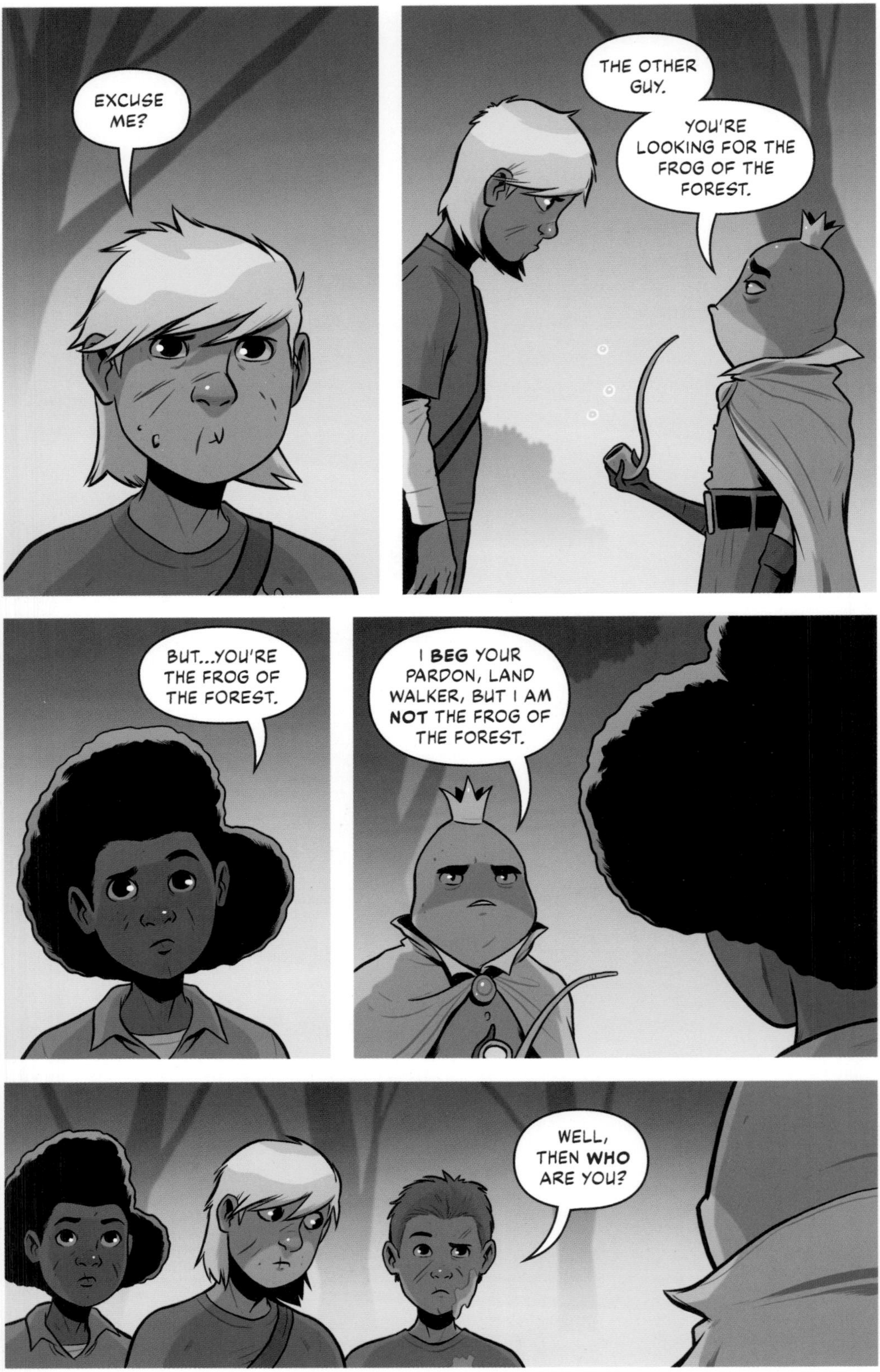
EXCUSE ME?
THE OTHER GUY.
YOU'RE LOOKING FOR THE FROG OF THE FOREST.
BUT...YOU'RE THE FROG OF THE FOREST.
I **BEG** YOUR PARDON, LAND WALKER, BUT I AM **NOT** THE FROG OF THE FOREST.
WELL, THEN **WHO** ARE YOU?

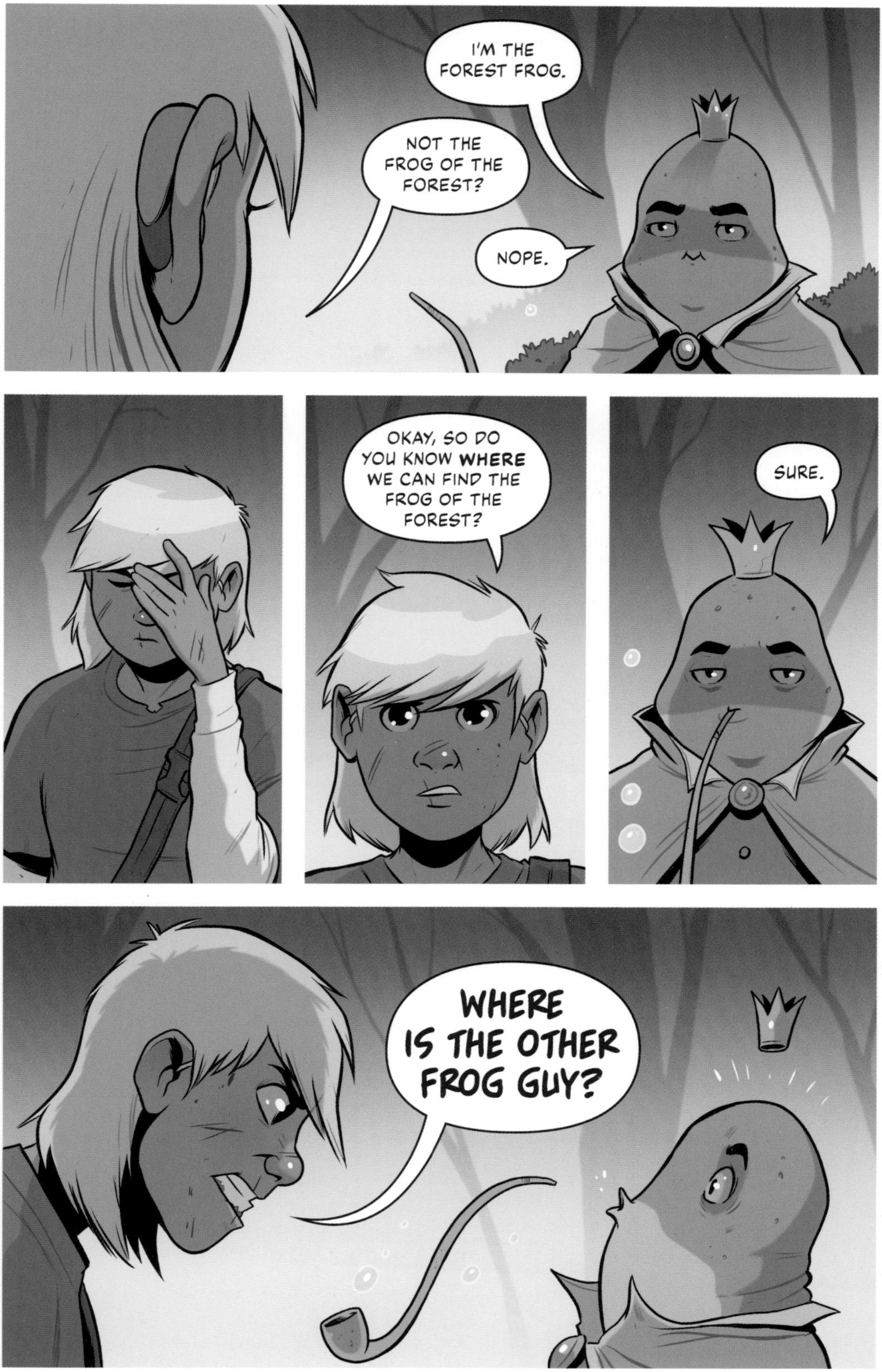
I'M THE FOREST FROG.
NOT THE FROG OF THE FOREST?
NOPE.
OKAY, SO DO YOU KNOW **WHERE** WE CAN FIND THE FROG OF THE FOREST?
SURE.
WHERE IS THE OTHER FROG GUY?

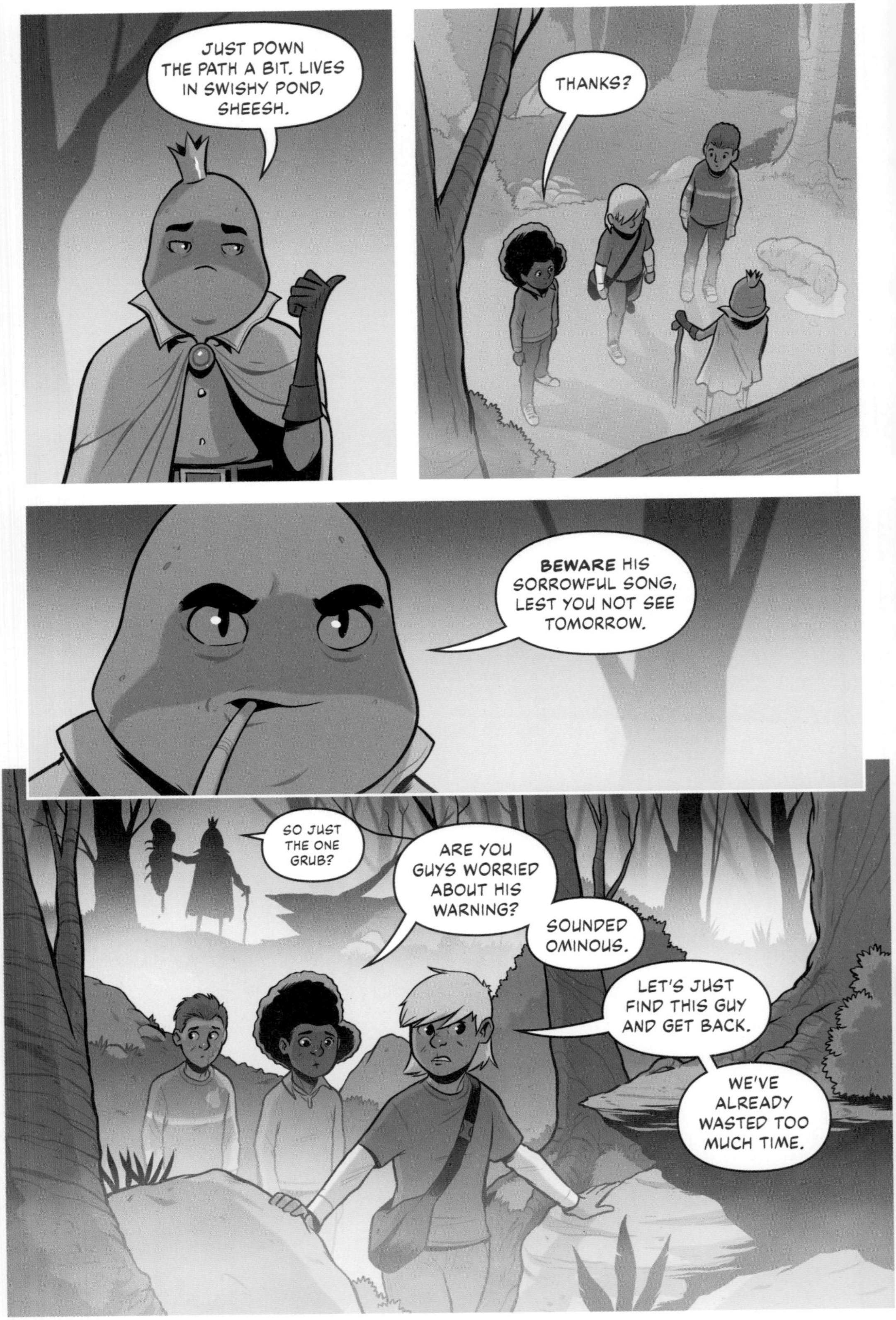
JUST DOWN THE PATH A BIT. LIVES IN SWISHY POND, SHEESH.
THANKS?
BEWARE HIS SORROWFUL SONG, LEST YOU NOT SEE TOMORROW.
SO JUST THE ONE GRUB?
ARE YOU GUYS WORRIED ABOUT HIS WARNING?
SOUNDED OMINOUS.
LET'S JUST FIND THIS GUY AND GET BACK.
WE'VE ALREADY WASTED TOO MUCH TIME.

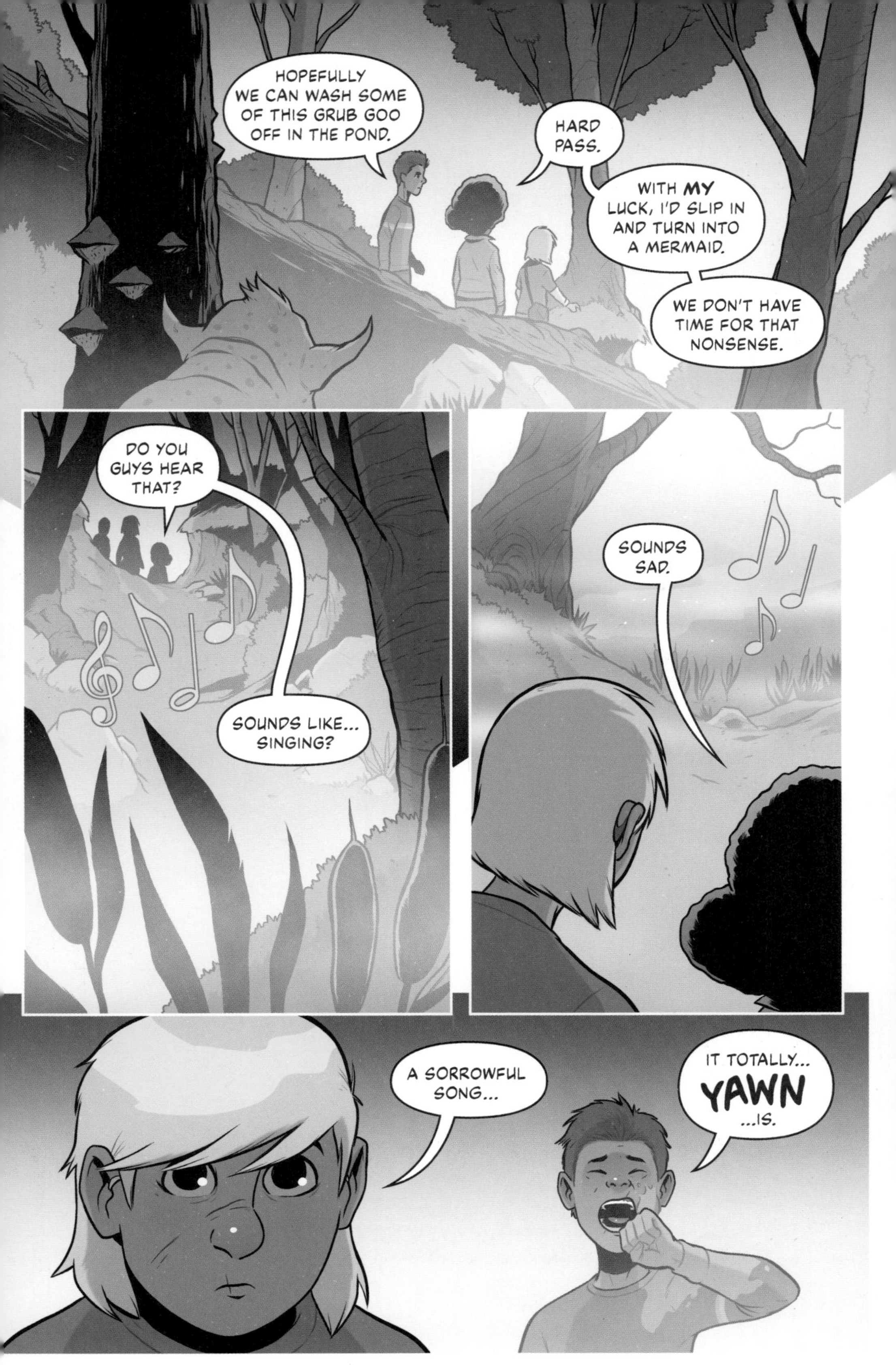
HOPEFULLY WE CAN WASH SOME OF THIS GRUB GOO OFF IN THE POND.
HARD PASS.
WITH MY LUCK, I'D SLIP IN AND TURN INTO A MERMAID.
WE DON'T HAVE TIME FOR THAT NONSENSE.
DO YOU GUYS HEAR THAT?
SOUNDS LIKE... SINGING?
SOUNDS SAD.
A SORROWFUL SONG...
IT TOTALLY... YAWN ...IS.

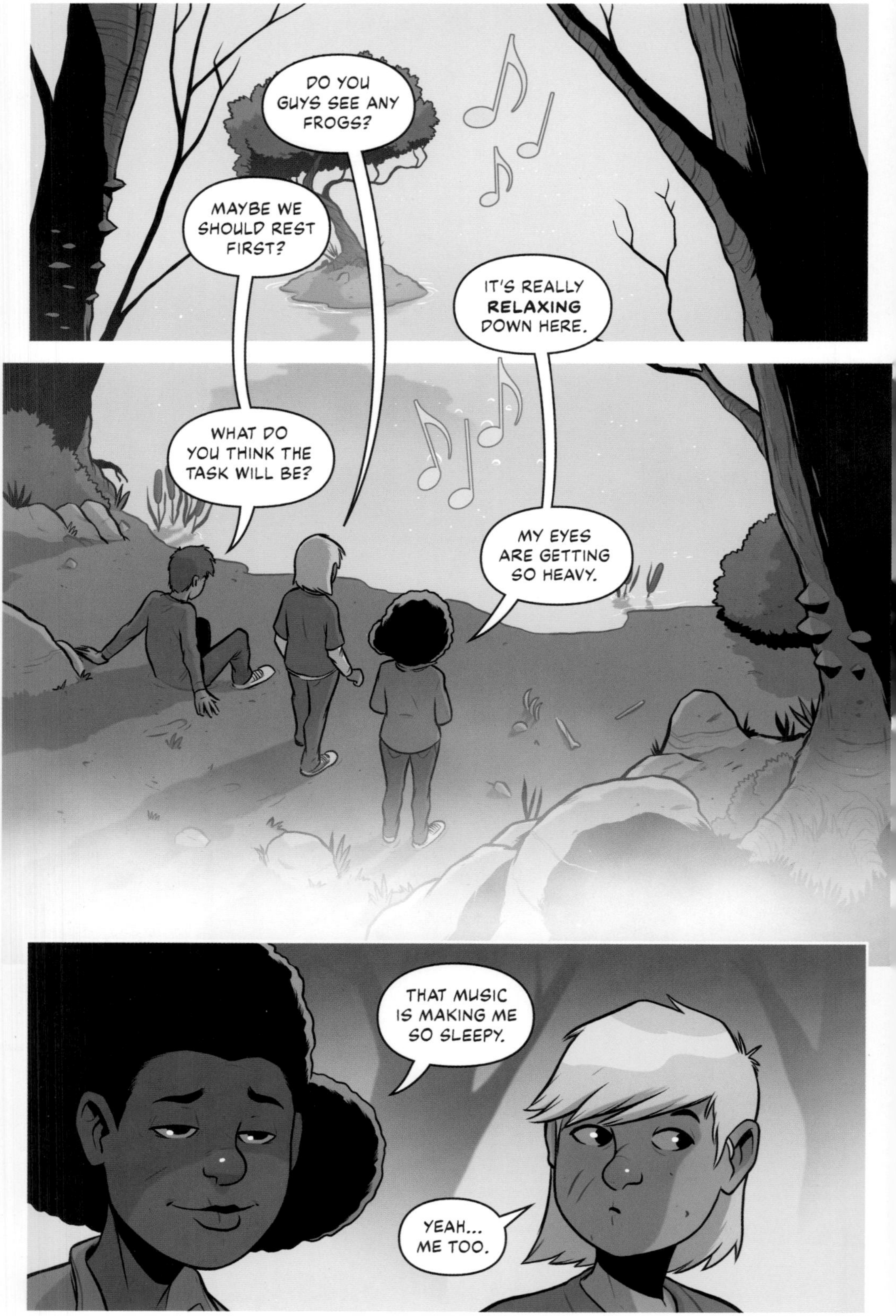
DO YOU GUYS SEE ANY FROGS?
MAYBE WE SHOULD REST FIRST?
IT'S REALLY **RELAXING** DOWN HERE.
WHAT DO YOU THINK THE TASK WILL BE?
MY EYES ARE GETTING SO HEAVY.
THAT MUSIC IS MAKING ME SO SLEEPY.
YEAH... ME TOO.

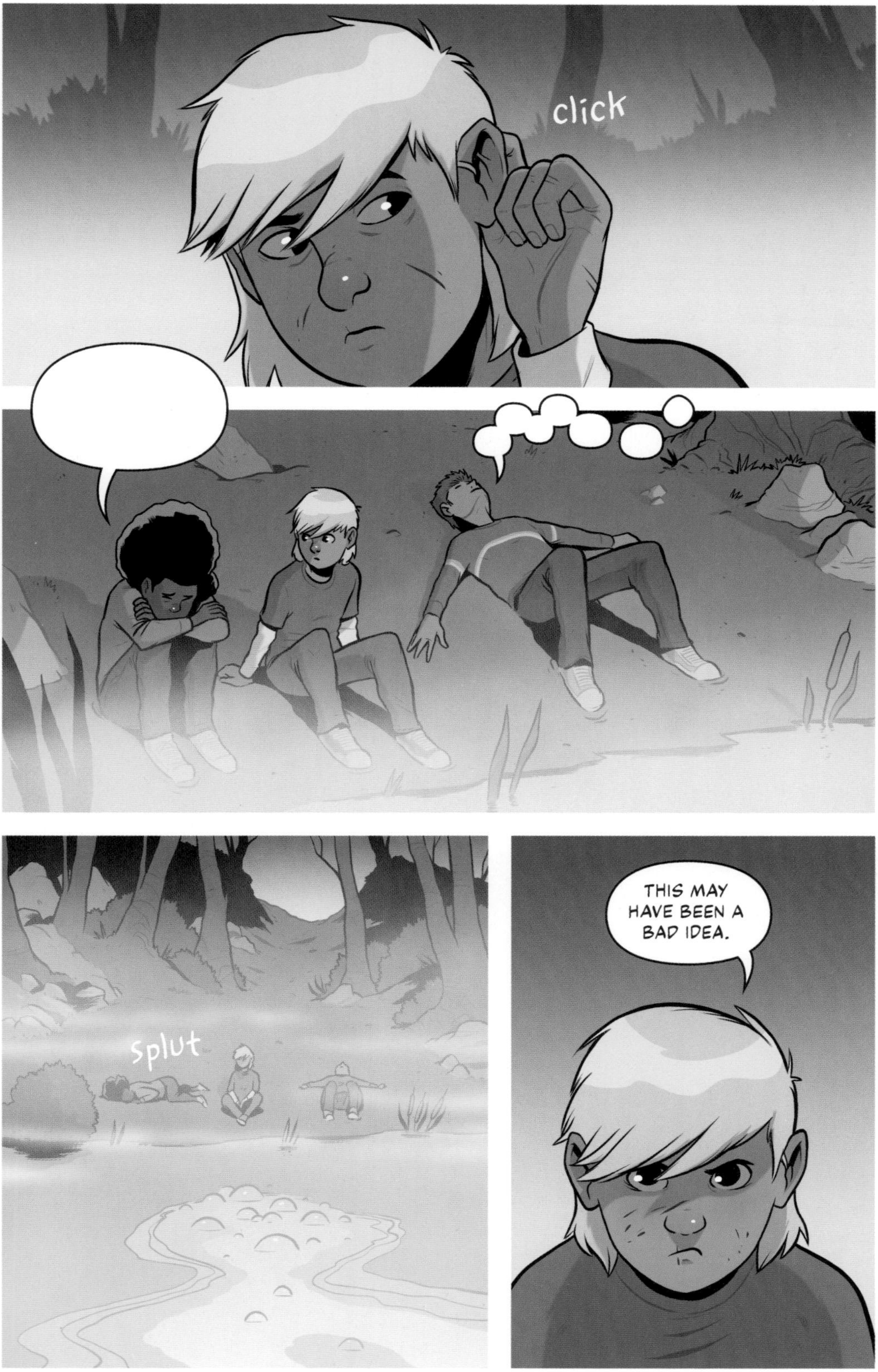
click
splut
THIS MAY HAVE BEEN A BAD IDEA.

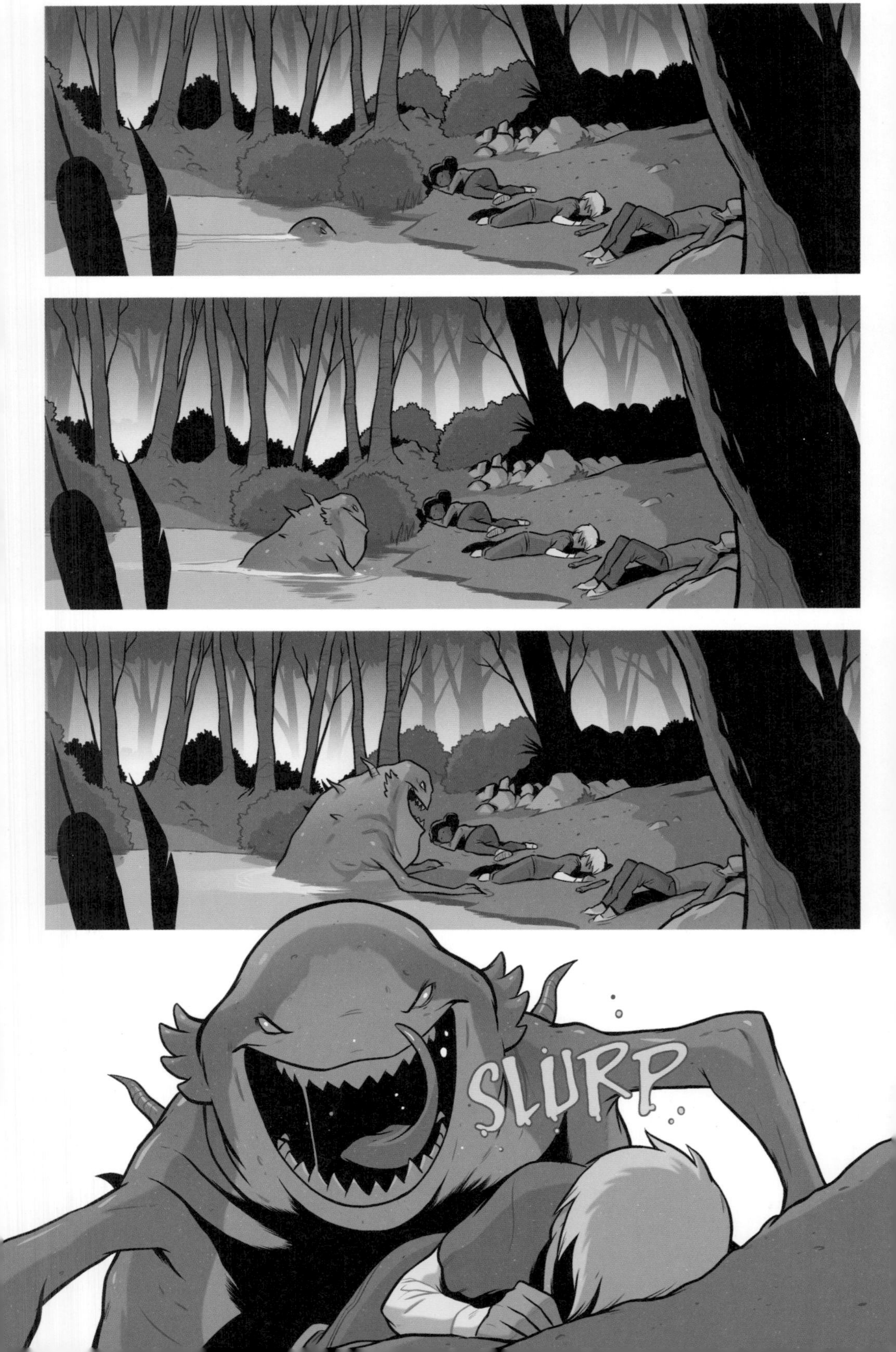
SLURP

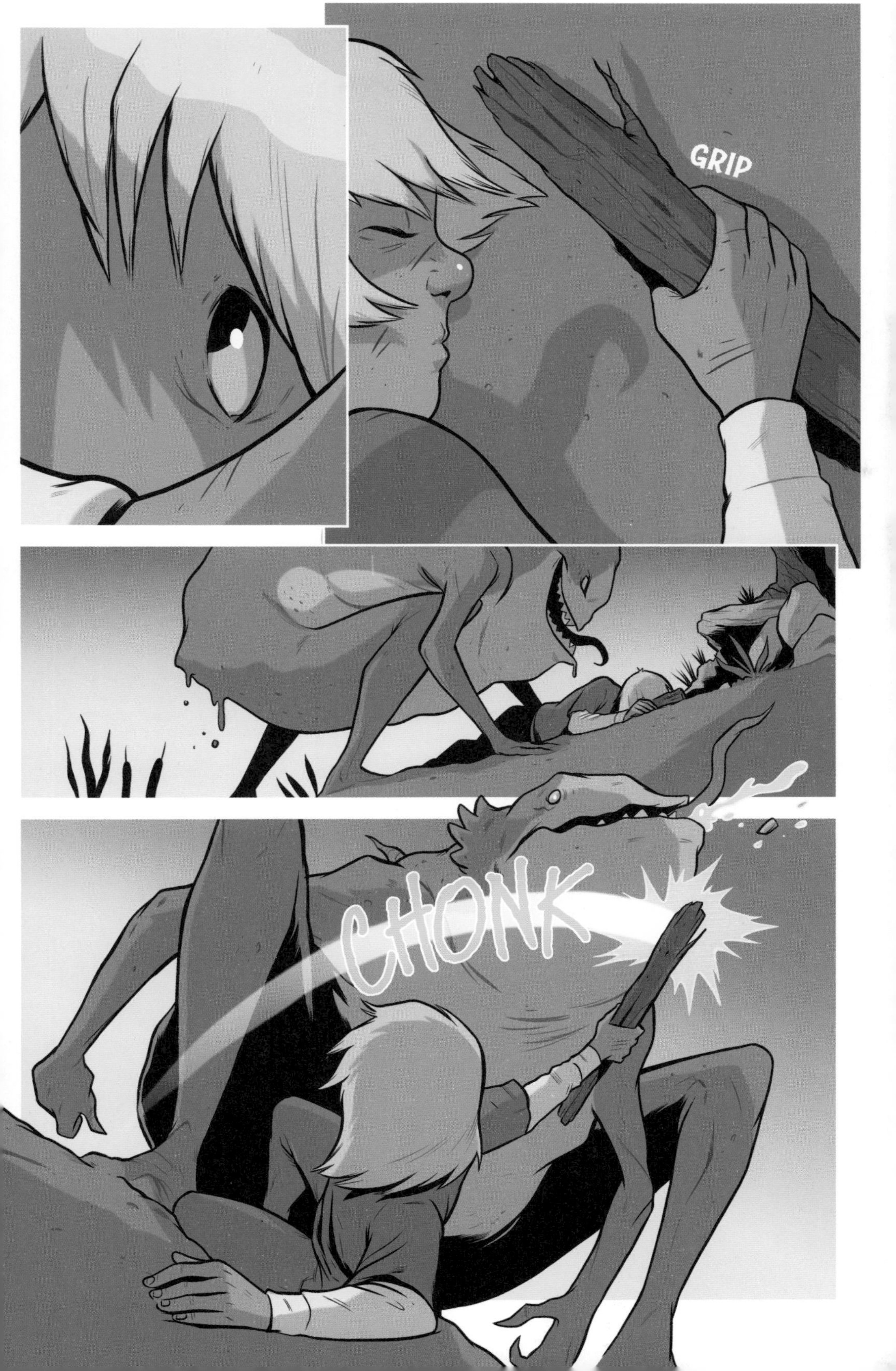
GRIP
CHONK

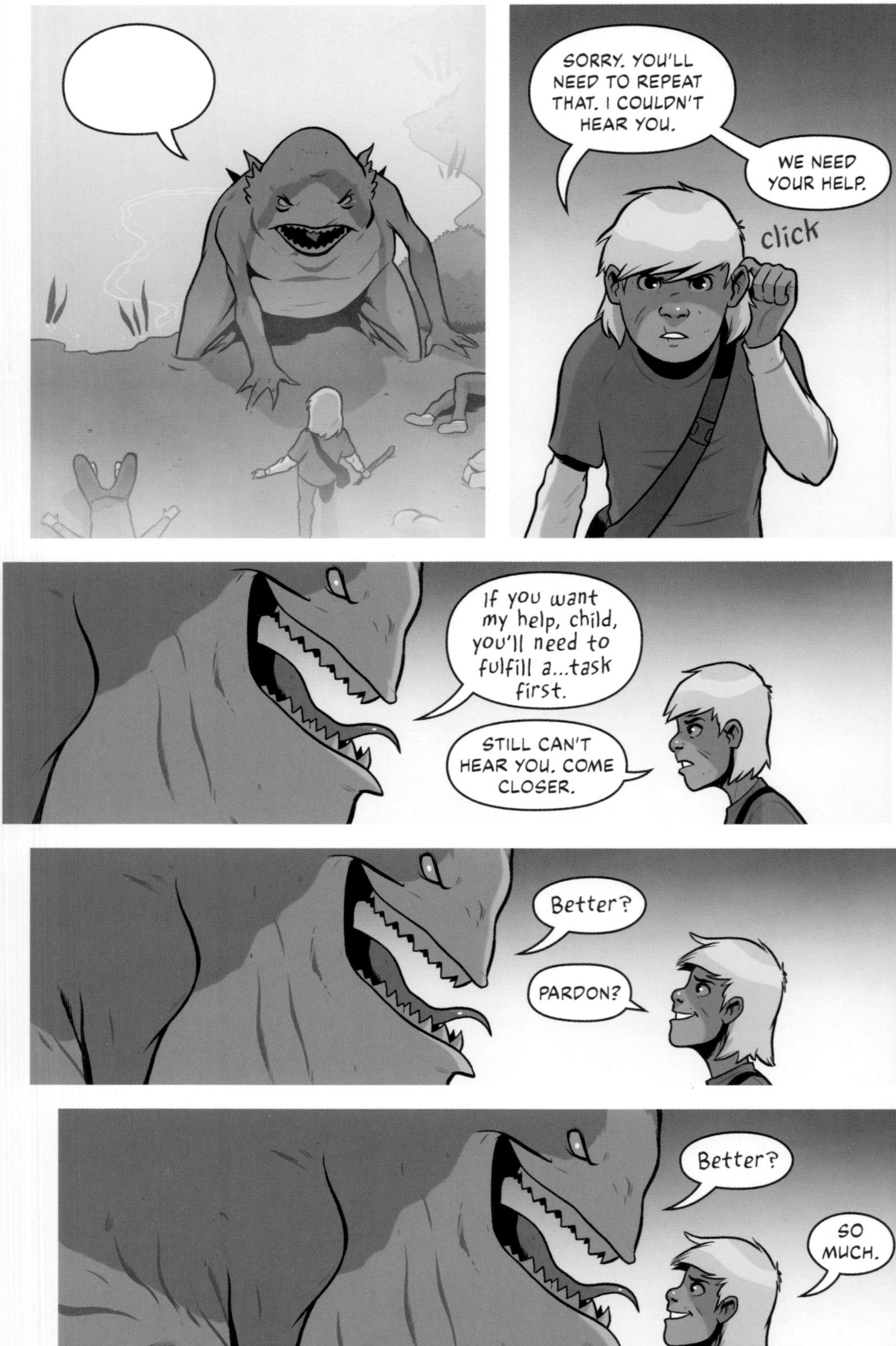
SORRY. YOU'LL NEED TO REPEAT THAT. I COULDN'T HEAR YOU.
WE NEED YOUR HELP.
click
If you want my help, child, you'll need to fulfill a...task first.
STILL CAN'T HEAR YOU. COME CLOSER.
Better?
PARDON?
Better?
SO MUCH.

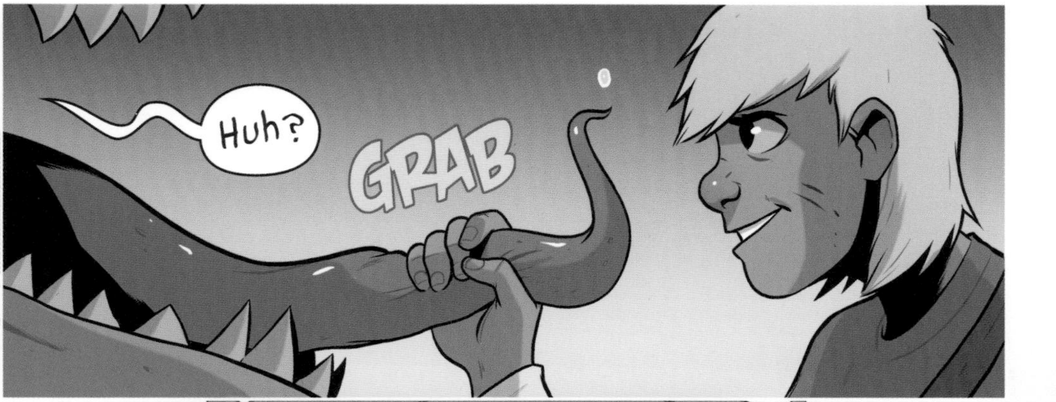
Huh?
GRAB

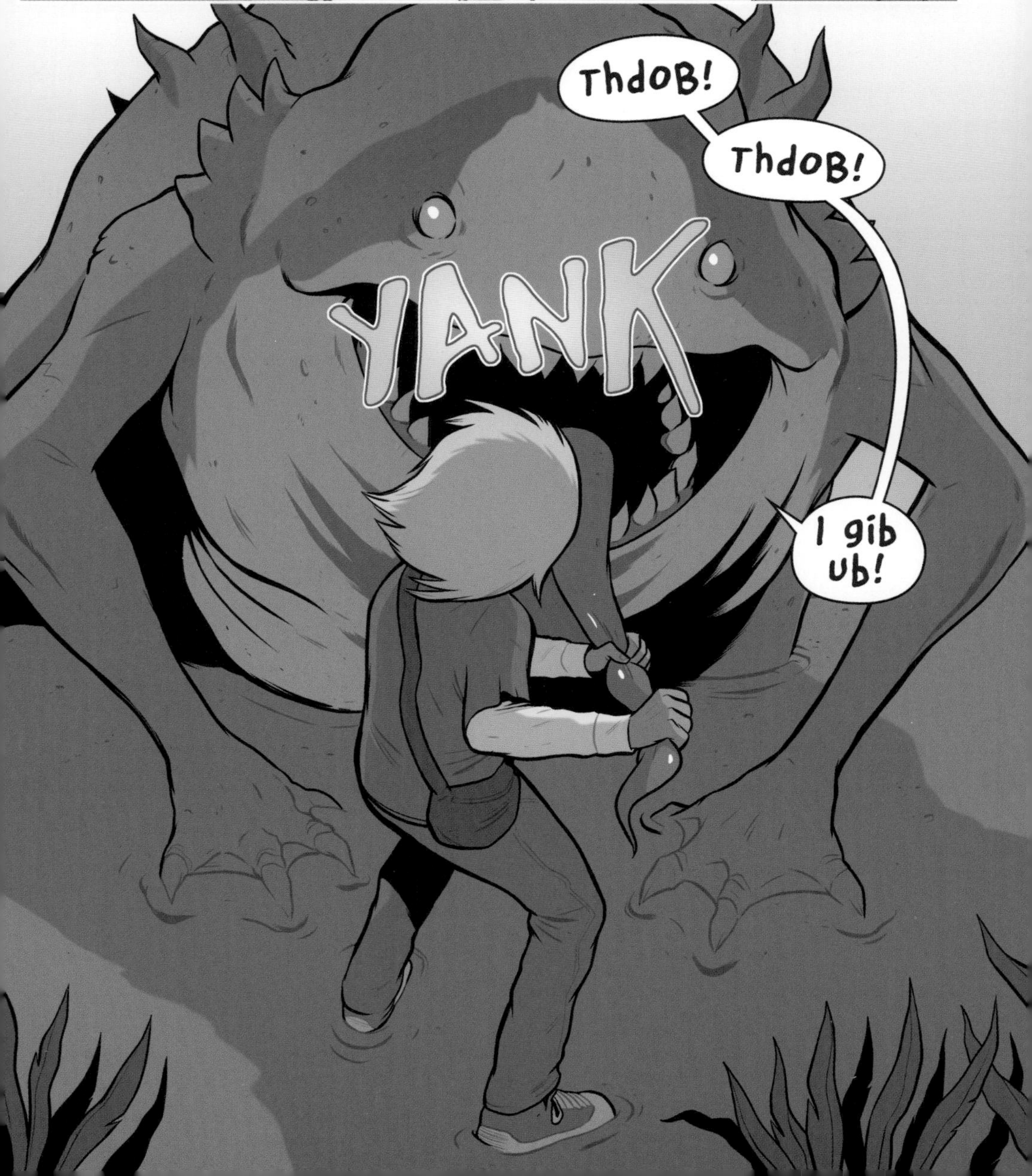
ThdoB!
ThdoB!
YANK
I gib ub!

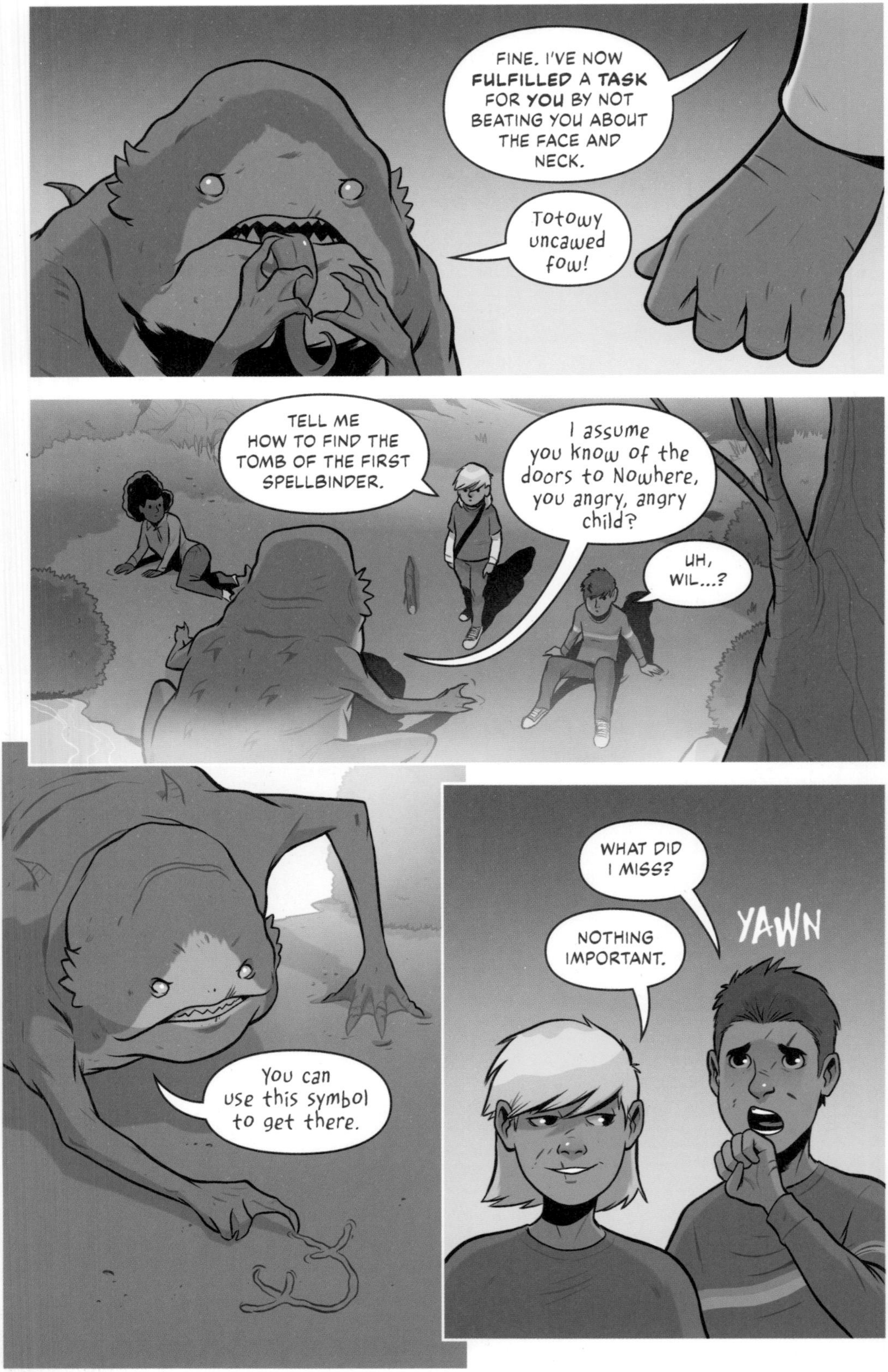
FINE. I'VE NOW **FULFILLED A TASK** FOR **YOU** BY NOT BEATING YOU ABOUT THE FACE AND NECK.
Totowy uncawed fow!
TELL ME HOW TO FIND THE TOMB OF THE FIRST SPELLBINDER.
I assume you know of the doors to Nowhere, you angry, angry child?
UH, WIL...?
You can use this symbol to get there.
WHAT DID I MISS?
YAWN
NOTHING IMPORTANT.

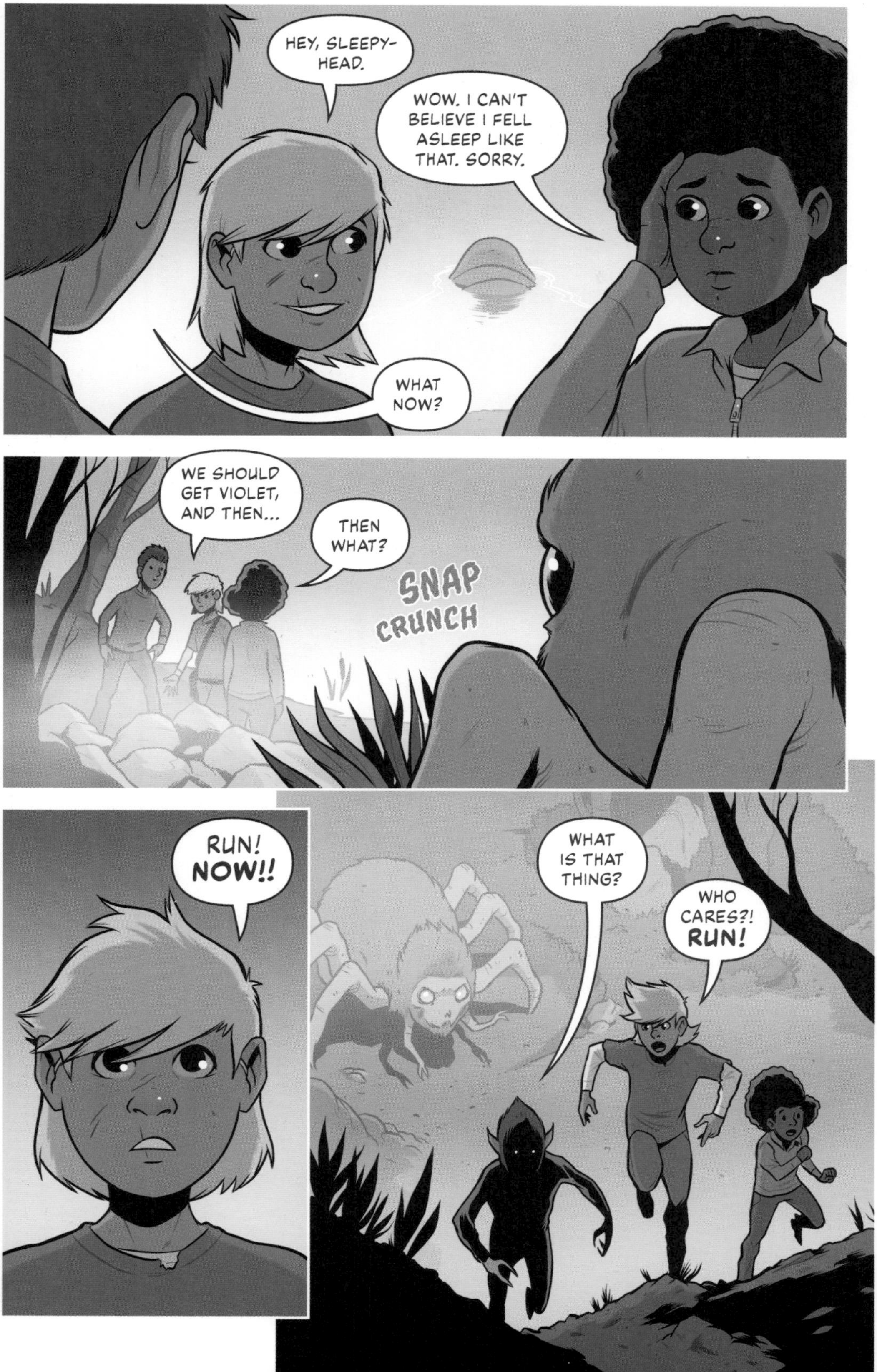
HEY, SLEEPY-HEAD.
WOW. I CAN'T BELIEVE I FELL ASLEEP LIKE THAT. SORRY.
WHAT NOW?
WE SHOULD GET VIOLET, AND THEN...
THEN WHAT?
SNAP
CRUNCH
RUN! NOW!!
WHAT IS THAT THING?
WHO CARES?! RUN!

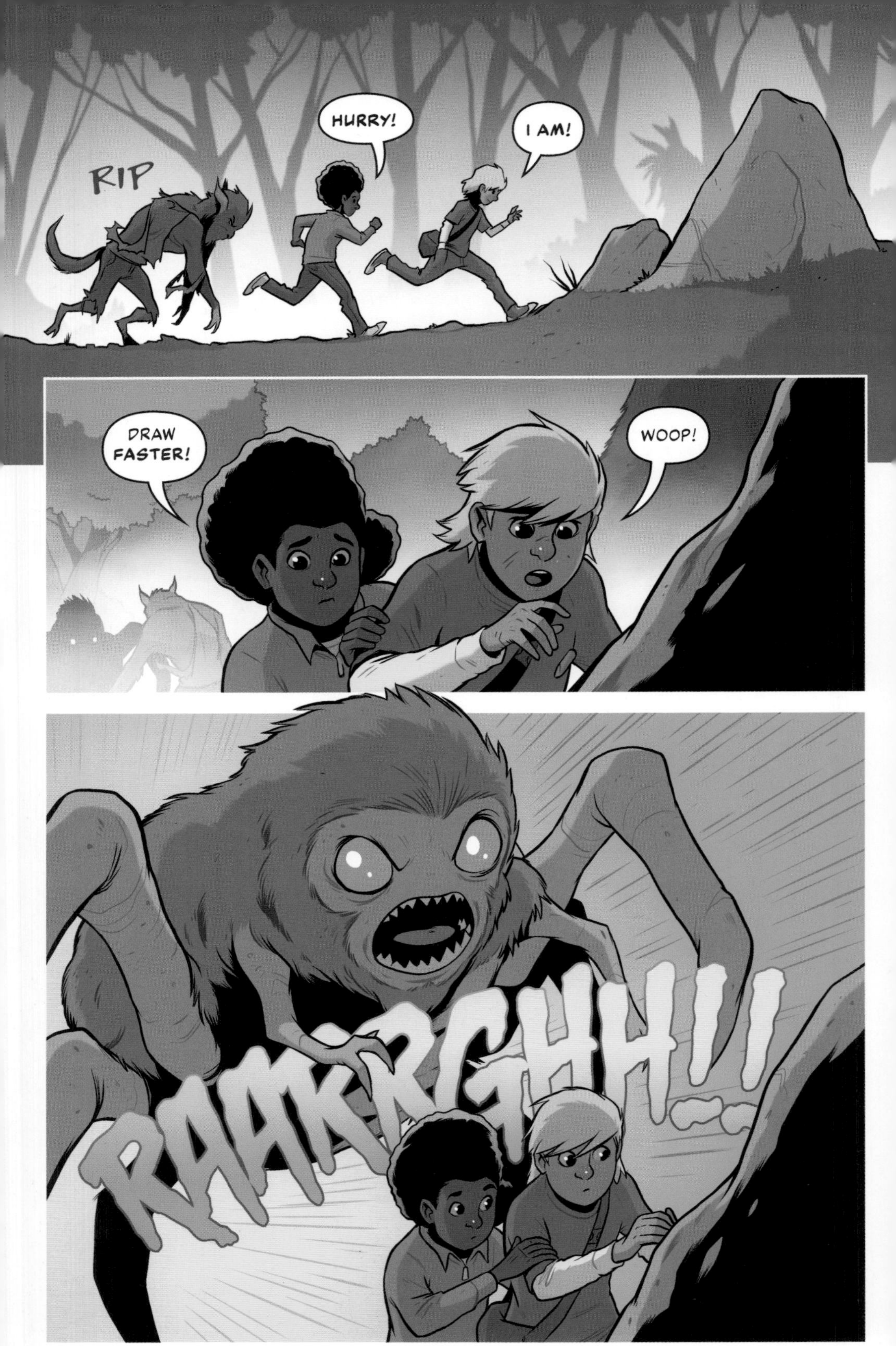
RIP
HURRY!
I AM!
DRAW FASTER!
WOOP!
RAAARGHH!!

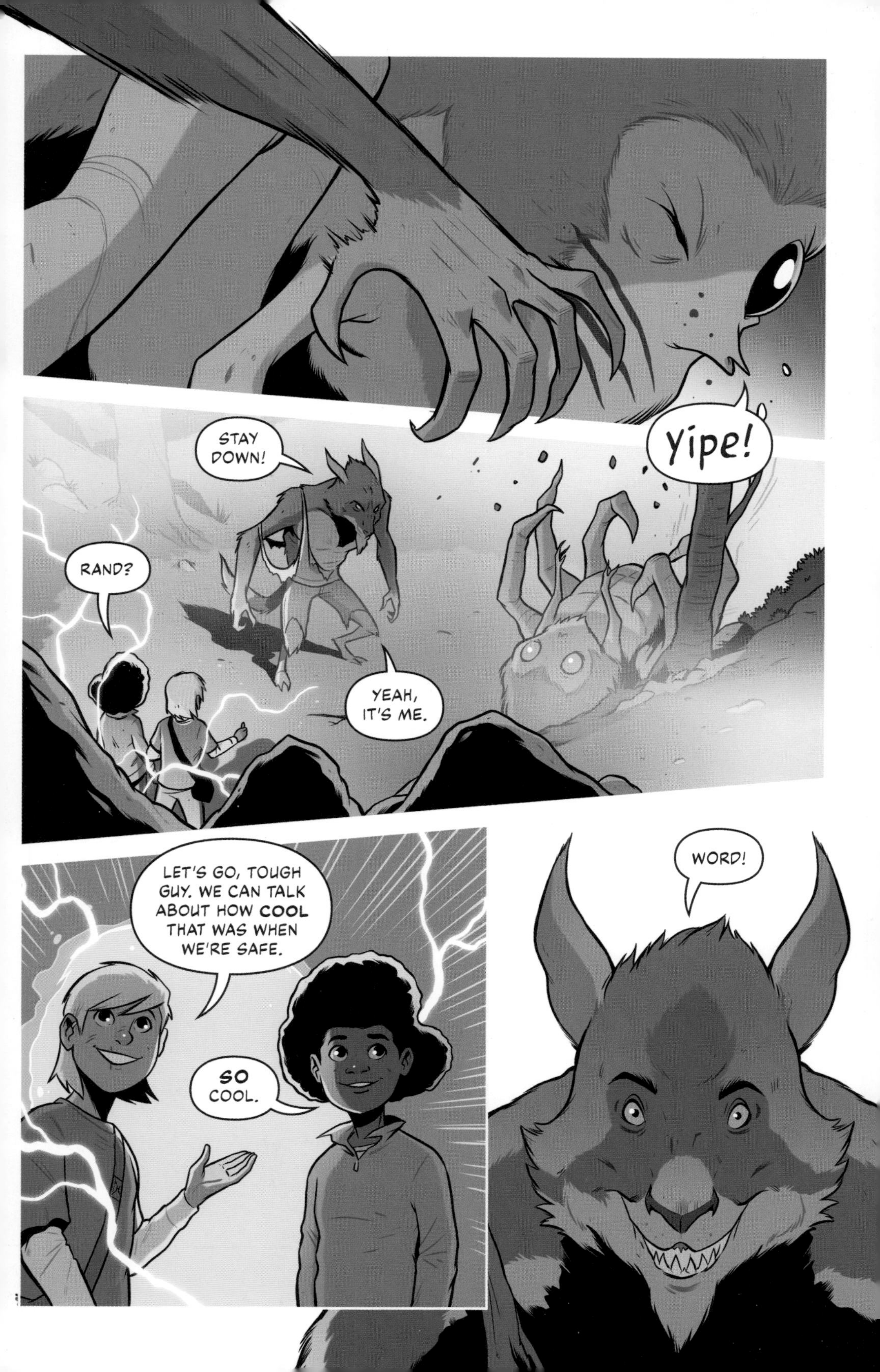
yipe!
STAY DOWN!
RAND?
YEAH, IT'S ME.
LET'S GO, TOUGH GUY. WE CAN TALK ABOUT HOW COOL THAT WAS WHEN WE'RE SAFE.
SO COOL.
WORD!

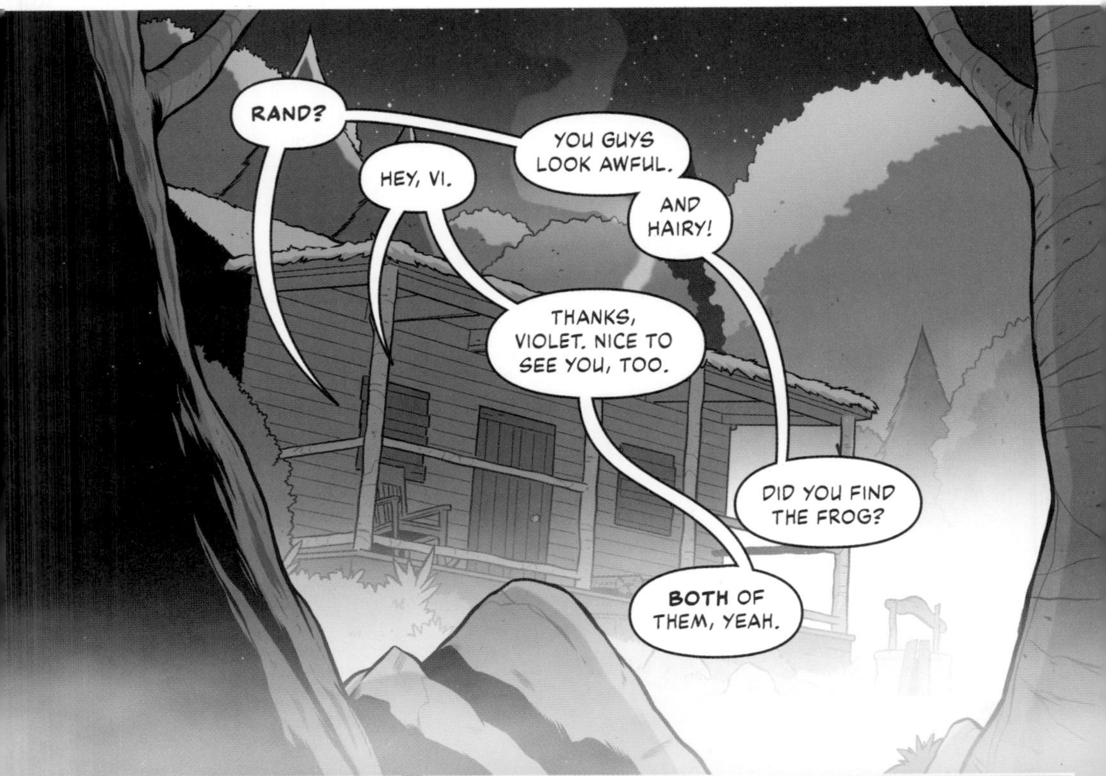
RAND?
YOU GUYS LOOK AWFUL.
AND HAIRY!
HEY, VI.
THANKS, VIOLET. NICE TO SEE YOU, TOO.
DID YOU FIND THE FROG?
BOTH OF THEM, YEAH.

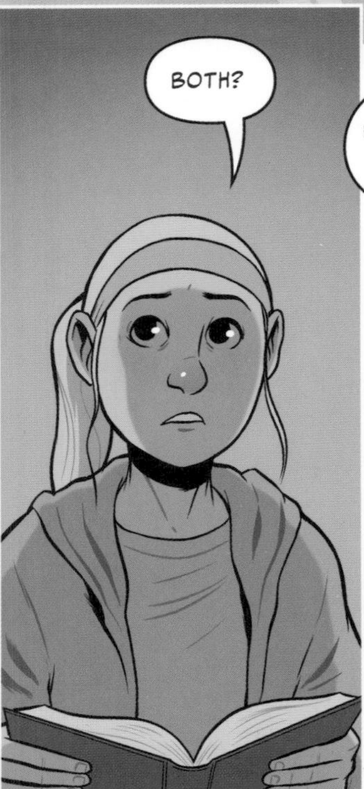
BOTH?

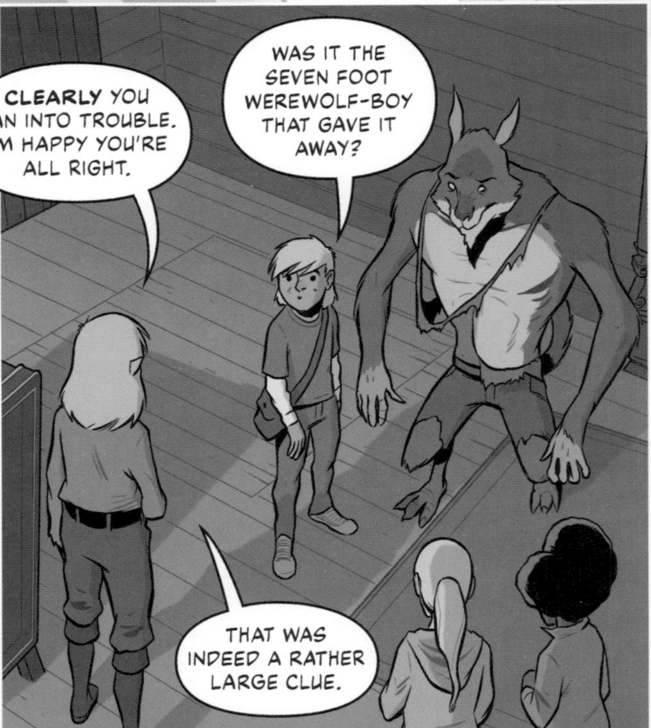
CLEARLY YOU RAN INTO TROUBLE. I'M HAPPY YOU'RE ALL RIGHT.
WAS IT THE SEVEN FOOT WEREWOLF-BOY THAT GAVE IT AWAY?
THAT WAS INDEED A RATHER LARGE CLUE.

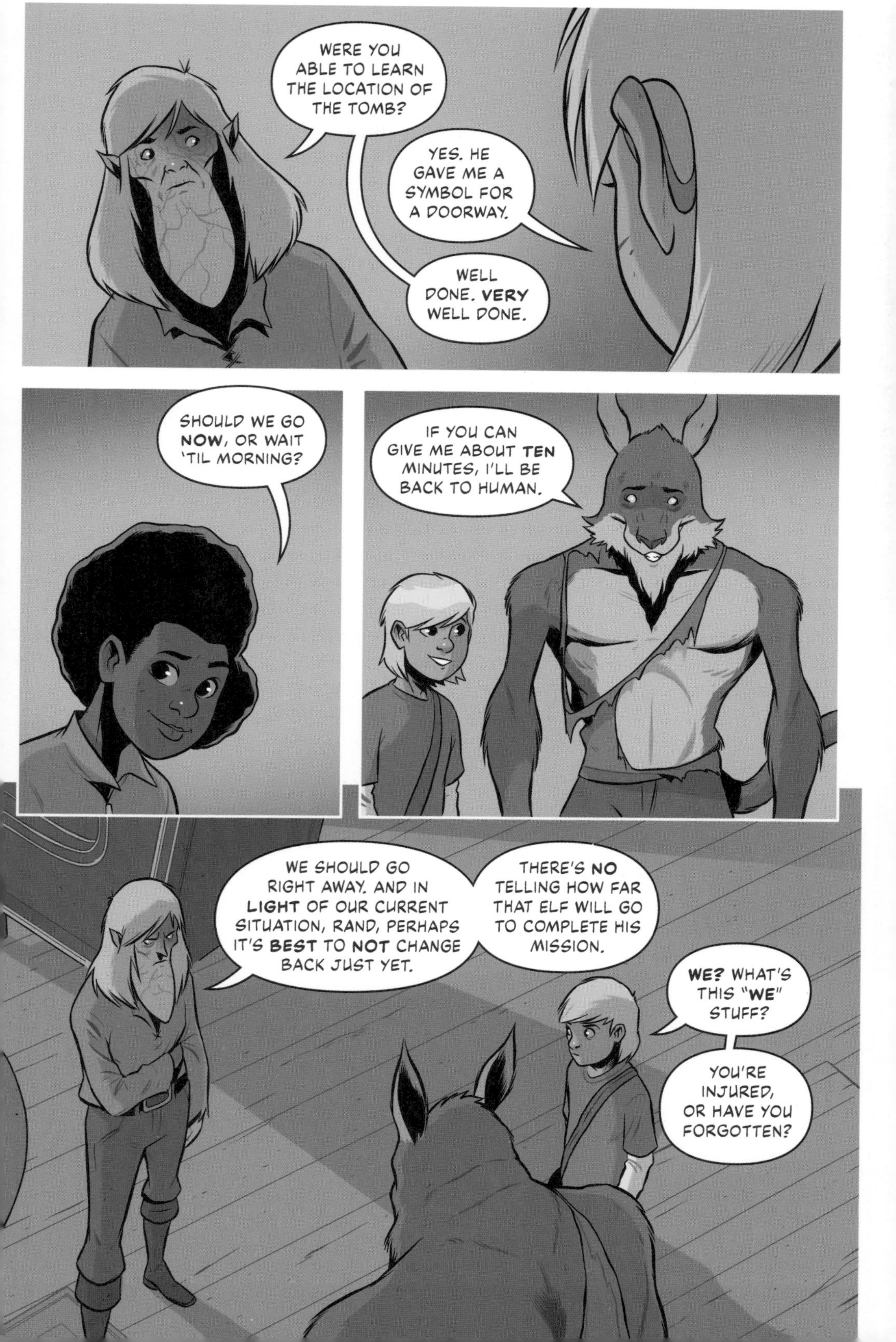
WERE YOU ABLE TO LEARN THE LOCATION OF THE TOMB?
YES. HE GAVE ME A SYMBOL FOR A DOORWAY.
WELL DONE. **VERY** WELL DONE.
SHOULD WE GO **NOW**, OR WAIT 'TIL MORNING?
IF YOU CAN GIVE ME ABOUT **TEN** MINUTES, I'LL BE BACK TO HUMAN.
WE SHOULD GO RIGHT AWAY. AND IN **LIGHT** OF OUR CURRENT SITUATION, RAND, PERHAPS IT'S **BEST** TO **NOT** CHANGE BACK JUST YET.
THERE'S **NO** TELLING HOW FAR THAT ELF WILL GO TO COMPLETE HIS MISSION.
WE? WHAT'S THIS "**WE**" STUFF?
YOU'RE INJURED, OR HAVE YOU FORGOTTEN?

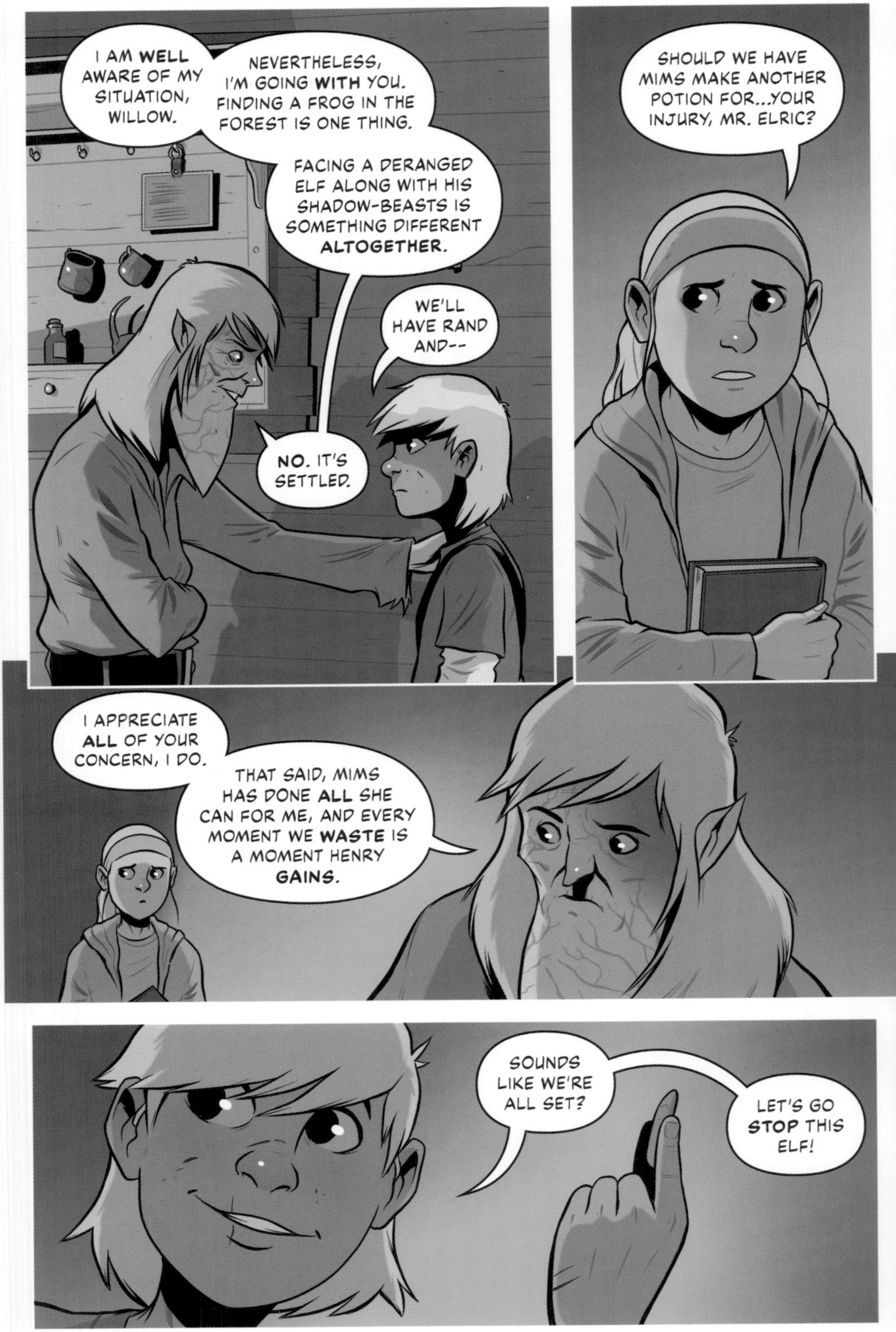
I AM **WELL** AWARE OF MY SITUATION, WILLOW.
NEVERTHELESS, I'M GOING **WITH** YOU. FINDING A FROG IN THE FOREST IS ONE THING.
FACING A DERANGED ELF ALONG WITH HIS SHADOW-BEASTS IS SOMETHING DIFFERENT **ALTOGETHER.**
WE'LL HAVE RAND AND--
NO. IT'S SETTLED.
SHOULD WE HAVE MIMS MAKE ANOTHER POTION FOR...YOUR INJURY, MR. ELRIC?
I APPRECIATE **ALL** OF YOUR CONCERN, I DO.
THAT SAID, MIMS HAS DONE **ALL** SHE CAN FOR ME, AND EVERY MOMENT WE **WASTE** IS A MOMENT HENRY **GAINS.**
SOUNDS LIKE WE'RE ALL SET?
LET'S GO **STOP** THIS ELF!

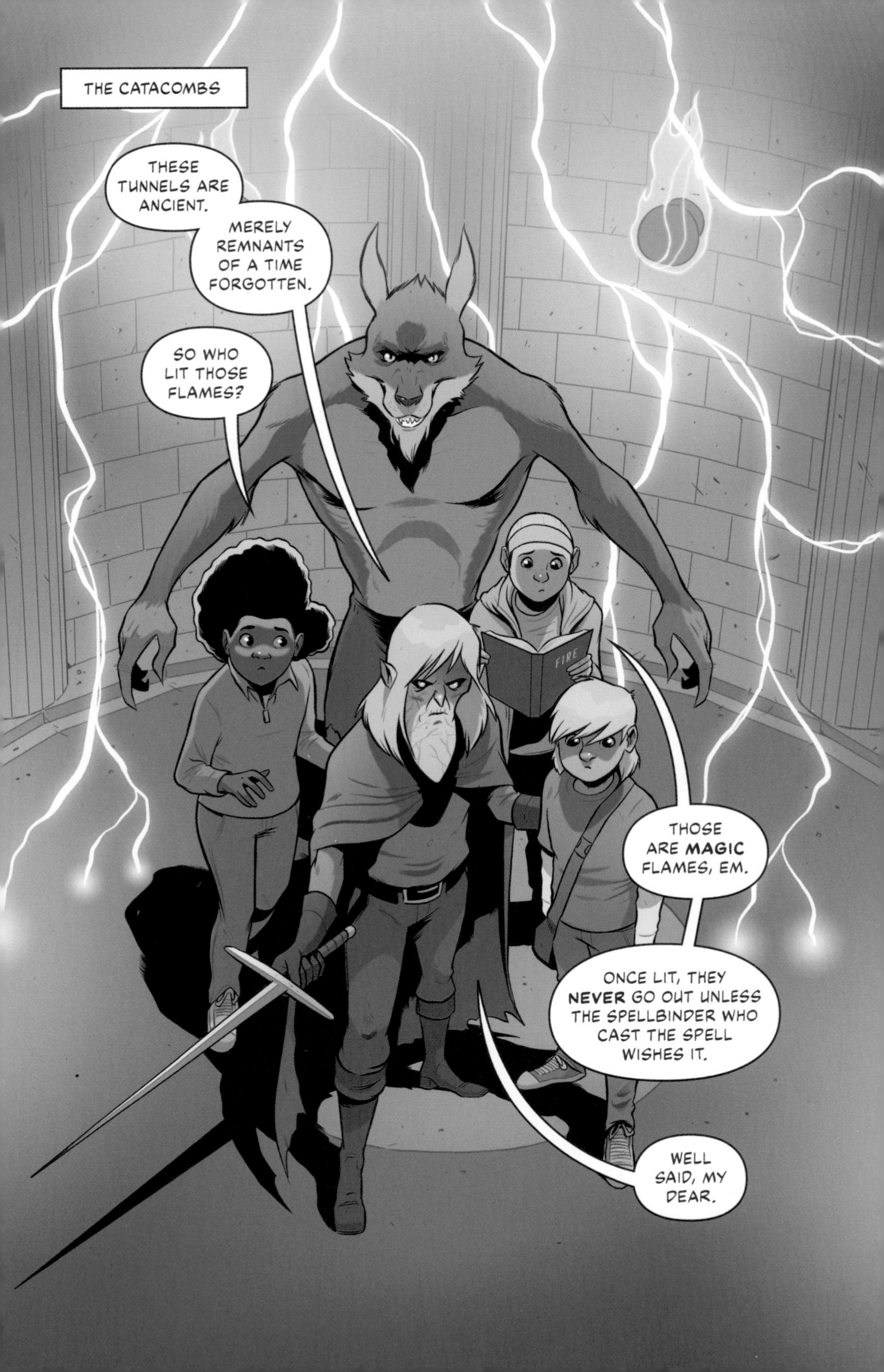
THE CATACOMBS
THESE TUNNELS ARE ANCIENT.
MERELY REMNANTS OF A TIME FORGOTTEN.
SO WHO LIT THOSE FLAMES?
FIRE
THOSE ARE **MAGIC** FLAMES, EM.
ONCE LIT, THEY **NEVER** GO OUT UNLESS THE SPELLBINDER WHO CAST THE SPELL WISHES IT.
WELL SAID, MY DEAR.

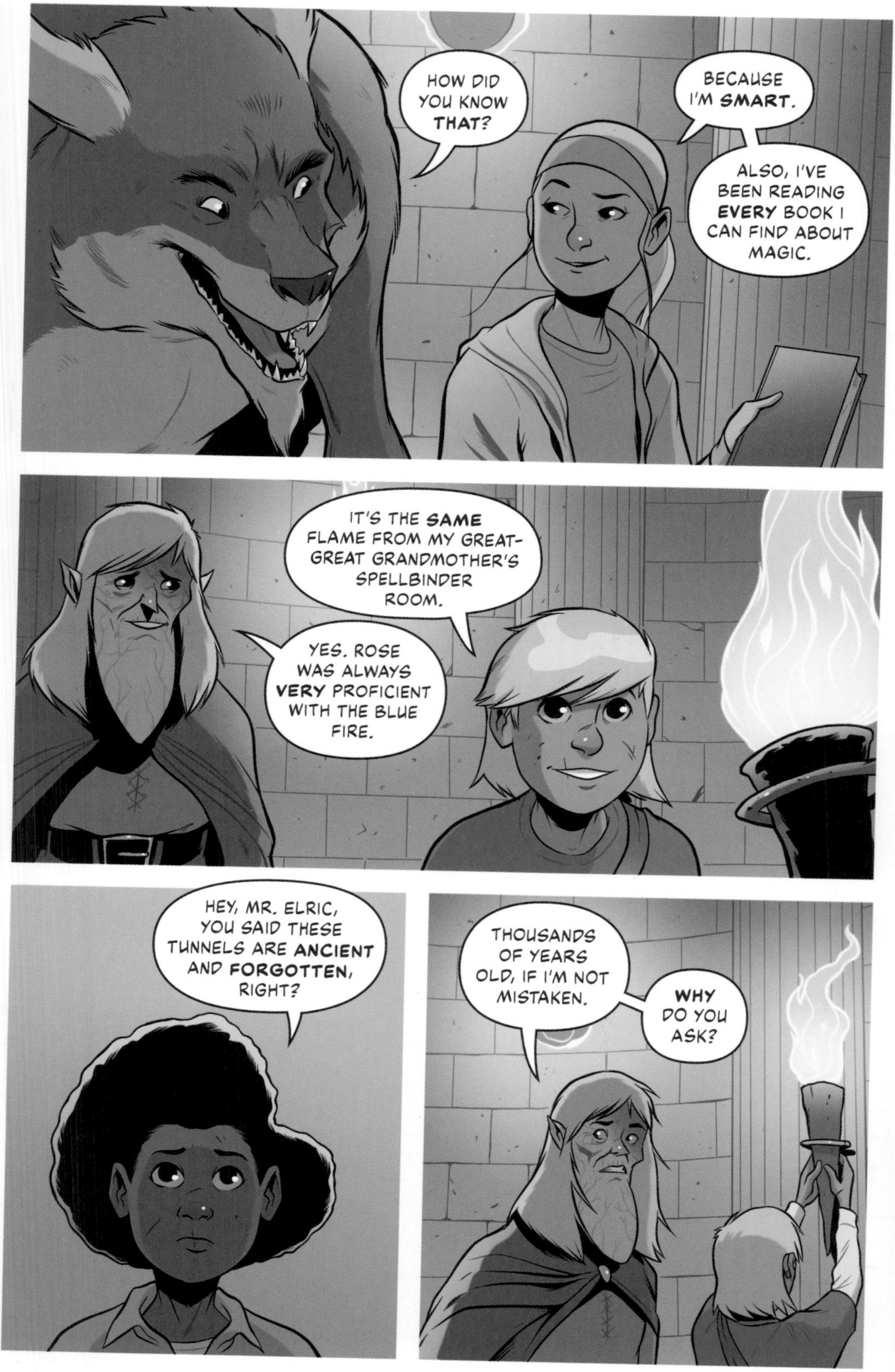
HOW DID YOU KNOW THAT?
BECAUSE I'M SMART.
ALSO, I'VE BEEN READING EVERY BOOK I CAN FIND ABOUT MAGIC.
IT'S THE SAME FLAME FROM MY GREAT-GREAT GRANDMOTHER'S SPELLBINDER ROOM.
YES. ROSE WAS ALWAYS VERY PROFICIENT WITH THE BLUE FIRE.
HEY, MR. ELRIC, YOU SAID THESE TUNNELS ARE ANCIENT AND FORGOTTEN, RIGHT?
THOUSANDS OF YEARS OLD, IF I'M NOT MISTAKEN.
WHY DO YOU ASK?

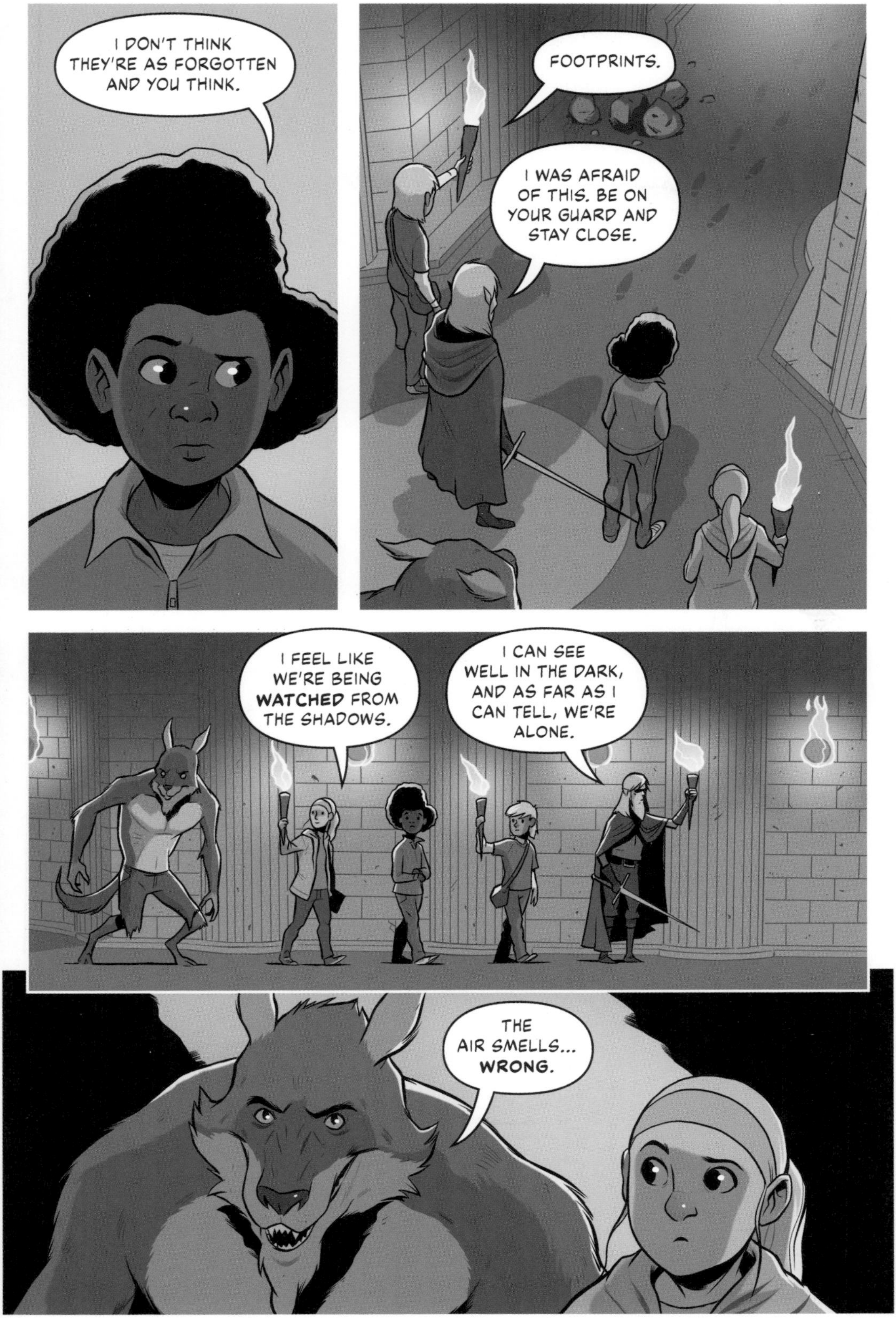

I DON'T THINK THEY'RE AS FORGOTTEN AND YOU THINK.
FOOTPRINTS.
I WAS AFRAID OF THIS. BE ON YOUR GUARD AND STAY CLOSE.
I FEEL LIKE WE'RE BEING **WATCHED** FROM THE SHADOWS.
I CAN SEE WELL IN THE DARK, AND AS FAR AS I CAN TELL, WE'RE ALONE.
THE AIR SMELLS... **WRONG.**

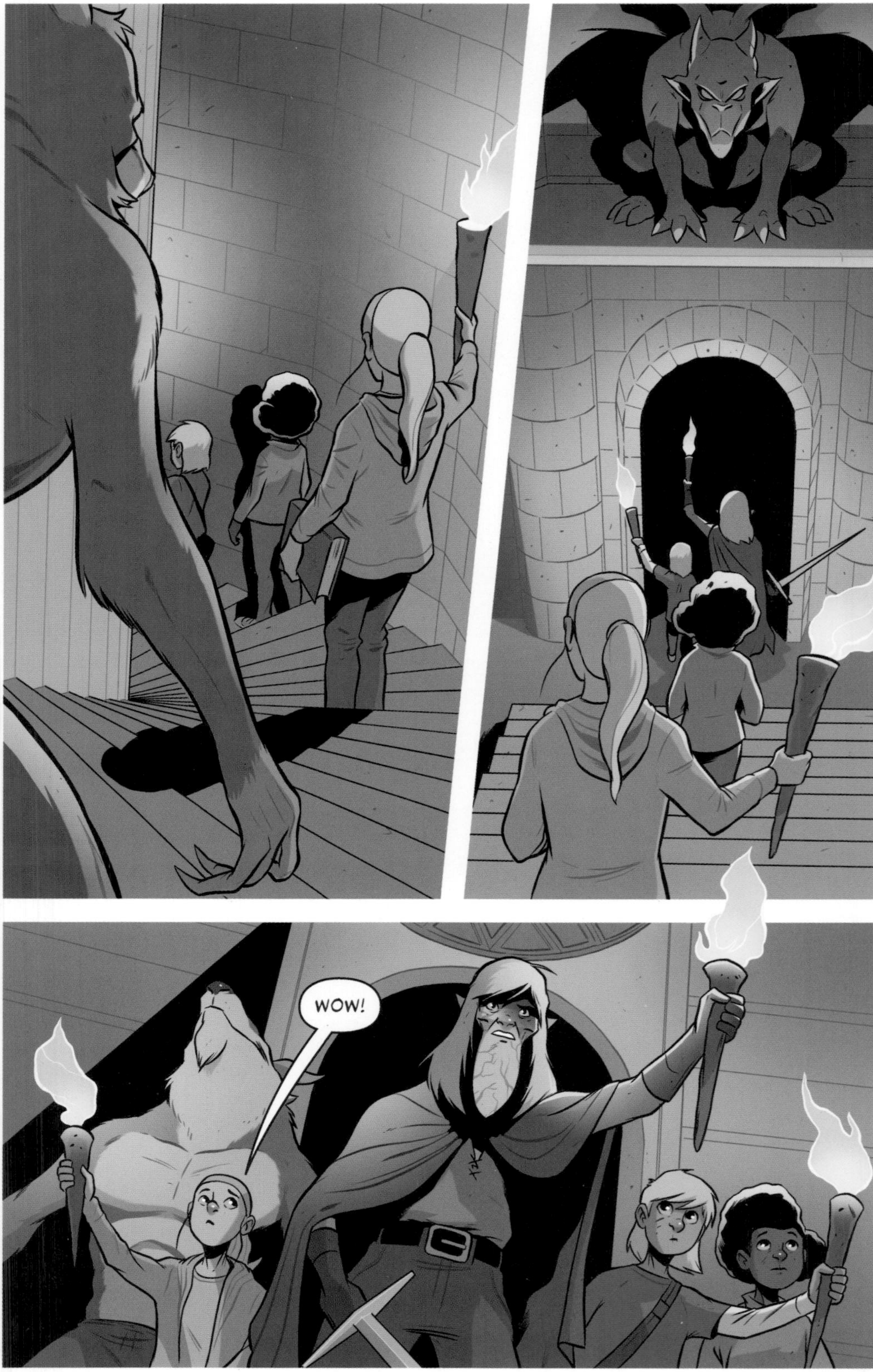
WOW!

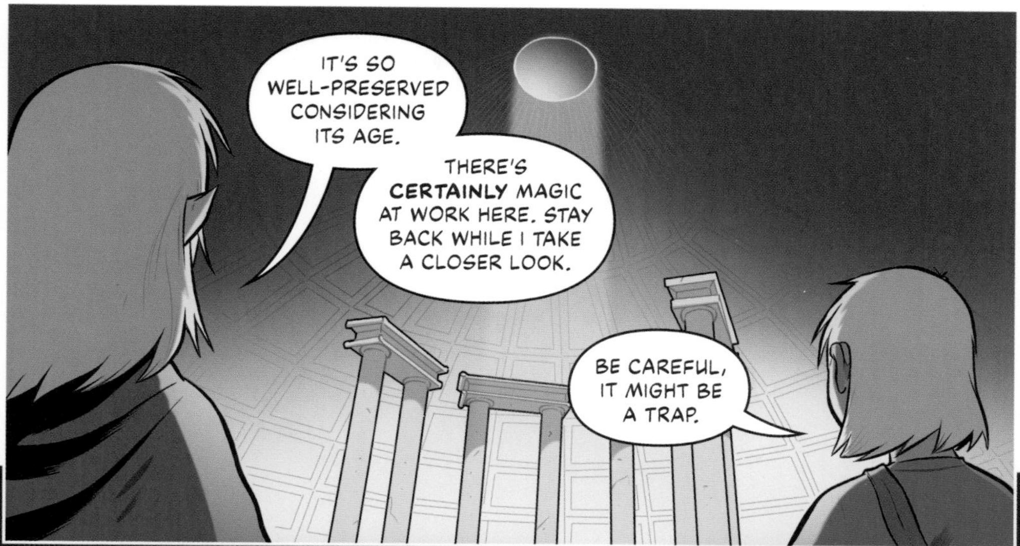
IT'S SO WELL-PRESERVED CONSIDERING ITS AGE.
THERE'S **CERTAINLY** MAGIC AT WORK HERE. STAY BACK WHILE I TAKE A CLOSER LOOK.
BE CAREFUL, IT MIGHT BE A TRAP.

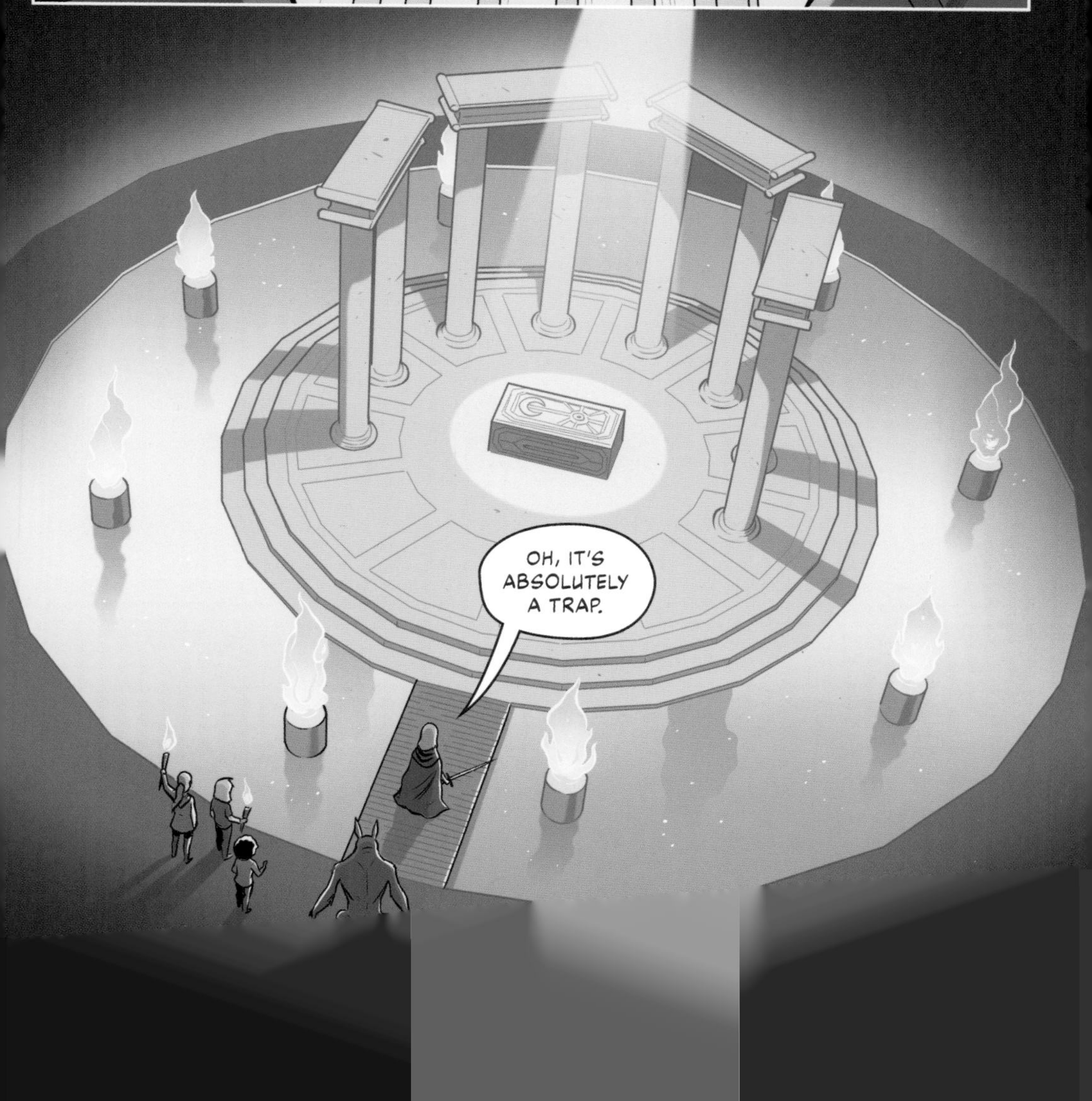
OH, IT'S ABSOLUTELY A TRAP.

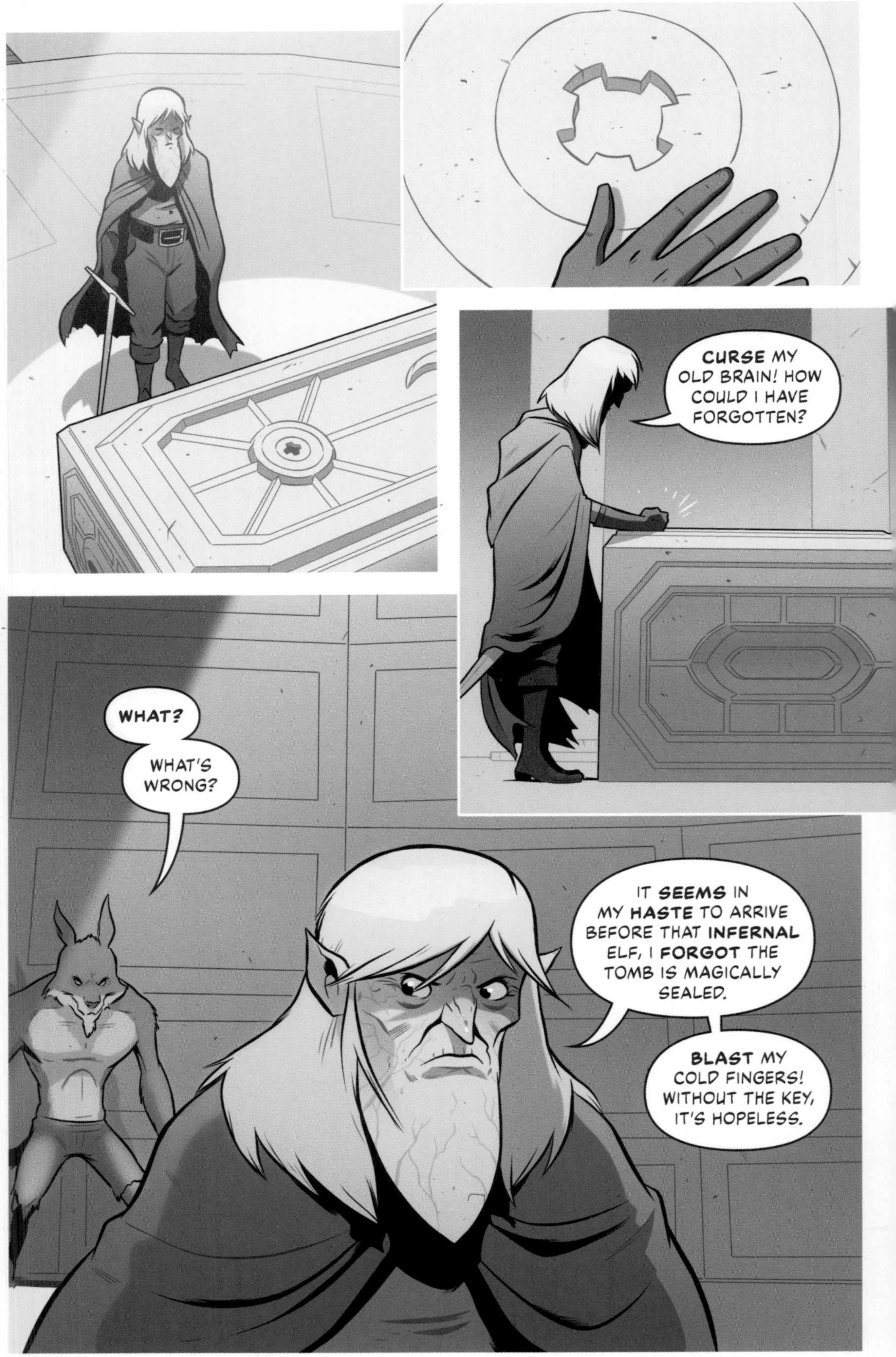
CURSE MY OLD BRAIN! HOW COULD I HAVE FORGOTTEN?
WHAT?
WHAT'S WRONG?
IT SEEMS IN MY HASTE TO ARRIVE BEFORE THAT INFERNAL ELF, I FORGOT THE TOMB IS MAGICALLY SEALED.
BLAST MY COLD FINGERS! WITHOUT THE KEY, IT'S HOPELESS.

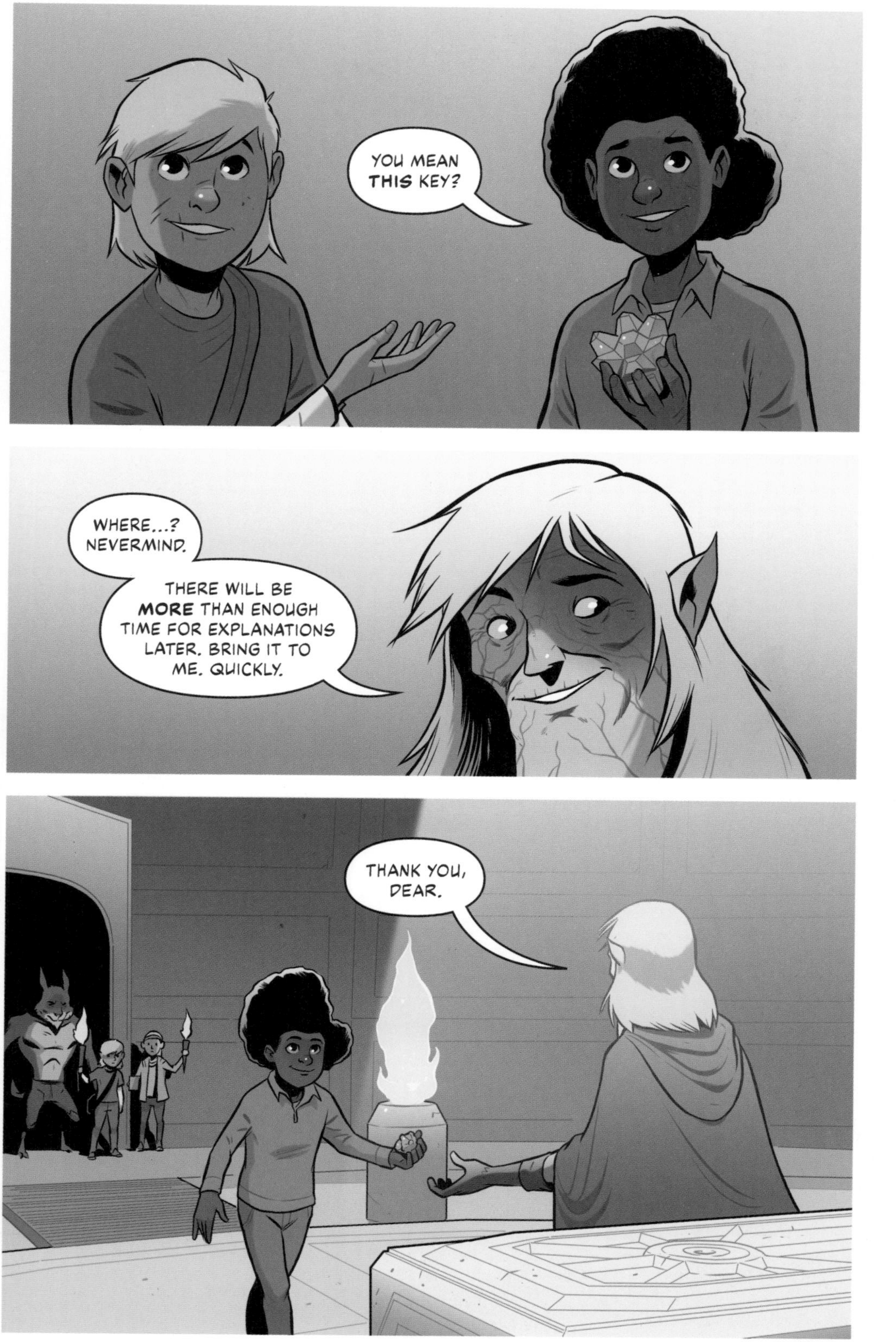
YOU MEAN THIS KEY?
WHERE...? NEVERMIND.
THERE WILL BE MORE THAN ENOUGH TIME FOR EXPLANATIONS LATER. BRING IT TO ME. QUICKLY.
THANK YOU, DEAR.

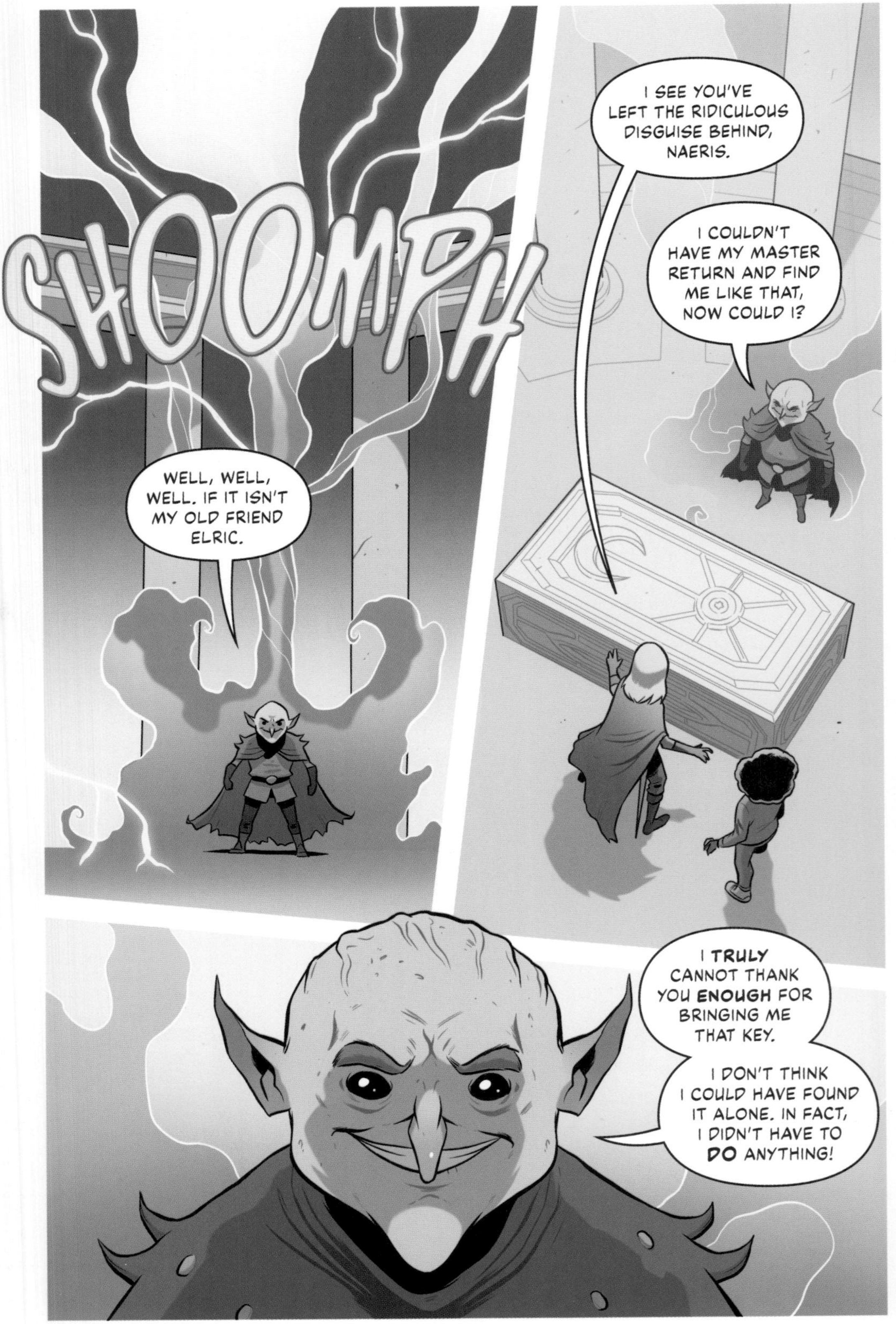

SHOOMPH
WELL, WELL, WELL. IF IT ISN'T MY OLD FRIEND ELRIC.
I SEE YOU'VE LEFT THE RIDICULOUS DISGUISE BEHIND, NAERIS.
I COULDN'T HAVE MY MASTER RETURN AND FIND ME LIKE THAT, NOW COULD I?
I **TRULY** CANNOT THANK YOU **ENOUGH** FOR BRINGING ME THAT KEY.
I DON'T THINK I COULD HAVE FOUND IT ALONE. IN FACT, I DIDN'T HAVE TO **DO** ANYTHING!

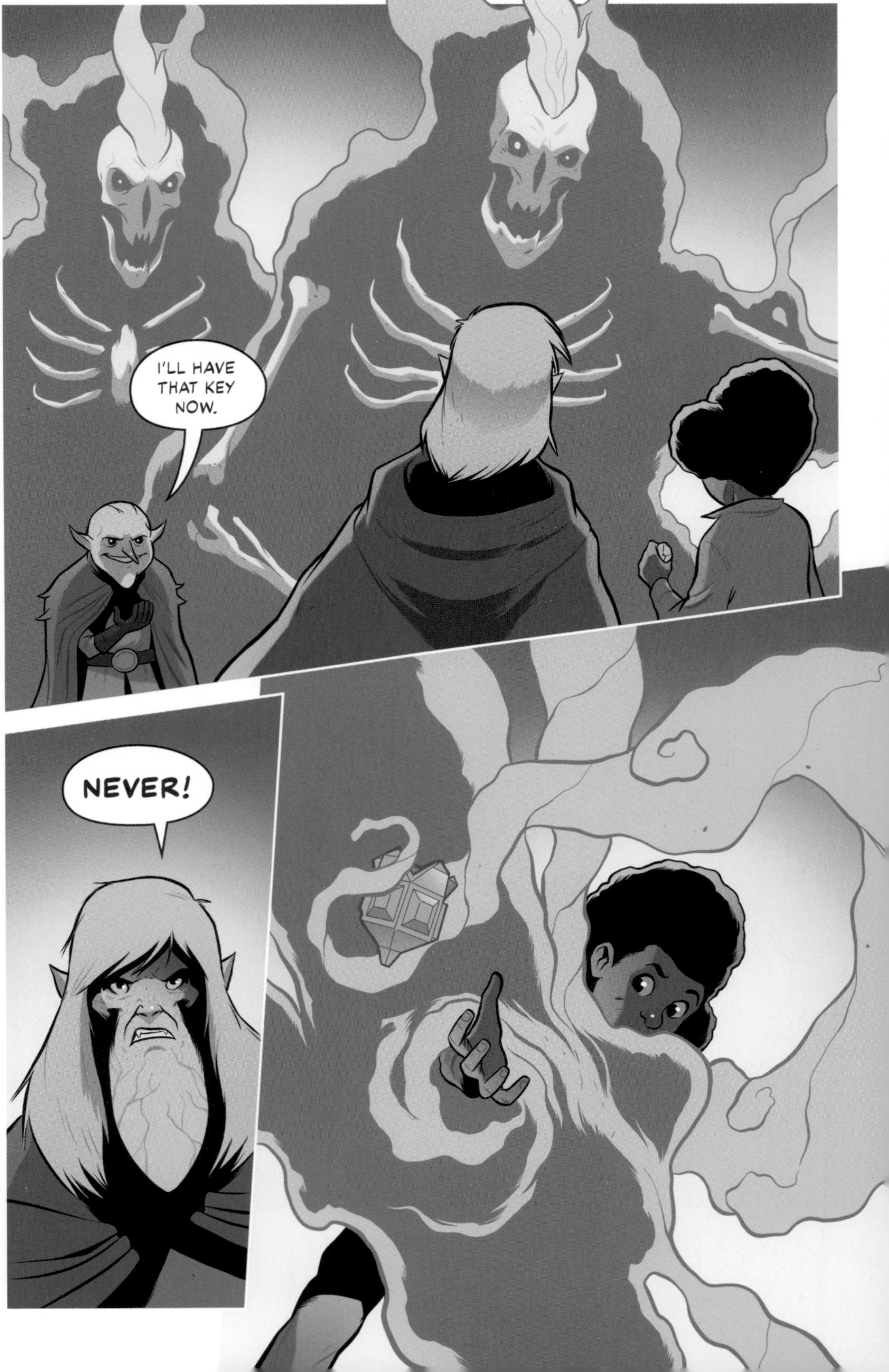
I'LL HAVE THAT KEY NOW.
NEVER!

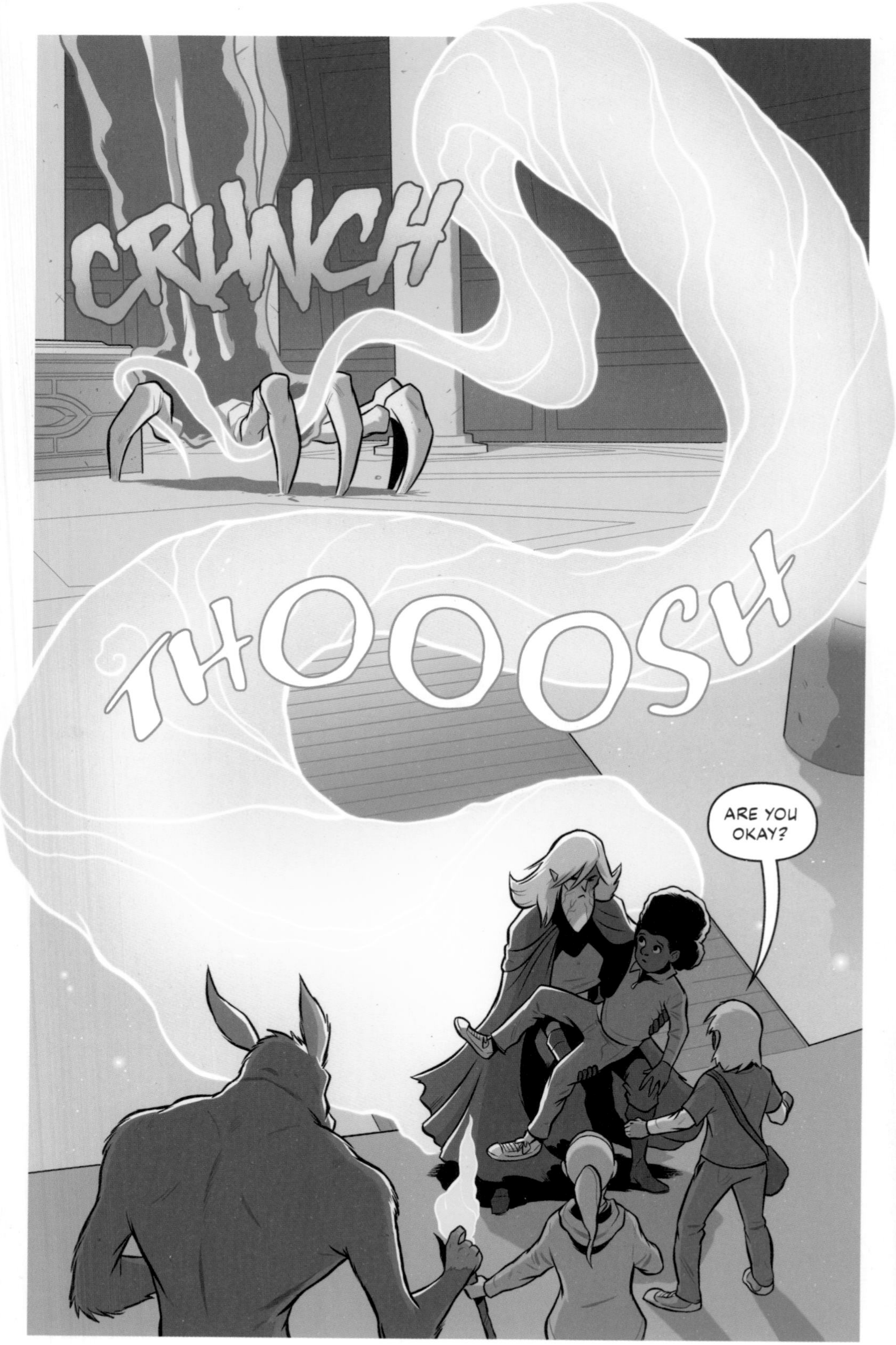
CRUNCH
THOOOSH
ARE YOU OKAY?

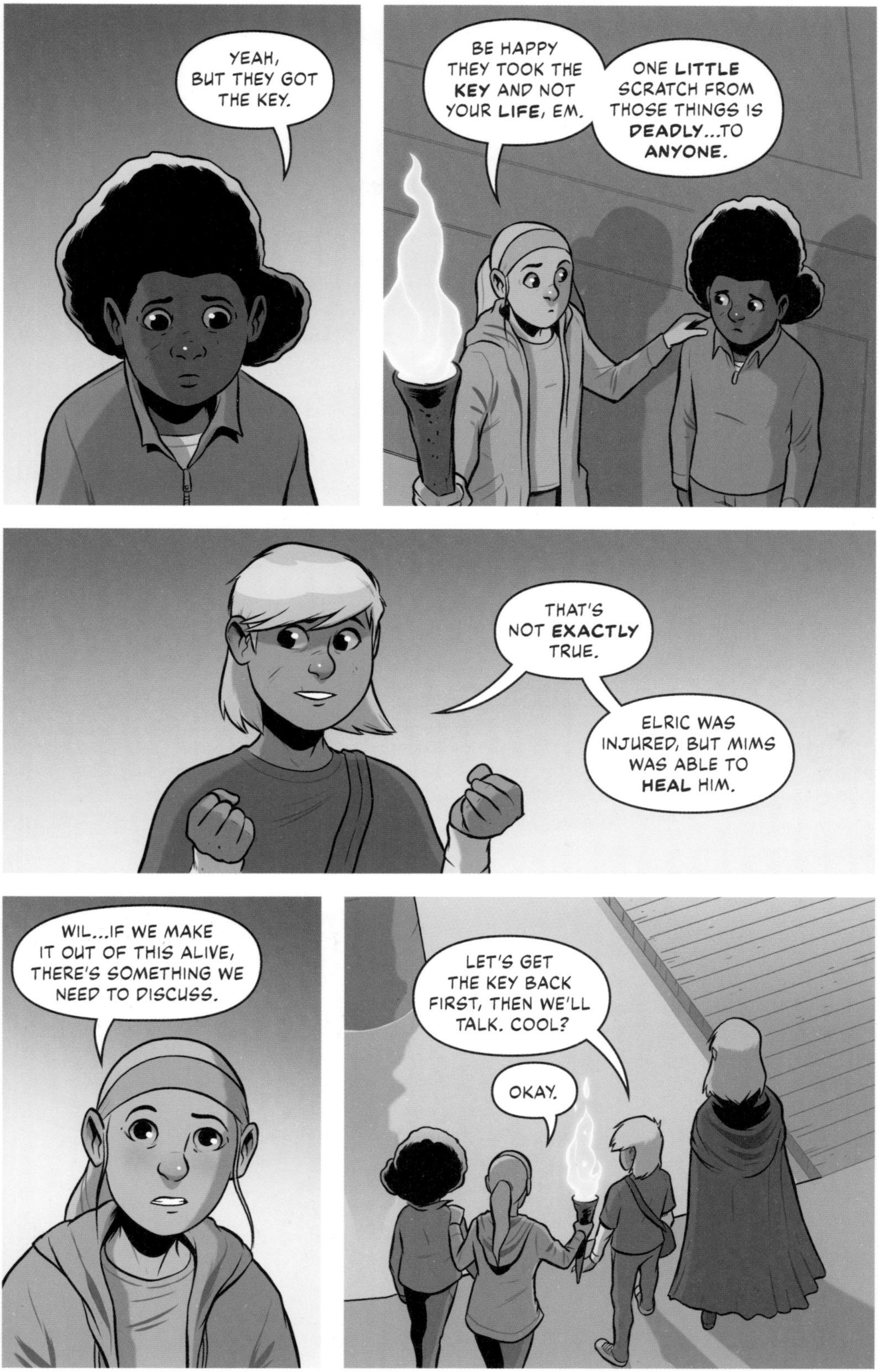
YEAH, BUT THEY GOT THE KEY.
BE HAPPY THEY TOOK THE KEY AND NOT YOUR LIFE, EM.
ONE LITTLE SCRATCH FROM THOSE THINGS IS DEADLY...TO ANYONE.
THAT'S NOT EXACTLY TRUE.
ELRIC WAS INJURED, BUT MIMS WAS ABLE TO HEAL HIM.
WIL...IF WE MAKE IT OUT OF THIS ALIVE, THERE'S SOMETHING WE NEED TO DISCUSS.
LET'S GET THE KEY BACK FIRST, THEN WE'LL TALK. COOL?
OKAY.

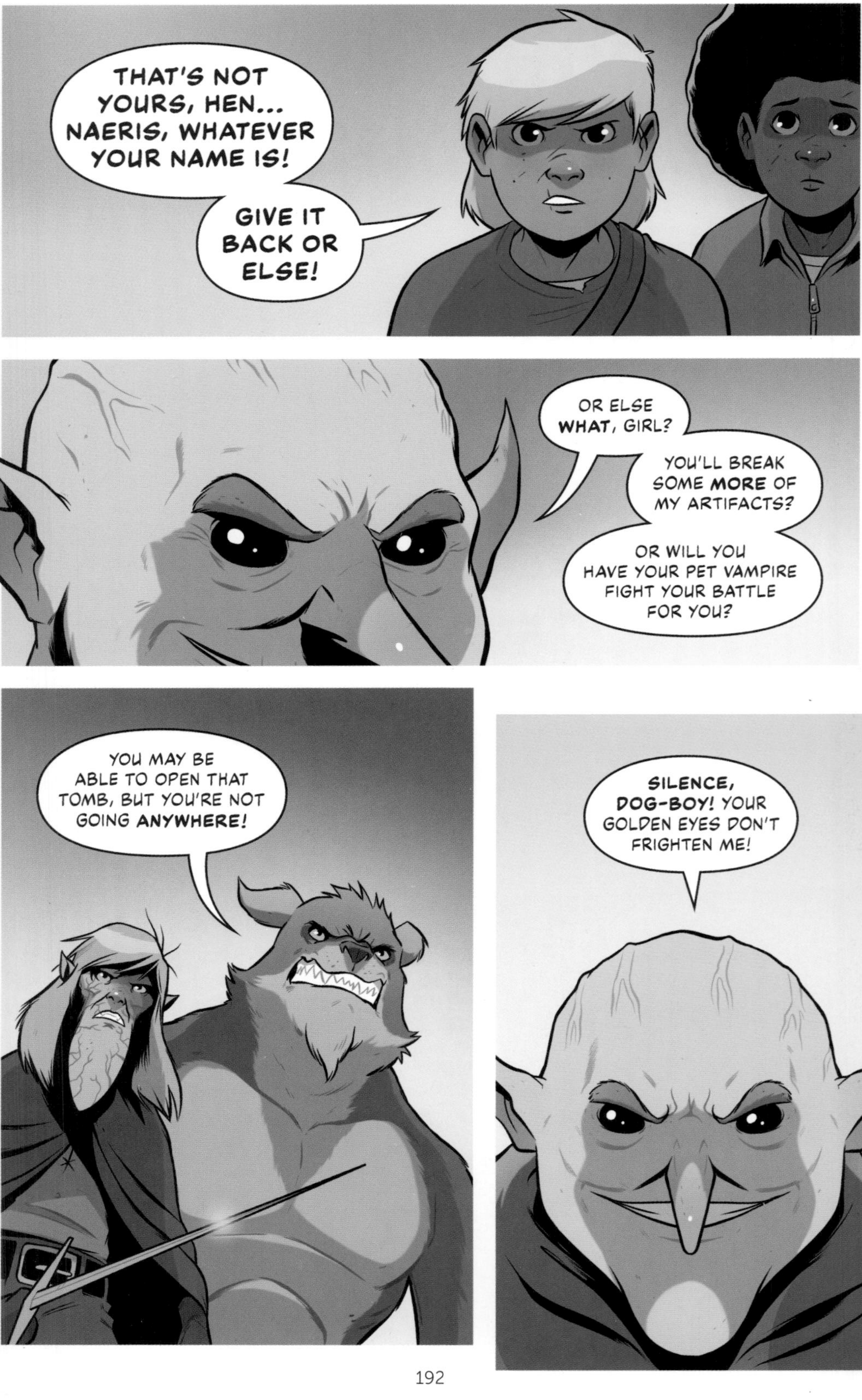
THAT'S NOT YOURS, HEN... NAERIS, WHATEVER YOUR NAME IS!
GIVE IT BACK OR ELSE!
OR ELSE WHAT, GIRL?
YOU'LL BREAK SOME MORE OF MY ARTIFACTS?
OR WILL YOU HAVE YOUR PET VAMPIRE FIGHT YOUR BATTLE FOR YOU?
YOU MAY BE ABLE TO OPEN THAT TOMB, BUT YOU'RE NOT GOING ANYWHERE!
SILENCE, DOG-BOY! YOUR GOLDEN EYES DON'T FRIGHTEN ME!

I'VE LONG KNOWN THE LOCATION OF THIS TOMB. I'VE BEEN HERE **SEVERAL** TIMES OVER THE YEARS, BUT I WAS NEVER ABLE TO **FIND** THIS PESKY KEY.

BUT THANKS TO **ALL OF YOUR HARD WORK, I'LL** BE ABLE TO **RESURRECT** MY MASTER AND BRING AN **END** TO THE RULE OF MORTALS.

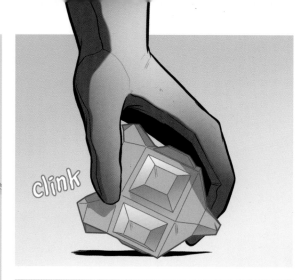

clink

BECAUSE OF **YOU,** I'LL BE ABLE TO USE THE BOOK CONTAINED WITHIN THIS TOMB TO BECOME MORE POWERFUL THAN ANY SPELLBINDER THAT HAS EVER--OR WILL EVER EXIST!

FOOM

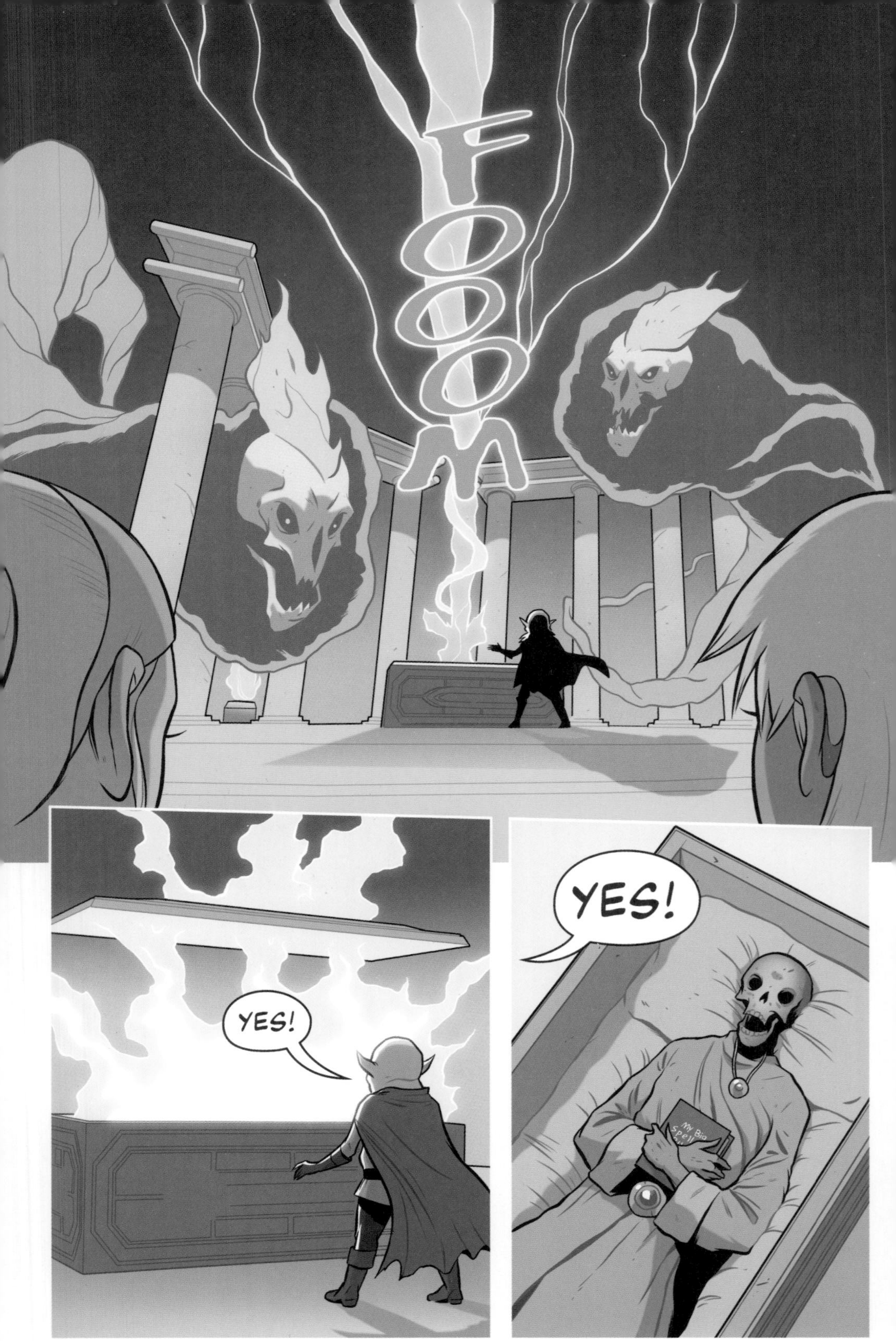
FOOOM
YES!
YES!

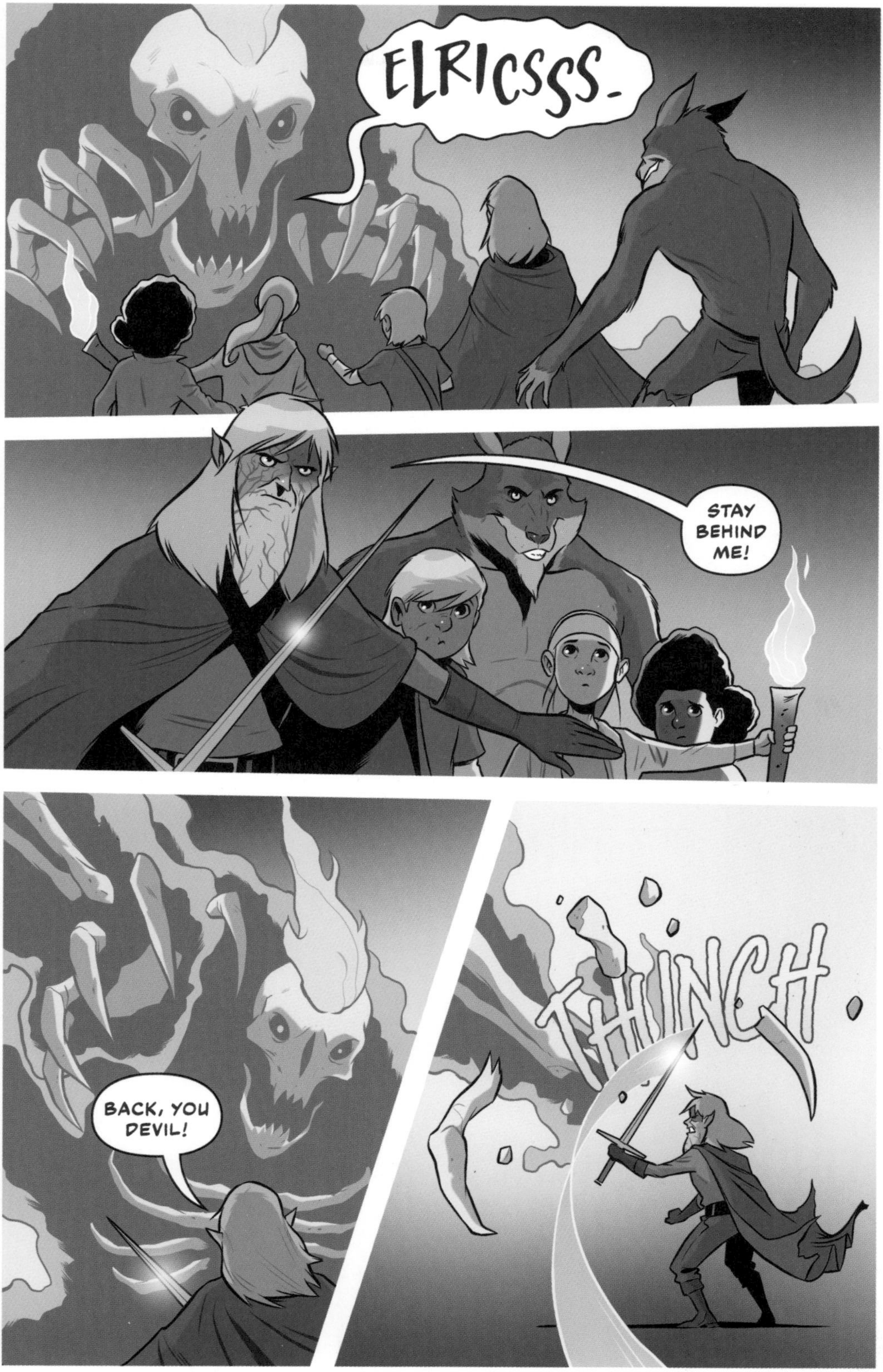
ELRICSSS.
STAY BEHIND ME!
BACK, YOU DEVIL!
THUNCH

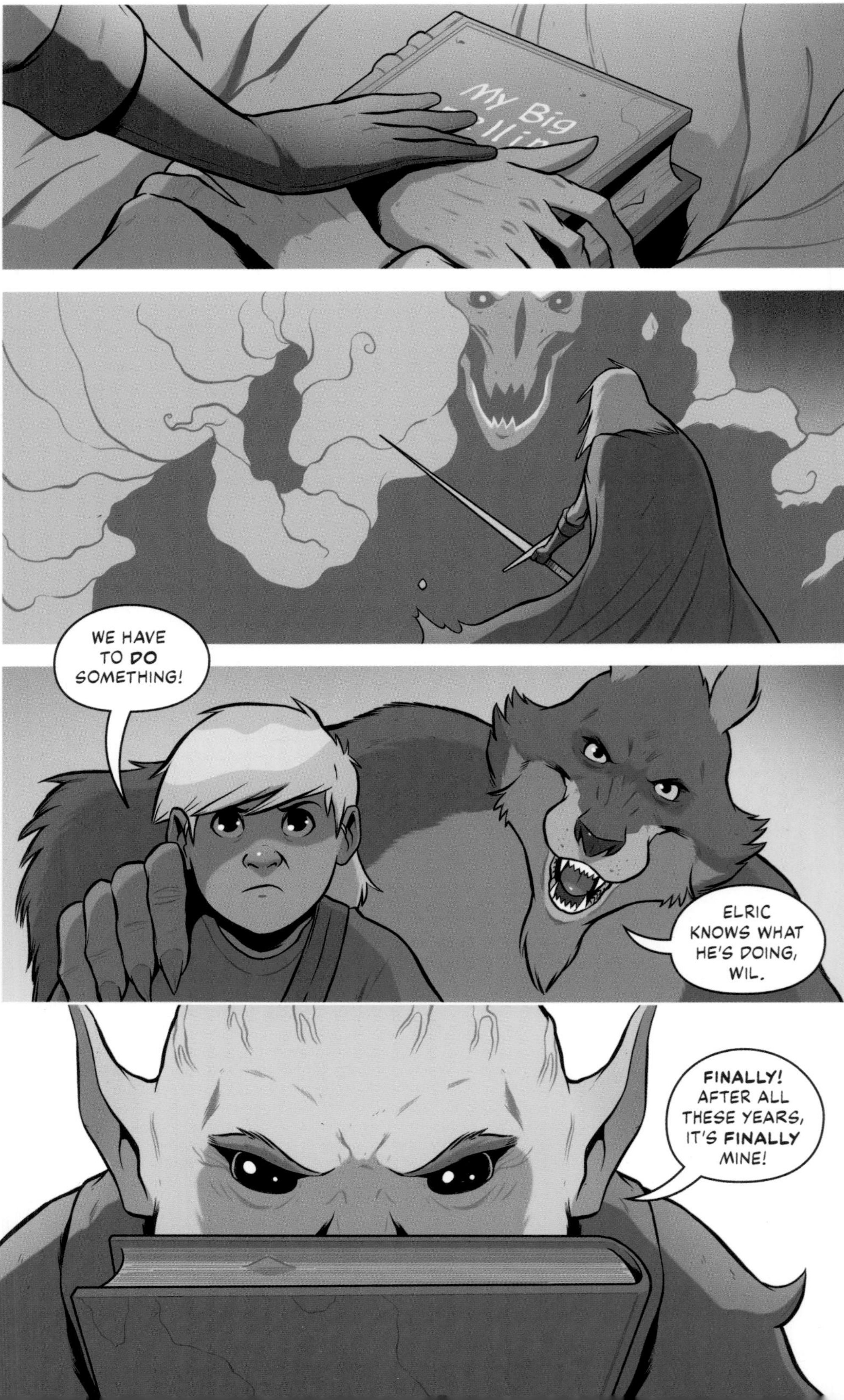
My Big
WE HAVE TO DO SOMETHING!
ELRIC KNOWS WHAT HE'S DOING, WIL.
FINALLY! AFTER ALL THESE YEARS, IT'S FINALLY MINE!

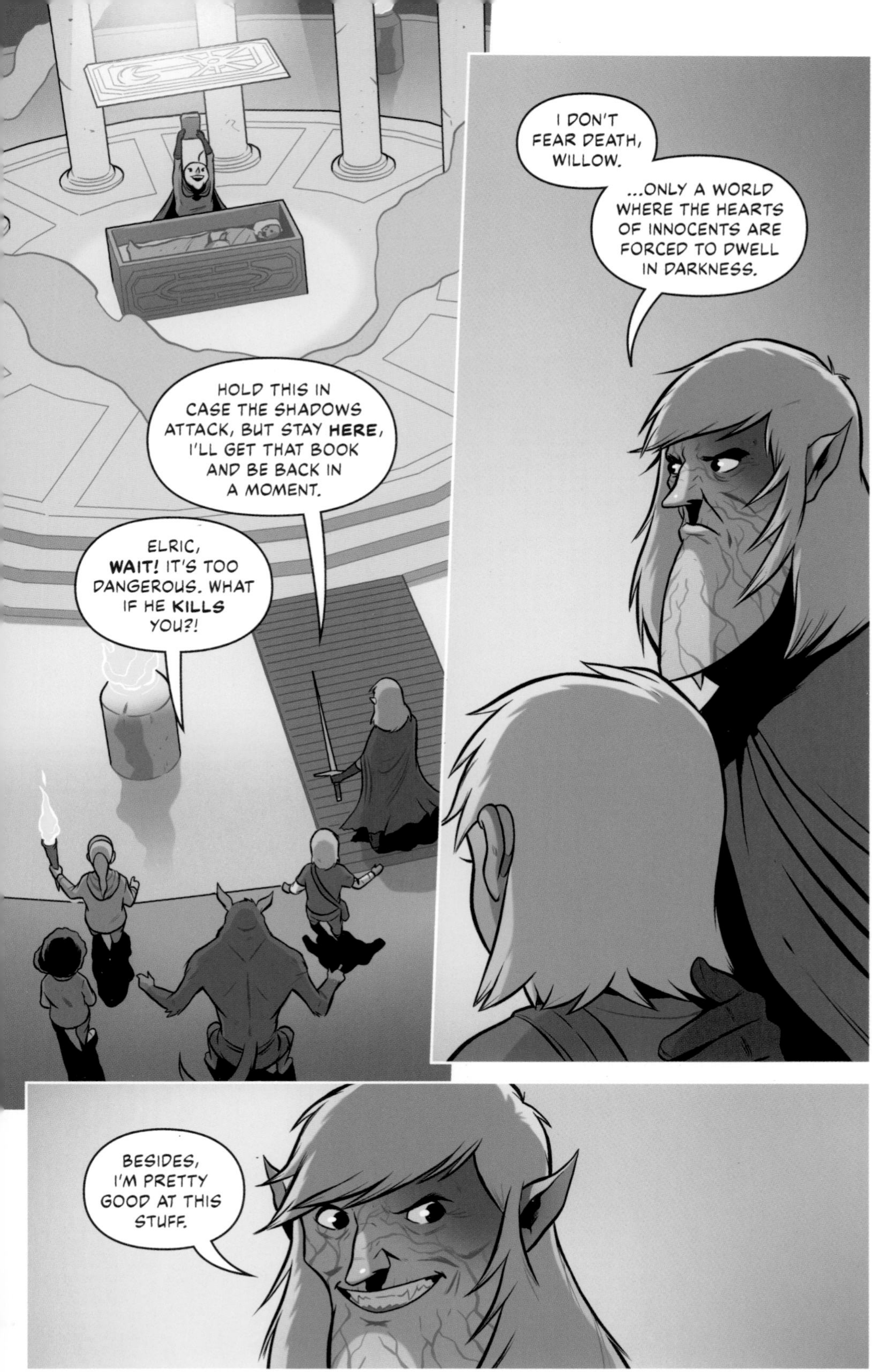
HOLD THIS IN CASE THE SHADOWS ATTACK, BUT STAY **HERE**, I'LL GET THAT BOOK AND BE BACK IN A MOMENT.
ELRIC, **WAIT!** IT'S TOO DANGEROUS. WHAT IF HE **KILLS** YOU?!
I DON'T FEAR DEATH, WILLOW.
...ONLY A WORLD WHERE THE HEARTS OF INNOCENTS ARE FORCED TO DWELL IN DARKNESS.
BESIDES, I'M PRETTY GOOD AT THIS STUFF.

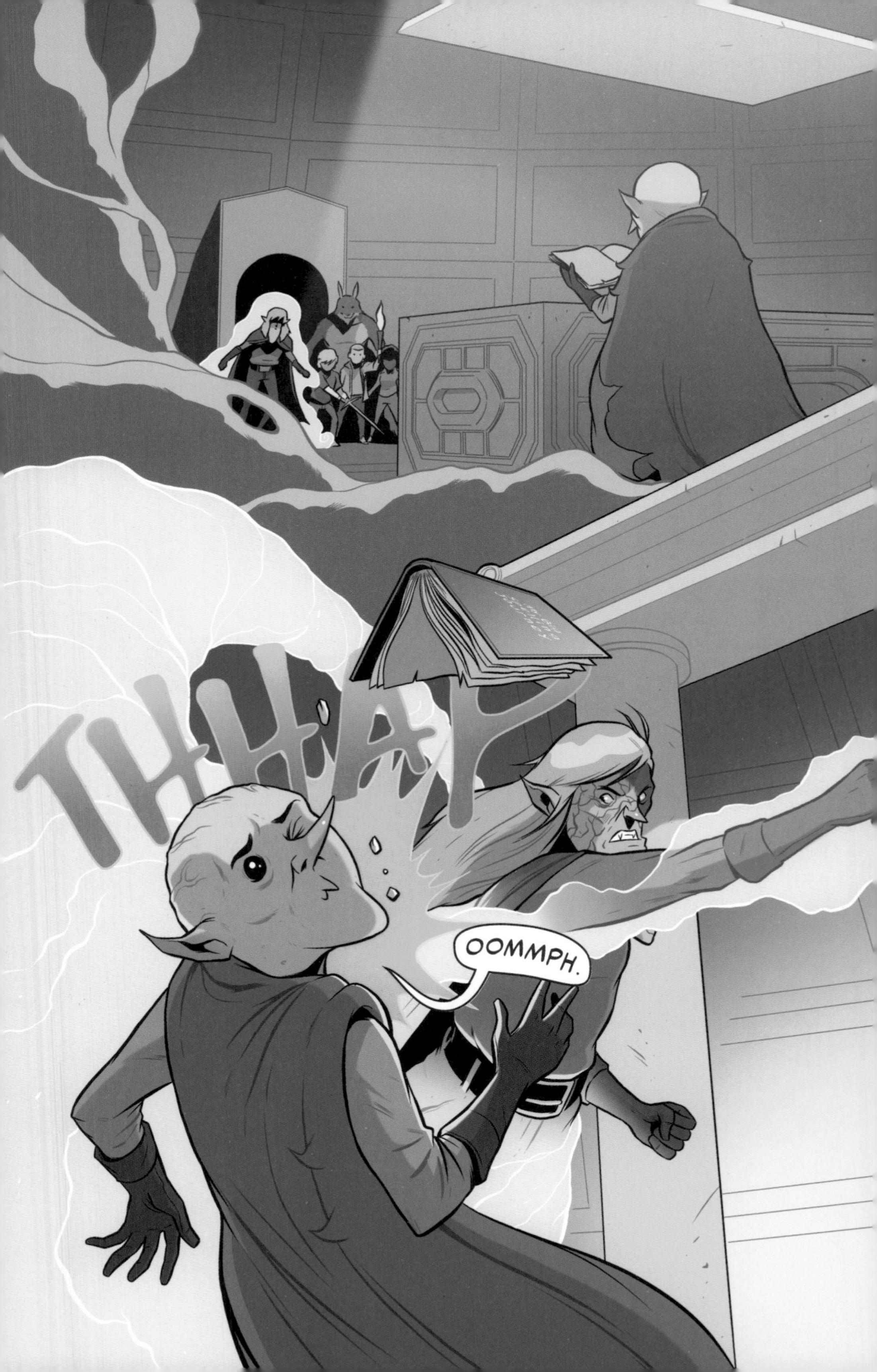
THHAP
OOMMPH.

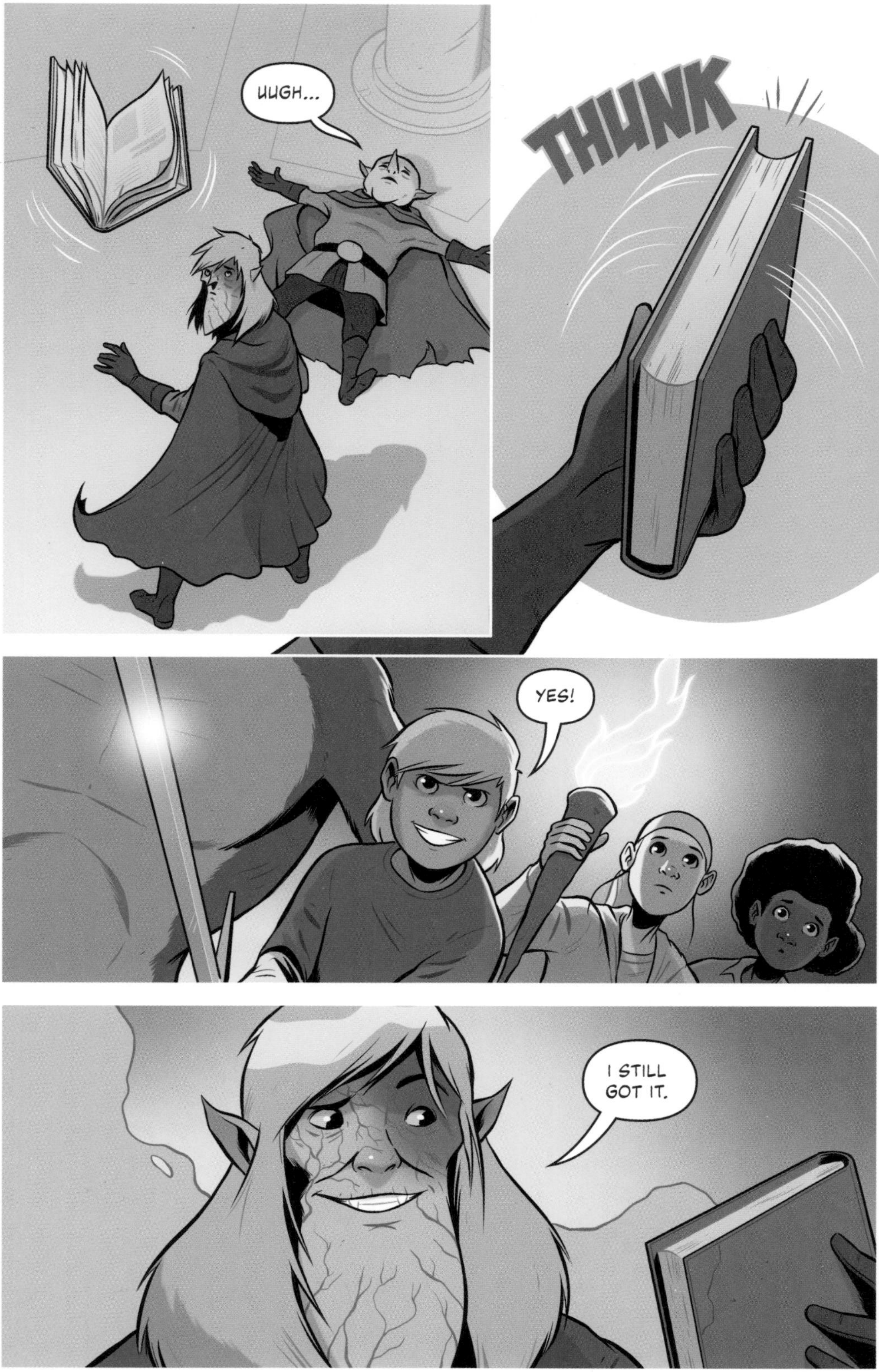
UUGH...
THUNK
YES!
I STILL GOT IT.

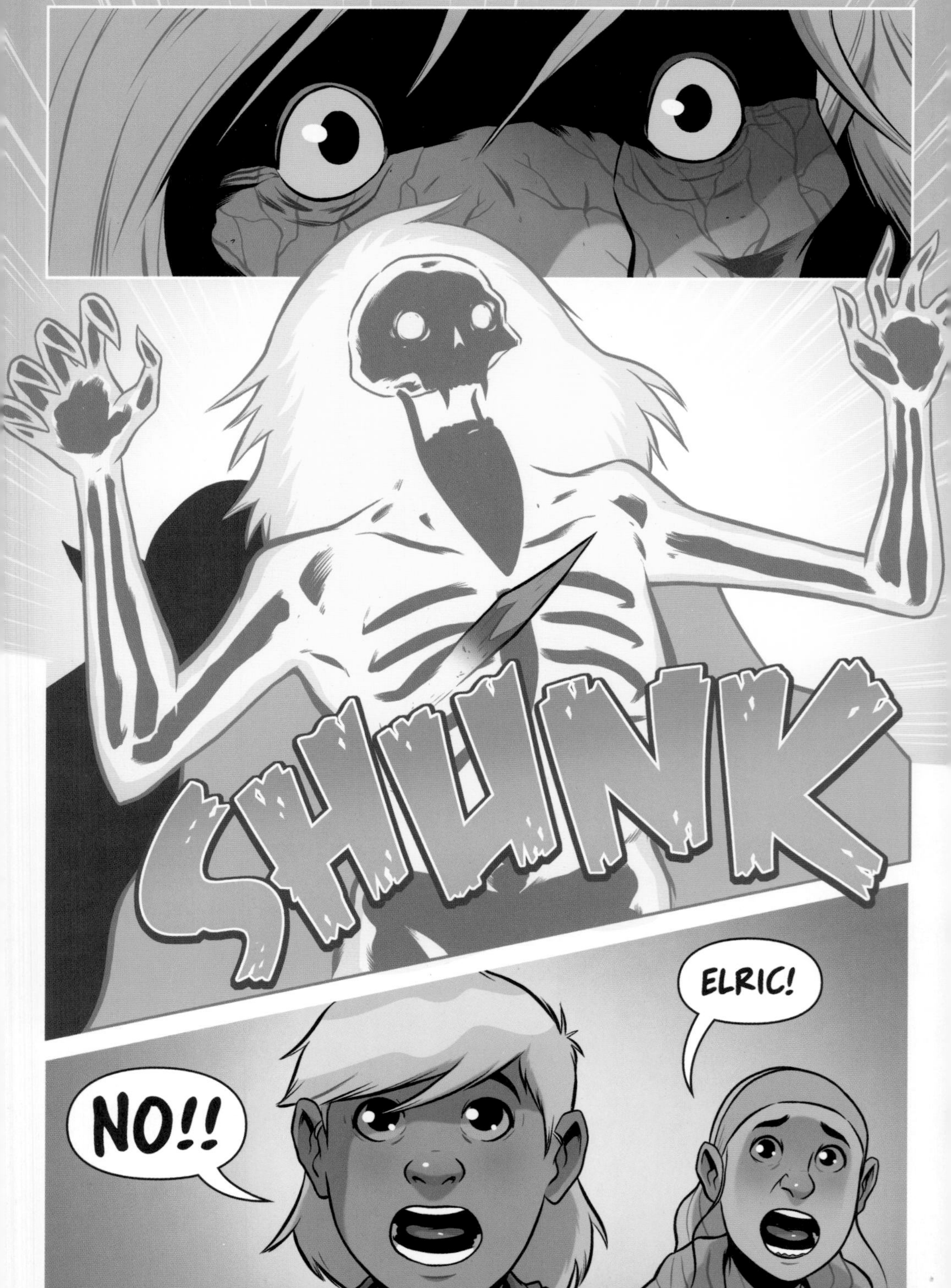
SHUNK
ELRIC!
NO!!

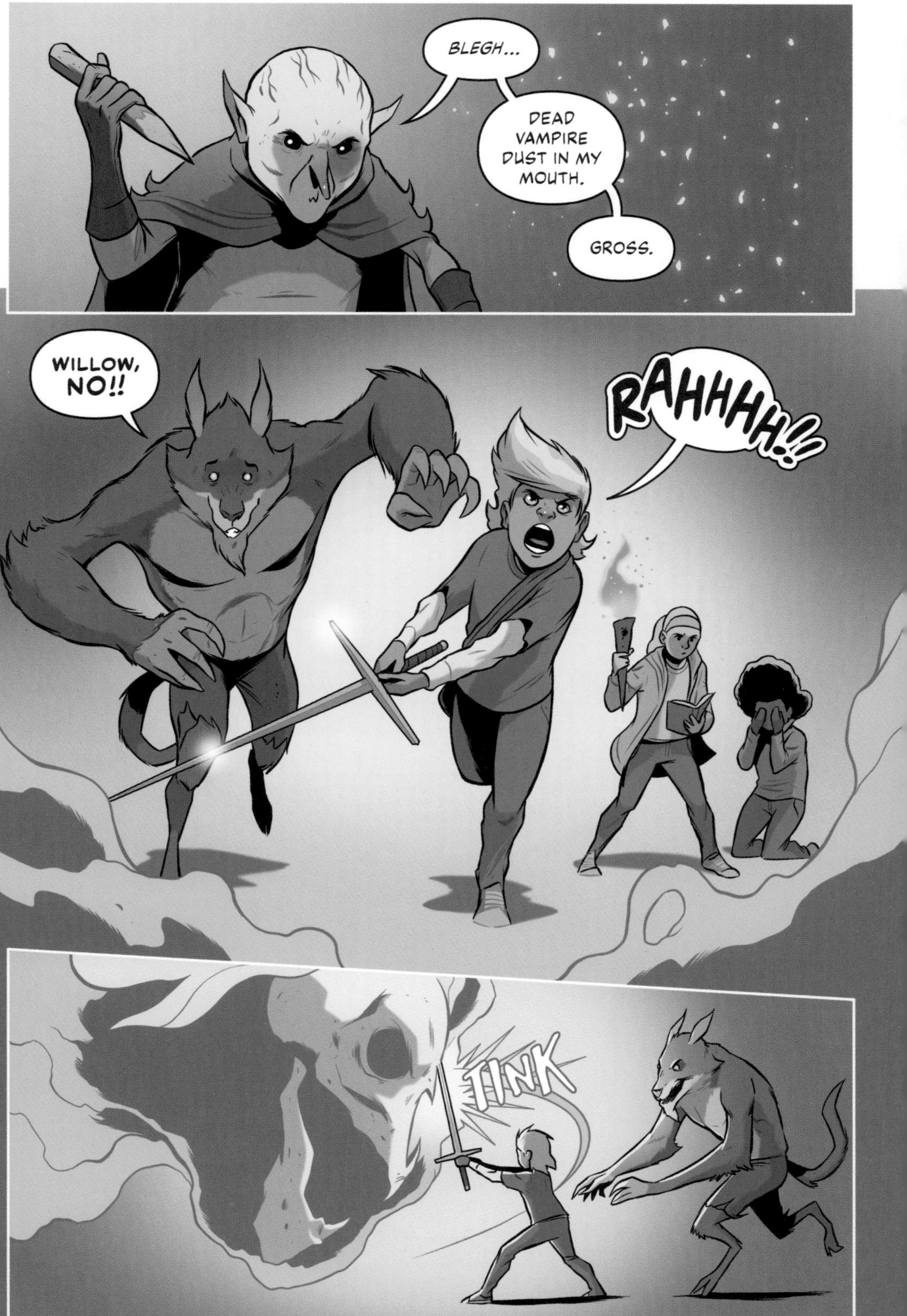

BLEGH...
DEAD VAMPIRE DUST IN MY MOUTH.
GROSS.
WILLOW, NO!!
RAHHHH!!!
TINK

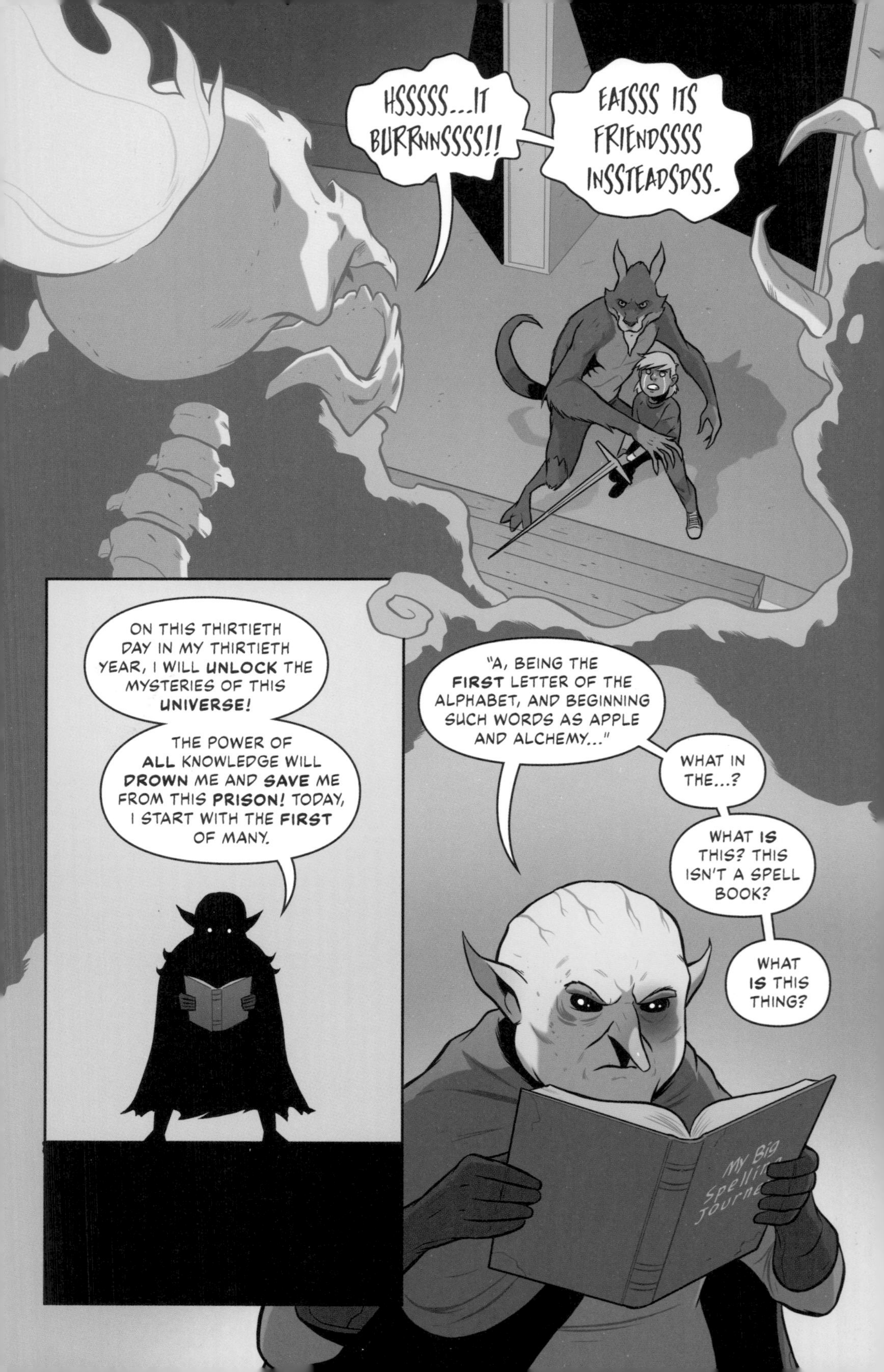
HSSSSS...IT BURRNNSSSS!!
EATSSS ITS FRIENDSSSS INSSTEADSDSS.
ON THIS THIRTIETH DAY IN MY THIRTIETH YEAR, I WILL UNLOCK THE MYSTERIES OF THIS UNIVERSE!
THE POWER OF ALL KNOWLEDGE WILL DROWN ME AND SAVE ME FROM THIS PRISON! TODAY, I START WITH THE FIRST OF MANY.
"A, BEING THE FIRST LETTER OF THE ALPHABET, AND BEGINNING SUCH WORDS AS APPLE AND ALCHEMY..."
WHAT IN THE...?
WHAT IS THIS? THIS ISN'T A SPELL BOOK?
WHAT IS THIS THING?

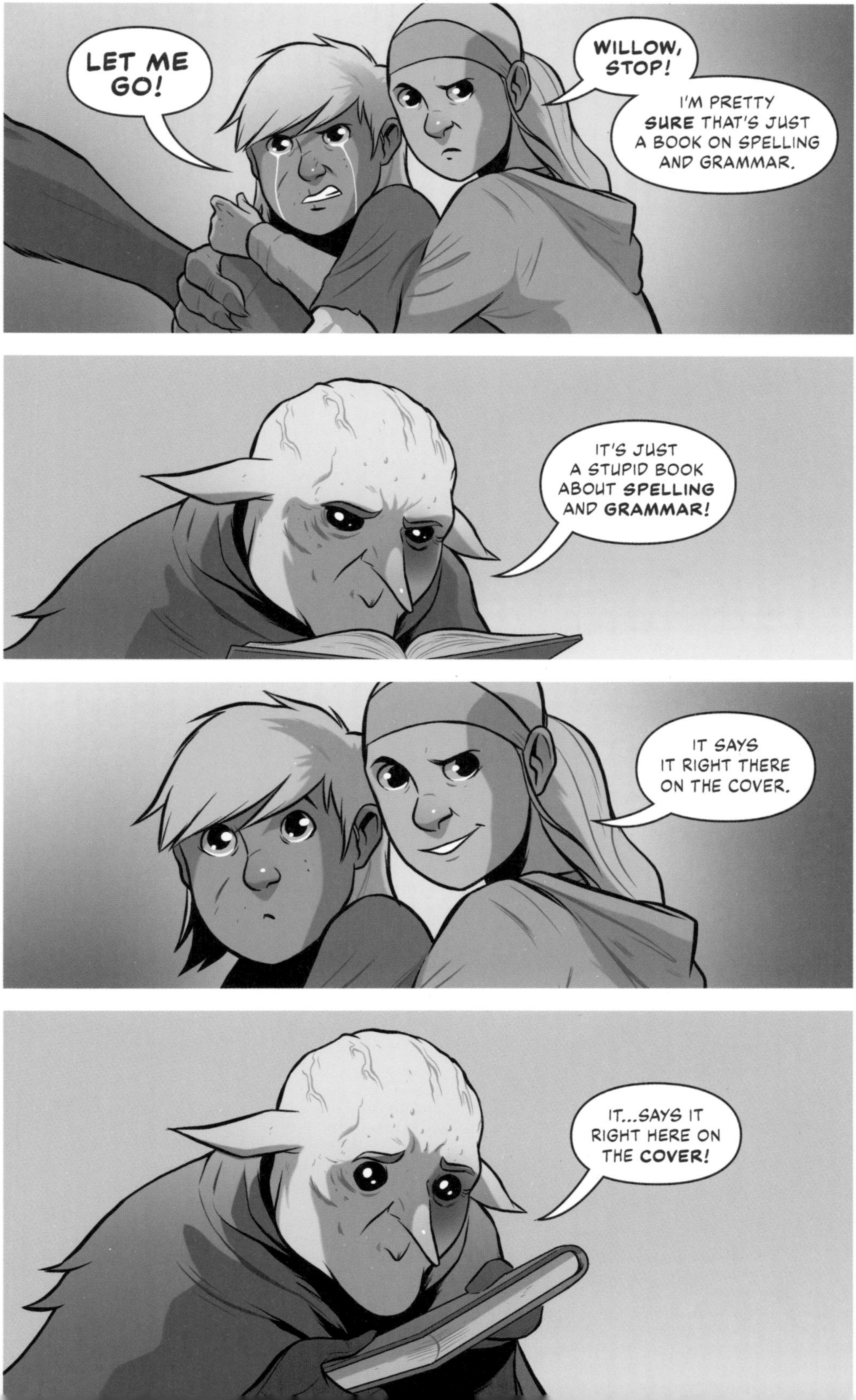
LET ME GO!
WILLOW, STOP!
I'M PRETTY **SURE** THAT'S JUST A BOOK ON SPELLING AND GRAMMAR.
IT'S JUST A STUPID BOOK ABOUT **SPELLING** AND **GRAMMAR!**
IT SAYS IT RIGHT THERE ON THE COVER.
IT...SAYS IT RIGHT HERE ON THE **COVER!**

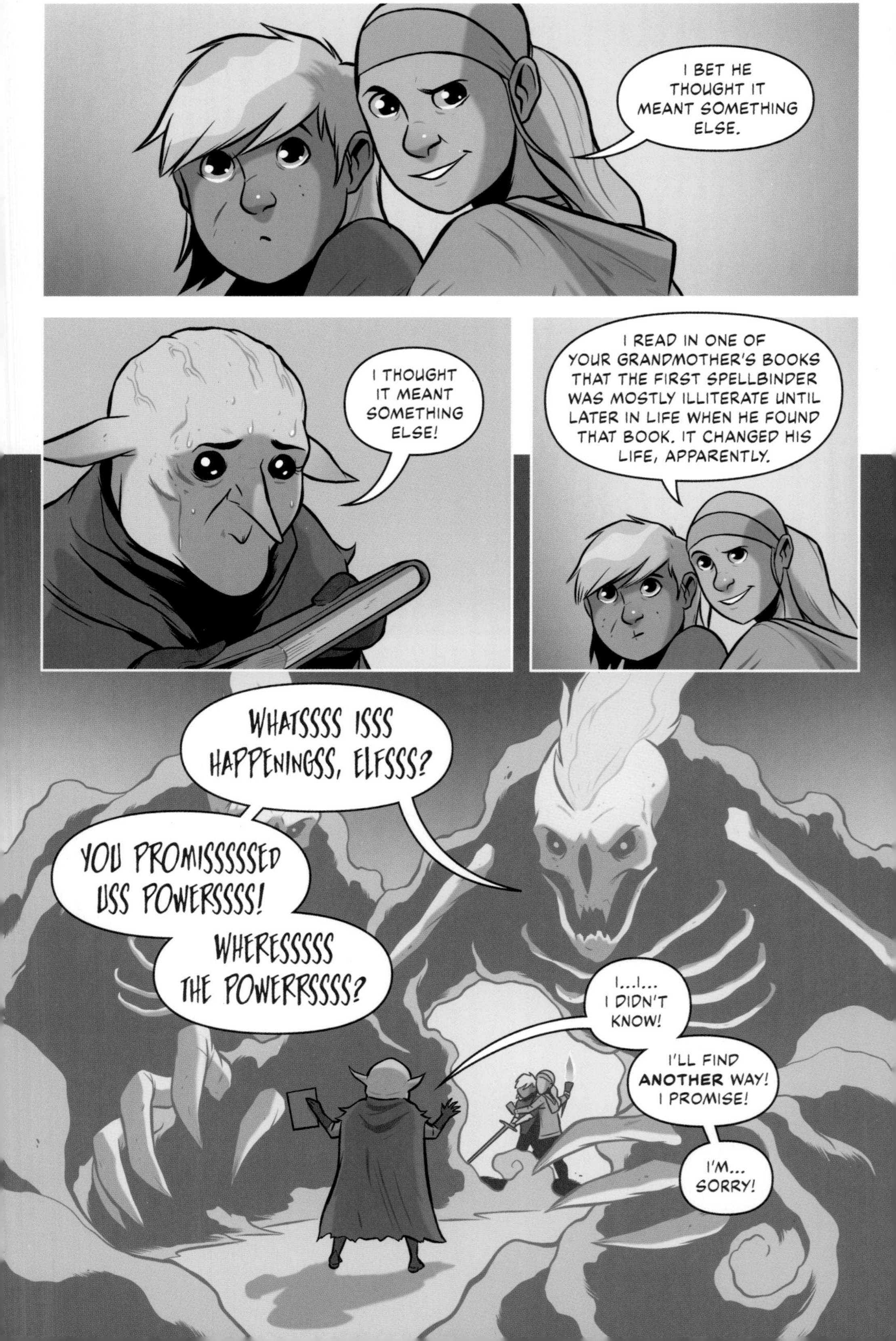
I BET HE THOUGHT IT MEANT SOMETHING ELSE.
I THOUGHT IT MEANT SOMETHING ELSE!
I READ IN ONE OF YOUR GRANDMOTHER'S BOOKS THAT THE FIRST SPELLBINDER WAS MOSTLY ILLITERATE UNTIL LATER IN LIFE WHEN HE FOUND THAT BOOK. IT CHANGED HIS LIFE, APPARENTLY.
WHATSSSS ISSS HAPPENINGSS, ELFSSS?
YOU PROMISSSSSED USS POWERSSSS!
WHERESSSSS THE POWERRSSSS?
I...I... I DIDN'T KNOW!
I'LL FIND ANOTHER WAY! I PROMISE!
I'M... SORRY!

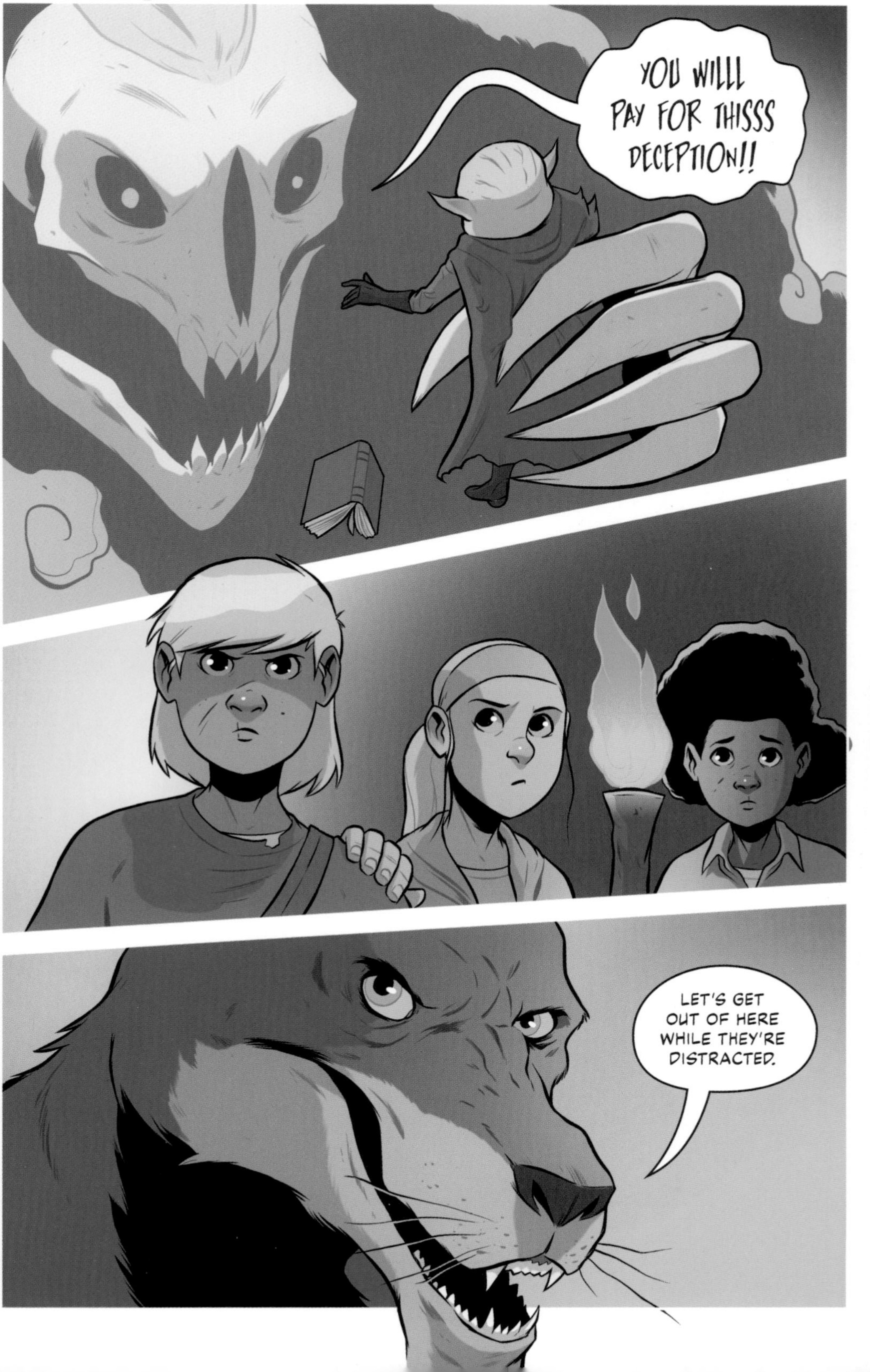
YOU WILLL PAY FOR THISSS DECEPTION!!
LET'S GET OUT OF HERE WHILE THEY'RE DISTRACTED.

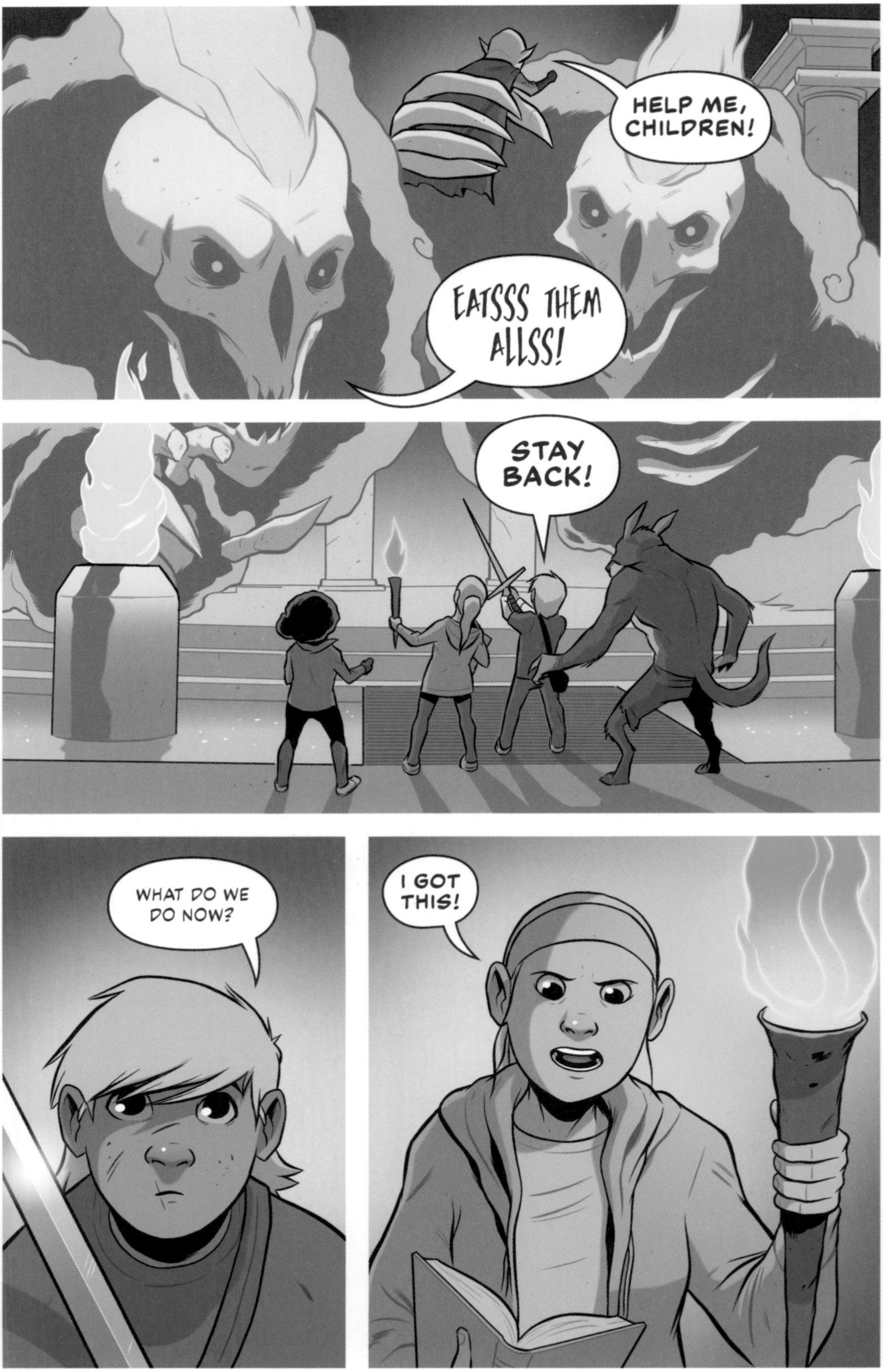
HELP ME, CHILDREN!
EATSSS THEM ALLSS!
STAY BACK!
WHAT DO WE DO NOW?
I GOT THIS!

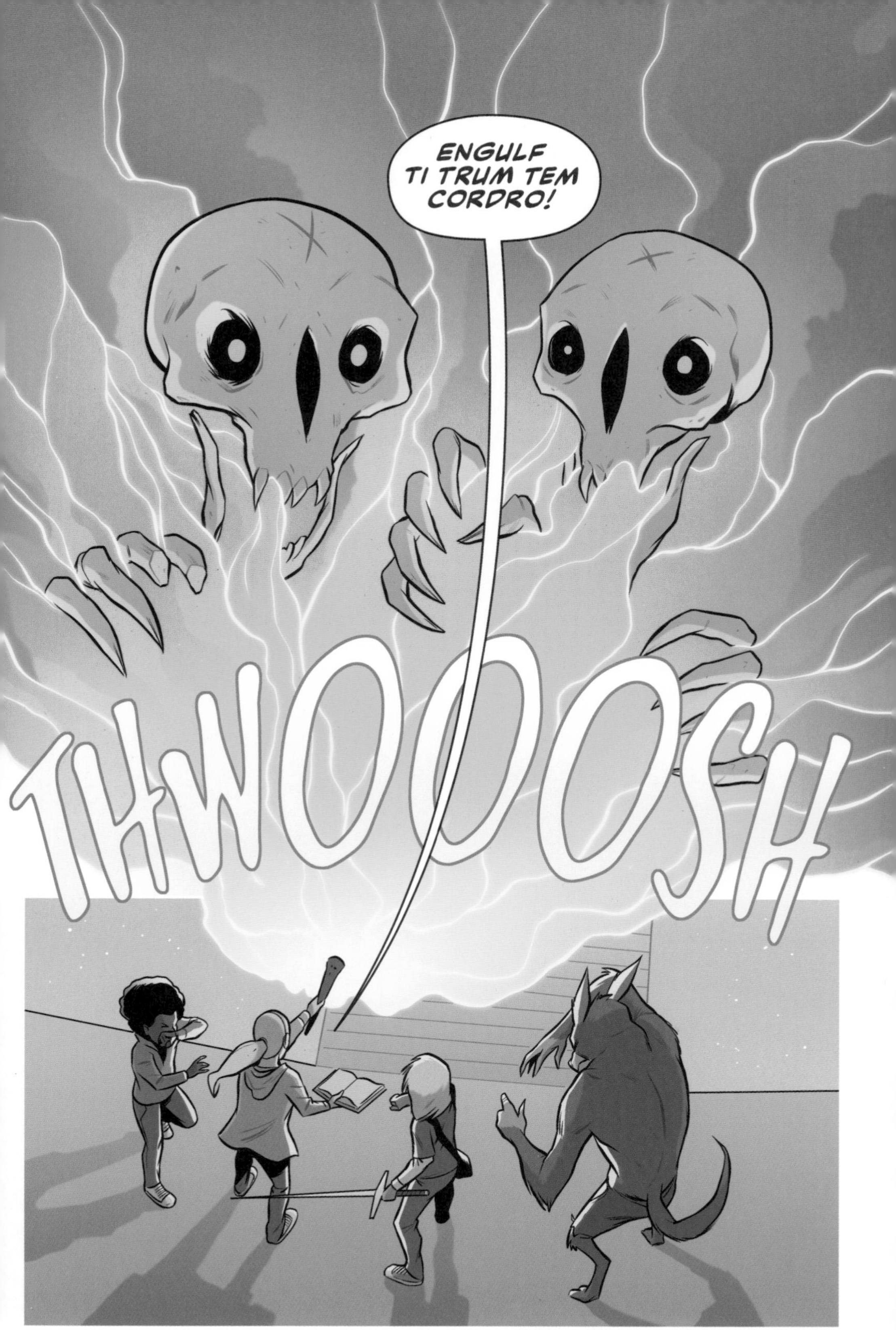
ENGULF TI TRUM TEM CORDRO!
THWOOOSH

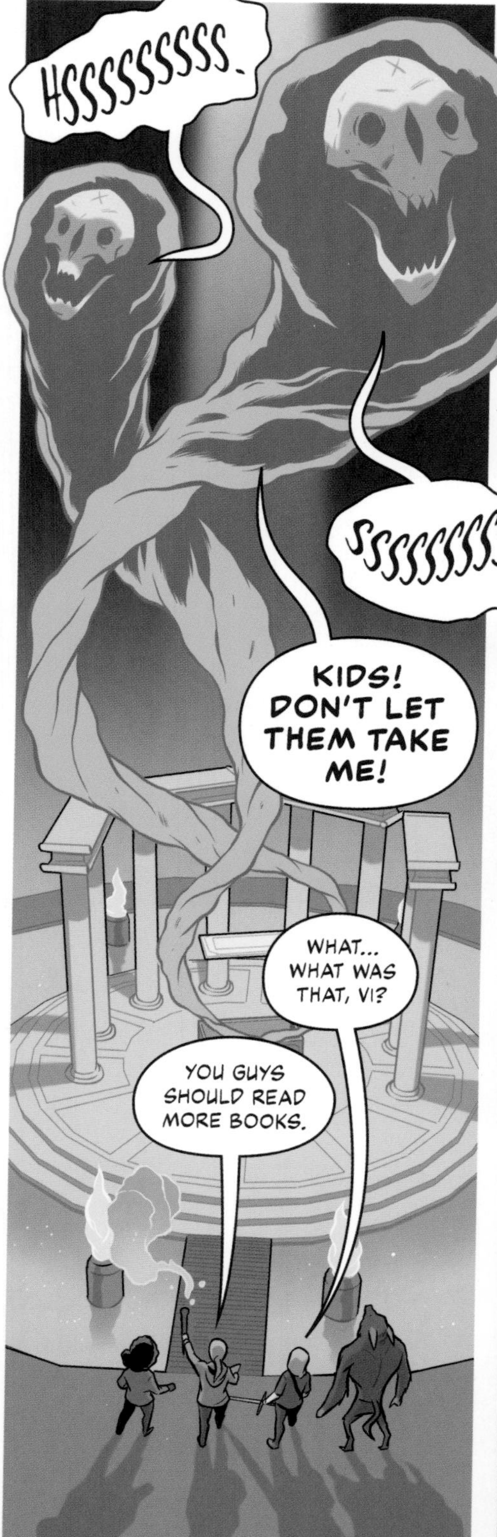
HSSSSSSSSS.
SSSSSSSSSSSSS.
KIDS! DON'T LET THEM TAKE ME!
WHAT... WHAT WAS THAT, VI?
YOU GUYS SHOULD READ MORE BOOKS.

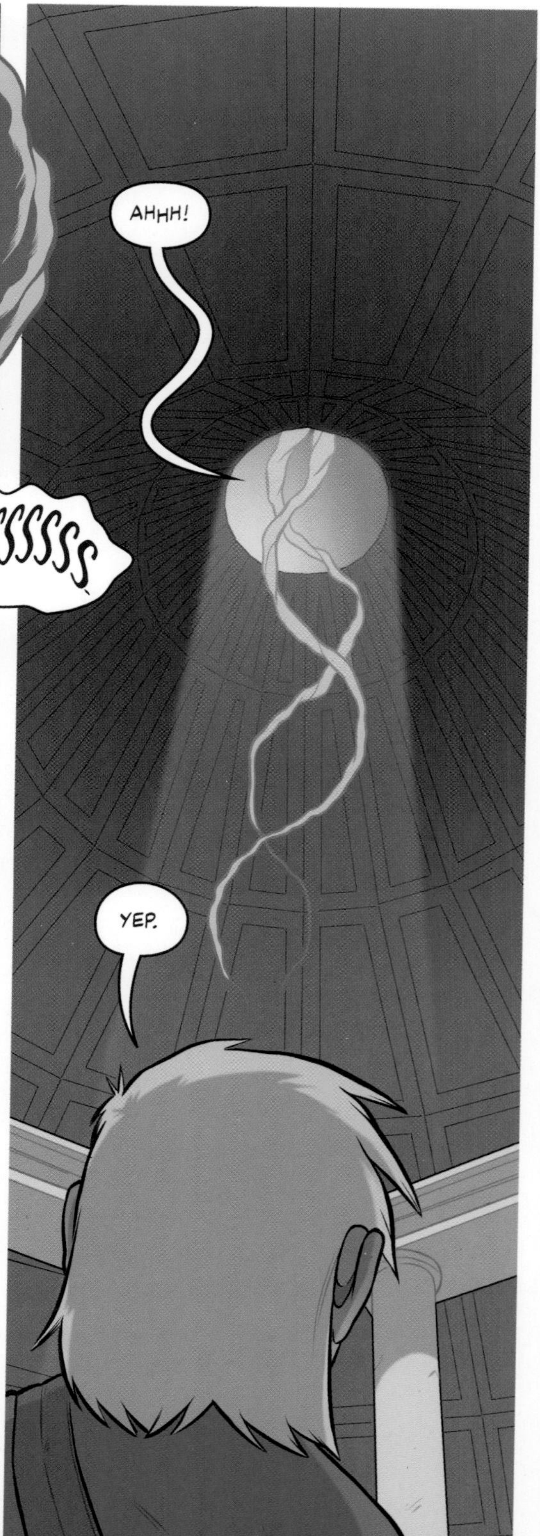
AHHH!
YEP.

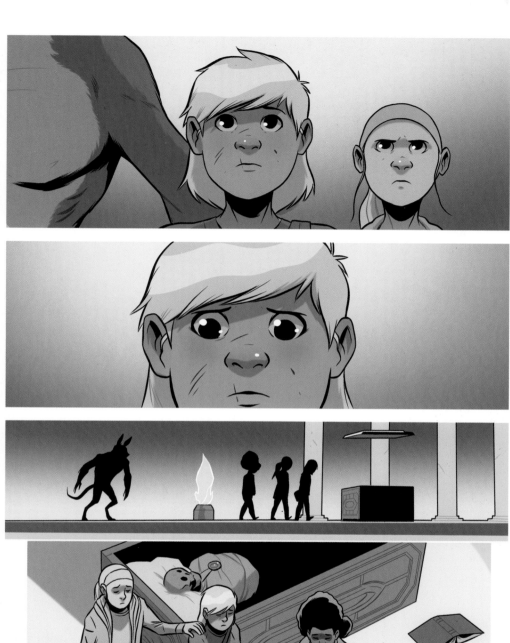

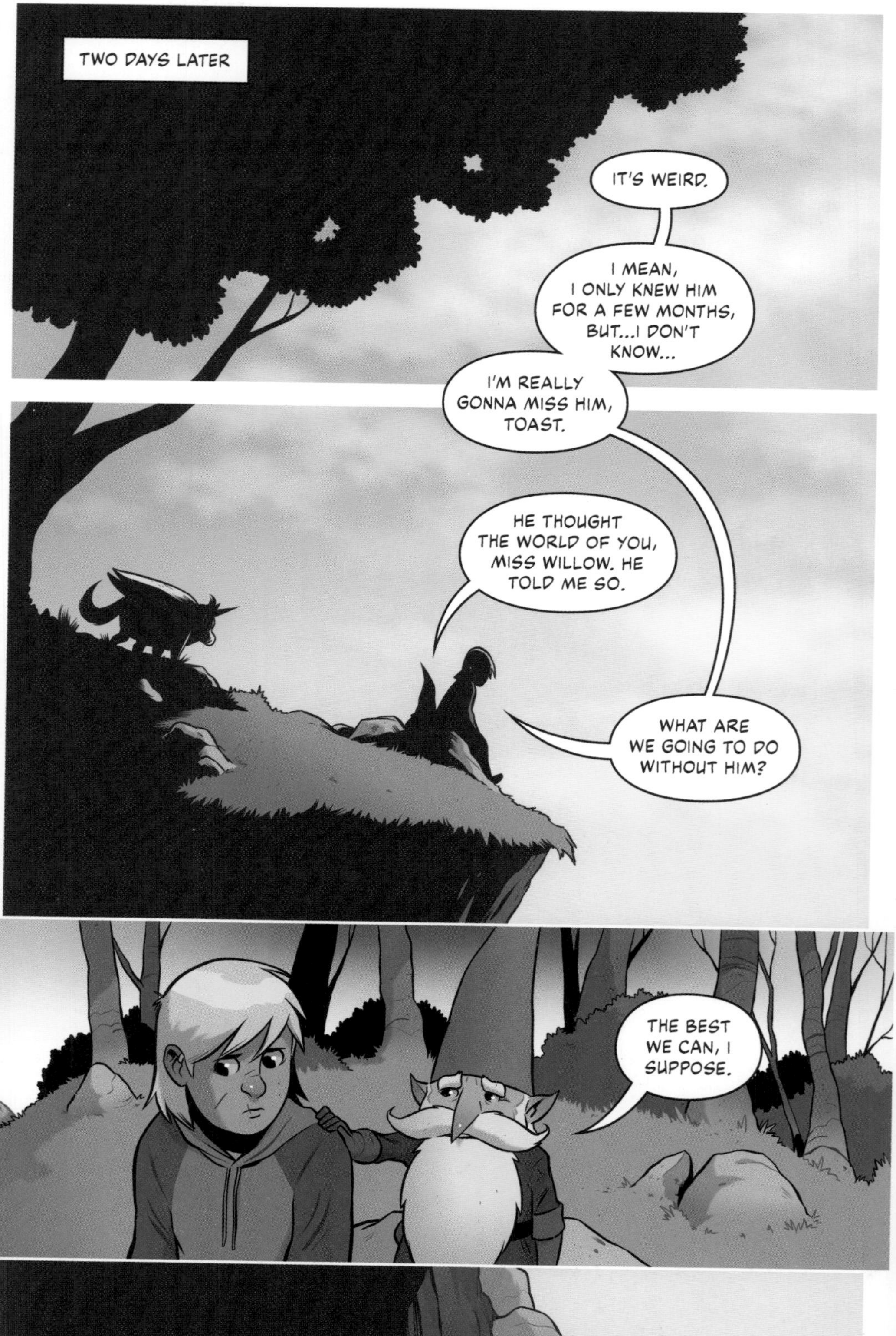
TWO DAYS LATER
IT'S WEIRD.
I MEAN, I ONLY KNEW HIM FOR A FEW MONTHS, BUT...I DON'T KNOW...
I'M REALLY GONNA MISS HIM, TOAST.
HE THOUGHT THE WORLD OF YOU, MISS WILLOW. HE TOLD ME SO.
WHAT ARE WE GOING TO DO WITHOUT HIM?
THE BEST WE CAN, I SUPPOSE.

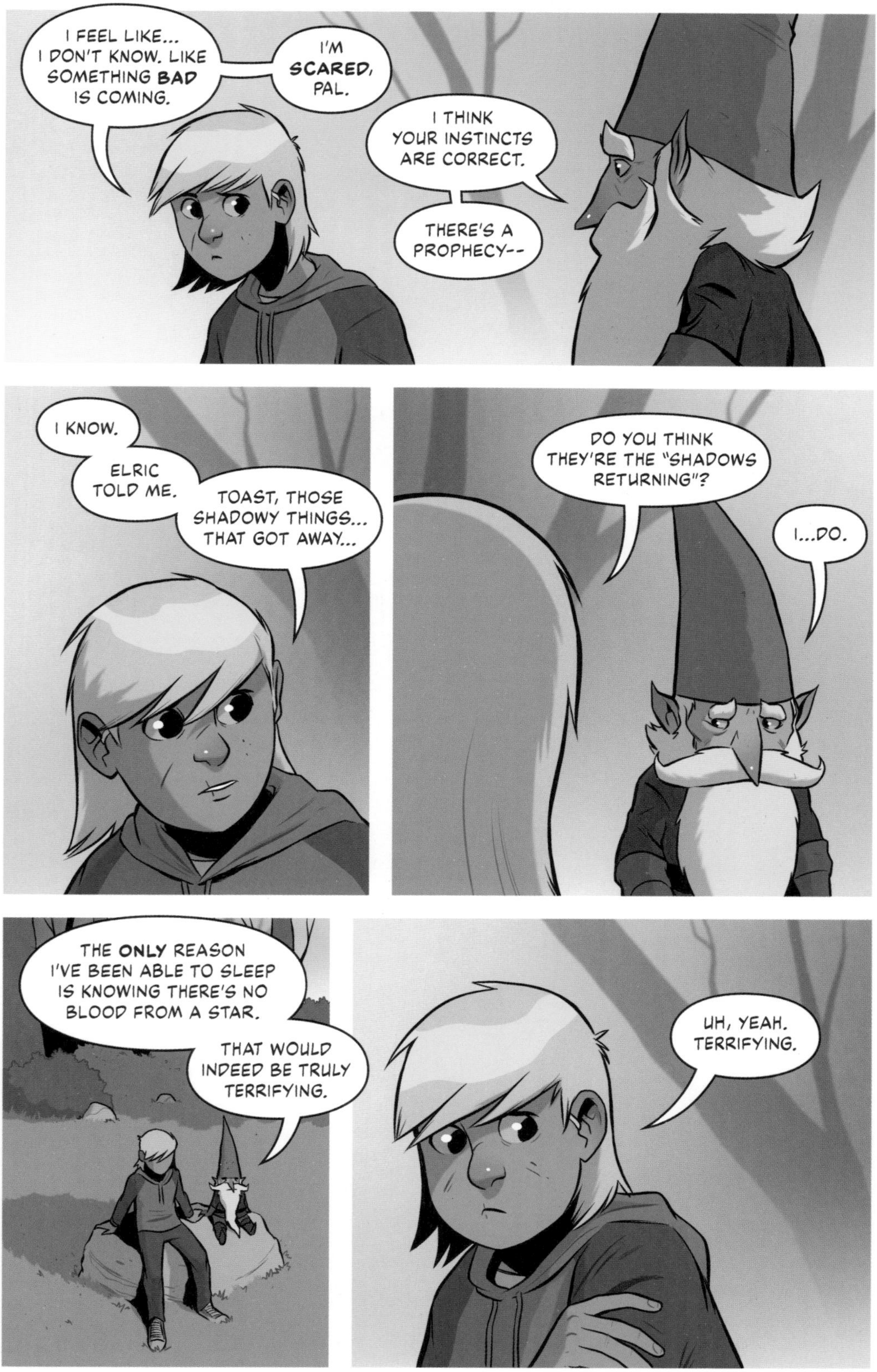

I FEEL LIKE... I DON'T KNOW. LIKE SOMETHING **BAD** IS COMING.
I'M **SCARED**, PAL.
I THINK YOUR INSTINCTS ARE CORRECT.
THERE'S A PROPHECY--
I KNOW.
ELRIC TOLD ME.
TOAST, THOSE SHADOWY THINGS... THAT GOT AWAY...
DO YOU THINK THEY'RE THE "SHADOWS RETURNING"?
I...DO.
THE **ONLY** REASON I'VE BEEN ABLE TO SLEEP IS KNOWING THERE'S NO BLOOD FROM A STAR.
THAT WOULD INDEED BE TRULY TERRIFYING.
UH, YEAH. TERRIFYING.

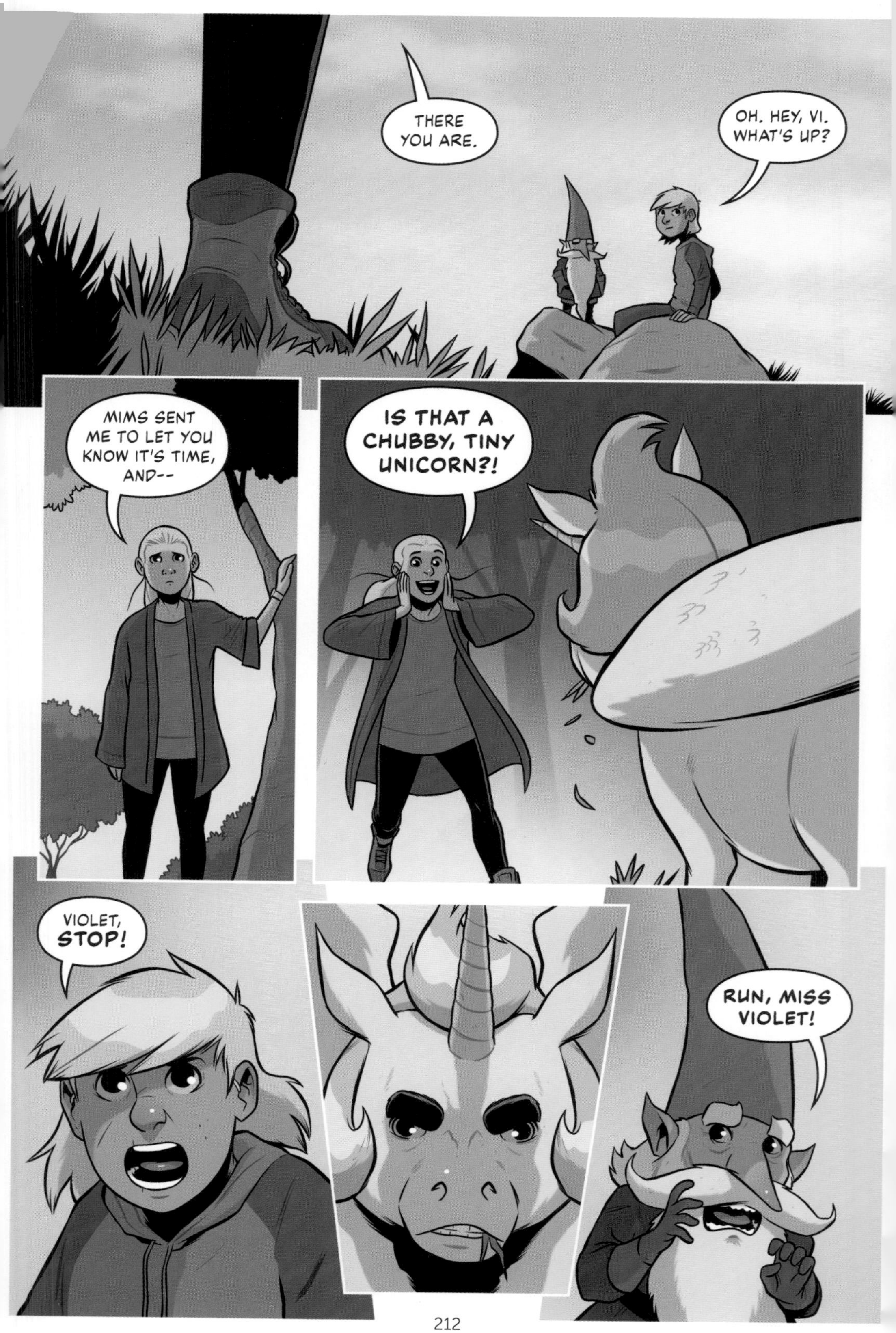
THERE YOU ARE.
OH. HEY, VI. WHAT'S UP?
MIMS SENT ME TO LET YOU KNOW IT'S TIME, AND--
IS THAT A CHUBBY, TINY UNICORN?!
VIOLET, STOP!
RUN, MISS VIOLET!

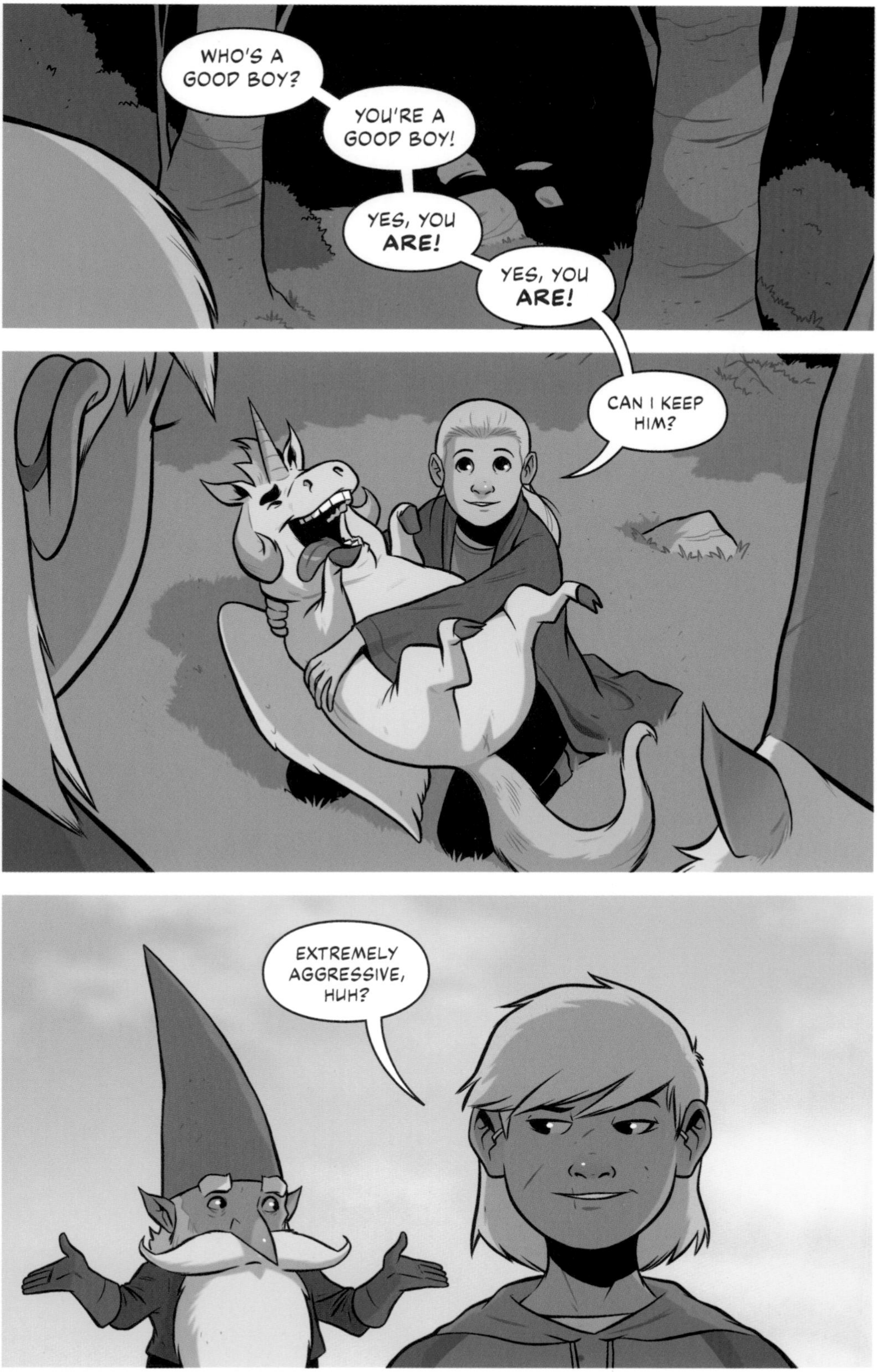
WHO'S A GOOD BOY?
YOU'RE A GOOD BOY!
YES, YOU ARE!
YES, YOU ARE!
CAN I KEEP HIM?
EXTREMELY AGGRESSIVE, HUH?

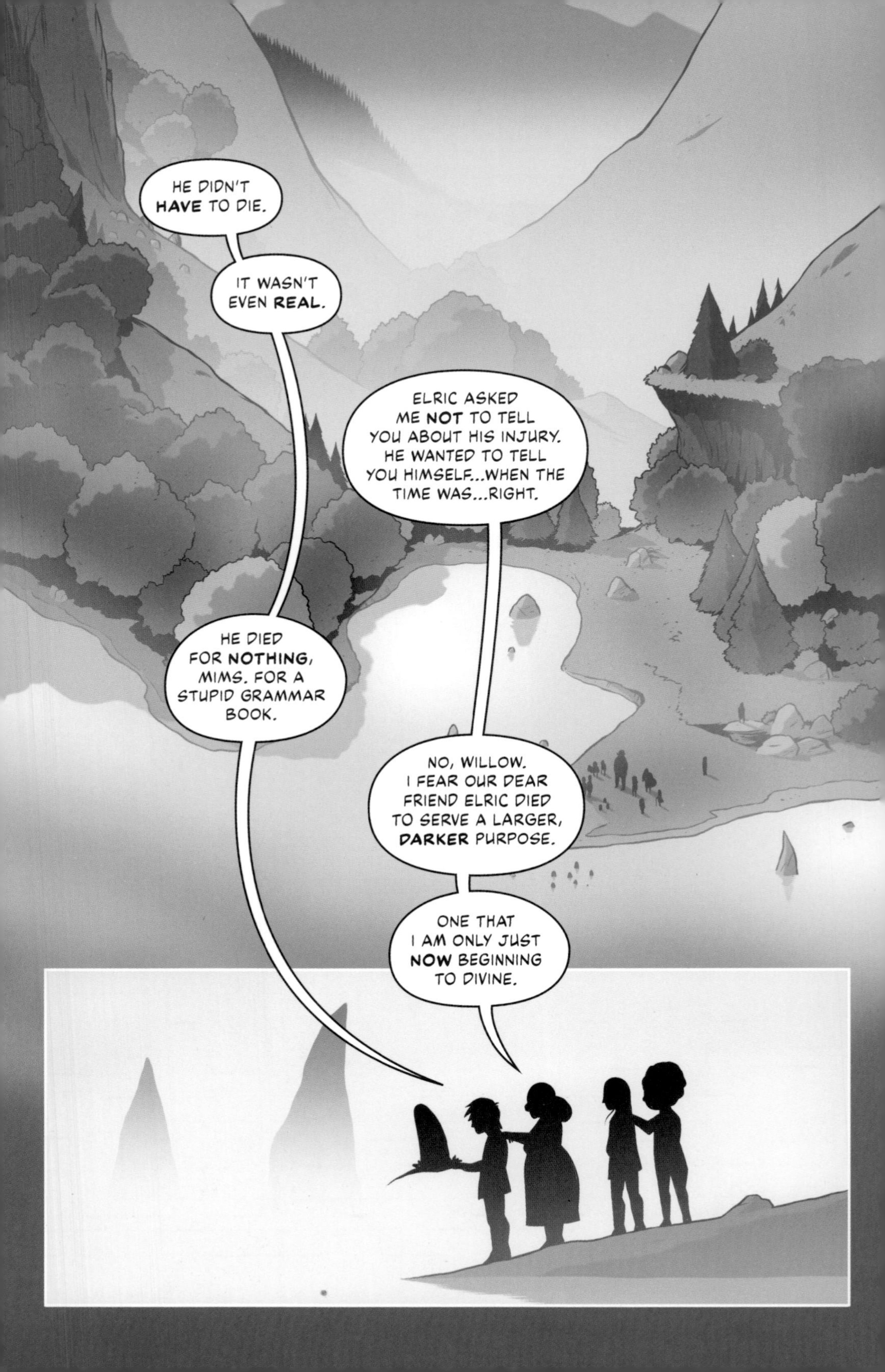

HE DIDN'T **HAVE** TO DIE.
IT WASN'T EVEN **REAL.**
ELRIC ASKED ME **NOT** TO TELL YOU ABOUT HIS INJURY. HE WANTED TO TELL YOU HIMSELF...WHEN THE TIME WAS...RIGHT.
HE DIED FOR **NOTHING**, MIMS. FOR A STUPID GRAMMAR BOOK.
NO, WILLOW. I FEAR OUR DEAR FRIEND ELRIC DIED TO SERVE A LARGER, **DARKER** PURPOSE.
ONE THAT I AM ONLY JUST **NOW** BEGINNING TO DIVINE.

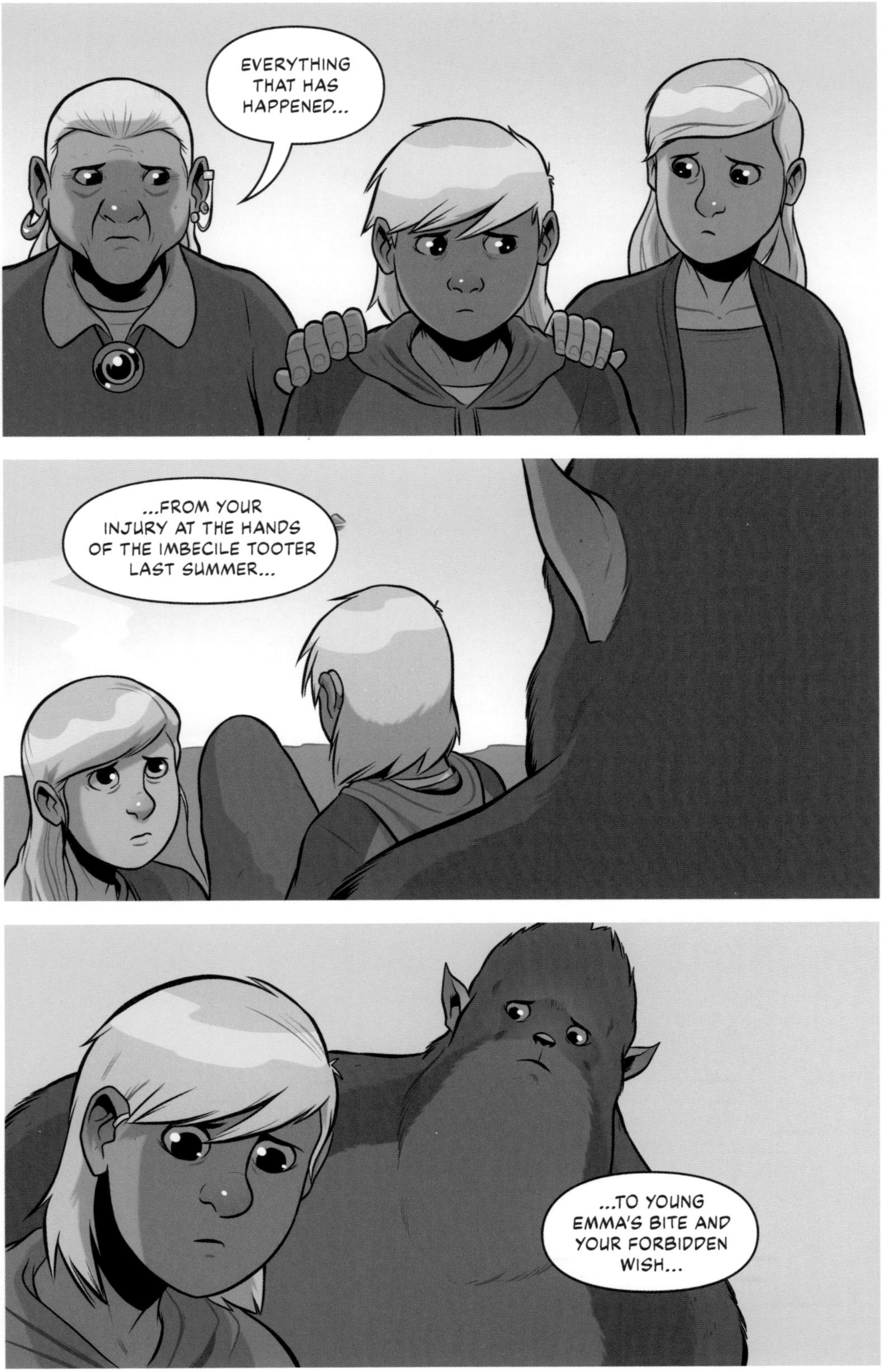
EVERYTHING THAT HAS HAPPENED...
...FROM YOUR INJURY AT THE HANDS OF THE IMBECILE TOOTER LAST SUMMER...
...TO YOUNG EMMA'S BITE AND YOUR FORBIDDEN WISH...

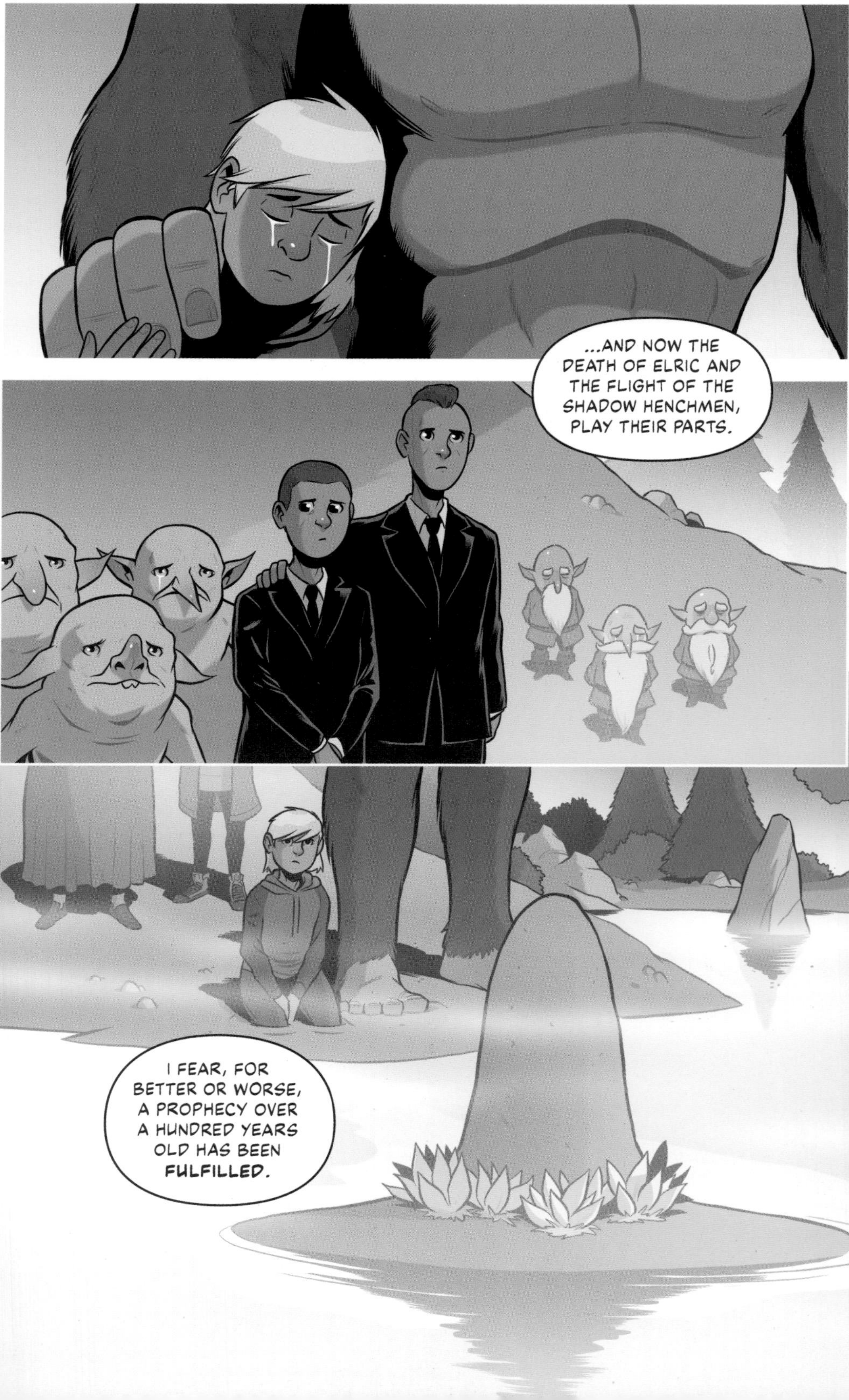
...AND NOW THE DEATH OF ELRIC AND THE FLIGHT OF THE SHADOW HENCHMEN, PLAY THEIR PARTS.
I FEAR, FOR BETTER OR WORSE, A PROPHECY OVER A HUNDRED YEARS OLD HAS BEEN **FULFILLED**.

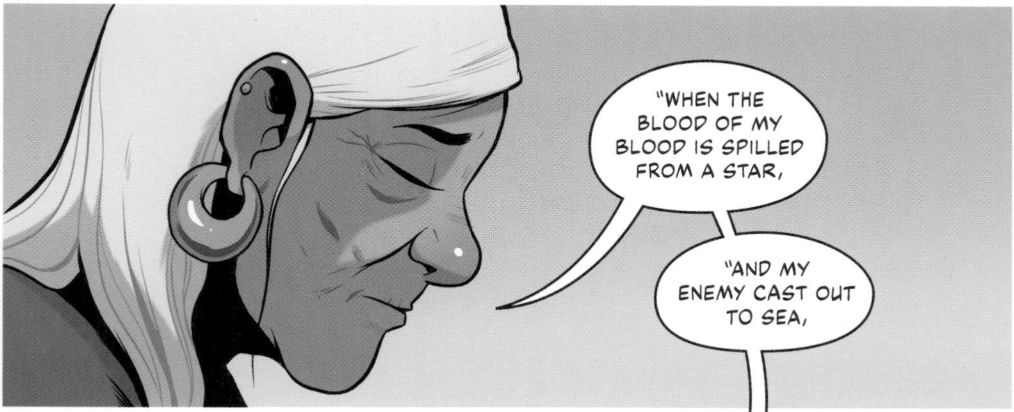
"WHEN THE BLOOD OF MY BLOOD IS SPILLED FROM A STAR,
"AND MY ENEMY CAST OUT TO SEA,

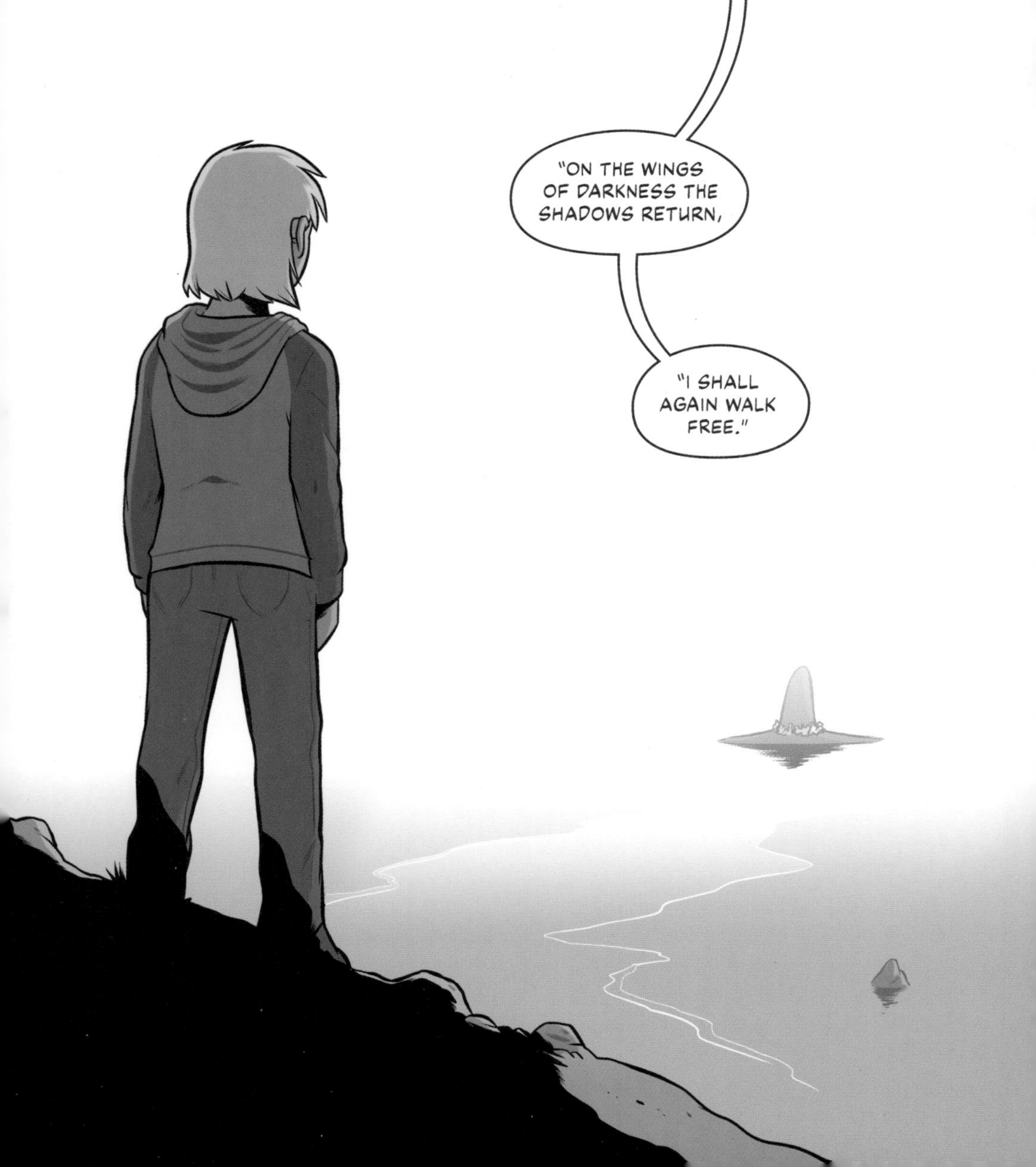
"ON THE WINGS OF DARKNESS THE SHADOWS RETURN,
"I SHALL AGAIN WALK FREE."

Epilogue

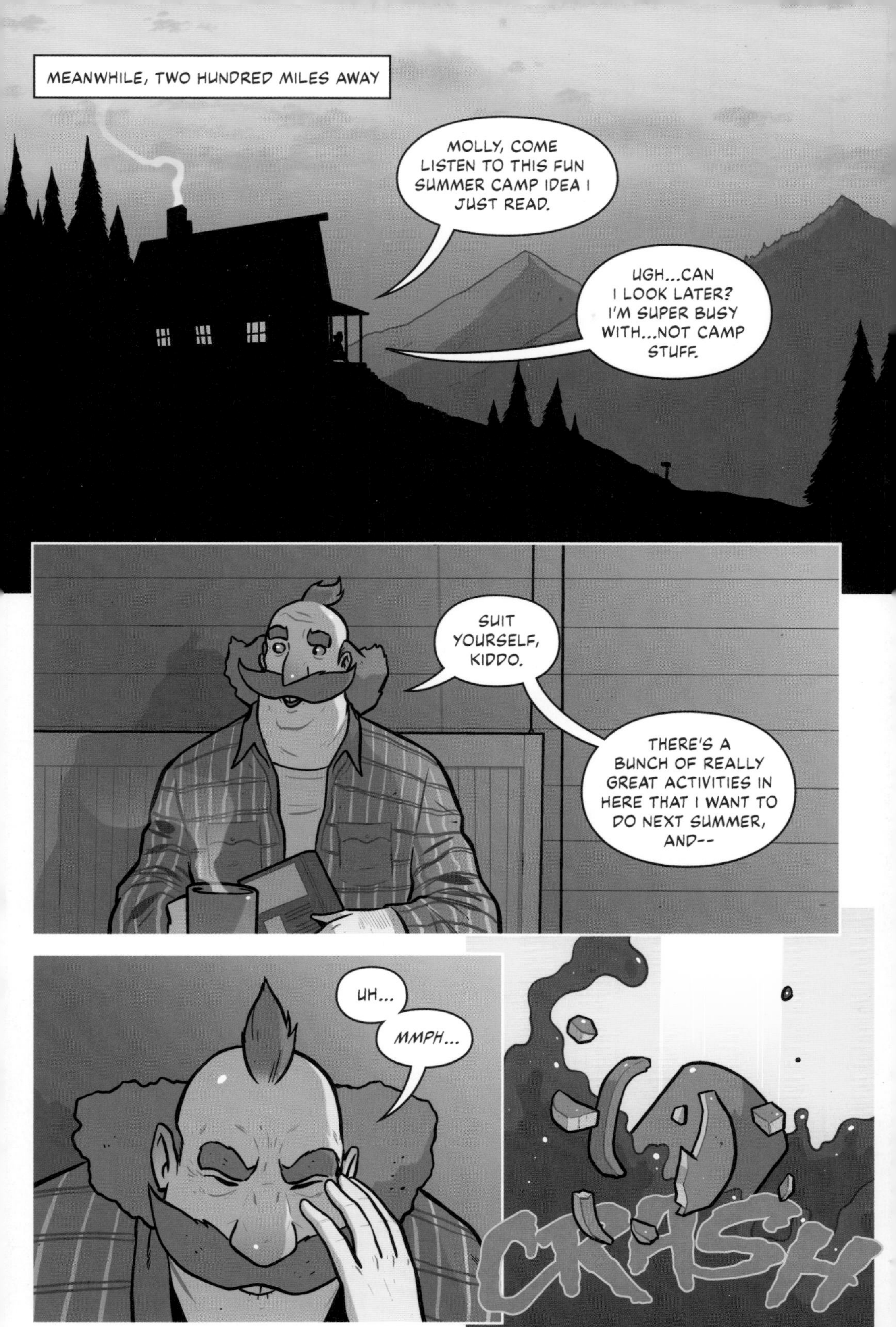
MEANWHILE, TWO HUNDRED MILES AWAY
MOLLY, COME LISTEN TO THIS FUN SUMMER CAMP IDEA I JUST READ.
UGH...CAN I LOOK LATER? I'M SUPER BUSY WITH...NOT CAMP STUFF.
SUIT YOURSELF, KIDDO.
THERE'S A BUNCH OF REALLY GREAT ACTIVITIES IN HERE THAT I WANT TO DO NEXT SUMMER, AND--
UH...
MMPH...
CRASH

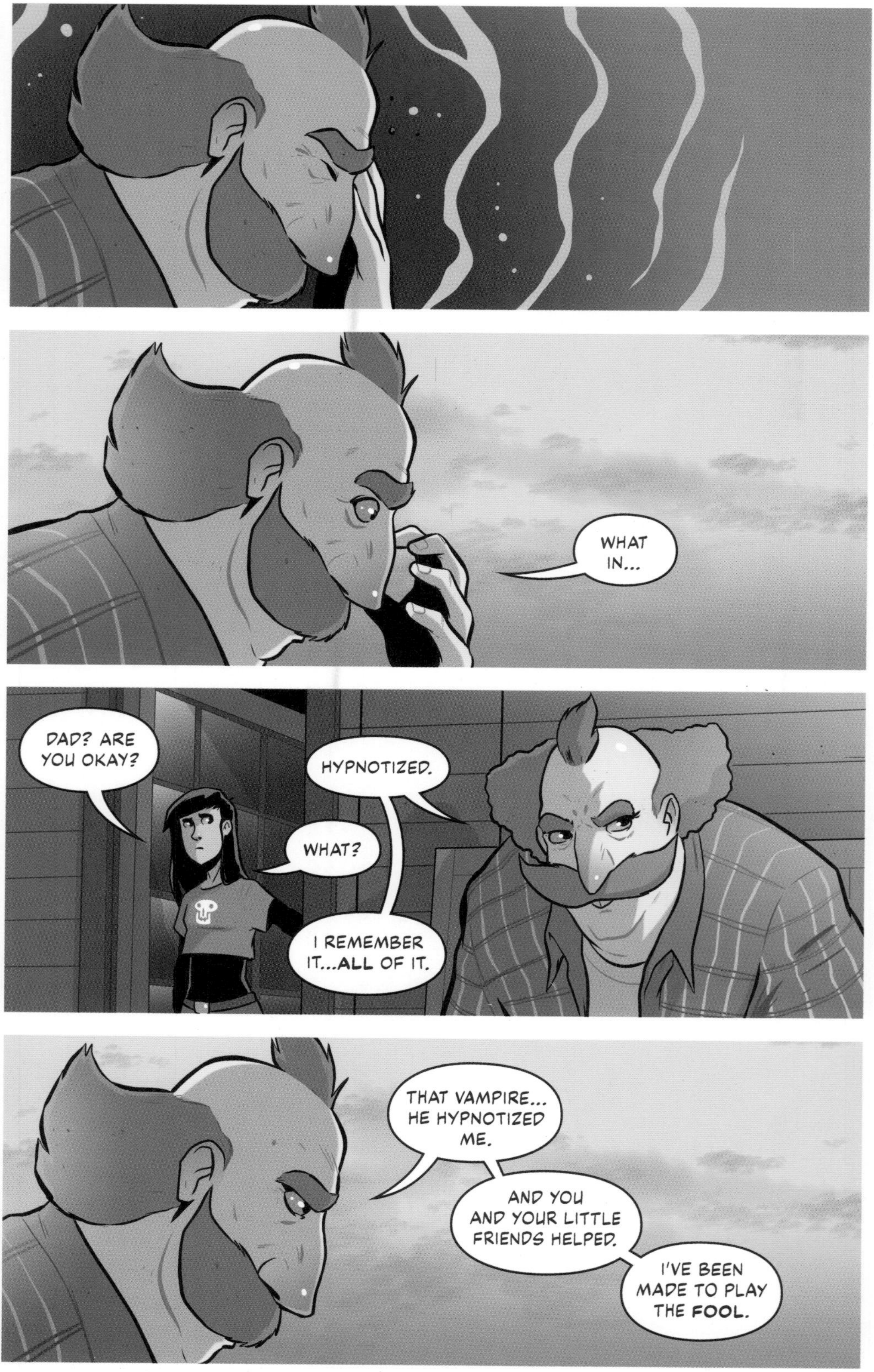
WHAT IN...
DAD? ARE YOU OKAY?
HYPNOTIZED.
WHAT?
I REMEMBER IT...ALL OF IT.
THAT VAMPIRE... HE HYPNOTIZED ME.
AND YOU AND YOUR LITTLE FRIENDS HELPED.
I'VE BEEN MADE TO PLAY THE **FOOL**.

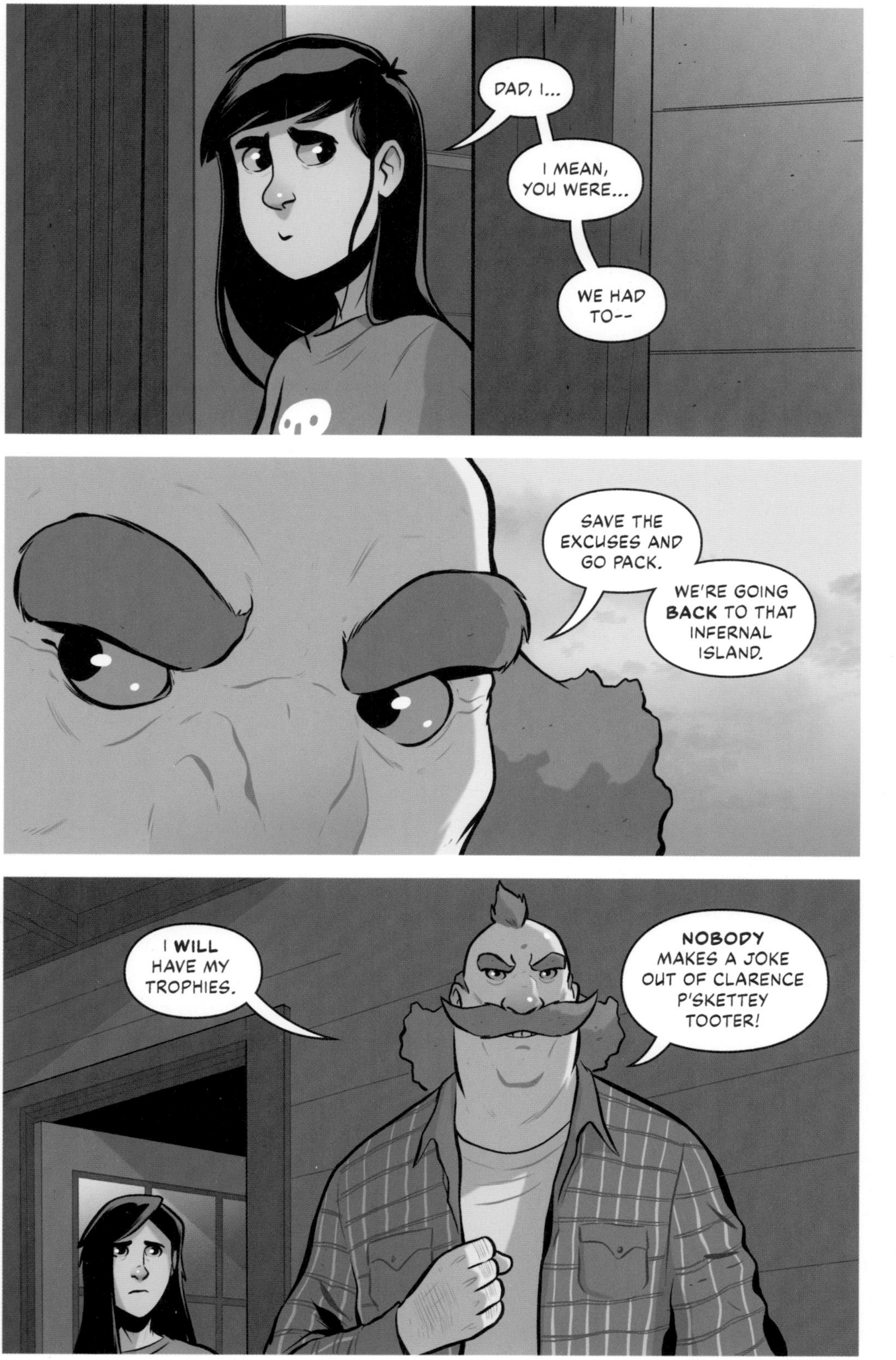
DAD, I...
I MEAN, YOU WERE...
WE HAD TO--
SAVE THE EXCUSES AND GO PACK.
WE'RE GOING **BACK** TO THAT INFERNAL ISLAND.
I **WILL** HAVE MY TROPHIES.
NOBODY MAKES A JOKE OUT OF CLARENCE P'SKETTEY TOOTER!